Collected Fiction: 1911–1937

ARTHUR MACHEN

Collected Fiction

Volume 3: 1911–1937

Edited by S. T. Joshi

Hippocampus Press

New York

Published by Hippocampus Press
P.O. Box 641, New York, NY 10156.
www.hippocampuspress.com

Cover illustration © 2019 by Matthew Jaffe, MatthewRJaffe.com.
Frontispiece photograph by John Gawsworth, provided by Mark Valentine.
Cover design by Daniel V. Sauer, DanSauerDesign.com
Hippocampus Press logo designed by Anastasia Damianakos.

First edition, 2019
1 3 5 7 9 8 6 4 2

ISBN 978-1-61498-285-2 three-volume set
ISBN 978-1-61498-250-0 volume 3
ISBN 978-1-61498-254-8 ebook

Contents

Introduction

The tales in this volume are of extraordinary diversity in tone, subject matter, and other elements, although a consistent thread of strangeness is evident in a great many of them; the tales also cover a chronological range of more than two and a half decades. During this period Machen was compelled to write voluminously as a journalist for a variety of newspapers and magazines, chiefly the London *Evening News* (1910–21), to which he contributed hundreds of pieces; he also wrote extensively for *T.P.'s Weekly*, the *Independent*, and others. Most of this work took the form of articles, reviews, and other miscellany, but Machen generated the occasional short story—sometimes disguised as work of a very different sort.

It was this tendency to write fiction that was more of the nature of a hoax that led to his most celebrated—or notorious—tale, "The Bowmen" (1914). It is evident that the trauma of the new world war affected Machen as it affected nearly everyone in Europe; and his writing of several war narratives with a supernatural twist—and, more importantly, their appearance in the *Evening News* as if they were news articles—manifestly led to their being taken as fact, or at least as the reporting of eyewitness accounts. So, in spite of Machen's frequently professed deprecation of those who took "The Bowmen" and analogous tales as literal truth, he bears some responsibility for that result. A British publisher was quick to take advantage of the furore, publishing four of Machen's short war tales as *The Angels of Mons: The Bowmen and Other Legends of the War* (1915); a subsequent edition included two further tales.

The novella "The Great Return" is also a war tale, of a sort; and, although it too appeared in the *Evening News* as a serial, its wistful mysticism led to its publication in book form by a religious press. Yet another war tale, "Munitions of War," was (according to a note by

Machen when he reprinted the story in *Holy Terrors*) written in 1915, although it was first published only in 1926.

In 1916 a few more war tales appeared, culminating in the powerful short novel *The Terror*, serialised in October 1916 in the *Evening News* and appearing in book form the next year. Thereafter, Machen's fiction-writing went into abeyance. In the 1920s, perhaps because he was freed from the onus of writing for the *Evening News*, he resumed fiction-writing on an occasional basis. Several of his tales appeared in anthologies of original fiction edited by Cynthia Asquith, most notably *The Ghost Book* (1926), *The Black Cap* (1927), and *Shudders* (1928). A few of these were stories for children, including "Johnny Double" and "Awaking."

In spite of numerous publications in the 1920s, notably of his three autobiographies—*Far Off Things* (1922), *Things Near and Far* (1923), and *The London Adventure* (1924)—and various volumes of essays, and in spite of the enormous popularity of his work in the United States as demonstrated by the reprints of his novels, tales, and essays by Alfred A. Knopf beginning in 1922, Machen had by the late 1920s fallen into dire poverty. He was rescued first by the poet Robert Hillyer, who provided financial assistance for several years, and then by a Civil List pension of £100 per year provided by the British government.

By this time, however, Machen's fiction-writing had all but ceased. He did write the short novel *The Green Round* in 1932 (it was published the following year), but it is a pale reflection of the dynamic work he had produced at the turn of the century. Two late collections appeared in 1936: *The Cosy Room and Other Stories* and *The Children of the Pool and Other Stories;* but their contents are highly uneven. Significantly, neither volume appeared in an American edition, being published only by second-tier British publishers. Machen did assemble an interesting volume of his rare work for a Penguin paperback, *Holy Terrors* (1946); and presumably he had some input on *Tales of Horror and the Supernatural* (1948), issued some months after his death on December 15, 1947. That latter volume remained in print for decades and kept the best of Machen's fiction alive until other presses, toward the end of the century, began a revival of his work that continues to the present day.

In terms of the textual status of the tales in this volume, it can be stated that the texts of the war stories are taken from *The Angels of*

Mons, the Faith Press edition of *The Great Return,* and the *Evening News* appearances of stories uncollected in Machen's lifetime. The text of *The Terror* is taken from the Caerleon Edition of Machen's *Works* (Martin Secker, 1923), Volume 7. The text of "Out of the Earth" is taken from *The Shining Pyramid* (1925). The texts of "Awaking," "The Compliments of the Season," "The Gift of Tongues," "The Islington Mystery," "N," and "A New Christmas Carol" are taken from *The Cosy Room and Other Stories;* "Change," "The Children of the Pool," "The Exalted Omega," and "Out of the Picture" are taken from *The Children of the Pool and Other Stories;* "The Bright Boy," "The Cosy Room," "The Happy Children," "Munitions of War," "Opening the Door," and "The Tree of Life" are taken from *Holy Terrors.* The late stories "The Dover Road" and "Ritual" were uncollected in Machen's lifetime and are taken from the anthologies in which they originally appeared.

In the Appendix I print Machen's lengthy introduction to *The Angels of Mons,* his brief introduction to *The Shining Pyramid,* and the abridgment of *The Terror* (which Machen confessed was done very skilfully) that appeared in *Century Magazine* (October 1917).

—S. T. JOSHI

Ten Thousand and One Nights

The Sultan of the Isles of Ebony expressed himself delighted with the narrative of the Vale of Serpents, and as his vizier, turning to the people, asked whether any person had complaint to make, petition to present, or audience to crave, a stranger burst through the crowd and, prostrating himself before the Sultan, begged that his heart might find utterance.

The Vizier, not knowing the man, would have beckoned to the guards that they might beat him from the presence of the Sultan. But the monarch, rising from his throne, gave orders that the stranger should have full and free audience, repeating the verses:—

> The Sultan gave command: the whole empire was interrogated.
> There was no reply; in vain they asked those who dwelt about the capital.
> The wise men of the city confessed themselves perplexed;
> And counsel was lacking to the council of the Vizier,
> But a poor man came from a far land,
> And, by the mercy of the Compassionate, he was the Resolver of Doubts.

The stranger again did obeisance, and informed the Sultan that he had indeed come from a far region, and that he had the most extraordinary matters to relate.

"Yet," he said, "though I have wandered, I have not gone astray, since I have come to Your Majesty's Court. For what says the poet?—

> How say ye that I was lost? I wandered amongst roses.
> The Lover in the House of the Beloved is not forlorn.
> Can he go astray that enters the rose garden?

"Your Majesty must know," he continued, "that more than a year's journey from this exalted court there is a rich and prosperous island in the ocean of the West. The capital of this island is answerable in wealth and splendour to the rest of the dominion, and is inhabited by many myriads of people. And in this city there is a palace inhabited en-

tirely by magicians, who are endowed with greater and more marvellous knowledge than that possessed by Suleiman-ben-Daoud (on whom
be peace!) and by all the wonder workers of the empire of the East.

"For, marvellous though it may appear, it is certainly true that
these magicians, sitting in their palace, hear all the murmurs and exul-
tations and lamentations of the whole world, since great secrets have
been revealed to them. They have laid enchantments upon wires of
metal, and on these wires intelligence is brought from all the four quarters of the earth to this one place, so that word comes of Sultans who
go forth to war, and of cities stricken by the plague, and of the devas-
tations wrought by fire, and of the upheaval of mountains, and of the
swelling of great floods; and all in a few moments of time.

"Nay, more; not only do these wires bring tidings across the land;
they have been laid in the depths of the sea to such a distance that a
strong ship with good sails should scarcely attain it in a year's voyaging.
So that if a man should utter a word in the furthest confines of the
Empire of China at the beginning of prayer, it would be delivered in
the city of Bagdad ere the faithful had risen from their prostrations.
Such is the power of the enchantment.

"Furthermore, it is to be noted that there are yet greater marvels.
They have other magic wires on which the voice of those who speak is
borne from far away, so that one man will converse with another freely,
though there be more than a hundred leagues distance between them.

"And that I may say all, they have procured a mystery to make the
djinns tremble from fear. For besides these wires they have magical instruments which cast forth voices and sentences upon the air, and by a
hidden art, the air receives these sounds and utters them across the
oceans and the deserts, into the ears of the enchanters of the palace.
By these methods everything that takes place on the entire earth is
quickly known in this place, where, as I have already said, all the voices
of the world must come to audience.

"Nor is this enough. For it is the business of these wonder-
workers that all the people of the city shall be made aware of the
events of the world, night by night. So, having written down all the intelligence that has been borne to them they cause their sentences and
proclamations to be moulded in strong metal. Then the blackest ink is
brought, and fine white paper; and contrivances with huge wheels and

cylinders begin to roar and shake the earth, revolving so violently and with so loud a noise that strangers are afflicted with perturbation as by the noise of stormy waters, so that when they go past the palace and the earth trembles and shakes and there is a great roaring as of ten thousand ferocious lions, they say to one another, 'He is the merciful, the Compassionate, the King of the Day of Judgment!' And shudder visibly.

"But when these cylinders have revolved many times, marvellous to relate, all that which has come by magic and by voices of the air from the ends of the world, and has been written down by the scribes, and moulded in metal, is now visible in fair characters on the white paper, and has been multiplied by ten thousand and by fifty times ten thousand, and it may be by a hundred times ten thousand. Lo! for each one that desires here is a scroll of paper and all the wonder and entertainment of the world appears on it, clearly written, as if by a scribe of Your Majesty's Palace. And so they do and execute this work day by day and night by night in this place; and so they have done for ten thousand nights. And thus some call this work the Entertainment of Ten Thousand Nights; but others name it The Evening News."

The Bowmen

It was during the Retreat of the Eighty Thousand, and the authority of the Censorship is sufficient excuse for not being more explicit. But it was on the most awful day of that awful time, on the day when ruin and disaster came so near that their shadow fell over London far away; and, without any certain news, the hearts of men failed within them and grew faint; as if the agony of the army in the battle-field had entered into their souls.

On this dreadful day, then, when three hundred thousand men in arms with all their artillery swelled like a flood against the little English company, there was one point above all other points in our battle line that was for a time in awful danger, not merely of defeat, but of utter annihilation. With the permission of the Censorship and of the military expert, this corner may, perhaps, be described as a salient, and if this angle were crushed and broken, then the English force as a whole would be shattered, the Allied left would be turned, and Sedan would inevitably follow.

All the morning the German guns had thundered and shrieked against this corner, and against the thousand or so of men who held it. The men joked at the shells, and found funny names for them, and had bets about them, and greeted them with scraps of music-hall songs. But the shells came on and burst, and tore good Englishmen limb from limb, and tore brother from brother, and as the heat of the day increased so did the fury of that terrific cannonade. There was no help, it seemed. The English artillery was good, but there was not nearly enough of it; it was being steadily battered into scrap iron.

There comes a moment in a storm at sea when people say to one another, "It is at its worst; it can blow no harder," and then there is a blast ten times more fierce than any before it. So it was in these British trenches.

There were no stouter hearts in the whole world than the hearts of these men; but even they were appalled as this seven-times-heated hell of the German cannonade fell upon them and overwhelmed them and destroyed them. And at this very moment they saw from their trenches that a tremendous host was moving against their lines. Five hundred of the thousand remained, and as far as they could see the German infantry was pressing on against them, column upon column, a grey world of men, ten thousand of them, as it appeared afterwards.

There was no hope at all. They shook hands, some of them. One man improvised a new version of the battle-song, "Good-bye, good-bye to Tipperary", ending with "And we shan't get there." And they all went on firing steadily. The officers pointed out that such an opportunity for high-class, fancy shooting might never occur again; the Germans dropped line after line; the Tipperary humorist asked, "What price Sidney Street?" And the few machine-guns did their best. But everybody knew it was of no use. The dead grey bodies lay in companies and battalions, as others came on and on and on, and they swarmed and stirred and advanced from beyond and beyond.

"World without end. Amen," said one of the British soldiers with some irrelevance as he took aim and fired. And then he remembered— he says he cannot think why or wherefore—a queer vegetarian restaurant in London where he had once or twice eaten eccentric dishes of cutlets made of lentils and nuts that pretended to be steak. On all the plates in this restaurant there was printed a figure of St. George in blue, with the motto, *Adsit Anglis Sanctus Georgius*—May St. George be a present help to the English. This soldier happened to know Latin and other useless things, and now, as he fired at his man in the grey advancing mass—300 yards away—he uttered the pious vegetarian motto. He went on firing to the end, and at last Bill on his right had to clout him cheerfully over the head to make him stop, pointing out as he did so that the King's ammunition cost money and was not lightly to be wasted in drilling funny patterns into dead Germans.

For as the Latin scholar uttered his invocation he felt something between a shudder and an electric shock pass through his body. The roar of the battle died down in his ears to a gentle murmur; instead of it, he says, he heard a great voice and a shout louder than a thunder-peal crying, "Array, array, array!"

His heart grew hot as a burning coal, it grew cold as ice within him, as it seemed to him that a tumult of voices answered to his summons. He heard, or seemed to hear, thousands shouting: "St. George! St. George!"

"Ha! messire; ha! sweet Saint, grant us good deliverance!"

"St. George for merry England!"

"Harow! Harow! Monseigneur St. George, succour us."

"Ha! St. George! Ha! St. George! a long bow and a strong bow."

"Heaven's Knight, aid us!"

And as the soldier heard these voices he saw before him, beyond the trench, a long line of shapes, with a shining about them. They were like men who drew the bow, and with another shout, their cloud of arrows flew singing and tingling through the air towards the German hosts.

$$* \qquad * \qquad * \qquad * \qquad *$$

The other men in the trench were firing all the while. They had no hope; but they aimed just as if they had been shooting at Bisley.

Suddenly one of them lifted up his voice in the plainest English.

"Gawd help us!" he bellowed to the man next to him, "but we're blooming marvels! Look at those grey . . . gentlemen, look at them! D'ye see them? They're not going down in dozens, nor in 'undreds; it's thousands, it is. Look! look! There's a regiment gone while I'm talking to ye."

"Shut it!" the other soldier bellowed, taking aim, "what are ye gassing about?"

But he gulped with astonishment even as he spoke, for, indeed, the grey men were falling by the thousands. The English could hear the guttural scream of the German officers, the crackle of their revolvers as they shot the reluctant; and still line after line crashed to the earth.

$$* \qquad * \qquad * \qquad * \qquad *$$

All the while the Latin-bred soldier heard the cry:

"Harow! Harow! Monseigneur, dear saint, quick to our aid! St. George help us!"

"High Chevalier, defend us!"

The singing arrows fled so swift and thick that they darkened the air; the heathen horde melted from before them.

*   *   *   *   *

"More machine-guns!" Bill yelled to Tom.

"Don't hear them," Tom yelled back. "But, thank God, anyway, they've got it in the neck."

In fact, there were ten thousand dead German soldiers left before that salient of the English army, and consequently there was no Sedan. In Germany, a country ruled by scientific principles, the Great General Staff decided that the contemptible English must have employed shells containing an unknown gas of a poisonous nature, as no wounds were discernible on the bodies of the dead German soldiers. But the man who knew what nuts tasted like when they called themselves steak knew also that St. George had brought his Agincourt Bowmen to help the English.

The Soldiers' Rest

The soldier with the ugly wound in the head opened his eyes at last and looked about him with an air of pleasant satisfaction.

He still felt drowsy and dazed with some fierce experience through which he had passed, but so far he could not recollect much about it. But an agreeable glow began to steal about his heart—such a glow as comes to people who have been in a tight place and have come through it better than they had expected. In its mildest form this set of emotions may be observed in passengers who have crossed the Channel on a windy day without being sick. They triumph a little internally, and are suffused with vague, kindly feelings.

The wounded soldier was somewhat of this disposition as he opened his eyes, pulled himself together, and looked about him. He felt a sense of delicious ease and repose in bones that had been racked and weary, and deep in the heart that had so lately been tormented there was an assurance of comfort—of the battle won. The thundering, roaring waves were passed; he had entered into the haven of calm waters. After fatigues and terrors that as yet he could not recollect he seemed now to be resting in the easiest of all easy chairs in a dim, low room.

In the hearth there was a glint of fire and a blue, sweet-scented puff of wood smoke; a great black oak beam roughly hewn crossed the ceiling. Through the leaded panes of the windows he saw a rich glow of sunlight, green lawns, and against the deepest and most radiant of all blue skies the wonderful far-lifted towers of a vast, Gothic cathedral—mystic, rich with imagery.

"Good Lord!" he murmured to himself. "I didn't know they had such places in France. It's just like Wells. And it might be the other day when I was going past the Swan, just as it might be past that window, and asked the ostler what time it was, and he says, 'What time? Why, summer-time'; and there outside it looks like summer that would last

18

for ever. If this was an inn they ought to call it 'The Soldiers' Rest'."

He dozed off again, and when he opened his eyes once more a kindly looking man in some sort of black robe was standing by him.

"It's all right now, isn't it?" he said, speaking in good English.

"Yes, thank you, sir, as right as can be. I hope to be back again soon."

"Well, well; but how did you come here? Where did you get that?" He pointed to the wound on the soldier's forehead.

The soldier put his hand up to his brow and looked dazed and puzzled.

"Well, sir," he said at last, "it was like this, to begin at the beginning. You know how we came over in August, and there we were in the thick of it, as you might say, in a day or two. An awful time it was, and I don't know how I got through it alive. My best friend was killed dead beside me as we lay in the trenches. By Cambrai, I think it was.

"Then things got a little quieter for a bit, and I was quartered in a village for the best part of a week. She was a very nice lady where I was, and she treated me proper with the best of everything. Her husband he was fighting; but she had the nicest little boy I ever knew, a little fellow of five, or six it might be, and we got on splendid. The amount of their lingo that kid taught me—'We, we' and 'Bong swor' and 'Commong voo porty voo', and all—and I taught him English. You should have heard that nipper say ''Arf a mo', old un!' It was a treat.

"Then one day we got surprised. There was about a dozen of us in the village, and two or three hundred Germans came down on us early one morning. They got us; no help for it. Before we could shoot.

   *   *   *   *   *

"Well, there we were. They tied our hands behind our backs, and smacked our faces and kicked us a bit, and we were lined up opposite the house where I'd been staying.

"And then that poor little chap broke away from his mother, and he run out and saw one of the Boshes, as we call them, fetch me one over the jaw with his clenched fist. Oh dear! oh dear! he might have done it a dozen times if only that little child hadn't seen him.

"He had a poor bit of a toy I'd bought him at the village shop; a toy gun it was. And out he came running, as I say, crying out something in French like 'Bad man! bad man! don't hurt my Anglish or I shoot you'; and he pointed that gun at the German soldier. The German, he took his bayonet, and he drove it right through the poor little chap's throat."

The soldier's face worked and twitched and twisted itself into a sort of grin, and he sat grinding his teeth and staring at the man in the black robe. He was silent for a little. And then he found his voice, and the oaths rolled terrible, thundering from him, as he cursed that murderous wretch, and bade him go down and burn for ever in hell. And the tears were raining down his face, and they choked him at last.

"I beg your pardon, sir, I'm sure," he said, "especially you being a minister of some kind, I suppose; but I can't help it, he was such a dear little man."

The man in black murmured something to himself: *"Pretiosa in conspectu Domini mors innocentium ejus"*—Dear in the sight of the Lord is the death of His innocents. Then he put a hand very gently on the soldier's shoulder.

"Never mind," said he; "I've seen some service in my time, myself. But what about that wound?"

"Oh, that; that's nothing. But I'll tell you how I got it. It was just like this. The Germans had us fair, as I tell you, and they shut us up in a barn in the village; just flung us on the ground and left us to starve seemingly. They barred up the big door of the barn, and put a sentry there, and thought we were all right.

"There were sort of slits like very narrow windows in one of the walls, and on the second day it was, I was looking out of these slits down the street, and I could see those German devils were up to mischief. They were planting their machine guns everywhere handy where an ordinary man coming up the street would never see them, but I see them, and I see the infantry lining up behind the garden walls. Then I had a sort of a notion of what was coming; and presently, sure enough, I could hear some of our chaps singing 'Hullo, hullo, hullo!' in the distance; and I says to myself, 'Not this time.'

"So I looked about me, and I found a hole under the wall; a kind of a drain I should think it was, and I found I could just squeeze through. And I got out and crept round, and away I goes running down the street, yelling for all I was worth, just as our chaps were getting round the corner at the bottom. 'Bang, bang!' went the guns, behind me and in front of me, and on each side of me, and then—bash! something hit me on the head and over I went; and I don't remember anything more till I woke up here just now."

The soldier lay back in his chair and closed his eyes for a moment. When he opened them he saw that there were other people in the room besides the minister in the black robes. One was a man in a big black cloak. He had a grim old face and a great beaky nose. He shook the soldier by the hand.

"By God! sir," he said, "you're a credit to the British Army; you're a damned fine soldier and a good man, and, by God! I'm proud to shake hands with you."

And then some one came out of the shadow, some one in queer clothes such as the soldier had seen worn by the heralds when he had been on duty at the opening of Parliament by the King.

"Now, by Corpus Domini," this man said, "of all knights ye be noblest and gentlest, and ye be of fairest report, and now ye be a brother of the noblest brotherhood that ever was since this world's beginning, since ye have yielded dear life for your friends' sake."

The soldier did not understand what the man was saying to him. There were others, too, in strange dresses, who came and spoke to him. Some spoke in what sounded like French. He could not make it out; but he knew that they all spoke kindly and praised him.

"What does it all mean?" he said to the minister. "What are they talking about? They don't think I'd let down my pals?"

"Drink this," said the minister, and he handed the soldier a great silver cup, brimming with wine.

The soldier took a deep draught, and in that moment all his sorrows passed from him.

"What is it?" he asked.

"Vin nouveau du Royaume," said the minister. "New Wine of the Kingdom, you call it." And then he bent down and murmured in the soldier's ear.

"What," said the wounded man, "the place they used to tell us about in Sunday School? With such drink and such joy—"

His voice was hushed. For as he looked at the minister the fashion of his vesture was changed. The black robe seemed to melt away from him. He was all in armour, if armour be made of starlight, of the rose of dawn, and of sunset fires; and he lifted up a great sword of flame.

> *Full in the midst, his Cross of Red*
> *Triumphant Michael brandished,*
>   *And trampled the Apostate's pride.*

The Monstrance

Then it fell out in the sacring of the Mass that right as the priest heaved up the Host there came a beam redder than any rose and smote upon it, and then it was changed bodily into the shape and fashion of a Child having his arms stretched forth, as he had been nailed upon the Tree.—OLD ROMANCE.

So far things were going very well indeed. The night was thick and black and cloudy, and the German force had come three-quarters of their way or more without an alarm. There was no challenge from the English lines; and indeed the English were being kept busy by a high shell-fire on their front. This had been the German plan; and it was coming off admirably. Nobody thought that there was any danger on the left; and so the Prussians, writhing on their stomachs over the ploughed field, were drawing nearer and nearer to the wood. Once there they could establish themselves comfortably and securely during what remained of the night; and at dawn the English left would be hopelessly enfiladed—and there would be another of those movements which people who really understand military matters call "readjustments of our line".

The noise made by the men creeping and crawling over the fields was drowned by the cannonade, from the English side as well as the German. On the English centre and right things were indeed very brisk; the big guns were thundering and shrieking and roaring, the machine guns were keeping up the very devil's racket; the flares and illuminating shells were as good as the Crystal Palace in the old days, as the soldiers said to one another. All this had been thought of and thought out on the other side. The German force was beautifully organised. The men who crept nearer and nearer to the wood carried quite a number of machine guns in bits on their backs; others of them had small bags full of sand; yet others big bags that were empty. When the wood was reached the sand from the small bags was to be emptied into the big bags; the machine-gun parts were to be put together, the guns mounted behind the sandbag redoubt, and then, as Major Von und Zu pleasantly observed, "the English pigs shall to gehenna-fire quickly come."

The major was so well pleased with the way things had gone that he permitted himself a very low and guttural chuckle; in another ten minutes success would be assured. He half turned his head round to whisper a caution about some detail of the sandbag business to the big sergeant-major, Karl Heinz, who was crawling just behind him. At that instant Karl Heinz leapt into the air with a scream that rent through the night and through all the roaring of the artillery. He cried in a terrible voice, "The Glory of the Lord!" and plunged and pitched forward, stone dead. They said that his face as he stood up there and cried aloud was as if it had been seen through a sheet of flame.

"They" were one or two out of the few who got back to the German lines. Most of the Prussians stayed in the ploughed field. Karl Heinz's scream had frozen the blood of the English soldiers, but it had also ruined the major's plans. He and his men, caught all unready, clumsy with the burdens that they carried, were shot to pieces; hardly a score of them returned. The rest of the force were attended to by an English burying party. According to custom the dead men were searched before they were buried, and some singular relics of the campaign were found upon them, but nothing so singular as Karl Heinz's diary.

He had been keeping it for some time. It began with entries about bread and sausage and the ordinary incidents of the trenches; here and there Karl wrote about an old grandfather, and a big china pipe, and pinewoods and roast goose. Then the diarist seemed to get fidgety about his health. Thus:

April 17.—Annoyed for some days by murmuring sounds in my head. I trust I shall not become deaf, like my departed uncle Christopher.

April 20.—The noise in my head grows worse; it is a humming sound. It distracts me; twice I have failed to hear the captain and have been reprimanded.

April 22.—So bad is my head that I go to see the doctor. He speaks of *tinnitus,* and gives me an inhaling apparatus that shall reach, he says, the middle ear.

April 25.—The apparatus is of no use. The sound is now become like the booming of a great church bell. It reminds me of the bell at St. Lambart on that terrible day of last August.

April 26.—I could swear that it is the bell of St. Lambart that I hear all the time. They rang it as the procession came out of the church.

The man's writing, at first firm enough, begins to straggle unevenly over the page at this point. The entries shew that he became convinced that he heard the bell of St. Lambart's Church ringing, though (as he knew better than most men) there had been no bell and no church at St. Lambart's since the summer of 1914. There was no village either—the whole place was a rubbish-heap.

Then the unfortunate Karl Heinz was beset with other troubles.

May 2.—I fear I am becoming ill. To-day Joseph Kleist, who is next to me in the trench, asked me why I jerked my head to the right so constantly. I told him to hold his tongue; but this shews that I am noticed. I keep fancying that there is something white just beyond the range of my sight on the right hand.

May 3.—This whiteness is now quite clear, and in front of me. All this day it has slowly passed before me. I asked Joseph Kleist if he saw a piece of newspaper just beyond the trench. He stared at me solemnly—he is a stupid fool—and said, "There is no paper."

May 4.—It looks like a white robe. There was a strong smell of incense to-day in the trench. No one seemed to notice it. There is decidedly a white robe, and I think I can see feet, passing very slowly before me at this moment while I write.

There is no space here for continuous extracts from Karl Heinz's diary. But to condense with severity, it would seem that he slowly gathered about himself a complete set of sensory hallucinations. First the auditory hallucination of the sound of a bell, which the doctor called *tinnitus*. Then a patch of white growing into a white robe, then the smell of incense. At last he lived in two worlds. He saw his trench, and the level before it, and the English lines; he talked with his comrades and obeyed orders, though with a certain difficulty; but he also heard the deep boom of St. Lambart's bell, and saw continually advancing towards him a white procession of little children, led by a boy who was swinging a censer. There is one extraordinary entry: "But in August those children carried no lilies; now they have lilies in their hands. Why should they have lilies?"

It is interesting to note the transition over the border line. After

May 2 there is no reference in the diary to bodily illness, with two nota-ble exceptions. Up to and including that date the sergeant knows that he is suffering from illusions; after that he accepts his hallucinations as ac-tualities. The man who cannot see what he sees and hear what he hears is a fool. So he writes: "I ask who is singing 'Ave Maria Stella'. That blockhead Friedrich Schumacher raises his crest and answers insolently that no one sings, since singing is strictly forbidden for the present."

A few days before the disastrous night expedition the last figure in the procession appeared to those sick eyes.

> The old priest now comes in his golden robe, the two boys holding each side of it. He is looking just as he did when he died, save that when he walked in St. Lambart there was no shining round his head. But this is illusion and contrary to reason, since no one has a shining about his head. I must take some medicine.

Note here that Karl Heinz absolutely accepts the appearance of the martyred priest of St. Lambart as actual, while he thinks that the halo must be an illusion; and so he reverts again to his physical condition.

The priest held up both his hands, the diary states, "as if there were something between them. But there is a sort of cloud or dimness over this object, whatever it may be. My poor Aunt Kathie suffered much from her eyes in her old age."

*   *   *   *   *

One can guess what the priest of St. Lambart carried in his hands when he and the little children went out into the hot sunlight to im-plore mercy, while the great resounding bell of St. Lambart boomed over the plain. Karl Heinz knew what happened then; they said that it was he who killed the old priest and helped to crucify the little child against the church door. The baby was only three years old. He died calling piteously for "mummy" and "daddy".

*   *   *   *   *

And those who will may guess what Karl Heinz saw when the mist cleared from before the monstrance in the priest's hands. Then he shrieked and died.

The Dazzling Light

*The new head-covering is made of heavy steel, which has been specially treated to increase its resisting power. The walls protecting the skull are particularly thick, and the weight of the helmet renders its use in open warfare out of the question. The rim is large, like that of the headpiece of Mambrino, and the soldier can at will either bring the helmet forward and protect his eyes or wear it so as to protect the base of the skull. . . . Military experts admit that continuance of the present trench warfare may lead to those engaged in it, especially bombing parties and barbed wire cutters, being more heavily armoured than the knights who fought at Bouvines and at Agincourt.—*THE TIMES, *July 22, 1915.*

The war is already a fruitful mother of legends. Some people think that there are too many war legends, and a Croydon gentleman—or lady, I am not sure which—wrote to me quite recently telling me that a certain particular legend, which I will not specify, had become the "chief horror of the war". There may be something to be said for this point of view, but it strikes me as interesting that the old myth-making faculty has survived into these days, a relic of noble, far-off Homeric battles. And after all, what do we know? It does not do to be too sure that this, that, or the other hasn't happened and couldn't have happened.

What follows, at any rate, has no claim to be considered either as legend or as myth. It is merely one of the odd circumstances of these times, and I have no doubt it can easily be "explained away". In fact, the rationalistic explanation of the whole thing is patent and on the surface. There is only one little difficulty, and that, I fancy, is by no means insuperable. In any case this one knot or tangle may be put down as a queer coincidence and nothing more.

Here, then, is the curiosity or oddity in question. A young fellow, whom we will call for avoidance of all identification Delamere Smith— he is now Lieutenant Delamere Smith—was spending his holidays on the coast of west South Wales at the beginning of the war. He was something or other not very important in the City, and in his leisure hours he smattered lightly and agreeably a little literature, a little art, a little antiquarianism. He liked the Italian primitives, he knew the difference between first, second, and third pointed, he had looked through Boutell's *Engraved Brasses.* He had been heard indeed to speak with enthusiasm of the brasses of Sir Robert de Septvans and Sir Roger de Trumpington.

One morning—he thinks it must have been the morning of August 16, 1914—the sun shone so brightly into his room that he woke early, and the fancy took him that it would be fine to sit on the cliffs in the pure sunlight. So he dressed and went out, and climbed up Giltar Point, and sat there enjoying the sweet air and the radiance of the sea, and the sight of the fringe of creaming foam about the grey foundations of St. Margaret's Island. Then he looked beyond and gazed at the new white monastery on Caldy, and wondered who the architect was, and how he had contrived to make the group of buildings look exactly like the background of a mediaeval picture.

After about an hour of this and a couple of pipes, Smith confesses that he began to feel extremely drowsy. He was just wondering whether it would not be pleasant to stretch himself out on the wild thyme that scented the high place and go to sleep till breakfast, when the mounting sun caught one of the monastery windows, and Smith stared sleepily at the darting flashing light till it dazzled him. Then he felt "queer". There was an odd sensation as if the top of his head were dilating and contracting, and then he says he had a sort of shock, something between a mild current of electricity and the sensation of putting one's hand into the ripple of a swift brook.

Now, what happened next Smith cannot describe at all clearly. He knew he was on Giltar, looking across the waves to Caldy; he heard all the while the hollow, booming tide in the caverns of the rocks far below him, And yet he saw, as if in a glass, a very different country—a level fenland cut by slow streams, by long avenues of trimmed trees.

"It looked," he says, "as if it ought to have been a lonely country, but it was swarming with men; they were thick as ants in an anthill. And they were all dressed in armour; that was the strange thing about it.

"I thought I was standing by what looked as if it had been a farmhouse; but it was all battered to bits, just a heap of ruins and rubbish. All that was left was one tall round chimney, shaped very much like the fifteenth-century chimneys in Pembrokeshire. And thousands and tens of thousands went marching by.

"They were all in armour, and in all sorts of armour. Some of them had overlapping tongues of bright metal fastened on their clothes, others were in chain mail from head to foot, others were in heavy plate armour.

"They wore helmets of all shapes and sorts and sizes. One regiment had steel caps with wide brims, something like the old barbers' basins. Another lot had knights' tilting helmets on, closed up so that you couldn't see their faces. Most of them wore metal gauntlets, either of steel rings or plates, and they had steel over their boots. A great many had things like battle-maces swinging by their sides, and all these fellows carried a sort of string of big metal balls round their waist. Then a dozen regiments went by, every man with a steel shield slung over his shoulder. The last to go by were cross-bowmen."

In fact, it appeared to Delamere Smith that he watched the passing of a host of men in mediaeval armour before him, and yet he knew— by the position of the sun and of a rosy cloud that was passing over the Worm's Head—that this vision, or whatever it was, only lasted a second or two. Then that slight sense of shock returned, and Smith returned to the contemplation of the physical phenomena of the Pembrokeshire coast—blue waves, grey St. Margaret's, and Caldy Abbey white in the sunlight.

It will be said, no doubt, and very likely with truth, that Smith fell asleep on Giltar, and mingled in a dream the thought of the great war just begun with his smatterings of mediaeval battle and arms and armour. The explanation seems tolerable enough.

But there is the one little difficulty. It has been said that Smith is now Lieutenant Smith. He got his commission last autumn, and went out in May. He happens to speak French rather well, and so he has become what is called, I believe, an officer of liaison, or some such term. Anyhow, he is often behind the French lines.

He was home on short leave last week, and said:

"Ten days ago I was ordered to ——. I got there early in the morning, and had to wait a bit before I could see the General. I looked about me, and there on the left of us was a farm shelled into a heap of ruins, with one round chimney standing, shaped like the 'Flemish' chimneys in Pembrokeshire. And then the men in armour marched by, just as I had seen them—French regiments. The things like battle-maces were bomb-throwers, and the metal balls round the men's waists were the bombs. They told me that the cross-bows were used for bomb-shooting.

"The march I saw was part of a big movement; you will hear more of it before long."

The Great Return

I. THE RUMOUR OF THE MARVELLOUS

There are strange things lost and forgotten in obscure corners of the newspaper. I often think that the most extraordinary item of intelligence that I have read in print appeared a few years ago in the London press. It came from a well-known and most respected news agency; I imagine it was in all the papers. It was astounding.

The circumstances necessary—not to the understanding of this paragraph, for that is out of the question—but, we will say, to the understanding of the events which made it possible, are these. We had invaded Thibet, and there had been trouble in the hierarchy of that country, and a personage known as the Tashi Lama had taken refuge with us in India. He went on pilgrimage from one Buddhist shrine to another, and came at last to a holy mountain of Buddhism, the name of which I have forgotten. And thus the morning paper:

> "His Holiness the Tashi Lama then ascended the Mountain and was transfigured—Reuter."

That was all. And from that day to this I have never heard a word of explanation or comment on this amazing statement.

There was no more, it seemed, to be said. "Reuter," apparently, thought he had made his simple statement of the facts of the case, had thereby done his duty, and so it all ended. Nobody, so far as I know, ever wrote to any paper asking what Reuter meant by it, or what the Tashi Lama meant by it. I suppose the fact was that nobody cared twopence about the matter; and so this strange event—if there were any such event—was exhibited to us for a moment, and the lantern show revolved to other spectacles.

This is an extreme instance of the manner in which the marvellous is flashed out to us and then withdrawn behind its black veils and concealments; but I have known of other cases. Now and again, at intervals of a few years, there appear in the newspapers strange stones of the strange doings of what are technically called *poltergeists*. Some house, often a lonely farm, is suddenly subjected to an infernal bombardment. Great stones crash through the windows, thunder down the chimneys, impelled by no visible hand. The plates and cups and saucers are whirled from the dresser into the middle of the kitchen, no one can say how or by what agency. Upstairs the big bedstead and an old chest or two are heard bounding on the floor as if in a mad ballet. Now and then such doings as these excite a whole neighbourhood; sometimes a London paper sends a man down to make an investigation. He writes half a column of description on the Monday, a couple of paragraphs on the Tuesday, and then returns to town. Nothing has been explained, the matter vanishes away; and nobody cares. The tale trickles for a day or two through the Press, and then instantly disappears, like an Australian stream, into the bowels of darkness. It is possible, I suppose, that this singular incuriousness as to marvellous events and reports is not wholly unaccountable. It may be that the events in question are, as it were, psychic accidents and misadventures. They are not meant to happen, or, rather, to be manifested. They belong to the world on the other side of the dark curtain; and it is only by some queer mischance that a corner of that curtain is twitched aside for an instant. Then—for an instant—we see; but the personages whom Mr. Kipling calls the Lords of Life and Death take care that we do not see too much. Our business is with things higher and things lower, with things different, anyhow; and on the whole we are not suffered to distract ourselves with that which does not really concern us. The Transfiguration of the Lama and the tricks of the *poltergeist* are evidently no affairs of ours; we raise an uninterested eyebrow and pass on—to poetry or to statistics.

Be it noted: I am not professing any fervent personal belief in the reports to which I have alluded. For all I know, the Lama, in spite of Reuter, was not transfigured, and the *poltergeist,* in spite of the late Mr. Andrew Lang, may in reality be only mischievous Polly, the servant girl at the farm. And to go farther: I do not know that I should be justified in putting either of these cases of the marvellous in line with a chance paragraph that caught my eye last summer; for this had not, on the face of it at all events, anything wildly out of the common. Indeed, I dare say that I should not have read it, should not have seen it, if it had not contained the name of a place which I had once visited, which had then moved me in an odd manner that I could not understand. Indeed, I am sure that this particular paragraph deserves to stand alone, for even if the *poltergeist* be a real *poltergeist,* it merely reveals the psychic whimsicality of some region that is not our region. There were better things and more relevant things behind the few lines dealing with Llantrisant, the little town by the sea in Arfonshire.

Not on the surface, I must say, for the cutting—I have preserved it—reads as follows:

"LLANTRISANT.—The season promises very favourably: temperature of the sea yesterday at noon, 65 deg. Remarkable occurrences are supposed to have taken place during the recent Revival. The lights have not been observed lately. The Crown. The Fisherman's Rest."

The style was odd certainly; knowing a little of newspapers, I could see that the figure called, I think, *tmesis,* or cutting, had been generously employed; the exuberances of the local correspondent had been pruned by a Fleet Street expert. And these poor men are often hurried; but what did those "lights" mean? What strange matters had the vehement blue pencil blotted out and brought to naught?

That was my first thought, and then, thinking still of Llantrisant and how I had first discovered it and found it strange, I read the paragraph again, and was saddened almost to see, as I thought, the obvious explanation. I had forgotten for the moment that it was war-time, that scares and rumours and terrors about traitorous signals and flashing lights were current everywhere by land and sea; some one, no doubt, had been watching innocent farmhouse windows and thoughtless fan-lights of lodging-houses; these were the "lights" that had not been observed lately.

I found out afterwards that the Llantrisant correspondent had no such treasonous lights in his mind, but something very different. Still; what do we know? He may have been mistaken, "the great rose of fire" that came over the deep may have been the port light of a coasting-ship. Did it shine at last from the old chapel on the headland? Possibly; or possibly it was the doctor's lamp at Sarnau, some miles away. I have had wonderful opportunities lately of analysing the marvels of lying, conscious and unconscious; and indeed almost incredible feats in this way can be performed. If I incline to the less likely explanation of the "lights" at Llantrisant, it is merely because this explanation seems to me to be altogether congruous with the "remarkable occurrences" of the newspaper paragraph.

After all, if rumour and gossip and hearsay are crazy things to be utterly neglected and laid aside: on the other hand, evidence is evidence, and when a couple of reputable surgeons assert, as they do assert in the case of Olwen Phillips, Croeswen, Llantrisant, that there has been a "kind of resurrection of the body", it is merely foolish to say that these things don't happen. The girl was a mass of tuberculosis, she was within a few hours of death; she is now full of life. And so, I do not believe that the rose of fire was merely a ship's light, magnified and transformed by dreaming Welsh sailors.

But now I am going forward too fast. I have not dated the paragraph, so I cannot give the exact day of its appearance, but I think it was somewhere between the second and third week of June. I cut it out partly because it was about Llantrisant, partly because of the "remarkable occurrences". I have an appetite for these matters, though I also have this misfortune, that I require evidence before I am ready to credit them, and I have a sort of lingering hope that some day I shall be able to elaborate some scheme or theory of such things.

But in the meantime, as a temporary measure, I hold what I call the doctrine of the jig-saw puzzle. That is: this remarkable occurrence, and that, and the other may be, and usually are, of no significance. Coincidence and chance and unsearchable causes will now and again make clouds that are undeniable fiery dragons, and potatoes that resemble Eminent Statesmen exactly and minutely in every feature, and rocks that are like eagles and lions. All this is nothing; it is when you get your set of odd shapes and find that they fit into one another, and at last that they are but parts of a large design; it is then that research grows interesting and indeed amazing, it is then that one queer form confirms the other, that the whole plan displayed justifies, corroborates, explains each separate piece.

So; it was within a week or ten days after I had read the paragraph about Llantrisant and had cut it out that I got a letter from a friend who was taking an early holiday in those regions.

"You will be interested," he wrote, "to hear that they have taken to ritualistic practices at Llantrisant. I went into the church the other day, and instead of smelling like a damp vault as usual, it was positively reeking with incense."

I knew better than that. The old parson was a firm Evangelical; he would rather have burnt sulphur in his church than incense any day. So I could not make out this report at all; and went down to Arfon a few weeks later determined to investigate this and any other remarkable occurrence at Llantrisant.

II. Odours of Paradise

I went down to Arfon in the very heat and bloom and fragrance of the wonderful summer that they were enjoying there. In London there was no such weather; it rather seemed as if the horror and fury of the war had mounted to the very skies and were there reigning. In the mornings the sun burnt down upon the city with a heat that scorched and consumed; but then clouds heavy and horrible would roll together from all quarters of the heavens, and early in the afternoon the air would darken, and a storm of thunder and lightning, and furious, hissing rain would fall upon the streets. Indeed, the torment of the world was in the London weather. The city wore a terrible vesture; within our hearts was dread; without we were clothed in black clouds and angry fire.

It is certain that I cannot shew in any words the utter peace of that Welsh coast to which I came; one sees, I think, in such a change a figure of the passage from the disquiets and the fears of earth to the peace of paradise. A land that seemed to be in a holy, happy dream, a sea that changed all the while from olivine to emerald, from emerald to sapphire, from sapphire to amethyst, that washed in white foam at the bases of the firm, grey rocks, and about the huge crimson bastions that hid the western bays and inlets of the waters; to this land I came, and to hollows that were purple and odorous with wild thyme, wonderful with many tiny, exquisite flowers. There was benediction in centaury, pardon in eyebright, joy in lady's slipper; and so the weary eyes were refreshed, looking now at the little flowers and the happy bees about them, now on the magic mirror of the deep, changing from marvel to marvel with the passing of the great white clouds, with the brightening of the sun. And the ears, torn with jangle and racket and idle, empty noise, were soothed and comforted by the ineffable, unutterable, unceasing murmur, as the tides swam to and fro, uttering mighty, hollow voices in the caverns of the rocks.

For three or four days I rested in the sun and smelt the savour of the blossoms and of the salt water, and then, refreshed, I remembered that there was something queer about Llantrisant that I might as well investigate. It was no great thing that I thought to find, for, it will be remembered, I had ruled out the apparent oddity of the reporter's—or commissioner's?—reference to lights, on the ground that he must have been referring to some local panic about signalling to the enemy; who had certainly torpedoed a ship or two off Lundy in the Bristol Channel. All that I had to go upon was the reference to the "remarkable occurrences" at some revival, and then that letter of Jackson's, which spoke of Llantrisant church as "reeking" with incense, a wholly incredible and impossible state of things. Why, old Mr. Evans, the rector, looked upon coloured stoles as the very robe of Satan and his angels, as things dear to the heart of the Pope of Rome. But as to incense! As I have already familiarly observed, I knew better.

But as a hard matter of fact, this may be worth noting: when I went over to Llantrisant on Monday, August 9th, I visited the church, and it was still fragrant and exquisite with the odour of rare gums that had fumed there.

Now I happened to have a slight acquaintance with the rector. He was a most courteous and delightful old man, and on my last visit he had come across me in the churchyard, as I was admiring the very fine Celtic cross that stands there. Besides the beauty of the interlaced ornament there is an inscription in Ogham on one of the edges, concerning which the learned dispute; it is altogether one of the more famous crosses of Celtdom. Mr. Evans, I say, seeing me looking at the cross, came up and began to give me, the stranger, a résumé—somewhat of a shaky and uncertain résumé, I found afterwards—of the various debates and questions that had arisen as to the exact meaning of the inscription, and I was amused to detect an evident but underlying belief of his own: that the supposed Ogham characters were, in fact, due to boys' mischief and weather and the passing of the ages. But then I happened to put a question as to the sort of stone of which the cross was made, and the rector brightened amazingly. He began to talk geology, and, I think, demonstrated that the cross or the material for it must have been brought to Llantrisant from the south-west coast of Ireland. This struck me as interesting, because it was curious evidence of the migrations of the Celtic saints, whom the rector, I was delighted to find, looked upon as good Protestants, though shaky on the subject of crosses; and so, with concessions on my part, we got on very well. Thus, with all this to the good, I was emboldened to call upon him.

I found him altered. Not that he was aged; indeed, he was rather made young, with a singular brightening upon his face, and something of joy upon it that I had not seen before, that I have seen on very few faces of men. We talked of the war, of course, since that is not to be avoided; of the farming prospects of the country; of general things, till I ventured to remark that I had been in the church, and had been surprised to find it perfumed with incense.

"You have made some alterations in the service since I was here last? You use incense now?"

The old man looked at me strangely, and hesitated.

"No," he said, "there has been no change. I use no incense in the church. I should not venture to do so."

"But," I was beginning, "the whole church is as if High Mass had just been sung there, and—"

He cut me short, and there was a certain grave solemnity in his manner that struck me almost with awe.

"I know you are a railer," he said, and the phrase coming from this mild old gentleman astonished me unutterably. "You are a railer and a bitter railer; I have read articles that you have written, and I know your contempt and your hatred for those you call Protestants in your derision; though your grandfather, the vicar of Caerleon-on-Usk, called himself Protestant and was proud of it, and your great-grand-uncle

Hezekiah, *ffeiriad coch yr Castletown*—the Red Priest of Castletown—was a great man with the Methodists in his day, and the people flocked by their thousands when he administered the Sacrament. I was born and brought up in Glamorganshire, and old men have wept as they told me of the weeping and contrition that there was when the Red Priest broke the Bread and raised the Cup. But you are a railer, and see nothing but the outside and the show. You are not worthy of this mystery that has been done here."

I went out from his presence rebuked indeed, and justly rebuked; but rather amazed. It is curiously true that the Welsh are still one people, one family almost, in a manner that the English cannot understand, but I had never thought that this old clergyman would have known anything of my ancestry or their doings. And as for my articles and suchlike, I knew that the country clergy sometimes read, but I had fancied my pronouncements sufficiently obscure, even in London, much more in Arfon.

But so it happened, and so I had no explanation from the rector of Llantrisant of the strange circumstance, that his church was full of incense and odours of paradise.

I went up and down the ways of Llantrisant wondering, and came to the harbour, which is a little place, with little quays where some small coasting trade still lingers. A brigantine was at anchor here, and very lazily in the sunshine they were loading it with anthracite; for it is one of the oddities of Llantrisant that there is a small colliery in the heart of the wood on the hillside. I crossed a causeway which parts the outer harbour from the inner harbour, and settled down on a rock beach hidden under a leafy hill. The tide was going out, and some children were playing on the wet sand, while two ladies—their mothers, I suppose—talked together as they sat comfortably on their rugs at a little distance from me.

At first they talked of the war, and I made myself deaf, for of that talk one gets enough, and more than enough, in London. Then there was a period of silence, and the conversation had passed to quite a different topic when I caught the thread of it again. I was sitting on the further side of a big rock, and I do not think that the two ladies had noticed my approach. However, though they spoke of strange things, they spoke of nothing which made it necessary for me to announce my presence.

"And, after all," one of them was saying, "what is it all about? I can't make out what is come to the people."

This speaker was a Welshwoman; I recognised the clear, over-emphasised consonants, and a faint suggestion of an accent. Her friend came from the Midlands, and it turned out that they had only known each other for a few days. Theirs was a friendship of the beach and of bathing; such friendships are common at small seaside places.

"There is certainly something odd about the people here. I have never been to Llantrisant before, you know; indeed, this is the first time we've been in Wales for our holidays, and knowing nothing about the ways of the people and not being accustomed to hear Welsh spoken, I thought, perhaps, it must be my imagination. But you think there really is something a little queer?"

"I can tell you this: that I have been in two minds whether I should not write to my husband and ask him to take me and the children away. You know where I am at Mrs. Morgan's, and the Morgans' sitting-room is just the other side of the passage, and sometimes they leave the door open, so that I can hear what they say quite plainly. And you see I understand the Welsh, though they don't know it. And I hear them saying the most alarming things!"

"What sort of things?"

"Well, indeed, it sounds like some kind of a religious service, but it's not Church of England, I know that. Old Morgan begins it, and the wife and children answer. Something like: 'Blessed be God for the messengers of Paradise.' 'Blessed be His Name for Paradise in the meat and in the drink.' 'Thanksgiving for the old offering.' 'Thanksgiving for the appearance of the old altar.' 'Praise for the joy of the ancient garden.' 'Praise for the return of those that have been long absent.' And all that sort of thing. It is nothing but madness."

"Depend upon it," said the lady from the Midlands, "there's no real harm in it. They're Dissenters; some new sect, I dare say. You know some Dissenters are very queer in their ways."

"All that is like no Dissenters that I have ever known in all my life whatever," replied the Welsh lady somewhat vehemently, with a very distinct intonation of the land. "And have you heard them speak of the bright light that shone at midnight from the church?"

III. A Secret in a Secret Place

Now here was I altogether at a loss and quite bewildered. The children broke into the conversation of the two ladies and cut it short, just as the midnight lights from the church came on the field, and when the little girls and boys went back again to the sands whooping, the tide of talk had turned, and Mrs. Harland and Mrs. Williams were quite safe and at home with Janey's measles, and a wonderful treatment for infantile earache, as exemplified in the case of Trevor. There was no more to be got out of them, evidently, so I left the beach, crossed the harbour causeway, and drank beer at the Fisherman's Rest till it was time to climb up two miles of deep lane and catch the train for Penvro, where I was staying. And I went up the lane, as I say, in a kind of amazement; and not so much, I think, because of evidences and hints of things strange to the senses, such as the savour of incense where no incense had smoked for three hundred and fifty years and more, or the story of bright light shining from the dark, closed church at dead of night, as because of that sentence of thanksgiving "for paradise in meat and in drink".

For the sun went down and the evening fell as I climbed the long hill through the deep woods and the high meadows, and the scent of all the green things rose from the earth and from the heart of the wood, and at a turn of the lane far below was the misty glimmer of the still sea, and from far below its deep murmur sounded as it washed on the little hidden, enclosed bay where Llantrisant stands. And I thought, if there be paradise in meat and in drink, so much the more is there paradise in the scent of the green leaves at evening and in the appearance of the sea and in the redness of the sky; and there came to me a certain vision of a real world about us all the while, of a language that was only secret because we would not take the trouble to listen to it and discern it.

It was almost dark when I got to the station, and here were the few feeble oil lamps lit, glimmering in that lonely land, where the way is long from farm to farm. The train came on its way, and I got into it; and just as we moved from the station I noticed a group under one of those dim lamps. A woman and her child had got out, and they were being welcomed by a man who had been waiting for them. I had not noticed his face as I stood on the platform, but now I saw it as he pointed down the hill towards Llantrisant, and I think I was almost frightened.

He was a young man, a farmer's son, I would say, dressed in rough brown clothes, and as different from old Mr. Evans, the rector, as one man might be from another. But on his face, as I saw it in the lamp-light, there was the like brightening that I had seen on the face of the rector. It was an illuminated face, glowing with an ineffable joy, and I thought it rather gave light to the platform lamp than received light from it. The woman and her child, I inferred, were strangers to the place, and had come to pay a visit to the young man's family. They had looked about them in bewilderment, half alarmed, before they saw him; and then his face was radiant in their sight, and it was easy to see that all their troubles were ended and over. A wayside station and a darkening country; and it was as if they were welcomed by shining, immortal gladness—even into paradise.

But though there seemed in a sense light all about my ways, I was my-self still quite bewildered. I could see, indeed, that something strange had happened or was happening in the little town hidden under the hill, but there was so far no clue to the mystery, or rather, the clue had been offered to me, and I had not taken it, I had not even known that it was there; since we do not so much as see what we have determined, without judging, to be incredible, even though it be held up before our eyes. The dialogue that the Welsh Mrs. Williams had reported to her English friend might have set me on the right way; but the right way was outside all my limits of possibility, outside the circle of my thought. The palæontologist might see monstrous, significant marks in the slime of a river bank, but he would never draw the conclusions that his own peculiar science would seem to suggest to him; he would choose any explanation rather than the obvious, since the obvious would also be the outrageous—according to our established habit of thought, which we deem final.

The next day I took all these strange things with me for consideration to a certain place that I knew of not far from Penvro. I was now in the early stages of the jig-saw process, or rather I had only a few pieces before me, and—to continue the figure—my difficulty was this: that though the markings on each piece seemed to have design and significance, yet I could not make the wildest guess as to the nature of the whole picture, of which these were the parts. I had clearly seen that there was a great secret; I had seen that on the face of the young farmer on the platform of Llantrisant station; and in my mind there was all the while the picture of him going down the dark, steep, winding lane that led to the town and the sea, going down through the heart of the wood, with light about him.

But there was bewilderment in the thought of this, and in the endeavour to match it with the perfumed church and the scraps of talk that I had heard and the rumour of midnight brightness; and though Penvro is by no means populous, I thought I would go to a certain solitary place called the Old Camp Head, which looks towards Cornwall and to the great deeps that roll beyond Cornwall to the far ends of the world; a place where fragments of dreams—they seemed such then—might, perhaps, be gathered into the clearness of vision.

It was some years since I had been to the Head, and I had gone on that last time and on a former visit by the cliffs, a rough and difficult path. Now I chose a landward way, which the county map seemed to justify, though doubtfully, as regarded the last part of the journey. So I went inland and climbed the hot summer by-roads, till I came at last to a lane which gradually turned turfy and grass-grown, and then on high ground, ceased to be. It left me at a gate in a hedge of old thorns; and across the field beyond there seemed to be some faint indications of a track. One would judge that sometimes men did pass by that way, but not often.

It was high ground but not within sight of the sea. But the breath of the sea blew about the hedge of thorns, and came with a keen savour to the nostrils. The ground sloped gently from the gate and then rose again to a ridge, where a white farmhouse stood all alone. I passed by this farmhouse, threading an uncertain way, followed a hedgerow doubtfully; and saw suddenly before me the Old Camp, and beyond it the sapphire plain of waters and the mist where sea and sky met. Steep from my feet the hill fell away, a land of gorse-blossom, red-gold and mellow, of glorious purple heather. It fell into a hollow that went down, shining with rich green bracken, to the glimmering sea; and before me and beyond the hollow rose a height of turf, bastioned at the summit with the awful, age-old walls of the Old Camp; green, rounded circumvallations, wall within wall, tremendous, with their myriad years upon them.

Within these smoothed, green mounds, looking across the shining and changing of the waters in the happy sunlight, I took out the bread and cheese and beer that I had carried in a bag, and ate and drank, and lit my pipe, and set myself to think over the enigmas of Llantrisant. And I had scarcely done so when, a good deal to my annoyance, a man came climbing up over the green ridges, and took up his stand close by, and stared out to sea. He nodded to me, and began with "Fine weather for the harvest" in the approved manner, and so sat down and engaged me in a net of talk. He was of Wales, it seemed, but from a different part of the country, and was staying for a few days with relations—at the white farmhouse which I had passed on my way. His tale of nothing flowed on to his pleasure and my pain, till he fell suddenly on Llantrisant and its doings. I listened then with wonder, and here is his tale condensed. Though it must be clearly understood that the man's evidence was only second-hand; he had heard it from his cousin, the farmer.

So, to be brief, it appeared that there had been a long feud at Llantrisant between a local solicitor, Lewis Prothero (we will say), and a farmer named James. There had been a quarrel about some trifle, which had grown more and more bitter as the two parties forgot the merits of the original dispute, and by some means or other, which I could not well understand, the lawyer had got the small freeholder "under his thumb". James, I think, had given a bill of sale in a bad season, and Prothero had bought it up; and the end was that the farmer was turned out of the old house, and was lodging in a cottage. People said he would have to take a place on his own farm as a labourer; he went about in dreadful misery, piteous to see. It was thought by some that he might very well murder the lawyer, if he met him.

They did meet, in the middle of the market-place at Llantrisant one Saturday in June. The farmer was a little black man, and he gave a shout of rage, and the people were rushing at him to keep him off Prothero.

"And then," said my informant, "I will tell you what happened. This lawyer, as they tell me, he is a great big brawny fellow, with a big jaw and a wide mouth, and a red face and red whiskers. And there he was in his black coat and his high hard hat, and all his money at his back, as you may say. And, indeed, he did fall down on his knees in the dust there in the street in front of Philip James, and every one could see that terror was upon him. And he did beg Philip James's pardon, and beg of him to have mercy, and he did implore him by God and man and the saints of paradise. And my cousin, John Jenkins, Penmawr, he do tell me that the tears were falling from Lewis Prothero's eyes like the rain. And he put his hand into his pocket and drew out the deed of Pantyreos, Philip James's old farm that was, and did give him the farm back and a hundred pounds for the stock that was on it, and two hundred pounds, all in notes of the bank, for amendment and consolation.

"And then, from what they do tell me, all the people did go mad, crying and weeping and calling out all manner of things at the top of their voices. And at last nothing would do but they must all go up to the churchyard, and there Philip James and Lewis Prothero they swear friendship to one another for a long age before the old cross, and every one sings praises. And my cousin he do declare to me that there were men standing in that crowd that he did never see before in Llantrisant in all his life, and his heart was shaken within him as if it had been in a whirlwind."

I had listened to all this in silence. I said then:

"What does your cousin mean by that? Men that he had never seen in Llantrisant? What men?"

"The people," he said very slowly, "call them the Fishermen."

And suddenly there came into my mind the "Rich Fisherman" who in the old legend guards the holy mystery of the Graal.

IV. THE RINGING OF THE BELL

So far I have not told the story of the things of Llantrisant, but rather the story of how I stumbled upon them and among them, perplexed and wholly astray, seeking, but yet not knowing at all what I sought; bewildered now and again by circumstances which seemed to me wholly inexplicable; devoid, not so much of the key to the enigma, but of the key to the nature of the enigma. You cannot begin to solve a puzzle till you know what the puzzle is about. "Yards divided by minutes," said the mathematical master to me long ago, "will give neither pigs, sheep, nor oxen." He was right; though his manner on this and on all other occasions was highly offensive. This is enough of the personal process, as I may call it; and here follows the story of what happened at Llantrisant last summer, the story as I pieced it together at last.

It all began, it appears, on a hot day, early in last June; so far as I can make out, on the first Saturday in the month. There was a deaf old woman, a Mrs. Parry, who lived by herself in a lonely cottage a mile or so from the town. She came into the market-place early on the Saturday morning in a state of some excitement, and as soon as she had taken up her usual place on the pavement by the churchyard, with her ducks and eggs and a few very early potatoes, she began to tell her neighbours about her having heard the sound of a great bell. The good women on each side smiled at one another behind Mrs. Parry's back, for one had to bawl into her ear before she could make out what one meant; and Mrs. Williams, Penycoed, bent over and yelled: "What bell should that be, Mrs. Parry? There's no church near you up at Penrhiw. Do you hear what nonsense she talks?" said Mrs. Williams in a low voice, to Mrs. Morgan. "As if she could hear any bell, whatever."

"What makes you talk nonsense yourself?" said Mrs. Parry, to the amazement of the two women. "I can hear a bell as well as you, Mrs. Williams, and as well as your whispers either."

And there is the fact, which is not to be disputed; though the deductions from it may be open to endless disputations; this old woman who had been all but stone deaf for twenty years—the defect had always been in her family—could suddenly hear on this June morning as well as anybody else. And her two old friends stared at her, and it was some time before they had appeased her indignation, and induced her to talk about the bell.

It had happened in the early morning, which was very misty. She had been gathering sage in her garden, high on a round hill looking over the sea. And there came in her ears a sort of throbbing and singing and trembling, "as if there were music coming out of the earth", and then something seemed to break in her head, and all the birds began to sing and make melody together, and the leaves of the poplars round the garden fluttered in the breeze that rose from the sea, and the cock crowed far off at Twyn, and the dog barked down in Kemeys Valley. But above all these sounds, unheard for so many years, there thrilled the deep and chanting note of the bell, "like the bell and a man's voice singing at once".

They stared again at her and at one another. "Where did it sound from?" asked one. "It came sailing across the sea," answered Mrs. Parry quite composedly, "and I did hear it coming nearer and nearer to the land."

"Well, indeed," said Mrs. Morgan, "it was a ship's bell then, though I can't make out why they would be ringing like that."

"It was not ringing on any ship, Mrs. Morgan," said Mrs. Parry.

"Then where do you think it was ringing?"

"*Ym mharadwys,*" replied Mrs. Parry. Now that means "in Paradise", and the two others changed the conversation quickly. They thought that Mrs. Parry had got back her hearing suddenly—such things did happen now and then—and that the shock had made her "a bit queer". And this explanation would no doubt have stood its ground, if it had not been for other experiences. Indeed, the local doctor (who had treated Mrs. Parry for a dozen years, not for her deafness, which he took to be hopeless and beyond cure, but for a tiresome and recurrent winter cough) sent an account of the case to a colleague at Bristol, suppressing, naturally enough, the reference to Paradise. The Bristol physician gave it as his opinion that the symptoms were absolutely what might have been expected. "You have here, in all probability," he wrote, "the sudden breaking down of an old obstruction in the aural passage, and I should quite expect this process to be accompanied by tinnitus of a pronounced and even violent character."

But for the other experiences? As the morning wore on and drew to noon, high market, and to the utmost brightness of that summer day, all the stalls and the streets were full of rumours and of awed faces. Now from one lonely farm, now from another, men and women came and told the story of how they had listened in the early morning with thrilling hearts to the thrilling music of a bell that was like no bell ever heard before. And it seemed that many people in the town had been roused, they knew not how, from sleep; waking up, as one of them said, as if bells were ringing and the organ playing, and a choir of sweet voices singing all together: "There were such melodies and songs that my heart was full of joy."

And a little past noon some fishermen who had been out all night returned, and brought a wonderful story into the town of what they had heard in the mist; and one of them said he had seen something go by at a little distance from his boat. "It was all golden and bright," he said, "and there was glory about it." Another fisherman declared "there was a song upon the water that was like heaven."

And here I would say in parenthesis that on returning to town I sought out a very old friend of mine, a man who has devoted a lifetime to strange and esoteric studies. I thought that I had a tale that would interest him profoundly, but I found that he heard me with a good deal of indifference. And at this very point of the sailors' stories I remember saying. "Now what do you make of that? Don't you think it's extremely curious?" He replied: "I hardly think so. Possibly the sailors were lying; possibly it happened as they say. Well; that sort of thing has always been happening." I give my friend's opinion; I make no comment on it.

Let it be noted that there was something remarkable as to the manner in which the sound of the bell was heard—or supposed to be heard. There are, no doubt, mysteries in sounds as in all else; indeed, I am informed that during one of the horrible outrages that have been perpetrated on London during this autumn there was an instance of a great block of workmen's dwellings in which the only person who heard the crash of a particular bomb falling was an old deaf woman, who had been fast asleep till the moment of the explosion. This is strange enough of a sound that was entirely in the natural (and horrible) order; and so it was at Llantrisant, where the sound was either a collective auditory hallucination or a manifestation of what is conveniently, if inaccurately, called the supernatural order.

For the thrill of the bell did not reach to all ears—or hearts. Deaf Mrs. Parry heard it in her lonely cottage garden, high above the misty sea; but then, in a farm on the other or western side of Llantrisant, a little child, scarcely three years old, was the only one out of a household of ten people who heard anything. He called out in stammering baby Welsh something that sounded like *"Clychau fawr, clychau fawr"*— the great bells, the great bells—and his mother wondered what he was talking about. Of the crews of half a dozen trawlers that were swinging from side to side in the mist, not more than four men had any tale to tell. And so it was that for an hour or two the men who had heard nothing suspected his neighbour, who had heard marvels, of lying; and it was some time before the mass of evidence coming from all manners of diverse and remote quarters convinced the people that there was a true story here. A might suspect B, his neighbour, of making up a tale; but when C, from some place on the hills five miles away, and D, the fisherman on the waters, each had a like report, then it was clear that something had happened.

And even then, as they told me, the signs to be seen upon the people were stranger than the tales told by them and among them. It has struck me that many people in reading some of the phrases that I have reported will dismiss them with laughter as very poor and fantastic inventions; fishermen, they will say, do not speak of "a song like heaven" or of "a glory about it". And I dare say this would be a just enough criticism if I were reporting English fishermen; but, odd though it may be, Wales has not yet lost the last shreds of the grand manner. And let it be remembered also that in most cases such phrases are translated from another language, that is, from the Welsh.

So they come trailing, let us say, fragments of the cloud of glory in their common speech; and so, on this Saturday, they began to display, uneasily enough in many cases, their consciousness that the things that were reported were of their ancient right and former custom. The comparison is not quite fair; but conceive Hardy's old Durbeyfield suddenly waking from long slumber to find himself in a noble thirteenth-century hall, waited on by kneeling pages, smiled on by sweet ladies in silken cotehardies.

So by evening time there had come to the old people the recollection of stories that their fathers had told them as they sat round the hearth of winter nights, fifty, sixty, seventy years ago; stories of the wonderful bell of Teilo Sant, that had sailed across the glassy seas from Syon, that was called a portion of Paradise, "and the sound of its ringing was like the perpetual choir of the angels".

Such things were remembered by the old and told to the young that evening, in the streets of the town and in the deep lanes that climbed far hills. The sun went down to the mountain red with fire like a burnt offering, the sky turned violet, the sea was purple, as one told another of the wonder that had returned to the land after long ages.

V. THE ROSE OF FIRE

It was during the next nine days, counting from that Saturday early in June—the first Saturday in June, as I believe—that Llantrisant and all the regions about became possessed either by an extraordinary set of hallucinations or by a visitation of great marvels.

This is not the place to strike the balance between the two possibilities. The evidence is, no doubt, readily available; the matter is open to systematic investigation.

But this may be said: The ordinary man, in the ordinary passages of his life, accepts in the main the evidence of his senses, and is entirely right in doing so. He says that he sees a cow, that he sees a stone wall, and that the cow and the stone wall are "there". This is very well for all the practical purposes of life, but I believe that the metaphysicians are by no means so easily satisfied as to the reality of the stone wall and the cow. Perhaps they might allow that both objects are "there" in the sense that one's reflection is in a glass; there is an actuality, but is there a reality external to oneself? In any event, it is solidly agreed that, supposing a real existence, this much is certain—it is not in the least like our conception of it. The ant and the microscope will quickly convince us that we do not see things as they really are, even supposing that we see them at all. If we could "see" the real cow she would appear utterly incredible, as incredible as the things I am to relate.

Now, there is nothing that I know much more unconvincing than the stories of the red light on the sea. Several sailors, men on small coasting ships, who were working up or down the Channel on the Saturday night, spoke of "seeing" the red light, and it must be said that there is a very tolerable agreement in their tales. All make the time as between midnight of the Saturday and one o'clock on the Sunday morning. Two of those sailormen are precise as to the time of the apparition; they fix it by elaborate calculations of their own as occurring at 12.20 A.M. And the story?

A red light, a burning spark seen far away in the darkness, taken at the first moment of seeing for a signal, and probably an enemy signal. Then it approached at a tremendous speed, and one man said he took it to be the port light of some new kind of navy motor-boat which was developing a rate hitherto unheard of, a hundred or a hundred and fifty knots an hour. And then, in the third instant of the sight, it was clear that this was no earthly speed. At first a red spark in the farthest distance; then a rushing lamp; and then, as if in an incredible point of time, it swelled into a vast rose of fire that filled all the sea and all the sky and hid the stars and possessed the land. "I thought the end of the world had come," one of the sailors said.

And then, an instant more, and it was gone from them, and four of them say that there was a red spark on Chapel Head, where the old grey chapel of St. Teilo stands, high above the water, in a cleft of the limestone rocks.

And thus the sailors; and thus their tales are incredible; but *they* are not incredible. I believe that men of the highest eminence in physical science have testified to the occurrence of phenomena every whit as marvellous, to things as absolutely opposed to all natural order, as we conceive it; and it may be said that nobody minds them. "That sort of thing has always been happening," as my friend remarked to me. But the men, whether or no the fire had ever been without them, there was no doubt that it was now within them, for it burned in their eyes. They were purged as if they had passed through the Furnace of the Sages governed with Wisdom that the alchemists know. They spoke without much difficulty of what they had seen, or had seemed to see, with their eyes, but hardly at all of what their hearts had known when for a moment the glory of the fiery rose had been about them.

For some weeks afterwards they were still, as it were, amazed; almost, I would say, incredulous. If there had been nothing more than the splendid and fiery appearance, shewing and vanishing, I do believe that they themselves would have discredited their own senses and denied the truth of their own tales. And one does not dare to say whether they would not have been right. Men like Sir William Crookes and Sir Oliver Lodge are certainly to be heard with respect, and they bear witness to all manner of apparent eversions of laws which we, or most of us, consider far more deeply founded than the ancient hills. They may be justified; but in our hearts we doubt. We cannot wholly believe in inner sincerity that the solid table did rise, without mechanical reason or cause, into the air, and so defy that which we name the "law of gravitation". I know what may be said on the other side; I know that there is no true question of "law" in the case; that the law of gravitation really means just this: that I have never seen a table rising without mechanical aid, or an apple, detached from the bough, soaring to the skies instead of falling to the ground. The so-called law is just the sum of common observation and nothing more; yet I say, in our hearts we do not believe that the tables rise; much less do we believe in the rose of fire that for a moment swallowed up the skies and seas and shores of the Welsh coast last June.

And the men who saw it would have invented fairy tales to account for it, I say again, if it had not been for that which was within them.

They said, all of them, and it was certain now that they spoke the truth, that in the moment of the vision, every pain and ache and malady in their bodies had passed away. One man had been vilely drunk on venomous spirit, procured at Jobson's Hole down by the Cardiff Docks. He was horribly ill; he had crawled up from his bunk for a little fresh air; and in an instant his horrors and his deadly nausea had left him. Another man was almost desperate with the raging hammering pain of an abscess on a tooth; he says that when the red flame came near he felt as if a dull, heavy blow had fallen on his jaw, and then the pain was quite gone; he could scarcely believe that there had been any pain there.

And they all bear witness to an extraordinary exaltation of the senses. It is indescribable, this; for they cannot describe it. They are amazed, again; they do not in the least profess to know what happened; but there is no more possibility of shaking their evidence than there is a possibility of shaking the evidence of a man who says that water is wet and fire hot.

"I felt a bit queer afterwards," said one of them, "and I steadied myself by the mast, and I can't tell how I felt as I touched it. I didn't know that touching a thing like a mast could be better than a big drink when you're thirsty, or a soft pillow when you're sleepy."

I heard other instances of this state of things, as I must vaguely call it, since I do not know what else to call it. But I suppose we can all agree that to the man in average health, the average impact of the external world on his senses is a matter of indifference. The average impact; a harsh scream, the bursting of a motor tyre, any violent assault on the aural nerves will annoy him, and he may say "damn". Then, on the other hand, the man who is not "fit" will easily be annoyed and irritated by some one pushing past him in a crowd, by the ringing of a bell, by the sharp closing of a book.

But so far as I could judge from the talk of these sailors, the average impact of the external world had become to them a fountain of pleasure. Their nerves were on edge, but an edge to receive exquisite sensuous impressions. The touch of the rough mast, for example; that was a joy far greater than is the joy of fine silk to some luxurious skins; they drank water and stared as if they had been *fins gourmets* tasting an amazing wine; the creak and whine of their ship on its slow way were as exquisite as the rhythm and song of a Bach fugue to an amateur of music.

And then, within; these rough fellows have their quarrels and strifes and variances and envyings like the rest of us; but that was all over between them that had seen the rosy light; old enemies shook hands heartily, and roared with laughter as they confessed one to another what fools they had been.

"I can't say how it has happened or what has happened at all," said one, "but if you have all the world and the glory of it, how can you fight for fivepence?"

The church of Llantrisant is a typical example of a Welsh parish church, before the evil and horrible period of "restoration".

This lower world is a palace of lies, and of all foolish lies there is none more insane than a certain vague fable about the mediaeval freemasons, a fable which somehow imposed itself upon the cold intellect of Hallam the historian. The story is, in brief, that throughout the Gothic period, at any rate, the art and craft of church building were executed by wandering guilds of "freemasons", possessed of various secrets of building and adornment, which they employed wherever they went. If this nonsense were true, the Gothic of Cologne would be as the Gothic of Colne, and the Gothic of Arles like to the Gothic of Abingdon. It is so grotesquely untrue that almost every county, let alone every country, has its distinctive style in Gothic architecture. Arfon is in the west of Wales; its churches have marks and features which distinguish them from the churches in the east of Wales.

The Llantrisant church has that primitive division between nave and chancel which only very foolish people decline to recognise as equivalent to the Oriental iconostasis and as the origin of the Western rood-screen. A solid wall divided the church into two portions; in the centre was a narrow opening with a rounded arch, through which those who sat towards the middle of the church could see the small, red-carpeted altar and the three roughly shaped lancet windows above it.

The "reading pew" was on the outer side of this wall of partition, and here the rector did his service, the choir being grouped in seats about him. On the inner side were the pews of certain privileged houses of the town and district.

On the Sunday morning the people were all in their accustomed places, not without a certain exultation in their eyes, not without a certain expectation of they knew not what. The bells stopped ringing, the rector, in his old-fashioned, ample surplice, entered the reading-desk, and gave out the hymn: "My God, and is Thy table spread."

And, as the singing began, all the people who were in the pews within the wall came out of them and streamed through the archway into the nave. They took what places they could find up and down the church, and the rest of the congregation looked at them in amazement.

Nobody knew what had happened. Those whose seats were next to the aisle tried to peer into the chancel, to see what had happened or what was going on there. But somehow the light flamed so brightly from the windows above the altar, those being the only windows in the chancel, one small lancet in the south wall excepted, that no one could see anything at all.

"It was as if a veil of gold adorned with jewels was hanging there," one man said; and indeed there are a few odds and scraps of old painted glass left in the eastern lancets.

But there were few in the church who did not hear now and again voices speaking beyond the veil.

VI. OLWEN'S DREAM

The well-to-do and dignifed personages who left their pews in the chancel of Llantrisant Church and came hurrying into the nave could give no explanation of what they had done. They felt, they said, that they "had to go", and to go quickly; they were driven out, as it were, by a secret, irresistible command. But all who were present in the church that morning were amazed, though all exulted in their hearts; for they, like the sailors who saw the rose of fire on the waters, were filled with a joy that was literally ineffable, since they could not utter it or interpret it to themselves.

And they too, like the sailors, were transmuted, or the world was transmuted for them. They experienced what the doctors call a sense of *bien être*, but a *bien être* raised to the highest power. Old men felt young again, eyes that had been growing dim now saw clearly, and saw a world that was like Paradise, the same world, it is true, but a world rectified and glowing, as if an inner flame shone in all things, and behind all things.

And the difficulty in recording this state is this, that it is so rare an experience that no set language to express it is in existence. A shadow of its raptures and ecstasies is found in the highest poetry; there are phrases in ancient books telling of the Celtic saints that dimly hint at it; some of the old Italian masters of painting had known it, for the light of it shines in their skies and about the battlements of their cities that are founded on magic hills. But these are but broken hints.

It is not poetic to go to Apothecaries' Hall for similes. But for many years I kept by me an article from the *Lancet* or the *British Medical Journal*—I forget which—in which a doctor gave an account of certain experiments he had conducted with a drug called the Mescal Button, or *Anhelonium Lewinii*. He said that while under the influence of the drug he had but to shut his eyes, and immediately before him there would rise incredible Gothic cathedrals, of such majesty and splendour and glory that no heart had ever conceived. They seemed to surge from the depths to the very heights of heaven, their spires swayed amongst the clouds and the stars, they were fretted with admirable imagery. And as he gazed, he would presently become aware that all the stones were living stones, that they were quickening and palpitating, and then that they were glowing jewels, say, emeralds, sapphires, rubies, opals, but of hues that the mortal eye had never seen.

That description gives, I think, some faint notion of the nature of the transmuted world into which these people by the sea had entered, a world quickened and glorified and full of pleasures. Joy and wonder were on all faces; but the deepest joy and the greatest wonder were on the face of the rector. For he had heard through the veil the Greek word for "holy", three times repeated. And he, who had once been a horrified assistant at High Mass in a foreign church, recognised the perfume of incense that filled the place from end to end.

It was on that Sunday night that Olwen Phillips of Croeswen dreamed her wonderful dream. She was a girl of sixteen, the daughter of small farming people, and for many months she had been doomed to certain death. Consumption, which flourishes in that damp, warm climate, had laid hold of her; not only her lungs but her whole system was a mass of tuberculosis. As is common enough, she had enjoyed many fallacious brief recoveries in the early stages of the disease, but all hope had long been over, and now for the last few weeks she had seemed to rush vehemently to death. The doctor had come on the Saturday morning, bringing with him a colleague. They had both agreed that the girl's case was in its last stages. "She cannot possibly last more than a day or two," said the local doctor to her mother. He came again on the Sunday morning and found his patient perceptibly worse, and soon afterwards she sank into a heavy sleep, and her mother thought that she would never wake from it.

The girl slept in an inner room communicating with the room occupied by her father and mother. The door between was kept open, so that Mrs. Phillips could hear her daughter if she called to her in the night. And Olwen called to her mother that night, just as the dawn was breaking. It was no faint summons from a dying bed that came to the mother's ears, but a loud cry that rang through the house, a cry of great gladness. Mrs. Phillips started up from sleep in wild amazement, wondering what could have happened. And then she saw Olwen, who had not been able to rise from her bed for many weeks past, standing in the doorway in the faint light of the growing day. The girl called to her mother: "Mam! mam! It is all over. I am quite well again."

Mrs. Phillips roused her husband, and they sat up in bed staring, not knowing on earth, as they said afterwards, what had been done with the world. Here was their poor girl wasted to a shadow, lying on her death-bed, and the life sighing from her with every breath, and her voice, when she last uttered it, so weak that one had to put one's ear to her mouth. And here in a few hours she stood up before them; and even in that faint light they could see that she was changed almost beyond knowing. And, indeed, Mrs. Phillips said that for a moment or two she fancied that the Germans must have come and killed them in their sleep, and so they were all dead together. But Olwen called out again, so the mother lit a candle and got up and went tottering across the room, and there was Olwen all gay and plump again, smiling with shining eyes. Her mother led her into her own room, and set down the candle there, and felt her daughter's flesh, and burst into prayers and tears of wonder and delight, and thanksgivings, and held the girl again to be sure that she was not deceived. And then Olwen told her dream, though she thought it was not a dream.

She said she woke up in the deep darkness, and she knew the life was fast going from her. She could not move so much as a finger, she tried to cry out, but no sound came from her lips. She felt that in another instant the whole world would fall from her—her heart was full of agony. And as the last breath was passing her lips, she heard a very faint, sweet sound, like the tinkling of a silver bell. It came from far away, from over by Ty-newydd. She forgot her agony and listened, and even then, she says, she felt the swirl of the world as it came back to her. And the sound of the bell swelled and grew louder, and it thrilled all through her body, and the life was in it. And as the bell rang and trembled in her ears, a faint light touched the wall of her room and reddened, till the whole room was full of rosy fire. And then she saw standing before her bed three men in blood-coloured robes with shining faces. And one man held a golden bell in his hand. And the second man held up something shaped like the top of a table. It was like a great jewel, and it was of a blue colour, and there were rivers of silver and of gold running through it and flowing as quick streams flow, and there were pools in it as if violets had been poured out into water, and then it was green as the sea near the shore, and then it was the sky at night with all the stars shining, and then the sun and the moon came down and washed in it. And the third man held up high above this a cup that was like a rose on fire; "there was a great burning in it, and a dropping of blood in it, and a red cloud above it, and I saw a great secret. And I heard a voice that sang nine times: 'Glory and praise to the Conqueror of Death, to the Fountain of Life immortal.' Then the red light went from the wall, and it was all darkness, and the bell rang faint again by Capel Teilo, and then I got up and called to you."

The doctor came on the Monday morning with the death certificate in his pocket-book, and Olwen ran out to meet him. I have quoted his phrase in the first chapter of this record: "A kind of resurrection of the body." He made a most careful examination of the girl; he has stated that he found that every trace of disease had disappeared. He left on the Sunday morning a patient entering into the coma that precedes death, a body condemned utterly and ready for the grave. He met at the garden gate on the Monday morning a young woman in whom life sprang up like a fountain, in whose body life laughed and rejoiced as if it had been a river flowing from an unending well.

Now this is the place to ask one of those questions—there are many such—which cannot be answered. The question is as to the continuance of tradition; more especially as to the continuance of tradition among the Welsh Celts of to-day. On the one hand, such waves and storms have gone over them. The wave of the heathen Saxons went over them, then the wave of Latin mediaevalism, then the waters of Anglicanism; last of all the flood of their queer Calvinistic Methodism, half Puritan, half pagan. It may well be asked whether any memory can possibly have survived such a series of deluges. I have said that the old people of Llantrisant had their tales of the bell of Teilo Sant; but these were but vague and broken recollections. And then there is the name by which the "strangers" who were seen in the market-place were known; that is more precise. Students of the Graal legend know that the keeper of the Graal in the romances is the "King Fisherman", or the "Rich Fisherman"; students of Celtic hagiology know that it was prophesied before the birth of Dewi (or David) that he should be "a man of aquatic life", that another legend tells how a little child, destined to be a saint, was discovered on a stone in the river, how through his childhood a fish for his nourishment was found on that stone every day, while another saint, Ilar, if I remember, was expressly known as "The Fisherman". But has the memory of all this persisted in the church-going and chapel-going people of Wales at the present day? It is difficult to say. There is the affair of the Healing Cup of Nant Eos, or Tregaron Healing Cup, as it is also called. It is only a few years ago since it was shewn to a wandering harper, who treated it lightly, and then spent a wretched night, as he said, and came back penitently and was left alone with the sacred vessel to pray over it, till "his mind was at rest". That was in 1887.

Then for my part—I only know modern Wales on the surface, I am sorry to say—I remember three or four years ago speaking to my temporary landlord of certain relics of Saint Teilo, which are supposed to be in the keeping of a particular family in that country. The landlord is a very jovial, merry fellow, and I observed with some astonishment that his ordinary, easy manner was completely altered as he said, gravely, "That will be over there, up by the mountain," pointing vaguely to the north. And he changed the subject, as a Freemason changes the subject.

There the matter lies, and its appositeness to the story of Llantrisant is this: that the dream of Olwen Phillips was, in fact, the vision of the Holy Graal.

VII. The Mass of the Sangraal

"*Ffeiriadwyr Melcisidec! Ffeiriadwyr Melcisidec!*" shouted the old Calvinistic Methodist deacon with the grey beard. "Priesthood of Melchizedek! Priesthood of Melchizedek!"

And he went on:

"The Bell that is like *y glwys yr angel ym mharadwys*—the joy of the angels in Paradise—is returned; the Altar that is of a colour that no men can discern is returned, the Cup that came from Syon is returned, the ancient Offering is restored, the Three Saints have come back to the church of the *tri sant*, the Three Holy Fishermen are amongst us, and their net is full. *Gogoniant, gogoniant*—glory, glory!"

Then another Methodist began to recite in Welsh a verse from Wesley's hymn.

> God still respects Thy sacrifice,
>> Its savour sweet doth always please;
> The Offering smokes through earth and skies,
>> Diffusing life and joy and peace;
> To these Thy lower courts it comes
> And fills them with Divine perfumes.

The whole church was full, as the old books tell, of the odour of the rarest spiceries. There were lights shining within the sanctuary, through the narrow archway.

This was the beginning of the end of what befell at Llantrisant. For it was the Sunday after that night on which Olwen Phillips had been restored from death to life. There was not a single chapel of the Dissenters open in the town that day. The Methodists with their minister and their deacons and all the Nonconformists had returned on this Sunday morning to "the old hive". One would have said, a church of the Middle Ages, a church in Ireland to-day. Every seat—save those in the chancel—was full, all the aisles were full, the churchyard was full; everyone on his knees, and the old rector kneeling before the door into the holy place.

Yet they can say but very little of what was done beyond the veil. There was no attempt to perform the usual service; when the bells had stopped the old deacon raised his cry, and priest and people fell down on their knees as they thought they heard a choir within singing "Alleluya, alleluya, alleluya." And as the bells in the tower ceased ringing, there sounded the thrill of the bell from Syon, and the golden veil of sunlight fell across the door into the altar, and the heavenly voices began their melodies.

A voice like a trumpet cried from within the brightness:

Agyos, Agyos, Agyos.

And the people, as if an age-old memory stirred in them, replied:

Agyos yr Tâd, agyos yr Mab, agyos yr Yspryd Glan. Sant, sant, sant, Drindod sant vendigeid. Sanctus Arglwydd Dduw Sabaoth, Dominus Deus.

There was a voice that cried and sang from within the altar; most of the people had heard some faint echo of it in the chapels; a voice rising and falling and soaring in awful modulations that rang like the trumpet of the Last Angel. The people beat upon their breasts, the tears were like rain of the mountains on their cheeks; those that were able fell down on their faces before the glory of the veil. They said afterwards that men of the hills, twenty miles away, heard that cry and that singing, rushing upon them on the wind, and they fell down on their faces and cried, "The offering is accomplished," knowing nothing of what they said.

There were a few who saw three come out of the door of the sanctuary, and stand for a moment on the pace before the door. These three were in dyed vesture, red as blood. One stood before two, looking to the west, and he rang the bell. And they say that all the birds of the wood, and all the waters of the sea, and all the leaves of the trees, and all the winds of the high rocks uttered their voices with the ringing of the bell. And the second and the third; they turned their faces one to another. The second held up the lost altar that they once called *Sapphirus,* which was like the changing of the sea and of the sky, and like the immixture of gold and silver. And the third heaved up high over the altar a cup that was red with burning and the blood of the offering.

And the old rector cried aloud then before the entrance:

Bendigeid yr Offeren yn oes oesoedd—blessed be the Offering unto the ages of ages.

And then the Mass of the Sangraal was ended, and then began the passing out of that land of the holy persons and holy things that had returned to it after the long years. It seemed, indeed, to many that the thrilling sound of the bell was in their ears for days, even for weeks after that Sunday morning. But thenceforth neither bell nor altar nor cup was seen by any one; not openly, that is, but only in dreams by day and by night. Nor did the people see Strangers again in the market of Llantrisant, nor in the lonely places where certain persons oppressed by great affliction and sorrow had once or twice encountered them.

But that time of visitation will never be forgotten by the people. Many things happened in the nine days that have not been set down in this record—or legend. Some of them were trifling matters, though strange enough in other times. Thus a man in the town who had a fierce dog that was always kept chained up found one day that the beast had become mild and gentle.

And this is stranger: Edward Davies, of Lanafon, a farmer, was roused from sleep one night by a queer yelping and barking in his yard. He looked out of the window and saw his sheep-dog playing with a big fox; they were chasing each other by turns, rolling over and over one another, "cutting such capers as I did never see the like", as the astonished farmer put it. And some of the people said that during this season of wonder the corn shot up, and the grass thickened, and the fruit was multiplied on the trees in a very marvellous manner.

More important, it seemed, was the case of Williams, the grocer; though this may have been a purely natural deliverance. Mr. Williams was to marry his daughter Mary to a smart young fellow from Carmarthen, and he was in great distress over it. Not over the marriage itself, but because things had been going very badly with him for some time, and he could not see his way to giving anything like the wedding entertainment that would be expected of him. The wedding was to be on the Saturday—that was the day on which the lawyer, Lewis Prothero, and the farmer, Philip James, were reconciled—and this John Williams, without money or credit, could not think how shame would not be on him for the meagreness and poverty of the wedding feast. And then on the Tuesday came a letter from his brother, David Williams, Australia, from whom he had not heard for fifteen years. And David, it seemed, had been making a great deal of money, and was a bachelor, and here was with his letter a paper good for a thousand pounds: "You may as well enjoy it now as wait till I am dead." This was enough, indeed, one might say; but hardly an hour after the letter had come the lady from the big house (Plas Mawr) drove up in all her grandeur, and went into the shop and said, "Mr. Williams, your daughter Mary has always been a very good girl, and my husband and I feel that we must give her some little thing on her wedding, and we hope she'll be very happy." It was a gold watch worth fifteen pounds. And after, Lady Watcyn advances the old doctor with a dozen of port, forty years upon it, and a long sermon on how to decant it. And the old rector's old wife brings to the beautiful dark girl two yards of creamy lace, like an enchantment, for her wedding veil, and tells Mary how she wore it for her own wedding fifty years ago; and the squire, Sir Watcyn, as if his wife had not been already with a fine gift, calls from his horse, and brings out Williams and barks like a dog at him, "Goin' to have a weddin', eh, Williams? Can't have a weddin' without champagne, y' know; wouldn't be legal, don't y' know. So look out for a couple of cases." So Williams tells the story of the gifts; and certainly there was never so famous a wedding in Llantrisant before.

All this, of course, may have been altogether in the natural order; the "glow", as they call it, seems more difficult to explain. For they say that all through the nine days, and indeed after the time had ended, there never was a man weary or sick at heart in Llantrisant, or in the country round it. For if a man felt that his work of the body or the mind was going to be too much for his strength, then there would come to him of a sudden a warm glow and a thrilling all over him, and he felt as strong as a giant, and happier than he had ever been in his life before, so that lawyer and hedger each rejoiced in the task that was before him, as if it were sport and play.

And, much more wonderful than this or any other wonders was forgiveness, with love to follow it. There were meetings of old enemies in the market-place and in the street that made the people lift up their hands and declare that it was as if one walked the miraculous streets of Syon.

But as to the "phenomena", the occurrences for which, in ordinary talk, we should reserve the word "miraculous"? Well, what do we know? The question that I have already stated comes up again, as to the possible survival of old tradition in a kind of dormant, or torpid, semi-conscious state. In other words, did the people "see" and "hear" what they expected to see and hear? This point, or one similar to it, occurred in a debate between Andrew Lang and Anatole France as to the visions of Joan of Arc. M. France stated that when Joan saw St. Michael, she saw the traditional archangel of the religious art of her day, but to the best of my belief Andrew Lang proved that the vision-ary figure Joan described was not in the least like the fifteenth-century conception of St. Michael. So, in the case of Llantrisant, I have stated that there was a sort of tradition about the holy bell of Teilo Sant; and it is, of course, barely possible that some vague notion of the Graal Cup may have reached even Welsh country folks through Tennyson's *Idylls*. But so far I see no reason to suppose that these people had ever heard of the portable altar (called Sapphirus in William of Malmesbury) or of its changing colours "that no man could discern".

And then there are the other questions of the distinction between hallucination and vision, of the average duration of one and the other, and of the possibility of collective hallucination. If a number of people all see (or think they see) the same appearances, can this be merely hallucination? I believe there is a leading case on the matter, which concerns a number of people seeing the same appearance on a church wall in Ireland; but there is, of course, this difficulty, that one may be hallucinated and communicate his impression to the others, telepathically.

But at the last, what do we know?

The Little Nations

There is a certain type of English cleric who may be regarded as a translation—if one may use the term—of the now extinct and forgotten French *abbé*. The two types are, of course, very different, just as a French word is in reality utterly different in its connotations from the English word which the dictionary supplies as its exact equivalent. Still, in certain loose but practical sense, the one word does translate the other, and so the English clergyman of whom I am thinking is a very rough translation of the French *abbé* of the old régime.

The two varieties of the cleric have this one mark in common: that neither is at heart a cleric at all.

The French *abbé* approximated to the French layman of his time; he was a Parisian in canonicals. And so with us, we have or had many ecclesiastics whose chief interests are not ecclesiastical. There was Dr. King, for example, ordained on his Fellowship; he really lived for Roman antiquities and Gnostic gems. I had an uncle, vicar of Llantrisant, who was sedulous in parochial visits—in that part of his parish where there were two or three limestone quarries. To these, after somewhat perfunctory ghostly work, he would carry his leather wallet and his hammers, and be happy; for he was a geologist rather than a priest.

I knew a fine specimen of the English *abbé* when I was at school at Herford. This was Dr. Duthoit, Prebendary of *Consumpta per Sabulum* in Herford Cathedral, Rector of St. Owen's, bookworm, and, chiefly, rose-grower. He was a middle-aged man when I was a little boy; but he suffered me to walk with him in his garden sloping down to the Wye, near the pleasaunce of the Vicars Choral, reciting sometimes the poems of Traherne, which he had in manuscript, sometimes alluding darkly to the secrets contained in *Lumen de Lumine* but for the most part demonstrating his progress in the art of growing a coal-black rose. This was the true work of his life, and nearly forty years ago he could shew blooms whose copper or crimson tints were very near to utter darkness. I believe that his ideal was never attained in absolute perfection; and perhaps the perfect end and attaining of desire do not bring happiness here below.

After 1880 Prebendary Duthoit and I rarely saw each other and rarely wrote. He was at rest among his roses by the quiet Wye and I was dashed to and fro in wilder waters. But each contrived at long intervals to let the other know that he was alive, and so I was not altogether surprised to see the Prebendary's queer, niggly writing on an envelope a week or two ago. He said he had heard a good deal of talk about . . . well, about a popular legend with which I am understood to be in some way concerned, and he thought that an odd experience of his might possibly interest me. I do not give the text of his letter chiefly because it is full of Latin phrases which I might be called upon to translate.

But the matter is as follows: On the 4th of August, the day of the service at St. Paul's, Dr. Duthoit was walking up and down and about that pleasant garden on the slopes of the Wye. Just above the water his gardener had prepared, under direction and instruction, a plot of ground in a very special manner. I do not gather the precise purpose of the operation; but it seems that the soil had been made very fine and level over a superficies of about ten yards. To this place the Prebendary walked slowly and reflectively, wishing to assure himself that his orders had been exactly carried out. The plot had been perfectly level the night before, but Dr. Duthoit wanted to be more than sure about it. But to his extreme annoyance, when he turned by the fig-tree, he saw that the plot was very far from even. He is an old man, but his sight is good, and at a distance of several yards he could discern quite plainly that there had been mischief

The chosen plot was in a disgraceful state. At first the Prebendary thought that the Custos's sandy tom-cat had scaled the wire entanglement on top of the dividing wall; then he felt inclined to set the ruin down to Scamp, the Bishop's wire-haired fox-terrier. And then coming close, he put on his spectacles, and wondered what had been at work.

For the level which had been so carefully established was all undone. At first the Doctor thought it was the mischief of some random, dancing beast, this confusion of hills and valleys which had taken the

place of the billiard-table surface of the night before. And then it reminded him of certain raised maps which he had seen in Diocesan
Training Schools. And then it reminded him, more distinctly, of a sort
of picture map which had illustrated his morning paper a day or two
before. And then he wondered violently, because he saw that somebody had with infinite pains made this garden plot of his into an exact
model of the Gallipoli Peninsula.

It was all so ingenious and perfect that the old clergyman held his
wrath for a moment, and peered into this miniature intricacy of peaks
and steeps and gullies and valleys. He had scarcely gathered himself together to wonder who had had the ingenious impudence for the mischief, when amazement once more seized him. For he saw now,
stooping down, that this garden Gallipoli was swarming with life.
There were hosts on it and about it; and then Dr. Duthoit forgot all
about what we call the realities and facts of life, forgot that this sort of
thing doesn't happen, and gasped and watched what was happening.

He writes that, queerly enough, he lost his sense of size. He was
not a Gulliver looking down on Lilliput; the mountains ten inches high
became to him actual and lofty summits; the tiny precipices were tremendous. And the red ants swarmed to attack the black ants who held
the heights with savage and desperate fury. He says that he panted with
excitement as he watched the courage of the attack and defence, the
savagery of the "hand-to-hand" fighting. Black and red fell by myriads;
and the Doctor has persuaded himself that he observed amazing instances of individual heroism. One particular range seemed the especial aim of the red forces; and they swarmed up victorious and held it
for awhile, and then retreated; the Doctor could not quite make out
the reason of this.

He started violently when his man called to him. Roberts said he
had called for five minutes without getting an answer, and that the
Dean was in a hurry, with only five minutes to spare. So the Prebendary went into the house in a kind of dwam, as the Scots put it, and
had no notion of what the Dean had to say. And when he got back to
the garden, he found the gardener smoothing plot with a long rake,
and raking in lot of dead ants with the mould. The gardener said it was
boys; but the Doctor talked in such a way to the Custos that night that

the Custos, reading his paper a fortnight later, began to think that the old Prebendary was a prophet.

And the Prebendary? He ends his letter: "Quod superius est sicut quod inferius (that which is above is as that which is below) as the Smaragdine Tablet of Hermes Trismegistus testifies; and it is my belief that this is a world-battle in a sense which we do not appreciate. There have been some who have held that the earthly conflict is but a reflection of the war in heaven; what if it be reflected infinitely, if it penetrate to the uttermost depths of creation? And if a speck of dust be a cosmos—a universe of revolving worlds? There may be battle between creatures that no microscope shall ever discover."

Out of the Earth

There was some sort of confused complaint during last August of the ill-behaviour of the children at certain Welsh watering-places. Such reports and vague rumours are most difficult to trace to their heads and fountains; none has better reason to know that than myself. I need not go over the old ground here, but I am afraid that many people are wishing by this time that they had never heard my name; again, a considerable number of estimable persons are concerning themselves gloomily enough, from my point of view, with my everlasting welfare. They write me letters, some in kindly remonstrance, begging me not to deprive poor, sick-hearted souls of what little comfort they possess amidst their sorrows. Others send me tracts and pink leaflets with allusions to "the daughter of a well-known canon"; others again are violently and anonymously abusive. And then in open print, in fair book-form, Mr. Begbie has dealt with me righteously but harshly, as I cannot but think.

Yet, it was all so entirely innocent, nay casual, on my part. A poor linnet of prose, I did but perform my indifferent piping in the *Evening News* because I wanted to do so, because I felt that the story of "The Bowmen" ought to be told. An inventor of fantasies is a poor creature, heaven knows, when all the world is at war; but I thought that no harm would be done, at any rate, if I bore witness, after the fashion of the fantastic craft, to my belief in the heroic glory of the English host who went back from Mons fighting and triumphing.

And then, somehow or other, it was as if I had touched a button and set in action a terrific, complicated mechanism of rumours that pretended to be sworn truth, of gossip that posed as evidence, of wild tarradiddles that good men most firmly believed. The supposed testimony of that "daughter of a well-known canon" took parish magazines by storm, and equally enjoyed the faith of dissenting divines.

The "daughter" denied all knowledge of the matter, but people still quoted her supposed sure word; and the issues were confused with tales, probably true, of painful hallucinations and deliriums of our retreating soldiers, men fatigued and shattered to the very verge of death. It all became worse than the Russian myths, and as in the fable of the Russians, it seemed impossible to follow the streams of delusion to their fountain-head—or heads. Who was it who said that "Miss M. knew two officers who, etc., etc."? I suppose we shall never know his lying, deluding name.

And so, I dare say, it will be with this strange affair of the troublesome children of the Welsh seaside town, or rather of a group of small towns and villages lying within a certain section or zone, which I am not going to indicate more precisely than I can help, since I love that country, and my recent experience with "The Bowmen" have taught me that no tale is too idle to be believed. And, of course, to begin with, nobody knew how this odd and malicious piece of gossip originated. So far as I know, it was more akin to the Russian myth than to the tale of "The Angels of Mons". That is, rumour preceded print; the thing was talked of here and there and passed from letter to letter long before the papers were aware of its existence. And—here it resembles rather the Mons affair—London and Manchester, Leeds and Birmingham were muttering vague unpleasant things while the little villages concerned basked innocently in the sunshine of an unusual prosperity.

In this last circumstance, as some believe, is to be sought the root of the whole matter. It is well known that certain East Coast towns suffered from the dread of air-raids, and that a good many of their usual visitors went westward for the first time. So there is a theory that the East Coast was mean enough to circulate reports against the West Coast out of pure malice and envy. It may be so; I do not pretend to know. But here is a personal experience, such as it is, which illustrated the way in which the rumour was circulated. I was lunching one day at my Fleet Street tavern—this was early in July—and a friend of mine, a solicitor, of Serjeants' Inn, came in and sat at the same table. We began to talk of holidays and my friend Eddis asked me where I was going. "To the same old place," I said. "Manavon. You know we always go there." "Are you really?" said the lawyer; "I thought that coast had gone off a lot. My wife has a friend who's heard that it's not at all that it was."

I was astonished to hear this, not seeing how a little village like Manavon could have "gone off". I had known it for ten years as having accommodation for about twenty visitors, and I could not believe that rows of lodging houses had sprung up since the August of 1914. Still I put the question to Eddis: "Trippers?" I asked, knowing firstly that trippers hate the solitudes of the country and the sea; secondly, that there are no industrial towns within cheap and easy distance, and thirdly, that the railways were issuing no excursion tickets during the war.

"No, not exactly trippers," the lawyer replied. "But my wife's friend knows a clergyman who says that the beach at Tremaen is not at all pleasant now, and Tremaen's only a few miles from Manavon, isn't it?"

"In what way not pleasant?" I carried on my examination. "Pierrots and shows, and that sort of thing?" I felt that it could not be so, for the solemn rocks of Tremaen would have turned the liveliest Pierrot to stone. He would have frozen into a crag on the beach, and the seagulls would carry away his song and make it a lament by lonely, booming caverns that look on Avalon. Eddis said he had heard nothing about showmen; but he understood that since the war the children of the whole district had gone quite out of hand.

"Bad language, you know," he said, "and all that sort of thing, worse than London slum children. One doesn't want one's wife and children to hear foul talk at any time, much less on their holiday. And they say that Castell Coch is quite impossible; no decent woman would be seen there!"

I said: "Really, that's a great pity," and changed the subject. But I could not make it out at all. I knew Castell Coch well—a little bay bastioned by dunes and red sandstone cliffs, rich with greenery. A stream of cold water runs down there to the sea; there is the ruined Norman Castle, the ancient church and the scattered village; it is altogether a place of peace and quiet and great beauty. The people there, children and grown-ups alike, were not merely decent but courteous folk: if one thanked a child for opening a gate, there would come the inevitable response: "And welcome kindly, sir." I could not make it out at all. I didn't believe the lawyer's tales; for the life of me I could not see what he could be driving at. And, for the avoidance of all unnecessary mystery, I may as well say that my wife and child and myself went down to Manavon last August and had a most delightful holiday. At the time we were certainly conscious of no annoyance or unpleasantness of any kind. Afterwards, I confess, I heard a story that puzzled and still puzzles me, and this story, if it be received, might give its own interpretation to one or two circumstances which seemed in themselves quite insignificant.

But all through July I came upon traces of evil rumours affecting this most gracious corner of the earth. Some of these rumours were repetitions of Eddis's gossip; others amplified his vague story and made it more definite. Of course, no first-hand evidence was available. There never is any first-hand evidence in these cases. But A knew B who had heard from C that her second cousin's little girl had been set upon and beaten by a pack of young Welsh savages. Then people quoted "a doctor in large practice in a well-known town in the Midlands", to the effect that Tremaen was a sink of juvenile depravity. They said that a responsible medical man's evidence was final and convincing; but they didn't bother to find out who the doctor was, or whether there was any doctor at all—or any doctor relevant to the issue. Then the thing began to get into the papers in a sort of oblique, by-the-way sort of manner. People cited the case of these imaginary bad children in support of their educational views. One side said that "these unfortunate little ones" would have been quite well-behaved if they had had no education at all; the opposition declared that continuation schools would speedily reform them and make them into admirable citizens. Then the poor Arfonshire children seemed to become involved in quarrels about Welsh Disestablishment and in the question of the miners; and all the while they were going about behaving politely and admirably as they always do behave. I knew all the time that it was all nonsense, but I couldn't understand in the least what it meant, or who was pulling the wires of rumour, or their purpose in so pulling. I began to wonder whether the pressure and anxiety and suspense of a terrible war had unhinged the public mind, so that it was ready to believe any fable, to debate the reasons for happenings which had never happened. At last, quite incredible things began to be whispered: visitors' children had not only been beaten, they had been tortured; a little boy had been found impaled on a stake in a lonely field near Manavon; another child had been lured to destruction over the cliffs at Castell Coch. A London paper sent a good man down quietly to Arfon to in-

vestigate. He was away for a week, and at the end of that period returned to his office and in his own phrase, "threw the whole story
down". There was not a word of truth, he said, in any of these rumours; no vestige of a foundation for the mildest forms of all this gossip. He had never seen such a beautiful country; he had never met
pleasanter men, women or children; there was not a single case of anyone having been annoyed or troubled in any sort or fashion.

Yet all the while the story grew, and grew more monstrous and incredible. I was too much occupied in watching the progress of my own
mythological monster to pay much attention. The Town Clerk of
Tremaen, to which the legend had at length penetrated, wrote a brief
letter to the press indignantly denying that there was the slightest
foundation for "the unsavoury rumours" which, he understood, were
being circulated; and about this time we went down to Manavon and,
as I say, enjoyed ourselves extremely. The weather was perfect: blues
of paradise in the skies, the seas all a shimmering wonder, olive greens
and emeralds, rich purples, glassy sapphires changing by the rocks; far
away a haze of magic lights and colours at the meeting of sea and sky.
Work and anxiety had harried me; I found nothing better than to rest
on the thymy banks by the shore, finding an infinite balm and refreshment in the great sea before me, in the tiny flowers beside me. Or
we would rest all the summer afternoon on a "shelf" high on the grey
cliffs and watch the tide creaming and surging about the rocks, and listen to it booming in the hollows and caverns below. Afterwards, as I
say, there were one or two things that struck cold. But at the time
those were nothing. You see a man in an odd white hat pass by and
think little or nothing about it. Afterwards, when you hear that a man
wearing just such a hat had committed murder in the next street five
minutes before, then you find in that hat a certain interest and significance. "Funny children," was the phrase my little boy used; and I began to think they were "funny" indeed.

If there be a key at all to this queer business, I think it is to be
found in a talk I had not long ago with a friend of mine named Morgan. He is a Welshman and a dreamer, and some people say he is like a
child who has grown up and yet has not grown up like other children
of men. Though I did not know it, while I was at Manavon, he was
spending his holiday time at Castell Coch. He was a lonely man and he

liked lonely places, and when we met in the autumn he told me how, day after day, he would carry his bread and cheese and beer in a basket to a remote headland on that coast known as the Old Camp. Here, far above the waters, are solemn, mighty walls, turf-grown; circumvallations rounded and smooth with the passing of many thousand years. At one end of this most ancient place there is a tumulus, a tower of observation, perhaps, and underneath it slinks the green, deceiving ditch that seems to wind into the heart of the camp, but in reality rushes down to sheer rock and a precipice over the waters.

Here came Morgan daily, as he said, to dream of Avalon, to purge himself from the fuming corruption of the streets.

And so, as he told me, it was with singular horror that one afternoon as he dozed and dreamed and opened his eyes now and again to watch the miracle and magic of the sea, as he listened to the myriad murmurs of the waves, his meditation was broken by a sudden burst of horrible raucous cries—and the cries of children, too, but children of the lowest type. Morgan says that the very tones made him shudder— "They were to the ear what slime is to the touch," and then the words: every foulness, every filthy abomination of speech; blasphemies that struck like blows at the sky, that sank down into the pure, shining depths, defiling them! He was amazed. He peered over the green wall of the fort, and there in the ditch he saw a swarm of noisome children, horrible little stunted creatures with old men's faces, with bloated faces, with little sunken eyes, with leering eyes. It was worse than uncovering a brood of snakes or a nest of worms.

No; he would not describe what they were about. "Read about Belgium," said Morgan, "and think they couldn't have been more than five or six years old." There was no infamy, he said, that they did not perpetrate; they spared no horror of cruelty. "I saw blood running in streams, as they shrieked with laughter, but I could not find the mark of it on the grass afterwards."

Morgan said he watched them and could not utter a word; it was as if a hand held his mouth tight. But at last he found his voice and shrieked at them, and they burst into a yell of obscene laughter and shrieked back at him, and scattered out of sight. He could not trace them; he supposes that they hid in the deep bracken behind the Old Camp.

"Sometimes I can't understand my landlord at Castell Coch," Morgan went on. "He's the village postmaster and has a little farm of his own—a decent, pleasant, ordinary sort of chap. But now and again he will talk oddly. I was telling him about these beastly children and wondering who they could be when he broke into Welsh, something like 'the battle that is for age unto ages; and the People take delight in it'."

So far Morgan, and it was evident that he did not understand at all. But this strange tale of his brought back an odd circumstance or two that I recollected: a matter of our little boy straying away more than once, and getting lost among the sand dunes and coming back screaming, evidently frightened horribly, and babbling about "funny children". We took no notice; did not trouble, I think, to look whether there were any children wandering about the dunes or not. We were accustomed to his small imaginations.

But after hearing Morgan's story I was interested and I wrote an account of the matter to my friend, old Doctor Duthoit, of Hereford. And he:

"They were only visible, only audible to children and the childlike. Hence the explanation of what puzzled you at first; the rumours, how did they arise? They arose from nursery gossip, from scraps and odds and ends of half-articulate children's talk of horrors that they didn't understand, of words that shamed their nurses and their mothers.

"These little people of the earth rise up and rejoice in these times of ours. For they are glad, as the Welshman said, when they know that men follow their ways."

The Men from Troy

"Creep? And crawl? I believe you. I should never have said it could be done unless I'd seen it. I tell you those little men are fair marvels. Now, suppose you were on sentry-go at night, and standing there as it might be by that geranium bed, and you had your eyes open pretty wide, well knowing, as you would know, that it was as much as your life was worth to be caught winking. Well, I tell you, sir, that one of those little men if he set out to do it, moon or no moon, he'd creep out of that shrubbery and he'd crawl round to your back, and give an imitation of a shadow if you looked round. And then there'd be a bit of fancy work, a shriek owl letting off within an inch of your ear, and when you'd done wondering your throat'ld be cut and you'ld be dead. They have a nasty kind of knives, cookeries they call them. And quite right."

The wounded man was giving the chaplain his impressions of the war. He had lost an arm in the Gallipoli fighting, and had been invalided home. The two were sitting in deck-chairs in the hospital garden on a sunny afternoon. And between his bursts of information the soldier sucked gratefully at his pipe, drawing in rich fumes of shag tobacco. And then he looked out over shrubs and flowers on a deep, blue sea.

The chaplain had been trying a little Kipling on the soldier. He had experimented with "The Drums of the Fore and Aft", and he observed that the man listened with decent politeness and attention, as indeed he would have listened to Ezekiel's Vision of the Chariot. But the holy man noted that the true gleam of interest was lacking in the invalid's eye, till the Gurkhas were mentioned. He beamed then, and spoke with enthusiasm of the wiles and crafts and deadly works of the little hillmen—"have they got a touch of the Jap in them, do you think, sir? They look a bit like it; not like the other Indian troop. A different style of thing altogether."

So the soldier told of the devices of the men with the cookeries (or *kukris* as pedants spell the word); how it was impossible to hear them or to see them as they lurked in shadows or slid like snakes upon the ground, how they could throw those curving knives of theirs with sure deadly aim.

"'They've got ways that seem a bit queer to us," he said; "but they're wonderful fighting men; there's no denying it."

And, having summed up the Gurkhas, the soldier lapsed into sweet enjoyment of security and summer air, blue seas and blue skies, and shag tobacco.

"But there's no doubt," he went on, after a pause, "that the British Army's a wonderful body of men altogether. The Kaiser made a bit of a mistake when he called it contemptible, it seems to me. Look at the Australians and New Zealanders and Canadians what they've done, and the Indians too, and those Gurkhas I was telling you about. I don't know that there's ever been an army like it for real hard fighting."

Now a great white cloud, like a mighty galleon, came sailing up over the sky from the south-west and passed across the sun. And beneath, the sea changed from fairy olive-garths and emerald waters to a deep violet blue. The soldier blinked as he watched the change.

"And we've got other men," he began anew, "that you don't hear much about in the papers. There's lots of odd corners in the British Empire that hardly anyone does know anything about, and the best of it is they're all full of first-rate fighting men. The fact is we've the knack of training them black or white, or yellow or mixed; it don't matter. I've known niggers from I don't know where or which way that were fine soldiers."

The chaplain allowed the soldier to run on, acting on the pastoral direction of George Herbert as to the wisdom and kindness of letting a body talk.

"And there's many people that think a nigger and an Indian's the same thing. Of course that's nonsense. Some of them are dark enough, but plenty are no darker than many a Welshman from the hills that I've seen, and now and then you will see them as white as you or me. There was that lot I came across by Teddy Bear." This was said for jocosely for Sid-ul-Bahr.

"They were the queerest I've ever touched, and I do believe the finest fighters. It's odd that dark patch over there on the sea reminding me of them."

"Patch on the sea?" said the chaplain. 'What patch? Oh, that purple bit over there. Yes, I see. Fine colour. But what has that got to do with our fellows at Gallipoli, or these Indians or whatever they were?"

"Well, it's like this. 'Struck the wine-dark sea with our oars,' their sergeant, or whatever they call him, says to me, and a minute or two ago when that cloud came over and the sea got dark that brought that man and his queer way of talking back to my mind. So it is, I said to myself, and I've drunk wine just that colour at Marseilles down in the View Port, and not bad drink either if you get enough of it."

The chaplain was no longer the patient listener. He started as a terrier starts when he suspects rats at hand, and he said:

"What did the native call the sea?"

"The wine-dark sea, as I told you, sir—just his silly way of talking. You know, a lot of them natives can talk English of a sort, pidgin English and all sorts of funny patter, but you can make out what they mean. This native sergeant he had a sort of lingo that he thought was English all right, and I could understand what he was driving at more or less, as you may say. I liked to listen to him when he got to his swear-words. I never heard the like. 'By Harris!' he'd say, as if he were talking of a Welshman, and then it would be 'By cloud-gathering Zoos', and 'rosy-fingered dawn child of the morn' and I don't know what else. He could curse. He was worse than old 'Damn-my-blanky-guts' in the Artillery."

The chaplain gasped. And he stared very straight at the soldier, having seen, as the soldier's friend might have put it, many cities of men. He knew, too, that the best of soldiers are not always the bond slaves of truth.

"And I tell you what," the wounded man began anew, "those Maoris are hot stuff. I've seen them in a tight place—"

"Look here," said the chaplain, "never mind about the Maoris just now. I want to hear about the other lot. They seem interesting. 'By Harris!' you say their sergeant swore. Wasn't it more like 'Ares'?" and he gave the vowels the broad "Continental" value.

"Now you mention it, that was more the way of it. A fine, tall man he was, too, with yellow hair, as English as English to look at, and a straight nose."

"How did you come across him?"

"It was like this. It was a darkish, cloudy sort of night. We'd captured a ridge the morning before, and we'd dug in. The word was

'Look out'; we knew the Turks—there's fighters for you—would have a good shot to get the ridge back again. A cloudy night it was, and there was a sort of white mist rising, and now and again there'd be a pale sort of light from what was left of the moon, coming out from behind a cloud. I won't deny that I wasn't too comfortable; I wasn't easy about our supports, and then in that roasting sort of country it came over quite chilly, and I shivered a bit and looked behind me.

"Well, then I was all right, and I saw we were all right and no mistake. There were the supports and the reserve right down the slope of the hill and below in the valley; thousands of them. It was misty, as I said, and I couldn't make things out very clear, but so far as I could see these fellows were all in white, something like what the Moors wear. That struck me as funny, but I know we have to be pleasant to some of these tribesmen and let them have a lot of their own way.

"And then, when I turned round, one of them, the man I told you about, that is, was by me in the trench, and we started to chat. He had his spear in his hand and his short sword by his side, and he carried his shield on his arm. A wonderful bit of work that shield was, covered with all sons of queer figures; regular native work, that takes about a hundred years to finish. They don't care, they've plenty of time and nothing to do. There was a man with thunderbolts in his hand sitting on a throne, and a naked woman coming out of the sea and a little chap hammering away like a blacksmith, and a fellow with the sun behind him shooting with a bow and arrows; all of them his native gods, I suppose. He was a savage man, of course, but a fine man and a good man, I believe."

"Did you make out the name of the tribe?" said the chaplain, speaking with a sort of desperate calm.

"Galeenies I think, he said they were."

"Not Hellenes?"

"That was it. I see you've come across them yourself, sir."

"In a sort of way. Did the sergeant say where they came from?"

"Well, you know the way those fellows talk, a sort of flowery way of putting it that's difficult to make out. They're straight men, very likely, but they don't seem as if they could give a straight answer to a straight question. He said, he and his pals were heroes—and by gum! he was right, though it isn't our way to talk like that—and they came from happy fields and the houses of the immortals, and the meadows of Arundel [the chaplain reads "asphodel" for "Arundel"], and a lot of stuff like that; I don't think they mean any harm by it. He said he and his people had fought some time ago not far from where we were. Ilion he said the place was.

"Still, all that don't matter. About two o'clock in the morning the Turks tried to rush us; tens of thousands of them. It looked ugly for a minute or two.

"Then my pal got up and he shouted and sang out, and he let off one of his worst. There was something like 'Now, O Pollo, lord of the far-shining bow', and 'drive their souls squeaking like bats down to Hades'—and I knew quite well what he meant by that word, though I daresay he flattered himself I didn't. And then he and his men let off a howl that fairly scared the life out of me.

"Well, there it was. They poured over our trench like a big white wave, and off they go straight for the Turks. Now, look here, sir; this is straight. I knew these native chaps were on our side. I knew they'd made it all right for us; but I tell you I went cold as death.

"I don't know what it was. It may have been that frightful yell those natives let off. It may have been their way of fighting, and you can believe me or not as you like, but as sure as I'm here I saw those long spears of theirs go like lightning flashes; I mean it. And I've seen men draw their swords many a time; but I'll take my oath to this: I've never seen before hell-fire coming out of a scabbard. But I see it then in Gallipoli.

"But I believe what frightened me was the fright of the Turks, and you know they are difficult people to frighten. They screamed out 'Ginny! Ginny!'—which is queer enough, when you come to think of it—and then, poor fellows, there were no Turks. They were gone; and I knew I was as white as paper. But it was like flaming, burning fire eating them up alive.

"What makes me sorry is that in the confusion of it all I couldn't make out what happened to my pal and his lot; the mist came on very thick, and I lost sight of them."

"But, look here," began the chaplain. "Do you mean—"

And then the nurse came and smiled and beckoned the soldier in-doors.

Munitions of War

There was a thick fog, acrid and abominable, all over London when I set out for the West. And at the heart of the fog, as it were, was the shudder of the hard frost that made one think of those winters in Dickens that had seemed to have become fabulous. It was a day on which to hear in dreams the iron ring of the horses' hoofs on the Great North Road, to meditate on the old inns with blazing fires, the coach going onward into the darkness, into a frozen world.

A few miles out of London the fog lifted. The horizon was still vague in a purple mist of cold, but the sun shone brilliantly from a pale clear sky of blue, and all the earth was a magic of whiteness: white fields stretched to that dim violet mist far away, white hedges divided them, and the trees were all snowy white with the winter blossom of the frost. The train had been delayed a little by the thick fog about London; now it was rushing at a tremendous speed through this strange white world.

My business with the famous town in the West was to attempt to make some picture of it as it faced the stress of war, to find out whether it prospered or not. From what I had seen in other large towns, I expected to find it all of a bustle on the Saturday, its shops busy, its streets thronged and massed with people. Therefore, it was with no small astonishment that I found the atmosphere of Westpool wholly different from anything I had observed at Sheffield or Birmingham. Hardly anybody seemed to leave the train at the big station, and the broad road into the town wore a shy, barred-up air; it reminded one somewhat of the streets by which the traveller passes into forgotten places, little villages that once were great cities. I remember how in the town of my birth, Caerleon-on-Usk, the doctor's wife would leave the fire and run to the window if a step sounded in the main street outside; and strangely I was reminded of this as I walked from the Westpool station. Save for one thing: at intervals there were silent parties huddled together as if for help and comfort, and all making for the outskirts of the city.

There is a fair quarter of an hour's walk between Westpool station and the centre of the town. And here I would say that though West-pool is one of the biggest and busiest cities in England, it is also, in my judgment, one of the most beautiful. Not only on account of the ancient timbered houses that still overhang many of its narrower streets, not only because of its glorious churches and noble old traditions of splendour—I am known to be weak and partial where such things are concerned—but rather because of its site. For through the very heart of the great town a narrow, deep river runs, full of tall ships, bordered by bustling quays; and so you can often look over your garden wall and see a cluster of masts, and the shaking out of sails for a fair wind. And this bringing of deep-sea business into the middle of the dusty streets has always seemed to me an enchantment; there is something of Sind-bad and Basra and Bagdad and the Nights in it. But this is not all the delight of Westpool; from the very quays of the river the town rushes up to great heights, with streets so steep that often they are flights of steps as in St. Peter Port, and ladder-like ascents. And as I came to Middle Quay in Westpool that winter day, the sun hovered over the violet mists, and the windows of the houses on the heights flamed and flashed red, vehement fires.

But the slight astonishment with which I had noted the shuttered and dismal aspect of the station road now became bewilderment. Middle Quay is the heart of Westpool, and all its business. I had always seen it swarm like an anthill. There were scarcely half a dozen people there on Saturday afternoon; and they seemed to be hurrying away. The Vintry and the Little Vintry, those famous streets, were deserted. I saw in a moment that I had come on a fool's errand: in Westpool as-suredly there was no hurry or rush of war-business, no swarm of eager shoppers for me to describe. I had an introduction to a well-known Westpool man. "Oh, no," he said, "we are very slack in Westpool. We are doing hardly anything. There's an aëroplane factory out at Oldham, and they're making high explosives by Portdown, but that doesn't af-fect us. Things are quiet, very quiet." I suggested that they might brighten up a little at night. "No," he said, "it really wouldn't be worth your while to stay on; you wouldn't find anything to write about, I assure you."

I was not satisfied. I went out and about the desolate streets of the great city; I made enquiries at random, and always heard the same story—"Things were very slack." And I began to receive an extraordinary impression: that the few I met were frightened, and were making the best of their way, either out of the town, or to the safety of their own bolted doors and barred shutters. It was only the very special mention of a friendly commercial traveller of my acquaintance that got me a room for the night at the Pineapple on Middle Quay, overlooking the river. The landlord assented with difficulty, after praising the express to town. "It's a noisy place, this," he said, "if you're not used to it." I looked at him. It was as quiet as if we were in the heart of the forest or the desert. "You see," he said, "we don't do much in munitions, but there's a lot of night transport for the docks at Portdown. You know those climbing motors that they use in the Army, caterpillars or whatever they call them. We get a lot of them through Westpool; we get all sorts of heavy stuff, and I expect they'll wake you at night. I wouldn't go to the window, if I were you, if you do wake up. They don't like anybody peering about."

And I woke up in the dead of night. There was a thundering and a rumbling and a trembling of the earth such as I had never heard. And shouting too; and rolling oaths that sounded like judgment. I got up and drew the blind a little aside, in spite of the landlord's warning, and there was that desolate Middle Quay swarming with men, and the river full of great ships, faint and huge in the frosty mist, and sailing-ships too. Men were rolling casks by the hundred down to the ships. "Hurry up, you lazy lubbers, you damned sons of guns, damn ye!" bellowed a huge voice. "Shall the King's Majesty lack powder?" "No, by God, he shall not!" roared the answer. "I rolled it aboard for old King George, and young King George shall be none the worse for me."

"And who the devil are you to speak so bold?"

"Blast ye, bos'n; I fell at Trafalgar."

The Light That Can Never Be Put Out

All public lights at Stratford-on-Avon have been extinguished by order of the Mayor.—Daily Paper.

A friend of mine—whose name I shall, of course, be prepared to give, in confidence, to any serious enquirer—has just come back from the Midlands with an extraordinary story of his adventures there. I pass it on to readers of *The Evening News* with all reserve and all caution; it is theirs to make what they will of it.

My friend is a commercial traveller, and goes his rounds usually in the west and south-west of England. His "line" is cheap blouses, and since the beginning of the war he has been doing extremely well. Working people have been a lot of money—for them—and, strange to say, they like to see their women folk in pretty things. They cannot be induced to imitate the austere economies of their betters; and so they have been buying five shilling blouses eagerly enough. The firm which employs my friend saw that the great munition centres of the North and of the Midlands would be more profitable than the districts of the south and west, and so they arranged that their "star" traveller should break new ground.

The plan turned out a great success. There was tremendous business to be done from Warwickshire to Yorkshire, from Lancashire to Lincolnshire; my friend, beaming, told me that he had never sent up such orders in the whole of his career. "And," said he, "I am going to give the small towns a chance after I've finished with the big ones. I believe there's money there; everywhere."

So a few days ago he found himself in a small town in Warwickshire. He had visited three or four of these little places in the course of the day and had done very well. It was nine o'clock at night, and he discovered that he would have to wait for two hours for the Birmingham train—unless he liked to send on his samples and walk to a certain junction, three miles off, where he could catch a good train to Birmingham. They told him the road was straight ahead; he couldn't miss the way. But he did miss the way.

It was a pitch-dark night; "straight ahead" in the country is sometimes a loose phrase; roads often run into one another and slide off from one another in a queer fashion; a townsman is easily bewildered by black woods and dead silence. Anyhow, the traveller went on and on, but found no junction. He struck a match under a hedge and looked at his watch: it was eleven o'clock, and he was lost and hopeless in the darkness. There was not a light to be seen anywhere; there was nothing for it but to walk on and on till he came to the dawn or a town of some sort, where he could wake up a cross landlord or landlady.

It was midnight when he turned out of the deep shadow of a murmurous wood, and to his utter amazement saw the sky blaze before him.

"Like the lights of London in the old days?" he said. "Not a bit of it. Ten times brighter. It was more like getting out of the beastly black London streets that we're getting used to new into a music-hall or a restaurant, all lighted up. I was looking down into a valley with river running through it, and a smallish town on the river. And I saw it all quite plainly, as if it had been in the daytime. I don't know how I saw it; there were no electric lamps or anything of the kind that I could see, but there it was, as if the stones were shining.

"I came to a big church with a spire by the river, and that was all light. Some sort of service seemed to be going on; the lights were shining through the stained glass, and the organ was rolling and thundering away, and the choir was singing; it sounded like Gregorians, which I don't like in a general way. I just peeped in at the door, and there were three clergymen before the Communion Table togged up to the nines, and the place all red and green and gold and full of images; so I went out. I wondered what was the matter.

"The streets were worse. I couldn't see a single lamp lighted; but everything was all alight. The houses were all old-looking, whitewash and black timbers, and leaning over the street, and I never saw such a crowd. It was like a fancy-dress ball turned out of Covent Garden. Everybody was dressed up; it was a splendid sight. All the Kings of England seemed to be there with their gold crowns on their heads, and men in bright armour riding with them, and men with spears, and men with bows and arrows. Then there was a wild-looking king walking with his queen, and she was holding up her hands all red with blood. Then there was a man got up like Hamlet all in black, and a girl in white with water dripping from her clothes came just behind him.

"And then I did feel a bit funny. Just after the Hamlet and Ophelia couple, I could have sworn I saw old George Weir, who used to be with F. R. Benson, with the spade in his hand and everything, just as he used to do the Gravedigger, and I knew he'd been dead five or six years.

"But they came swarming on, one on the top of the other, a perfect host of them. There was a great big red-faced fellow, rolling in his walk, and leering all about him, and smelling like a wine-barrel, and a pack of awful cut-throats at his heels, sneaking and snarling; and then came alone an old man with a white beard, with his hands up, and a fellow dressed like Jack Point, in red and yellow patches, follows him, with the tears streaming from his eyes. Then there was a kind of transformation scene, girls in green with silver wings; fairies I suppose they were meant to be.

"And then they all began to sing. I wrote it down that night in my bedroom:—

> To holy Church now fare we all,
> That we may keep high festival,
> So Alman fiend shall not appal,
> > Neither by night nor day.
>
> For we be come, of earth and sea,
> Of heaven and hell and of faerie,
> Of high and low and each degree,
> Both king and clown in this meinie,
> So shall we hear with mirth and glee
> > Missam pro Anglia.

"Then everything went black. I was staggering about, and saying, 'Where am I?' And then there was a policeman, steadying me by the shoulder, and saying, 'I don't wonder you've lost your way, sir. All public lights out by the Mayor's orders, and Stratford's a puzzling place in the dark for strangers."

I heard my friend's story as a parable, and understood by it that there is a light at Stratford-on-Avon that shall never be put out.

The Ghost of Whit-Monday

(After Charles Dickens)

It was a wild, wet morning. The trees in the parks and squares were tossing and shivering before a fierce and bitter wind. Grey clouds drove across the sky, and the rain scourged the dismal streets.

It was as miserable a morning as any man had seen in the month of June, since June was invented. When black night turned by degrees into a dismal, dirty grey the few people who were compelled to be abroad saw no difference, and wondered when the dawn was coming. The Special Constables thought that something must have happened to the Calendar, in consequence, probably, of the Radicals having meddled with the clock. The sparrows wouldn't believe that the sun had risen, and slept all the faster. Still, in spite of all, it really grew a little lighter, and at last everybody had to wake up and confess that it was Whit-Monday.

The boys who took down the shutters of the shops felt that there was something very queer abroad. One of them, a pale, thin lad employed at a shop in the Strand, told a friend that he had "seen something". He said that an elderly gentleman in an enormous great coat, with capes to it like those worn by the stage-coachmen in the old days, and six shawls round his neck and the largest umbrella ever seen held over his head (which was also protected by a sou'wester), had walked briskly towards him from the City and had then disappeared shuddering and wailing dismally, "Where am I? Where am I? What has become of me?" The other apprentices told the thin lad that that was what came of drinking too much cocoa overnight, and didn't believe a word of it.

Nevertheless, the thin apprentice was quite right. He did see the old gentleman shivering in his capes and shawls, and it was quite true about his disappearing as near as can be ascertained in front of the tobacco shop at the corner of Bedford Street. For the old gentleman was a phantom. *He was the Ghost of Whit-Monday.*

He spent a wretched morning. He floated up to Hampstead Heath and looked for his swings, his roundabouts, his coconut shies. The Heath was all bare, there was not a sign of merrymaking of any kind. The Spirit groaned. The wind blew savagely right through him. The Spirit shivered. A few flakes of snow, half melted, drifted into his spectral features, and he fled, wailing, southwards.

He went to the big station where the troops of merry children and cheery fathers and happy mothers and glad young people should have been rushing to catch their trains for the seaside and a day's pleasuring. They were not there, not one of them. All that he saw was the usual workaday crowd hurrying out of the station to their shops and offices. They looked cold.

The Ghost of Whit-Monday resolved to make quite sure, and being a Ghost he was at Brighton and Margate and Folkstone and Hastings in no time. And yet, though he was in all these places, he wasn't in any of them. No signs of a holiday, no signs of the sun, there were no crowds. He saw nothing but wet pebbles and rain falling into the sea.

The Phantom was puzzled by one thing. Though there was no holiday there were no gloomy faces, and there was no grumbling. Everybody had a quiet, determined look. The Ghost saw a swarm of people going into a great yard, and he listened. He heard one man say to another, "After all, this is better than a holiday." And the other man answered, "There's only one way of taking a holiday now, and that's making shells to kill Germans." And the Spirit knew that these men were munition-makers; and he understood everything.

The Ghost of Whit-Monday was a very sensible phantom. He melted into thin sleet immediately without causing anybody the slightest annoyance. And he no longer wailed.

"I really am not here to-day," he observed cheerfully. "But when I come next year, what larks!"

The ghost chuckled.

A New Christmas Carol

Scrooge was undoubtedly getting on in life, to begin with. There is no doubt whatever about that. Ten years had gone by since the spirit of old Jacob Marley had visited him, and the Ghost of Christmas Past, Christmas Present, and Christmas Yet to Come had shewn him the error of his mean, niggardly, churlish ways, and had made him the merriest old boy that ever walked on 'Change with a chuckle, and was called "Old Medlar" by the young dogs who never reverenced anybody or anything.

And, not a doubt of it, the young dogs were in the right. Ebenezer Scrooge *was* a meddler. He was always ferreting about into other people's business; so that he might find out what good he could do them. Many a hard man of affairs softened as he thought of Scrooge and of the old man creeping round to the counting-house where the hard man sat in despair, and thought of the certain ruin before him.

"My dear Mr. Hardman," old Scrooge had said, "not another word. Take this draft for thirty thousand pounds, and use it as none knows better. Why, you'll double it for me before six months are out."

He would go out chuckling on that, and Charles the waiter, at the old City tavern where Scrooge dined, always said that Scrooge was a fortune for him and to the house. To say nothing of what Charles got by him; everybody ordered a fresh supply of hot brandy and water when his cheery, rosy old face entered the room.

It was Christmastide. Scrooge was sitting before his roaring fire, sipping at something warm and comfortable, and plotting happiness for all sorts of people.

"I won't bear Bob's obstinacy," he was saying to himself—the firm was Scrooge and Cratchit now—"he does all the work, and it's not fair for a useless old fellow like me to take more than a quarter share of the profits."

A dreadful sound echoed through the grave old house. The air grew chill and sour. The something warm and comfortable grew cold and tasteless as Scrooge sipped it nervously. The door flew open, and a vague but fearful form stood in the doorway.

"Follow me," it said.

Scrooge is not at all sure what happened then. He was in the streets. He recollected that he wanted to buy some sweetmeats for his little nephews and nieces, and he went into a shop.

"Past eight o'clock, sir," said the civil man. "I can't serve you."

He wandered on through the streets that seemed strangely altered. He was going westward, and he began to feel faint. He thought he would be the better for a little brandy and water, and he was just turning into a tavern when all the people came out and the iron gates were shut in his face.

"What's the matter?" he asked feebly of the man who was closing the doors.

"Gone ten," the fellow said shortly, and turned out all the lights.

Scrooge felt sure that the second mince-pie had given him indigestion, and that he was in a dreadful dream. He seemed to fall into a deep gulf of darkness, in which all was blotted out. When he came to himself again it was Christmas Day, and the people were walking about the streets.

Scrooge, somehow or other, found himself among them. They smiled and greeted one another cheerfully, but it was evident that they were not happy. Marks of care were on their faces, marks that told of past troubles and future anxieties. Scrooge heard a man sigh heavily just after he had wished a neighbour a Merry Christmas. There were tears on a woman's face as she came down the church steps, all in black.

"Poor John!" she was murmuring. "I am sure it was the wearing cark of money troubles that killed him. Still, he is in heaven now. But the clergyman said in his sermon that heaven was only a pretty fairy tale." She wept anew.

All this disturbed Scrooge dreadfully. Something seemed to be pressing on his heart.

"But," said he, "I shall forget all this when I sit down to dinner with Nephew Fred and my niece and their young rascals."

It was late in the afternoon; four o'clock and dark, but in capital time for dinner. Scrooge found his nephew's house. It was as dark as the sky; not a window was lighted up. Scrooge's heart grew cold.

He knocked and knocked again, and rang a bell that sounded as faint and far as if it had rung in a grave.

At last a miserable old woman opened the door a few inches and looked out suspiciously.

"Mr. Fred?" said she. "Why, he and his missus have gone off to the Hotel Splendid, as they call it, and they won't be home till midnight. They got their table six weeks ago! The children are away at Eastbourne."

"Dining in a tavern on Christmas Day!" Scrooge murmured. "What terrible fate is this? Who is so miserable, so desolate, that he dines at a tavern on Christmas Day? And the children at Eastbourne!"

The air grew misty about him. He seemed to hear as though from a great distance the voice of Tiny Tim, saying "God help us, every one!"

Again the Spirit stood before him. Scrooge fell upon his knees.

"Terrible Phantom!" he exclaimed. "Who and what are thou? Speak, I entreat thee."

"Ebenezer Scrooge," replied the Spirit in awful tones. "I am the Ghost of the Christmas of 1920. With me I bring the demand note of the Commissioners of Income Tax!"

Scrooge's hair bristled as he saw the figures. But it fell out when he saw that the Apparition had feet like those of a gigantic cat.

"My name is Pussyfoot. I am also called Ruin and Despair," said the Phantom, and vanished.

With that Scrooge awoke and drew back the curtains of his bed.

"Thank God!" he uttered from his heart. "It was but a dream!"

Scrooge and the Spirit—
of Psycho-analysis

Scrooge woke up with a sudden start. He heard the bell toll one.
He remembered that it was Christmas Eve, and that he was going to make a tremendous day of it with his nephew and his niece by marriage.

There was a woman for you! As hearty as old Christmas itself, and the very wife for Fred.

He had a trifle or two in the pocket-book in the old desk at the foot of the bed that he thought would please her: a diamond and ruby ring that would look well on her plump finger, and a watch with curious enamels on its case that had taken his fancy a full month ago.

And as for Fred: the portly gentleman who had called on Scrooge just a year before turned out to be an old-fashioned wine merchant in an old-fashioned place right down by the river, where they burnt candles in the counting-house all the year round, including the sunniest days in August; and he had supplied Scrooge with a dozen of most particular port, which had been sent to Fred by the earlier.

And Bob Cratchit and Tiny Tim were to enjoy such a Christmas as they had never dreamed of.

So, on the whole, Scrooge had gone to bed in a happy humour, feeling that he was entitled to a good night's rest.

And yet he woke up with a start and a shudder as the old clock in the old church tower hard by tolled one.

"Dear me!" said Scrooge; "I wonder what woke me. But what a horrible smell! Odd I never noticed it, before. There must be a dead rat behind the wainscoting. Really, this is dreadful!"

"It is not a rat," said a voice at his elbow. And a dismal and hideous figure stood by his bed.

"I," said the Phantom, for such was the form, "am the Spirit of

Christmas as it will appear when psycho-analysed. Follow me."

With a dreadful sinking at his heart, and involuntarily stopping his nose with his fingers, Scrooge accompanied the spectral presence. They were out in the streets.

It was Christmas morning.

The people were hurrying to church with cheerful faces.

The merry bells filled the air with happy sound.

The Phantom drew Scrooge into one of the churches.

It was all gay with ivy and green holly and shining red berries and bright tapers. The organ was playing, and they were singing of Peace on Earth and Goodwill to Men.

"Amen!" said Scrooge under his breath.

"Look," muttered the Spectre, "this is a cultural festival. You see, it is the period of the year when vegetation is at its lowest ebb. The ancestors of these people, seeing that the ground was hard and the leaves fallen and that everything seemed dead, were afraid that nothing would ever grow again."

"Phantom!" gasped Scrooge, with trembling accents. "Spirit! speak the truth, I adjure you! Is it possible that even ancestors were such infernal fools as that'?"

"Certainly," replied the Spectre. "You will find it all in the text-books. Mark the result. The cultural feast called Christmas was instituted. The green boughs and the red berries are a mimetic appeal for the revivification of Nature, similar to the mimetic appeal of the may-pole. The organ is an imitation of the warm south-west wind; and the singing mimics the twittering of the birds in spring."

"But what are those candles on the altar for?" said Scrooge in his bewilderment.

"You seem a most obtuse person," answered the Ghost. "Midwinter is the darkest time in the year. Candles are lighted to make the sun shine again."

"There *must* be a dead rat somewhere," murmured Scrooge under his breath. He was still holding his nose firmly between his two fingers.

The church with its bright tapers and red berries and green leaves faded away.

The Spectre and Scrooge were again in the streets.

A poor woman, wan and thin, shivered in the cold December air, and drew her scanty shawl closely about her. She looked sadly at the happy people hurrying to their Christmas dinners.

Scrooge seemed to hear her murmur to herself about the happy Christmases when she was a child, and her poor father and mother were still alive. Just then a kindly-looking old gentleman went up to her, spoke a few words in her ear, and put something bright and chinking into her timid palm.

The tears were rolling down his cheeks as he hurried away to avoid her grateful words of thanks.

"That," said the Spectre, "is an instance of the Terror-Complex. Rich people are in continual dread of a rising of the class-conscious proletariat, and such gifts are an attempt to buy off the infuritated people."

"It is odd," thought Scrooge to himself, "how that dead rat—and he must have been dead a very long time—seems to follow us everywhere."

Again the scene changed. The Spirit and his companion were in a cheerfully lighted drawing-room.

A happy-looking woman drew her two little boys about her knees as she sat by the blazing hearth, and began to tell them of the Shepherds and the Wise Men and the singing Angels.

A rosy-faced man came in at the door, humming an old Christmas carol.

"Oh, do hush, papa," said one of the little boys. "Mamma is telling us such a beautiful story."

"Aha!" chuckled the Ghost. "There you have the Œdipus Complex. Note the hatred of the sons for the father; note also—" And he whispered in Scrooge's ear.

"I'll swear there are a dozen dead rats somewhere," thought Scrooge, as his gorge rose.

And then Scrooge woke up, and this time in real earnest. He leapt out of the bed and found a little book on psycho-analysis, that had somehow got into the room, lying on the floor.

"And I thought it was only a poor dead rat," said Scrooge, as he took up the book with the tongs and flung it out of the window into the gutter.

The Terror

I

After two years we are turning once more to the morning's news with a sense of appetite and glad expectation. There were thrills at the beginning of the war; the thrill of horror and of a doom that seemed at once incredible and certain; this was when Namur fell and the German host swelled like a flood over the French fields, and drew very near to the walls of Paris. Then we felt the thrill of exultation when the good news came that the awful tide had been turned back, that Paris and the world were safe; for a while at all events.

Then for days we hoped for more news as good as this or better. Has Von Kluck been surrounded? Not to-day, but perhaps he will be surrounded to-morrow. But the days became weeks, the weeks drew out to months; the battle in the West seemed frozen. Now and again things were done that seemed hopeful, with promise of events still better. But Neuve Chapelle and Loos dwindled into disappointments as their tale was told fully; the lines in the West remained, for all practical purposes of victory, immobile. Nothing seemed to happen, there was nothing to read save the record of operations that were clearly trifling and insignificant. People speculated as to the reason of this inaction; the hopeful said that Joffre had a plan, that he was "nibbling", others declared that we were short of munitions, others again that the new levies were not yet ripe for battle. So the months went by, and almost two years of war had been completed before the motionless English line began to stir and quiver as if it awoke from a long sleep, and began to roll onward, overwhelming the enemy.

The secret of the long inaction of the British Armies has been well kept. On the one hand it was rigorously protected by the censorship, which severe, and sometimes severe to the point of absurdity—"the captains and the . . . depart", for instance—became in this particular matter ferocious. As soon as the real significance of that which was happening, or beginning to happen, was perceived by the authorities, an underlined circular was issued to the newspaper proprietors of Great Britain and Ireland. It warned each proprietor that he might impart the contents of this circular to one other person only, such person being the responsible editor of his paper, who was to keep the communication secret under the severest penalties. The circular forbade any mention of certain events that had taken place, that might take place; it forbade any kind of allusion to these events or any hint of their existence, or of the possibility of their existence, not only in the Press, but in any form whatever. The subject was not to be alluded to in conversation, it was not to be hinted at, however obscurely, in letters; the very existence of the circular, its subject apart, was to be a dead secret.

These measures were successful. A wealthy newspaper proprietor of the North, warmed a little at the end of the Throwsters' Feast (which was held as usual, it will be remembered), ventured to say to the man next to him: "How awful it would be, wouldn't it, if . . ." His words were repeated, as proof, one regrets to say, that it was time for "old Arnold" to "pull himself together"; and he was fined a thousand pounds. Then, there was the case of an obscure weekly paper published in the county town of an agricultural district in Wales. The *Meiros Observer* (we will call it) was issued from a stationer's back premises, and filled its four pages with accounts of local flower shows, fancy fairs at vicarages, reports of parish councils, and rare bathing fatalities. It also issued a visitors' list, which has been known to contain six names.

This enlightened organ printed a paragraph, which nobody noticed, which was very like paragraphs that small country newspapers have long been in the habit of printing, which could hardly give so much as a hint to any one—to any one, that is, who was not fully instructed in the secret. As a matter of fact, this piece of intelligence got into the paper because the proprietor, who was also the editor, incautiously left the last processes of this particular issue to the staff, who was the Lord-High-Everything-Else of the establishment; and the staff put in a bit of gossip he had heard in the market to fill up two inches on the back page. But the result was that the *Meiros Observer* ceased to appear, owing to "untoward circumstances" as the proprietor said; and he would say no more. No more, that is, by way of explanation, but a great deal more by way of execration of "damned, prying busybodies".

Now a censorship that is sufficiently minute and utterly remorseless can do amazing things in the way of hiding . . . what it wants to hide. Before the war, one would have thought otherwise; one would have said that, censor or no censor, the fact of the murder at X or the fact of the bank robbery at Y would certainly become known; if not through the Press, at all events through rumour and the passage of the news from mouth to mouth. And this would be true—of England three hundred years ago, and of savage tribelands of to-day. But we have grown of late to such a reverence for the printed word and such a reliance on it, that the old faculty of disseminating news by word of mouth has become atrophied. Forbid the Press to mention the fact that Jones has been murdered, and it is marvellous how few people will hear of it, and of those who hear how few will credit the story that they have heard. You meet a man in the train who remarks that he has been told something about a murder in Southwark; there is all the difference in the world between the impression you receive from such a chance communication and that given by half a dozen lines of print with name, and street and date and all the facts of the case. People in trains repeat all sorts of tales, many of them false; newspapers do not print accounts of murders that have not been committed.

Then another consideration that has made for secrecy. I may have seemed to say that the old office of rumour no longer exists; I shall be reminded of the strange legend of "the Russians" and the mythology of the "Angels of Mons". But let me point out, in the first place, that both these absurdities depended on the papers for their wide dissemination. If there had been no newspapers or magazines Russians and Angels would have made but a brief, vague appearance of the most shadowy kind—a few would have heard of them, fewer still would have believed in them, they would have been gossiped about for a bare week or two, and so they would have vanished away.

And, then, again, the very fact of these vain rumours and fantastic tales having been so widely believed for a time was fatal to the credit of any stray mutterings that may have got abroad. People had been taken in twice; they had seen how grave persons, men of credit, had preached and lectured about the shining forms that had saved the British Army at Mons, or had testified to the trains, packed with grey-coated Muscovites, rushing through the land at dead of night; and now there was a hint of something more amazing than either of the discredited legends. But this time there was no word of confirmation to be found in daily paper, or weekly review, or parish magazine, and so the few that heard either laughed, or, being serious, went home and jotted down notes for essays on "War-time Psychology: Collective Delusions".

I followed neither of these courses. For before the secret circular had been issued my curiosity had somehow been aroused by certain paragraphs concerning a "Fatal Accident to Well-known Airman". The propeller of the airplane had been shattered, apparently by a collision with a flight of pigeons; the blades had been broken and the machine had fallen like lead to the earth. And soon after I had seen this account, I heard of some very odd circumstances relating to an explosion in a great munition factory in the Midlands. I thought I saw the possibility of a connection between two very different events.

It has been pointed out to me by friends who have been good enough to read this record, that certain phrases I have used may give the impression that I ascribe all the delays of the war on the Western front to the extraordinary circumstances which occasioned the issue of the Secret Circular. Of course this is not the case; there were many reasons for the immobility of our lines from October 1914 to July 1916. These causes have been evident enough and have been openly discussed and deplored. But behind them was something of infinitely greater moment. We lacked men, but men were pouring into the new army; we were short of shells, but when the shortage was proclaimed the nation set itself to mend this matter with all its energy. We could undertake to supply the defects of our army both in men and munitions—*if* the new and incredible danger could be overcome. It has been overcome; rather, perhaps, it has ceased to exist; and the secret may now be told.

I have said my attention was attracted by an account of the death of a well-known airman. I have not the habit of preserving cuttings, I am sorry to say, so that I cannot be precise as to the date of this event.

To the best of my belief it was either towards the end of May or the beginning of June 1915. The newspaper paragraph announcing the death of Flight-Lieutenant Western-Reynolds was brief enough; accidents, and fatal accidents, to the men who are storming the air for us are, unfortunately, by no means so rare as to demand an elaborated notice. But the manner in which Western-Reynolds met his death struck me as extraordinary, inasmuch as it revealed a new danger in the element that we have lately conquered. He was brought down, as I said, by a flight of birds; of pigeons, as appeared by what was found on the blood-stained and shattered blades of the propeller. An eye-witness of the accident, a fellow-officer, described how Western-Reynolds set out from the aerodrome on a fine afternoon, there being hardly any wind. He was going to France; he had made the journey to and fro half a dozen times or more, and felt perfectly secure and at ease.

"'Wester' rose to a great height at once, and we could scarcely see the machine. I was turning to go when one of the fellows called out, 'I say! What's this?' He pointed up, and we saw what looked like a black cloud coming from the south at a tremendous rate. I saw at once it wasn't a cloud; it came with a swirl and a rush quite different from any cloud I've ever seen. But for a second I couldn't make out exactly what it was. It altered its shape and turned into a great crescent, and wheeled and veered about as if it was looking for something. The man who had called out had got his glasses, and was staring for all he was worth. Then he shouted that it was a tremendous flight of birds, 'thousands of them'. They went on wheeling and beating about high up in the air, and we were watching them, thinking it was interesting, but not supposing that they would make any difference to 'Wester', who was just about out of sight. His machine was just a speck. Then the two arms of the crescent drew in as quick as lightning, and these thousands of birds shot in a solid mass right up there across the sky, and flew away somewhere about nor'-nor'-west. Then Henley, the man with the glasses, called out: 'He's down!' and started running, and I went after him. We got a car and as we were going along Henley told me that he'd seen the machine drop dead, as if it came out of that cloud of birds. He thought then that they must have mucked up the propeller somehow. That turned out to be the case. We found the propeller blades all broken and covered with blood and pigeon feathers, and carcasses of the birds had got wedged in between the blades, and were sticking to them."

This was the story that the young airman told one evening in a small company. He did not speak "in confidence", so I have no hesitation in reproducing what he said. Naturally, I did not take a verbatim note of his conversation, but I have something of a knack of remembering talk that interests me, and I think my reproduction is very near to the tale that I heard. And let it be noted that the flying man told his story without any sense or indication of a sense that the incredible, or all but the incredible, had happened. So far as he knew, he said, it was the first accident of the kind. Airmen in France had been bothered once or twice by birds—he thought they were eagles—flying viciously at them, but poor old 'Wester' had been the first man to come up against a flight of some thousands of pigeons.

"And perhaps I shall be the next," he added, "but why look for trouble? Anyhow, I'm going to see *Toodle-oo* to-morrow afternoon."

Well, I heard the story, as one hears all the varied marvels and terrors of the air; as one heard some years ago of "air pockets", strange gulfs or voids in the atmosphere into which airmen fell with great peril; or as one heard of the experience of the airman who flew over the Cumberland mountains in the burning summer of 1911, and as he swam far above the heights was suddenly and vehemently blown upwards, the hot air from the rocks striking his plane as if it had been a blast from a furnace chimney. We have just begun to navigate a strange region; we must expect to encounter strange adventures, strange perils. And here a new chapter in the chronicles of these perils and adventures had been opened by the death of Western-Reynolds; and no doubt invention and contrivance would presently hit on some way of countering the new danger.

It was, I think, about a week or ten days after the airman's death that my business called me to a northern town, the name of which, perhaps, had better remain unknown. My mission was to enquire into certain charges of extravagance which had been laid against the working people, that is, the munition workers of this especial town. It was said that the men who used to earn £2 10s. a week were now getting from seven to eight pounds, that "bits of girls" were being paid two pounds instead of seven or eight shillings, and that, in consequence, there was an orgy of foolish extravagance. The girls, I was told, were eating chocolates at four, five, and six shillings a pound, the women were ordering thirty-pound pianos which they couldn't play, and the men bought gold chains at ten and twenty guineas apiece.

I dived into the town in question and found, as usual, that there was a mixture of truth and exaggeration in the stories that I had heard. Gramophones, for example: they cannot be called in strictness necessaries, but they were undoubtedly finding a ready sale, even in the more expensive brands. And I thought that there were a great many very spick and span perambulators to be seen on the pavement; smart perambulators, painted in tender shades of colour and expensively fitted.

"And how can you be surprised if people will have a bit of a fling?" a worker said to me. "We're seeing money for the first time in our lives, and it's bright. And we work hard for it, and we risk our lives to get it. You've heard of the explosion yonder?"

He mentioned certain works on the outskirts of the town. Of course, neither the name of the works nor of the town had been printed; there had been a brief notice of "Explosion at Munition Works in the Northern District: Many Fatalities." The working man told me about it, and added some dreadful details.

"They wouldn't let their folks see bodies; screwed them up in coffins as they found them in shop. The gas had done it."

"Turned their faces black, you mean?"

"Nay. They were all as if they had been bitten to pieces."

This was a strange gas.

I asked the man in the northern town all sorts of questions about the extraordinary explosion of which he had spoken to me. But he had very little more to say. As I have noted already, secrets that may not be printed are often deeply kept; last summer there were very few people outside high official circles who knew anything about the "Tanks", of which we have all been talking lately, though these strange instruments of war were being exercised and tested in a park not far from London. So the man who told me of the explosion in the munition factory was most likely genuine in his profession that he knew nothing more of the disaster. I found out that he was a smelter employed at a furnace on the other side of the town to the ruined factory; he didn't know even what they had been making there; some very dangerous high explosive, he supposed. His information was really nothing more than a bit of gruesome gossip, which he had heard probably at third or fourth or fifth hand. The horrible detail of faces "as if they had been bitten to pieces" had made its violent impression on him, that was all.

I gave him up and took a tram to the district of the disaster; a sort of industrial suburb, five miles from the centre of the town. When I asked for the factory, I was told that it was no good my going to it as there was nobody there. But I found it, a raw and hideous shed with a walled yard about it, and a shut gate. I looked for signs of destruction, but there was nothing. The roof was quite undamaged; and again it struck me that this had had been a strange accident. There had been an explosion of sufficient violence to kill work-people in the building, but the building itself shewed no wounds or scars.

A man came out of the gate and locked it behind him. I began to ask him some sort of question, or rather, I began to "open" for a question with "A terrible business here, they tell me," or some such phrase of convention. I got no farther. The man asked me if I saw a police-man walking down the street. I said I did, and I was given the choice of getting about my business forthwith or of being instantly given in charge as a spy. "Th'ast better be gone and quick about it," was, I think, his final advice, and I took it.

Well, I had come literally up against a brick wall. Thinking the problem over, I could only suppose that the smelter or his informant had twisted the phrases of the story. The smelter had said the dead men's faces were "bitten to pieces"; this might be an unconscious per-version of "eaten away". That phrase might describe well enough the effect of strong acids, and, for all I knew of the processes of munition-making, such acids might be used and might explode with horrible re-sults in some perilous stage of their admixture.

It was a day or two later that the accident to the airman, Western-Reynolds, came into my mind. For one of those instants which are far shorter than any measure of time there flashed out the possibility of a link between the two disasters. But here was a wild impossibility, and I drove it away. And yet I think the thought, mad as it seemed, never left me; it was the secret light that at last guided me through a sombre grove of enigmas.

It was about this time, so far as the date can be fixed, that a whole district, one might say a whole county, was visited by a series of extraordinary and terrible calamities, which were the more terrible inasmuch
as they continued for some time to be inscrutable mysteries. It is, indeed, doubtful whether these awful events do not still remain mysteries to many of those concerned; for before the inhabitants of this part
of the country had time to join one link of evidence to another the circular was issued, and thenceforth no one knew how to distinguish undoubted fact from wild and extravagant surmise.

The district in question is in the far west of Wales; I shall call it, for
convenience, Meirion. In it there is one seaside town of some repute
with holiday-makers for five or six weeks in the summer, and dotted
about the county there are three or four small old towns that seem
drooping in a slow decay, sleepy and grey with age and forgetfulness.
They remind me of what I have read of towns in the west of Ireland.
Grass grows between the uneven stones of the pavements, the signs
above the shop windows decline, half the letters of these signs are
missing, here and there a house has been pulled down, or has been allowed to slide into ruin, and wild greenery springs up through the fallen
stones, and there is silence in all the streets. And, it is to be noted, these
are not places that were once magnificent. The Celts have never had the
art of building, and so far as I can see, such towns as Towy and Merthyr
Tegveth and Meiros must have been always much as they are now,
clusters of poorish, meanly-built houses, ill-kept and down at heel.

And these few towns are thinly scattered over a wild country
where north is divided from south by a wilder mountain range. One of
these places is sixteen miles from any station; the others are doubtfully
and deviously connected by single-line railways served by rare trains
that pause and stagger and hesitate on their slow journey up mountain
passes, or stop for half an hour or more at lonely sheds called stations,
situated in the midst of desolate marshes. A few years ago I travelled
with an Irishman on one of these queer lines, and he looked to right and
saw the bog with its yellow and blue grasses and stagnant pools, and he
looked to left and saw a ragged hillside, set with grey stone walls. "I
can hardly believe," he said, "that I'm not still in the wilds of Ireland."

Here, then, one sees a wild and divided and scattered region, a land
of outland hills and secret and hidden valleys. I know white farms on

this coast which must be separate by two hours of hard, rough walking from any other habitation, which are invisible from any other house. And inland, again, the farms are often ringed about by thick groves of ash, planted by men of old days to shelter their roof-trees from rude winds of the mountain and stormy winds of the sea; so that these places, too, are hidden away, to be surmised only by the wood smoke that rises from the green surrounding leaves. A Londoner must see them to believe in them; and even then he can scarcely credit their utter isolation.

Such, then, in the main is Meirion, and on this land in the early summer of last year terror descended—a terror without shape, such as no man there had ever known.

It began with the tale of a little child who wandered out into the lanes to pick flowers one sunny afternoon, and never came back to the cottage on the hill.

II

The child who was lost came from a lonely cottage that stands on the slope of a steep hillside called the Allt, or the height. The land about it is wild and ragged; here the growth of gorse and bracken, here a marshy hollow of reeds and rushes, marking the course of the stream from some hidden well, here thickets of dense and tangled undergrowth, the outposts of the wood. Down through this broken and uneven ground a path leads to the lane at the bottom of the valley; then the land rises again and swells up to the cliffs over the sea, about a quarter of a mile away. The little girl, Gertrude Morgan, asked her mother if she might go down to the lane and pick the purple flowers—these were orchids—that grew there, and her mother gave her leave, telling her she must be sure to be back by tea-time, as there was apple-tart for tea.

She never came back. It was supposed that she must have crossed the road and gone to the cliff's edge, possibly in order to pick the sea-pinks that were then in full blossom. She must have slipped, they said, and fallen into the sea, two hundred feet below. And, it may be said at once, that there was no doubt some truth in this conjecture, though it stopped very far short of the whole truth. The child's body must have been carried out by the tide, for it was never found.

The conjecture of a false step or of a fatal slide on the slippery turf that slopes down to the rocks was accepted as being the only explanation possible. People thought the accident a strange one because, as a rule, country children living by the cliffs and the sea become wary at an early age, and Gertrude Morgan was almost ten years old. Still, as the neighbours said, "that's how it must have happened, and it's a great pity, to be sure." But this would not do when in a week's time a strong young labourer failed to come to his cottage after the day's work. His body was found on the rocks six or seven miles from the cliffs where the child was supposed to have fallen; he was going home by a path that he had used every night of his life for eight or nine years, that he used of dark nights in perfect security, knowing every inch of it. The police asked if he drank, but he was a teetotaller; if he were subject to fits, but he wasn't. And he was not murdered for his wealth, since agricultural labourers are not wealthy. It was only possible again to talk of slippery turf and a false step: but people began to be frightened. Then a woman was found with her neck broken at the bottom of a disused quarry near Llanfihangel, in the middle of the county. The "false step" theory was eliminated here, for the quarry was guarded with a natural hedge of gorse bushes. One would have to struggle and fight through sharp thorns to destruction in such a place as this; and indeed the gorse bushes were broken as if some one had rushed furiously through them, just above the place where the woman's body was found. And this was strange: there was a dead sheep lying beside her in the pit, as if the woman and the sheep together had been chased over the brim of the quarry. But chased by whom, or by what? And then there was a new form of terror.

This was in the region of the marshes under the mountain. A man and his son, a lad of fourteen or fifteen, set out early one morning to work and never reached the farm where they were bound. Their way skirted the marsh, but it was broad, firm and well metalled, and it had been raised about two feet above the bog. But when search was made in the evening of the same day Phillips and his son were found dead in the marsh, covered with black slime and pond-weed. And they lay some ten yards from the path, which, it would seem, they must have left deliberately. It was useless, of course, to look for tracks in the black ooze, for if one threw a big stone into it a few seconds removed all marks of the disturbance. The men who found the two bodies beat about the verges and purlieus of the marsh in hope of finding some trace of the murderers; they went to and fro over the rising ground where the black cattle were grazing, they searched the alder thickets by the brook; but they discovered nothing.

Most horrible of all these horrors, perhaps, was the affair of the Highway, a lonely and unfrequented by-road that winds for many miles on high and lonely land. Here, a mile from any other dwelling, stands a cottage on the edge of a dark wood. It was inhabited by a labourer named Williams, his wife, and their three children. One hot summer's evening, a man who had been doing a day's gardening at a rectory three or four miles away passed the cottage, and stopped for a few minutes to chat with Williams, the labourer, who was pottering about his garden, while the children were playing on the path by the door. The two talked of their neighbours and of the potatoes till Mrs. Williams appeared at the doorway and said supper was ready, and Williams turned to go into the house. This was about eight o'clock, and in the ordinary course the family would have their supper and be in bed by nine, or by half-past nine at latest. At ten o'clock that night the local doctor was driving home along the Highway. His horse shied violently and then stopped dead just opposite the gate to the cottage. The doctor got down, frightened at what he saw; and there on the roadway lay Williams, his wife, and the three children, stone dead, all of them, Their skulls were battered in as if by some heavy iron instrument; their faces were beaten into a pulp.

III

It is not easy to make any picture of the horror that lay dark on the hearts of the people of Meirion. It was no longer possible to believe or to pretend to believe that these men and women and children met their deaths through strange accidents. The little girl and the young labourer might have slipped and fallen over the cliffs, but the woman who lay dead with the dead sheep at the bottom of the quarry, the two men who had been lured into the ooze of the marsh, the family who were found murdered on the Highway before their own cottage door; in these cases there could be no room for the supposition of accident.

It seemed as if it were impossible to frame any conjecture or outline of a conjecture that would account for these hideous and, as it seemed, utterly purposeless crimes. For a time people said that there must be a madman at large, a sort of country variant of Jack the Ripper, some horrible pervert who was possessed by the passion of death, who prowled darkling about that lonely land, hiding in woods and in wild places, always watching and seeking for the victims of his desire.

Indeed, Dr. Lewis, who found poor Williams, his wife and children miserably slaughtered on the Highway, was convinced at first that the presence of a concealed madman in the countryside offered the only possible solution to the difficulty.

"I felt sure," he said to me afterwards, "that the Williams's had been killed by a homicidal maniac. It was the nature of the poor creatures' injuries that convinced me that this was the case. Some years ago—thirty-seven or thirty-eight years ago as a matter of fact—I had something to do with a case which on the face of it had a strong likeness to the Highway murder. At that time I had a practice at Usk, in Monmouthshire. A whole family living in a cottage by the roadside were murdered one evening; it was called, I think, the Llangibby murder; the cottage was near the village of that name. The murderer was caught in Newport: he was a Spanish sailor, named Garcia, and it appeared that he had killed father, mother, and the three children for the sake of the brass works of an old Dutch clock, which were found on him when he was arrested.

"Garcia had been serving a month's imprisonment in Usk Gaol for some small theft, and on his release he set out to walk to Newport, nine or ten miles away; no doubt to get another ship. He passed the cottage and saw the man working in his garden. Garcia stabbed him with his sailor's knife. The wife rushed out; he stabbed her. Then he went into the cottage and stabbed the three children, tried to set the place on fire, and made off with the clockworks. That looked like the deed of a madman, but Garcia wasn't mad—they hanged him, I may say—he was merely a man of a very low type, a degenerate who hadn't the slightest value for human life. I am not sure, but I think he came from one of the Spanish islands, where the people are said to be degenerates, very likely from too much inter-breeding.

"But my point is that Garcia stabbed to kill and did kill, with one blow in each case. There was no senseless hacking and slashing. Now those poor people on the Highway had their heads smashed to pieces by what must have been a storm of blows. Any one of them would have been fatal, but the murderer must have gone on raining blows with his iron hammer on people who were already stone dead. And *that* sort of thing is the work of a madman, and nothing but a madman. That's how I argued the matter out to myself just after the event.

"I was utterly wrong, monstrously wrong. But who could have suspected the truth?"

Thus Dr. Lewis, and I quote him, or the substance of him, as representative of most of the educated opinion of the district at the beginnings of the terror. People seized on this theory largely because it offered at least the comfort of an explanation, and any explanation, even the poorest, is better than an intolerable and terrible mystery. Besides, Dr. Lewis's theory was plausible; it explained the lack of purpose that seemed to characterise the murders. And yet—there were difficulties even from the first. It was hardly possible that a strange madman should be able to keep hidden in a countryside where any stranger is instantly noted and noticed; sooner or later he would be seen as he prowled along the lanes or across the wild places. Indeed, a drunken, cheerful, and altogether harmless tramp was arrested by a farmer and his man in the fact and act of sleeping off beer under a hedge; but the vagrant was able to prove complete and undoubted alibis, and was soon allowed to go on his wandering way.

Then another theory, or rather a variant of Dr. Lewis's theory, was started. This was to the effect that the person responsible for the outrages was, indeed, a madman; but a madman only at intervals. It was one of the members of the Porth Club, a certain Mr. Remnant, who was supposed to have originated this more subtle explanation. Mr. Remnant was a middle-aged man, who, having nothing particular to do, read a great many books by way of conquering the hours. He talked to the club—doctors, retired colonels, parsons, lawyers—about "personality", quoted various psychological text-books in support of his contention that personality was sometimes fluid and unstable, went back to "Dr. Jekyll and Mr. Hyde" as good evidence of this proposition, and laid stress on Dr. Jekyll's speculation that the human soul, so far from being one and indivisible, might possibly turn out to be a mere polity, a state in which dwelt many strange and incongruous citizens, whose characters were not merely unknown but altogether unsurmised by that form of consciousness which so rashly assumed that it was not only the president of the republic but also its sole citizen.

"The long and the short of it is," Mr. Remnant concluded, "that any one of us may be the murderer, though he hasn't the faintest notion of the fact. Take Llewelyn there."

Mr. Payne Llewelyn was an elderly lawyer, a rural Tulkinghorn. He was the hereditary solicitor to the Morgans of Pentwyn. This does not sound anything tremendous to the Saxons of London; but the style is far more than noble to the Celts of west Wales: it is immemorial; Teilo Sant was of the collaterals of the first known chief of the race. And Mr. Payne Llewelyn did his best to look like the legal adviser of this ancient house. He was weighty, he was cautious, he was sound, he was secure. I have compared him to Mr. Tulkinghorn of Lincoln's Inn Fields; but Mr. Llewelyn would most certainly never have dreamed of employing his leisure in peering into the cupboards where the family skeletons were hidden. Supposing such cupboards to have existed, Mr. Payne Llewelyn would have risked large out-of-pocket expenses to furnish them with double, triple, impregnable locks. He was a new man, an *advena*, certainly; for he was partly of the Conquest, being descended on one side from Sir Payne Turberville; but he meant to stand by the old stock.

"Take Llewelyn now," said Mr. Remnant. "Look here, Llewelyn, can you produce evidence to shew where you were on the night those people were murdered on the Highway? I thought not."

Mr. Llewelyn, an elderly man, as I have said, hesitated before speaking.

"I thought not," Remnant went on. "Now I say that it is perfectly possible that Llewelyn may be dealing death throughout Meirion, although in his present personality he may not have the faintest suspicion that there is another Llewelyn within him, a Llewelyn who follows murder as a fine art."

Mr. Payne Llewelyn did not at all relish Mr. Remnant's suggestion that he might well be a secret murderer, ravening for blood, remorseless as a wild beast. He thought the phrase about his following murder as a fine art was both nonsensical and in the worst taste, and his opinion was not changed when Remnant pointed out that it was used by De Quincey in the title of one of his most famous essays.

"If you had allowed me to speak," he said with some coldness of manner, "I would have told you that on Tuesday last, the night on which those unfortunate people were murdered on the Highway, I was staying at the Angel Hotel, Cardiff. I had business in Cardiff, and I was detained till Wednesday afternoon."

Having given this satisfactory alibi, Mr. Payne Llewelyn left the club, and did not go near it for the rest of the week.

Remnant explained to those who stayed in the smoking-room that, of course, he had merely used Mr. Llewelyn as a concrete example of his theory, which, he persisted, had the support of a considerable body of evidence.

"There are several cases of double personality on record," he declared. "And I say again that it is quite possible that these murders may have been committed by one of us in his secondary personality. Why, I may be the murderer in my Remnant B. state, though Remnant A. knows nothing whatever about it, and is perfectly convinced that he could not kill a fowl, much less a whole family. Isn't it so, Lewis?"

Dr. Lewis said it was so, in theory, but he thought not in fact.

"Most of the cases of double or multiple personality that have been investigated," he said, "have been in connection with the very dubious experiments of hypnotism, or the still more dubious experiments of spiritualism. All that sort of thing, in my opinion, is like tinkering with the works of a clock—amateur tinkering, I mean. You fumble about with the wheels and cogs and bits of mechanism that you don't really know anything about; and then you find your clock going backwards or striking 240 at tea-time. And I believe it's just the same thing with these psychical research experiments; the secondary personality is very likely the result of the tinkering and fumbling with a very delicate apparatus that we know nothing about. Mind, I can't say that it's impossible for one of us to be the Highway murderer in his B. state, as Remnant puts it. But I think it's extremely improbable. Probability is the guide of life, you know, Remnant," said Dr. Lewis, smiling at that gentleman, as if to say that he also had done a little reading in his day. "And it follows, therefore, that improbability is also the guide of life. When you get a very high degree of probability, that is, you are justified in taking it as a certainty; and on the other hand, if a supposition is highly improbable, you are justified in treating it as an impossible one. That is, in nine hundred and ninety-nine cases out of a thousand."

"How about the thousandth case?" said Remnant. "Supposing these extraordinary crimes constitute the thousandth case?"

The doctor smiled and shrugged his shoulders, being tired of the subject. But for some little time highly respectable members of Porth society would look suspiciously at one another wondering whether, after all, there mightn't be "something in it". However, both Mr. Remnant's somewhat crazy theory and Dr. Lewis's plausible theory became untenable when two more victims of an awful and mysterious death were offered up in sacrifice, for a man was found dead in the Llanfihangel quarry, where the woman had been discovered. And on the same day a girl of fifteen was found broken on the jagged rocks under the cliffs near Porth. Now, it appeared that these two deaths must have occurred at about the same time, within an hour of one another, certainly; and the distance between the quarry and the cliffs by Black Rock is certainly twenty miles.

"A motor could do it," one man said.

But it was pointed out that there was no high road between the two places; indeed, it might be said that there was no road at all between them. There was a network of deep, narrow, and tortuous lanes that wandered into one another at all manner of queer angles for, say, seventeen miles; this in the middle, as it were, between Black Rock and the quarry at Llanfihangel. But to get to the high land of the cliffs one had to take a path that went through two miles of fields; and the quarry lay a mile away from the nearest by-road in the midst of gorse and bracken and broken land. And, finally, there was no track of motor-car or motor-bicycle in the lanes which must have been followed to pass from one place to the other.

"What about an airplane, then?" said the man of the motor-car theory. Well, there was certainly an aerodrome not far from one of the two places of death; but somehow, nobody believed that the Flying Corps harboured a homicidal maniac. It seemed clear, therefore, that there must be more than one person concerned in the terror of Meirion. And Dr. Lewis himself abandoned his own theory.

"As I said to Remnant at the club," he remarked, "improbability is the guide of life. I can't believe that there are a pack of madmen or even two madmen at large in the country. I give it up."

And now a fresh circumstance or set of circumstances became manifest to confound judgment and to awaken new and wild surmises. For at about this time people realised that none of the dreadful events that were happening all about them was so much as mentioned in the Press. I have already spoken of the fate of the *Meiros Observer*. This paper was suppressed by the authorities because it had inserted a brief paragraph about some person who had been "found dead under mysterious circumstances"; I think that paragraph referred to the first death of Llanfihangel quarry. Thenceforth, horror followed on horror, but no word was printed in any of the local journals. The curious went to the newspaper offices—there were two left in the county—but found nothing save a firm refusal to discuss the matter. And the Cardiff papers were drawn and found blank; and the London Press was apparently ignorant of the fact that crimes that had no parallel were terrorising a whole countryside. Everybody wondered what could have happened, what was happening; and then it was whispered that the coroner would allow no enquiry to be made as to these deaths of darkness.

"In consequence of instructions received from the Home Office," one coroner was understood to have said, "I have to tell the jury that their business will be to hear the medical evidence and to bring in a verdict immediately in accordance with that evidence. I shall disallow all questions."

One jury protested. The foreman refused to bring in any verdict at all.

"Very good," said the coroner. "Then I beg to inform you, Mr. Foreman and gentlemen of the jury, that under the Defence of the Realm Act I have power to supersede your functions, and to enter a verdict according to the evidence which has been laid before the Court as if it had been the verdict of you all."

The foreman and jury collapsed and accepted what they could not avoid. But the rumours that got abroad of all this, added to the known fact that the terror was ignored in the Press, no doubt by official command, increased the panic that was now arising, and gave it a new direction. Clearly, people reasoned, these Government restrictions and prohibitions could only refer to the war, to some great danger in connection with the war. And that being so, it followed that the outrages which must be kept so secret were the work of the enemy, that is of concealed German agents.

IV

It is time, I think, for me to make one point clear. I began this history with certain references to an extraordinary accident to an airman whose machine fell to the ground after collision with a huge flock of pigeons; and then to an explosion in a northern munition factory, an explosion, as I noted, of a very singular kind. Then I deserted the neighbourhood of London, and the northern district, and dwelt on a mysterious and terrible series of events which occurred in the summer of 1915 in a Welsh county, which I have named, for convenience, Meirion.

Well, let it be understood at once that all this detail that I have given about the occurrences in Meirion does not imply that the county in the far west was alone or especially afflicted by the terror that was over the land. They tell me that in the villages about Dartmoor the stout Devonshire hearts sank as men's hearts used to sink in the time of plague and pestilence. There was horror, too, about the Norfolk Broads, and far up by Perth no one would venture on the path that leads by Scone to the wooded heights above the Tay. And in the industrial districts: I met a man by chance one day in an odd London corner who spoke with horror of what a friend had told him.

"'Ask no questions, Ned,' he says to me, 'but I tell yaw a' was in Bairnigan t'other day, and a' met a pal who'd seen three hundred coffins going out of a works not far from there.'"

And then the ship that hovered outside the mouth of the Thames with all sails set and beat to and fro in the wind, and never answered any hail, and shewed no light! The forts shot at her and brought down one of the masts, but she went suddenly about with a change of wind under what sail still stood, and then veered down Channel, and drove ashore at last on the sandbanks and pinewoods of Arcachon, and not a man alive on her, but only rattling heaps of bones! That last voyage of the *Semiramis* would be something horribly worth telling; but I only heard it at a distance as a yarn, and only believed it because it squared with other things that I knew for certain.

This, then, is my point; I have written of the terror as it fell on Meirion, simply because I have had opportunities of getting close there to what really happened. Third or fourth or fifth hand in the other places; but round about Porth and Merthyr Tegveth I have spoken with people who have seen the tracks of the terror with their own eyes.

Well, I have said that the people of that far western county realised, not only that death was abroad in their quiet lanes and on their peaceful hills, but that for some reason it was to be kept all secret. Newspapers might not print any news of it, the very juries summoned to investigate it were allowed to investigate nothing. And so they concluded that this veil of secrecy must somehow be connected with the war; and from this position it was not a long way to a further inference: that the murderers of innocent men and women and children were either Germans or agents of Germany. It would be just like the Huns, everybody agreed, to think out such a devilish scheme as this; and they always thought out their schemes beforehand. They hoped to seize Paris in a few weeks, but when they were beaten on the Marne they had their trenches on the Aisne ready to fall back on: it had all been prepared years before the war. And so, no doubt, they had devised this terrible plan against England in case they could not beat us in open fight; there were people ready, very likely, all over the country, who were prepared to murder and destroy everywhere as soon as they got the word. In this way the Germans intended to sow terror throughout England and fill our hearts with panic and dismay, hoping so to weaken their enemy at home that he would lose all heart over the war abroad. It was the Zeppelin notion, in another form; they were committing these horrible and mysterious outrages thinking that we should be frightened out of our wits.

It all seemed plausible enough; Germany had by this time perpetrated so many horrors and had so excelled in devilish ingenuities that no abomination seemed too abominable to be probable, or too ingeniously wicked to be beyond the tortuous malice of the Hun. But then came the questions as to who the agents of this terrible design were, as to where they lived, as to how they contrived to move unseen from field to field, from lane to lane. All sorts of fantastic attempts were made to answer these questions; but it was felt that they remained unanswered. Some suggested that the murderers landed from submarines, or flew from hiding places on the West Coast of Ireland, coming and going by night; but there were seen to be flagrant impossibilities in both these suggestions. Everybody agreed that the evil work was no doubt the work of Germany; but nobody could begin to guess how it was done. Somebody at the club asked Remnant for his theory.

"My theory," said that ingenious person, "is that human progress is simply a long march from one inconceivable to another. Look at that airship of ours that came over Porth yesterday; ten years ago that would have been an inconceivable sight. Take the steam engine, take printing, take the theory of gravitation: they were all inconceivable till somebody thought of them. So it is, no doubt, with this infernal dodgery that we're talking about: the Huns have found it out, and we haven't; and there you are. We can't conceive how these poor people have been murdered, because the method's inconceivable to us."

The club listened with some awe to this high argument. After Remnant had gone, one member said: "Wonderful man, that."

"Yes," said Dr. Lewis. "He was asked whether he knew something. And his reply really amounted to 'No, I don't.' But I have never heard it better put."

It was, I suppose, at about this time when the people were puzzling their heads as to the secret methods used by the Germans or their agents to accomplish their crimes that a very singular circumstance became known to a few of the Porth people. It related to the murder of the Williams family on the Highway in front of their cottage door. I do not know that I have made it plain that the old Roman road called the Highway follows the course of a long, steep hill that goes steadily westward till it slants down and droops towards the sea. On either side of the road the ground falls away, here into deep shadowy woods, here to high pastures, now and again into a field of corn, but for the most part into the wild and broken land that is characteristic of Arfon. The fields are long and narrow, stretching up the steep hillside; they fall into sudden dips and hollows, a well springs up in the midst of one and a grove of ash and thorn bends over it, shading it; and beneath it the ground is thick with reeds and rushes. And then may come on either side of such a field territories glistening with the deep growth of bracken, and rough with gorse and rugged with thickets of blackthorn, green lichen hanging strangely from the branches; such are the lands on either side of the Highway.

Now on the lower slopes of it, beneath the Williams's cottage, some three or four fields down the hill, there is a military camp. The place has been used as a camp for many years, and lately the site has been extended and huts have been erected. But a considerable number of the men were under canvas here in the summer of 1915.

On the night of the Highway murder, this camp, as it appeared afterwards, was the scene of the extraordinary panic of the horses.

A good many men in the camp were asleep in their tents soon after 9.30, when the Last Post was sounded. They woke up in panic. There was a thundering sound on the steep hillside above them, and down upon the tents came half a dozen horses, mad with fright, trampling the canvas, trampling the men, bruising dozens of them and killing two.

Everything was in wild confusion, men groaning and screaming in the darkness, struggling with the canvas and the twisted ropes, shouting out, some of them, raw lads enough, that the Germans had landed, others wiping the blood from their eyes, a few, roused suddenly from heavy sleep, hitting out at one another, officers coming up at the double roaring out orders to the sergeants, a party of soldiers who were just returning to camp from the village seized with fright at what they could scarcely see or distinguish, at the wildness of the shouting and cursing and groaning that they could not understand, bolting out of the camp again and racing for their lives back to the village: everything in the maddest confusion of wild disorder.

Some of the men had seen the horses galloping down the hill as if terror itself was driving them. They scattered off into the darkness, and somehow or another found their way back in the night to their pasture above the camp. They were grazing there peacefully in the morning, and the only sign of the panic of the night before was the mud they had scattered all over themselves as they pelted through a patch of wet ground. The farmer said they were as quiet a lot as any in Meirion; he could make nothing of it.

"Indeed," he said, "I believe they must have seen the devil himself to be in such a fright as that: save the people!"

Now all this was kept as quiet as might be at the time when it happened; it became known to the men of the Porth Club in the days when they were discussing the difficult question of the German outrages, as the murders were commonly called. And this wild stampede of the farm horses was held by some to be evidence of the extraordinary and unheard-of character of the dreadful agency that was at work. One of the members of the club had been told by an officer who was in the camp at the time of the panic that the horses that came charging down were in a perfect fury of fright, that he had never seen horses in such a state, and so there was endless speculation as to the nature of the sight or the sound that had driven half a dozen quiet beasts into raging madness.

Then, in the middle of this talk, two or three other incidents, quite as odd and incomprehensible, came to be known, borne on chance trickles of gossip that came into the towns from outland farms, or were carried by cottagers tramping into Porth on market-day with a fowl or two and eggs and garden stuff; scraps and fragments of talk gathered by servants from the country folk and repeated to their mistresses. And in such ways it came out that up at Plas Newydd there had been a terrible business over swarming the bees; they had turned as wild as wasps and much more savage. They had come about the people who were taking the swarm like a cloud. They settled on one man's face so that you could not see the flesh for the bees crawling all over it, and they had stung him so badly that the doctor did not know whether he would get over it, and they had chased a girl who had come out to see the swarming, and settled on her and stung her to death. Then they had gone off to a brake below the farm and got into a hollow tree there, and it was not safe to go near it, for they would come out at you by day or by night.

And much the same thing had happened, it seemed, at three or four farms and cottages where bees were kept. And there were stories, hardly so clear or so credible, of sheepdogs, mild and trusted beasts, turning as savage as wolves and injuring the farm boys in a horrible manner—in one case it was said with fatal results. It was certainly true that old Mrs. Owen's favourite Brahma-Dorking cock had gone mad; she came into Porth one Saturday morning with her face and her neck all bound up and plastered. She had gone out to her bit of a field to feed the poultry the night before, and the bird had flown at her and attacked her most savagely, inflicting some very nasty wounds before she could beat it off.

"There was a stake handy, lucky for me," she said, "and I did beat him and beat him till the life was out of him. But what is come to the world, whatever?"

Now Remnant, the man of theories, was also a man of extreme leisure. It was understood that he had succeeded to ample means when he was quite a young man, and after tasting the savours of the law, as it were, for half a dozen terms at the board of the Middle Temple, he had decided that it would be senseless to bother himself with passing examinations for a profession which he had not the faintest intention of practising. So he turned a deaf ear to the call of "Manger" ringing through the Temple Courts, and set himself out to potter amiably through the world. He had pottered all over Europe, he had looked at Africa, and had even put his head in at the door of the East, on a trip which included the Greek isles and Constantinople. Now, getting into the middle fifties, he had settled at Porth for the sake, as he said, of the Gulf Stream and the fuchsia hedges, and pottered over his books and his theories and the local gossip. He was no more brutal than the general public, which revels in the details of mysterious crime; but it must be said that the terror, black though it was, was a boon to him. He peered and investigated and poked about with the relish of a man to whose life a new zest has been added. He listened attentively to the strange tales of bees and dogs and poultry that came into Porth with the country baskets of butter, rabbits, and green peas; and he evolved at last a most extraordinary theory.

Full of this discovery, as he thought it, he went one night to see Dr. Lewis and take his view of the matter.

"I want to talk to you," said Remnant to the doctor, "about what I have called, provisionally, the Z Ray."

V

Dr. Lewis, smiling indulgently, and quite prepared for some monstrous piece of theorising, led Remnant into the room that overlooked the terraced garden and the sea.

The doctor's house, though it was only ten minutes' walk from the centre of the town, seemed remote from all other habitations. The drive to it from the road came through a deep grove of trees and a dense shrubbery, trees were about the house on either side, mingling with neighbouring groves, and below, the garden fell down, terrace by green terrace, to wild growth, a twisted path amongst red rocks, and at last to the yellow sand of a little cove. The room to which the doctor took Remnant looked over these terraces and across the water to the dim boundaries of the bay. It had French windows that were thrown wide open, and the two men sat in the soft light of the lamp—this was before the days of severe lighting regulations in the far west—and enjoyed the sweet odours and the sweet vision of the summer evening. Then Remnant began:

"I suppose, Lewis, you've heard these extraordinary stories of bees and dogs and things that have been going about lately?"

"Certainly I have heard them. I was called in at Plas Newydd, and treated Thomas Trevor, who's only just out of danger, by the way. I certified for the poor child, Mary Trevor. She was dying when I got to the place. There was no doubt she was stung to death by bees, and I believe there were other very similar cases at Llantarnam and Morwen; none fatal, I think. What about them?"

"Well: then there are the stories of good-tempered old sheepdogs turning wicked and 'savaging' children?"

"Quite so. I haven't seen any of these cases professionally; but I believe the stories are accurate enough."

"And the old woman assaulted by her own poultry?"

"That's perfectly true. Her daughter put some stuff of their own concoction on her face and neck, and then she came to me. The wounds seemed going all right, so I told her to continue the treatment, whatever it might be."

"Very good," said Mr. Remnant. He spoke now with an italic impressiveness. *"Don't you see the link between all this and the horrible things that have been happening about here for the last month?"*

Lewis stared at Remnant in amazement. He lifted his red eyebrows and lowered them in a kind of scowl. His speech shewed traces of his native accent.

"Great burning!" he exclaimed. "What on earth are you getting at now? It is madness. Do you mean to tell me that you think there is some connection between a swarm or two of bees that have turned nasty, a cross dog, and a wicked old barn-door cock and these poor people that have been pitched over the cliffs and hammered to death on the road? There's no sense in it, you know."

"I am strongly inclined to believe that there is a great deal of sense in it," replied Remnant with extreme calmness. "Look here, Lewis, I saw you grinning the other day at the club when I was telling the fellows that in my opinion all these outrages had been committed, certainly by the Germans, but by some method of which we have no conception. But what I meant to say when I talked about inconceivables was just this: that the Williams's and the rest of them have been killed in some way that's not in theory at all, not in our theory, at all events, some way we've not contemplated, not thought of for an instant. Do you see my point?"

"Well, in a sort of way. You mean there's an absolute originality in the method? I suppose that is so. But what next?"

Remnant seemed to hesitate, partly from a sense of the portentous nature of what he was about to say, partly from a sort of half-unwillingness to part with so profound a secret.

"Well," he said, "you will allow that we have two sets of phenomena of a very extraordinary kind occurring at the same time. Don't you think that it's only reasonable to connect the two sets with one another?"

"So the philosopher of Tenterden steeple and the Goodwin Sands thought, certainly," said Lewis. "But what is the connection? Those poor folks on the Highway weren't stung by bees or worried by a dog. And horses don't throw people over cliffs or stifle them in marshes."

"No; I never meant to suggest anything so absurd. It is evident to me that in all these cases of animals turning suddenly savage the cause has been terror, panic, fear. The horses that went charging into the camp were mad with fright, we know. And I say that in the other instances we have been discussing the cause was the same. The creatures were exposed to an infection of fear, and a frightened beast or bird or insect uses its weapons, whatever they may be. If, for example, there had been anybody with those horses when they took their panic they would have lashed out at him with their heels."

"Yes, I dare say that that is so. Well."

"Well; my belief is that the Germans have made an extraordinary discovery. I have called it the Z Ray. You know that the ether is merely an hypothesis; we have to suppose that it's there to account for the passage of the Marconi current from one place to another. Now, suppose that there is a psychic ether as well as a material ether, suppose that it is possible to direct irresistible impulses across this medium, suppose that these impulses are towards murder or suicide; then I think that you have an explanation of the terrible series of events that have been happening in Meirion for the last few weeks. And it is quite clear to my mind that the horses and the other creatures have been exposed to this Z Ray, and that it has produced on them the effect of terror, with ferocity as the result of terror. Now what do you say to that? Telepathy, you know, is well established: so is hypnotic suggestion. You have only to look in the 'Encyclopædia Britannica' to see that, and suggestion is so strong in some cases as to be an irresistible imperative. Now don't you feel that putting telepathy and suggestion together, as it were, you have more than the elements of what I call the Z Ray? I feel myself that I have more to go on in making my hypothesis than the inventor of the steam-engine had in making his hypothesis when he saw the lid of the kettle bobbing up and down. What do you say?"

Dr. Lewis made no answer. He was watching the growth of a new, unknown tree in his garden.

The doctor made no answer to Remnant's question. For one thing, Remnant was profuse in his eloquence—he has been rigidly condensed in this history—and Lewis was tired of the sound of his voice. For another thing, he found the Z Ray theory almost too extravagant to be bearable, wild enough to tear patience to tatters. And then as the tedious argument continued Lewis became conscious that there was something strange about the night.

It was a dark summer night. The moon was old and faint, above the Dragon's Head across the bay, and the air was very still. It was so still that Lewis had noted that not a leaf stirred on the very tip of a high tree that stood out against the sky; and yet he knew that he was listening to some sound that he could not determine or define. It was not the wind in the leaves, it was not the gentle wash of the water of the sea against the rocks; that latter sound he could distinguish quite

easily. But there was something else. It was scarcely a sound; it was as
if the air itself trembled and fluttered, as the air trembles in a church
when they open the great pedal pipes of the organ.

The doctor listened intently. It was not an illusion, the sound was
not in his own head, as he had suspected for a moment; but for the life
of him he could not make out whence it came or what it was. He
gazed down into the night over the terraces of his garden, now sweet
with the scent of the flowers of the night; tried to peer over the tree-
tops across the sea towards the Dragon's Head. It struck him suddenly
that this strange fluttering vibration of the air might be the noise of a
distant airplane or airship; there was not the usual droning hum, but
this sound might be caused by a new type of engine. A new type of engine? Possibly it was an enemy airship; their range, it had been said,
was getting longer; and Lewis was just going to call Remnant's attention to the sound, to its possible cause, and to the possible danger that
might be hovering over them, when he saw something that caught his
breath and his heart with wild amazement and a touch of terror.

He had been staring upward into the sky, and, about to speak to
Remnant, he had let his eyes drop for an instant. He looked down towards the trees in the garden, and saw with utter astonishment that
one had changed its shape in the few hours that had passed since the
setting of the sun. There was a thick grove of ilexes bordering the lowest terrace, and above them rose one tall pine, spreading its head of
sparse, dark branches dark against the sky.

As Lewis glanced down over the terraces he saw that the tall pine
tree was no longer there. In its place there rose above the ilexes what
might have been a greater ilex; there was the blackness of a dense
growth of foliage rising like a broad and far-spreading and rounded
cloud over the lesser trees.

Here, then, was a sight wholly incredible, impossible. It is doubtful
whether the process of the human mind in such a case has ever been
analysed and registered; it is doubtful whether it ever can be registered.
It is hardly fair to bring in the mathematician, since he deals with absolute truth (so far as mortality can conceive absolute truth); but how
would a mathematician feel if he were suddenly confronted with a two-
sided triangle? I suppose he would instantly become a raging madman;
and Lewis, staring wide-eyed and wild-eyed at a dark and spreading

tree which his own experience informed him was not there, felt for an instant that shock which should affront us all when we first realise the intolerable antinomy of Achilles and the Tortoise. Common sense tells us that Achilles will flash past the tortoise almost with the speed of the lightning; the inflexible truth of mathematics assures us that till the earth boils and the heavens cease to endure the Tortoise must still be in advance; and thereupon we should, in common decency, go mad. We do not go mad, because, by special grace, we are certified that, in the final court of appeal, all science is a lie, even the highest science of all; and so we simply grin at Achilles and the Tortoise, as we grin at Darwin, deride Huxley, and laugh at Herbert Spencer.

Dr. Lewis did not grin. He glared into the dimness of the night, at the great spreading tree that he knew could not be there. And as he gazed he saw that what at first appeared the dense blackness of foliage was fretted and starred with wonderful appearances of lights and colours.

Afterwards he said to me: "I remember thinking to myself: 'Look here, I am not delirious; my temperature is perfectly normal. I am not drunk; I only had a pint of Graves with my dinner, over three hours ago. I have not eaten any poisonous fungus; I have not taken *Anhelonium Lewinii* experimentally. So, now then! What is happening?'"

The night had gloomed over; clouds obscured the faint moon and the misty stars. Lewis rose, with some kind of warning and inhibiting gesture to Remnant, who, he was conscious, was gaping at him in astonishment. He walked to the open French window, and took a pace forward on the path outside, and looked, very intently, at the dark shape of the tree, down below the sloping garden, above the washing of the waves. He shaded the light of the lamp behind him by holding his hands on each side of his eyes.

The mass of the tree—the tree that couldn't be there—stood out against the sky, but not so clearly, now that the clouds had rolled up. Its edges, the limits of its leafage, were not so distinct. Lewis thought that he could detect some sort of quivering movement in it; though the air was at a dead calm. It was a night on which one might hold up a lighted match and watch it burn without any wavering or inclination of the flame.

"You know," said Lewis, "how a bit of burnt paper will sometimes hang over the coals before it goes up the chimney, and little worms of fire will shoot through it. It was like that, if you should be standing some distance away. Just threads and hairs of yellow light I saw, and specks and sparks of fire, and then a twinkling of a ruby no bigger than a pin point, and a green wandering in the black, as if an emerald were crawling, and then little veins of deep blue. 'Woe is me!' I said to myself in Welsh. 'What is all this colour and burning?'

"And, then, at that very moment there came a thundering rap at the door of the room inside, and there was my man telling me that I was wanted directly up at the Garth, as old Mr. Trevor Williams had been taken very bad. I knew his heart was not worth much, so I had to go off directly, and leave Remnant to make what he could of it all."

VI

Dr. Lewis was kept some time at the Garth. It was past twelve when he got back to his house. He went quickly to the room that overlooked the garden and the sea and threw open the French window and peered into the darkness. There, dim indeed against the dim sky but unmistakable, was the tall pine with its sparse branches, high above the dense growth of the ilex trees. The strange boughs which had amazed him had vanished; there was no appearance now of colours or of fires.

He drew his chair up to the open window and sat there gazing and wondering far into the night, till brightness came upon the sea and sky, and the forms of the trees in the garden grew clear and evident. He went up to his bed at last filled with a great perplexity, still asking questions to which there was no answer.

The doctor did not say anything about the strange tree to Remnant. When they next met, Lewis said that he had thought there was a man hiding amongst the bushes—this in explanation of that warning gesture he had used, and of his going out into the garden and staring into the night. He concealed the truth because he dreaded the Remnant doctrine that would undoubtedly be produced; indeed, he hoped that he had heard the last of the theory of the Z Ray. But Remnant firmly reopened this subject.

"We were interrupted just as I was putting my case to you," he said. "And to sum it all up, it amounts to this: that the Huns have made one of the great leaps of science. They are sending 'suggestions' (which amount to irresistible commands) over here, and the persons affected are seized with suicidal or homicidal mania. The people who were killed by falling over the cliffs or into the quarry probably committed suicide; and so with the man and the boy who were found in the bog. As to the Highway case, you remember that Thomas Evans said that he stopped and talked to Williams on the night of the murder. In my opinion Evans was the murderer. He came under the influence of the Ray, became a homicidal maniac in an instant, snatched Williams's spade from his hand and killed him and the others."

"The bodies were found by me on the road."

"It is possible that the first impact of the Ray produces violent nervous excitement, which would manifest itself externally. Williams might have called to his wife to come and see what was the matter with Evans. The children would naturally follow their mother. It seems to me simple. And as for the animals—the horses, dogs, and so forth, they, as I say, were no doubt panic-stricken by the Ray, and hence driven to frenzy."

"Why should Evans have murdered Williams instead of Williams murdering Evans? Why should the impact of the Ray affect one and not the other?"

"Why does one man react violently to a certain drug, while it makes no impression on another man? Why is A able to drink a bottle of whisky and remain sober, while B is turned into something very like a lunatic after he has drunk three glasses?"

"It is a question of idiosyncrasy," said the doctor.

"Is 'idiosyncrasy' Greek for 'I don't know'?" asked Remnant.

"Not at all," said Lewis, smiling blandly. "I mean that in some diatheses whisky—as you have mentioned whisky—appears not to be pathogenic, or at all events not immediately pathogenic. In other cases, as you very justly observed, there seems to be a very marked cachexia associated with the exhibition of the spirit in question, even in comparatively small doses."

Under this cloud of professional verbiage Lewis escaped from the club and from Remnant. He did not want to hear any more about that dreadful Ray, because he felt sure that the Ray was all nonsense. But asking himself why he felt this certitude in the matter, he had to confess that he didn't know. An airplane, he reflected, was all nonsense before it was made; and he remembered talking in the early 'nineties to a friend of his about the newly discovered X Rays. The friend laughed incredulously, evidently didn't believe a word of it, till Lewis told him that there was an article on the subject in the current number of the *Saturday Review;* whereupon the unbeliever said, "Oh, is that so? Oh, really, I *see,*" and was converted on the X Ray faith on the spot. Lewis, remembering this talk, marvelled at the strange processes of the human mind, its illogical and yet all-compelling *ergos,* and wondered whether he himself was only waiting for an article on the Z Ray in the *Saturday Review* to become a devout believer in the doctrine of Remnant.

But he wondered with far more fervour as to the extraordinary thing he had seen in his own garden with his own eyes. The tree that changed all its shape for an hour or two of the night, the growth of strange boughs, the apparition of secret fires among them, the sparkling of emerald and ruby lights: how could one fail to be afraid with great amazement at the thought of such a mystery?

Dr. Lewis's thoughts were distracted from the incredible adventure of the tree by the visit of his sister and her husband. Mr. and Mrs. Merritt lived in a well-known manufacturing town of the Midlands, which was now, of course, a centre of munition work. On the day of their arrival at Porth, Mrs. Merritt, who was tired after the long, hot journey, went to bed early, and Merritt and Lewis went into the room by the garden for their talk and tobacco. They spoke of the year that had passed since their last meeting, of the weary dragging of the war, of friends that had perished in it, of the hopelessness of an early ending of all this misery. Lewis said nothing of the terror that was on the land. One does not greet a tired man who is come to a quiet, sunny place for relief from black smoke and work and worry with a tale of horror. Indeed, the doctor saw that his brother-in-law looked far from well. And he seemed "jumpy"; there was an occasional twitch of his mouth that Lewis did not like at all.

"Well," said the doctor, after an interval of silence and port wine, "I am glad to see you here again. Porth always suits you. I don't think you're looking quite up to your usual form. But three weeks of Meirion air will do wonders."

"Well, I hope it will," said the other. "I am not up to the mark. Things are not going well at Midlingham."

"Business is all right, isn't it?"

"Yes. Business is all right. But there are other things that are all wrong. We are living under a reign of terror. It comes to that."

"What on earth do you mean?"

"Well, I suppose I may tell you what I know. It's not much. I didn't dare write it. But do you know that at every one of the munition works in Midlingham and all about it there's a guard of soldiers with drawn bayonets and loaded rifles day and night? Men with bombs, too. And machine-guns at the big factories."

"German spies?"

"You don't want Lewis guns to fight spies with. Nor bombs. Nor a platoon of men. I woke up last night. It was the machine-gun at Benington's Army Motor Works. Firing like fury. And then bang! bang! bang! That was the hand bombs."

"But what against?"

"Nobody knows.

"Nobody knows what is happening," Merritt repeated, and he went on to describe the bewilderment and terror that hung like a cloud over the great industrial city in the Midlands, how the feeling of concealment, of some intolerable secret danger that must not be named, was worst of all.

"A young fellow I know," he said, "was on short leave the other day from the front, and he spent it with his people at Belmont—that's about four miles out of Midlingham, you know. 'Thank God,' he said to me, 'I am going back to-morrow. It's no good saying that the Wipers salient is nice, because it isn't. But it's a damned sight better than this. At the front you know what you're up against, anyhow.' At Midlingham everybody has the feeling that we're up against something awful and we don't know what; it's that that makes people inclined to whisper. There's terror in the air."

Merritt made a sort of picture of the great town cowering in its fear of an unknown danger.

"People are afraid to go about alone at nights in the outskirts. They make up parties at the stations to go home together if it's anything like dark, or if there are any lonely bits on their way."

"But why? I don't understand. What are they afraid of?"

"Well, I told you about my being woke up the other night with the machine-guns at the motor works rattling away, and the bombs exploding and making the most terrible noise. That sort of thing alarms one, you know. It's only natural."

"Indeed, it must be very terrifying. You mean, then, there is a general nervousness about, a vague sort of apprehension that makes people inclined to herd together?"

"There's that, and there's more. People have gone out that have never come back. There were a couple of men in the train to Holme, arguing about the quickest way to get to Northend, a sort of outlying part of Holme where they both lived. They argued all the way out of Midlingham, one saying that the high road was the quickest though it was the longest way. 'It's the quickest going because it's the cleanest going,' he said.

"The other chap fancied a short cut across the fields, by the canal. 'It's half the distance,' he kept on. 'Yes, if you don't lose your way,' said the other. Well, it appears they put an even half-crown on it, and each was to try his own way when they got out of the train. It was arranged that they were to meet at the 'Waggon' in Northend. 'I shall be at the "Waggon" first,' said the man who believed in the short cut, and with that he climbed over the stile and made off across the fields. It wasn't late enough to be really dark, and a lot of them thought he might win the stakes. But he never turned up at the 'Waggon'—or anywhere else for the matter of that."

"What happened to him?"

"He was found lying on his back in the middle of a field—some way from the path. He was dead. The doctors said he'd been suffocated. Nobody knows how. Then there have been other cases. We whisper about them at Midlingham, but we're afraid to speak out."

Lewis was ruminating all this profoundly. Terror in Meirion and terror far away in the heart of England; but at Midlingham, so far as he could gather from these stories of soldiers on guard, of crackling machine-guns, it was a case of an organised attack on the munitioning of the army. He felt that he did not know enough to warrant his deciding that the terror of Meirion and of Stratfordshire were one.

Then Merritt began again:

"There's a queer story going about, when the door's shut and the curtain's drawn, that is, as to a place right out in the country over the other side of Midlingham; on the opposite side to Dunwich. They've built one of the new factories out there, a great red brick town of sheds they tell me it is, with a tremendous chimney. It's not been finished more than a month or six weeks. They plumped it down right in the middle of the fields, by the line, and they're building huts for the workers as fast as they can, but up to the present the men are billeted all about, up and down the line.

"About two hundred yards from this place there's an old footpath, leading from the station and the main road up to a small hamlet on the hillside. Part of the way this path goes by a pretty large wood, most of it thick undergrowth. I should think there must be twenty acres of wood, more or less. As it happens, I used this path once long ago; and I can tell you it's a black place of nights.

"A man had to go this way one night. He got along all right till he came to the wood. And then he said his heart dropped out of his body. It was awful to hear the noises in that wood. Thousands of men were in it, he swears that. It was full of rustling, and pattering of feet trying to go dainty, and the crack of dead boughs lying on the ground as some one trod on them, and swishing of the grass, and some sort of chattering speech going on that sounded, so he said, as if the dead sat in their bones and talked! He ran for his life, anyhow; across fields, over hedges, through brooks. He must have run, by his tale, ten miles out of his way before he got home to his wife, and beat at the door, and broke in, and bolted it behind him."

"There is something rather alarming about any wood at night," said Dr. Lewis.

Merritt shrugged his shoulders.

"People say that the Germans have landed, and that they are hiding in underground places all over the country."

VII

Lewis gasped for a moment, silent in contemplation of the magnificence of rumour. The Germans already landed, hiding underground, striking by night, secretly, terribly, at the power of England! Here was a conception which made the myth of "the Russians" a paltry fable; before which the Legend of Mons was an ineffectual thing.

It was monstrous. And yet—

He looked steadily at Merritt; a square-headed, black-haired, solid sort of man. He had symptoms of nerves about him for the moment, certainly, but one could not wonder at that, whether the tales he told were true, or whether he merely believed them to be true. Lewis had known his brother-in-law for twenty years or more, and had always found him a sure man in his own small world. "But then," said the doctor to himself, "those men, if they once get out of the ring of that little world of theirs, they are lost. Those are the men that believed in Madame Blavatsky."

"Well," he said, "what do you think yourself? The Germans landed and hiding somewhere about the country: there's something extravagant in the notion, isn't there?"

"I don't know what to think. You can't get over the facts. There are the soldiers with their rifles and their guns at the works all over Stratfordshire, and those guns go off. I told you I'd heard them. Then who are the soldiers shooting at? That's what we ask ourselves at Midlingham."

"Quite so; I quite understand. It's an extraordinary state of things."

"It's more than extraordinary; it's an awful state of things. It's terror in the dark, and there's nothing worse than that. As that young fellow I was telling you about said, 'At the front you do know what you're up against.'"

"And people really believe that a number of Germans have somehow got over to England and have hid themselves underground?"

"People say they've got a new kind of poison-gas. Some think that they dig underground places and make the gas there, and lead it by secret pipes into the shops; others say that they throw gas bombs into the factories. It must be worse than anything they've used in France, from what the authorities say."

"The authorities? Do *they* admit that there are Germans in hiding about Midlingham?"

"No. They call it 'explosions'. But we know it isn't explosions. We know in the Midlands what an explosion sounds like and looks like. And we know that the people killed in these 'explosions' are put into their coffins in the works. Their own relations are not allowed to see them."

"And so you believe in the German theory?"

"If I do, it's because one must believe in something. Some say they've seen the gas. I heard that a man living in Dunwich saw it one night like a black cloud with sparks of fire in it floating over the tops of the trees by Dunwich Common."

The light of an ineffable amazement came into Lewis's eyes. The night of Remnant's visit, the trembling vibration of the air, the dark tree that had grown in his garden since the setting of the sun, the strange leafage that was starred with burning, with emerald and ruby fires, and all vanished away when he returned from his visit to the Garth; and such a leafage had appeared as a burning cloud far in the heart of England: what intolerable mystery, what tremendous doom was signified in this? But one thing was clear and certain: that the terror of Meirion was also the terror of the Midlands.

Lewis made up his mind most firmly that if possible all this should be kept from his brother-in-law. Merritt had come to Porth as to a city of refuge from the horrors of Midlingham; if it could be managed he should be spared the knowledge that the cloud of terror had gone before him and hung black over the western land. Lewis passed the port and said in an even voice:

"Very strange, indeed; a black cloud with sparks of fire?"

"I can't answer for it, you know; it's only a rumour."

"Just so; and you think or you're inclined to think that this and all the rest you've told me is to be put down to the hidden Germans?"

"As I say; because one must think something."

"I quite see your point. No doubt, if it's true, it's the most awful blow that has ever been dealt at any nation in the whole history of man. The enemy established in our vitals! But it is possible, after all? How could it have been worked?"

Merritt told Lewis how it had been worked, or rather, how people said it had been worked. The idea, he said, was that this was a part, and a most important part, of the great German plot to destroy England and the British Empire.

The scheme had been prepared years ago, some thought soon after the Franco-Prussian War. Moltke had seen that the invasion of England (in the ordinary sense of the term invasion) presented very great difficulties. The matter was constantly in discussion in the inner military and high political circles, and the general trend of opinion in these quarters was that at the best, the invasion of England would involve Germany in the gravest difficulties, and leave France in the position of the *tertius gaudens*. This was the state of affairs when a very high Prussian personage was approached by the Swedish professor, Huvelius.

Thus Merritt, and here I would say in parenthesis that this Huvelius was by all accounts an extraordinary man. Considered personally and apart from his writings he would appear to have been a most amiable individual. He was richer than the generality of Swedes, certainly far richer than the average university professor in Sweden. But his shabby green frock-coat, and his battered, furry hat were notorious in the university town where he lived. No one laughed, because it was well known that Professor Huvelius spent every penny of his private means and a large portion of his official stipend on works of kindness and charity. He hid his head in a garret, some one said, in order that others might be able to swell on the first floor. It was told of him that he restricted himself to a diet of dry bread and coffee for a month, in order that a poor woman of the streets, dying of consumption, might enjoy luxuries in hospital.

And this was the man who wrote the treatise *De Facinore Humano*, to prove the infinite corruption of the human race.

Oddly enough, Professor Huvelius wrote the most cynical book in the world—Hobbes preaches rosy sentimentalism in comparison— with the very highest motives. He held that a very large part of human misery, misadventure, and sorrow was due to the false convention that the heart of man was naturally and in the main well disposed and kindly, if not exactly righteous. "Murderers, thieves, assassins, violators, and all the host of the abominable," he says in one passage, "are created by the false pretence and foolish credence of human virtue. A lion in a cage is a fierce beast, indeed; but what will he be if we declare him to be a lamb and open the doors of his den? Who will be guilty of the deaths of the men, women, and children whom he will surely devour, save those who unlocked the cage?" And he goes on to shew that kings and the rulers of the peoples could decrease the sum of human misery to a vast extent by acting on the doctrine of human wickedness.

"War," he declares, "which is one of the worst of evils, will always continue to exist. But a wise king will desire a brief war rather than a lengthy one, a short evil rather than a long evil. And this not from the benignity of his heart towards his enemies, for we have seen that the human heart is naturally malignant, but because he desires to conquer, and to conquer easily, without a great expenditure of men or of treasure, knowing that if he can accomplish this feat his people will love him and his crown will be secure. So he will wage brief victorious wars, and not only spare his own nation, but the nation of the enemy, since in a short war the loss is less on both sides than in a long war. And so from evil will come good."

And how, asks Huvelius, are such wars to be waged? The wise prince, he replies, will begin by assuming the enemy to be infinitely corruptible and infinitely stupid, since stupidity and corruption are the chief characteristics of man. So the prince will make himself friends in the very councils of his enemy, and also amongst the populace, bribing the wealthy by proffering to them the opportunity of still greater wealth, and winning the poor by swelling words. "For, contrary to the common opinion, it is the wealthy who are greedy of wealth; while the populace are to be gained by talking to them about liberty, their unknown god. And so much are they enchanted by the words liberty, freedom, and such like, that the wise can go to the poor, rob them of what little they have, dismiss them with a hearty kick, and win their hearts and their votes for ever, if only they will assure them that the treatment which they have received is called liberty."

Guided by these principles, says Huvelius, the wise prince will entrench himself in the country that he desires to conquer; "nay, with but little trouble, he may actually and literally throw his garrisons into the heart of the enemy country before war has begun."

This is a long and tiresome parenthesis; but it is necessary as explaining the long tale which Merritt told his brother-in-law, he having received it from some magnate of the Midlands, who had travelled in Germany. It is probable that the story was suggested in the first place by the passage from Huvelius which I have just quoted.

Merritt knew nothing of the real Huvelius, who was all but a saint; he thought of the Swedish professor as a monster of iniquity, "worse," as he said, "than Neech"—meaning, no doubt, Nietzsche.

So he told the story of how Huvelius had sold his plan to the Germans; a plan for filling England with German soldiers. Land was to be bought in certain suitable and well-considered places, Englishmen were to be bought as the apparent owners of such land, and secret excavations were to be made, till the country was literally undermined. A subterranean Germany, in fact, was to be dug under selected districts of England: there were to be great caverns, underground cities, well drained, well ventilated, supplied with water, and in these places vast stores both of food and of munitions were to be accumulated, year after year, till "the Day" dawned. And then, warned in time, the secret garrison would leave shops, hotels, offices, villas, and vanish underground, ready to begin their work of bleeding England at the heart.

"That's what Henson told me," said Merritt at the end of his long story. "Henson, head of the Buckley Iron and Steel Syndicate. He has been a lot in Germany."

"Well," said Lewis, "of course, it may be so. If it is so, it is terrible beyond words."

Indeed, he found something horribly plausible in the story. It was an extraordinary plan, of course; an unheard-of scheme; but it did not seem impossible. It was the Trojan Horse on a gigantic scale; indeed, he reflected, the story of the horse with the warriors concealed within it which was dragged into the heart of Troy by the deluded Trojans themselves might be taken as a prophetic parable of what had happened to England—if Henson's theory were well founded. And this theory certainly squared with what one had heard of German preparations in Belgium and in France: emplacements for guns ready for the invader, German manufactories which were really German forts on Belgian soil, the caverns by the Aisne made ready for the cannon; indeed, Lewis thought he remembered something about suspicious concrete tennis-courts on the heights commanding London. But a German army hidden under English ground! It was a thought to chill the stoutest heart.

And it seemed from that wonder of the burning tree, that the enemy mysteriously and terribly present at Midlingham, was present also in Meirion. Lewis, thinking of the country as he knew it, of its wild and desolate hillsides, its deep woods, its wastes and solitary places, could not but confess that no more fit region could be found for the deadly enterprise of secret men. Yet, he thought again, there was but little harm to be done in Meirion to the armies of England or to their munitionment. They were working for panic terror? Possibly that might be so: but the camp under the Highway? That should be their first object, and no harm had been done there.

Lewis did not know that since the panic of the horses men had died terribly in that camp; that it was now a fortified place, with a deep, broad trench, a thick tangle of savage barbed wire about it, and a machine-gun planted at each corner.

VIII

Mr. Merritt began to pick up his health and spirits a good deal. For the first morning or two of his stay at the doctor's he contented himself with a very comfortable deck chair close to the house, where he sat under the shade of an old mulberry tree beside his wife and watched the bright sunshine on the green lawns, on the creamy crests of the waves, on the headlands of that glorious coast, purple even from afar with the imperial glow of the heather, on the white farmhouses gleaming in the sunlight, high over the sea, far from any turmoil, from any troubling of men.

The sun was hot, but the wind breathed all the while gently, incessantly, from the east, and Merritt, who had come to this quiet place, not only from dismay, but from the stifling and oily airs of the smoky Midland town, said that that east wind, pure and clear and like well water from the rock, was new life to him. He ate a capital dinner at the end of his first day at Porth and took rosy views. As to what they had been talking about the night before, he said to Lewis, no doubt there must be trouble of some sort, and perhaps bad trouble; still, Kitchener would soon put it all right.

So things went on very well. Merritt began to stroll about the garden, which was full of the comfortable spaces, groves, and surprises that only country gardens know. To the right of one of the terraces he found an arbour or summer-house covered with white roses, and he was as pleased as if he had discovered the Pole. He spent a whole day there, smoking and lounging and reading a rubbishy sensational story, and declared that the Devonshire roses had taken many years off his age. Then on the other side of the garden there was a filbert grove that he had never explored on any of this former visits; and again there was a find. Deep in the shadow of the filberts was a bubbling well, issuing from rocks, and all manner of green, dewy ferns growing about it and above it, and an angelica springing beside it. Merritt knelt on his knees, and hollowed his hand and drank the well water. He said (over his port) that night that if all water were like the water of the filbert well the world would turn to teetotalism. It takes a townsman to relish the manifold and exquisite joys of the country.

It was not till he began to venture abroad that Merritt found that something was lacking of the old rich peace that used to dwell in Meirion. He had a favourite walk which he never neglected, year after year. This walk led along the cliffs towards Meiros, and then one could turn inland and return to Porth by deep winding lanes that went over the Allt. So Merritt set out early one morning and got as far as a sentry-box at the foot of the path that led up to the cliff. There was a sentry pacing up and down in front of the box, and he called on Merritt to produce his pass, or to turn back to the main road. Merritt was a good deal put out, and asked the doctor about this strict guard. And the doctor was surprised.

"I didn't know they had put their bar up there," he said. "I suppose it's wise. We are certainly in the far West here; still, the Germans might slip round and raid us and do a lot of damage just because Meirion is the last place we should expect them to go for."

"But there are no fortifications, surely, on the cliff?"

"Oh, no; I never heard of anything of the kind there."

"Well, what's the point of forbidding the public to go on the cliff, then? I can quite understand putting a sentry on the top to keep a look-out for the enemy. What I don't understand is a sentry at the bottom who can't keep a look-out for anything, as he can't see the sea. And why warn the public off the cliffs? I couldn't facilitate a German landing by standing on Pengareg, even if I wanted to."

"It is curious," the doctor agreed. "Some military reasons, I suppose."

He let the matter drop, perhaps because the matter did not affect him. People who live in the country all the year round, country doctors certainly, are little given to desultory walking in search of the picturesque.

Lewis had no suspicion that sentries whose object was equally obscure were being dotted all over the country. There was a sentry, for
example, by the quarry at Llanfihangel, where the dead woman and the
dead sheep had been found some weeks before. The path by the quarry was used a good deal, and its closing would have inconvenienced
the people of the neighbourhood very considerably. But the sentry had
his box by the side of the track and had his orders to keep everybody
strictly to the path, as if the quarry were a secret fort.

It was not known till a month or two ago that one of these sentries
was himself a victim of the terror. The men on duty at this place were
given certain very strict orders, which, from the nature of the case,
must have seemed to them unreasonable. For old soldiers, orders are
orders; but here was a young bank clerk, scarcely in training for a couple of months, who had not begun to appreciate the necessity of hard,
literal obedience to an order which seemed to him meaningless. He
found himself on a remote and lonely hillside, he had not the faintest
notion that his every movement was watched; and he disobeyed a certain instruction that had been given him. The post was found deserted
by the relief; the sentry's dead body was found at the bottom of the
quarry.

This by the way; but Mr. Merritt discovered again and again that things
happened to hamper his walks and his wanderings. Two or three miles
from Porth there is a great marsh made by the Afon River before it
falls into the sea, and here Merritt had been accustomed to botanise
mildly. He had learned pretty accurately the causeways of solid ground
that led through the sea of swamp and ooze and soft yielding soil, and
he set out one hot afternoon determined to make a thorough explora-
tion of the marsh, and this time to find that rare Bog Bean that, he felt
sure, must grow somewhere in its wide extent.

He got into the by-road that skirts the marsh, and to the gate
which he had always used for entrance.

There was the scene as he had known it always, the rich growth of
reeds and flags and rushes, the mild black cattle grazing on the "islands" of firm turf, the scented procession of the meadowsweet, the
royal glory of the loosestrife, flaming pennons, crimson and golden, of
the giant dock.

But they were bringing out a dead man's body through the gate.

A labouring man was holding open the gate on the marsh. Merritt, horrified, spoke to him and asked who it was, and how it had happened.

"They do say he was a visitor at Porth. Somehow he has been drowned in the marsh, whatever."

"But it's perfectly safe. I've been all over it a dozen times."

"Well, indeed, we did always think so. If you did slip by accident, like, and fall into the water, it was not so deep; it was easy enough to climb out again. And this gentleman was quite young, to look at him, poor man; and he has come to Meirion for his pleasure and holiday and found his death in it!"

"Did he do it on purpose? Is it suicide?"

"They say he had no reasons to do that."

Here the sergeant of police in charge of the party interposed, according to orders, which he himself did not understand.

"A terrible thing, sir, to be sure, and a sad pity; and I am sure this is not the sort of sight you have come to see down in Meirion this beautiful summer. So don't you think, sir, that it would be more pleasant like, if you would leave us to this sad business of ours? I have heard many gentlemen staying in Porth say that there is nothing to beat the view from the hill over there, not in the whole of Wales."

Every one is polite in Meirion, but somehow Merritt understood that, in English, this speech meant "move on".

Merritt moved back to Porth—he was not in the humour for any idle, pleasurable strolling after so dreadful a meeting with death. He made some enquiries in the town about the dead man, but nothing seemed known of him. It was said that he had been on his honeymoon, that he had been staying at the Porth Castle Hotel; but the people of the hotel declared that they had never heard of such a person. Merritt got the local paper at the end of the week; there was not a word in it of any fatal accident in the marsh. He met the sergeant of police in the street. That officer touched his helmet with the utmost politeness and a "hope you are enjoying yourself, sir; indeed you do look a lot better already"; but as to the poor man who was found drowned or stifled in the marsh, he knew nothing.

The next day Merritt made up his mind to go to the marsh to see whether he could find anything to account for so strange a death. What he found was a man with an armlet standing by the gate. The armlet had the letters "C. W." on it, which are understood to mean Coast Watcher. The Watcher said he had strict instructions to keep everybody away from the marsh. Why? He didn't know, but some said that the river was changing its course since the new railway embankment was built, and the marsh had become dangerous to people who didn't know it thoroughly.

"Indeed, sir," he added, "it is part of my orders not to set foot on either side of that gate myself, not for one scrag-end of a minute."

Merritt glanced over the gate incredulously. The marsh looked as it had always looked; there was plenty of sound, hard ground to walk on; he could see the track that he used to follow as firm as ever. He did not believe in the story of the changing course of the river, and Lewis said he had never heard of anything of the kind. But Merritt had put the question in the middle of general conversation; he had not led up to it from any discussion of the death in the marsh, and so the doctor was taken unawares. If he had known of the connection in Merritt's mind between the alleged changing of the Afon's course and the tragical event in the marsh, no doubt he would have confirmed the official explanation. He was, above all things, anxious to prevent his sister and her husband from finding out that the invisible hand of terror that ruled at Midlingham was ruling also in Meirion.

Lewis himself had little doubt that the man who was found dead in the marsh had been struck down by the secret agency, whatever it was, that had already accomplished so much of evil; but it was a chief part of the terror that no one knew for certain that this or that particular event was to be ascribed to it. People do occasionally fall over cliffs through their own carelessness, and as the case of Garcia, the Spanish sailor, shewed, cottagers and their wives and children are now and then the victims of savage and purposeless violence. Lewis had never wandered about the marsh himself; but Remnant had pottered round it and about it, and declared that the man who met his death there—his name was never known, in Porth at all events—must either have committed suicide by deliberately lying prone in the ooze and stifling himself, or else must have been held down in it. There were no details available, so it was clear that the authorities had classified this death with the others; still, the man might have committed suicide, or he might have had a sudden seizure and fallen in the slimy water face downwards. And so on: it was possible to believe that case A *or* B *or* C was in the category of ordinary accidents or ordinary crimes. But it was not possible to believe that A *and* B *and* C were all in that category. And thus it was to the end, and thus it is now. We know that the terror reigned, and how it reigned, but there were many dreadful events ascribed to its rule about which there must always be room for doubt.

For example, there was the case of the *Mary Ann,* the rowing-boat which came to grief in so strange a manner, almost under Merritt's eyes. In my opinion he was quite wrong in associating the sorry fate of the boat and her occupants with a system of signalling by flashlights which he detected, or thought that he detected, on the afternoon in which the *Mary Ann* was capsized. I believe his signalling theory to be all nonsense, in spite of the naturalised German governess who was lodging with her employers in the suspected house. But, on the other hand, there is no doubt in my own mind that the boat was overturned and those in it drowned by the work of the terror.

IX

Let it be noted carefully that so far Merritt had not the slightest suspicion that the terror of Midlingham was quick over Meirion. Lewis had watched and shepherded him carefully. He had let out no suspicion of what had happened in Meirion, and before taking his brother-in-law to the club he had passed round a hint among the members. He did not tell the truth about Midlingham—and here again is a point of interest, that as the terror deepened the general public co-operated voluntarily, and, one would say, almost subconsciously, with the authorities in concealing what they knew from one another—but he gave out a desirable portion of the truth: that his brother-in-law was "nervy", not by any means up to the mark, and that it was therefore desirable that he should be spared the knowledge of the intolerable and tragic mysteries which were being enacted all about them.

"He knows about that poor fellow who was found in the marsh," said Lewis, "and he has a kind of vague suspicion that there is something out of the common about the case; but no more than that."

"A clear case of suggested, or rather commanded suicide," said Remnant. "I regard it as a strong confirmation of my theory."

"Perhaps so," said the doctor, dreading lest he might have to hear about the Z Ray all over again. "But please don't let anything out to him; I want him to get built up thoroughly before he goes back to Midlingham."

Then, on the other hand, Merritt was as still as death about the doings of the Midlands; he hated to think of them, much more to speak of them; and thus, as I say, he and the men at the Porth Club kept their secrets from one another; and thus, from the beginning to the end of the terror, the links were not drawn together. In many cases, no doubt, A and B met every day and talked familiarly, it may be confidentially, on other matters of all sorts, each having in his possession half of the truth, which he concealed from the other. So the two halves were never put together to make a whole.

Merritt, as the doctor guessed, had a kind of uneasy feeling—it scarcely amounted to a suspicion—as to the business of the marsh; chiefly because he thought the official talk about the railway embankment and the course of the river rank nonsense. But finding that nothing more happened, he let the matter drop from his mind, and settled himself down to enjoy his holiday.

He found to his delight that there were no sentries or watchers to hinder him from the approach to Larnac Bay, a delicious cove, a place where the ash-grove and the green meadow and the glistening bracken sloped gently down to red rocks and firm yellow sands. Merritt remembered a rock that formed a comfortable seat, and here he established himself of a golden afternoon, and gazed at the blue of the sea and the crimson bastions and bays of the coast as it bent inward to Sarnau and swept out again southward to the odd-shaped promontory called the Dragon's Head. Merritt gazed on, amused by the antics of the porpoises who were tumbling and splashing and gambolling a little way out at sea, charmed by the pure and radiant air that was so different from the oily smoke that often stood for heaven at Midlingham, and charmed, too, by the white farmhouses dotted here and there on the heights of the curving coast.

Then he noticed a little row-boat at about two hundred yards from the shore. There were two or three people aboard, he could not quite make out how many, and they seemed to be doing something with a line; they were no doubt fishing, and Merritt (who disliked fish) wondered how people could spoil such an afternoon, such a sea, such pellucid and radiant air by trying to catch white, flabby, offensive, evil-smelling creatures that would be excessively nasty when cooked. He puzzled over this problem and turned away from it to the contemplation of the crimson headlands. And then he says that he noticed that signalling was going on. Flashing lights of intense brilliance, he declares, were coming from one of those farms on the heights of the coast; it was as if white fire was spouting from it. Merritt was certain, as the light appeared and disappeared, that some message was being sent, and he regretted that he knew nothing of heliography. Three short flashes, a long and very brilliant flash, then two short flashes. Merritt fumbled in his pocket for pencil and paper so that he might record these signals, and, bringing his eyes down to the sea level, he became aware, with amazement and horror, that the boat had disappeared. All that he could see was some vague, dark object far to westward, running out with the tide.

Now it is certain, unfortunately, that the *Mary Ann* was capsized and that two schoolboys and the sailor in charge were drowned. The bones of the boat were found amongst the rocks far along the coast, and the three bodies were also washed ashore. The sailor could not swim at all, the boys only a little, and it needs an exceptionally fine swimmer to fight against the outward suck of the tide as it rushes past Pengareg Point.

But I have no belief whatever in Merritt's theory. He held (and still holds, for all I know) that the flashes of light which he saw coming from Penyrhaul, the farmhouse on the height, had some connection with the disaster to the *Mary Ann*. When it was ascertained that a family were spending their summer at the farm, and that the governess was a German, though a long-naturalised German, Merritt could not see that there was anything left to argue about, though there might be many details to discover. But, in my opinion, all this was a mere mare's nest: the flashes of brilliant light were caused, no doubt, by the sun lighting up one window of the farmhouse after the other.

Still, Merritt was convinced from the very first, even before the damning circumstance of the German governess was brought to light; and on the evening of the disaster, as Lewis and he sat together after dinner, he was endeavouring to put what he called the common sense of the matter to the doctor.

"If you hear a shot," said Merritt, "and you see a man fall, you know pretty well what killed him."

There was a flutter of wild wings in the room. A great moth beat to and fro and dashed itself madly against the ceiling, the walls, the glass bookcase. Then a sputtering sound, a momentary dimming of the lamp. The moth had succeeded in its mysterious quest.

"Can you tell me," said Lewis as if he were answering Merritt, "why moths rush into the flame?"

Lewis had put his question as to the strange habits of the common moth to Merritt with the deliberate intent of closing the debate on death by heliograph. The query was suggested, of course, by the incident of the moth in the lamp, and Lewis thought that he had said, "Oh, shut up!" in a somewhat elegant manner. And, in fact, Merritt looked dignified, remained silent, and helped himself to port.

That was the end that the doctor had desired. He had no doubt in his own mind that the affair of the *Mary Ann* was but one more item in a long account of horrors that grew larger almost with every day; and he was in no humour to listen to wild and futile theories as to the manner in which the disaster had been accomplished. Here was a proof that the terror that was upon them was mighty not only on the land but on the waters; for Lewis could not see that the boat could have been attacked by any ordinary means of destruction. From Merritt's story, it must have been in shallow water. The shore of Larnac Bay shelves very gradually, and the Admiralty charts shewed the depth of water two hundred yards out to be only two fathoms; this would be too shallow for a submarine. And it could not have been shelled, and it could not have been torpedoed; there was no explosion. The disaster might have been due to carelessness; boys, he considered, will play the fool anywhere, even in a boat; but he did not think so; the sailor would have stopped them. And, it may be mentioned, that the two boys were as a matter of fact extremely steady, sensible young fellows, not in the least likely to play foolish tricks of any kind.

Lewis was immersed in these reflections, having successfully silenced his brother-in-law; he was trying in vain to find some clue to the horrible enigma. The Midlingham theory of a concealed German force, hiding in places under the earth, was extravagant enough, and yet it seemed the only solution that approached plausibility; but then again even a subterranean German host would hardly account for this wreckage of a boat, floating on a calm sea. And then what of the tree with the burning in it that had appeared in the garden there a few weeks ago, and the cloud with a burning in it that had shewn over the trees of the Midland village?

I think I have already written something of the probable emotions of the mathematician confronted suddenly with an undoubted two-sided triangle. I said, if I remember, that he would be forced, in decency, to go mad; and I believe that Lewis was very near to this point. He felt himself confronted with an intolerable problem that most instantly demanded solution, and yet, with the same breath, as it were, denied the possibility of their being any solution. People were being killed in an inscrutable manner by some inscrutable means, day after day, and one asked "why" and "how"; and there seemed no answer. In the Midlands, where every kind of munitionment was manufactured, the explanation of German agency was plausible; and even if the subterranean notion was to be rejected as savouring altogether too much of the fairy-tale, or rather of the sensational romance, yet it was possible that the back-bone of the theory was true; the Germans might have planted their agents in some way or another in the midst of our factories. But here in Meirion, what serious effect could be produced by the casual and indiscriminate slaughter of a couple of schoolboys in a boat, of a harmless holiday-maker in a marsh? The creation of an atmosphere of terror and dismay? It was possible, of course, but it hardly seemed tolerable, in spite of the enormities of Louvain and of the *Lusitania*.

Into these meditations, and into the still dignified silence of Merritt, broke the rap on the door of Lewis's man and those words which harass the ease of the country doctor when he tries to take any ease: "You're wanted in the surgery, if you please, sir." Lewis bustled out, and appeared no more that night.

The doctor had been summoned to a little hamlet on the outskirts of Porth, separated from it by half a mile or three-quarters of road. One dignifies, indeed, this settlement without a name in calling it a hamlet; it was a mere row of four cottages, built about a hundred years ago for the accommodation of the workers in a quarry long since disused. In one of these cottages the doctor found a father and mother weeping and crying out to "doctor bach, doctor bach", and two frightened children, and one little body, still and dead. It was the youngest of the three, little Johnnie, and he was dead.

The doctor found that the child had been asphyxiated. He felt the clothes; they were dry; it was not a case of drowning. He looked at the neck; there was no mark of strangling. He asked the father how it had happened, and father and mother, weeping most lamentably, declared they had no knowledge of how their child had been killed: "unless it was the People that had done it". The Celtic fairies are still malignant. Lewis asked what had happened that evening; where had the child been?

"Was he with his brother and sister? Don't they know anything about it?"

Reduced into some sort of order from its original piteous confusion, this is the story that the doctor gathered.

All three children had been well and happy through the day. They had walked in with the mother, Mrs. Roberts, to Porth on a marketing expedition in the afternoon; they had returned to the cottage, had had their tea, and afterwards played about on the road in front of the house. John Roberts had come home somewhat late from his work, and it was after dusk when the family sat down to supper. Supper over, the three children went out again to play with other children from the cottage next door, Mrs. Roberts telling them that they might have half an hour before going to bed.

The two mothers came to the cottage gates at the same moment and called out to their children to come along and be quick about it. The two small families had been playing on the strip of turf across the road, just by the stile into the fields. The children ran across the road; all of them except Johnnie Roberts. His brother Willie said that just as their mother called them he heard Johnnie cry out:

"Oh, what is that beautiful shiny thing over the stile?"

X

The little Roberts's ran across the road, up the path, and into the lighted room. Then they noticed that Johnnie had not followed them. Mrs. Roberts was doing something in the back kitchen, and Mr. Roberts had gone out to the shed to bring in some sticks for the next morning's fire. Mrs. Roberts heard the children run in and went on with her work. The children whispered to one another that Johnnie would "catch it" when their mother came out of the back room and found him missing; but they expected he would run in through the open door any minute. But six or seven, perhaps ten, minutes passed, and there was no Johnnie. Then the father and mother came into the kitchen together, and saw that their little boy was not there.

They thought it was some small piece of mischief—that the two other children had hidden the boy somewhere in the room: in the big cupboard perhaps.

"What have you done with him then?" said Mrs. Roberts. "Come out, you little rascal, directly in a minute."

There was no little rascal to come out, and Margaret Roberts, the girl, said that Johnnie had not come across the road with them: he must be still playing all by himself by the hedge.

"What did you let him stay like that for?" said Mrs. Roberts. "Can't I trust you for two minutes together? Indeed to goodness, you are all of you more trouble than you are worth." She went to the open door:

"Johnnie! Come you in directly, or you will be sorry for it. Johnnie!"

The poor woman called at the door. She went out to the gate and called there:

"Come you, little Johnnie. Come you, bachgen, there's a good boy. I do see you hiding there."

She thought he must be hiding in the shadow of the hedge, and that he would come running and laughing—"he was always such a happy little fellow"—to her across the road. But no little merry figure danced out of the gloom of the still, dark night; it was all silence.

It was then, as the mother's heart began to chill, though she still called cheerfully to the missing child, that the elder boy told how Johnnie had said there was something beautiful by the stile: "and perhaps he did climb over, and he is running now about the meadow, and has lost his way."

The father got his lantern then, and the whole family went crying and calling about the meadow, promising cakes and sweets and a fine toy to the poor Johnnie if he would come to them.

They found the little body, under the ash-grove in the middle of the field. He was quite still and dead, so still that a great moth had settled on his forehead, fluttering away when they lifted him up.

Dr. Lewis heard this story. There was nothing to be done; little to be said to these most unhappy people.

"Take care of the two that you have left to you," said the doctor as he went away. "Don't let them out of your sight if you can help it. It is dreadful times that we are living in."

It is curious to record that all through these dreadful times the simple little "season" went through its accustomed course at Porth. The war and its consequences had somewhat thinned the numbers of the summer visitors; still a very fair contingent of them occupied the hotels and boarding-houses and lodging-houses and bathed from the old-fashioned machines on one beach, or from the new-fashioned tents on the other, and sauntered in the sun, or lay stretched out in the shade under the trees that grow down almost to the water's edge. Porth never tolerated Ethiopians or shows of any kind on its sands, but "the Rockets" did very well during that summer in their garden entertainment, given in the castle grounds, and the fit-up companies that came to the Assembly Rooms are said to have paid their bills to a woman and to a man.

Porth depends very largely on its midland and northern custom, custom of a prosperous, well-established sort. People who think Llandudno overcrowded and Colwyn Bay too raw and red and new, come year after year to the placid old town in the south-west and delight in its peace; and as I say, they enjoyed themselves much as usual there in the summer of 1915. Now and then they became conscious, as Mr. Merritt became conscious, that they could not wander about quite in the old way; but they accepted sentries and coast watchers and people who politely pointed out the advantages of seeing the view from this point rather than from that as very necessary consequences of the dreadful war that was being waged; nay, as a Manchester man said, after having been turned back from his favourite walk to Castell Coch, it was gratifying to think that they were so well looked after.

"So far as I can see," he added, "there's nothing to prevent a submarine from standing out there by Ynys Sant and landing half a dozen men in a collapsible boat in any of these little coves. And pretty fools we should look, shouldn't we, with our throats cut on the sands; or carried back to Germany in the submarine?" He tipped the coast watcher half a crown.

"That's right, lad," he said, "you give us the tip."

Now here was a strange thing. The north-countryman had his thoughts on elusive submarines and German raiders; the watcher had simply received instructions to keep people off the Castell Coch fields, without reason assigned. And there can be no doubt that the authorities themselves, while they marked out the fields as in the "terror zone", gave their orders in the dark and were themselves profoundly in the dark as to the manner of the slaughter that had been done there; for if they had understood what had happened, they would have understood also that their restrictions were useless.

The Manchester man was warned off his walk about ten days after Johnnie Roberts's death. The Watcher had been placed at his post because, the night before, a young farmer had been found by his wife lying in the grass close to the castle, with no scar on him, nor any mark of violence, but stone dead.

The wife of the dead man, Joseph Cradock, finding her husband lying motionless on the dewy turf, went white and stricken up the path to the village and got two men who bore the body to the farm. Lewis was sent for, and knew at once when he saw the dead man that he had perished in the way that the little Roberts boy had perished—whatever that awful way might be. Cradock had been asphyxiated; and here again there was no mark of a grip on the throat. It might have been a piece of work by Burke and Hare, the doctor reflected; a pitch plaster might have been clapped over the man's mouth and nostrils and held there.

Then a thought struck him; his brother-in-law had talked of a new kind of poison gas that was said to be used against the munition workers in the Midlands: was it possible that the deaths of the man and the boy were due to some such instrument? He applied his tests but could find no trace of any gas having been employed. Carbonic acid gas? A man could not be killed with that in the open air; to be fatal that required a confined space, such a position as the bottom of a huge vat or of a well.

He did not know how Cradock had been killed; he confessed it to himself. He had been suffocated; that was all he could say.

It seemed that the man had gone out at about half-past nine to look after some beasts. The field in which they were was about five minutes' walk from the house. He told his wife he would be back in a quarter of an hour or twenty minutes. He did not return, and when he had gone for three-quarters of an hour Mrs. Cradock went out to look for him. She went into the field where the beasts were, and everything seemed all right, but there was no trace of Cradock. She called out; there was no answer.

Now the meadow in which the cattle were pastured is high ground; a hedge divides it from the fields which fall gently down to the castle and the sea. Mrs. Cradock hardly seemed able to say why, having failed to find her husband among his beasts, she turned to the path which led to Castell Coch. She said at first that she had thought that one of the oxen might have broken through the hedge and strayed, and that Cradock had perhaps gone after it. And then, correcting herself, she said:

"There was that; and then there was something else that I could not make out at all. It seemed to me that the hedge did look different from usual. To be sure, things do look different at night, and there was a bit of sea-mist about, but somehow it did look odd to me, and I said to myself: "Have I lost my way then?""

She declared that the shape of the trees in the hedge appeared to have changed, and besides, it had a look "as if it was lighted up, somehow", and so she went on towards the stile to see what all this could be, and when she came near everything was as usual. She looked over the stile and called and hoped to see her husband coming towards her or to hear his voice; but there was no answer, and glancing down the path she saw, or thought she saw, some sort of brightness on the ground, "a dim sort of light like a bunch of glow-worms in a hedge-bank.

"And so I climbed over the stile and went down the path, and the light seemed to melt away; and there was my poor husband lying on his back, saying not a word to me when I spoke to him and touched him."

So for Lewis the terror blackened and became altogether intolerable, and others, he perceived, felt as he did. He did not know, he never asked whether the men at the club had heard of these deaths of the child and the young farmer; but no one spoke of them. Indeed, the change was evident; at the beginning of the terror men spoke of nothing else; now it had become all too awful for ingenious chatter or laboured and grotesque theories. And Lewis had received a letter from his brother-in-law at Midlingham; it contained the sentence, "I am afraid Fanny's health has not greatly benefited by her visit to Porth; there are still several symptoms I don't at all like." And this told him, in a phraseology that the doctor and Merritt had agreed upon, that the terror remained heavy in the Midland town.

It was soon after the death of Cradock that people began to tell strange tales of a sound that was to be heard of nights about the hills and valleys to the northward of Porth. A man who had missed the last train from Meiros and had been forced to tramp the ten miles between Meiros and Porth seems to have been the first to hear it. He said he had got to the top of the hill by Tredonoc, somewhere between half-past ten and eleven, when he first noticed an odd noise that he could not make out at all: it was like a shout, a long, drawn-out, dismal wail coming from a great way off, faint with distance. He stopped to listen, thinking at first that it might be owls hooting in the woods; but it was different, he said, from that; it was a long cry, and then there was silence and then it began over again. He could make nothing of it, and feeling frightened, he did not quite know of what, he walked on briskly and was glad to see the lights of Porth station.

He told his wife of this dismal sound that night, and she told the neighbours, and most of them thought that it was "all fancy"—or drink, or the owls after all. But the night after, two or three people, who had been to some small merrymaking in a cottage just off the Meiros road, heard the sound as they were going home, soon after ten. They, too, described it as a long, wailing cry, indescribably dismal in the stillness of the autumn night; "like the ghost of a voice", said one; "as if it came up from the bottom of the earth", said another.

XI

Let it be remembered, again and again, that, all the while that the terror lasted, there was no common stock of information as to the dreadful things that were being done. The press had not said one word upon it, there was no criterion by which the mass of the people could separate fact from mere vague rumour—no test by which ordinary misadventure or disaster could be distinguished from the achievements of the secret and awful force that was at work.

And so with every event of the passing day. A harmless commercial traveller might shew himself in the course of his business in the tumbledown main street of Meiros and find himself regarded with looks of fear and suspicion as a possible worker of murder, while it is likely enough that the true agents of the terror went quite unnoticed. And since the real nature of all this mystery of death was unknown, it followed easily that the signs and warnings and omens of it were all the more unknown. Here was horror, there was horror; but there was no link to join one horror with another; no common basis of knowledge from which the connection between this horror and that horror might be inferred.

So there was no one who suspected at all that this dismal and hollow sound that was now heard of nights in the region to the north of Porth, had any relation at all to the case of the little girl who went out one afternoon to pick purple flowers and never returned, or to the case of the man whose body was taken out of the peaty slime of the marsh, or to the case of Cradock, dead in his fields, with a strange glimmering of light about his body, as his wife reported. And it is a question as to how far the rumour of this melancholy, nocturnal summons got abroad at all. Lewis heard of it, as a country doctor hears of most things, driving up and down the lanes, but he heard of it without much interest, with no sense that it was in any sort of relation to the terror. Remnant had been given the story of the hollow and echoing voice of the darkness in a coloured and picturesque form; he employed a Tredonoc man to work in his garden once a week. The gardener had not heard the summons himself, but he knew a man who had done so.

"Thomas Jenkins, Pentoppin, he did put his head out late last night to see what the weather was like, and he was cutting a field of corn the next day, and he did tell me that when he was with the Methodists in Cardigan he did never hear no singing eloquence in the chapels that was like to it. He did declare it was like a wailing of Judgment Day."

Remnant considered the matter, and was inclined to think that the sound must be caused by a subterranean inlet of the sea; there might be, he supposed, an imperfect or half-opened or tortuous blow-hole in the Tredonoc woods, and the noise of the tide, surging up below, might very well produce that effect of a hollow wailing, far away. But neither he nor any one else paid much attention to the matter; save the few who heard the call at dead of night, as it echoed awfully over the black hills.

The sound had been heard for three or perhaps four nights, when the people coming out of Tredonoc church after morning service on Sunday noticed that there was a big yellow sheepdog in the church-yard. The dog, it appeared, had been waiting for the congregation; for it at once attached itself to them, at first to the whole body, and then to a group of half a dozen who took the turning to the right. Two of these presently went off over the fields to their respective houses, and four strolled on in the leisurely Sunday-morning manner of the country, and these the dog followed, keeping to heel all the time. The men were talking hay, corn, and markets and paid no attention to the animal, and so they strolled along the autumn lane till they came to a gate in the hedge, whence a roughly made farm road went through the fields, and dipped down into the woods and to Treff Loyne farm.

Then the dog became like a possessed creature. He barked furiously. He ran up to one of the men and looked up at him, "as if he were begging for his life", as the man said, and then rushed to the gate and stood by it, wagging his tail and barking at intervals. The men stared and laughed.

"Whose dog will that be?" said one of them.

"It will be Thomas Griffith's, Treff Loyne," said another.

"Well, then, why doesn't he go home? Go home then!" He went through the gesture of picking up a stone from the road and throwing it at the dog. "Go home, then! Over the gate with you."

But the dog never stirred. He barked and whined and ran up to the men and then back to the gate. At last he came to one of them, and crawled and abased himself on the ground and then took hold of the man's coat and tried to pull him in the direction of the gate. The farmer shook the dog off, and the four went on their way; and the dog stood in the road and watched them and then put up its head and uttered a long and dismal howl that was despair.

The four farmers thought nothing of it; sheepdogs in the country are dogs to look after sheep, and their whims and fancies are not studied. But the yellow dog—he was a kind of degenerate collie—haunted the Tredonoc lanes from that day. He came to a cottage door one night and scratched at it, and when it was opened lay down, and then, barking, ran to the garden gate and waited, entreating, as it seemed, the cottager to follow him. They drove him away and again he gave that long howl of anguish. It was almost as bad, they said, as the noise that they had heard a few nights before. And then it occurred to somebody, so far as I can make out with no particular reference to the odd conduct of the Treff Loyne sheepdog, that Thomas Griffith had not been seen for some time past. He had missed market day at Porth, he had not been at Tredonoc church, where he was a pretty regular attendant on Sunday; and then, as heads were put together, it appeared that nobody had seen any of the Griffith family for days and days.

Now in a town, even in a small town, this process of putting heads together is a pretty quick business. In the country, especially in a countryside of wild lands and scattered and lonely farms and cottages, the affair takes time. Harvest was going on, everybody was busy in his own fields, and after the long day's hard work neither the farmer nor his men felt inclined to stroll about in search of news or gossip. A harvester at the day's end is ready for supper and sleep and for nothing else.

And so it was late in that week when it was discovered that Thomas Griffith and all his house had vanished from this world.

I have often been reproached for my curiosity over questions which are apparently of slight importance, or of no importance at all. I love to enquire, for instance, into the question of the visibility of a lighted candle at a distance. Suppose, that is, a candle lighted on a still, dark night in the country; what is the greatest distance at which you can see that there is a light at all? And then as to the human voice; what is its carrying distance, under good conditions, as a mere sound, apart from any matter of making out words that may be uttered?

They are trivial questions, no doubt, but they have always interested me, and the latter point has its application to the strange business of Treff Loyne. That melancholy and hollow sound, that wailing summons that appalled the hearts of those who heard it was, indeed, a human voice, produced in a very exceptional manner; and it seems to have been heard at points varying from a mile and a half to two miles from the farm. I do not know whether this is anything extraordinary; I do not know whether the peculiar method of production was calculated to increase or diminish the carrying power of the sound.

Again and again I have laid emphasis in this story of the terror on the strange isolation of many of the farms and cottages in Meirion. I have done so in the effort to convince the townsman of something that he has never known. To the Londoner a house a quarter of a mile from the outlying suburban lamp, with no other dwelling within two hundred yards, is a lonely house, a place to fit with ghosts and mysteries and terrors. How can he understand, then, the true loneliness of the white farmhouses of Meirion, dotted here and there, for the most part not even on the little lanes and deep winding byways, but set in the very heart of the fields, or alone on huge bastioned headlands facing the sea, and whether on the high verge of the sea or on the hills or in the hollows of the inner country, hidden from the sight of men, far from the sound of any common call. There is Penyrhaul, for example, the farm from which the foolish Merritt thought he saw signals of light being made: from seaward it is, of course, widely visible; but from landward, owing partly to the curving and indented configuration of the bay, I doubt whether any other habitation views it from a nearer distance than three miles.

And of all these hidden and remote places, I doubt if any is so deeply buried as Treff Loyne. I have little or no Welsh, I am sorry to say, but I suppose that the name is corrupted from Trellwyn, or Tref-y-llwyn, "the place in the grove", and indeed, it lies in the very heart of dark, overhanging woods. A deep, narrow valley runs down from the high lands of the Allt, through these woods, through steep hillsides of bracken and gorse, right down to the great marsh, whence Merritt saw the dead man being carried. The valley lies away from any road, even from that by-road, little better than a bridlepath, where the four farmers, returning from church, were perplexed by the strange antics of the sheepdog. One cannot say that the valley is overlooked, even from a distance, for so narrow is it that the ash-groves that rim it on either side seem to meet and shut it in. I, at all events, have never found any high place from which Treff Loyne is visible; though, looking down from the Allt, I have seen blue wood-smoke rising from its hidden chimneys.

Such was the place, then, to which one September afternoon a party went up to discover what had happened to Griffith and his family. There were half a dozen farmers, a couple of policemen, and four soldiers, carrying their arms; those last had been lent by the officer commanding at the camp. Lewis, too, was of the party; he had heard by chance that no one knew what had become of Griffith and his family; and he was anxious about a young fellow, a painter, of his acquaintance, who had been lodging at Treff Loyne all the summer.

They all met by the gate of Tredonoc churchyard, and tramped solemnly along the narrow lane; all of them, I think, with some vague discomfort of mind, with a certain shadowy fear, as of men who do not quite know what they may encounter. Lewis heard the corporal and the three soldiers arguing over their orders.

"The captain says to me," muttered the corporal, "'Don't hesitate to shoot if there's any trouble.' 'Shoot what, sir?' I says. 'The trouble,' says he, and that's all I could get out of him."

The men grumbled in reply; Lewis thought he heard some obscure reference to rat-poison, and wondered what they were talking about.

They came to the gate in the hedge, where the farm road led down to Treff Loyne. They followed this track, roughly made, with grass growing up between its loosely laid stones, down by the hedge from field to wood, till at last they came to the sudden walls of the valley, and the sheltering groves of the ash trees. Here the way curved down the steep hillside, and bent southward, and followed henceforward the hidden hollow of the valley, under the shadow of the trees.

Here was the farm enclosure; the outlying walls of the yard and the barns and sheds and outhouses. One of the farmers threw open the gate and walked into the yard, and forthwith began bellowing at the top of his voice:

"Thomas Griffith! Thomas Griffith! Where be you, Thomas Griffith?"

The rest followed him. The corporal snapped out an order over his shoulder, and there was a rattling metallic noise as the men fixed their bayonets and became in an instant dreadful dealers out of death, in place of harmless fellows with a feeling for beer.

"Thomas Griffith!" again bellowed the farmer.

There was no answer to this summons. But they found poor Griffith lying on his face at the edge of the pond in the middle of the yard. There was a ghastly wound in his side, as if a sharp stake had been driven into his body.

XII

It was a still September afternoon. No wind stirred in the hanging woods that were dark all about the ancient house of Treff Loyne; the only sound in the dim air was the lowing of the cattle; they had wandered, it seemed, from the fields and had come in by the gate of the farmyard and stood there melancholy, as if they mourned for their dead master. And the horses; four great, heavy, patient-looking beasts they were there too, and in the lower field the sheep were standing, as if they waited to be fed.

"You would think they all knew there was something wrong," one of the soldiers muttered to another. A pale sun shewed for a moment and glittered on their bayonets. They were standing about the body of poor, dead Griffith, with a certain grimness growing on their faces and hardening there. Their corporal snapped something at them again; they were quite ready. Lewis knelt down by the dead man and looked closely at the great gaping wound in his side.

"He's been dead a long time," he said. "A week, two weeks, perhaps. He was killed by some sharp pointed weapon. How about the family? How many are there of them? I never attended them."

"There was Griffith, and his wife, and his son Thomas, and Mary Griffith, his daughter. And I do think there was a gentleman lodging with them this summer."

That was from one of the farmers. They all looked at one another, this party of rescue, who knew nothing of the danger that had smitten this house of quiet people, nothing of the peril which had brought them to this pass of a farmyard with a dead man in it, and his beasts standing patiently about him, as if they waited for the farmer to rise up and give them their food. Then the party turned to the house. It was an old, sixteenth-century building, with the singular round, "Flemish" chimney that is characteristic of Meirion. The walls were snowy with whitewash, the windows were deeply set and stone-mullioned, and a solid, stone-tiled porch sheltered the doorway from any winds that might penetrate to the hollow of that hidden valley. The windows were shut tight. There was no sign of any life or movement about the place. The party of men looked at one another, and the churchwarden amongst the farmers, the sergeant of police, Lewis, and the corporal drew together.

"What is it to goodness, doctor?" said the churchwarden.

"I can tell you nothing at all—except that that poor man there has been pierced to the heart," said Lewis.

"Do you think they are inside and they will shoot us?" said another farmer. He had no notion of what he meant by "they", and no one of them knew better than he. They did not know what the danger was, or where it might strike them, or whether it was from without or from within. They stared at the murdered man, and gazed dismally at one another.

"Come!" said Lewis, "we must do something. We must get into the house and see what is wrong."

"Yes, but suppose they are at us while we are getting in," said the sergeant. "Where shall we be then, Doctor Lewis?"

The corporal put one of his men by the gate at the top of the farmyard, another at the gate by the bottom of the farmyard, and told them to challenge and shoot. The doctor and the rest opened the little gate of the front garden and went up to the porch and stood listening by the door. It was all dead silence. Lewis took an ash stick from one of the farmers and beat heavily three times on the old, black, oaken door studded with antique nails.

He struck three thundering blows, and then they all waited. There was no answer from within. He beat again, and still silence. He shouted to the people within, but there was no answer. They all turned and looked at one another, that party of quest and rescue who knew not what they sought, what enemy they were to encounter. There was an iron ring on the door. Lewis turned it but the door stood fast; it was evidently barred and bolted. The sergeant of police called out to open, but again there was no answer.

They consulted together. There was nothing for it but to blow the door open, and some one of them called in a loud voice to anybody that might be within to stand away from the door, or they would be killed. And at this very moment the yellow sheepdog came bounding up the yard from the woods and licked their hands and fawned on them and barked joyfully.

"Indeed now," said one of the farmers, "he did know that there was something amiss. A pity it was, Thomas Williams, that we did not follow him when he implored us last Sunday."

The corporal motioned the rest of the party back, and they stood looking fearfully about them at the entrance to the porch. The corporal disengaged his bayonet and shot into the keyhole, calling out once more before he fired. He shot and shot again; so heavy and firm was the ancient door, so stout its bolts and fastenings. At last he had to fire at the massive hinges, and then they all pushed together and the door lurched open and fell forward. The corporal raised his left hand and stepped back a few paces. He hailed his two men at the top and bottom of the farmyard. They were all right, they said. And so the party climbed and struggled over the fallen door into the passage, and into the kitchen of the farmhouse.

Young Griffith was lying dead before the hearth, before a dead fire of white wood ashes. They went on towards the "parlour", and in the doorway of the room was the body of the artist, Secretan, as if he had fallen in trying to get to the kitchen. Upstairs the two women, Mrs. Griffith and her daughter, a girl of eighteen, were lying together on the bed in the big bedroom, clasped in each other's arms.

They went about the house, searched the pantries, the back kitchen, and the cellars; there was no life in it.

"Look!" said Dr. Lewis, when they came back to the big kitchen, "look! It is as if they had been besieged. Do you see that piece of bacon, half gnawed through?"

Then they found these pieces of bacon, cut from the sides on the kitchen wall, here and there about the house. There was no bread in the place, no milk, no water.

"And," said one of the farmers, "they had the best water here in all Meirion. The well is down there in the wood; it is most famous water. The old people did use to call it Ffynnon Teilo; it was Saint Teilo's Well, they did say."

"They must have died of thirst," said Lewis. "They have been dead for days and days."

The group of men stood in the big kitchen and stared at one another, a dreadful perplexity in their eyes. The dead were all about them, within the house and without it; and it was in vain to ask why they had died thus. The old man had been killed with the piercing thrust of some sharp weapon; the rest had perished, it seemed probable, of thirst; but what possible enemy was this that besieged the farm and shut in its inhabitants? There was no answer.

The sergeant of police spoke of getting a cart and taking the bodies into Porth, and Dr. Lewis went into the parlour that Secretan had used as a sitting-room, intending to gather any possessions or effects of the dead artist that he might find there. Half a dozen portfolios were piled up in one corner, there were some books on a side table, a fishing-rod and basket behind the door—that seemed all. No doubt there would be clothes and such matters upstairs, and Lewis was about to rejoin the rest of the party in the kitchen, when he looked down at some scattered papers lying with the books on the side table. On one of the sheets he read to his astonishment the words: "Dr. James Lewis, Porth." This was written in a staggering trembling scrawl, and examining the other leaves he saw that they were covered with writing.

The table stood in a dark corner of the room, and Lewis gathered up the sheets of paper and took them to the window-ledge and began to read, amazed at certain phrases that had caught his eye. But the manuscript was in disorder, as if the dead man who had written it had not been equal to the task of gathering the leaves into their proper sequence; it was some time before the doctor had each page in its place. This was the statement that he read, with ever-growing wonder, while a couple of the farmers were harnessing one of the horses in the yard to a cart, and the others were bringing down the dead women.

"I do not think that I can last much longer. We shared out the last drops of water a long time ago. I do not know how many days ago. We fall asleep and dream and walk about the house in our dreams, and I am often not sure whether I am awake or still dreaming, and so the days and nights are confused in my mind. I awoke not long ago, at least I suppose I awoke, and found I was lying in the passage. I had a confused feeling that I had had an awful dream which seemed horribly real, and I thought for a moment what a relief it was to know that it wasn't true, whatever it might have been. I made up my mind to have a good long walk to freshen myself up, and then I looked round and found that I had been lying on the stones of the passage; and it all came back to me. There was no walk for me.

"I have not seen Mrs. Griffith or her daughter for a long while. They said they were going upstairs to have a rest. I heard them moving about the room at first, now I can hear nothing. Young Griffith is lying in the kitchen, before the hearth. He was talking to himself about the harvest and the weather when I last went into the kitchen. He didn't seem to know I was there, as he went gabbling on in a low voice very fast, and then he began to call the dog, Tiger.

"There seems no hope for any of us. We are in the dream of death. . . ."

Here the manuscript became unintelligible for half a dozen lines. Secretan had written the words "dream of death" three or four times over. He had begun a fresh word and scratched it out and then followed strange, unmeaning characters, the script, as Lewis thought, of a terrible language. And then the writing became clear, clearer than it was at the beginning of the manuscript, and the sentences flowed more easily, as if the cloud on Secretan's mind had lifted for a while. There was a fresh start, as it were, and the writer began again, in ordinary letter form:

"DEAR LEWIS,

"I hope you will excuse all this confusion and wandering. I intended to begin a proper letter to you, and now I find all that stuff that you have been reading—if this ever gets into your hands. I have not the energy even to tear it up. If you read it you will know to what a sad pass I had come when it was written. It looks like delirium or a bad dream, and even now, though my mind seems to have cleared up a good deal, I have to hold myself in tightly to be sure that the experiences of the last days in this awful place are true, real things, not a long nightmare from which I shall wake up presently and find myself in my rooms at Chelsea.

"I have said of what I am writing, 'if it ever gets into your hands', and I am not at all sure that it ever will. If what is happening here is happening everywhere else, then I suppose, the world is coming to an end. I cannot understand it; even now I can hardly believe it. I know that I dream such wild dreams and walk in such mad fancies that I have to look out and look about me to make sure that I am not still dreaming.

"Do you remember that talk we had about two months ago when I dined with you? We got on, somehow or other, to space and time, and I think we agreed that as soon as one tried to reason about space and time one was landed in a maze of contradictions. You said something to the effect that it was very curious, but this was just like a dream. 'A man will sometimes wake himself from his crazy dream,' you said, "by realising that he is thinking nonsense." And we both wondered whether these contradictions that one can't avoid if one begins to think of time and space may not really be proofs that the whole of life is a dream, and the moon and the stars bits of nightmare. I have often thought over that lately. I kick at the walls as Dr. Johnson kicked at the stone, to make sure that the things about me are there. And then that other question gets into my mind—is the world really coming to an end, the world as we have always known it; and what on earth will this new world be like? I can't imagine it; it's a story like Noah's Ark and the Flood. People used to talk about the end of the world and fire, but no one ever thought of anything like this.

"And then there's another thing that bothers me. Now and then I wonder whether we are not all mad together in this house. In spite of what I see and know, or, perhaps, I should say, because what I see and know is so impossible, I wonder whether we are not all suffering from a delusion. Perhaps we are our own gaolers, and we are really free to go out and live. Perhaps what we think we see is not there at all. I believe I have heard of whole families going mad together, and I may have come under the influence of the house, having lived in it for the last four months. I know there have been people who have been kept alive by their keepers forcing food down their throats, because they are quite sure that their throats are closed, so that they feel they are unable to swallow a morsel. I wonder now and then whether we are all like this in Treff Loyne; yet in my heart I feel sure that it is not so.

"Still, I do not want to leave a madman's letter behind me, and so I will not tell you the full story of what I have seen, or believe I have seen. If I am a sane man you be able to fill in the blanks for yourself from your own knowledge. If I am mad, burn the letter and say nothing about it. Or perhaps—and indeed, I am not quite sure—I may wake up and hear Mary Griffith calling to me in her cheerful sing-song that breakfast will be ready 'directly, in a minute', and I shall enjoy it and walk over to Porth and tell you the queerest, most horrible dream that a man ever had, and ask what I had better take.

"I think that it was on a Tuesday that we first noticed that there was something queer about, only at the time we didn't know that there was anything really queer in what we noticed. I had been out since nine o'clock in the morning trying to paint the marsh, and I found it a very tough job. I came home about five or six o'clock and found the family at Treff Loyne laughing at old Tiger, the sheepdog. He was making short runs from the farmyard to the door of the house, barking, with quick, short yelps. Mrs. Griffith and Miss Griffith were standing by the porch, and the dog would go to them, look in their faces, and then run up the farmyard to the gate, and then look back with that eager yelping bark, as if he were waiting for the women to follow him. Then, again and again, he ran up to them and tugged at their skirts as if he would pull them by main force away from the house.

"Then the men came home from the fields and he repeated this performance. The dog was running all up and down the farmyard, in and out of the barn and sheds, yelping, barking; and always with that eager run to the person he addressed, and running away directly, and looking back as if to see whether we were following him. When the house-door was shut and they all sat down to supper, he would give them no peace, till at last they turned him out of doors. And then he sat in the porch and scratched at the door with his claws, barking all the while. When the daughter brought in my meal, she said: 'We can't think what is come to old Tiger, and indeed, he has always been a good dog, too.'

"The dog barked and yelped and whined and scratched at the door all through the evening. They let him in once, but he seemed to have become quite frantic. He ran up to one member of the family after another; his eyes were bloodshot and his mouth was foaming, and he tore at their clothes till they drove him out again into the darkness. Then he broke into a long, lamentable howl of anguish, and we heard no more of him.

XIII

"I slept ill that night. I woke again and again from uneasy dreams, and I seemed in my sleep to hear strange calls and noises and a sound of murmurs and beatings on the door. There were deep, hollow voices, too, that echoed in my sleep, and when I woke I could hear the autumn wind, mournful, on the hills above us. I started up once with a dreadful scream in my ears; but then the house was all still, and I fell again into uneasy sleep.

"It was soon after dawn when I finally roused myself. The people in the house were talking to each other in high voices, arguing about something that I did not understand.

"'It is those damned gypsies, I tell you,' said old Griffith.

"'What would they do a thing like that for?' asked Mrs. Griffith. 'If it was stealing now—'

"'It is more likely that John Jenkins has done it out of spite,' said the son. 'He said that he would remember you when we did catch him poaching.'

"They seemed puzzled and angry, so far as I could make out, but not at all frightened. I got up and began to dress. I don't think I looked out of the window. The glass on my dressing-table is high and broad, and the window is small; one would have to poke one's head round the glass to see anything.

"The voices were still arguing downstairs. I heard the old man say, 'Well, here's for a beginning anyhow,' and then the door slammed.

"A minute later the old man shouted, I think, to his son. Then there was a great noise which I will not describe more particularly, and a dreadful screaming and crying inside the house and a sound of rushing feet. They all cried out at once to each other. I heard the daughter crying, 'it is no good, mother, he is dead, indeed they have killed him,' and Mrs. Griffith screaming to the girl to let her go. And then one of them rushed out of the kitchen and shot the great bolts of oak across the door, just as something beat against it with a thundering crash.

"I ran downstairs. I found them all in wild confusion, in an agony of grief and horror and amazement. They were like people who had seen something so awful that they had gone mad.

"I went to the window looking out on the farmyard. I won't tell you all that I saw. But I saw poor old Griffith lying by the pond, with blood pouring out of his side.

"I wanted to go out to him and bring him in. But they told me that he must be stone dead, and such things also that it was quite plain that any one who went out of the house would not live more than a moment. We could not believe it, even as we gazed at the body of the dead man; but it was there. I used to wonder sometimes what one would feel like if one saw an apple drop from the tree and shoot up into the air and disappear. I think I know now how one would feel.

"Even then we couldn't believe that it would last. We were not seriously afraid for ourselves. We spoke of getting out in an hour or two, before dinner anyhow. It couldn't last, because it was impossible. Indeed, at twelve o'clock young Griffith said he would go down to the well by the back way and draw another pail of water. I went to the door and stood by it. He had not gone a dozen yards before they were on him. He ran for his life, and we had all we could do to bar the door in time. And then I began to get frightened.

"Still we could not believe in it. Somebody would come along shouting in an hour or two and it would all melt away and vanish. There could not be any real danger. There was plenty of bacon in the house, and half the weekly baking of loaves and some beer in the cellar and a pound or so of tea, and a whole pitcher of water that had been drawn from the well the night before. We could do all right for the day and in the morning it would have all gone away.

"But day followed day and it was still there. I knew Treff Loyne was a lonely place—that was why I had gone there, to have a long rest from all the jangle and rattle and turmoil of London, that makes a man alive and kills him too. I went to Treff Loyne because it was buried in the narrow valley under the ash trees, far away from any track. There was not so much as a footpath that was near it; no one ever came that way. Young Griffith had told me that it was a mile and a half to the nearest house, and the thought of the silent peace and retirement of the farm used to be a delight to me.

"And now this thought came back without delight, with terror. Griffith thought that a shout might be heard on a still night up away on the Allt, 'if a man was listening for it', he added, doubtfully. My voice was clearer and stronger than his, and on the second night I said I would go up to my bedroom and call for help through the open window. I waited till it was all dark and still, and looked out through the window before opening it. And when I saw over the ridge of the long barn across the yard what looked like a tree, though I knew there was no tree there. It was a dark mass against the sky, with wide-spread boughs, a tree of thick, dense growth. I wondered what this could be, and I threw open the window, not only because I was going to call for help, but because I wanted to see more clearly what the dark growth over the barn really was.

"I saw in the depth of the dark of it points of fire, and colours in light, all glowing and moving, and the air trembled. I stared out into the night, and the dark tree lifted over the roof of the barn and rose up in the air and floated towards me. I did not move till at the last moment when it was close to the house; and then I saw what it was and banged the window down only just in time. I had to fight, and I saw the tree that was like a burning cloud rise up in the night and sink again and settle over the barn.

"I told them downstairs of this. They sat with white faces, and Mrs. Griffith said that ancient devils were let loose and had come out of the trees and out of the old hills because of the wickedness that was on the earth. She began to murmur something to herself, something that sounded to me like broken-down Latin.

"I went up to my room again an hour later, but the dark tree swelled over the barn. Another day went by, and at dusk I looked out, but the eyes of fire were watching me. I dared not open the window.

"And then I thought of another plan. There was the great old fireplace, with the round Flemish chimney going high above the house. If I stood beneath it and shouted I thought perhaps the sound might be carried better than if I called out of the window; for all I knew the round chimney might act as a sort of megaphone. Night after night, then, I stood in the hearth and called for help from nine o'clock to eleven. I thought of the lonely place, deep in the valley of the ash trees, of the lonely hills and lands about it. I thought of the little cottages far away and hoped that my voice might reach to those within them. I thought of the winding lane high on the Allt, and of the few men that came there of nights; but I hoped that my cry might come to one of them.

"But we had drunk up the beer, and we would only let ourselves have water by little drops, and on the fourth night my throat was dry, and I began to feel strange and weak; I knew that all the voice I had in my lungs would hardly reach the length of the field of the farm.

"It was then we began to dream of wells and fountains, and water coming very cold, in little drops, out of rocky places in the middle of a cool wood. We had given up all meals; now and then one would cut a lump from the sides of bacon on the kitchen wall and chew a bit of it, but the saltness was like fire.

"There was a great shower of rain one night. The girl said we might open a window and hold out bowls and basins and catch the rain. I spoke of the cloud with burning eyes. She said 'we will go to the window in the dairy at the back, and one of us can get some water at all events.' She stood up with her basin on the stone slab in the dairy and looked out and heard the plashing of the rain, falling very fast. And she unfastened the catch of the window and had just opened it gently with one hand, for about an inch, and had her basin in the other hand. 'And then,' said she, 'there was something that began to tremble and shudder and shake as it did when we went to the Choral Festival at St. Teilo's, and the organ played, and there was the cloud and the burning close before me.'

"And then we began to dream, as I say. I woke up in my sitting-room one hot afternoon when the sun was shining, and I had been looking and searching in my dream all through the house, and I had gone down to the old cellar that wasn't used, the cellar with the pillars and the vaulted roof, with an iron pike in my hand. Something said to me that there was water there, and in my dream I went to a heavy stone by the middle pillar and raised it up, and there beneath was a bubbling well of cold, clear water, and I had just hollowed my hand to drink it when I woke. I went into the kitchen and told young Griffith. I said I was sure there was water there. He shook his head, but he took up the great kitchen poker and we went down to the old cellar. I shewed him the stone by the pillar, and he raised it up. But there was no well.

"Do you know, I reminded myself of many people whom I have met in life? I would not be convinced. I was sure that, after all, there was a well there. They had a butcher's cleaver in the kitchen and I took it down to the old cellar and hacked at the ground with it. The others didn't interfere with me. We were getting past that. We hardly ever spoke to one another. Each one would be wandering about the house, upstairs and downstairs, each one of us, I suppose, bent on his own foolish plan and mad design, but we hardly ever spoke. Years ago, I was an actor for a bit, and I remember how it was on first nights; the actors treading softly up and down the wings, by their entrance, their lips moving and muttering over the words of their parts, but without a word for one another. So it was with us. I came upon young Griffith one evening evidently trying to make a subterranean passage under one of the walls of the house. I knew he was mad, as he knew I was mad when he saw me digging for a well in the cellar; but neither said anything to the other.

"Now we are past all this. We are too weak. We dream when we are awake and when we dream we think we wake. Night and day come and go and we mistake one for another; I hear Griffith murmuring to himself about the stars when the sun is high at noonday, and at midnight I have found myself thinking that I walked in bright sunlit meadows beside cold, rushing streams that flowed from high rocks.

"Then at the dawn figures in black robes, carrying lighted tapers in their hands, pass slowly about and about; and I hear great rolling organ music that sounds as if some tremendous rite were to begin, and voices crying in an ancient song shrill from the depths of the earth.

"Only a little while ago I heard a voice which sounded as if it were at my very ears, but rang and echoed and resounded as if it were rolling and reverberating from the vault of some cathedral, chanting in terrible modulations. I heard the words quite clearly.

"*Incipit liber iræ Domini Dei nostri*. (Here beginneth The Book of the Wrath of the Lord our God.)

"And then the voice sang the word *Aleph*, prolonging it, it seemed through ages, and a light was extinguished as it began the chapter:

"*In that day, saith the Lord, there shall be a cloud over the land, and in the cloud a burning and a shape of fire, and out of the cloud shall issue forth my messengers; they shall run all together, they shall not turn aside; this shall be a day of exceeding bitter-*

ness, without salvation. And on every high hill, saith the Lord of Hosts, I will set my sentinels, and my armies shall encamp in the place of every valley; in the house that is amongst rushes I will execute judgment, and in vain shall they fly for refuge to the munitions of the rocks. In the groves of the woods, in the places where the leaves are as a tent above them, they shall find the sword of the slayer; and they that put their trust in walled cities shall be confounded. Woe unto the armed man, woe unto him that taketh pleasure in the strength of his artillery, for a little thing shall smite him, and by one that hath no might shall he be brought down into the dust. That which is low shall be set on high; I will make the lamb and the young sheep to be as the lion from the swellings of Jordan; they shall not spare, saith the Lord, and the doves shall be as eagles on the hill Engedi; none shall be found that may abide the onset of their battle.

"Even now I can hear the voice rolling far away, as if it came from the altar of a great church and I stood at the door. There are lights very far away in the hollow of a vast darkness, and one by one they are put out. I hear a voice chanting again with that endless modulation that climbs and aspires to the stars, and shines there, and rushes down to the dark depths of the earth, again to ascend; the word is *Zain*."

Here the manuscript lapsed again, and finally into utter, lamentable confusion. There were scrawled lines wavering across the page on which Secretan seemed to have been trying to note the unearthly music that swelled in his dying ears. As the scrapes and scratches of ink shewed, he had tried hard to begin a new sentence. The pen had dropped at last out of his hand upon the paper, leaving a blot and a smear upon it.

Lewis heard the tramp of feet along the passage; they were carrying out the dead to the cart.

XIV

Dr. Lewis maintained that we should never begin to understand the real significance of life until we began to study just those aspects of it which we now dismiss and overlook as utterly inexplicable, and therefore, unimportant.

We were discussing a few months ago the awful shadow of the terror which at length had passed away from the land. I had formed my opinion, partly from observation, partly from certain facts which had been communicated to me, and the passwords having been exchanged,

I found that Lewis had come by very different ways to the same end.

"And yet," he said, "it is not a true end, or rather, it is like all the ends of human enquiry, it leads one to a great mystery. We must confess that what has happened might have happened at any time in the history of the world. It did not happen till a year ago as a matter of fact, and therefore we made up our minds that it never could happen; or, one would better say, it was outside the range even of imagination. But this is our way. Most people are quite sure that the Black Death— otherwise the Plague—will never invade Europe again. They have made up their complacent minds that it was due to dirt and bad drainage. As a matter of fact the Plague had nothing to do with dirt or with drains; and there is nothing to prevent its ravaging England tomorrow. But if you tell people so, they won't believe you. They won't believe in anything that isn't there at the particular moment when you are talking to them. As with the Plague, so with the Terror. We could not believe that such a thing could ever happen. Remnant said truly enough, that whatever it was, it was outside theory, outside our theory. Flatland cannot believe in the cube or the sphere."

I agreed with all this. I added that sometimes the world was incapable of seeing, much less believing, that which was before its own eyes.

"Look," I said, "at any eighteenth century print of a Gothic cathedral. You will find that the trained artistic eye even could not behold in any true sense the building that was before it. I have seen an old print of Peterborough Cathedral that looks as if the artist had drawn it from a clumsy model, constructed of bent wire and children's bricks."

"Exactly; because Gothic was outside the aesthetic theory (and therefore vision) of the time. You can't believe what you don't see: rather, you can't see what you don't believe. It was so during the time of the Terror. All this bears out what Coleridge said as to the necessity of having the idea before the facts could be of any service to one. Of course, he was right; mere facts, without the correlating idea, are nothing and lead to no conclusion. We had plenty of facts, but we could make nothing of them. I went home at the tail of that dreadful procession from Treff Loyne in a state of mind very near to madness. I heard one of the soldiers saying to the other: 'There's no rat that'll spike a man to the heart, Bill.' I don't know why, but I felt that if I heard any more of such talk as that I should go crazy; it seemed to me that the anchors of reason were parting. I left the party and took the short cut across the fields into Porth. I looked up Davies in the High Street and arranged with him that he should take on any cases I might have that evening, and then I went home and gave my man his instructions to send people on. And then I shut myself up to think it all out—if I could.

"You must not suppose that my experiences of that afternoon had afforded me the slightest illumination. Indeed, if it had not been that I had seen poor old Griffith's body lying pierced in his own farmyard, I think I should have been inclined to accept one of Secretan's hints, and to believe that the whole family had fallen a victim to a collective delusion or hallucination, and had shut themselves up and died of thirst through sheer madness. I think there have been such cases. It's the insanity of inhibition, the belief that you can't do something which you are really perfectly capable of doing. But; I had seen the body of the murdered man and the wound that had killed him.

"Did the manuscript left by Secretan give me no hint? Well, it seemed to me to make confusion worse confounded. You have seen it; you know that in certain places it is evidently mere delirium, the wanderings of a dying mind. How was I to separate the facts from the phantasms—lacking the key to the whole enigma. Delirium is often a sort of cloud-castle, a sort of magnified and distorted shadow of actualities, but it is a very difficult thing, almost an impossible thing, to reconstruct the real house from the distortion of it, thrown on the clouds of the patient's brain. You see, Secretan in writing that extraordinary document almost insisted on the fact that he was not in his proper senses; that for days he had been part asleep, part awake, part delirious. How was one to judge his statement, to separate delirium from fact? In one thing he stood confirmed; you remember he speaks of calling for help up the old chimney of Treff Loyne; that did seem to fit in with the tales of a hollow, moaning cry that had been heard upon the Allt: so far one could take him as a recorder of actual experiences. And I looked in the old cellars of the farm and found a frantic sort of rabbit-hole dug by one of the pillars; again he was confirmed. But what was one to make of that story of the chanting voice, and the letters of the Hebrew alphabet, and the chapter out of some unknown Minor Prophet? When one has the key it is easy enough to sort out the facts, or the hints of facts from the delusions; but I hadn't the key on that September evening. I was forgetting the 'tree' with lights and fires in it; that, I think, impressed me more than anything with the feeling that Secretan's story was, in the main, a true story. I had seen a like appearance down there in my own garden; but what was it?

"Now, I was saying that, paradoxically, it is only by the inexplicable things that life can be explained. We are apt to say, you know, 'a very odd coincidence' and pass the matter by, as if there were no more to be said, or as if that were the end of it. Well, I believe that the only real path lies through the blind alleys."

"How do you mean?"

"Well, this is an instance of what I mean. I told you about Merritt, my brother-in-law, and the capsizing of that boat, the *Mary Ann*. He had seen, he said, signal lights flashing from one of the farms on the coast, and he was quite certain that the two things were intimately connected as cause and effect. I thought it all nonsense, and I was wondering how I was going to shut him up when a big moth flew into the room through that window, fluttered about, and succeeded in burning itself alive in the lamp. That gave me my cue; I asked Merritt if he knew why moths made for lamps or something of the kind; I thought it would be a hint to him that I was sick of his flashlights and his half-baked theories. So it was—he looked sulky and held his tongue.

"But a few minutes later I was called out by a man who had found his little boy dead in a field near his cottage about an hour before. The child was so still, they said, that a great moth had settled on his forehead and only fluttered away when they lifted up the body. It was absolutely illogical; but it was this odd 'coincidence' of the moth in my lamp and the moth on the dead boy's forehead that first set me on the track. I can't say that it guided me in any real sense; it was more like a great flare of red paint on a wall: it rang up my attention, if I may say so; it was a sort of shock like a bang on the big drum. No doubt Merritt was talking great nonsense that evening so far as his particular instance went; the flashes of light from the farm had nothing to do with the wreck of the boat. But his general principle was sound; when you hear a gun go off and see a man fall it is idle to talk of 'a mere coincidence'. I think a very interesting book might be written on this question: I would call it 'A Grammar of Coincidence'.

"But as you will remember, from having read my notes on the matter, I was called in about ten days later to see a man named Cradock, who had been found in a field near his farm quite dead. This also was at night. His wife found him, and there were some very queer things in her story. She said that the hedge of the field looked as if it were changed: she began to be afraid that she had lost her way and got into the wrong field. Then she said the hedge was lighted up as if there were a lot of glow-worms in it, and when she peered over the stile there seemed to be some kind of glimmering upon the ground, and then the glimmering melted away, and she found her husband's body near where this light had been. Now this man Cradock had been suffocated just as the little boy Roberts had been suffocated, and as that man in the Midlands who took a short cut one night had been suffocated. Then I remembered that poor Johnnie Roberts had called out about 'something shiny' over the stile just before he played truant. Then, on my part, I had to contribute the very remarkable sight I witnessed here, as I looked down over the garden; the appearance as of a spreading tree where I knew there was no such tree, and then the shining and burning of lights and moving colours. Like the poor child and Mrs. Cradock, I had seen something shiny, just as some man in Stratfordshire had seen a dark cloud with points of fire in it floating over the trees. And Mrs. Cradock thought that the shape of the trees in the hedge had changed.

"My mind almost uttered the word that was wanted; but you see the difficulties. This set of circumstances could not, so far as I could see, have any relation with the other circumstances of the Terror. How could I connect all this with the bombs and machine-guns of the Midlands, with the armed men who kept watch about the munition shops by day and night? Then there was the long list of people here who had fallen over the cliffs or into the quarry; there were the cases of the men stifled in the slime of the marshes; there was the affair of the family murdered in front of their cottage on the Highway; there was the capsized *Mary Ann*. I could not see any thread that could bring all these incidents together; they seemed to me to be hopelessly disconnected. I could not make out any relation between the agency that beat out the brains of the Williams's and the agency that overturned the boat. I don't know, but I think it's very likely if nothing more had happened that I should have put the whole thing down as an unaccountable series of crimes and accidents which chanced to occur in Meirion in the summer of 1915. Well, of course, that would have been an impossible standpoint in view of certain incidents in Merritt's story. Still, if one is confronted by the insoluble, one lets it go at last. If the mystery is inexplicable, one pretends that there isn't any mystery. That is the justification for what is called free thinking.

"Then came that extraordinary business of Treff Loyne. I couldn't put that on one side. I couldn't pretend that nothing strange or out of the way had happened. There was no getting over it or getting round it. I had seen with my eyes that there was a mystery, and a most horrible mystery. I have forgotten my logic, but one might say that Treff Loyne demonstrated the existence of a mystery in the figure of Death.

"I took it all home, as I have told you, and sat down for the evening before it. It appalled me, not only by its horror, but here again by the discrepancy between its terms. Old Griffith, so far as I could judge, had been killed by the thrust of a pike or perhaps of a sharpened stake: how could one relate this to the burning tree that had floated over the ridge of the barn? It was as if I said to you: 'here is a man drowned, and here is a man burned alive: shew that each death was caused by the same agency!' And the moment that I left this particular case of Treff Loyne, and tried to get some light on it from other instances of the Terror, I would think of the man in the Midlands who heard the feet of a thousand men rustling in the wood, and their voices as if dead men sat up in their bones and talked. And then I would say to myself, 'and how about that boat overturned in a calm sea?' There seemed no end to it, no hope of any solution.

"It was, I believe, a sudden leap of the mind that liberated me from the tangle. It was quite beyond logic. I went back to that evening when Merritt was boring me with his flashlights, to the moth in the candle, and to the moth on the forehead of poor Johnnie Roberts. There was no sense in it; but I suddenly determined that the child and Joseph Cradock the farmer, and that unnamed Stratfordshire man, all found at night, all asphyxiated, had been choked by vast swarms of moths. I don't pretend even now that this is demonstrated, but I'm sure it's true.

"Now suppose you encounter a swarm of these creatures in the dark. Suppose the smaller ones fly up your nostrils. You will gasp for breath and open your mouth. Then, suppose some hundreds of them fly into your mouth, into your gullet, into your windpipe, what will happen to you? You will be dead in a very short time, choked, asphyxiated."

"But the moths would be dead too. They would be found in the bodies."

"The moths? Do you know that it is extremely difficult to kill a moth with cyanide of potassium? Take a frog, kill it, open its stomach. There you will find its dinner of moths and small beetles, and the 'dinner' will shake itself and walk off cheerily, to resume an entirely active existence. No; that is no difficulty.

"Well, now I came to this. I was shutting out all the other cases. I was confining myself to those that came under the one formula. I got to the assumption, or conclusion, whichever you like, that certain people had been asphyxiated by the action of moths. I had accounted for that extraordinary appearance of burning or coloured lights that I had witnessed myself, when I saw the growth of that strange tree in my garden. That was clearly the cloud with points of fire in it that the Stratfordshire man took for a new and terrible kind of poison-gas, that was the shiny something that poor little Johnnie Roberts had seen over the stile, that was the glimmering light that had led Mrs. Cradock to her husband's dead body, that was the assemblage of terrible eyes that had watched over Treff Loyne by night. Once on the right track I understood all this, for coming into this room in the dark, I have been amazed by the wonderful burning and the strange fiery colours of the eyes of a single moth, as it crept up the pane of glass, outside. Imagine the effect of myriads of such eyes, of the movement of these lights and fires in a vast swarm of moths, each insect being in constant motion while it kept its place in the mass: I felt that all this was clear and certain.

"Then the next step. Of course, we know nothing really about moths; rather, we know nothing of moth reality. For all I know there may be hundreds of books which treat of moth and nothing but moth. But these are scientific books, and science only deals with surfaces; it has nothing to do with realities—it is impertinent if it attempts to do with realities. To take a very minor matter; we don't even know why the moth desires the flame. But we do know what the moth does not do; it does not gather itself into swarms with the object of destroying human life. But here, by the hypothesis, were cases in which the moth had done this very thing; the moth race had entered, it seemed, into a malignant conspiracy against the human race. It was quite impossible, no doubt—that is to say, it had never happened before—but I could see no escape from this conclusion.

"These insects, then, were definitely hostile to man; and then I stopped, for I could not see the next step, obvious though it seems to me now. I believe that the soldiers' scraps of talk on the way to Treff Loyne and back flung the next plank over the gulf. They had spoken of 'rat poison', of no rat being able to spike a man through the heart; and then, suddenly, I saw my way clear. If the moths were infected with hatred of men, and possessed the design and the power of combining against him; why not suppose this hatred, this design, this power shared by other non-human creatures?

"The secret of the Terror might be condensed into a sentence: the animals had revolted against men.

"Now, the puzzle became easy enough: one had only to classify. Take the cases of the people who met their deaths by falling over cliffs or over the edge of quarries. We think of sheep as timid creatures, who always run away. But suppose sheep that don't run away: and, after all, in reason why should they run away? Quarry or no quarry, cliff or no cliff; what would happen to you if a hundred sheep ran after you instead of running from you? There would be no help for it; they would have you down and beat you to death or stifle you. Then suppose man, woman, or child near a cliff's edge or a quarryside, and a sudden rush of sheep. Clearly there is no help; there is nothing for it but to go over. There can be no doubt that that is what happened in all these cases.

"And again; you know the country and you know how a herd of cattle will sometimes pursue people through the fields in a solemn, stolid sort of way. They behave as if they wanted to close in on you. Townspeople sometimes get frightened and scream and run; you or I would take no notice, or at the utmost, wave our sticks at the herd, which will stop dead or lumber off. But suppose they don't lumber off. The mildest old cow, remember, is stronger than any man. What can one man or half a dozen men do against half a hundred of these beasts no longer restrained by that mysterious inhibition, which has made for ages the strong the humble slaves of the weak? But if you are botanising in the marsh, like that poor fellow who was staying at Porth, and forty or fifty young cattle gradually close round you, and refuse to move when you shout and wave your stick, but get closer and closer instead, and get you into the slime. Again, where is your help? If you haven't got an automatic pistol, you must go down and stay down, while the beasts lie quietly on you for five minutes. It was a quicker death for poor Griffith of Treff Loyne—one of his own beasts gored him to death with one sharp thrust of its horn into his heart. And from that morning those within the house were closely besieged by their own cattle and horses and sheep; and when those unhappy people within opened a window to call for help or to catch a few drops of rain water to relieve their burning thirst, the cloud waited for them with its myriad eyes of fire. Can you wonder that Secretan's statement reads in places like mania? You perceive the horrible position of those people in Treff Loyne; not only did they see death advancing on them, but advancing with incredible steps, as if one were to die not only in nightmare but by nightmare. But no one in his wildest, most fiery dreams had ever imagined such a fate. I am not astonished that Secretan at one moment suspected the evidence of his own senses, at another surmised that the world's end had come."

"And how about the Williams's who were murdered on the Highway near here?"

"The horses were the murderers; the horses that afterwards stampeded the camp below. By some means which is still obscure to me they lured that family into the road and beat their brains out; their shod hoofs were the instruments of execution. And, as for the *Mary Ann*, the boat that was capsized, I have no doubt that it was overturned by a sudden rush of the porpoises that were gambolling about in the water of Larnac Bay. A porpoise is a heavy beast—half a dozen of them could easily upset a light rowing-boat. The munition works? Their enemy was rats. I believe that it has been calculated that in 'Greater London' the number of rats is about equal to the number of human beings, that is, there are about seven million of them. The proportion would be about the same in all the great centres of population; and the rat, moreover, is, on occasion, migratory in its habits. You can understand now that story of the *Semiramis*, beating about the mouth of the Thames, and at last cast away by Arcachon, her only crew dry heaps of bones. The rat is an expert boarder of ships. And so one can understand the tale told by the frightened man who took the path by the wood that led up from the new munition works. He thought he heard a thousand men treading softly through the wood and chattering to one another in some horrible tongue; what he did hear was the marshalling of an army of rats—their array before the battle.

"And conceive the terror of such an attack. Even one rat in a fury is said to be an ugly customer to meet; conceive, then, the irruption of these terrible, swarming myriads, rushing upon the helpless, unprepared, astonished workers in the munition shops."

There can be no doubt, I think, that Dr. Lewis was entirely justified in these extraordinary conclusions. As I say, I had arrived at pretty much the same end, by different ways; but this rather as to the general situation, while Lewis had made his own particular study of those circumstances of the Terror that were within his immediate purview, as a physician in large practice in the southern part of Meirion. Of some of the cases which he reviewed he had, no doubt, no immediate or firsthand knowledge; but he judged these instances by their similarity to the facts which had come under his personal notice. He spoke of the affairs of the quarry at Llanfihangel on the analogy of the people who were found dead at the bottom of the cliffs near Porth, and he was no doubt justified in doing so. He told me that, thinking the whole matter over, he was hardly more astonished by the Terror in itself than by the strange way in which he had arrived at his conclusions.

"You know," he said, "those certain evidences of animal malevolence which we knew of, the bees that stung the child to death, the trusted sheepdog's turning savage, and so forth. Well, I got no light whatever from all this; it suggested nothing to me—simply because I had not got that 'idea' which Coleridge rightly holds necessary in all enquiry; facts *qua* facts, as we said, mean nothing and come to nothing. You do not believe, therefore you cannot see.

"And then, when the truth at last appeared it was through the whimsical 'coincidence', as we call such signs, of the moth in my lamp and the moth on the dead child's forehead. This, I think, is very extraordinary."

"And there seems to have been one beast that remained faithful; the dog at Treff Loyne. That is strange."

"That remains a mystery."

It would not be wise, even now, to describe too closely the terrible scenes that were to be seen in the munition areas of the north and the Midlands during the black months of the Terror. Out of the factories issued at black midnight the shrouded dead in their coffins, and their very kinsfolk did not know how they had come by their deaths. All the towns were full of houses of mourning, were full of dark and terrible rumours; incredible, as the incredible reality. There were things done and suffered that perhaps never will be brought to light, memories and secret traditions of these things will be whispered in families, delivered from father to son, growing wilder with the passage of the years, but never growing wilder than the truth.

It is enough to say that the cause of the Allies was for awhile in deadly peril. The men at the front called in their extremity for guns and shells. No one told them what was happening in the places where these munitions were made.

At first the position was nothing less than desperate; men in high places were almost ready to cry "mercy" to the enemy. But, after the first panic, measures were taken such as those described by Merritt in his account of the matter. The workers were armed with special weapons, guards were mounted, machine-guns were placed in position, bombs and liquid flame were ready against the obscene hordes of the enemy, and the "burning clouds" found a fire fiercer than their own. Many deaths occurred amongst the airmen; but they, too, were given special guns, arms that scattered shot broadcast, and so drove away the dark flights that threatened the airplanes.

And, then, in the winter of 1915–16, the Terror ended suddenly as it had begun. Once more a sheep was a frightened beast that ran instinctively from a little child; the cattle were again solemn, stupid creatures, void of harm; the spirit and the convention of malignant design passed out of the hearts of all the animals. The chains that they had cast off for awhile were thrown again about them.

And, finally, there comes the inevitable "why?" Why did the beasts who had been humbly and patiently subject to man, or affrighted by his presence, suddenly know their strength and learn how to league together, and declare bitter war against their ancient master?

It is a most difficult and obscure question. I give what explanation I have to give with very great diffidence, and an eminent disposition to be corrected, if a clearer light can be found.

Some friends of mine, for whose judgment I have very great respect, are inclined to think that there was a certain contagion of hate. They hold that the fury of the whole world at war, the great passion of death that seems driving all humanity to destruction, infected at last these lower creatures, and in place of their native instinct of submission, gave them rage and wrath and ravening.

This may be the explanation. I cannot say that it is not so, because I do not profess to understand the working of the universe. But I confess that the theory strikes me as fanciful. There may be a contagion of hate as there is a contagion of smallpox; I do not know, but I hardly believe it.

In my opinion, and it is only an opinion, the source of the great revolt of the beasts is to be sought in a much subtler region of enquiry. I believe that the subjects revolted because the king abdicated. Man has dominated the beasts throughout the ages, the spiritual has reigned over the rational through the peculiar quality and grace of spirituality that men possess, that makes a man to be that which he is. And when he maintained this power and grace, I think it is pretty clear that between him and the animals there was a certain treaty and alliance. There was supremacy on the one hand, and submission on the other; but at the same time there was between the two that cordiality which exists between lords and subjects in a well-organised state. I know a socialist who maintains that Chaucer's *Canterbury Tales* give a picture of true democracy. I do not know about that, but I see that knight and miller were able to get on quite pleasantly together, just because the knight knew that he was a knight and the miller knew that he was a miller. If the knight had had conscientious objections to his knightly grade, while the miller saw no reason why he should not be a knight, I am sure that their intercourse would have been difficult, unpleasant, and perhaps murderous.

So with man. I believe in the strength and truth of tradition. A learned man said to me a few weeks ago: "When I have to choose between the evidence of tradition and the evidence of a document, I always believe the evidence of tradition. Documents may be falsified, and often are falsified; tradition is never falsified." This is true; and, therefore, I think, one may put trust in the vast body of folklore which asserts that there was once a worthy and friendly alliance between man and the beasts. Our popular tale of Dick Whittington and his Cat no doubt represents the adaptation of a very ancient legend to a comparatively modern personage, but we may go back into the ages and find the popular tradition asserting that not only are the animals the subjects, but also the friends of man.

All that was in virtue of that singular spiritual element in man which the rational animals do not possess. Spiritual does not mean respectable, it does not even mean moral, it does not mean "good" in the ordinary acceptation of the word. It signifies the royal prerogative of man, differencing him from the beasts.

For long ages he has been putting off this royal robe, he has been wiping the balm of consecration from his own breast. He has declared, again and again, that he is not spiritual, but rational, that is, the equal of the beasts over whom he was once sovereign. He has vowed that he is not Orpheus but Caliban.

But the beasts also have within them something which corresponds to the spiritual quality in men—we are content to call it instinct. They perceived that the throne was vacant—not even friendship was possible between them and the self-deposed monarch. If he were not king he was a sham, an impostor, a thing to be destroyed.

Hence, I think, the Terror. They have risen once—they may rise again.

The Happy Children

A day after the Christmas of 1915, my professional duties took me up North; or to be as precise as our present conventions allow, to "the North-Eastern district". There was some singular talk; mad gossip of the Germans having a "dug-out" somewhere by Malton Head. Nobody seemed to be quite clear as to what they were doing there or what they hoped to do there; but the report ran like wildfire from one foolish mouth to another, and it was thought desirable that the whole silly tale should be tracked down to its source and exposed or denied once and for all.

I went up, then, to that North-Eastern district on Sunday, December 26th, 1915, and pursued my investigations from Helmsdale Bay, which is a small watering-place within a couple of miles of Malton Head. The people of the dales and the moors had just heard of the fable, I found, and regarded it all with supreme and sour contempt. So far as I could make out, it originated from the games of some children who had stayed at Helmsdale Bay in the summer. They had acted a rude drama of German spies and their capture, and had used Helby Cavern, between Helmsdale and Malton Head, as the scene of their play. That was all; the fools apparently had done the rest; the fools who believed with all their hearts in "the Russians", and got cross with anyone who expressed a doubt as to "the Angels of Mons".

"Gang oop to beasten and tell them sike a tale and they'll not believe it," said one dalesman to me; and I have a suspicion that he thought that I, who had come so many hundred miles to investigate the story, was but little wiser than those who credited it. He could not be expected to understand that a journalist has two offices—to proclaim the truth and to denounce the lie.

I had finished with "the Germans" and their dug-out early in the afternoon of Monday, and I decided to break the journey home at

Banwick, which I had often heard of as a beautiful and curious old place. So I took the one-thirty train, and went wandering inland, and stopped at many unknown stations in the midst of great levels, and changed at Marishes Ambo, and went on again through a strange land in the dimness of the winter afternoon. Somehow the train left the level and glided down into a deep and narrow dell, dark with winter woods, brown with withered bracken, solemn in its loneliness. The only thing that moved was the swift and rushing stream that foamed over the boulders and then lay still in brown pools under the bank.

The dark woods scattered and thinned into groups of stunted, ancient thorns; great grey rocks, strangely shaped, rose out of the ground; crenellated rocks rose on the heights on either side. The brooklet swelled and became a river, and always following this river we came to Banwick soon after the setting of the sun.

I saw the wonder of the town in the light of the afterglow that was red in the west. The clouds blossomed into rose-gardens; there were seas of fairy green that swam about isles of crimson light; there were clouds like spears of flame, like dragons of fire. And under the mingling lights and colours of such a sky Banwick went down to the pools of its land-locked harbour and climbed again across the bridge towards the ruined abbey and the great church on the hill.

I came from the station by an ancient street, winding and narrow, with cavernous closes and yards opening from it on either side, and flights of uneven steps going upward to high terraced houses, or downward to the harbour and the incoming tide. I saw there many gabled houses, sunken with age far beneath the level of the pavement, with dipping roof-trees and bowed doorways, with traces of grotesque carving on their walls. And when I stood on the quay, there on the other side of the harbour was the most amazing confusion of red-tiled roofs that I had ever seen, and the great grey Norman church high on the bare hill above them; and below them the boats swinging in the swaying tide, and the water burning in the fires of the sunset. It was the town of a magic dream. I stood on the quay till the shining had gone from the sky and the waterpools, and the winter night came down dark upon Banwick.

I found an old snug inn just by the harbour, where I had been standing. The walls of the rooms met each other at odd and unexpected angles; there were strange projections and juttings of masonry, as if one room were trying to force its way into another; there were indications as of unthinkable staircases in the corners of the ceilings. But there was a bar where Tom Smart would have loved to sit, with a roaring fire and snug, old elbow chairs about it and pleasant indications that if "something warm" were wanted after supper it could be generously supplied.

I sat in this pleasant place for an hour or two and talked to the pleasant people of the town who came in and out. They told me of the old adventures and industries of the town. It had once been, they said, a great whaling port, and then there had been a lot of shipbuilding, and later Banwick had been famous for its amber-cutting. "And now there's nowt," said one of the men in the bar; "but we get on none so badly."

I went out for a stroll before my supper. Banwick was now black, in thick darkness. For good reasons not a single lamp was lighted in the streets, hardly a gleam shewed from behind the closely-curtained windows. It was as if one walked a town of the Middle Ages, and with the ancient overhanging shapes of the houses dimly visible I was reminded of those strange, cavernous pictures of mediæval Paris and Tours that Doré drew.

Hardly anyone was abroad in the streets; but all the courts and alleys seemed alive with children. I could just see little white forms fluttering to and fro as they ran in and out. And I never heard such happy children's voices. Some were singing, some were laughing; and peering into one black cavern, I made out a ring of children dancing round and round and chanting in clear voices a wonderful melody; some old tune of local tradition, as I supposed, for its modulations were such as I had never heard before.

I went back to my tavern and spoke to the landlord about the number of children who were playing about the dark streets and courts, and how delightfully happy they all seemed to be.

He looked at me steadily for a moment, and then said:

"Well, you see, sir, the children have got a bit out of hand of late; their fathers are out at the front, and their mothers can't keep them in order. So they're running a bit wild."

There was something odd about his manner. I could not make out exactly what the oddity was, or what it meant. I could see that my remark had somehow made him uncomfortable; but I was at a loss to know what I had done. I had my supper, and then sat down for a couple of hours to settle "the Germans" of Malton Head.

I finished my account of the German myth, and instead of going to bed, I determined that I would have one more look at Banwick in its wonderful darkness. So I went out and crossed the bridge, and began to climb up the street on the other side, where there was that strange huddle of red roofs mounting one above the other that I had seen in the afterglow. And to my amazement I found that these extraordinary Banwick children were still about and abroad, still revelling and carolling, dancing and singing, standing, as I supposed, on the top of the flights of steps that climbed from the courts up the hillside, and so having the appearance of floating in mid-air. And their happy laughter rang out like bells on the night.

It was a quarter past eleven when I had left my inn, and I was just thinking that the Banwick mothers had indeed allowed indulgence to go too far, when the children began again to sing that old melody that I had heard in the evening. And now the sweet, clear voices swelled out into the night, and, I thought, must be numbered by hundreds. I was standing in a dark alley-way, and I saw with amazement that the children were passing me in a long procession that wound up the hill towards the abbey. Whether a faint moon now rose, or whether clouds passed from before the stars, I do not know; but the air lightened, and I could see the children plainly as they went by singing, with the rapture and exultation of them that sing in the woods in springtime.

They were all in white, but some of them had strange marks upon them which, I supposed, were of significance in this fragment of some traditional mystery-play that I was beholding. Many of them had wreaths of dripping seaweed about their brows; one shewed a painted scar on her throat; a tiny boy held open his white robe, and pointed to a dreadful wound above his heart, from which the blood seemed to flow; another child held out his hands wide apart and the palms looked torn and bleeding, as if they had been pierced. One of the children held up a little baby in her arms, and even the infant shewed the appearance of a wound on its face.

The procession passed me by, and I heard it still singing as if in the sky as it went on its steep way up the hill to the ancient church. I went back to my inn, and as I crossed the bridge it suddenly struck me that this was the eve of the Holy Innocents'. No doubt I had seen a confused relic of some mediæval observance, and when I got back to the inn I asked the landlord about it.

Then I understood the meaning of the strange expression I had seen on the man's face. He was sick and shuddering with terror; he drew away from me as though I were a messenger from the dead.

Some weeks after this I was reading in a book called *The Ancient Rites of Banwick*. It was written in the reign of Queen Elizabeth by some anonymous person who had seen the glory of the old abbey, and then the desolation that had come to it. I found this passage:

"And on Childermas Day, at midnight, there was done there a marvellous solemn service. For when the monks had ended their singing of Te Deum at their Mattins, there came unto the altar the lord abbot, gloriously arrayed in a vestment of cloth of gold, so that it was a great marvel to behold him. And there came also into the church all the children that were of tender years of Banwick, and they were all clothed in white robes. And then began the lord abbot to sing the Mass of the Holy Innocents. And when the sacring of the Mass was ended, then there came up from the church into the quire the youngest child that there was present that might hold himself aright. And this child was borne up to the high altar, and the lord abbot set the little child upon a golden and glistering throne afore the high altar, and bowed down and worshipped him, singing, 'Talium Regnum Coelorum, Alleluya. Of such is the Kingdom of Heaven. Alleluya,' and all the quire answered singing, 'Amicti sunt stolis albis, Alleluya, Alleluya; They are clad in white robes, Alleluya, Alleluya.' And then the prior and all the monks in their order did like worship and reverence to the little child that was upon the throne."

I had seen the White Order of the Innocents. I had seen those who came singing from the deep waters that are about the *Lusitania;* I had seen the innocent martyrs of the fields of Flanders and France rejoicing as they went up to hear their Mass in the spiritual place.

The Islington Mystery

I

The public taste in murders is often erratic, and sometimes, I think, fallible enough. Take, for example, that Crippen business. It happened seventeen years ago, and it is still freshly remembered and discussed with interest. Yet it was by no means a murder of the first rank. What was there in it? The outline is crude enough; simple, easy, and disgusting, as Dr. Johnson observed of another work of art. Crippen was cursed with a nagging wife of unpleasant habits; and he cherished a passion for his typist. Whereupon he poisoned Mrs. Crippen, cut her up and buried the pieces in the coal-cellar. This was well enough, though elementary; and if the foolish little man had been content to lie quietly and do nothing, he might have lived and died peaceably. But he must needs disappear from his house—the action of a fool—and cross the Atlantic with his typist absurdly and obviously disguised as a boy: sheer, bungling imbecility. Here, surely, there is no single trace of the master's hand; and yet, as I say, the Crippen Murder is reckoned amongst the masterpieces. It is the same tale in all the arts: the low comedian was always sure of a laugh if he cared to tumble over a pin; and the weakest murderer is sure of a certain amount of respectful attention if he will take the trouble to dismember his subject. And then, with respect to Crippen: he was caught by means of the wireless device, then in its early stages. This, of course, was utterly irrelevant to the true issue; but the public wallows in irrelevance. A great art critic may praise a great picture, and make his criticism a masterpiece in itself. He will be unread; but let some asinine paragraphist say that the painter always sings "Tom Bowling" as he sets his palette, and dines on boiled fowl and apricot sauce three times a week—then the world will proclaim the artist great.

II

The success of the second-rate is deplorable in itself; but it is more deplorable in that it very often obscures the genuine masterpiece. If the crowd runs after the false, it must neglect the true. The intolerable *Romola* is praised; the admirable *Cloister and the Hearth* is waived aside. So, while the very indifferent and clumsy performance of Crippen filled the papers, the extraordinary Battersea Murder was served with a scanty paragraph or two in obscure corners of the Press. Indeed, we were so shamefully starved of detail that I only retain a bare outline of this superb crime in my memory; but, roughly, the affair was shaped as follows: In the first floor of one of the smaller sets of flats in Battersea a young fellow (?18–20) was talking to an actress, a "touring" actress of no particular fame, whose age, if I recollect, was drawing on from thirty to forty. A shot, a near shot, broke in suddenly on their talk. The young man dashed out of the flat, down the stairs, and there, in the entry of the flats, found his own father, shot dead. The father, it should be remarked, was a touring actor, and an old friend of the lady upstairs. But here comes the magistral element in this murder. Beside the dead man, or in the hand of the dead man, or in a pocket of the dead man's coat—I am not sure how it was—there was found a weapon made of heavy wire—a vile and most deadly contraption, fashioned with curious and malignant ingenuity. It was night-time, but the bright light of a moon ten days old was shining, and the young man said he saw someone running and leaping over walls.

But mark the point: the dead actor was hiding beneath his friend's flat, hiding and lying in wait, with his villainous weapon to his hand. He was expecting an encounter with some enemy, on whom he was resolved to work at least deadly mischief, if not murder.

Who was that enemy? Whose bullet was it that was swifter than the dead man's savage and premeditated desire?

We shall probably never know. A murder that might have stood in the very first rank, that might have vied with the affair of Madeleine Smith—there were certain indications that made this seem possible—was suffered to fade into obscurity, while the foolish crowd surged about elementary Crippen and his bungling imbecilities. So there were once people who considered *Robert Elsmere* as a literary work of palmary significance.

III

Naturally, and with some excuse, the war was responsible for a good deal of this sort of neglect. In those appalling years there was but one thing in men's heads; all else was blotted out. So little attention was paid to the affair of the woman's body, carefully wrapped in sacking, which was found in Regent's Square, by the Gray's Inn Road. A man was hanged without phrases, but there were one or two curious points in the case.

Then, again, there was the Wimbledon Murder, a singular business. A well-to-do family had just moved into a big house facing the Common, so recently that many of their goods and chattels were still in the packing-cases. The master of the house was murdered one night by a man who made off with his booty. It was a curious haul, consisting of a mackintosh worth, perhaps, a couple of pounds, and a watch which would have been dear at ten shillings. This murderer, too, was hanged without comment; and yet, on the face of it, his conduct seems in need of explanation. But the most singular case of all those that suffered from the preoccupations of the war was, there is no doubt, the Islington Mystery, as the Press called it. It was a striking headline, but the world was too busy to attend. The affair got abroad, so far as it did get abroad, about the time of the first employment of the tanks; and people were trying not to see through the war correspondents, not to perceive that the inky fandangoes and corroborees of these gentlemen hid a sense of failure and disappointment.

IV

But as to the Islington Mystery—this is how it fell out. There is an odd street, not far from the region which was once called Spa Fields, not far from Pentonville or Islington Fields, where Grimaldi the clown was once accused of inciting the mob to chase an overdriven ox. It goes up a steep hill, and the rare adventurer who pierces now and then into this unknown quarter of London is amazed and bewildered at the very outset, since there are no steep hills in the London of his knowledge, and the contours of the scene remind him of the cheap lodging-house area at the back of hilly seaside resorts. But if the site is strange, the buildings on it are far stranger. They were no doubt set up at the high tide of Sir Walter Scott Gothic, which has left such queer memorials behind it. The houses of Lloyd Street are in couples, and the architect, combining the two into one design, desired to create an illusion of a succession of churches, in the Perpendicular or Third Pointed manner, climbing up the hill. The detail is rich, there are finials to rejoice the heart, and gargoyles of fine fantasy, all carried out in the purest stucco. At the lowest house on the right-hand side lived Mr. Harold Boale and his wife, and a brass plate on the Gothic door said, "Taxidermist: Skeletons Articulated". As it chanced, this lowest house of Lloyd Street had a longer garden than its fellows, giving on a contractor's yard, and at the end of the garden Mr. Boale had set up the apparatus of his craft in an outhouse, away from the noses of his fellow-men.

So far as can be gathered, the stuffer and articulator was a harmless and inoffensive little fellow. His neighbours liked him, and he and the Boule cabinet-maker from next door, the Shell box-maker over the way, the seal-engraver and the armourer from Baker Square at the top of the hill, and the old mercantile marine skipper who lived round the corner in Marchmont Street, at the house with the ivory junk in the window, used to spend many a genial evening together in the parlour of the Quill in the days before everything was spoilt by the war.

They did not drink very much or talk very much, any of them; but they enjoyed their moderate cups and the snug comfort of the place, and stared solemnly at the old coaching prints that were upon the walls, and at the large glass painting depicting the landing of England's Injured Queen, which hung over the mantelpiece, between two Pink Dogs with gold collars. Mr. Boale passed as a very nice sort of man in this circle, and everybody was sorry for him. Mrs. Boale was a tartar and a scold. The men of the quarter kept out of her way; the women were afraid of her. She led poor Boale the devil's own life. Her voice, often enough, would be heard at the Quill door, vomiting venom at her husband's address; and he, poor man, would tremble and go forth, lest some worse thing might happen. Mrs. Boale was a short dark woman. Her hair was coal-black, her face wore an expression of acid malignity, and she walked quickly but with a decided limp. She was full of energy and the pest of the neighbourhood, and more than a pest to her husband.

The war, with its scarcity and its severe closing-hours, made the meetings at the Quill rarer than before, and deprived them of a good deal of their old comfort. Still, the circle was not wholly broken up, and one evening Boale announced that his wife had gone to visit relations in Lancashire and would most likely be away for a considerable time.

"Well, there's nothing like a change of air, so they say," said the skipper, "though I've had more than enough of it myself."

The others said nothing, but congratulated Boale in their hearts. One of them remarked afterwards that the only change that would do Mrs. Boale good was a change to Kingdom Come, and they all agreed. They were not aware that Mrs. Boale was enjoying the advantages of the recommended treatment.

V

As I recollect, Mr. Boale's worries began with the appearance of Mrs. Boale's sister, Mary Aspinall, a woman almost as ill-tempered and malignant as Mrs. Boale herself. She had been for some years a nurse with a family in Capetown, and had come home with her mistress. In the first place, the woman had written two or three letters to her sister, and there had been no reply. This struck her as odd, for Mrs. Boale had been a very good correspondent, filling her letters with "nasty things" about her husband. So, on her first afternoon off after her return, Mary Aspinall called at the house in Lloyd Street to get the truth of the matter from her sister's own lips. She strongly suspected Boale of having suppressed her letters. "The dirty little tyke; I'll serve him," she said to herself. So came Miss Aspinall to Lloyd Street and brought out Boale from his workshop. And when he saw her his heart sank. He had read her letters. But the decision to return to England had been taken suddenly; Miss Aspinall had therefore said not a word about it. Boale had thought of his wife's sister as established at the other end of the world for the next ten, twenty years, perhaps; and he meant to go away and lose himself under a new name in a year or two. And so when he saw the woman his heart sank.

Mary Aspinall went straight to the point.

"Where's Elizabeth?" she asked. "Upstairs? I wonder she didn't come down when she heard the bell."

"No," said Boale. He comforted himself with the thought of the curious labyrinth he had drawn about his secret; he felt secure in the centre of it.

"No, she's not upstairs. She's not in the house."

"Oh, indeed. Not in the house. Gone to see some friends, I suppose. When do you expect her back?"

"The truth is, Mary, that I don't expect her back. She's left me—three months ago, it is."

"You mean to tell me that! Left you! Shewed her sense, I think. Where has she gone?"

"Upon my word, Mary, I don't know. We had a bit of a to-do one evening, though I don't think I said much. But she said she'd had enough, and she packed a few things in a bag and off she went. I ran after her and called to her to come back, but she wouldn't so much as turn her head, and went off King's Cross way. And from that day to this I've never seen her, nor had a word from her. I've had to send all of her letters back to the post office."

Mary Aspinall stared hard at her brother-in-law and pondered. Beyond telling him that he had brought it on himself, there seemed nothing to say. So she dealt with Boale on those lines very thoroughly, and made an indignant exit from the parlour. He went back to stuff peacocks, for all I know. He was feeling comfortable again. There had been a very unpleasant sensation in the stomach for a few seconds—a very horrible fear at the moment that one of the outer walls of that labyrinth of his had been breached; but now all was well again.

And all might have been permanently well if Miss Aspinall had not happened to meet Mrs. Horridge in the main road, close to the bottom of Lloyd Street. Mrs. Horridge was the wife of the Shell box-maker, and the two had met once or twice long ago at Mrs. Boale's tea-table. They recognised each other, and after a few unmeaning remarks Mrs. Horridge asked Miss Aspinall if she had seen her sister since her return to England.

"How could I see her when I don't know where she is?" asked Miss Aspinall with some ferocity.

"Dear me, you haven't seen Mr. Boale, then?"

"I've just come from him this minute."

"But he can't have lost the Lancashire address, surely?"

And so one thing led to another, and Mary Aspinall gathered quite clearly that Boale had told his friends that his wife was paying a long visit to relations in Lancashire. In the first place, the Aspinalls had no relations in Lancashire—they came from Suffolk—and secondly, Boale had informed her that Elizabeth had gone away in a rage, he knew not where. She did not pay him another visit then and there, as she had at first intended. It was growing late, and she took her considerations back with her to Wimbledon, determined on thinking the matter out.

Next week she called again at Lloyd Street. She charged Boale with deliberate lying, placing frankly before him the two tales he had told. Again that horrid sinking sensation lay heavy upon Boale. But he had reserves.

"Indeed," he said, "I've told you no lies, Mary. It all happened just as I said before. But I did make up that tale about Lancashire for the people about here. I didn't like them to have my troubles to talk over, especially as Elizabeth is bound to come back some time, and I hope it will be soon."

Miss Aspinall stared at the little man in a doubtful, threatening fashion for a moment, and then hurried upstairs. She came down soon afterwards.

"I've gone through Elizabeth's drawers," she said with defiance. "There's a good many things missing. I don't see those bits of lace she had from Granny, and the set of jet is gone, and so is the garnet necklace, and the coral brooch. I couldn't find the ivory fan, either."

"I found all the drawers wide open after she'd gone," sighed Mr. Boale. "I suppose she'd taken the things away with her."

It must be confessed that Mr. Boale, taught, perhaps, by the nicety of his craft, had paid every attention to detail. He had realised that it would be vain to tell a tale of his wife going away and leaving her treasures behind her. And so the treasures had disappeared.

Really, the Aspinall vixen did not know what to say. She had to confess that Boale had explained the difficulty of his two stories quite plausibly. So she informed him that he was more like a worm than a man, and banged the hall door. Again Boale went back to his workshop with a warmth about his heart. His labyrinth was still secure, its secret safe. At first, when confronted again by the accusing Aspinall, he had thought of bolting the moment he got the woman out of the house; but that was unreasoning panic. He was in no danger. And he remembered, like the rest of us, the Crippen case. It was running away that brought Crippen to ruin; if he had sat tight he would have sat secure, and the secret of the cellar would never have been known. Though, as Mr. Boale reflected, anybody was welcome to search his cellar, to search here and there and anywhere on his premises, from the hall door in front to the workshop at the back. And he proceeded to give his calm, whole-souled attention to a fine raven that had been sent round in the morning.

Miss Aspinall took the extraordinary disappearance of her sister back with her to Wimbledon and thought it over. She thought it over again and again, and she could make nothing of it. She did not know that people are constantly disappearing for all sorts of reasons; that nobody hears anything about such cases unless some enterprising paper sees matter for a "stunt", and rouses all England to hunt for John Jones or Mrs. Carraway. To Miss Aspinall, the vanishing of Elizabeth Boale seemed a portent and a wonder, a unique and terrible event; and she puzzled her head over it, and still could find no exit from her labyrinth—a different structure from the labyrinth maintained by the serene Boale. The Aspinall had no suspicions of her brother-in-law; both his manner and his matter were straightforward, clear, and square. He was a worm, as she had informed him, but he was certainly telling the truth. But the woman was fond of her sister, and wanted to know where she had gone and what had happened to her; and so she put the matter into the hands of the police.

VI

She furnished the best description that she could of the missing woman, but the officer in charge of the case pointed out that she had not seen her sister for many years, and that Mr. Boale was obviously the person to be consulted in the matter. So the taxidermist was once again drawn from his scientific labours. He was shewn the information laid by Miss Aspinall and the description furnished by her. He told his simple story once more, mentioning the incident of his lying to his neighbours to avoid unpleasant gossip, and added several details to Miss Aspinall's picture of his wife. He then furnished the constable with two photographs, pointed out the better likeness of the two, and saw his visitor off his premises with cheerful calm.

In due course, the "Missing" bill, garnished with a reproduction of the photograph selected by Mr. Boale, with minute descriptive details, including the "marked limp", was posted up at the police-stations all over the country, and glanced at casually by a few passers-by here and there. There was nothing sensational about the placard; and the statement, "Last seen going in the direction of King's Cross," was not a very promising clue for the amateur detective. No hint of the matter got into the Press; as I have pointed out, hardly one per cent of these cases of "missing" does get into the Press. And just then we were all occupied in reading the paeans of the war correspondents, who were proving that an advance of a mile and a half on a nine-mile front constituted a victory which threw Waterloo into the shade. There was no room for discussing the whereabouts of an obscure woman whom Islington knew no more.

It was sheer accident that brought about the catastrophe. James Curry, a medical student who had rooms in Percy Street, Tottenham Court Road, was prowling about his quarter one afternoon in an indefinite and idle manner, gazing at shop windows and mooning at street corners. He knew that he would never want a cash register, but he inspected the stock with the closest attention, and chose a fine specimen listed at £75. Again, he invested heavily in costly Oriental rugs, and furnished a town mansion in the Sheraton manner at very considerable expense. And so his tour of inspection brought him to the police-station; and there he proceeded to read the bills posted outside, including the bill related to Elizabeth Boale.

"Walks with a marked limp."

James Curry felt his breath go out of his body in a swift gasp. He put out a hand towards the railing to steady himself as he read that amazing sentence over again. And then he walked straight into the police-station.

The fact was that he had bought from Harold Boale, three weeks after the date on which Elizabeth Boale was last seen, a female skeleton. He had got it comparatively cheaply because of the malformation of one of the thigh-bones. And now it struck him that the late owner of that thigh-bone must have walked with a very marked limp.

VII

M'Aulay made his reputation at the trial. He defended Harold Boale with magnificent audacity. I was in court—it was a considerable part of my business in those days to frequent the Old Bailey—and I shall never forget the opening phrases of his speech for the prisoner. He rose slowly, and let his glance go slowly round the court. His eyes rested at last with grave solemnity on the jury. At length he spoke, in a low, clear, deliberate voice, weighing, as it seemed, every word he uttered.

"Gentleman," he began, "a very great man, and a very wise man, and a very good man once said that probability is the guide of life. I think you will agree with me that this is a weighty utterance. When we once leave the domain of pure mathematics, there is very little that is certain. Supposing we have money to invest: we weigh the pros and cons of this scheme and that, and decide at last on probable grounds. Or it may be our lot to have to make an appointment; we have to choose a man to fill a responsible position in which both honesty and sagacity are of the first consequence. Again probability must guide us to a decision. No one man can form a certain and infallible judgment of another. And so through all the affairs of life: we must be content with probability, and again and again with probability. Bishop Butler was right.

"But every rule has its exception. The rule which we have just laid down has its exception. That exception confronts you terribly, tremendously, at this very moment. You may think—I do not say that you do think—but you may think that Harold Boale, the prisoner at the bar, in all probability murdered his wife, Elizabeth Boale."

There was a long pause at this point. Then:

"*If* you think that, then it is your imperative duty to acquit the prisoner at the bar. The only verdict which you dare give is a verdict of 'Not Guilty'."

Up to this moment, Counsel had maintained the low, deliberate utterance with which he had begun his speech, pausing now and again and seeming to consider within himself the precise value of every word that came to his lips. Suddenly his voice rang out, resonant, piercing. One word followed swiftly on another:

"This, remember, is not a court of probability. Bishop Butler's maxim does not apply here. Here there is no place for probability. This is a court of certainty. And unless you are certain that my client is guilty, unless you are as certain of his guilt as you are certain that two and two make four, then you must acquit him.

"Again, and yet again—this is a court of certainty. In the ordinary affairs of life, as we have seen, we are guided by probability. We sometimes make mistakes; in most cases these mistakes may be rectified. A disastrous investment may be counter balanced by a prosperous investment; a bad servant may be replaced by a good one. But in this place, where life and death may hang in the balances which are in your hands, there is no room for mistakes, since here mistakes are irreparable. You cannot bring a dead man back to life. You must not say, 'This man is probably a murderer, and therefore he is guilty.' Before you bring in such a verdict, you must be able to say, 'This man is certainly a murderer.' And *that* you cannot say, and I will tell you why."

M'Aulay then took the evidence piece by piece. Scientific witnesses had declared that the malformation of the thigh-bone in the skeleton exhibited would produce exactly the sort of limp which had characterised Elizabeth Boale. Counsel for the defence had worried the doctors, had made them admit that such a malformation was by no means unique. It was uncommon. Yes, but not very uncommon? Perhaps not. Finally, one doctor admitted that in the course of thirty years of hospital and private practice he had known of five such cases of malformation of the thigh-bone. M'Aulay gave an inaudible sigh of relief; he felt that he had got his verdict.

He made all this quite clear to the jury. He dwelt on the principle that no one can be condemned unless the *corpus delicti,* the body, or some identifiable portion of the body of the murdered person can be produced. He told them the story of the Campden Wonder; how the "murdered" man walked into his village two years after the three people had been hanged for murdering him. "Gentlemen," he said, "for all I know, and for all you know, Elizabeth Boale may walk into this court at any moment. I say boldly that we have no earthly right to assume that she is dead."

Of course Boale's defence was a very simple one. The skeleton which he sold to Mr. Curry had been gradually assembled by him in the course of the last three years. He pointed out that the two hands were not a very good match; and, indeed, this was a little detail that he had not overlooked.

The jury took half an hour to consider their verdict. Harold Boale was found "Not Guilty".

He was seen by an old friend a couple of years ago. He had emigrated to America, and was doing prosperously in his old craft in a big town of the Middle West. He had married a pleasant girl of Swedish extraction.

"You see," he explained, "the lawyers told me I should be safe in presuming poor Elizabeth's death."

He smiled amiably.

And finally, I beg to state that this account of mine is a grossly partial narrative. For all I know, assuming for a moment the severe standards of M'Aulay, Boale was an innocent man. It is possible that his story was a true one. Elizabeth Boale may, after all, be living; she may return after the fashion of the "murdered" man in the Campden Wonder. All the thoughts, devices, meditations that I have put into the heart and mind of Boale may be my own malignant inventions without a shadow of true substance behind them.

In theory, then, the Islington Mystery is an open question. Certainly; but in fact?

The Gift of Tongues

More than a hundred years ago a simple German maid-of-all-work caused a great sensation. She became subject to seizures of a very singular character, of so singular a character that the family inconvenienced by these attacks were interested and, perhaps, a little proud of a servant whose fits were so far removed from the ordinary convulsion. The case was thus. Anna, or Gretchen, or whatever her name might be, would suddenly become oblivious of soup, sausage, and the material world generally.

But she neither screamed, nor foamed, nor fell to earth after the common fashion of such seizures. She stood up, and from her mouth rolled sentence after sentence of splendid sound, in a sonorous tongue, filling her hearers with awe and wonder. Not one of her listeners understood a word of Anna's majestic utterances, and it was useless to question her in her uninspired moments, for the girl knew nothing of what had happened.

At length, as it fell out, some scholarly personage was present during one of these extraordinary fits; and he at once declared that the girl was speaking Hebrew, with a pure accent and perfect intonation. And, in a sense, the wonder was now greater than ever. How could the simple Anna speak Hebrew? She had certainly never learnt it. She could barely read and write her native German. Everyone was amazed, and the occult mind of the day began to formulate theories and speak of possession and familiar spirits. Unfortunately (as I think, for I am a lover of all insoluble mysteries), the problem of the girl's Hebrew speech was solved; solved, that is, to a certain extent.

The tale got abroad, and so it became known that some years before Anna had been servant to an old scholar. This personage was in the habit of declaiming Hebrew as he walked up and down his study and the passages of his house, and the maid had unconsciously stored the chanted words in some cavern of her soul; in that receptacle, I suppose, which we are content to call the subconsciousness. I must confess that the explanation does not strike me as satisfactory in all respects. In the first place, there is the extraordinary tenacity of memory; but I suppose that other instances of this, though rare enough, might be cited. Then, there is the association of this particular storage of the subconscious with a species of seizure; I do not know whether any similar instances can be cited.

Still, minor puzzles apart, the great mystery was mysterious no more: Anna spoke Hebrew because she had heard Hebrew and, in her odd fashion, had remembered it.

To the best of my belief, cases that offer some points of similarity are occasionally noted at the present day. Persons ignorant of Chinese deliver messages in that tongue; the speech of Abyssinia is heard from lips incapable, in ordinary moments, of anything but the pleasing idiom of the United States of America, and untaught Cockneys suddenly become fluent in Basque.

But all this, so far as I am concerned, is little more than rumour; I do not know how far these tales have been subjected to strict and systematic examination. But in any case, they do not interest me so much as a very odd business that happened on the Welsh border more than sixty years ago. I was not very old at the time, but I remember my father and mother talking about the affair, just as I remember them talking about the Franco-Prussian War in the August of 1870, and coming to the conclusion that the French seemed to be getting the worst of it. And later, when I was growing up and the mysteries were beginning to exercise their fascination upon me, I was able to confirm my vague recollections and add to them a good deal of exact information. The odd business to which I am referring was the so-called "Speaking with Tongues" at Bryn Sion Chapel, Treowen, Monmouthshire, on a Christmas Day of the early 'seventies.

Treowen is one of a chain of horrible mining villages that wind in and out of the Monmouthshire and Glamorganshire valleys. Above are the great domed heights, quivering with leaves (like the dear Zacynthus of Ulysses), on their lower slopes, and then mounting by far stretches of deep bracken, glittering in the sunlight, to a golden land of gorse, and at last to wild territory, bare and desolate, that seems to surge upward for ever. But beneath, in the valley, are the black pits and the blacker mounds, and heaps of refuse, vomiting chimneys, mean rows and ranks of grey houses faced with red brick; all as dismal and detestable as the eye can see.

Such a place is Treowen; uglier and blacker now than it was sixty years ago; and all the worse for the contrast of its vileness with those glorious and shining heights above it. Down in the town there are three great chapels of the Methodists and Baptists and Congregationalists; architectural monstrosities all three of them, and a red brick church does not do much to beautify the place. But above all this, on the hillside, there are scattered white-washed farms, and a little hamlet of white, thatched cottages, remnants all of a pre-industrial age, and here is situated the old meeting-house called Bryn Sion, which means, I believe, the Brow of Zion. It must have been built about 1790–1800, and, being a simple, square building, devoid of crazy ornament, is quite inoffensive.

Here came the mountain farmers and cottagers, trudging, some of them, long distances on the wild tracks and paths of the hillside; and here ministered, from 1860 to 1880, the Reverend Thomas Beynon, a bachelor, who lived in the little cottage next to the chapel, where a grove of beech trees was blown into a thin straggle of tossing boughs by the great winds of the mountain.

Now, Christmas Day falling on a Sunday in this year of long ago, the usual service was held at Bryn Sion Chapel, and, the weather being fine, the congregation was a large one—that is, something between forty and fifty people. People met and shook hands and wished each other "Merry Christmas", and exchanged the news of the week and prices at Newport market, till the elderly, white-bearded minister, in his shining black, went into the chapel. The deacons followed him and took their places in the big pew by the open fireplace, and the little meeting-house was almost full. The minister had a windsor chair, a red hassock, and a pitch-pine table in a sort of raised pen at the end of the chapel, and from this place he gave out the opening hymn. Then followed a long portion of Scripture, a second hymn, and the congregation settled themselves to attend to the prayer.

It was at this moment that the service began to vary from the accustomed order. The minister did not kneel down in the usual way; he stood staring at the people, very strangely, as some of them thought. For perhaps a couple of minutes he faced them in dead silence, and here and there people shuffled uneasily in their pews. Then he came down a few paces and stood in front of the table with bowed head, his back to the people. Those nearest to the ministerial pen or rostrum heard a low murmur coming from his lips. They could not make out the words.

Bewilderment fell upon them all, and, as it would seem, a confusion of mind, so that it was difficult afterwards to gather any clear account of what actually happened that Christmas morning at Bryn Sion Chapel. For some while the mass of the congregation heard nothing at all; only the deacons in the Big Seat could make out the swift mutter that issued from their pastor's lips; now a little higher in tone, now sunken so as to be almost inaudible. They strained their ears to discover what he was saying in that low, continued utterance; and they could hear words plainly, but they could not understand. It was not Welsh.

It was neither Welsh—the language of the chapel—nor was it English. They looked at one another, those deacons, old men like their minister most of them; looked at one another with something of strangeness and fear in their eyes. One of them, Evan Tudor, Torymynydd, ventured to rise in his place and to ask the preacher, in a low voice, if he were ill. The Reverend Thomas Beynon took no notice; it was evident that he did not hear the question: swiftly the unknown words passed his lips.

"He is wrestling with the Lord in prayer," one deacon whispered to another, and the man nodded—and looked frightened.

And it was not only this murmured utterance that bewildered those who heard it; they, and all who were present, were amazed at the pastor's strange movements. He would stand before the middle of the table and bow his head, and go now to the left of the table, now to the right of it, and then back again to the middle. He would bow down his head, and raise it, and look up, as a man said afterwards, as if he saw the heavens opened. Once or twice he turned round and faced the people, with his arms stretched wide open, and a swift word on his lips, and his eyes staring and seeing nothing, nothing that anyone else could see. And then he would turn again. And all the while the people were dumb and stricken with amazement; they hardly dared to look at each other; they hardly dared to ask themselves what could be happening before them. And then, suddenly, the minister began to sing.

It must be said that the Reverend Thomas Beynon was celebrated all through the valley and beyond it for his "singing religious eloquence", for that singular chant which the Welsh call the *hwyl*. But his congregation had never heard so noble, so aweful a chant as this before. It rang out and soared on high, and fell, to rise again with wonderful modulations; pleading to them and calling them and summoning them; with the old voice of the *hwyl*, and yet with a new voice that they had never heard before: and all in those sonorous words that they could not understand. They stood up in their wonder, their hearts shaken by the chant; and then the voice died away. It was as still as death in the chapel. One of the deacons could see that the minister's lips still moved; but he could hear no sound at all. Then the minister raised up his hands as if he held something between them; and knelt down, and rising, again lifted his hands. And there came the faint tinkle of a bell from the sheep grazing high up on the mountain side.

The Reverend Thomas Beynon seemed to come to himself out of a dream, as they said. He looked about him nervously, perplexed, noted that his people were gazing at him strangely, and then, with a stammering voice, gave out a hymn and afterwards ended the service. He discussed the whole matter with the deacons and heard what they had to tell him. He knew nothing of it himself and had no explanation to offer. He knew no languages, he declared, save Welsh and English. He said that he did not believe there was evil in what had happened, for he felt that he had been in heaven before the Throne. There was a great talk about it all, and that queer Christmas service became known as the Speaking with Tongues of Bryn Sion.

Years afterwards, I met a fellow-countryman, Edward Williams, in London, and we fell talking, in the manner of exiles, of the land and its stories. Williams was many years older than myself, and he told me of an odd thing that had once happened to him.

"It was years ago," he said, "and I had some business—I was a mining-engineer in those days—at Treowen, up in the hills. I had to stay over Christmas, which was on a Sunday that year, and talking to some people there about the *hwyl*, they told me that I ought to go up to Bryn Sion if I wanted to hear it done really well. Well, I went, and it was the queerest service I ever heard of. I don't know much about the Methodists' way of doing things, but before long it struck me that the minister was saying some sort of Mass. I could hear a word or two of the Latin service now and again, and then he sang the Christmas Preface right through: *'Quia per incarnati Verbi mysterium'*—you know."

Very well; but there is always a loophole by which the reasonable, or comparatively reasonable, may escape. Who is to say that the old preacher had not strayed long before into some Roman Catholic Church at Newport or Cardiff on a Christmas Day, and there heard Mass with exterior horror but interior love?

The Cosy Room

I

And he found to his astonishment that he came to the appointed place with a sense of profound relief. It was true that the window was somewhat high up in the wall, and that, in case of fire, it might be difficult, for many reasons, to get out that way; it was barred like the basement windows that one sees now and then in London houses, but as for the rest it was an extremely snug room. There was a gay flowering paper on the walls, a hanging bookshelf—his stomach sickened for an instant—a little table under the window with a board and draughtsmen on it, two or three good pictures, religious and ordinary, and the man who looked after him was arranging the tea-things on the table in the middle of the room. And there was a nice wicker chair by a bright fire. It was a thoroughly pleasant room; cosy you would call it. And, thank God, it was all over, anyhow.

II

It had been a horrible time for the last three months, up to an hour ago. First of all there was the trouble; all over in a minute, that was, and couldn't be helped, though it was a pity, and the girl wasn't worth it. But then there was the getting out of the town. He thought at first of just going about his ordinary business and knowing nothing about it; he didn't think that anybody had seen him following Joe down to the river. Why not loaf about as usual, and say nothing, and go into the Ringland Arms for a pint? It might be days before they found the body under the alders; and there would be an inquest, and all that. Would it be the best plan just to stick it out, and hold his tongue if the police came asking him questions? But then, how could he account for himself and his doings that evening? He might say he went for a stroll in Bleadon Woods and home again without meeting anybody. There was nobody who could contradict him that he could think of.

And now, sitting in the snug room with the bright wallpaper, sitting in the cosy chair by the fire—all so different from the tales they told of such places—he wished he had stuck it out and faced it out, and let them come on and find out what they could. But, then, he had got frightened. Lots of men had heard him swearing it would be outing does for Joe if he didn't leave the girl alone. And he had shewn his revolver to Dick Haddon, and "Lobster" Carey, and Finniman, and others, and then they would be fitting the bullet into the revolver, and it would be all up. He got into a panic and shook with terror, and knew he could never stay in Ledham, not another hour.

III

Mrs. Evans, his landlady, was spending the evening with her married daughter at the other side of the town, and would not be back till eleven. He shaved off his stubbly black beard and moustache, and slunk out of the town in the dark and walked all through the night by a lonely by-road, and got to Darnley, twenty miles away, in the morning in time to catch the London excursion. There was a great crowd of people, and, so far as he could see, nobody that he knew, and the carriages packed full of Darnleyites and Lockwood weavers all in high spirits and taking no notice of him. They all got out at King's Cross, and he strolled about with the rest, and looked round here and there as they did and had a glass of beer at a crowded bar. He didn't see how anybody was to find out where he had gone.

IV

He got a back room in a quiet street off the Caledonian Road, and waited. There was something in the evening paper that night, something that you couldn't very well make out. By the next day Joe's body was found, and they got to Murder—the doctor said it couldn't be suicide. Then his own name came in, and he was missing and was asked to come forward. And then he read that he was supposed to have gone to London, and he went sick with fear. He went hot and he went cold. Something rose in his throat and choked him. His hands shook as he held the paper, his head whirled with terror. He was afraid to go home to his room, because he knew he could not stay still in it; he would be tramping up and down, like a wild beast, and the landlady would wonder. And he was afraid to be in the streets, for fear a policeman would come behind him and put a hand on his shoulder. There was a kind of small square round the corner and he sat down on one of the benches there and held up the paper before his face, with the children yelling and howling and playing all about him on the asphalt paths. They took no notice of him, and yet they were company of a sort; it was not like being all alone in that little, quiet room. But it soon got dark and the man came to shut the gates.

V

And after that night; nights and days of horror and sick terrors that he never had known a man could suffer and live. He had brought enough money to keep him for a while, but every time he changed a note he shook with fear, wondering whether it would be traced. What could he do? Where could he go? Could he get out of the country? But there were passports and papers of all sorts; that would never do. He read that the police held a clue to the Ledham Murder Mystery; and he trembled to his lodgings and locked himself in and moaned in his agony, and then found himself chattering words and phrases at random, without meaning or relevance; strings of gibbering words: "all right, all right, all right . . . yes, yes, yes, yes . . . there, there, there . . . well, well, well, well . . ." just because he must utter something, because he could not bear to sit still and silent, with that anguish tearing his heart, with that sick horror choking him, with that weight of terror pressing on his breast. And then, nothing happened; and a little, faint, trembling hope fluttered in his breast for a while, and for a day or two he felt he might have a chance after all.

One night he was in such a happy state that he ventured round to the little public-house at the corner, and drank a bottle of Old Brown Ale with some enjoyment, and began to think of what life might be again, if by a miracle—he recognised even then that it would be a miracle—all this horror passed away, and he was once more just like other men, with nothing to be afraid of. He was relishing the Brown Ale, and quite plucking up a spirit, when a chance phrase from the bar caught him: "looking for him not far from here, so they say". He left the glass of beer half full, and went out wondering whether he had the courage to kill himself that night. As a matter of fact the men at the bar were talking about a recent and sensational cat burglar; but every such word was doom to this wretch. And ever and again, he would check himself in his horrors, in his mutterings and gibberings, and wonder with amazement that the heart of a man could suffer such bitter agony, such rending torment. It was as if he had found out and discovered, he alone of all men living, a new world of which no man before had ever dreamed, in which no man could believe, if he were told the story of it. He had woken up in his past life from such nightmares, now and again, as most men suffer. They were terrible, so terrible that he re-membered two or three of them that had oppressed him years before; but they were pure delight to what he now endured. Not endured, but writhed under as a worm twisting amidst red, burning coals.

He went out into the streets, some noisy, some dull and empty, and considered in his panic-stricken confusion which he should choose. They were looking for him in that part of London; there was deadly peril in every step. The streets where people went to and fro and laughed and chattered might be the safer; he could walk with the others and seem to be of them, and so be less likely to be noticed by those who were hunting on his track. But then, on the other hand, the great electric lamps made these streets almost as bright as day, and every feature of the passers-by was clearly seen. True, he was clean-shaven now, and the pictures of him in the papers shewed a bearded man, and his own face in the glass still looked strange to him. Still, there were sharp eyes that could penetrate such disguises; and they might have brought down some man from Ledham who knew him well, and knew the way he walked; and so he might be hailed and held at any moment. He dared not walk under the clear blaze of the electric lamps. He would be safe in the dark, quiet by-ways.

He was turning aside, making for a very quiet street close by, when he hesitated. This street, indeed, was still enough after dark, and not over well lighted. It was a street of low, two-storied houses of grey brick that had grimed, with three or four families in each house. Tired men came home here after working hard all day, and people drew their blinds early and stirred very little abroad, and went early to bed; footsteps were rare in this street and in other streets into which it led, and the lamps were few and dim compared with those in the big thoroughfares. And yet, the very fact that few people were about made such as were all the more noticeable and conspicuous. And the police went slowly on their beats in the dark streets as in the bright, and with few people to look at no doubt they looked all the more keenly at such as passed on the pavement. In his world, that dreadful world that he had discovered and dwelt in, alone, the darkness was brighter than the daylight, and solitude more dangerous than a multitude of men. He dared not go into the light, he feared the shadows, and went trembling to his room and shuddered there as the hours of the night went by; shuddered and gabbled to himself his infernal rosary: "all right, all right, all right . . . splendid, splendid . . . that's the way, that's the way, that's the way, that's the way . . . yes, yes, yes . . . first rate, first rate . . . all right . . . one, one, one, one"—gabbled in a low mutter to keep himself from howling like a wild beast.

VI

It was somewhat in the manner of a wild beast that he beat and tore against the cage of his fate. Now and again it struck him as incredible. He would not believe that it was so. It was something that he would wake from, as he had waked from those nightmares that he remembered, for things did not really happen so. He could not believe it, he would not believe it. Or, if it were so indeed, then all these horrors must be happening to some other man into whose torments he had mysteriously entered. Or he had got into a book, into a tale which one read and shuddered at, but did not for one moment credit; all makebelieve, it must be, and presumably everything would be all right again. And then the truth came down on him like a heavy hammer, and beat him down, and held him down—on the burning coals of his anguish.

Now and then he tried to reason with himself. He forced himself to be sensible, as he put it; not to give way, to think of his chances. After all, it was three weeks since he had got into the excursion train at

Darnley, and he was still a free man, and every day of freedom made his chances better. These things often die down. There were lots of cases in which the police never got the man they were after. He lit his pipe and began to think things over quietly. It might be a good plan to give his landlady notice, and leave at the end of the week, and make for somewhere in South London, and try to get a job of some sort: that would help to put them off his track. He got up and looked thought-fully out of the window; and caught his breath. There, outside the little newspaper shop opposite, was the bill of the evening paper: New Clue in Ledham Murder Mystery.

VII

The moment came at last. He never knew the exact means by which he was hunted down. As a matter of fact, a woman who knew him well happened to be standing outside Darnley station on the Excursion Day morning, and she had recognised him, in spite of his beardless chin. And then, at the other end, his landlady, on her way upstairs, had heard his mutterings and gabblings, though the voice was low. She was interested, and curious, and a little frightened, and wondered whether her lodger might be dangerous, and naturally she talked to her friends. So the story trickled down to the ears of the police, and the police asked about the date of the lodger's arrival. And there you were. And there was our nameless friend, drinking a good, hot cup of tea, and polishing off the bacon and eggs with rare appetite; in the cosy room with the cheerful paper; otherwise the Condemned Cell.

Johnny Double

I

The worst of it was that Johnny Marchant had nothing particular to complain of. He did not live in a slum in the most miserable part of London. He lived in a beautiful old house in the country. His father did not beat him when he came home drunk, because his father very rarely left his house and therefore he couldn't come home. And besides, his father never got drunk. His old grandmother never thought of shutting him up in dark cupboards. All the cupboards at Johnny's home were full of books and of curious and beautiful things, so there was no room for Johnny. Besides, his grandmother, who came on visits about twice a year, would never have dreamt of doing such a silly thing. In the first place she was as kind as kind could be; and then she was not the sort of woman to take a lot of rare china out of a cupboard for the sake of putting a little boy into it; in fact, as I say, Johnny Marchant had nothing whatever to complain of, and that's a pity. People are not interested in a child who isn't shut up in the dark, starved, or beaten. It is true that Johnny's mother had died when he was a year old. But he never remembered her, and his nurse Mary knew what a boy's feelings are, and generally had gooseberry jam for tea. Or if not, blackberry jelly in the blue Chinese pot with the yellow dragons.

II

So, since we cannot pretend that Johnny Marchant had a rough time, we may as well make the best of the smooth things that he enjoyed. To begin with, the house that he lived in was old and odd and beautiful. It was in a hollow looking over a quiet bay of a calm blue sea. About it were groves of dark ilex trees, green all the year round; and then there were huge old laurels of a brighter green that blossomed and bore a crimson-purple fruit. There was a lawn in front of the house with fuchsia hedges twenty feet high. On one side was the kitchen garden, where the peaches grew from pale green to yellow, and from yellow to pink, and from pink to crimson all through the spring and summer. On the other side were the dessert apples and pears in an orchard sloping to the south and the sea. Then from the first lawn steps went down to the second lawn, called Johnny Summerhouse Lawn, for here was a summer house that had tried to look like a Chinese temple, before the white roses had grown all over it. And then another flight of steps went down to Well Lawn, where a tall pine tree grew off a red rock, and all manner of green boughs shaded a bubbling well, with white sand always stirring at the bottom of it, as the water rose clear and cold out of the heart of the hill. And, after that, below again was the wild place where all the trees grew thick together and the ground was rich with ferns, and a steep path twisted in and out of the wildness down to the sea.

III

As for the house; it was about a hundred and twenty years old. There was a ground floor and a first floor, and that was all, and then a thatched roof. The walls were painted white, and the veranda was painted green, and purple clematis covered it. And on the path, in front of the house, were six great green tubs, and in the six great green tubs there were six great green bushes of box, as old as the house. The man who had built it was a captain in the Navy, who had fought in all the fights against Napoleon and had sailed all over the world besides. He had made the builders paint the walls white, and had called his house Casabianca, or White House. But when the box trees in the tubs grew big and round, as they soon did, the country people called the place "The Bunches", and at last it was known as Casabianca Bunches, and Johnny never heard the last of it when he went to school and told his best friend where he lived. In fact he was called "Bunches" at Oxford; and for all I know his fellow-judges call him "Brother Bunches" to this day—except when they are all dressed in scarlet and white and wear great wigs.

IV

So there were all sorts of nice things outside the house, and one could always get lost in the wild place. And when it rained, there were all sorts of nice things inside the house. There were Chinese monsters and junks and temples made of ivory and lacquer cabinets, rich red and gold and mother-of-pearl, and Japanese pictures in deep fine colours, with people making horrible faces in the front, and blue mountains and rivers and bridges in the distance, and Indian gods with too many arms, and elephants' heads, and serpents and everything a boy can want. As for books, there were plenty everywhere: Baxter's *Saints' Rest, The Arabian Nights,* Jeremy Taylor, *Roderick Random,* the Poetical Works of Akenside, the Waverley Novels, *Gil Blas, Gulliver's Travels,* all Dickens', Jortin's *Sermons,* and *Don Quixote.* In due time Johnny tried them all—very small bits of some of them, and, as his father said, gave himself a liberal education. And yet his father and his grandmother and his Aunt Letitia were sometimes "quite uneasy" about him. He was so very odd at times. The old doctor came over from Nantgaron and heard all about it, and looked at Johnny's tongue, and pinched him in the proper places, and sent powders; and that was no good. Then Johnny was taken to the doctor at Bristol, who said he must live on cream and mutton chops done pink; and that was no good. Then Johnny was taken to the doctor in London, and he said that raw carrots, finely sliced, with plenty of nuts, would make an immense change for the better; but that did no good. Though his doctor spoke of "irritability of the nervous system", "marked psychological cachexia", "idiosyncrasy", and "pathogenic" at considerable length.

V

Johnny's trouble was a very odd one, and for some time his relations didn't think much about it. It began by his telling long stories about where he had been and what he had seen, all the most wonderful things that he hadn't seen and couldn't have seen. Mary, the nurse, heard most of these tales in the morning and at tea-time and at bed-time, and she only said, "Yes, dear"; "Of course, darling"; "I see, Master Johnny"; and "Well, I'm sure!" not heeding a word of it. So she heard how Johnny had been a long way off to a big town, ever so much bigger than Nantgaron, and there were houses and houses, and then a sort of country in the middle of the houses, full of trees and grass, and there all the wild beasts in the picture-books came alive, elephants and everything. And Mary cut more bread-and-butter, for this was at tea, and said, "Beautiful, I'm sure." Another time there was a story of a great place, full of lights, and seats rising one behind another; and then something dark went away, and there was a wood beyond, and people in queer dresses talking and singing. "That's the way," said Mary, "and here's your nightshirt, Master Johnny, nice and warm, as I've aired it myself by the kitchen fire." Then it was a tale about another country in the middle of the big town, not the country where the beasts in the picture-book came to life, but a different one, and big soldiers in scarlet and gold with bright swords in their hands riding through the country, and a band playing. And Mary went on cutting the bread-and-butter and helping the jam and brushing Johnny's hair, and not putting herself out a bit. Sometimes Johnny would tell his adventures to his father, who let him run on as he liked. Imaginative children, he said to himself, will always "make up" and "make believe", and it is absurd to punish them for lying. So he would listen almost as quietly as Mary; and one night Johnny told him a long and confused story of one of the bright places with rows of seats rising one above another and the dark place getting bright, and then all sorts of wonderful things happening: a man all white and misty, who talked in a deep voice and seemed to frighten everybody very much, and a king and queen sat on thrones, and a man in a black cloak, who seemed very miserable, talked to them, and at last they all killed each other, and so everybody was dead, and there was a great noise. Mr. Marchant went on reading his paper, and said, "I see," and "Very good, and what did they do then?" "Did you say a churchyard and a rather cross clergyman with a bald head? Dear me! About your bedtime, isn't it?" He thought nothing about it, and he didn't think anything about it when his cousin Anna—one of the "Dawson girls", aged fifty-five—wrote to him from London and said amongst many other things: "Do you think *Hamlet* quite a suitable play for Johnny? He is surely very young for all the horrors. I must say he seemed to be enjoying himself when I saw him two or three weeks ago at the Lyceum. Irving is certainly very fine.

Was Johnny staying with the Gascoignes? I did not recognise the lady next to him." Mr. Marchant simply said, "Tut, tut, tut: Anna talking nonsense as usual," and paid no more attention to the matter. He had not listened to half Johnny's story of the misty man and the miserable man and the king and queen and the cross clergyman, and he had forgotten all about the rest. And, anyhow, he knew that Johnny had been at Casabianca Bunches all the summer, and Anna had always been a muddlehead.

VI

Mr. Marchant only began to get seriously disturbed about the boy one hot day in August, when Johnny was about nine. There was some business to be done at Nantgaron, the market town, eight miles away, and Mr. Marchant drove over in the dogcart. As he was lunching in the coffee-room of The Three Salmons, his friend, Captain Lloyd, came in and sat down at another table and began to munch bread and cheese and to drink beer out of a great silver tankard with a lid. At first he talked of the harvest, which, as he said, was the earliest for twenty years, and then he remarked:

"What have you done with Johnny? Turned him loose in the tuck shop?"

"Johnny?" said Mr. Marchant. "What d'you mean? I left him at home. Nothing to amuse him at Nantgaron."

"Nonsense, I saw him in the High Street ten minutes ago. He was staring at those steeplejacks mending the weathercock on the spire of St. Mary's."

"I left Johnny reading on the veranda at home an hour and a half ago, and I've only just come. He could hardly have walked the distance in the time. You must have mistaken some other boy for him."

"Well, that's very strange. I was quite close to him. He was wearing a straw hat with a green ribbon and a pheasant's feather stuck in it."

Mr. Marchant looked very oddly at Captain Lloyd.

"Queer things boys will wear," was all he said, and that was not much to the point. But the fact was that he had noticed the pheasant's feather in the straw hat with the green ribbon on Johnny's head when he said good-bye to him on the veranda, and had told Johnny that that style of hat was very little worn in town just now. Clearly Johnny had managed to get a lift into Nantgaron, and the only thing to do was to ask him what he meant by it. And so when Mr. Marchant got home about tea-time, the first thing he did was to ask Mary, the nurse, whether Master Johnny had come back.

"He's not been away, sir. He's reading in the Rose Bower, and I'm just going to call him for his tea."

"Not been away, Mary? Do you mean he was in to dinner?"

"As usual, sir, at one o'clock. Roast chicken and raspberry tart. And I thought to myself how children can eat so well and the weather so hot."

Mr. Marchant looked hard at the nurse and then said:

"Oh, I see. Thank you, Mary. That's all right, then."

He didn't see at all. But he thought the matter over, and decided that it was quite possible that some other little boy might have a straw hat with a green ribbon and stick a pheasant's tail feather in it. Soon after tea Mr. Marchant was enjoying his hollyhocks and his pipe on the Summerhouse Lawn, and Johnny was helping, and putting in a word about the Templar in *Ivanhoe*. And then he said: "Daddy! weren't those men wonderful to-day, right up on the very top of the church?"

And Mr. Marchant's pipe dropped out of his mouth.

VII

It was no good to try to get Johnny to explain. He didn't seem to think that there was anything to explain. He said he wondered what his father was doing at Nantgaron, so he thought he would go and see; and that was all, and that was how all his relations got "quite uneasy", as they said. And the doctors' medicines and chopped carrots and nuts made no difference whatever. Till at last the parson said there was nothing for it but school, and the boy was "packed off", first of all to a big preparatory school, and then to a bigger public school. Odd things happened once or twice at both places. He began to tell the other boys one of his queer stories and was promptly kicked and clouted as a young liar. Then he got into trouble for being about the town at midnight, and things looked extremely serious. But as he was able to prove that he was fast asleep in the dormitory at the time, his house-master only gave him lines on general principles. Johnny was cured, or so his father and the people at home thought.

VIII

But many years afterwards, only three years ago as a matter of fact, and some time after Johnny had become Mr. Justice Marchant, it was appointed that he should try Henry Farmer, who was accused of the dreadful Hetton murder. When the court was opened, and the judge and the prisoner faced each other, a few people noticed that the two men in their different places "looked as if they had seen a ghost". The prisoner in the dock gasped and shuddered, and muttered something about "the man in scarlet", and the judge on the bench turned ghastly white, and his head almost fell on the desk before him. Mr. Justice Marchant said in a faint voice that he feared a somewhat severe indisposition would prevent him trying the case. The prisoner was put back: it was another judge who sentenced Farmer to death a few days later. Mr. Justice Marchant never told any one that he had seen the man in the dock before—and with the red knife in his hand.

Awaking: A Children's Story

I

Far up on the hillside Johnny sat on the stile in his garden hedge, and looked out on the rough lands, the marshes with rushes, the thickets of ash and thorn, the little glittering stream, and on the twinkling town below and the dark forest far away. The sun had just set behind him on the huge hill in the west, and at first there were red lights in the river that wound about the town, and the thorns and thickets blossomed as if they were rose-gardens. Then the glow grew dim on the earth and in the sky, and the dusk came on, and after it the night. But the town in the valley twinkled all the more as the lights came out one after another; and more lights still on the level meadow by the river.

For to-morrow was the great Midsummer Fair, and to this, as Johnny believed, there came all the people of the world, bringing with them the world's wonders, and he had a groat to spend, which was as good as five shillings of our money, or much better. And there, in the Fair meadow, as he looked from his high perch on the steep hillside, he could see the lamps and lights dancing to and fro, moving here, moving there, going together like a swarm of golden flies, scattering apart, swimming through the darkness, and here and there flames shooting up from a bonfire. For all the Fair folk were setting up their booths and stalls and tents and tabernacles, getting ready for the business of the next day.

Johnny gazed on and on, down the dark hillside, where the bats were shrilling on their thin, high pipes, where the owls cried "Hoo, hoo, hoo," as if they were afraid, and the fern owl, hidden in bracken, drove his whirring rattle round and round. And in the field of corn the crake cried in a harsh voice "Jar, jar." Johnny sat still on the stile, and

215

listened to these strange sounds and voices, and watched the hurrying and floating of the lights in the Fair meadow, till at last his mother called him, and he went in to the house, and to his cot under the thatch, and then to such happy sleep as comes on a hillside on still summer nights.

II

Very early the next morning Johnny got up from his bed, and saw the sun come dancing over the trees of the forest, and shining on all the round world. The owl and the bat, the crake and the jar were all hidden and asleep, deep in the thickets and in stony places, but the birds of the day were singing together as Johnny ran down the twisting path that led into the valley and the town. And there all was stirring and awaking, and shouts and cries mingling in the streets: there trumpets calling, and horns blowing, and drums beating, and clear pipes sounding like the wind, and bread and wine set out by the gate of Paradise, and by the door of Heaven, according to the custom of the manor, on the Fair of Midsummer Day. Paradise and Heaven, I must say, were the names of the two high taverns of the town, and the people meant no harm. But Johnny, who had eaten bread and meat and had drunk milk before he set out, went into the church and heard Mass and rejoiced in the white-robed men singing in the choir, and in the red beam, redder than any rose, that came down upon the priest from the painted window over the altar. And bells were rung, and deep voices spoke from the organ, and the singing men cried out "Hosanna."

III

Then went Johnny leaping to the Fair, through the streets garlanded with green boughs, with rich carpets hanging out of the windows, and so to the field by the river and the old walls of the Romans. Here was, first of all, the encampment of the Knights, jewelled with pavilions of gold and green, of silver and crimson, of scarlet and purple; the banners all figured with lions and dragons, wyverns and leopards, flying over them; and the place prepared for the joust, with palisades and bars. Presently, the ringing trumpets echoed from the hill and the thunder of the horses' hoofs answered, and the two knights in their glittering armour crashed together. Johnny saw a lance fly in splinters into the air, and a knight falling headlong, and then the people all rushed together, shouting, and he saw no more, but turned to the Fair. And here were all the good and fine things in the world. There was silken and rich stuff blazing in the sunlight; there was a man with birds of all colours that spoke and uttered words and sentences. There were cups of gold and silver and vessels of brass; there were puppets that went dancing and did a mystery before all; there were swords and armour, and jars of wine, and meat roasting, and horns calling, and a man that came with a pipe and a drum and morris men following him, and a fool in gold and green, arm in arm with a grisly Death. And such a singing and a ringing, such shouts and tumult, that Johnny felt his head turn round and he went out of the Fair, and walked all alone far along the meadows by the river. And there was a very old and twisted thorn tree that threw a shadow on a green bank. And here Johnny lay down and fell asleep for a long while.

IV

When he woke up all the world had changed. He thought that the sun must have struck him before he lay down under the thorn. For he recollected broken dreams, and pains all over him, and fallings into darkness, and waking again into a room with a twinkling light and black shadows in it, and voices, half heard, murmuring about him, and the last music of the Fair dying down very far away. And when he could get up, everything that he knew had passed away. The clothes people wore were different from those that he remembered; there seemed to be no knights in glittering armour; the shops had no such treasures as he had seen at the Fair; all the wonder and the glory had gone from the world. When he tried to speak of what he remembered, nobody would listen to him.

He ended as a poet. His family did not care to have it mentioned. They said that it all began with the sunstroke he got when he was a little boy, and that it was a great pity.

As his Aunt Elizabeth always said:

"He would go off to that horrible, common Fair, all alone, and just like a boy, he left his cap in the hall, though it was blazing Midsummer. Then, there was the Salvation Army holding a meeting in the market-place, bawling and banging in their usual way; and I'm sure the cornet, as old Sam Smith plays it, is enough to split anybody's head in two. Then off to the Fair, that, I say, ought to have been put down a hundred years ago; and in and out of the tents; boxing and prize-fighting, and 'Maria Marten' and the rest of it, and the Performing Parrots and Punch and Judy, and Potter's Perfect Pierrots, and the Flying Serpents, and that burning sun all the time. No wonder he got a sunstroke, and has been very queer ever since."

Opening the Door

The newspaper reporter, from the nature of the case, has generally to deal with the commonplaces of life. He does his best to find something singular and arresting in the spectacle of the day's doings; but, in spite of himself, he is generally forced to confess that whatever there may be beneath the surface, the surface itself is dull enough.

I must allow, however, that during my ten years or so in Fleet Street, I came across some tracks that were not devoid of oddity. There was that business of Campo Tosto, for example. That never got into the papers. Campo Tosto, I must explain, was a Belgian, settled for many years in England, who had left all his property to the man who looked after him.

My news editor was struck by something odd in the brief story that appeared in the morning paper, and sent me down to make enquiries. I left the train at Reigate; and there I found that Mr. Campo Tosto had lived at a place called Burnt Green—which is a translation of his name into English—and that he shot at trespassers with a bow and arrows. I was driven to his house, and saw through a glass door some of the property which he had bequeathed to his servant: fifteenth-century triptychs, dim and rich and golden; carved statues of the saints; great spiked altar candlesticks; storied censers in tarnished silver; and much more of old church treasure. The legatee, whose name was Turk, would not let me enter; but, as a treat, he took my newspaper from my pocket and read it upside down with great accuracy and facility. I wrote this very queer story, but Fleet Street would not suffer it. I believe it struck them as too strange a thing for their sober columns.

And then there was the affair of the J.H.V.S. Syndicate, which dealt with a Cabalistic cipher, and the phenomenon, called in the Old Testament "the Glory of the Lord", and the discovery of certain objects buried under the site of the Temple at Jerusalem; that story was left half told, and I never heard the ending of it. And I never understood the affair of the hoard of coins that a storm disclosed on the Suffolk coast near Aldeburgh. From the talk of the longshoremen, who were on the look-out amongst the dunes, it appeared that a great wave came in and washed away a slice of the sand cliff just beneath them. They saw glittering objects as the sea washed back, and retrieved what they could. I viewed the treasure—it was a collection of coins, the earliest of the twelfth century, the latest, pennies, three or four of them, of Edward VII, and a bronze medal of Charles Spurgeon. There are, of course, explanations of the puzzle; but there are difficulties in the way of accepting any one of them. It is very clear, for example, that the hoard was not gathered by a collector of coins; neither the twentieth-century pennies nor the medal of the great Baptist preacher would appeal to a numismatologist.

But perhaps the queerest story to which my newspaper connections introduced me was the affair of the Reverend Secretan Jones, the "Canonbury Clergyman", as the headlines called him.

To begin with, it was a matter of sudden disappearance. I believe people of all sorts disappear by dozens in the course of every year, and nobody hears of them or their vanishings. Perhaps they turn up again, or perhaps they don't; anyhow, they never get so much as a line in the papers, and there is an end of it. Take, for example, that unknown man in the burning car, who cost the amorous commercial traveller his life. In a certain sense, we all heard of him; but he must have disappeared from somewhere in space, and nobody knew that he had gone from his world. So it is often; but now and then there is some circumstance that draws attention to the fact that A. or B. was in his place on Monday and missing from it on Tuesday and Wednesday, and then enquiries are made and usually the lost man is found, alive or dead, and the explanation is often simple enough.

But as to the case of Secretan Jones. This gentleman, a cleric as I have said, but seldom, it appeared, exercising his sacred office, lived retired in a misty, 1830–40 square in the recesses of Canonbury. He was understood to be engaged in some kind of scholarly research, was a well-known figure in the Reading Room of the British Museum, and looked anything between fifty and sixty. It seems probable that if he had been content with that achievement he might have disappeared as often as he pleased, and nobody would have troubled; but one night as he sat late over his books in the stillness of that retired quarter, a motor-lorry passed along a road not far from Tollit Square, breaking the silence with a heavy rumble and causing a tremor of the ground that penetrated into Secretan Jones's study. A teacup and saucer on a side-table trembled slightly, and Secretan Jones's attention was taken from his authorities and note-books.

This was in February or March of 1907, and the motor industry was still in its early stages. If you preferred a horse-bus, there were plenty left in the streets. Motor coaches were non-existent, hansom cabs still jogged and jingled on their cheerful way; and there were very few heavy motor-vans in use. But to Secretan Jones, disturbed by the rattle of his cup and saucer, a vision of the future, highly coloured, was vouchsafed, and he began to write to the papers. He saw the London streets almost as we know them today; streets where a horse-vehicle would be almost a matter to shew one's children for them to remember in their old age; streets in which a great procession of huge omnibuses carrying fifty, seventy, a hundred people was continually passing; streets in which vans and trailers loaded far beyond the capacity of any manageable team of horses would make the ground tremble without ceasing.

The retired scholar, with the happy activity which does sometimes, oddly enough, distinguish the fish out of water, went on and spared nothing. Newton saw the apple fall, and built up a mathematical universe; Jones heard the teacup rattle, and laid the universe of London in ruins. He pointed out that neither the roadways nor the houses beside them were constructed to withstand the weight and vibration of the coming traffic. He crumbled all the shops in Oxford Street and Piccadilly into dust; he cracked the dome of St. Paul's, brought down Westminster Abbey, reduced the Law Courts to a fine powder. What was left was dealt with by fire, flood and pestilence. The prophetic Jones demonstrated that the roads must collapse, involving the various services beneath them. Here, the water-mains and the main drainage would flood the streets; there, huge volumes of gas would escape, and electric wires fuse; the earth would be rent with explosions, and the myriad streets of London would go up in a great flame of fire. Nobody really believed that it would happen, but it made good reading, and Secretan Jones gave interviews, started discussions, and enjoyed himself thoroughly. Thus he became the "Canonbury Clergyman". "Canonbury Clergyman Says That Catastrophe Is Inevitable"; "Doom of London Pronounced by Canonbury Clergyman"; "Canonbury Clergyman's Forecast: London a Carnival of Flood, Fire and Earthquake"—that sort of thing.

And thus Secretan Jones, though his main interests were liturgical, was able to secure a few newspaper paragraphs when he disappeared—rather more than a year after his great campaign in the press, which was not quite forgotten, but not very clearly remembered.

A few paragraphs, I said, and stowed away, most of them, in out-of-the-way corners of the papers. It seemed that Mrs. Sedger, the woman who shared with her husband the business of looking after Secretan Jones, brought in tea on a tray to his study at four o'clock as usual, and came, again as usual, to take it away at five. And, a good deal to her astonishment, the study was empty. She concluded that her master had gone out for a stroll, though he never went out for strolls between tea and dinner. He didn't come back for dinner; and Sedger, inspecting the hall, pointed out that the master's hats and coats and sticks and umbrellas were all on their pegs and in their places. The Sedgers conjectured this, that, and the other, waited a week, and then went to the police, and the story came out and perturbed a few learned friends and correspondents: Prebendary Lincoln, author of *The Roman Canon in the Third Century;* Dr. Brightwell, wise on the Rite of Malabar; and Stokes, the Mozarabic man. The rest of the populace did not take very much interest in the affair, and when, at the end of six weeks, there was a line or two stating that "the Rev. Secretan Jones, whose disappearance at the beginning of last month from his house in Tollit Square, Canonbury, caused some anxiety to his friends, returned yesterday", there was neither enthusiasm nor curiosity. The last line of the paragraph said that the incident was supposed to be the result of a misunderstanding; and nobody even asked what that statement meant.

And there would have been the end of it—if Sedger had not gossiped to the circle in the private bar of The King of Prussia. Some mysterious and unofficial person, in touch with this circle, insinuated himself into the presence of my news editor and told him Sedger's tale.

Mrs. Sedger, a careful woman, had kept all the rooms tidy and well dusted. On the Tuesday afternoon she had opened the study door and saw, to her amazement and delight, her master sitting at his table with a great book open beside him and a pencil in his hand. She exclaimed:

"Oh, sir, I *am* glad to see you back again!"

"Back again?" said the clergyman. "What do you mean? I think I should like some more tea."

"I don't know in the least what it's all about," said the news editor, "but you might go and see Secretan Jones and have a chat with him. There may be a story in it." There was a story in it, but not for my paper, or any other paper.

I got into the house in Tollit Square on some unhandsome pretext connected with Secretan Jones's traffic scare of the year before. He looked at me in a dim, abstracted way at first—the "great book" of his servant's story, and other books, and many black quarto notebooks were about him—but my introduction of the proposed design for a "mammoth carrier" clarified him, and he began to talk eagerly, and as it seemed to me lucidly, of the grave menace of the new mechanical transport.

"But what's the use of talking?" he ended. "I tried to wake people up to the certain dangers ahead. I seemed to succeed for a few weeks; and then they forgot all about it. You would really say that the great majority are like dreamers, like sleepwalkers. Yes, like men walking in a dream, shutting out all the actualities, all the facts of life. They know that they are, in fact, walking on the edge of a precipice; and yet they are able to believe, it seems, that the precipice is a garden path; and they behave as if it were a garden path, as safe as that path you see down there, going to the door at the bottom of my garden."

The study was at the back of the house, and looked on the long garden, heavily overgrown with shrubs run wild, mingling with one another, some of them flowering richly, and altogether and happily obscuring and confounding the rigid grey walls that doubtless separated each garden from its neighbours. Above the tall shrubs, taller elms and planes and ash trees grew unlopped and handsomely neglected; and under this deep concealment of green boughs the path went down to a green door, just visible under a cloud of white roses.

"As safe as that path you see there," Secretan Jones repeated, and, looking at him, I thought his expression changed a little; very slightly, indeed, but to a certain questioning, one might say to a meditative doubt. He suggested to me a man engaged in an argument, who puts his case strongly, decisively; and then hesitates for the fraction of a second as a point occurs to him of which he had never thought before; a point as yet unweighed, unestimated; dimly present, but more as a shadow than a shape.

The newspaper reporter needs the gestures of the serpent as well as its wisdom. I forget how I glided from the safe topic of the traffic peril to the dubious territory which I had been sent to explore. At all events, my contortions were the most graceful that I could devise; but they were altogether vain. Secretan Jones's kind, lean, clean-shaven face took on an expression of distress. He looked at me as one in perplexity; he seemed to search his mind not for the answer that he should give me, but rather for some answer due to himself.

"I am extremely sorry that I cannot give you the information you want," he said, after a considerable pause. "But I really can't go any farther into the matter. In fact, it is quite out of the question to do so. You must tell your editor—or sub-editor; which is it?—that the whole business is due to a misunderstanding, a misconception, which I am not at liberty to explain. But I am really sorry that you have come all this way for nothing."

There was real apology and regret, not only in his words, but in his tones and in his aspect. I could not clutch my hat and get on my way with a short word in the character of a disappointed and somewhat disgusted emissary; so we fell on general talk, and it came out that we both came from the Welsh borderland, and had long ago walked over the same hills and drunk of the same wells. Indeed, I believe we proved cousinship, in the seventh degree or so, and tea came in, and before long Secretan Jones was deep in liturgical problems, of which I knew just enough to play the listener's part. Indeed, when I had told him that the *hwyl*, or chanted eloquence, of the Welsh Methodists was, in fact, the Preface Tone of the Roman Missal, he overflowed with grateful interest, and made a note in one of his books, and said the point was most curious and important. It was a pleasant evening, and we strolled through the french windows into the green-shadowed, blossoming garden, and went on with our talk, till it was time—and high time—for me to go. I had taken up my hat as we left the study, and as we stood by the green door in the wall at the end of the garden, I suggested that I might use it.

"I'm so sorry," said Secretan Jones, looking, I thought, a little worried, "but I am afraid it's jammed, or something of that kind. It has always been an awkward door, and I hardly ever use it."

So we went through the house, and on the doorstep he pressed me to come again, and was so cordial that I agreed to his suggestion of the Saturday sennight. And so at last I got an answer to the question with which my newspaper had originally entrusted me; but an answer by no means for newspaper use. The tale, or the experience, or the impression, or whatever it may be called, was delivered to me by very slow degrees, with hesitations, and in a manner of tentative suggestion that often reminded me of our first talk together. It was as if Jones were again and again questioning himself as to the matter of his utterances, as if he doubted whether they should not rather be treated as dreams, and dismissed as trifles without consequence.

He said once to me: "People do tell their dreams, I know; but isn't it usually felt that they are telling nothing? That's what I am afraid of."

I told him that I thought we might throw a great deal of light on very dark places if more dreams were told.

"But there," I said, "is the difficulty. I doubt whether the dreams that I am thinking of *can* be told. There are dreams that are perfectly lucid from beginning to end, and also perfectly insignificant. There are others which are blurred by a failure of memory, perhaps only on one point: you dream of a dead man as if he were alive. Then there are dreams which are prophetic: there seems, on the whole, no doubt of that. Then you may have sheer clotted nonsense; I once chased Julius Cæsar all over London to get his recipe for curried eggs. But, besides these, there is a certain dream of another order: utter lucidity up to the moment of waking, and then perceived to be beyond the power of words to express. It is neither sense nor nonsense; it has, perhaps, a notation of its own, but . . . well, you can't play Euclid on the violin."

Secretan Jones shook his head. "I am afraid my experiences are rather like that," he said. It was clear, indeed, that he found great difficulty in finding a verbal formula which should convey some hint of his adventures.

But that was later. To start with, things were fairly easy; but, characteristically enough, he began his story before I realised that the story was begun. I had been talking of the queer tricks a man's memory sometimes plays him. I was saying that a few days before, I was suddenly interrupted in some work I was doing. It was necessary that I should clear my desk in a hurry. I shuffled a lot of loose papers together and put them away, and awaited my caller with a fresh writing-pad before me. The man came. I attended to the business with which he was concerned, and went back to my former affair when he had gone. But I could not find the sheaf of papers. I thought I had put them in a drawer. They were not in the drawer; they were not in any drawer, or in the blotting-book, or in any place where one might reasonably expect to find them. They were found next morning by the servant who dusted the room, stuffed hard down into the crevice between the seat and the back of an arm-chair, and carefully hidden under a cushion.

"And," I finished, "I hadn't the faintest recollection of doing it. My mind was blank on the matter."

"Yes," said Secretan Jones, "I suppose we all suffer from that sort of thing at times. About a year ago I had a very odd experience of the same kind. It troubled me a good deal at the time. It was soon after I had taken up that question of the new traffic and its probable—its certain—results. As you may have gathered, I have been absorbed for most of my life in my own special studies, which are remote enough from the activities and interests of the day. It hasn't been at all my way to write to the papers to say there are too many dogs in London, or to denounce street musicians. But I must say that the extraordinary dangers of using our present road system for a traffic for which it was not designed did impress themselves very deeply upon me; and I dare say I allowed myself to be over-interested and over-excited.

"There is a great deal to be said for the Apostolic maxim: 'Study to be quiet and to mind your own business.' I am afraid I got the whole thing on the brain, and neglected my own business, which at that particular time, if I remember, was the investigation of a very curious question—the validity or non-validity of the Consecration Formula of the *Grand Saint Graal: Car chou est li sanc di ma nouviele loy, li miens meismes.* Instead of attending to my proper work, I allowed myself to be drawn into the discussion I had started, and for a week or two I thought of very little else; even when I was looking up authorities at the British Museum, I couldn't get the rumble of the motor-van out of my head. So, you see, I allowed myself to get harried and worried and distracted, and I put down what followed to all the bother and excitement I was going through. The other day, when you had to leave your work in the middle and start on something else, I dare say you felt annoyed and put out, and shoved those papers of yours away without really thinking of what you were doing, and I suppose something of the same kind happened to me. Though it was still queerer, I think."

He paused, and seemed to meditate doubtfully, and then broke out with an apologetic laugh, and: "It really sounds quite crazy!" And then: "I forgot where I lived."

"Loss of memory, in fact, through overwork and nervous excitement?"

"Yes, but not quite in the usual way. I was quite clear about my name and my identity. And I knew my address perfectly well: Thirty-nine, Tollit Square, Canonbury."

"But you said you forgot where you lived."

"I know; but there's the difficulty of expression we were talking about the other day. I am looking for the notation, as you called it. But it was like this: I had been working till the morning in the Reading Room with the motor danger at the back of my mind, and as I left the Museum, feeling a sort of heaviness and confusion, I made up my mind to walk home. I thought the air might freshen me a little. I set out at a good pace. I knew every foot of the way, as I had often done the walk before, and I went ahead mechanically, with my mind wrapt up in a very important matter relating to my proper studies. As a matter of fact, I had found in a most unexpected quarter a statement that threw an entirely new light on the Rite of the Celtic Church, and I felt that I might be on the verge of an important discovery. I was lost in a maze of conjectures, and when I looked up I found myself standing on the pavement by the Angel, Islington, totally unaware of where I was to go next.

"Yes, quite so: I knew the Angel when I saw it, and I knew I lived in Tollit Square; but the relation between the two had entirely vanished from my consciousness. For me, there were no longer any points of the compass; there was no such thing as direction, neither north nor south, nor left nor right, an extraordinary sensation, which I don't feel I have made plain to you at all. I was a good deal disturbed, and felt that I must move somewhere, so I set off—and found myself at King's Cross railway station. Then I did the only thing there was to be done: took a hansom and got home, feeling shaky enough."

I gathered that this was the first incident of significance in a series of odd experiences that befell this learned and amiable clergyman. His memory became thoroughly unreliable, or so he thought at first.

He began to miss important papers from his table in the study. A series of notes, on three sheets lettered A, B, and C, were placed by him on the table under a paperweight one night, just before he went up to bed. They were missing when he went into his study the next morning. He was certain that he had put them in that particular place, under the bulbous glass weight with the pink roses embedded in its depths, but they were not there. Then Mrs. Sedger knocked at the door and entered with the papers in her hand. She said she had found them between the bed and the mattress in the master's bedroom, and thought they might be wanted.

Secretan Jones could not make it out at all. He supposed he must have put the papers where they were found and then forgotten all about it, and he was uneasy, feeling afraid that he was on the brink of a nervous breakdown. Then there were difficulties about his books, as to which he was very precise, every book having its own place. One morning he wanted to consult the *Missale de Arbuthnott,* a big red quarto, which lived at the end of a bottom shelf near the window. It was not there. The unfortunate man went up to his bedroom, and felt the bed all over and looked under his shirts in the chest of drawers, and searched all the room in vain. However, determined to get what he wanted, he went to the Reading Room, verified his reference, and returned to Canonbury: and there was the red quarto in its place. Now here, it seemed certain, there was no room for loss of memory; and Secretan Jones began to suspect his servants of playing tricks with his possessions, and tried to find a reason for their imbecility or villainy— he did not know what to call it. But it would not do at all. Papers and books disappeared and reappeared, or now and then vanished without return. One afternoon, struggling, as he told me, against a growing sense of confusion and bewilderment, he had with considerable difficulty filled two quarto sheets of ruled paper with a number of extracts necessary to the subject he had in hand. When this was done, he felt his bewilderment thickening like a cloud about him: "It was, physically and mentally, as if the objects in the room became indistinct, were presented in a shimmering mist or darkness." He felt afraid, and rose, and went out into the garden. The two sheets of paper he had left on his table were lying on the path by the garden door.

I remember he stopped dead at this point. To tell the truth, I was thinking that all these instances were rather matter for the ear of a mental specialist than for my hearing. There was evidence enough of a bad nervous breakdown, and it seemed to me, of delusions. I wondered whether it was my duty to advise the man to go to the best doctor he knew, and without delay. Then Secretan Jones began again:

"I won't tell you any more of these absurdities. I know they are drivel, pantomime tricks and traps, children's conjuring; contemptible, all of it.

"But it made me afraid. I felt like a man walking in the dark, beset with uncertain sounds and faint echoes of his footsteps that seem to come from a vast depth, till he begins to fear that he is treading by the edge of some awful precipice. There was something unknown about me; and I was holding on hard to what I knew, and wondering whether I should be sustained.

"One afternoon I was in a very miserable and distracted state. I could not attend to my work. I went out into the garden, and walked up and down trying to calm myself. I opened the garden door and looked into the narrow passage which runs at the end of all the gardens on this side of the square. There was nobody there—except three children playing some game or other. They were queer, stunted little creatures, and I turned back into the garden and walked into the study. I had just sat down, and had turned to my work hoping to find relief in it, when Mrs. Sedger, my servant, came into the room and cried out, in an excited sort of way, that she was glad to see me back again.

"I made up some story. I don't know whether she believes it. I suppose she thinks I have been mixed up in something disreputable."

"And what had happened?"

"I haven't the remotest notion."

We sat looking at each other for some time.

"I suppose what happened was just this," I said at last. "Your nervous system had been in a very bad way for some time. It broke down utterly; you lost your memory, your sense of identity—everything. You may have spent the six weeks in addressing envelopes in the City Road."

He turned to one of the books on the table and opened it. Between the leaves there were the dimmed red and white petals of some flower that looked like an anemone.

"I picked this flower," he said, "as I was walking down the path that afternoon. It was the first of its kind to be in bloom—very early. It was still in my hand when I walked back into this room, six weeks later, as everybody declares. But it was quite fresh."

There was nothing to be said. I kept silent for five minutes, I suppose, before I asked him whether his mind was an utter blank as to the six weeks during which no known person had set eyes on him; whether he had no sort of recollection, however vague.

"At first, nothing at all. I could not believe that more than a few seconds came between my opening the garden door and shutting it. Then in a day or two there was a vague impression that I had been somewhere where everything was absolutely right. I can't say more than that. No fairyland joys, or bowers of bliss, or anything of that kind; no sense of anything strange or unaccustomed. But there was no care there at all. *Est enim magnum chaos.*"

But that means "For there is a great void", or "a great gulf".

We never spoke of the matter again. Two months later he told me that his nerves had been troubling him, and that he was going to spend a month or six weeks at a farm near Llanthony, in the Black Mountains, a few miles from his old home. In three weeks I got a letter, addressed in Secretan Jones's hand. Inside was a slip of paper on which he had written the words:

Est enim magnum chaos.

The day on which the letter was posted he had gone out in wild autumn weather, late one afternoon, and had never come back. No trace of him has ever been found.

The Green Round

PROLOGUE

Is there to be no end of this spoiling of all the beauties of our lovely country?" wrote Brown of Clapham or Smith of Wimbledon—the name is of no consequence—to a London paper at the beginning of the summer of 1929. And having asked his rhetorical question, Smith or Brown proceeded to give his instance.

"For some years past," he wrote, "I have been accustomed to take my family for the annual holiday to the picturesque little watering-place of Porth, in the west of Wales. The place has always commended itself to me, not only for the beauty of the rocky coast, the excellent sands with their facilities for safe bathing, and the capital golf course, but also for the quiet, so valuable for those whose nerves have been set on edge by the inevitable racket and hurry of modern life. Within ten minutes' stroll of the centre of the town, it was always possible to secure perfect peace on the dunes, where I have been accustomed to spend many hours, greatly to the benefit of my health.

"Last week, I was unexpectedly called to Porth on a matter of business. Judge of my disgust when, on the first day of my visit, finding myself at leisure for a couple of hours, I took my usual stroll on the dunes, and found myself in the midst of a scene far noisier than Piccadilly Circus or Charing Cross. A hideous building, of staring red brick and grotesque design, has been erected in the midst of what was once a grassy amphitheatre, sweet with the growth of the wild thyme. On a balcony, a jazz band was emitting ear-splitting cacophonies, and dancing was in full swing. Coconut shies, swings, roundabouts, and shooting galleries were all in evidence and seemed fully patronised. The more popular entertainments were surrounded by a surging mass of people; the noise was deafening. The whole effect was that of a country fair on a Saturday night. I walked back. to my hotel at once, horrified at the growth of a crude commercialism which has vulgarised and destroyed the peace and beauty of what was once one of the most charming spots in the island."

Thus Smith of Wimbledon—I think we will let him have the credit of the deed—and thus began the famous Beauty Spot correspondence and controversy.

For, of course, Smith was not allowed to have it all his own way. A good many people agreed with him and confirmed his complaint. One man wrote from "a typical old English town in the midlands". The Town Hall, he said, a beautiful specimen of sixteenth-century half-timber architecture, had stood in the middle of the town, and gave character to the place. "With the object, I suppose, of enabling motorists to dash through the town at an even greater speed than that to which they have been accustomed, this beautiful building has been destroyed. Moreover, the Watch House, a fine example of Queen Anne brickwork, has been pulled down, and its place taken by the new Town Hall, a square monstrosity in white concrete, adorned (?) with grotesque sculptures in the manner of Easter Island."

Then there was the sad story of Dix Regis, famous formerly for its thatched cottages and its brook running down the middle of the winding village way: now much more famous for its motor factory, and its blocks of workers' dwellings; "all of them strictly functional in design", as a lover of the new order of things protested, There was Morrow End, with its ancient avenue of walnut-trees; these had been cut down, every one of them, because the residents, as a whole, considered that they made the houses damp. An F.S.A. was in a very bad temper about the doings at Polters Ambo, on the Yorkshire coast. This was a little place that had been a maze of old red brick courts and alleys and backways with narrow, steep flights of steps leading from one winding street to another, and an interesting chapel of St. Michael, in very fair preservation, built in the thirteenth century on a jagged rock in the middle of the harbour. Ambo was strangely transmuted. Few of the old courts and alleys survived. Their place had been taken by rows of lodging houses in glazed brick and tasty tiles, by big hotels in concrete and lots of glass. There were lifts from the harbour to the High Town. It had been found necessary to destroy St. Michael's Chapel, and to blast away the upper part of the rock, the lower portion of which helped to support the pier and its cheerful pavilion. The F.S.A., as I have remarked, wrote very crossly about these Ambo doings; and the like complaints came from all over the country about other doings of the same kind: the making of deep, ferny, oak-shadowed lanes into ditches like railway cuttings, setting up aerodromes in ancient solitudes, and erecting "prehistoric beastliness"—as the enemy called it—as sculptured memorials on quiet village greens.

"I have to pass this horrible group," wrote a country parson, "every time I enter the church. I sometimes think I must be in Nbanga—Nbanga Land, not in Sussex."

And, of course, there was the other side—plenty of it. Mrs. Partington was quoted a great deal. The merits of modern architecture were explained, very patiently; with dissertations on the suitability of steel and glass for structural work. It was pointed out, again and again, that we were not living in the sixteenth century, but in the twentieth; and that the traffic of the present could not move on the bridle-paths and water-tracks of the past. The F.S.A., who had shewn temper over the alterations at Ambo, was convicted of selfishness. "An insanitary and tortuous village," wrote the Mayor, "has been converted into a happy, cheerful resort, where thousands of poor workers wash away the smoke of the mills in the health-giving, ozone-laden breezes of the north sea. The pier, of which 'F.S.A.' makes such bitter complaint, brings the weary toilers into close quarters with the sea; and the round of entertainments given in the Pavilion, most of them of very high quality, offer an alternative to the dubious pleasures of the public-house. It was, no doubt, unfortunate that the old chapel had to be destroyed; but many feel that the Pier and Pavilion correspond more closely with the ideas and requirements of the present time." Another correspondent addressed himself briefly to the question at large. "We have become a poor nation," he said. "Poor people cannot afford luxuries. Crooked roads and ruined chapels are, no doubt, luxuries to some of us; but we must learn to do without them." An artist, with a curiously exotic name, declared that the brick-sculpture, "The Birth of the Calf", executed in yellow bricks, which adorned the village green at Little Pedlington, marked an epoch. Somebody wrote to say that he didn't like it at all; but the artist simply replied, "O God! O Montreal!" and was considered to have scored heavily.

It was a highly entertaining correspondence, and went on for weeks. So far as I remember, very little notice was taken of an indignant letter from the Town Clerk of Porth, the Welsh watering-place where all the row began. It was, I say, an indignant letter, with signs of suppressed spluttering about it, but, considering the provocation, laudably restrained.

"I am at a loss to understand the letter of your correspondent, Mr. Smith of Wimbledon.

"He informs your readers that an unsightly and blatant building has been erected on the dunes—I presume he refers to the Burrows—near Porth.

"He adds that a band played jazz music, that dancing was in progress, that coconut shies, roundabouts, swings and shooting galleries had attracted throngs of people, and that the noise was deafening. In short, he gives your readers to understand that the amenities of Porth have been completely ruined.

"My reply to this, is that there is not one word of truth in your correspondent's allegations. No such building as he describes has been erected on the Burrows. No band plays or has played there or anywhere in the neighbourhood. The ground is quite unsuited for dancing, and, in fact, no dancing has taken place in the position indicated. No booths, coconut shies, shooting galleries, swings, or roundabouts would be permitted on the Burrows; and there was nothing of the kind there on the date indicated. The majority of the visitors to Porth betake themselves to the sands, the finest in Europe, and avail themselves of the bathing facilities provided by the Municipality. The natural golf course (eighteen holes), second to none in the island, attracts many, while others are glad to visit the beautiful scenery, coastal and inland, and the ancient castles for which the county is famous. For these, an admirable service of luxurious motor coaches is provided.

"In no case, and under no circumstances, will surging masses of people be found on the Burrows, where those who desire quiet and solitude will always be able to gratify their wishes.

"It is true that the Annual Fair, held under a charter of Henry III, took, place on June 1st and 2nd, as usual. But the fair is held in a field, near the railway station, at the other side of the town; the site it has occupied since 1860. Before that date the booths, roundabouts, etc., were set up in the High Street, opposite the church.

"I can only conclude that' your correspondent, under the influence of some slight temporary confusion, mistook his right hand for his left, and thus took the wrong turning; afterwards forgetting the direction in which his steps had led him.

"At the same time I find it difficult to understand how your correspondent contrived to confuse the level expanse of the station meadow with the miniature Switzerland of the Burrows."

Very little notice was taken of the Town Clerk's letter, since the controversy had sailed off from particular instances to general principles. Smith might have been mistaken; but, anyhow, that sort of thing was being done all over the country; and was it an infamous scandal, or was it a sign that England was waking up and seeing straight? It made a luxurious and luxuriant quarrel.

At the end, everybody was pleased, even the indignant Town Clerk, for visitors were arriving at Porth in large numbers, and the season promised prosperously. Everybody was pleased—excepting Smith of Wimbledon. The poor man had devoted a week-end to another visit to the town. He had popped out of the train, tired as he was from the long journey, and had made straight for the dunes, as he still called them. There they were, silent in the golden peace of a summer evening; undisturbed, solitary, blest, The feet of Smith pressed on the short, sweet turf, and trod down the fragrant circles of the wild thyme, passed among the burnet roses, passed by pink centaury and tiny eyebright. The sun was sinking, and no breeze stirred, and Smith, standing on one of the highest of the Burrows, saw the sea as a luminous blue jewel. Beneath him, the sandhills about it, was the green round, where, he could have sworn, and could still swear, he had seen the red brick building, the centre of horrible noise and vulgar gaiety. Indignant in his set conviction, he descended from his height and went exploring in and out among the hills and valleys, expecting every moment to light upon the horror he had witnessed a week or ten days before. There was nothing of the kind to be found; he was forced to admit it. He returned to the town and dined in a state of sullen amazement and then went out and about, and was sly and crafty; asking guileless questions of the policeman, and the barmaids of the Rose and the Red Dragon, and chance passengers on the pavement. "Could you tell me the way . . . ?" "Does the Dance Hall on the dunes, the Burrows, stay open . . . ?" "I suppose the new Dance Hall down on the Burrows is a great success?"—all that sort of clever, detective talk. But without result: people said they didn't know what he was driving at. Smith spent the next day in his traffics and enquiries. He went over the dunes and round the dunes in rings, perplexing the few quiet people who were enjoying the solitude by appearing and reappearing over their lairs. Further enquiries in the town and about it were fruitless. Some people in the lounge of his hotel were discussing the matter, and he listened eagerly with his face turned away from them. He heard, firstly, that you couldn't believe a word you saw in the papers, and secondly, to his rage, that he, Smith, of Wimbledon, must have been drunk. He came to the conclusion, he was forced to it, that he had been mistaken.

And yet, at breakfast, the next morning, as he mingled his perplexity with coffee and bacon and eggs, he heard a fragment of conversation from two men, pausing for a moment by the open door of the coffee-room. ". . . infernal row; about two o'clock in the morning."

" You don't say so!"

"Noise like a brass band in full blast woke me up, I tell you. I looked out of my window, and there was some damned *tamasha* going on on the Burrows: all lit up . . ."

The hotel door opened and shut with a crash. Two well-set-up men passed the window by Smith's table. He would have liked to follow and question; but they looked too trim, tweedy, and self-contained for that.

In a cloud of bewilderment he took train from Porth. He never returned; for the summer holiday of the Smiths from that year onwards was spent at some place on the Wash, where it is so bracing.

CHAPTER I

1.

It was at the end of a dreary spring day when Mr. Lawrence Hillyer came to the uneasy conclusion that something was amiss, and that it was time to pull himself together. It was in May, and summer-time had come in, and the sun should still be shining brightly. But all the day long it had been grey and dismal, with hardly a gleam of sunlight; only now and again a watery light above, and a pallor on grey walls; and the wind blew in gusts, coldish, as if it had been March instead of May. In the middle of the road, in front of Hillyer's rooms, where Layburn Street branched to right and left and became Layburn Square, there was a triangular enclosure of dingy grass and soot-infected beds, where flower-growing had been abandoned many years before, in the seventies perhaps, when the last carriage company abandoned the region. Here, the spotted laurel bushes were at their dreariest, and the blotched boughs of the plane-trees had hardly broken into their sickly yellow buds. The only hope in this horrid patch came from an elder-bush, doubtless a stray chance-comer, which had put on a lively festal green, a witness in the grey heart of London that there was a world of country outside; just as the vine on a neighbouring wall of Pentonville and the great fig-tree that had filled a dank area in the Gray's Inn Road, testified to sunny hills in France and Syrian gardens.

All the weary day with its gloomy heaven and ill wind had been neither good nor bad to Hillyer. He had been deep in books and papers at his old Japanese bureau, and thought no more of the weather than he thought of the golden figures engaged in unintelligible employments in the decorated scheme of the bureau. He had worked all the morning, and had gone out to lunch at an obscure tavern called "The Quill", which lurked in a tortuous passage near at hand, and had returned to his papers and to a long reverie, which was only broken by his landlady bringing up tea. The tea was over, the tray on the sideboard, and the pipe was lit. Hillyer strolled to the window and contemplated the misery and desolation of the scene. It did not move him to despair or to any other emotion, since he did not live in it, but in a secret science of his own making. The thoughtless and inconsiderate have been heard to say that they are hanged if they care if it snows pink. No one credits them; we all know that they would run howling to shelter if such an unlikely phenomenon were manifested; but Hillyer could have taken this oath with truth, if it had occurred to him to take it; which it never did. There are advantages in living for the most part outside the visible world; though there are, doubtless, items on the other side of the account. And Hillyer, turning from the ashen light of

the window, was not so utterly rapt from the phenomenal as not to
perceive that the fire was low and near to going out. He bent down to
take the shovel and put on more coal, and as he did so a sharp neural-
gic pain zigzagged through his head. There was nothing alarming about
it; most of us know these occasional momentary pangs that flicker un-
accountably over our nerves; and Hillyer, pondering the matter afterwards, decided that he had not been a bit frightened. It was what came
next that alarmed him. It was as he dug the shovel into the coal-scuttle,
as the black cat asleep on the hearth-rug rose up and hunched its back,
as he threw three or four lumps of coal on the fire, that he found himself murmuring: "Black cat . . . coal-scuttle . . . shovel . . . putting coals
on the fire . . . that was exactly what happened . . . when the Cardinal
. . . when I missed that great chance . . ."

He put the shovel back in its place, and straightened himself. He
looked about him, with a dumb, bewildered enquiry. What was he saying, what was he thinking, what was happening? What were these incoherences? What was the connection between this accustomed and
very ordinary action of putting coal on the fire, while a cat sat on the
hearth-rug, and the acute sense of a great chance neglected, of a supreme opportunity in life allowed to slip away, unembraced, unused? If
he had . . . uttered some word, performed some action . . . he knew not
what or which . . . the whole course of his days would have been
changed to a vague golden felicity . . . but . . . was it an incoherent
dream recollected? Had he read of something of the kind?

He slid into the saddle-bag arm-chair with the doubtful spring, and
took up the pipe he had laid on the small table beside him, and sat
there, the pipe dangling from his hand, in that state which the Scots
call a dwam, in which the mind questions its own authority and its own
process, and is ready to deny the evidence that the senses have laid before it. Seeing is no longer believing; not in any subtle, philosophical
significance of the words, but in their obvious, everyday meaning; the
universe collapses, and returns for a while into its first condition: it is
without form and void, and darkness is on the face of the deep. Or if
this be all too fine a way of putting it, let us say that there is no sense
any more; only nonsense remains. And, perhaps, only those who have
endured this experience know that is very awful.

Hillyer sat in his chair trembling a little. The horrid gibberish of cat, coal and cardinal became less vivid and threatening in his mind. He knocked the ash out of his pipe, and began slowly to refill it, and tried to collect himself. The suggested image is near enough to the facts of the case. Hillyer, sitting in his room on that dreary evening in the May of '29, might well be compared to a jigsaw puzzle that has been broken up and scattered abroad. The intelligible whole had been shattered; the parts that made it up, severally meaningless nonsense, were here, there, and every-where in amorphous confusion. He tried to gather them together to col-lect them, and for some time with poor enough success. Life seemed to have become all misty, uncertain; his own identity was blurred in his mind. There were things to be done, he knew, but he could not say for the moment exactly what they were; he saw neither the days behind with their finished work nor the tasks and interests of the days that were to come; he was pretty much, mentally, in the condition of a man in a thick London fog, whose own doorstep has been transmuted into a monstrous unfamiliarity, before whom open gulfs and caverns of smoking terror—where the streets and shops had been in the morning. It is a horrid state; summed up for common use in the familiar phrase, "suffering from loss of memory", lest the true description, loss of *ego*, loss of true being, should confuse and alarm. Hillyer certainly wondered what he was doing in his own sitting-room, and wondered, further, where he would get if he went out and turned to right or left. He confessed to himself that he didn't know. A heavy bewilderment clouded his mind all the rest of the evening. He read a little without making much of what he read; he looked through a notebook and grasped the points and questions that he had set down very dimly, as if he were poking into another man's work, and trying to appreciate interests that were foreign to him. He took something hot last thing, but slept ill enough in spite of his dose.

2.

The trouble was, very likely, due to over-absorption in a singular en-quiry, immensely aggravated by isolation. Scholars, men of research, high-priests of science are usually gregarious, both in body and mind. Very often, as Sidney Dobell said of poets, they grow in clumps, like primroses; they have their centres in the college, the university, the learned society, and medical school. If these people of the mind are merely men of letters, they are apt to meet one another in clubs and drawing-rooms; and for one reason or another they generally keep in touch with the main currents of life. Hillyer had gone another way; he had fallen out of the march, and had lost sight of his fellow-travellers. He was fifty-five and for thirty years he had been growing more and more a solitary. His relations in the country were all dead. His early friends—they were not many—had set to work, married, gone to China and California. Hillyer had a small income, and not entering any business, made no new friends or connections, and, perhaps, he lacked the sociable habit of mind, as he certainly lacked the equally valuable habit of being interested, if but mildly, in matters which interested the mass of his fellow-creatures. Now and then, in his early days in London, he found himself in company—and invariably wondered what he did there. When people meet, there is always something of a simple game at ball, and most of us who miss one ball make a fair catch of another. Now, when a lady asked Hillyer what he thought of Polenska's new dance, he didn't know what he thought, for he had never seen it. Very well; but he was just as bad when a man asked him what he thought of Chamberlain now. And, then, in literary society, the talk of "rates per thou", and "£500 down on account of royalties" failed to move him: he didn't care; and we know that "Don't Care" was eaten by lions. It is possible that these lions had begun to snuff the track of Hillyer on that cold May evening. At all events, it is clear that he had not the social gift which is the capacity for being interested, or simulating interest—it doesn't matter which—in all the small change that passes in company. And, it could not be said that, even if he had possessed the necessary confidence, he was in a position to make conversation out of his own topics. He was in the beginning of his researches, treading doubtfully in a dubious region, wondering as to whether he were on the right way, wondering sometimes whether there were a way at all. As to his secret science, he was much in the position of Ashmole as to other secret sciences: he knew enough to hold his tongue, but not enough to speak. He had made an entry in one of his first notebooks.

"I am moved to wonder, whether what we call 'fairy-tales' do not, in fact, contain a strange wisdom and the secrets of a very strange, and mysterious psychology. Take the old tale of the fairy gold and its transmutation into ugly rubbish, as an example. To most of us it is a tale and nothing more than a tale; without any reason, without any meaning, without any sort of sense or significance in it. We accept it just as a piece of picturesque fancy and nothing more; the turning of the magic gold into dry leaves was just a happy notion of the unknown and remote individual who made up the story. But suppose that there is something more than this; rather, something quite different from this? Is it possible that there is, now and then, a more hidden and interior sense in some of the tales of the fairylands and the fairies? I am inclined to think that this may be so; that the stories are—occasionally, not always by any means—the veils of certain rare interior experiences of mankind; dangerous experiences, perhaps. The gold faded into dead leaves; it may be more than a pretty story.

"And the way to find the Fairy Queen—*in occlusum Regina palatium?*"

Now that sort of thing may be sense or nonsense; but it is, clearly, not the current coinage of general conversation. Anyhow, there is no need to enquire into the value of Hillyer's researches; but being absorbed in them, and sometimes visited by gleams of a light in which he hardly dared believe, it is not much wonder that he gradually drew apart from the crowd, and became a hermit, a solitary, in the midst of myriads. At first he had rooms in Little Russell Street, quiet and handy for the Museum Reading Room; but he felt rather than saw that Bloomsbury had changed and was changing every day, that dimness was departing from it, that it began to glitter and to shine and to be manifested. He withdrew himself. He had the habit of aimless walking, finding out by instinct quiet places fit for his strange meditations, and had thus discovered the unknown region that lies beyond the Gray's Inn Road: a world where only the unknown live, which never gets into the papers, which is never traversed by steps familiar with Piccadilly and Kensington. He found out rooms on the height of Layburn Street facing the dank enclosure of spotted laurels and blotched plane-trees. Nothing has been altered in this quarter for eighty or ninety years; Hillyer felt himself at ease in it, and lapsed into deeper, stranger dreams.

3.

They were roughly broken by the unpleasant experience that came upon him so suddenly. This was the intrusion of a very different order from that to which he was accustomed. There was something physically wrong; and he went the next day to Dr. Flanagan, whose brass plate he had often observed in Layburn Square. The doctor, a cheerful man, listened to the symptoms and shook his head.

"Indeed, all that's not much in my way," he said, very frankly. "It's your nerves that are all wrong, and we don't have much to do with nerves in this part of the world. I'll send you to a specialist, but first I'll just give you a sedative that'll make you feel more comfortable."

Whereupon, the amazed Hillyer was taken into a sitting-room, furnished in the seventies of the last century, and given Irish whiskey hot, with sugar, at eleven o'clock in the morning; the doctor joining him. The specialist was interested, and a little alarming. He spoke of the dangers of continued solitude. "I had chambers in Gray's Inn when I was a young man, and there were men there that had got into the habit of living alone: they mostly ended with suicide. Just as it is in Dickens; he knew the Inns. A wonderful observer, Dickens, whatever the young people may say.

"Well, you've been living a great deal too much alone, and I gather you don't get about much, and don't go in for any outside interests or amusements, and the result is that you're getting jumpy. If you aren't careful you'll begin to see things, and that won't do at all. You want change—change of air, change of scene, change of habit, change of everything. So the sooner you get out of town, the better."

The doctor advised sea air, preferably in the west, Hillyer remembered going with his parents to Porth when he was a small boy; and so he stood in the golden sunlight over the sea in the calm evenings, and it may well be that he and Mr. Smith passed each other in the streets of Porth.

4.

At the end of a week Hillyer felt distinctly the better for the change. He sat on the sands, and listened to the chatter of the children of their fathers, mothers, sisters, brothers and nurses. He heard the tones of Manchester and Birmingham, of the London suburb with its curious compound vowels, listening with rapt attention to the manner in which the simple "me" was enriched to "mah-eh-ee" in a wonderful fashion. And as a relief, came the chant of the native speech, a rich melody, a relic of the age when all speech was song. He would stroll up and down, making his way between sand-castles with their flooded moats, children dancing in rings as they came out of the sea, and earnest men talking of cotton; getting as much noise and chatter into his ears as he could, feeling that to be the best remedy for the deep silence in which he had lived so long. In the hotel smoking-room in the evening he did his best to break himself into the habit of speech, and to amend the errors of his youth. He tried his utmost to answer the question that he had refused in his earlier years: "What do you think of Chamberlain now?" It was a different Chamberlain, but Hillyer read—with pain it must be confessed—all the leading articles every morning directly after breakfast, and was able to say a few words in the evening on the subject of derating to Mr. Sykes, a pleasant man from the north; though he felt strongly inclined to quote Mr. Cleaver, in *Our Mutual Friend*: "'Deration, oh, don't." There were all sorts of topics, he found, which he could acquire by a careful study of the paper; and he got them up as well as he could, though he found it almost impossible at his age to acquire the complicated technique of the racing news. But as he advanced in his studies he began to be seriously interested, and found that even here there were minor mysteries that entertained him. For example, he was sitting one evening with Mr. and Mrs. Sykes in the hotel lounge over coffee and cigarettes. After some cogitation he thought of a brilliant opening and asked Mrs. Sykes about her jewelled pipes.

"What on earth are you talking about?" said Mrs. Sykes, in a state of amazement; and Hillyer explained, abashed a little, that he had read only that morning in the woman's page of a popular paper, that fashionable women were all smoking briar pipes heavily jewelled, and that rubies and emeralds were the most popular combination. The lady laughed and told him that nobody paid any attention to that nonsense—"except very young typists, perhaps, and they may try to believe in it". Then there was another party, with a very pretty dark daughter in it. He asked her why she hadn't painted her caste-mark on her forehead; and was horrified at the storm of fury which burst from her father, General Clinton, who had served for many years in India. Yet Hillyer had seen a paragraph to the effect that with smart women the caste-mark on the forehead had become a craze. He apologised humbly to the lady and her father; but putting two and two together, he came to the most interesting conclusion that a great part of the daily paper dealt with a world of pure fiction, reporting its news with all the gravity of one who deals with the plain and common facts of life. Women did not smoke jewelled briars, they did not paint Hindoo caste-marks on their brows, they did not clothe their legs and feet with gold-leaf in place of stockings. The reason of these strange inventions puzzled Hillyer profoundly; they seemed to him shapes in a magic lantern show; and, passing to the "Personal" column, he carried his new scepticism so far as to doubt the very existence of Captain "Sam" Hurlingham and Lady "Billy" Donkin, who were always being seen lunching together at the Grandeur. If he had ever thought of the mysteries as things hidden away and apart, remote from the general stream of life, he saw now that he was mistaken. The mysteries were part of the very tissue and being of man; they were not to be avoided. The quest for that which was concealed by the golden and jewelled world of the *Arabian Nights* was conducted in the columns of the daily press: behind Persian lattice-work, in a tiled court, deep azure, where the music of falling water rang from the fountain, he saw the appearance of the dark lady with the jewelled pipe, the caste-mark on her forehead, her feet gleaming golden on the rose-marble floor.

Hillyer shook his head; these images were leading him back to old and too familiar ground: he had come to Porth to escape from dreams, not to cherish them. He directed his attention to the League of Nations, to Unemployment, to the Indian troubles, to the Labour Policy, to the Problems of Canada and Australia. He borrowed solid novels from the Library, and read them with infinite satisfaction and benefit, since they seemed to him more free than the daily record of the press from the elements which he recognised as dangerous—during the period of his cure, at all events. They shut out wonder from their picture of existence; they gave him the rest that would be afforded by an old, terraced, brick-walled garden to a man who has been in peril in a land of rocks and desert places. So the treatment went on prosperously; and Hillyer never failed to attend the performances of the excellent town orchestra—not the jazz band of Smith's fevered imagination—which played twice daily. He was not a learned lover of good music, but he recognised the enormous benefit of listening to it. For the one sure effect of all music good or bad is to destroy thought for the time being. It is comparatively easy to think in mere noise: a man will soon accustom himself to the jar and jangle of trams, the rattle of passing trains, the song that the sirens sing down by the docks, the hubbub of a busy street, the loud brisk squabbles of the slum round the corner. He can look for the fifth figure in Logic in the midst of all this, invent an original plot for a detective story, or plan a poem and write it. But when music—sound in order and rhythm—is heard, thought is forthwith extinguished. The quality of the music has nothing to do with this effect of it, which will be produced as surely by a Bach fugue as by the silliest song of the Halls or the cabarets. Hillyer found the two hours spent daily in listening to the Porth orchestra a most valuable part of his course; since it was a two hours abstinence from thinking, of immersion in an element which negatived thought.

5.

For some weeks Hillyer, remembering the doctor's warnings against the solitary habit, kept well in touch with company. If the weather were wet, he frequented the lounge of his hotel, first reading the papers and then discussing the news with any acquaintance who seemed ready for conversation. If it were fine, there was a little garden across the road reserved for the hotel guests and pleasantly provided with deck-chairs. Here, sitting in comfort, well in the world of the living, he smoked and played the game at Lords', or trembled at the situation in the Balkans, and gazed out on the glittering waters of the bay, and the coast curving round to the Dragon's Head in the east. Every day, he felt better, renewed in body and spirit; and he became confident; he began to go farther afield, to walk along the cliffs one day, to lose himself in deep inland lanes on another. And then he discovered the attraction of the dunes, of their sand mountains, of their valleys of flowery turf and of wild thyme in purple circles of bloom. The desire of this region grew upon him, and by degrees he spent more and more of his time in wandering in and out among the hills of sand, in taking his place in the green round that Mr. Smith had once frequented. There was a ledge of turf on one side of this place that made an easy seat. There was solitude without desolation; every now and again explorers like himself would pass by, delay a little and look about them, botanise, and go onwards in search of an appetite for lunch or dinner.

Hillyer began to be conscious that the Labour Policy, the situation in Australia, and the economics of the Balkans, had served their turn; he was glad to be silent, and yet to see that his fellows were at hand. There was a charm about this hollow, with its glimpse of blue sea and a misty coast far away, seen through a cleft in the sandhills, that won him more and more; and hour after hour, he would delay here, morning and evening. He felt that his health was quite restored, that his nerves were in splendid order; but he could not make up his mind to leave these happy shores for the grey lodgings on the grim hillside in desert London. It was an obscure set of circumstances, that at last made up his mind for him, and sent him hurrying back to town in a very pitiable state of terror and bewilderment. In a way, it all began with the story of a missing woman, though this business and its ending were rather of the accidents not of the essence of Hillyer's trouble.

The case was thus. A few miles from Porth, going eastward, the coast rises slowly from the sea into high sloping land covered with heather. Here and there on these heights clearings have been made, and two or three white farmhouses face the sea and the cliffs on which Porth stands. Hillyer, sitting in the little hotel garden, had often rejoiced in the sight of the white walls, shining in the sun, amidst their few fields of corn and meadows of rough pasture, islands with the heathery steeps all about them and dividing them from one another. To him, looking across the sea, the farms seemed close enough together; but, in fact, each was separated from its nearest neighbour by at least a mile of steep ascent and descent, through rough land, difficult walking, and the best way little better than a sheep track. In one of these lonely farms, with the odd name of Ty Captain (which means Captain's House), there was living a man named Prothero with his wife and two children, a boy and girl of eight and eleven. Mrs. Prothero was a handsome, red-cheeked, black-haired woman of thirty or a little over. Early one Saturday morning, about a fortnight before Hillyer's visit, Mrs. Prothero set out for market at Porth, her basket, with a couple of fowls and some eggs, on her arm.

She took her usual way, which was the only way; the rough track through the heather that trailed across the hillside, then down on the other side by a farm road, and so to the main road and St. Fagan's station, about ten miles from Porth, and between two and three miles from Ty Captain farm. Her husband saw her climbing up the path as he stood by the garden gate, and then he went to his work in the fields, and thought no more of her till the evening. The time passed by and she did not return; Prothero and the children waited by the gate till it grew dark, and she did not come. The man told the frightened children some story about their mother staying with her friend, Mrs. Evans at Porth, and got them hot milk and sent them off to bed. He put the lamp in the window and kept watch all night. Two or three times he took his lantern and went out on the track that his wife had taken; looking to left and right into the black darkness; stopping, calling her name, and then going on a little, and calling again. The only thing that he could think was that she had slipped and fallen and broken a leg, and was now lying helpless in the heather. There was no answer to his shouts, his lantern shewed him nothing but the wild growth; and he went back to the farm hoping that, somehow or other, he might find her there. As soon as it was light he took the two children and set out for St. Fagan's. He knocked up the people at the first house he passed, told them his story and left the children in their care. Then, at St. Fagan's, he woke the station-master—there were no trains till the afternoon on Sundays—and heard that Mrs. Prothero had not been seen at the station the day before; the station-master had thought she must be ill, since she took the 8.40 for Porth every Saturday. Prothero got a lift in a car and went to the police at Porth. The usual thing followed; search-parties, official and unofficial, the "missing" broadcast, the summons of Scotland Yard, vain clues that led nowhere, idle theories that led to the combing of Camden Town, and a sharp look-out at Northampton. A month after Mrs. Prothero's disappearance her body, shamefully torn and mutilated, was found hidden in a dense thicket of blackthorn about a hundred yards from the farm-track that went to the main road and the station. The poor woman's murderer was never discovered; he had left no trace behind him, save his horrible violence; there was no thread for the police to hold or follow. The case of Mrs. Prothero simply went down on the tolerably long list of undiscovered murders; there was nothing to be done or said.

Nothing, indeed, to be said in reason; but horrors make many people hysterical and therefore highly unreasonable; and the people at Porth, both the natives and the visitors, talked an incredible amount of nonsense about the murder. And their nonsense affected Hillyer in a very strange manner. Though, if we begin to talk of strangeness . . .

Hillyer was not what is called, I believe, a noticing man. He had roused himself so far that he was ready to take part in the casual conversation of the hotel lounge or the sands; he no longer hid himself away from his fellow-men. But he stood on no watch-tower, and kept no sharp look-out; he was not curious in minute shades of manner, nor ready to deduce this or that from the raising of an eyebrow or the compression of a lip. He was not acutely interested in any of the agreeable chance acquaintances he had made; and so for some time he failed to perceive that anything was amiss. And then, after four or five days, during which a sharper, or perhaps, a more deeply interested man, would have scented some thing a little queer in the social air, Hillyer did begin to be aware of a difference. People were distinctly less genial where he was concerned. The hitherto friendly groups on the sands answered his greetings drily. If he attempted to discuss the architecture of sand castles with the builders, there was apt to be a cry from a deck-chair: "Peter, Betty! come here for a minute; I want you." He found that his approach was apt to break up the small after-dinner circles of the lounge; Mrs. Sykes would remind Mr. Sykes that they had arranged to stroll to the Black Rock before it got dark; and General Clinton, though he had seemed to forgive the caste-mark business, glared and said nothing. Once or twice, perceiving that a brisk and eager conversation became an awkward silence on his approach, he guessed that he had been the subject of the talk; and wondered, but not very much. If he supposed anything, he supposed that these people, having given him a fair trial, found him dull company, and were happier among themselves with their own interests. He had no objection to this, no defence to make: very likely they were right. It was only when Bradshaw, the analytical chemist from Birmingham, addressed him one day as he was coming back to lunch after a morning spent in the green round of the Burrows, that he began to wonder seriously, and to ask himself what was amiss. Bradshaw was waiting for him at the top of the flight of steps leading from the sands and the Burrows to the Front, or Esplanade. He looked very oddly at Hillyer, though Hillyer noted nothing of this.

"I saw you on the Burrows, just now," he remarked.

"Yes," replied Hillyer cheerfully, "I spend a lot of time there. I like it."

"But what have you done with your friend? Why don't you bring him along to the Dragon?"

Hillyer stared at Bradshaw.

"Friend," said he, ". . . friend? I beg your pardon . . . friend . . . done with my friend? I am very sorry, but I don't know what you're talking about."

"You don't? Very good," and Bradshaw walked away without more words, leaving Hillyer confused and a little troubled. He sat down for a few minutes on one of the seats on the front, and wondered what Bradshaw was driving at with this talk of "your friend". He could make nothing of it, and went on to his lunch at the Red Dragon. He entered the coffee-room and took his usual place at a small table by one of the windows; and was perplexed anew as he noticed that his entrance made a distinct sensation and by no means an agreeable one. Bradshaw was talking eagerly to some friends at the other side of the room. They leaned across the table, evidently so that they might miss nothing, and one of them looked towards Hillyer with a glance of great abhorrence. And afterwards he saw a shade of much the same kind on many faces, as he went through the lounge into the street. He met it again, two or three hours later. He was sitting on the ledge of turf in his favourite hollow in the Burrows, still feeling a little upset, and vastly puzzled, by what had happened in the morning, when glancing up, he saw a man named Davies, another acquaintance of the hotel, standing on the sandy height opposite, and staring towards him with an extraordinary intentness. There was violent dislike and amazement too, and something of fear in the man's expression. Hillyer gaped at him blankly for a few moments, and then called out, to break the scene: "Why don't you come down here? Very pleasant in the shade."

Davies opened his mouth to speak, and then turned and hurried away towards the town, looking backward once, with dread in his gaze, with an awful surmise written on his countenance. That night the people in the hotel threw away ceremony and form, and cut Hillyer to his face. The next morning, Poggi, the manager, beckoned him into the office, and expressed his regret that No. 23 was booked in advance from that date onward, and wished he had not forgotten to mention the fact on Hillyer's arrival.

"There is something the matter," said Hillyer. "Of course, I shall make no trouble about going. But, in strict: confidence, tell me what it is all about. I shall be very much obliged, if you will."

Poggi raised his broad and benignant shoulders, and began to do wonderful things with the fingers of his left hand.

"Not a word, no? Good. I think they are mad; but they say you are a friend of that murderer of the woman Prothero; that you are hiding him, and that very likely you will hang also. I know they are mad; but—" and the fingers and the hand executed an amazing fantasia in the air.

6.

Hillyer packed his bag, paid his bill, and left the hotel ten minutes later. He saw the half-dozen people who were about eyeing him curiously and furiously, and he took his way at a brisk pace towards the station; the morning train for Paddington was due in twenty minutes. He walked on to the platform—the station was an open one—bought a paper at the bookstall, and paced up and down in sight of everyone.

Passengers for London thickened about him; huge piles of luggage were piled up at intervals on the platform; then when the train came in, country people who were going to the market poured out of the carriages, obstructing the entrance of those who were Paddington bound, and burned for corner places facing the engine. In the midst of all this confusion, Hillyer stole out of the station by a side path, and fetching a compass, made his way to a second-rate street at the back of the town, and secured two small rooms without difficulty. He thought it most unlikely that the people in this obscure street would know his face or be familiar with the rumours of the Red Dragon on the front; and he wanted to lie latent for a day or two, that he might study his problem in peace, and see if he could discover any materials for its solution. For three days he lay snug and hidden; perplexed and pondering, and quite unable to pitch on any explanation that was at all tolerable to his common-sense. He had a bad half-hour soon after he was established in his retreat, for, looking at certain strange and terrifying pictures confronting him, in which moonlight was indicated by an inlay of mother-of-pearl, it suddenly struck him that he must be suffering from delusions, that the change of air and scene had failed to effect a cure of his nervous trouble, and that all the alarms of the last few days were figments of his disordered brain. But he cast this from him. At times, every man is infallible, and, in spite of philosophic doubts, is able to say "I know." You cannot, for instance, persuade a country farmer who has been going to market every Saturday for thirty or forty years that he is uncertain as to market day: on that point at least he is ready with fast assurance to defy all the schools of the sceptics. He knows. So Hillyer knew that he had been confronted with facts, not fancies; and with this moderate satisfaction he was left to find out what these facts signified. Looking back he made his calculation: first of all, as he saw now more clearly than he had done at the time, the friendly people of the hotel had begun to edge off from his company, to make excuses for retreat when he appeared, to become deaf when he spoke of lawn tennis, or the Labour policy, or the Balkans. Then, there had been that Birmingham chemist, who asked him what he had done with his friend; why he didn't bring his friend to the Dragon. He could find no explanation of these extraordinary questions. There was something offensive, almost threatening about the man's manner; for this he could find no explanation. And then, as he sat alone in the peaceful circle of the green amphitheatre, Davies appearing on the sandy summit staring at him aghast, in horror, and making off in frightened haste; here again he came dead against a blank wall. And as for the manager of the hotel, and his talk of hiding the Ty Captain murderer, what on earth could that mean? So far as Hillyer could see, it implied, first of all that the police had made up their minds as to the identity of the murderer, that they were unable to lay hands on the suspect, and that, somehow or other—he could not conceive how—these transitory birds, these visitors, his fellow-guests at the hotel, knew the supposed miscreant, and had seen him in Hillyer's company. All of which was a string of nonsense, and absolutely intolerable.

It would still have been intolerable; but the burden would have been lightened a little, if Hillyer's newspaper studies had been more thorough and more prolonged. He would have been familiar with certain processes of the public mind when confronted with a murder mystery; his recollections would have furnished him with many enlightening instances and examples. An old woman is murdered in her sweet shop: Mrs. Bunkin, which clear starches, is sure to come forward and describe a man with a black moustache, in a blue serge suit, who was loafing about the street between eleven and twelve. The supposed villain turns out to be a builder in a small way, who had an appointment with a bookmaker; but Mrs. Bunkin is convinced to the end that he was the very murderer. She felt, at the time, she says, that he was up to no good, and that is considered conclusive evidence. That is the way it is done, and if Hillyer had been acquainted with the method he might have guessed at the manner in which one of the minor links in his puzzle was forged. There had been muttered confabulations in snug corners of the Dragon: "one of the most horrible-looking fellows I've ever seen", "made my blood run cold", "something quite ghastly about him", "my notion of a murderer", "a dwarf, you said?" "Yes, but those deformed creatures are often tremendously strong: looked as if murder would be child's play to him"—and so forth and so forth; and after two or three such conferences, the unknown was firmly established as the Ty Captain murderer. Still, if Hillyer had divined all this it would not have helped him much as to the major problem. He had not been in company with anyone during his stay at Porth, excepting these hotel people, who had become rabid; and so . . . It was impossible to finish the sentence.

On the fourth day, Hillyer emerged from his retreat. Meditation had done nothing to elucidate the dark riddle that perplexed him; he would try action, if going abroad and shewing himself could be called action. He walked up and down the town, strolled about the sands, and sat on the front gazing blandly out to sea. He met two or three of his former associates of the Dragon. They stared at him amazed, threatening, furious; stopped dead, as if stricken suddenly, glared helpless astonishment. Hillyer was as if he saw them not, passed and repassed, and betook himself, after his usual routine, to the green round in the Burrows. He repeated these proceedings after lunch, taking some pains as to his goings and comings, so that possible sleuths, watchers and trackers of the company of the Red Dragon might be thrown off the scent. The next day he followed the same procedure; and in the late afternoon, whether wind fell, he thought, as he sat on his seat in the green round that he could distinguish stealthy rustlings in the coarse grass that grew about the encircling dunes; and once or twice, keeping a sharp look-out, he noted appearances that were neither grass nor sand. He guessed that prone watchers, half buried in sand, were observing him all the while. "And the devil knows why," he said to himself.

The next morning the crisis came. He had been sitting for an hour or more in the usual place, and the sunlight and blue sky, and the faint breeze from the east was so enchanting that he had almost forgotten the maniacs that beset his ways. It was fortunate that his stay at Porth had really and effectively restored the apparatus of his nerves. There was a sudden shrill excruciating whistle: from every tussock in the circle of the dunes a man shot up, raging, and then flung himself headlong down the slope. In an instant Hillyer, stupid with surprise, found himself in the midst of a circle of men, shouting, foaming, cursing, yelling incoherences. Two of them had poured down at his back and held him tightly, one on each arm; and then, as suddenly as it rose, the tumult died away, and stupefaction and silence fell upon this strange assembly. They glared at Hillyer, they glared at one another. There were about a dozen of them. Some of them Hillyer recognised as his former acquaintances of the Red Dragon. Davies and Bradshaw held him by the arms. There was General Clinton, open-eyed, open-mouthed, staring at him; there was the face of Sykes, as of one confounded; a man named Sullivan held a heavy cane above his head, as if it were a broad-sword in a stage combat. Others he had seen on the sands; some faces were altogether strange to him; and all of them, in furious action and furious utterance a moment before, now stood silent, motionless, frozen in sheer amazement; as their faces declared.

The General at last found speech:

"Hold him tight," he said to Hillyer's guards, "or he'll get away like the other. Take him a few yards off, you fellows; there's some infernal hanky-panky here. There must be a trap-door hidden in the turf, and we've got to find it."

One man had a stick with a long iron ferule. Under the General's direction, he poked and prodded the bank of turf where Hillyer had been sitting, and the turf all around. The stick went in easily; there was hardly more than an inch of soil over a depth of sand. Others climbed the banks and looked round and about, in the hopes of seeing a creeping or a flying figure. The General marched up and down, stamping at intervals; he would be able to detect a hollow beneath. There was a thick growth of brambles in one spot; it was all beaten down to the sand in no time. The poking, prodding, beating, stamping went on for twenty minutes.

"Stop!" the General called out. "They're too many for us. I never saw the Rope Trick. I never believed in it. I always thought it was a damned lie. This is worse. Let that fellow go; we can't do anything to him."

And then, after a pause:

"But, by God! I saw that infernal, murdering scoundrel with my own eyes."

He turned and walked away towards the town, and the others followed him in dead silence.

Hillyer was left standing; he also said nothing. He had no notion of threatening an action for assault and violent constraint; it did not occur to him to demand a humble apology from General Clinton, from Davies, from Bradshaw, from the whole pack of them. Utter stupor overwhelmed him and pressed down his tongue like the great ox of the Greek proverb. The actions and the words of these raging people gave him some inkling of his supposed offences; in a way his problem was answered; but the answer was worse than the enigma; in itself an enigma and a chaos.

"And I haven't the remotest notion what has happened," that was all he could find to say to himself, as he in his turn walked away from this scene of a wild experience. But he decided that any benefit that Porth could give him was exhausted; and he left the town by the earliest possible train, glad to think of the refuge waiting him on the remoter side of the Gray's Inn Road.

He settled down peacefully to his old routine and scheme of daily life. In spite of the unpleasantness which had spoilt the end of his visit, he was glad he had made it, since it happened his eyes to the significance of the daily paper, a source of information he had hitherto scandalously neglected, He recalled now, with a free mind, those mysterious news items concerning jewelled pipes, Hindu caste-marks, gilded feet. Immediately on his return he gave an order to the local news agent to send him two popular papers every day; and he was overjoyed to read at once in one of them the remarkable intelligence that the "lastest fad of the Seaside Girl" was to enamel her toe-nails in brilliant colours. The other paper reported that one of the smartest women in society had been seen wearing a fez at lunch. All this struck Hillyer as most important. The idea evidently was, as he had seen from the first, to suggest the gorgeous symbolism of the *Arabian Nights;* that great vision of a world which all men desire, to which few attain. Here, indeed, were "fairy-tales" of profound significance.

CHAPTER II

1.

Hillyer did not intend to lapse into his former state of dark absorption in his studies, meditations and researches. The odd seizure that had befallen him, and the grave warning of the nerve specialist, had not failed of their effect; he made up his mind to go warily and take care of his paths for the future. He would give the evening and perhaps a goodly portion of the night to his work; in the morning he would stir about and move with men, and survey the infinite world of London: in itself, he reflected, the study of a lifetime. No longer a self-sentenced prisoner in the narrow compass of his lodgings, he began to discover what strange regions might be reached by the wise expenditure of a few pence on an omnibus ride. Nay, to turn a corner, or to take a way hitherto neglected, might unlock the doors of a new region; and he was reminded of one of the old tales that were the subject of his constant meditations—the story of the man who, passing along some street that he has trodden a hundred times, sees a door before unnoticed, and opening it enters a world of marvel and strange experience, that has been unsuspected but close at hand all his days. On one of these voyages through the ocean of myriad-streeted London, he came one day upon a little square or oasis of greenery in the very heart of a grey and dismal quarter. The racket of King's Cross was not far off, trams jangled near at hand, and a cloud of depression hung like a mist on the surrounding streets. But Belmore Square had lived on from another age. It was composed of little two-storied houses, on whose walls the vine and the fig-tree mingled and brought Syria to the heart of London; and each little house had its little garden, with palings of faded green, and flowers fit for cottage gardens by a country lane. In the green centre, the town supremacy of the plane was disputed by the mystic ash, by wych elm, by birch and hornbeam, and in their shade were a few seats, on which a few old people sat when the sun shone. Hillyer came round a corner that he had never turned before, and saw the green and the quiet of the place and delighted in it. He made a perambulation, wondered who were so fortunate as to enjoy this humble peace and pleasantness, and sat down to smoke beneath green boughs for half an hour or more, then passed on his way. He had been gone five minutes when two old men who had been sitting on a bench at the upper end of the enclosure began to discourse:

"That was a queer-looking customer," said old Tom Bryce.

"Who was that then?" asked old Sam Simmons.

"Why, him down over on the seat opposite, that's just gone."

"The one in grey clothes? I didn't see anything very queer about him. Quiet-looking man; might be a schoolmaster, I should say."

"I don't mean him. I mean the little chap sitting by him."

"I never saw anyone sitting by him."

"Of course you did; how could you help seeing of him?"

"Well, I didn't see him."

"Do you mean to tell me, you sitting there next to me, at my elbow, as you might say, you say you didn't see that short chap, sitting on that bench, over there, not so much as forty foot off from where us two are sitting now? Don't talk such nonsense, Sam Simmons."

"Don't you talk nonsense then. There was that quiet grave sort of gentleman, like a schoolmaster, or you might say a man who might have retired from something; might have been a clerk who'd come into a bit of money from what I could see; very nice grey suit of clothes he was wearing. There he was sitting and he put on his pipe, and he looked pleased with himself. And he's the only man I see, or you either, if it comes to that."

Mr. Bryce stared at his old friend in angry amazement. He called down a meaningless curse upon himself, and continued his argument:

"Now, are you sure we mean the same seat? I mean that bench, over there, opposite, under that tree with spiky leaves. And there's white chalk-marks on the top of the back of the bench on the left hand. Do you see what I tell you?"

"Yes, I do; as plain as I see you. I've got eyes in my head. I can see that bench all right. What about it?"

"I'll tell you. There was two men sitting on that bench not ten minutes ago."

"I say there was one man, and no more than one."

"There was two, I tell you. There was that quiet-looking man in the grey suit you've been gassing about; and there was another small man sitting a foot off him, or thereabouts. A foot, you might say, or it might be a foot and a half. But not two foot."

"So there was another man, was there? And what sort of a man might he be, as you saw him so plain?"

"Well, that's the funny thing," said Brice, soothed by what he considered old Sam's admission. He pondered.

"It is a funny thing," he went on, after consideration of the case, "I saw him, as I tell you, as plain as I see you now. But if you ask me what he was like . . ."

"Of course I ask you. You saw him plain, didn't you?"

"I did see him plain. No doubt about it. But there's some people . . . well, you know them all right when you see them, and yet it's hard to say how you know them, if you take my meaning. Now, there's Harry Jackson. You know Harry Jackson in the Caledonian Road? Next door to Puller's coffee-house?"

"Never mind about him. I know him. I want to hear about this other chap that you say you see sitting over there just opposite."

"Well, that's a difficult proposal. It isn't so easy as it sounds, not by a long way. You know the Private Bar at the Belmore; but I dare say you might find it not so easy to hit it off so that another man would recognise it as soon as he went in."

"If you saw this man at all, you can tell what you saw. That's what I say."

Old Mr. Bryce was profoundly disturbed. He wagged his short white beard from side to side. He tried to speak, but gibbered meaningless syllables. At last, "I did see him, I'll take my oath, and there was something wrong about him, and I'm blest if I can tell you any more than that."

Sam Simmons looked at his old friend with some apprehension in his glance.

"Come along," he said. "Them children will be swarming out of school in a minute and I don't want to listen to their noise. What about a pint at the Belmore? There's chop toad at Puller's. Saw it up in the window as I went by this morning."

They went off together. Old Bryce's face was working, and he looked nervously away as they passed the bench with the chalk-marks on its back.

2.

Twenty-nine, Layburn Street, Hillyer's abode, was a very quiet house. In the basement, the landlady, Mrs. Jolly, and her daughter, a young woman of twenty or a little more or a little less, dwelt in a gentle gloom; on the ground floor there was a middle-aged clerk, who got up early in the morning and made off for somewhere in the far east, down by the docks. Hillyer had the first floor, and the two rooms above held two young men who followed skilled crafts in Soho workshops. One was supposed to be a bookbinder, the other a worker in gold and silver; but this was more conjecture and doubtful rumour than ascertained fact. There was no bond that held the inhabitants of the house together; they were all quiet, keeping little company and never banging doors. The two craftsmen strolled in and out of each other's rooms sometimes of an evening; and Hillyer and the clerk just knew each other by sight, after the passage of a good many years. Once upon a time, more than twenty years before, there had been a reveller on the ground floor, who had gathered his young friends about him once or twice, and had endeavoured to revive the tradition of the late-sitting, jovial party with an occasional chorus. But he was given to understand that doings forbidden in the green tree of Mrs. Raddle were anathema in the dry day of Mrs. Jolly. He slunk away: to look for Bob Sawyer and Ben Allen possibly in another world; and since his exit peace had reigned profound on every landing.

That peace was broken, and with it the heavy moonless silence of a summer night, not long after Hillyer's return from his seaside visit. It was on the stroke of two in the morning, as afterwards appeared, that a tremendous crash rent the air. The day had been faint with burning heavy heat, and the little breeze that had sprung up at sunset had died away. Leaden clouds covered the sky and shut in the hot breath of the innumerable streets. A man strolling up Layburn Street, seeking perhaps for fresh air on the eminences of Sadlers Wells and Islington, stopped a moment, lit a match and watched the flame burn without quavering. Even in that region where old fashions linger, where forgotten prints hang on the walls, where lustres are common enough, and at least one example of the right Victorian wax-flowers school has been observed; even there windows had been thrown open and suffered to stay open, in spite of the general belief in the mysterious venoms of the air of night.

The roar of London has long ceased to exist. It was dead silence, or all but dead silence. A late car or taxi in the Gray's Inn Road, a late footfall on a distant pavement made no more sound than a stirring of leaves before a feeble momentary breath of wind, or the patter of a few scarce drops of rain on a laurel bush. And then, a tremendous splintering crash tore the stillness into tatters; and on it fell the two broken thunders of Big Ben.

After this, there was a pause of a few seconds. Thereupon, the confused noise of people jumping out of bed, pattering over the floor, stumbling and fumbling on their way to the gas, upsetting chairs and small tables: *fragor et strepitus*. The clerk on the ground floor woke up with a sonorous shout, as though he occupied his business in deep waters, instead of in a warehouse near the Docks. One of the young men on the top floor opened his door and made a Slavonic noise. Mrs. Jolly left her daughter trembling in bed, came up in set silence, stood at Hillyer's door, and called on him for goodness' sake to say what he was doing.

And at that moment, he appeared; confounded by sleep and the shock of his awakening. He stared about him, inarticulate. His fellow-lodgers came up the stairs, came down the stairs and in their odd costumes gathered and gaped: a group for the last act of a farcical comedy.

"What was that noise?" gasped Hillyer at last. "Is it the gas? Is anybody hurt?"

"It was in your room," said Mr. Pytle, the clerk from downstairs. "I thought the house was coming down on me. Front room," he added, as Hillyer gaped at the bedroom he had just left. Hillyer threw open the door of his sitting-room, and they all trooped in.

"Take care of the glass," shouted the man who had cried out words of Slavonic sound, going with a cautious step towards the gas. They checked, and as the two jets flamed, stared at the ruin about them.

Above the mantelpiece there had stood a vast mirror with a heavily decorated gold frame, in the most ornate manner of the 'sixties. Mrs. Jolly and her friends thought it very handsome, costly, and in these degenerate days, rare. This horrible thing had, somehow, escaped from its cords, and had fallen forward on the table, and had shattered itself into two or three hundred pieces, that now glittered insanely on the floor. Mrs. Jolly lamented the ruin of the mirror, which had come from her Aunt Bessy, of Nuneaton; the rest of the party gaped and jabbered for a while, till one of the young craftsmen climbed from a chair to the white marble mantelpiece, and examined the cord, which had given in two places.

"Perfectly sound, it is," he said, testing what remained unbroken. "Looks as if it had been regular torn apart. Funny."

"Don't try to set things right to-night," said Hillyer, to the afflicted Mrs. Jolly, "and, whatever you do, don't go down on your knees; you'll cut yourself to pieces. Bring up a broom or something in the morning. And you needn't bother about my breakfast; I'll go out and get something."

They all agreed that there was nothing to be done till the next day, and crept back to their beds, yawning. Hillyer thought no more of the matter, save to be somewhat glad that the vulgar and pretentious state of the huge mirror was no more. He made an excellent breakfast at a station hotel the next morning, and came back to find his room in neat order, "Bolton Abbey in the Olden Time" hanging in the place of the monstrous glass, and his landlady mournful but calm. She was slightly uneasy as to the supposed bad luck indicated or caused by a broken mirror; but comforted herself by saying that there were many who didn't believe in that sort of thing now.

A few days later he was tempted into making a morning excursion of a farther range than usual. The wind had changed to the north and had blown away the heavy oppression that had hung over London. The freshness and sweetness of the country floated about the grey walls of Layburn Street, and the sunlight danced and glittered on a poplar that rose, a huge billow of green, from a wilderness of grim yards at the back of the house. Hillyer sallied forth, and with favouring 'buses found himself on Wimbledon Common, in a radiant, rejoicing air. He was strolling slowly along, by a road lined with houses of a rich and prosperous aspect, conjectured rather than seen through groves and shrubberies, when his steps were arrested for a moment by the sudden noise of smashing glass. He walked on again without curiosity; but a rapid patter of feet, a shout of "Stop!" came behind him, and a rough hand grasped his shoulder and twisted him round. He was in strong keeping. The person of well-to-do appearance who had captured him was thickset and muscular, with features resembling those of the late Professor Huxley: benevolent in repose, no doubt, but at the moment erupting indignation.

"Did you do that?" he ejaculated.

"Do what?" said doubting Hillyer.

"Smash my greenhouse. You might have killed me!"

"I say!" exclaimed Hillyer. "Do I look as if I would smash your greenhouse or anybody else's? Besides, I haven't seen a greenhouse this morning; I haven't been off this path for the last ten minutes. What do you mean by talking like this?"

The angry man glared at Hillyer for a moment; then snatched his hands, right and left, and inspected the open palms.

"I beg your pardon. I see I've made a mistake. I apologise. But would you mind coming with me for a moment? I should like to shew you what's happened."

Hillyer turned back, and Mr. Horncastle, as he introduced himself, led the way by a postern gate into his demesne. A winding path through deodars, wellingtonias, box, cypress and yew led them to the gravelled space on one side of the large suburban mansion, and Mr. Horncastle pointed eloquently. There was a big greenhouse, as ugly as its tribe or a trifle uglier, and the bulge of its pretentious dome shewed a large and jagged hole. And on the floor inside, with broken flower-pots, scattered mould, and sad blossoms about it, was a huge lump of coal.

Hillyer understood the fierce examination of his hands.

"And where the devil could that have come from?" asked Mr. Horncastle, as the two returned to the open.

Hillyer pointed out that it was too far a cast from the roadway, unless one posited the presence of a Celtic Champion at hurling things through the air; a soured man, of a malicious and mischievous habit of mind. This seemed most unlikely.

"It must have been someone hiding in those laurels, at the edge of your plantation. He popped out, threw the lump of coal, and went back into hiding. He may be there now."

"It's possible. Suppose we have a hunt for him."

"I'm afraid he waited for you to rush out, and made off as soon as he saw us both safe in the greenhouse. But we might try."

They went to and fro amongst the evergreens, and beat about, and peered and poked and pried into the recesses of the dose-growing box and cypress. The result was nothing. It seemed quite possible that the offender had indeed watched the outward rush of Mr. Horncastle, his return with Hillyer and the entrance of the two into the greenhouse, and had then taken flight. There was whiskey and soda in the billiard-room after the futile search. Mr. Horncastle said he had dismissed an under-gardener six months before. It seemed possible that he might have taken his revenge. Mr. Horncastle said he would have a talk to the local detective, apologised once more, and saw Hillyer off the premises. And Hillyer went on his way, entertained on the whole with the small adventure. He had lived so long in obscure retirement that little things diverted him, as the movement of a dull street seems gaiety to the man who has spent years in prison. He found himself speculating as to what manner of rich occupation in the City nurtured Mr. Horncastle, as to the possible guilt of the dismissed under-gardener, as to the result of the conference with the police. Johnson was inclined to wonder at the disuse of smoking at the latter end of the eighteenth century, since, as he pointed out, it was a relief from mere vacuity. But there are many substitutes for tobacco.

3.

The skies were of a calm and even grey, the air was still and a little mournful, as with a prophecy of the autumn to come; and Hillyer made his way back from one of his visits to the Reading Room of the British Museum—now become rarer than in former years—and climbed the steps to the house in Layburn Street. He was in a satisfied and happy mood; for his two or three hours of research had gone prosperously and he had by sheer lucky chance found an unexpected treasure in turning over the pages of the catalogue. His main object in visiting Great Russell Street, once dim and rich in its suggestion, now grown red and rancid, was to investigate the relation between the legends of the Seven Sleepers class and those that tell of mortals who have dwelt for a while with the Queen of the Fairies; to query the identity of the Fairy Queen with Tannhauser's Venus, to determine the exact shade of guilt imputed to personages like Thomas of Ercildoune and the British King in the Mapp Story. And then, another point: what was the relation, if any, between these fables and the singular Story of the Entertainment of the Venerable Head in the Mabinogion? Did they all symbolise the same experience? Or, were there two experiences, one supernal, and the other, if not infernal, as in Tannhauser, then at least, dubious, suspect, perilous? All the legends in their essence, no doubt, were pre-Christian: might one take it that those in which the implied experience was held up to reprobation were the stories which had come under the review of the Church; while the Mabinogion mythos (for example) had, for one reason or another, escaped ecclesiastical censure, coming down to us in its original form with its original feeling? Very interesting questions, these, Hillyer thought; and he reviewed them thoughtfully, verified his impressions of the sources, noted down this and that point.

"Query," he wrote, "whether the Church's condemnation, as implied in some of the legends, may not arise from confounding the nature of the sign with the things signified: the Fairy Queen and Venus being taken as sexual symbols, and therefore condemned. Yet this objection should lie equally against the imagery of the Song of Songs. Here the symbolism is undoubtedly and definitely sexual, but the book had not been excluded from the Canon on that account, nor had the nature of the sign been permitted to obscure or tarnish the thing signified. Moderns, of course, have questioned the existence of any symbolism whatever, and are content to hold the book as a passionate love song and nothing more. This position is negligible, as not only opposed to the tradition and doctrine of the whole of Christendom, but to the entire consensus of the East on this matter. The Song of Solomon is written in a symbolical language which would be understood by Easterns of every faith and of all ages.

"All this seems fairly plain and straightforward; but there are perplexed and difficult questions in the background. Putting the Song with its authorised and orthodox interpretation on one side, it is to be enquired whether it be lawful to regain or to attempt to regain the *Earthly* Paradise; to pass, as it were, under the guard of the flaming swords; to recover a state which is represented as definitely ended, so far as bodily existence is concerned. In the Mabinogion story, it may be noted, there is a marked analogy with the Eden story of Genesis. The eating of a certain forbidden fruit in this case, and the opening of a certain forbidden door in that break the enchantment for ever. Adam and Eve know that the gates of Paradise are finally closed against them; the companions of Bendigeid Vran, when the door that looked towards Cornwall and Aber Henvelen was thrown open, saw that all their felicity was accomplished and ended, 'And when they had looked, they were as conscious of all the evils they had ever sustained, and of all the friends and companions they had lost, and of all the misery that had befallen them, as if all had happened in that very spot.' The 'Entertaining of the Noble Head' was finished.

"There was no hope or possibility of renewing it: never would they hear again the three fairy birds of Rhiannon 'singing unto them a certain song'.

"Of course it may he said that the Fairy Queen tales are to be taken in the same sense, and as referring to the same mysterious loss as the Genesis story and the Welsh story; they may all be understood to refer to the *Parens Protoplastus,* to Adam, the archetypal or Platonic man, not to any actual man; though in this or that legend an individual and actual man, such as Thomas of Ercildoune, is made to achieve the adventure of fairyland. This is a point worth noting: it may or may not be valid."

He had made his notes and practically finished the work of the afternoon, when, as he glanced through one of the volumes of the catalogue, he came upon a title which, somehow, attracted him. The author was the Reverend Thomas Hampole, and the book was called *A London Walk: Meditations in the Streets of the Metropolis.* It bore the date 1853. Hillyer could scarcely say what it was that drew him in this sententious title, with its hint of moralising: perhaps his own recent walks abroad made him desire to compare his experiences with those of a fellow-traveller of long ago. At all events, he made out his form, and got the book, a thinnish octavo, bound in faded brown cloth stamped with blind tools of weak invention. There was a frontispiece entitled, "The Old Wells, Canonbury", a steel engraving by J. Rospickx, after the well-known painting by R. Landon: not a great performance, and yet hinting that curious sense of enchantment that is often lacking in the cleverer work of to-day. In the distance, a glimpse of a classic façade; umbrageous trees drooped over smooth lawns in the middle distance; and in the foreground fashionable ladies and gentlemen, dressed in the habit of the Regency, gathered about a glassy waterpool, admiring a marble nymph who rose from its depths. Glancing at this odd performance, Hillyer turned to the book, found himself addressed as "Courteous Reader", but persevered.

"Has it ever been your fortune, courteous reader," the author enquired, "to rise in the earliest dawning of a summer day, ere yet the radiant beams of the sun have done more than touch with light the domes and spires of the great city? Have you risen from your couch, weary, perchance, of sleepless hours of tossing to and fro, or, it may be, impelled by the call of business, and gone forth through the familiar street where your abode is situated, the street which had known your steps by day and by night, but never before at the hour of dawn? If this has been your lot, have you not observed that magic powers have apparently been at work? The accustomed scene has lost its familiar appearance. The houses which you have passed daily, it may be for many years, as you have issued forth on your avocations or your amusements, now seem as if you beheld them for the first time. They have suffered a mysterious change, into something rich and strange. Though they may have been designed by no extraordinary exertion of the art of architecture, though their materials may be of common brick and stone and plaster, though neither Pentelicus nor Ferrara has assisted in the adornment of these edifices; yet you have been ready to affirm that they now 'stand in glory, shine like stars, apparelled in a light serene'. They have become magical habitations, supernal dwellings; more desirable to the eye than the fabled pleasure dome of the Eastern potentate, or the bejewelled hall built by the Genie for Aladdin in the Arabian Tale."

And so forth, and so forth:

"And if the boughs of a tree chance to extend over a garden wall, you are ready to vow that its roots must flourish in the soil of Paradise." "Your perspective may be closed by the heights of Hampstead or of Highgate; but in the light of the Aurora these hills rise in the land that is very far off."

A good deal in this vein; and then a curious passage:

"But all these are transitory effects that soon disappear. As the sun mounts in the sky, the vision fades *into the light of common day;* buildings, trees, objects close at hand and distant vistas resume their ordinary aspect; the whole enchanting scene is now *a sullen street of common clay.* You may, perhaps, reproach yourself with having allowed your senses to be beguiled and your imagination to be overcome by the mere fact that you have gazed on a familiar scene in unusual circumstances. Yet, some have declared that it lies within our own choice to gaze continually upon a world of like beauty, or even greater. It is said by these that all the experiments of the alchemists of the Dark Ages, generally supposed to be 'dreams at the dawn of philosophy', the feeble gropings of an ignorant and superstitious time after the truths of philosophical knowledge, are, in fact, related not to the transmutation of metals, but to the transmutation of the entire Universe. The avowed aim of these *alchemical philosophers* was not always regarded with favour by those high in Church and State; but it is said, I do not know whether on good or bad authority, that their concealed principles and projects would have caused them to incur still greater odium, and indeed, have made them liable to persecution of the most rigorous kind. This seem probable enough, when we are reminded by the history of the famous Friar Bacon that those in authority during the period of the Middle Age had but little tolerance for unlicensed usual theories and experiments."

Hillyer skipped over a few pages. He felt that this discovery of his, this oddest of odd books, deserved a day's clear study; it was not to be taken as a mere epilogue to the afternoon's work. But before he returned the brown volume to the desk, his eye was arrested by a passage printed in italics:

"This method, or art, or science, or whatever we choose to call it (supposing that it really exists) is simply concerned to restore the delights of the primal Paradise; to enable men, if they will, to inhabit a world of joy and of splendour. I have no authority either to affirm or to deny that there is such an experiment, and that

some have made it. I therefore abandon the matter to the consideration and the enquiry of men of equal and ingenious mind."

Hillyer felt, as he shut the door of his room, that his afternoon had been exceptionally fruitful. He resolved to make a careful study of *A London Walk;* and to find out all that he could as to the author, this obscure Thomas Hampole, who dated his brief preface, Hillyer had observed, from Clifford's Inn. The apparatus of his tea, with the spirit-lamp, was set ready for him on the table, and this done, and the dusky tobacco well lighted, he settled down for the evening to enter up the notes he had made at the Reading Room, materials for the curious book that might be written—some day.

And while he was in the midst of these calm pursuits, all hell broke loose above him. With a terrific crash some heavy piece of furniture thundered to the floor, and a shower of plaster covered Hillyer, his table, and the carpet with white dust. One would have said that, in the room above, Badminton, fast Badminton, was being played with chairs for shuttlecocks; and a minor game was going on with the vases on the mantelpiece. Hillyer ran from his room and summoned the landlady from her depths.

"God help us!" she cried. "Mr. Zerny must have gone mad, and who's to pay?"

Indeed, the noise came from Mr. Zerny's room—he put a good many more letters into his name, but his English friends did not trouble about them—as was speedily evident, when Mrs. Jolly and Hillyer entered without ceremony. For the room was wreck and disaster. A great wardrobe cupboard had fallen on the floor. The two chairs were smashed out of shape. The china was in fragments. It was all a horrible spectacle of ruin. And when Mr. Zerny saw it he screamed. But the mischief was clearly not due to any madness of his, since he had been working overtime, and did not get home from his shop till an hour later. His neighbour, Haddock, was out of town, having been sent away on some job in the country. Doubt, anger and distraction fell upon the whole house. And that question that Mrs. Jolly had asked herself and the world, "Who's to pay?" bore upon her more heavily than the riddle of the Sphinx. "On the top of my beautiful glass smashed to bits the other night in Mr. Hillyer's room," as she said to her friends and neighbours, "what is one to make of it? Indeed, you may ask, and echo answers you, as they say: what is anybody to make of it? And who's to pay? Five pounds wouldn't buy me another glass like the one I've had broken to bits, and there's the chairs only good for firewood, and all that china just fit for the dustman to take away in his cart."

"But how did it happen? And who done it? That's what I should want to know if I was in your place, Mrs. Jolly. I should indeed."

"That's what I said to my husband last night," broke in another lady. "I said to him: 'Albert,' I said, 'there's something behind all this,' I said, 'that we don't know of. First of all,' I said, 'there's that beautiful glass that was over the mantelpiece in the front-room of Mrs. Jolly's first floor. You don't tell me,' I said, 'that that lovely mirror was broke natural. Mrs. Jolly gave me them cords to hold in me hand,' as you did, Mrs. Jolly, 'and anybody could see,' I said, 'that it wasn't no accident. Them cords was strong, like new, and they must have been torn and done on purpose, and it was a strong hand and arm that done it. And what I say is,' I said, "oo done it? That's what I should want to know,' I said to my husband. And now that top room; as if wild men had been fighting in it!"

And a third counsellor:

"I can't say as to that glass. I never saw it, and I never saw the cord that held it. Funny things do happen with cord; we know that. But chairs don't throw themselves about. That's certain. Then, who threw them? It's what I call a mystery. This is a mystery, I said to myself last night when I heard about it, if ever there was one. We know somebody upset that wardrobe, and threw those two chairs about and broke that china. Who was it? Was it somebody in the house or did they come in from the street? It must have been one or the other, it seems to me."

Mrs. Jolly explained the position:

"It was just on seven o'clock when it all happened," she began. "Mr. Pytle had been back for half an hour, or it might be a little over. I was frying a chop for his supper, and it was all ready and waiting in the oven, and Annie here"—indicating her daughter—"had just run round to the Quill in New Street for a pint of mild and bitter for Mr. Pytle's supper, and I was waiting by the window to see her come back, and dish up and take up his tray for him. And the minute I see her come down the steps, I put the plate on the tray and Annie come in with the jug, and then there came that awful bang and crash, and Mr. Hillyer calling out. I thought I should have dropped. So I don't see how anybody could have got into the house, with me watching up to the last minute."

"Not that minute," said one of the ladies, "no, certainly not. But they might have been hid somewhere for hours for all you know or we know either. In the very room, it might be, for all we can tell. I suppose you hadn't been in the room since the morning when you done the bed."

"Well!" exclaimed Mrs. Jolly, who found this possibility of hidden foes lurking concealed in her house a terrifying supposition. "To think of that! You're quite right, Mrs. Dolman. I get all my rooms nice and tidy as soon as ever I can, and I hadn't occasion to go up on that floor, let alone Mr. Zerny's room since ten in the morning."

"There, you see. Anybody might have been there. You can't be watching the street door all day long, and there's plenty of people that locks don't puzzle."

"But suppose they was in, how'd they get out?"

"Easy enough. Them as can get in and hide can hide and get out. I don't suppose, Mrs. Jolly, you troubled to look into the other room on your top floor."

"I never thought of it," gasped Mrs. Jolly. "Dear, oh dear!"

"That was the way, then. Waited till it was dark and all quiet, and you in your beds, and then slipped out as easy as easy."

It was felt that Mrs. Dolman had solved the enigma. But Mrs. Jolly propounded a new problem.

"But what on earth did they do such a wicked thing for? I haven't got an enemy in the world so far as I can say. And nothing taken. I can't see the sense of it."

They all confessed that they could make nothing of it. The police were consulted. They came, examined the house, questioned the lodgers, enquired as to the possibility of dismissed servants of a spiteful nature; and, like Mrs. Jolly and her friends, made nothing of it.

The Inspector, or Superintendent, or whatever he was, certainly had a suggestion, but it did not seem to lead anybody very far.

"I seem to remember," he said to Mrs. Jolly, "something of the same kind over Hornsey way, nine or ten years ago. It didn't come under our official notice at all, there being no suggestion of anything criminal. In consequence, we haven't any sort of record available for purposes of comparison. But it was all written up a good deal in the papers, especially the evening papers; columns of it there were. As far as I can remember, having read these newspaper articles as a member of the public, this Hornsey business was an affair of breakages: two or three pounds' worth of damage done, I believe. Things thrown about, you know. The family would be sitting round their fire comfortable of an evening, and there'd be a smash of glass and a lump of coal falling in the middle of the room. China and glass ornaments, too; they'd be flung from one side of the room to the other, in a very surprising manner, from what the papers said about it. There was a clergyman, a friend of the family, I believe, told one of the newspaper reporters that he'd seen a metal ash-tray fly off the mantelpiece and fall at his feet, right across the room. Very surprising, no doubt. I don't profess to have fathomed it out at all myself; speaking solely from what I read about it, it was my impression that there was some jiggery-pokery or other in the background, as I expect there is in your business, Mrs. Jolly.

"But one thing comes back to my mind; it struck me at the time as very singular. I must say, I couldn't make anything of it. There were some young people in the family, a couple of boys, thirteen to fifteen years old, I think they were. Well, it was announced three or four weeks after the disturbances had terminated, or it might be more, that one of these boys had become subject to epileptic fits. I must say, I don't see myself that fits are here or there, supposing these people and their friend the minister spoke the truth; but there it is. Now, Mrs. Jolly, I gather that your daughter's the only inhabitant of your house who might be termed young. That is so, I believe."

Mrs. Jolly grew red in the face before the policeman's interrogative eye.

"Not at all," she said briskly. "Mr. Zerny and Mr. Haddock are quite young."

"Now what age would you say they are? As far as you can judge, you know."

"Well, Mr. Zerny may be twenty-five, and Mr. Haddock a couple of years older—just about that, I should say, more or less."

"Ah, yes, Mrs. Jolly, but that isn't quite what I had in my mind when I was talking of young persons. Twenty-five, you may say, is grown up and a little bit over. No, I was thinking of something younger than that, more about in the 'teens, as they say. Now what age is your daughter that we were speaking of—if one may ask a young lady's age?"

Mrs. Jolly, as she said afterwards, looked very straight at the officer. She would have liked—she fervently desired—to tell him to mind his own business. But she held that it was no good to set their backs up; so she answered coldly:

"Annie is nineteen; nineteen next December, that is."

"Exactly, exactly. Now we're coming to cues, as a theatrical gentleman I knew once was in the habit of saying. That's much more like it. And—you'll excuse me, I'm sure—but has she ever had any trouble of the sort we were speaking of? You take my meaning?"

Mrs. Jolly was appalled. She was not a reader of detective fiction; but she had heard the almost miraculous powers of detectives discussed. She had not believed in these tales. "All make-up and a lot of nonsense, if you ask me," had expressed her attitude. Now she believed and trembled. Who would have thought it? Her goods and chattels had been maliciously damaged and destroyed; she had called in the police, and by tortuous and mysterious ways they had brought it round to Annie's fits. She had not the courage to deny.

"Not real fits," she distinguished. "And all over years ago. She fell down the kitchen stairs when she was thirteen and hurt her head. But the doctor said she would get over them. And she did. She's had no trouble at all since she was fifteen."

"Quite so, quite so," said the officer. "I quite understand. Well, I'm afraid we can't do anything further, Mrs. Jolly. Good morning."

He went off with the air of a man who has solved a dark and obscure mystery by the exertion of faculties verging on the super-human. And he left Mrs. Jolly a firm and awed believer in the miracle of the detective art. It was two or three hours before she was able to judge the situation with her usual sagacious commonsense. Indeed, it was with a shock that she at last realised that, in hard fact, the detective had really detected nothing. It was absolutely certain that Annie had nothing whatever to do either with the shattering of the picture or with the wrecking of Mr. Zerny's room. In the one case the girl had been asleep in bed beside her mother; in the other she had been standing by the kitchen table, with the beer-jug in her hand. Annie's alibis were undoubted, firm, above all question. "So that's that," said Mrs. Jolly to herself, in the deplorable idiom which she had, somehow, acquired.

And yet it hurt her a little to have to return to the flat sanity of her former attitude on the mystery and craft of detection.

"After all," she observed, to an old friend, consoling herself, "I will say it was a marvel the way he found out about my poor girl's illness. I don't know how he done it. Wonderful. Why, nobody's past life isn't safe from them, Mrs. Hemmons."

CHAPTER III

1.

I have often speculated, Hillyer wrote, in one of his note-books, as to the state of the human consciousness immediately after death. I am inclined to believe that the most salient feature of that extraordinary mode of existence, in its opening period, at all events, is confusion. Once or twice, I have found myself in a familiar room in total darkness; by the accident of having forgotten to take matches in my pocket, or by the accident of having omitted to place the box of matches in its usual position on shelf or table. It is extraordinary how easily and quickly all sense of direction and position are lost. Perhaps there may have been an initial mistake, in the nervous flurry of looking for those matches and not finding them. Dazzled with the darkness, if such a phrase may be allowed, I have gone to the right, intending the left, and after the first false step the confusion becomes more and more hopeless. The hands are stretched out to touch the expected object, and find nothingness; the feet stumble on obstacles which are not supposed to exist. Distances are misjudged, all reckonings are falsified; the arm-chair where I have sat day after day has become a terrifying enigma. I resolve to get out of this room that is confounding me, and I cannot find the door. I suffer from a kind of false panic; I am only sustained by the firm conviction that, in spite of all evidence to the contrary, I am in my own familiar room, though it seems through the well-used door that I have passed into a black unknown chaos. Yet, I know that this is a false report, and that I shall come out into the light at last. There may be something like this at the moment—but there are no longer moments—that succeeds death.

Or, it is possible that a better image is to be found in the dream state, and its interaction on the consciousness of the waking hours? There is a wonderful passage in De Quincey, describing the strange way in which some figure in his dreams would occasionally survive, as it were, the awakening. I think the particular instance he gives is of a dream of a dance. Cavaliers and their ladies tread an ancient, splendid measure: the dreamer awakes suddenly, and sees, dimly, the familiar forms of his own room. But there, standing on the floor at the bottom of his bed, is a beautiful woman, one of the figures of the dream, seen clearly for an instant in the light of dreamland. I have myself experienced something of this kind: the presence of the two worlds; the dark dome of the enchanted mountain and the dark mass of the dressing-table both seen at once. A man once told me a very curious experience of his, which illustrates this most singular confusion, or interaction, of the two states. He dreamed that he was in bed, fast asleep—as he was. He then dreamed that he woke up and remembered that the night before he had been engaged with certain papers of extraordinary and secret importance; and that he had been so careless as to leave them exposed on his desk. There was no truth, or semblance of truth in this; he had no papers of any consequence in his possession, and no secrets worth twopence. And then, this dreamer thought of another matter of anxiety. There were those papers teeming with their deadly secrets, lying open in the next room, and at half-past eight his brother-in-law would be coming round to breakfast: he of all men must never see those tremendous documents. They must be concealed before he came. And here truth again peeped in. He had a brother-in-law, who was expected to look in for breakfast. The man, deep asleep all the while, opened his eyes. It was quite dark and therefore early. Jack (the brother-in-law) would not be coming yet awhile. Still, he felt that he must make sure of the time, so he got up, and went to the chair where his coat was hanging; the matches were in one of the pockets. He felt in the pocket; it was empty. Then he remembered that the night before, out of his usual custom, he had left the box of matches on the dressing-table. He crossed the room, found the matches on the table, returned, and struck a match, and looked at the clock by his bedside. Five o'clock; more than three hours before Jack would be likely to turn up. He would hear the daily servant coming at a little before eight.

There would be plenty of time to hide the papers then; in the meantime, he would get back to bed and sleep. But all these manœuvres of his, the shufflings and stumblings about the room, and then the hiss and flare of the match, had woke up my friend's wife. She asked him, with some irritation, what on earth he was doing. He tried to explain the situation; the nature of the secrets, the importance, the dire importance of keeping them from Jack. She, half awake, and only dimly perceiving that nonsense was being talked, said tartly: "Oh, do get back to bed and go to sleep!" This impudent and careless contempt—so he took it—for matters of great moment filled my friend's heart with rage. He was furious; it was with difficulty that he restrained himself from uttering the bitterest reproaches. He went back to bed in savage silence, and, as he told me, it was only as he laid his head on the pillow that he woke up and realised that he had been thinking, acting, and talking nonsense of the wildest kind.

Here is an instance, then, of the two states, the waking state and the dream state, impinging on one another, mingling sheer fantasy and delusion with the plain facts of life. In some particulars, the memory was both sane and active: Jack, the brother-in-law, existed, and he was coming to breakfast. Moreover, he was actually a most inquisitive man; it might almost be said that, in his business, curiosity was a virtue. Further, there was the co-operation of the memory and the senses in the finding of the matchbox, after the initial forgetfulness, and in the inspection of the clock; and yet the whole operation was based on a vain figment. The man was asleep and dreaming; and yet he was awake; the one world was inextricably mingled with the other. It is, perhaps, in some such confusion that the newly dead may move. But what we should call their past life is, doubtless, the wild dream that troubles them. They cannot rouse themselves from the delusion that the weight of intolerable sorrows is pressing on their hearts; and then again, they are vexed at the first dawning of the thought—one must use mortal words—that those old ecstatic joys were also delusions and figments without significance.

But all this apart—and more than enough of a world for which we have no words; since, like music, it is beyond words, beyond ideas— there is another sense in which the dream world mingles with the world of actuality. There is a common phrase, which, perhaps, means more than it is intended to mean. "You must have dreamt it!" people say when they hear something that astonishes them a good deal. On the face of it, the phrase implies, "That's not true"; really, it simply means, "you surprise me very much." But, perhaps, in rare cases, the teller of the tale had dreamt "it", and had allowed it to trickle into his consciousness as a piece of actual experience or veritable knowledge. And, on the other hand, these may be impressions about which a man is uncertain; wondering whether this or that were an actual experience, a thing seen or heard, or read; or whether it did not come out of some dream of the night. Something of this kind happened to me, very much to my alarm at the time. I found myself repeating, internally, a string of senseless jargon, and beating about in my endeavour to find some rational source or origin for the gibberish I was repeating, trying vainly to connect it with actual experience . . . with something read . . . with a dream; inclining, on the whole, to the belief that it was a broken recollection of a dream, perhaps of many years ago. For dreams certainly remain in the memory under the same conditions and according to the same laws as those governing our waking impressions. I remember, vividly, every detail of a horrid nightmare that beset me when I cannot have been more than five years old. I can recall the awful oppression of formless terror with which I awoke with much greater distinctness than many actual events of far later years. Many of these, indeed, I have, as we say, forgotten—though, of course, nothing is really forgotten—but the horror that befell by that bend of the road close to my old home is as clear in my mind as the image of the houses opposite, or clearer; though I glanced at them ten minutes ago, and the nightmare must be nearly fifty years away. And there is another question which may open strange vistas of thought: whether it is only the dreams recollected on awakening that remain in our memories. These are but a few out of a great number. Some day, perhaps in the hour of death, the rest may return, and appear before us, a wild multitude.

But the experience which alarmed me, to which I have referred, was, I think, a morbid symptom. I had shut myself up with my books and my investigations for too long a time, and my nervous system must have been near the breaking point. The specialist whom I consulted advised me to go away to a new scene and fresher air, to be idle, to distract myself from my work, and to take things more lightly and easily for the future. I did as I was told, and found myself better; as well, indeed, as I hope to be for the rest of my day. And this, in spite of a very strange and unpleasant experience which happened towards the end of my stay at Porth, in South Wales. It was an experience which annoyed and puzzled me very much at the time. Now and again, I have been tempted to set it down as a grotesque and extremely ill-natured practical joke; but some of the circumstances were hardly patient of this explanation, and I am still bewildered whenever I think of the affair. However, I did not allow it to affect my health or my mental composure, either at the time or afterwards. My nervous trouble, or whatever it was, fell upon me in May. I spent most of June at the seaside, and came back feeling perfectly fit and well, as I have said. I am quite sure that my nerves were as sound as they ever had been. I was keeping in mind all the time the advice the doctor had given me. I no longer "shut myself up in a cupboard" with my books all day long and most of the night—I am using the specialist's phrases. I read the papers and went out and about every morning; and so gave mind and body the air; it was only in the afternoon and evening that I devoted myself to the fairy gold. In the course of these researches, now carried on with a little more sense than before, pure luck led me to a most interesting discovery. This was an odd little book, called *A London Walk*, published by some obscure firm nearly eighty years ago, and, so far as I can make out, utterly neglected and unknown. It was written by a clergyman, the Rev. Thomas Hampole, and is the author's only title in the British Museum Catalogue. The Rev. Thomas was sententious and occasionally pompous—after the manner of his tribe, as some might say—but his book had some extremely curious things in it which interested me immensely; they were things that, so far as I could see, were quite in the line of my studies and quests. Or, on parallel lines, perhaps: rather in the vein of: "There is a great experiment, and some there are that have made it": which is not quite what I am after, but something like it. The end may be the same in both cases; but I am not sure about that. Anyhow, there were some very striking things in this Hampole book; and I was inquisitive. I wanted, naturally, to know something about the man himself, where he came from, how he lived, what he had done besides writing *A London Walk;* but I was a good deal more interested to know where his book came from, what its literary sources were. The author did not strike me as having the creative, originating mind: he was rather of the "from information received" type, and I wanted to know where he had got his information. There were traces of the influence of Blake; but, one would have said, much stronger traces of Traherne's *Centuries of Meditations.* There was the difficulty. *A London Walk* was published in the early 'fifties, and the manuscript of the *Centuries* was not discovered till at least fifty years later. Of course, it was quite possible that this manuscript, which came to light at last on a bookstall in Farringdon Street, had not remained uninspected and unread since 1674 or thereabouts, when it was written. It was possible, if it came to that, that it had been in the possession of Hampole himself. Well, there were a good many odd questions connected with the book; and I have no doubt that they occupied my mind pretty constantly, I dare say that I had Hampole in my mind as I was sitting one night in my room, somewhere between nine and ten. It was one of the hot and heavy nights of the London summer, when any wind there may be falls with the sun, and the heat seems to swelter from the pavements and the walls. I had the window wide open, and I was sitting at my desk with a shaded candle lamp beside me; I always use one for working, and find it very much better than gas or electric light. There was a tap at the door, and thinking it was my landlady with some question of bacon and eggs, I said: "Come in," and turned round on my chair. I was a good deal surprised to see an old friend, Montonnier Hawkins, especially as he was a bibliographer of experience, and exactly the man I wanted to see. I welcomed him, put out my candle, turned on the gas, sat him down, and asked how he got in. "I didn't hear your knock."

"The door was open. About the time of going for the supper beer? So I walked up."

We talked a little of old times, of good event and ill event that had fallen to men we had known, twenty, thirty years ago; of some that had died, and of others that were sorry, perhaps, to be surviving. And then I came to the matter that was so much in my mind just then. I found Hawkins knew about Hampole—what there was to be known, and that not much. He came, it seemed, of an old yeoman family who had been long settled in a village near Northampton. His parents were well-to-do people, and they sent him to Oxford, where he took his de-

gree in 1830. He was ordained deacon and priest by the Bishop of Lichfield, was curate at Alfreton in Derbyshire, then in Stafford, and finally
at Altrincham, near Manchester. About 1840, he received a legacy from
an uncle, enough apparently to make him independent of his profession,
since shortly afterwards he took chambers at Clifford's Inn, and only did
occasional duty for the rest of his life. He died in 1871. Nothing much
more was known of him. He was supposed to have corresponded with
the author of *A Suggestive Inquiry into the Hermetic Mystery,* but, according
to Hawkins, none of his letters had been preserved.

It was not much. With the one exception of the reputed association between Hampole, and the author of a very singular book, it
threw little light on his literary origins. Hawkins, I found, knew nothing about the subject-matter of *A London Walk;* and indeed, his interests were purely bibliographical, It was a rare book, he said, but not
generally "collected": it would be worth four or five pounds, not more.
Many copies had been ruined by the work of Grangerisers, or extra-
illustrators, who had torn out the frontispiece.

I had been bending over the table, taking notes of such dates and
facts as Hawkins gave me. At the end of his remarks, I looked up from
the paper, and met his eye. I was struck at once by something strange
and unfamiliar in his expression. There was a look of fury in his face
that terrified me. He did not utter a word. There was dead silence in
the room. I thought he had suddenly gone mad, and I would have giv-
en anything to start to my feet, and shout and rush at him; but a ghastly oppression weighed on me and held me fast, and held my lips. It
was as if I had been gagged and bound; and as if a heavy weight had
been laid on my breast. I suffered an unutterable horror. The figure
opposite to me seemed to change into a dreadful and unspeakable and
most detestable shape, and then everything was black darkness.

I came to myself trembling with fear. I did not dare to move for
some time. Then I heard a clock strike eleven. I looked about the
room fearfully; saw there was nothing amiss, and ventured at last to my
feet, and crawled to the cupboard, and poured out and drank off half a
glass of whiskey. I felt myself slowly returning from a world of very
awful experience: the fiery mist out of which I seemed to have come
melted slowly away. For a long time I was afraid to go to bed. I drank
more whiskey, deliberately, not to raise my spirits, but to stupefy my-

self into sleep that I hoped would be dreamless. It was three o'clock in the morning when at last I went heavily to bed.

It was some days before I could shake off the terrible sense of fear. As soon as I began to think the matter over with some approach to calmness, I made up my mind that I had fallen asleep in my chair, and had been visited by violent nightmare; the weight and oppression I had experienced seemed to me decisive. And, indeed, these symptoms apart, there was no other explanation to be given. I wanted badly to write to Hawkins, shaping my letter in such a way that if, indeed, he had been to see me that night, the fact would appear in his reply, I was ashamed to do so. About a fortnight later, I ran across him in the Reading Room and managed to get out a question as to Hampole and *A London Walk*. He said he had just heard of the book as a minor rarity, that he believed that it was sought for to some extent in occult circles. Then I asked him about the author, and, to my glowing relief, Hawkins declared that he knew nothing about him. I felt that I had been a fool to want his assurance; but so it was. And the experience passed into the region of dreams.

And in spite of that, it still persisted vividly, with all the force and the impression of an actual experience. It would stay with me as though it had happened; and it stays with me still: a dream, and yet an event. I have to be on my guard against it; against the recognition of it as something that is, veritably, part of my life. And, no doubt, it is the panic terror, the deadly oppression of fear with which the dream ended that fortifies me against taking it as actuality. Here are the marks of nightmare, not to be mistaken. The first part of the dream; the tap on the door, Hawkins entering and explaining probably enough, that the street door had been left open for the return of somebody with a beer-jug—I have heard my landlady say that she always locks the area gate when it gets dark—all this was perfectly in the common order of things. And so were his replies to my questions; his account of Thomas Hampole's very ordinary and uninteresting career, his bibliographer's summing up of the rarity and comparatively small value of the book; his remark as to the imperfect state of many copies, owing to the tearing out of the frontispiece; again, everything is strictly according to common order. I must say that if it had all stopped there, or, rather, if Hawkins had stayed a little longer and chatted odds and ends before leaving, I should most certainly have believed that he had paid me an actual visit. I should have woke up, looked about me with the dazed bewilderment of the awaking sleeper, and concluded that I had fallen asleep in my chair after seeing Hawkins out at the street door. No doubt, as I say, there would be a sense of bewilderment, of questioning uncertainty; the 'Have I been dreaming, or what?' mood. The edges would have been a little misty and undecided; there would have been a certain vagueness, let us say, about the beginning and end of the dream. But, I make no doubt that if it had all kept within the lines I have mentioned, the whole thing would have passed into my mind as an ordinary bit of experience. I should have accepted Hawkins's somewhat bald data as entirely trustworthy, and probably have regarded them as a starting point for more searching enquiries. It was the fright in which I awoke, the instant recollection of the abominable transformation that I had witnessed, which convicted the whole of being a mere figment of the sleeping brain, stirred, no doubt, into this most disagreeable form of activity by something wrong with the digestion. No one can suspect true nightmare of being a part of actuality: its own evidence is destructive of any such claim. If Westminster Abbey turns into a cloud that descends upon you and chokes your breath and suffocates you, you know when you wake, panting and trembling, that it was all a dream and that you are safe. *Credo quia impossibile:* using the old phrase with a new twist.

And yet: that test may lead us to strange conclusions. "The impossible, the contradiction in terms must be a dream"; where shall we find ourselves if we allow that axiom to mark the distinction between dream and waking? To leave on one side our attempted definitions of time and space, which involve us in bottomless pits of absurdity and contradiction: think of the mark on the paper which we are told is a line; that which is length without breadth and therefore invisible for ever to the eye of flesh. Think also of Achilles in his vain chase of the tortoise; and see into what hideous nonsense the certainty of mathematics leads us. If the belief in monstrous absurdity and contradiction be the sure mark of dreaming, then what do we do daily? What world is it that we inhabit?

Let me note this. It is possible that those who find their way to the Queen of Fairyland are liberated from these dreams and monsters and delusions, and behold with a rapture of delight the real world. But it is agreed on all hands that such are forced to return, and the fairy gold is dust and ashes in the morning.

But all this is beside the mark; beside the present mark at all events. I said that it was the extravagant and monstrous ending that convinced me that Hawkins's visit was nothing but a dream: all that went before was rational and orderly enough, and dull enough, too, to be part of any day. But there was one singular circumstance which so far I have not noted. Before I went to bed on that evil night, I gathered up the loose papers that were about the room, and locked them in my desk. I have always had the good habit of leaving my sitting-room tidy at night. Loose papers are apt to go astray; and they are in the way of the landlady's daughter, when she comes to lay the table in the morning. When this particular morning came, and I had done my best with the breakfast before me, I felt that I needed a very liberal dose of fresh air. Indeed, I thought the case almost pointed to Brighton and back, but this seemed an extreme measure, so I went on 'bus outside to Wimbledon. I had found that the air blew freshly on the Common, and I meant to combine its benefits with an enquiry into an odd business which had happened when I was last there, a few weeks earlier. One of the prosperous people who live in the big houses on the Common had run out of his garden as I was passing by, and had accused me of smashing his greenhouse by throwing a lump of coal at it. I soon convinced him that I had nothing to do with the outrage, and that nobody could have hit the greenhouse from the road. Mr. Horncastle—or something northern of that kind—made up his mind that the criminal must be a gardener whom he had discharged some time before; and I thought I should like to hear what had happened. But it turned out that the gardener had been at Plymouth on that particular day, by clear evidence; and there was nothing more to be done. But at all events, I had my dose of fresh breezes, and I came back feeling all the better for the excursion. After tea, I went to my desk and began to set my papers in order—and was on the verge of a relapse. There, on one of the sheets of paper, were the notes concerning Thomas Hampole that I dreamed I had taken. "I dreamed I had taken!" But I had taken them. There they were; very plainly written by me:

"Thomas Hampole. b. The Lees, Hedgworth, nr. Northampton. c. 1809.

Queen's Coll. Oxon. A.D. 1830. Ordained, Bp. of Lichfield. D. 32. P. 33. Curate Alfreton, Derb. 32–35: Stafford 36–38: Altrincham, nr. Manchester, 38–40. Settled Clifford's Inn, 1842. Ob. 1871."

Then it all happened. That was my first thought, and I was sick with fear. Then it had all happened. And that abomination had been accomplished here before my eyes. For a moment, it was a relief to me to remember what the doctor had said to me a few weeks before: "If you don't take care you will be seeing things." It was a relief, that is, to think that I was going mad.

It was some time before I was able to calm myself and consider the whole business with sense, instead of panic. I remembered the affair of that friend of mine; his dream of the secret papers not to be seen by his brother-in-law; how, fast asleep all the while, he had hunted his matchbox from pocket to table, struck a light, inspected the clock, gone back to bed, not awaking till his head had touched the pillow. I found a great similarity between the two cases. If he could look at a clock and tell the time in his sleep, I might just as easily take pencil and paper, and put down the inventions of my dream. This was, no doubt, exactly what had happened, and—save for the senseless horror of the dream, which will haunt me, I suppose, as that nightmare of my childhood has haunted me—there the matter rests. I confess that I have made no further researches into the life of Thomas Hampole, or into the literary origins, if any, of *A London Walk*. I do not like to think how I might feel, if such research confirmed all the facts which I jotted down in my dream. I suppose I should have to fall back on the hypothesis that I had read it all, perhaps without attention, many years before, that it had sunk below the level of my conscious mind, and that it had risen from the depths of the subconscious during the dream. Such things do happen; I have found myself in a dream pattering Greek phrases far beyond my waking capacity. I have remembered these phrases on waking, and verified them with the aid of Liddell and Scott, finding to my astonishment that I was more learned by night than by day. I should be prepared, then, if I happened to discover that the bibliographer of the dream had been strictly accurate; and there I intend to let the matter rest. And as for Hampole's book and its connections, that is to rest too. I have a superstitious doubt whether the chance that led me to it were altogether a happy one.

2.

It seems probable that Hillyer made these personal notes and wrote down the accompanying reasonings and meditations by way of relief. He had very few friends, and nearly all of them, if not all, were less friends than acquaintances. He had lived alone for many years. He had lost the habit of ready speech; if he had ever possessed it. When he did talk, it was of external things, never of his own feelings or inner experiences. Still, it is to be supposed that he felt the need of expression; and so, apparently, he made a quarto manuscript book serve the office of an intimate friend. More men are in this case, perhaps, than is generally supposed. Pepys was familiar enough, in a sense, with plenty of jolly gossips, and *bona robas,* and men of state; but he held his real converse with himself in the shorthand cypher: Pepys was the only confidant of Pepys. Hillyer, whose mere acquaintances were few enough, had all the greater need of shewing his heart to himself. He wound up the odd affair of Hampole to his own satisfaction, but before long he was at work again.

Life has some strange satisfactions, alleviations, and escapes from trouble—the new page begins. I remember long ago, soon after I first came to London and before I had taken the final vows of solitude, or something very near solitude, being confronted by a queer experience in its trivial way. Some people I knew who lived at Highgate used to encourage their friends to drop in for coffee, whiskey, tobacco and talk on Sunday nights. I don't think they went so far as to say they were At Home. One cold winter night, with a wind roaring about the housetop and whining in the chimney, we all drew our chairs in a rough semi-circle about the fire. We had been sitting in this way for half an hour or more when there was a slight but intense sort of noise. I do not know whether to call it a puff, or a hiss, or a whiz; perhaps it was a combination of all three. With the noise, some object shot off the mantelpiece, and fell with a flop on the ground before us, in the centre of the semi-circle. One of the party picked up the object, and it turned out to be a matchbox. In it, there were four or five matches. They had been used; the wood was blackened; but they were quite cold. No doubt somebody out of range of the fireplace and the nearest ash-tray had used the matchbox in their stead, and had finally put it down on the mantelshelf. The man who picked up the box and examined it, flung it into the fire with an expression of faint contempt, as if he disapproved of the transaction. We speculated vaguely for a few minutes as to what had happened and how it had happened, and then dropped the subject. Some of the party, encountering one another a few days afterwards, did a little more wondering and suggesting of possible explanations; but nobody was much interested, because everybody knew there was some trick, and, it seemed, a clever one, since it remained undiscovered. But nobody was really curious, or puzzled, or perturbed; since nobody believed that the matchbox had been shot through the air by occult forces, hidden from man. Miracles are not on the modern map; and our disbelief in them is one of the escapes from trouble to which I have alluded. We see something that we do not understand; and we conclude that there is a trick somewhere. And usually, unless we are seriously affected by the event, we trouble no farther, not even to find out what the trick may have been.

I have been laying this consolation to my heart lately. For some weeks we have been vexed here in an odd manner enough, and I am afraid that my landlady, who does her best for us all, has been very considerably distressed. And I am afraid, too, that for some time, at all events, I bore the trouble lightly, since it did not greatly affect my comfort or convenience. It began with the fall of the mirror that used to hang over the mantelpiece in my room. The thing came down in the dead of night with a bang and a crash that woke up the house. One of the lodgers, a young workman of some kind, said that the cords were sound and that it looked as if they had been violently torn. I don't think anybody paid much attention to this very improbable conjecture. Mrs. Jolly, the landlady, was sorry to lose a handsome piece of furniture, as she considered it, and I think she feared the bad luck that is supposed to follow the breaking of a glass. And I was relieved to be rid of the horrid object. Then, not long afterwards, there was some more smashing. The furniture in a room on the floor above mine was thrown about in an extraordinary manner, and everything breakable was broken. Nobody could explain it. The police were called in, I believe quite ineffectually. The Inspector, or whatever he was, seems to have insinuated that Mrs. Jolly's daughter was somehow or other at the bottom of the mischief, but I believe the girl was down in the kitchen with her mother when the furniture was falling about over our heads. And again, I am afraid that beyond a general dislike of rows and disturbances of all kinds, I took no great interest in the affair. We are mostly selfish, not so much in an active as in a passive way. I was mildly sorry that a very decent woman should be harassed and be the worse off by three or four pounds; but my rest was not broken by the thought of Mrs. Jolly's troubles. When my own turn came, it is hardly necessary to state that I was moved more deeply.

I was working one afternoon at my desk. I wanted to consult a book which was on a shelf in my bedroom. I shut the door of the sitting-room behind me and went into the bedroom next door. I was delayed a little in getting the book I wanted, as I had carelessly put it back in a hurry on the wrong shelf some weeks before. But I could not have been out of my sitting-room for more than three minutes. When I got back I was amazed and horrified to find one of the note-books I had been using lying on the floor, torn to shreds and fragments. It might be possible, I thought, to piece it all together, at the cost of a great deal of time and trouble; but how on earth had it happened? I had not done it; that was certain. I am sometimes absent-minded. I juggle with small objects such as pipes and pens and pencils and look for them everywhere but in the place where I have laid them five minutes before: but I was very sure that I had not torn up my own note-book and forgotten all about it three minutes afterwards. Who had done it? I was the only lodger in the house at the time. I went down to the kitchen and found Mrs. Jolly asleep in her arm-chair and her daughter mending things by the window. I made some instruction about breakfast a little earlier to-morrow my excuse for disturbing them, and went back and stood bewildered in the middle of my room; not knowing in the least what to think of the scraps and fragments of paper littering the floor. "Look at the hangman when it comes home to him," I quoted somewhat harshly and irrelevantly from *Barnaby Rudge*. But I had been brought up hard against a blank wall. I gathered the torn pieces into a heap by the waste-paper basket, so that it might look probable, the result of an author's despair, when they brought up my tea-things; and I spent the rest of the evening and a good part of the night in doing a sort of jig-saw puzzle with the fragments, a bottle of gum, and a blank book. This was distraction of a kind; but, the one puzzle solved with tolerable success, the other presented itself again, and remained—intolerable and unsolvable. I had to invent a deadly enemy for Mrs. Jolly before I could go to bed with any hope of going to sleep. I made my figment as plausible as I could. I feigned two opposition letters of lodgings in the same street, many years before, borrowing pretty freely from *Mrs. Lirriper's Lodgings.* There was competition and deadly enmity between the two. Finally, Mrs. Jolly had triumphed all along the line, and Mrs. X. bankrupt, sold up and utterly defeated, had fled the country. She had returned after the long years, had tracked Mrs. Jolly down, and was now wreaking vengeance on her old foe. She had lived amongst the Blackfellows of Australia, and had learnt their stealthy secrets. Her plan was, no doubt, to make No. 29 uninhabitable, to drive the lodgers away, and thus reduce Mrs. Jolly to ruin and beggary. And, for the time, this strange story served its turn. Later, I picked holes in it, detected improbabilities, doubted whether that sort of thing really happened; and yet reflected that, after all, the strangest things did happen, and that plots and stratagems quite as unusual were on record. There was clearly a trick, a series of tricks somewhere: manuscript books do not tear themselves any more than matchboxes fly off mantelshelves of their own accord. My explanation of the note-book trick might not be altogether satisfactory; but it was good enough.

Within a few weeks, however, I was concerned in a number of misadventures, which, so far as I see, cannot be accounted for by the hypothesis I put forward to cover the incidents at 29 Layburn Street. I say I was concerned with these affairs, but this is not quite exact. I was present when they occurred; a different matter.

I was having my lunch—or rather dinner—at the Quill two days after the incident of the torn manuscript. I had just lit my pipe, when one of the big glass jars, used for holding spirits, standing on a shelf at the back of the bar, fell forward and smashed to pieces on the floor.

The next day, in the morning, I was going along Holborn on the top of a 'bus. A strong wind was blowing, and I was holding my hat. It was nearly blown away a few minutes before. On the south side of the street, near one of the Turnstiles into Lincoln's Inn Fields, I noticed a house, with high hoardings, and an elaborate galleried scaffolding in front of it. In a moment, just as we were going past, the whole structure seemed to fall to pieces and collapse, like a pagoda built of cards.

The hoardings fell out on the pavement; the poles and planks of the scaffolding fell to right and left. I believe that a man employed in the rebuilding work and a passer-by were injured, but not seriously.

On the afternoon of the same day I was walking back to my rooms by way of Oxford Street. I was passing a jeweller's shop when there was a crash of glass. There was a great jagged opening in one of the panes of the shop-front. There was a rush of people to the spot, yells and shouts, blowing of police whistles. Very much to my disgust I found myself in the centre of the scrummage, and got pretty roughly handled—or, rather, shoved. I heard that nothing was stolen, and that nobody had seen the "smash and grab" man get away.

Three days later I had to see my solicitor on some business. We were discussing it in his room, when there was a loud crack and then the noise of a heavy fall. In the next room, separated from the one in which we were sitting by a wooden partition, the Letter Books of the firm were kept on shelves. A clerk wanted to consult one of these volumes dated thirty or forty years back, and standing on a high shelf. The man had gone up a library ladder to get the book. He was a heavy man, and they said there was a defect in the wood. The ladder broke and the clerk went headlong. But he was not seriously hurt, I am glad to say.

Four days later. Collapse of a cellar flap in Soho Street, just after I had walked over it.

The same day, a couple of hours afterwards. Precisely similar accident in the Caledonian Road; but in this case I was on the other side of the street.

Five days later. I could not settle down to my work on this particular evening, and went round to see a friend who had a flat—or lower part of a "converted" house—in the Finchley Road. As we were talking, there was a noise like thunder above us, and a shower of plaster covered us and everything in the room. My friend ran upstairs, and found that an old-fashioned wardrobe had fallen forward—jarred out of place, the people supposed, by the heavy traffic.

Next morning, I was going under the covered space between the Great Central Hotel and Marylebone Station. There was a splintering crash of broken glass, and something fell to the ground five or six feet to my left. It was a butcher's weight of four pounds. I heard a man say that it must have been flung out of one of the hotel windows. I do not know whether this was found to be the case.

In the ten days following there were four more incidents of the same order, in which I was present, though as I have said, and maintain, I was in no way concerned.

And I draw no conclusions whatever. I do not believe that there is any conclusion to be drawn. A good many people would say, I suppose, that it is highly improbable that one man should be present at, or at least in the near neighbourhood of, so many disasters in the course of three weeks and four days. It is not in the least improbable when the vastness of London and its myriad movements and activities are considered. No doubt, it appears strange, but the strangeness is only in appearance. It appears strange when a man gets an entire suit dealt to him at cards; in reality that hand of his is no stranger than any other combination of thirteen cards. The world is full of these combinations, of events as well as of cards, which invite us to draw conclusions; to say, therefore, this, that or the other. But there is no "therefore". A man once thought it worth while writing to the paper to chronicle one of these odd coincidences. He bought a watch, he said. somewhere in the Straits Settlements. Thirty years later, he was in London. The watch was out of order, and he walked into a shop, I think in Holborn, to have it seen to. The man across the counter who took the watch, was the man who had sold the watch in the far east all those years before. It happened so; and again, there is no "therefore", no conclusion to be drawn.

Nor was there any connection between the broken bottles and smashed ladders and the events that have troubled us at the lodging-house in Layburn Street. In the latter case, I have no doubt that my fable was not far from the fact. Somebody had a grudge against my landlady and tried to scare away her lodgers and ruin her business. I don't profess to understand how the trick was done: I am puzzled. But then I am puzzled by the simplest card-trick—"choose a card. Put it back; don't shew me where, etc., etc."—till they tell me how it is done. But the great thing to remember when one is confronted with apparent impossibilities is: there is a trick somewhere. As for the other smashes and crashes—the affairs of tavern and street, lawyer's office, and cellar flap—as I have noted, there is no puzzle here, no improbability, even much less impossibility. Here, the only thing to remember is that London stretches for ten miles in every direction, and that it contains more than eight million inhabitants.

3.

It would appear that the last sentence in Hillyer's remarks on certain odd experiences that had befallen him—which he declined to consider odd—dwelt in his mind. He had evidently been thinking over the question of probabilities, and weighing their importance and their applicability to his own field of research. He continues his notes:

I was very much struck, when I was reading Whately's *Logic* for the first time, by a footnote on Probability. Indeed, I have forgotten the statement in the text thus annotated, but the note was to the effect that the Insurance Offices employed people whose business it was to estimate probability; to reduce it and transmute it from probability to certainty; and to do so with such nice exactness that the result of this marvellous process might be expressed in pounds, shillings, and pence—surely the utmost word of accuracy. Thus, if a man living near the Monument wanted to insure against the column falling on his house he will find, as I have been told, that the chances have been precisely reckoned, and that his yearly payment must be eighteenpence per cent. And to me, such a process seems to grapple almost with the infinite, to draw very near to the land where Achilles will race past the tortoise and all parallel straight lines will meet at last.

It must be confessed, however, that such a reckoning and most of those which are the matter of insurance calculations are material in their conditions and in their issues. There is a question whether a house will burn, a ship sink, or a tall column fall headlong. The likelihood of these events happening is estimated, and the chances are expressed in terms of money. But the material event and the monetary payments are not the process itself but the application of it to commercial purposes. By means of the process, the Insurance Office ascertains the exact degree of likelihood that the Monument will tumble down, and even the likelihood of its falling to east, west, north or south. And the result is expressed, for the special purposes of insurer and insured, in terms of eighteenpence per cent., per annum. But I see no reason why the method should not be applied to the things of the mind as well as the things of the body. And the question of money is accidental, not essential. Why is there not an office where, in return for a sufficient fee, one might be informed as to the exact chance of a man of the highest literary genius appearing in the next fifty years? We may be inclined to say that the question is incalculable, but this is probably not the case. There would be a difficulty, the affair would have to be in the hands of a college or society or brotherhood, since the highest genius is not always recognised in its own age. Shakespeare was, no doubt, held to be a very clever man in his own time, and was handsomely rewarded. His social position was, perhaps, something higher than that of a writer of successful farcical comedies in our day: he might be fairly equated in general esteem with the late W. S. Gilbert. Milton had to wait for some years: Wordsworth, Coleridge, Keats were not immediately acclaimed. Hence, the necessity of a college or permanent body, if we are to deal with the risk of a supreme genius being born: the college might have to wait a hundred years before the reply to its question could be tested. I like to think of some of the calculations to be made, of the strange reckonings that would go into the account. For example, suppose we simplify the problem, and deal only with England and with England merely from the time of Shakespeare onwards. How many have been born in that period? And then, what is the percentage of men of supreme literary genius? Supposing a hundred million lives: how many great masters should we expect? And, of course, apart from this drudgery of figures, there are the wider, vaguer, subtler, enquiries. Sometimes genius may depend to a certain extent on the attitude, atmosphere and fashion of the age; and it may be said that these are things that cannot be prophesied far in advance. But when Ascham denounced the *Morte d'Arthur* as a bad book, when the Elizabethan Puritans protested against holidays and feasts because it was written "six days shalt thou labour"—then Gradgrind and Bounderby rose clearly into view.

But there is one region into which the doctrine of probability cannot enter. That is the land where the Queen of the Fairies holds court, where they give gold that turns into dead leaves; into dead ashes. There is no list of those who have gone down into that valley; merely hints and rumours that go on from age to age. Those who have visited the enchanted region are either unable or unwilling to give any very definite account of their experiences on their return. But it is to be gathered that a certain transformation or transmutation of the world is effected; both within and without.

CHAPTER IV

1.

One of the strange matters of dreaming—Hillyer recurs here to what was perhaps a favourite subject—is the manner in which the dream sometimes bears witness to itself. Indirectly, not directly. Nobody says: "This is all true, and it is actually happening." But the kind of dream of which I am speaking affirms its own reality by connecting itself with innumerable other experiences in the past, with a whole cycle of events, with a recognised group of characters, in fact, with life; but with a life that is wholly of dreamland. In our actual waking hours, we hear, or we read that our friend X is dead, or is appointed Governor of Kafiristan, or has discovered a new metal. But whatever fate may have befallen him, we are at once conscious of a whole circle of event emotions, recollections, in all of which X had some share. X's name brings X's world with it; to a greater or less extent we also are inhabitants of that world, and find ourselves in familiar, recognised company. And so with these dreams. The main action of the dream is confirmed by a hundred subsidiary recollections. Say, we are to descend into a dark and obscure valley, deeply wooded, silent save for a faint ripple of water that seems to come from far away. We are to go down into this valley; and there is a secret to be discovered there, in the darkness underneath the trees. But we have heard of all this before; the adventure is well known; it has been described again and again; what were A and C and E saying about it a week ago? That all who went into that valley returned with a mark on their breasts? Or were they changed into . . . ? And so on and so on: but however monstrous the matter of the dream, however mad its circumstances, all are entirely acceptable to the mind of the dreamer, and are perceived to be a part of daily and accustomed life, to be congruous with half a dozen or half a hundred associations and recollections. Sometimes, indeed, such a dream is so fixed and established in its (apparent) actuality, that it is with a very considerable effort that it is dismissed and discharged from the region of actual things when the sleeper awakes; and, as I have noted before, it may hang about the consciousness with a Strange persistence, and become perhaps, at last recognised as part of the waking world: "something I must have read long ago", "something I heard when I was a boy and got all mixed up". And I think also that it is the sense of continuity, of being a part of a familiar life, that leads some people to affirm that they dream of a certain place, of a certain event or adventure, over and over again. The dream suggestion: "I have been here before," "I know what is coming next," and so forth, is so strong that the sleeper awakened is convinced that this particular dream is recurrent; that it repeats itself at intervals. Of course, there may be dreams which do recur; I believe that the case of the Cornishman who dreamed on two (or three?) successive nights that he saw Percival the Prime Minister being assassinated is well attested; but I hold that the great majority of (apparently) recurring dreams are to be explained in the manner I have suggested.

The point interests me personally. I have no doubt that a short time ago—I cannot fix a precise date—I had a singularly vivid dream. I was walking pretty briskly on the pavement of a London street; of a street, rather, since I did not distinguish it, or recognise this feature or that; I simply took it for granted. I think I was conscious of a faint rustle as of leaves; but I am not sure of this. It was night-time, and evidently late since very few people were about. I was aware that I had an appointment, some end to my walk; but this end, whatever it was, was in the background of my mind, not continuously and sharply apprehended. I think this is often so in our waking hours. A man has settled that he is to meet Jones at a certain time and a certain place. He sets out to keep his appointment, and very likely dismisses it from his mind as he goes to that place. He may be thinking of politics or incunabula, or hybridising for most of the way; since the art of the young waterman, thinking of nothing at all, is a very difficult and rare achievement. So there was just this impression on my mind as I passed through the lighted street. Then I came to my journey's end. I was in Layburn Street. I knew it by the steep ascent of the road, and by the vague darkness of the group of trees at the top, where the way branches to left and right. And I was standing before number 29, the house in which I live. I was not in the least astonished to see the whole house blazing with light; shining out radiant into the night, and resonant with music. As it was, so it was accepted without question; in the manner after which St. Paul's Cathedral is accepted by people who go eastward up Ludgate Hill. I went up the steps, through the open door, and found myself not in Mrs. Jolly's extremely modest apartments, but in a gorgeous palace. Here, one would suppose, the absurdity should have arrested me, and brought the whole fabric of the dream crashing to the ground. It was not so. I knew that this was not the aspect of the place to which I was used. For an inappreciable instant of time, the jaundiced marble paper of the passage, the dingy carpet on the stairs, the sordid light that crept through the landing window were present to me; that, I recollected, was the accustomed greeting of the house. I quite appreciated the vast difference between that and this splendour into which I had entered; but I understood perfectly what had happened. For this, it seems, was one of those dreams which do not stand alone as solitary incidents, but are a part of a larger whole, and in relation to a whole world of circumstance. And so the palace of golden and glorious light in which I stood was utterly rational and acceptable. In the dream, I say, I was in the secret, I knew what had happened and how and why it had happened. It was all a part of a scheme which was perfectly familiar to me; I received it and rejoiced in it, not as one who is incredulous and all amazed at the coming of some tremendous unexpected good, saying to himself, scarcely daring to believe: "Then my dreams have come true!" but rather, as a man witnessing a happy ending which he has long foreseen in the fashioning of which he has, perhaps, played his part. I say, "a happy ending" for the figures about me were, I knew, possessed with the felicity that was in my heart. I was sharing in a great festival of ineffable joy. And the cause and reason of it were not hidden from me; I participated in the secret possessed by all, and could have uttered it in a word. But when I awoke, the word, though it was even then on my lips, was lost.

I find my recollection insisting very strongly on this master word. It was as if all the secret, all the magic of the adventure in which I supposed myself engaged were made by it and summed up in it. It was the cause of all and the end of all; the deep foundation stone and the highest pinnacle of the palace. If it were taken away, all would fall into ugly ruin. Indeed, I am reminded a little of the Lost Word which the Freemasons seek; and it is likely enough that the word of my dream arose from a confused recollection of the Masonic legend.

I have said that the dream was a singularly vivid one. So it was. Not so much in the recollection of its detail and imagery, as in my extraordinary conviction on awaking, and after awaking of having gone through a real and veritable experience. I can remember something of a certain ritual in which I joined, of which I was a witness. In the dream it all seemed just and right; in the awakening its strangeness was incredible. But not so much the external imagery as the inward felicity impressed itself upon me. And curiously (as I think) this felicity was very largely negative in its nature. Curiously, because I believe that most of us regard happiness, or joy, or well-being or what you will, as a positive thing, based on what a man has gained, or received or possessed himself of in one way or another: it is an affair of having. But in the dream my delight—and it was greater than words can utter—was founded not on what I had gained but on what I had lost. What I had lost was all the burden of life. I do not think that many of us realise what that amounts to. Perhaps it might be said that we do not know that it is there—till it has dropped off. And who can tell of this experience? Very few, I suppose; and I only of a belief in a dream.

For the burden of life is made up of an infinite number of little things. The great sorrows, the terrible losses, the horrible defeats, the remorse for grievous misdoings: these are in the pack, but there is much more. It is piled up with the trifles that we suppose we have forgotten. There are few days on which we do not do something amiss. There are few days on which something is not done amiss to us. There are few days on which something amiss does not happen, without our fault or the fault of another. I think if you put this to the next man he would probably admit that this is so. "But," he would add, "I've no time to think of trifles. Thingumbob did give me a nasty look in the train; and I'm afraid I was a bit short with Whatd'yecall; and the chop I had for lunch was as tough as hell. But I'm not bothering much about little things like that. I've got more serious matters to think of." He is perfectly sensible and perfectly right; and if he did otherwise he would in all probability go mad. Nevertheless, this wise neglect of trifles does not abolish them or annihilate them. They are, very properly, dismissed from the working, practical memory. But they sink down, one by one, into their appointed depths; and every day the burden grows a little heavier though the greater part of the small odds and ends that stuff it are forgotten. But all the time the weight is on the shoulders; a constant part of life. The trifles are forgotten, and so they survive. We have striven with the great troubles: the deadly wrongs and sins, the grievous sorrows and losses have been in greater or less measure encountered and accounted for; their measure has been taken, their sting drawn. And the odds and ends are set on one side, neglected and, as we say, forgotten; and yet surviving: the burden of life.

It was all this heavy burden that in my dream was taken from me, and I was raised up in an instant from thick darkness to shining light; knowing only in that instant how heavy the burden had been. And so I say that the felicity which I enjoyed was negative; and I remember vaguely receiving some intimation that this was but the first degree of a new life, that there were brighter enlightenments and far more intense joys to succeed in their order.

And I awoke out of all this astounding fantasy of sleep into our common actual world, which I, like most other men, had found bearable enough, and often enjoyable. I awoke into misery, as one who has been for the second time put out of Paradise. I had lost the word; the golden world had fallen into dust. And as I have noted, I could not persuade myself that it had been a solitary experience. It was rather the culmination of a long series of such dreams; not the same dream, perhaps, but all of the same order.

2.

Mrs. Jolly, the landlady of 29, Layburn Street, wished with all her heart that she had never called in the police. There had been no more breakages of furniture—she knew nothing of the affair of Hillyer's torn manuscript—and the house had regained its ancient peace. She gave no credit to the police on that account. She felt sure that it would have been just the same if they had never come near the place, prying and poking about, and talking a lot of nonsense, as if they knew all about it. Couldn't find out who was breaking up the home; never said a word as to how she was going to get her money back that she spent on new things for Mr. Zerny's room, nor about that beautiful glass of Aunt Bessie's, that was worth pounds—and if you had the money to spend, you wouldn't get anything a half or a quarter as good in these times; they couldn't make them like that now. All that policeman fellow did was to come round and ask a lot of impudent questions about her daughter, making his insinuations that were nothing better than falsehoods and lies; you couldn't call them nothing but lies, and the poor girl standing by that very table all the time. "Fits, indeed! I'd give him fits, and see how he liked it"—so Mrs. Jolly ended her secret; the last words spoken aloud, as if they had been: *Per omnia sæcula sæculorem, Amen.*

The fact was, that the Inspector had been stirring again. He had made up his mind firmly that the girl was, somehow or other, at the bottom of the trouble at No. 29. He did not know exactly how she had done it. He brushed aside the alibi that Mrs. Jolly had set up for her daughter: "The sort of woman who would say anything if she thought her daughter was likely to get into trouble." He remembered the dictum of a master detective to the effect that it would be a good thing if all girls between fifteen and twenty could be shut up somewhere, as the police would then be saved a lot of trouble. But, anyhow, the officer summed up in his mind, it was not a matter for police action, and that was all about it. And then, a month or so later, odd rumours came to his ears, information of a cloudy and perplexing kind was received, and the Inspector found that Mrs. Jolly's house was again his business; or looked as if it might possibly become his business.

A sort of forewarning of the trouble that was to come was vouchsafed to the landlady—if she could have taken it in that light. Marketing in Exeter Street, Islington, she met a neighbour and acquaintance, Mrs. Teed of Baker Street. They were politic for a while over cabbages and kippers, and then Mrs. Teed remarked:

"I always say it's pleasant to have cheerful people about you. You and I, Mrs. Jolly, we know well enough that there's no fortune in lodgings, and I'm sure there's plenty of work. So, as I say, if the lodgers are cheerful and like a bit of fun it's all the better for all concerned. Though some would call it burning the candle at both ends. There's your Mr. Pytle now. Up for the best part of the night, and off first thing in the morning. However can he do it? But there you are: one

man's meat is another man's poison, as granny used to say. Well, I've
got to buy a rabbit before I get home, so good morning to you, Mrs.
Jolly. Rather warm, I find it."

Mrs. Jolly received this farago in a dumb and gaping silence; stupid
with perplexity, with searching for meaning where, for her, no meaning
was. She had not the remote notion of what Mrs. Teed was talking
about. "Burning the candle at both ends!" Who burned it? Once or
twice, certainly, Mr. Zerny and the other young man on the top floor
had been to a Palais de Danse, and had not got home till late; but it
had not happened three times in the last six months, and not at all for
six weeks or more; she knew that. They were steady young fellows,
both of them. Came in from their work, brought home sausages for
her to cook sometimes, sometimes a tin of salmon, went out again as a
rule after supper, and had a pint of beer in the private bar of the Quill,
and mostly called "good night" to her down the stairs, as they came in.
And not a sound or a song from them till seven o'clock the next
morning. Whatever could Mrs. Teed be thinking of? As for Mr. Pytle,
at his time of life; the woman must be off her head to think of such a
thing. Every Sunday morning of his life regular at the Barnsbury Chapel, Baptist, and taught Sunday school till that bad cough took him last
winter. And Mr. Hillyer as quiet as quiet, and his nose never out of his
books. Revolving such things, Mrs. Jolly walked home in an indignant
daze. Again and again she sought for a clue and found none, and could
only wonder many times what on earth the woman was thinking about.
And Inspector Martin was making his stealthy enquiries as to her and
as to all the lodgers under her roof.

For the fact was that a man lodging in a house on the other side of
the street, a little higher up, was employed Fleet Street way, in the mechanical department of a newspaper, and thus was accustomed to get
back from his work at about three o'clock in the morning. And he had
been much astonished at strange things to be seen in Layburn Street at
that hour, for three or four nights running. He declared that No. 29
was blazing and bursting with light, the brightest, whitest light he had
ever seen. "Were the blinds all up, then?" he was asked. He couldn't
say about that, he hadn't noticed whether they were up or down. It was
all ablaze, that was all he could say; he didn't think anything of blinds
or curtains either. And as to seeing anybody through the windows,

there again, the man was drawn blank. He didn't know; there might be people inside, or there might not be. He thought he was dazzled with the light and could see nothing else. And this story, variegated, embroidered, illuminated in all colours, went abroad in the quarter in many versions. Mrs. Teed, as we may conjecture, had heard that there were such doings at Mrs. Jolly's, a party every night, and up to any hours, and people going home with the milk. "A gay lot, and no mistake," was the opinion of those who held this view of the case. But there were darker opinions. There was talk of clubs, more specifically of night-clubs; of gambling clubs, of drinking clubs, of dance instructresses—here were sneers and bitter laughter—of whiskey served in coffee cups, and—worst of all—"champagne galore". Mrs. Jolly, on her marketing excursions and perambulations grew conscious that things were, somehow, different from usual. She found herself coming in upon muttered confidences, which ceased at her approach. She would hear: "There she is! That's Mrs. Jolly," as she passed on her way. The shopmen received her orders with a new attention. Some of her friends greeted her with curious smiles, others frowned moral judgments; and smiles and frowns alike enraged and perplexed her, and she felt inclined to ask herself, in the Hillyer manner, whether she were asleep or awake.

And then, a very summit of annoyance and affliction, Inspector Martin called, with bland enquiries. Of course it was the night-club stories of the strange doings at 29, Layburn Street that had attracted his interest. These, in the course of a week or ten days, had assumed a remarkable solidity and consistency. The folk-lore imagination of the neighbourhood had been at work; details at first vague and conjectural, were now clear cut, precise, undoubted. Gaming dropped out of the account; drink and worse evils took its place. The Inspector was doubtful at first.

"There must be a lot of cars and taxis drawing up before the house, then," he remarked, to a voluble informant. "I should have thought we would have heard about it from the man on the beat."

"Not a bit of it; they're too artful for that. They don't come near the street. One pulls up at the corner of Theobald's Road, and another one may go right into King's Cross Station, d'you see? There may be a couple stop in Acton Street, and another in Lloyd's Square, and one more by the Free Hospital in Gray's Inn Road, that's how they do it. And the toffs don't mind a bit of a walk, so long as they can keep it snug."

The Inspector had heard of such unworthy dodges before; he began to think there was something in it. But there were grave improbabilities. Mrs. Jolly had been the tenant of 29, Layburn Street for many years; there was nothing against her or the house or any of her lodgers. He had looked into them, when the police were called in over that smash-up on the top floor; and there was nothing against any of them. Still, he went round and began to put his bland suggestions. Whereupon, to his amazement, Mrs. Jolly turned on him in her fury, and told her story. Of mutterings and whisperings in the market-place, of Mrs. Teed and her madness, of nods and scowls and smiles of innuendo. It was a vague tale enough, but there was bewildered rage behind it, and the landlady vowed she would have them up in the police court, if they went on with their wicked lies and backbiting. And the officer went away to make further enquiries, and they led him into quicksands and swamps of fabrications and contradictions, but to no certain ground of fact whatever. For the newspaper mechanic had been sent by his firm to Newcastle-on-Tyne; and no one else had seen the bright and shining appearances of Layburn Street. And so all the superstructures, the castles and domes and palaces of loose talk, and vain invention that had been built upon the man's story fell apart, were disintegrated, and dispersed into shapeless mists.

3.

Not long ago, a couple of years ago, perhaps—said the eminent nerve specialist—a rather queer case came my way. He had had a fright, and had gone to the first brass plate that he saw in his neighbourhood. The G.P. sent him on to me; and he came round in a very shaky condition. His eyes were in an odd state. I should have suspected opium, but he said that he had never taken hypnotics of any kind, and I believed him. Well, he told me his story. He had been putting coals on the fire or doing something equally ordinary, and he suddenly found himself, as he put it, thinking gibberish; forming in his mind sentences entirely wanting in sense of any sort, absolute incoherence, as far as I could make out. He gibbered to himself, and wondered whether he were dreaming, or quoting out of a book which he didn't remember reading. And then it struck him that he wasn't exactly clear as to who he was or where he was, or what he was doing there. I gathered that he wasn't quite sure whether he was alive or dead for the next hour or so.

I got him to tell me about himself; where he lived, and what he did, and how he passed his time generally. Well in the first place, it seemed he had been living for twenty years or more in some unearthly part of London that nobody had ever heard of or ever goes to; somewhere in the north, off the Gray's Inn Road or the King's Cross Road. He lived in two rooms in a lodging house, said "thank you" twice a day to his landlady, and "good evening" to a fellow-lodger about once a week. Hardly any friends, never went out except now and then to the B.M. Reading Room, and was absorbed in the study of some branch of folk-lore, as well as I could gather. He was a clear case of Claustrophilia. He had got into the way of shutting himself up, living alone, never speaking to anybody, avoiding the society of his fellow-creatures, dreading the very thought of society of any kind. And the result was, he'd got himself into a devil of a state. In a very few weeks, I should think he would have lost his memory and his identity and have been found wandering about, wondering who he was and where he lived. Or he might have killed himself. There's a great deal of sound observation, you know, in that chapter in *Pickwick* about the old Inns of Court, and the people who shut themselves up in them.

I told this patient of mine that he must have a thorough change; get away to the sea, stay somewhere where he would meet people and be pretty well forced to talk to them, read the papers, take an interest in things in general, and so on and so on. I warned him that if he stuck in his old rut, he'd be seeing things before he was much older. As a matter of fact, I didn't think the trouble would take that form; but I thought I'd better give him a bit of a fright. Anyhow, I gathered later that he had followed the prescription, and gone to a seaside place; and as he said, had felt very much better, in fact, quite well.

"And I feel quite well now," he told me, the next time I saw him. "But . . ."

It was a very big "but" indeed. I had seen him for the first time at the end of May. He came to me again in the beginning of the October of the same year. Before listening to what he had to say—I stopped him as he was beginning his story—I made the usual examination, and put him through the ordinary tests. He was right in saying that he felt well; he was well. Everything as sound as it could be in a man in the 'fifties; and a good deal sounder, I should say, than the average man of that age. But the fellow was frightened out of his life. What at? He suffered from a delusion; and it was the most extraordinary delusion that I've ever come across. His delusion was that he thought he was going mad. "You know," he said, "that you warned me that if I didn't take care I should be seeing things." And then he began to tell me all about it; but before he got very far, I stopped him. I saw that there were some very singular and, indeed, unique features about the case—so far as my experience goes. It was getting late in the morning, and I had an important consultation in half an hour, and I wanted to go into the case thoroughly, without bothering about the time. As it happened, my wife was going to some show that evening with friends; so I asked him if he would mind coming round after dinner to talk the whole thing over in comfort. And I told him to cheer up; there was nothing to be frightened about. "Nothing to be frightened about?" he repeated. "Then you think it was really there?"

In the evening I heard the whole story from first to last. I settled him in a comfortable chair, and he lit his pipe, and sipped at his whiskey and soda as if he enjoyed it. That told me something. I knew that his trouble, whatever it was, had nothing to do with alcohol. An alcoholic patient doesn't sip whiskey and soda as if he enjoyed it. He takes it as people take very nasty medicine: a shudder and a clutch and down it goes, with an ugly quiver of the face to follow.

The tale began with his stay at a seaside town in Wales, where he had gone to carry out my advice. He said he had enjoyed it very much. He read the papers every day as I had told him, and got up some sort of an interest in what he found in them; he even went through the social gossip and the "Woman's Page", I gathered—which is more than I can do. He talked to the people at the hotel, and tried to play with their children on the sands; in fact, he carried out my directions and took his medicine like a Briton. He said he felt better every day; so well indeed, after two or three weeks of the treatment that he felt it would be safe to relax a little. You see, I don't think he would ever be a sociable man at heart. He struck me as the sort of fellow who might have a few intimate friends—though, I gathered, this had not been the case—but casual come and go acquaintance and casual chatter would always represent a bit of an effort to him. So he thought that as he had been such a good boy, he might allow himself a holiday between breakfast and lunch, and he took to strolling about the dunes in the morning by himself, and finally fixed on a sort of natural amphitheatre, a pleasant turfy, flowery sort of place, where he sat and smoked and felt pleased with himself and everything. "And that was the beginning of the trouble," he said. He reproached himself for his over-confidence, and for disobeying my orders, as he put it. He felt quite sure that if he had stuck to instructions and kept among other people all the time, he would have been quite all right. He soon found, as he declared, the bad results of getting back even for two or three hours a day to his solitary habits. He began to have delusions. He was convinced, he said, that the people at his hotel were no longer friendly. He was sure they were talking about him among themselves. They looked at him in a very odd way. Parties broke up when he came near them. They spied on him when he was sitting in his favourite hollow in the dunes. One of them asked him why he didn't bring his friend to the hotel. At last, nobody would speak to him, and the manager asked him to leave. The man said the other guests accused him of consorting with a suspected murderer. My patient left the hotel and took lodgings in the town. And then, one day when he was at his old place, the green round, a whole gang rushed him and held him, while they looked for somebody who wasn't there, who, they were quite sure, had been there a moment before.

He went back to town after that, feeling naturally, a good deal upset. He assured me that he was absolutely convinced at the time that everything had happened just as he had told it to me.

"Once or twice," he said, "I had a horrible qualm. I remembered what you had told me about the state of my nerves, and your hint that things might get very much worse if I didn't take care of myself. I asked myself: 'Are you quite certain that all that really happened?' But I was quite certain; so certain that I was thoroughly reassured. I took it that for some reason or other, I didn't in the least know what, these people at the hotel had taken a dislike to me, and that the whole thing was a very ill-natured practical joke to get me out of the place. I tried to remember what I could have done to offend them. Then I recollected that I had said something that had annoyed an old general very much indeed. I hadn't the smallest intention of being offensive; in fact, I was trying to make myself agreeable to his daughter, but I saw afterwards that I had put my foot into it very badly. The general got into a foaming rage, and of course I apologised most humbly, and called myself the worst names I could think of. I thought I was forgiven, but when things turned out as they did, and I went back to town, I thought it all over, and came to the conclusion that the old man was still furious and had taken it out of me in his own way. And, in a way, that set my mind at ease."

"And now," I said to him, "you think the whole business was a delusion?"

"I am quite sure of that, I am sorry to say," he replied. And then he went on with his tale. It was certainly an odd one. The man was struggling you know, all the time against falling back into his foolish way of living, before I had warned him of what that sort of thing led to. He took a certain amount of exercise, I gathered; walked about London, went on 'bus rides, did no work in the morning. And he was almost morbidly over-anxious to avoid the mere suspicion of morbidity of any kind. When he found himself indulging in fancies that were a little off the main track of life, he pulled himself together and read the daily paper for all he was worth. That was all very well; but I can't help thinking that the subject in which he was interested, the psychology of certain folk-lore legends, so far as I could gather, was not exactly the best direction for his thoughts. I told him that the Queen of Fairyland—she seemed the principal bee in his bonnet—was rather of pathological than psychological interest; and I may say, by the way, that in my opinion, legends of this kind are simply confused and fanciful reports of cases of hyperæsthesia. Still, a man may have a crazy hobby and be quite sound apart from it; and that was the way this patient impressed me. But queer things happened to him. He had not been back in London long, when his morning walk took him to some God-forsaken little square somewhere near his rooms, and he sat down on one of the benches to smoke and meditate. There were two old men on another bench, and he noticed presently that one of them was staring at him in a very queer sort of way—as if he saw something that frightened him, as my patient put it. He turned away and looked at the houses of the square, and admired the gardens in front of him; but when he glanced towards the bench opposite, there was the old fellow glaring in terror: "Not exactly at me, but as though he saw something on the bench beside me. He looked so frightened that he frightened me. The other old chap was puffing at his pipe and seemed as cheerful as possible; but I got up and went away, feeling a little disturbed and uneasy. Then it struck me that one old man was, perhaps, a little queer in the head, and that the other was a friend who took him out and looked after him; and I thought no more of it."

Then he went on to tell me about things being smashed up in the house where he lodged. A big mirror over the fireplace in his sitting-room, some chairs and crockery on the floor above him, a note-book that he had left on his desk for two or three minutes, torn to pieces. And then a long list of breakages and smashes that had happened when he was about, in all sorts of places: in a public-house, in an office, in the street. I told him that there was nothing in all that beyond coincidence. London was a big place; hoardings would blow down, and things get broken and ladders give way—I am giving some of his misadventures. He told me that that was exactly the way he talked to himself; he wouldn't admit that there was anything queer, anything to be uneasy about. He stuck out against it, as he said, and accounted for everything on commonsense lines. He said he had made up a story about someone who had quarrelled with his landlady to explain her broken furniture and his torn notebook.

"Well," I said, "that sounds a likely story enough, so far as I can see. I don't make out the bearing of all this upon your case. The only advice I can give you is to change your rooms. I'm told there's very snug lying in Kensington."

He grinned at the allusion; but then it all came out. He had hinted at something of the kind at the beginning of his story. He was convinced that there was not a word of truth in it from beginning to end. He was sure that he was suffering from delusions; that nothing had happened as he had told it, that all that trouble at the seaside place was imaginary, and that nothing had been smashed, broken, or damaged in any way; either in his rooms or out of them. I reminded him of the torn note-book.

"You have evidence of that at least," I pointed out. "You told me you fitted the torn scraps together and pasted them into a new book." But he had his answer. No doubt, he had torn the book to pieces himself, and then had forgotten all about it.

I was beginning to get extremely interested in the man. There was something exceptional about him. It is not usual for paranoiacs to insist on their insanity. As a rule, they are quite certain that their wildest delusions are hard facts. You may have a man worth a hundred thousand pounds who is quite certain that he will be in the workhouse in a week. You shew him his bank-book with the hard figures. It's no good. Either the bank is in the plot or else there are huge debts which nobody knows about. The man is dead sure that he is a beggar; and that the figures in the bank-book are part of a conspiracy. And here was this patient insisting that a mass of experiences which he had taken for facts at the time were the creations of his diseased brain. I determined to settle the matter one way or the other by a very simple test. I got dates, places, and addresses out of him, and noted them down. "Now," I said, "I believe that your case is a very hopeful one. I am almost sure that it will yield to treatment. Go down to Brighton for a fortnight, and come and see me on October 17th, in the evening."

I proceeded to apply the test I had thought of. As it happened I knew the seaside place he had stayed at in the early summer, and I had stayed at the same hotel. I wrote to the manager and put the case to him just as I had heard it from the patient. I asked him to let me know, confidentially, whether anything of the kind had taken place, whether the circumstances were as represented. He wrote to me confirming the patient's story in every particular, so far as the facts came under his knowledge. He said that some of the people staying in his hotel declared that they had seen my patient in a certain spot on the Burrows, in company with a horrible-looking man, who, they were quite sure, was the man wanted by the police for the Ty Captain murder. He added, that he understood from some talk in his lounge that after my friend had left the hotel there had been some kind of scuffle on the Burrows, and he hoped that nothing would get into the papers.

That was one point. Then I took up the business of the breakages at his lodgings. There again the patient's story was absolutely confirmed; even to the torn note-book. The landlady's daughter remembered seeing the carpet all littered with bits of paper with writing on them one afternoon, when she took up the gentleman's tea-things. Then, he had told me that when he called on his solicitor, a library ladder with a clerk on it came to grief in the next room. It was perfectly true. I saw the clerk, who was still limping a bit, and I saw the lawyer. That was enough for me. A most extraordinary case; the absolute reverse of the conditions we are usually called on to deal with. Many mental cases think they are persecuted when they aren't; this man had been persecuted in a sort of a way, and was quite sure that his persecution was a delusion; in other words, that he was mad. He was as sane as I am. And, yet, was he? I began to wonder. We say that a man who sees a cow in the garden which isn't there is mad. What about the man who sees a cow in the garden which is there, and says it isn't; that it's the creation of his morbid brain? Theoretically, that's a nice point; but such cases are so rare that I don't think it has ever come up for judgment. Anyhow, my business was practical, and I thought I should be able to untie the knots into which the man had wound himself.

He kept his appointment. I told him what I had done. I put the facts before him, fair and square. I shewed him that in every instance in which I had tested his statements he had been proved veridical and accurate in the smallest particular. Of course I suppressed that odd query that had risen in my mind. I said:

"Let's take the principal case. You said you were cold-shouldered by those people at the hotel. Well; it's quite true. The whole hotel staff noticed it. You say the manager asked you to leave. He did. Here's his letter. You say you were attacked as you were sitting in your favourite place in the dunes—or Burrows, as they seem to call them. Look at the bottom of the page: 'some sort of a scuffle on the Burrows'. And now what have you got to say for yourself?"

I expected him to look intensely relieved. He didn't. He looked puzzled. He didn't speak for some time. He looked down at the carpet and seemed to be weighing something in his mind; going over it, and again going over it, in a maze of perplexity. At last he spoke. He looked at me. There was terror in his face.

"If you are right," he said, and the words were blurred together as he uttered them, "if you are right: who is that horrible child that follows me wherever I go?"

And the story came out. About three weeks or a month before his second visit to me, he became vaguely conscious, as he said, that he was watched. He couldn't be more exact. He felt that there was an eye on him; there was somebody just outside his line of vision. He felt sure that if he turned his head sharply, he would see the watcher, as he called him. And then again, he said to himself: "This is a mere fancy; liver trouble, or, perhaps, eye trouble. Of course there is nobody there." He did turn round at last, and there was nobody there. Still, the sense of being watched persisted; not throughout the whole day, but at intervals. He would be on one of his walks and suddenly have a very strong feeling that someone was "in attendance", walking on the other side of the street, a little to the rear, and keeping an intent eye on him all the time. Or he might be in his room, sitting at his desk, writing or reading; and he would get the same notion that he was being observed, and feel obliged to look under the sofa, or move the big arm-chair, to make sure that the room was empty, except for himself. And in five minutes the sensation would return; he was sure that "there was some-body there". On one occasion, he crept across the room on tiptoe, flung open the door with a crash, and rushed out—and, naturally, didn't find anyone on the landing. Then, with the liver notion in his head, he dosed himself with medicine; but that was no good. There was still that recurring sense of the attendant watcher, not seen, but felt to be present; sometimes only for a moment. One day, he said, he had taken out his latch-key and was just putting it into the lock of the front door, when the sudden conviction rushed on him that someone was standing immediately behind him. He spun round in an instant. The usual result: no one there. Another time, he had gone into the country, and was strolling along a Hertfordshire byeway, when it struck him that he was being followed by his persecutor, who crept along all the while on the other side of the hedge. He was sure that he would get the fellow this time. He jumped over the first stile he came to, and looked all along the straight hedge. And then pulled himself to-gether, asked himself why he had been such a fool. Of course, there was nobody on the other side of the hedge; there never had been. He was out of sorts. In a woman his condition would be called hysterical; he must exercise it out of him. So he walked ten miles at four miles an hour, got home and slept like a log—and woke up with a start at four in the morning and searched the wardrobe.

This state of things went on for about ten days. The man was getting distressed and a little shaky, but he held stoutly to his opinion that
the trouble was due to something wrong physically. Then one day
when he was wandering about the rather dreary part he lives in, he felt,
as he told me, that the whole thing was lifted from him, as if a heavy
pack had been taken off his back. He felt as if he must do something
festive; have a big drink or go to the British Museum and find somebody to talk to. And as he was hesitating, he saw a very ugly little boy
standing by a lamp-post on the other side of the road, and grinning at
him: "Something twisted and deformed about the creature; he had the
old face of a dwarf." He went on his way, to a pub or the Reading
Room, I don't know which. As he was walking up the steep street
where he lives on his way home, he saw the dwarfish child again. He
was standing in the middle of the road this time, with that evil grin still
on his face. My patient hated the sight of him, supposed he lived
somewhere in the neighbourhood, and thought no more about it. The
next day, he was wandering about Kew Gardens, and as he was going
along the rhododendron walk, he heard a rustle; and there was the imp
looking at him from a rhododendron bush. He didn't understand it at
all. He was on his way back on the top of a 'bus and looking about him
for an old inn he remembered years ago on the London side of Turnham Green. There was the little horror glaring at him from an open
window in the roof of one of the houses. For a moment he thought of
stopping the 'bus and going to the house—the ground floor was a grocer's shop—and making enquiries, under the pretence of warning the
people that their little boy was in a dangerous position at the open
window above. But then what he called a cold thrill at his heart warned
him to do nothing of the kind. He began to fear the possible solution
of the puzzle. For a week after that there was no trouble. Then one
morning, as he woke up, he saw that hideous little shape by his door. It
appeared to open the door. It went out and the door was closed. He
screamed in his terror, and the landlady ran up the stairs to his room.
He asked her, as soon as he could speak plainly, who that horrible
child was, and what it was doing in his room. He noticed the look of
shock and alarm on the woman's face. She mumbled something about
her sister's child, how they were afraid he wasn't quite so strong in the
head as he might be, and promised to keep the child downstairs. He

didn't believe a word of this; and not long after he broke down completely, and became quite sure that this hateful visitant was but one of the delusions from which he had suffered all the summer. And then he came to me.

I heard him to the end of his story. I was puzzled. It really looked as if this last business was a delusion. I asked him if he had been troubled at Brighton. He said he thought there had been something on the platform when he got out of the train on his arrival; otherwise he had been left in peace.

"But," he said, "as I was ringing your bell to-night, I looked round, and it walked away towards Cavendish Square."

The man was miserably depressed. I did what I could to cheer him a little. I said it was a very singular case—that was true enough. I told him that I was certain he could be cured. There was more hope than certainty about that pronouncement; but I pointed out that he had been almost if not quite free from the mischief at Brighton, and that a long sea voyage would most likely cure him for good and all. I made an appointment for him to see me in a week's time. As soon as he was gone, I wrote to his landlady. I didn't say too much. I told her that her lodger, my patient, was suffering from nervous depression, that I thought of ordering him a sea voyage, and I asked her if she could manage to keep her little nephew as much out of his way as possible for the next week or so. She answered me that the only nephew she had was a man of thirty who was a carpenter at Devizes; that she had made up the tale to try to make the gentleman more easy in his mind, but she was afraid he was in a bad way, and she was frightened about him. The patient did not keep his appointment, and I went round to his place that evening. He had walked out of the house the day before, carrying a brown paper parcel, not like luggage, more like a parcel for the post. He had left a note for the landlady on his table. There was a month's money instead of notice in it. A well-known firm would call for his books and store them, and the landlady could have his clothes. He said he was going abroad for his health.

I have seen nothing more of him. But I have heard, indirectly, that he is living somewhere in the near east; and I understand that he is quite well. An odd case, as I said.

EPILOGUE

Dr. William Brown, who is, I believe, reader in Psychology, at the University of Oxford, saw some very extraordinary things one evening at the National Laboratory for Psychical Research. The date was sometime in the spring of this year, 1932; and the occasion was a "sitting" to test the powers of the young Austrian, Rudi Schneider. Dr. Brown was immensely impressed at the time. If I remember rightly, he said he had seen things done of which he could find no explanation on ordinary physical lines. I have forgotten the exact nature of the phenomena, but, let us say, the law of gravity was flagrantly broken. Solid objects soared and floated instead of falling; all possibility of trickery or conjuring apparatus being excluded, in the judgment of the expert scientific observers, of whom Dr. Brown was one. Dr. Brown wrote two letters to *The Times* on the subject; and the second letter does not so much qualify the first, as make the necessary reservation of the immensity of our ignorance; a reservation which applies to all our experiences and all our knowledge. "I am still unable," Dr. Brown wrote, in this second letter, "to dispute the genuineness of the phenomena that I witnessed. On the other hand, the extensive *lacunæ* in my knowledge of this wider circle of facts prevents me from going sponsor for the phenomena, in spite of their immediate impressiveness." And that means, I take it, that the scientific mind is loath to accept isolated supernormal phenomena which have no theory behind them, no *logos* to rationalise them, no scheme in which they can be fitted. The man of science sees a phenomenon, which he judges to be a contravention of the laws of nature, as these laws are known to him. He cannot deny, he cannot explain away what he has seen; and yet he cannot unreservedly accept it, because of the *lacunæ*, the gaps in his knowledge. A mass of lead, ten pounds in weight, let us say, has floated gently up to the ceiling, hovered there, and slowly fluttered down again. Our scientific witness has seen it happen, and yet he will not accept it as an undoubted fact; because nobody can furnish him with an acceptable and reasoned theory explaining how lumps of lead, under certain conditions, will behave exactly in this way.

Such, to the scientific observer, was the case of Rudi Schneider; such, also, is the case of Lawrence Hillyer. The *lacunæ*, the gaps in the history are both wide and deep. And they are of two kinds; the gaps in any theory which can be constructed of what actually happened to Hillyer; and then the *lacunæ* in the actual story, gathered in odd pieces from here and from there, and put together doubtfully, conjecturally; without any very strong conviction, in some instances at any rate, that this jig goes into that saw.

A good deal of the material available is derived from Hillyer's note-books. His landlady, anxious to tell all that there was to be told, mentioned the brown paper parcel which he was seen carrying away with him. This contained the note-books in question; and I was the consignee. I had known Hillyer as most of his friends knew him, slightly, in the on-and-off fashion, for a good many years. He enclosed a letter to the effect that he thought some of his notes were in my way and might interest me. If not, I was to destroy them; he had no further use for them. He ended: "I have managed to get myself into a very extraordinary state, which I think is dangerous. I am going abroad, far abroad, to see if I can get free. I don't think of coming back to England, or of renewing any of my old interests."

I heard from him in the course of last summer. He has settled in Aleppo, where he has some interest in the sponge trade, and according to his own story, is doing very fairly well. He has never attempted to give me any account of what happened to him in the year 1929; chiefly, I think, because he doesn't know what did happen to him. Hence the fragments, hence the gaps, hence the rough, unfinished ends in the tale. Sometimes there has been frank reconstruction, in the manner of our modern historians. For example, there is that scene in the north London square, in which Hillyer and two old men were oddly engaged. There are foundations; something of the kind must have happened. The authorities are, partly Hillyer's statement to the specialist, and partly a puzzling and confused argument between the two old codgers, overheard fortuitously in a private bar somewhere deep in Barnsbury. Then there are uncertainties. There is that business of Hampole and his book, *A London Walk*, which melts into the story of Hillyer's mysterious visitor—or of a very bad dream. And the bright light which a man—and only one man, apparently—saw pouring from the house where Hillyer lodged, in the dead of night. That is a loose end, and I must leave it loose.

But there can be no doubt that Hillyer was subjected to a series of very horrible tricks, of varying orders. And here we come to the *lacunæ* of theory. At one time, as in the Green Round of the sandhills, and in the square by the Caledonian Road, his attendant was invisible to himself, but visible to others, or rather, to some others. Then, in the last stages, before his flight, the dwarfish child of his terror was seen by no eye but his own; so far as we know, at least. At other times, the power that troubled him converted him into an involuntary poltergeist: destruction was about all his ways. Here, however, the proceedings followed the established order, and we may even grasp at least the tail of a theory. For it is certain that the poltergeist—when it is not a naughty child, playing mischievous tricks—is always involuntary and unconscious of its own work. It has no more volition, control, or direction of the energy which it transmits than has the wire of the electric current which passes along it.

But as to the origin of the experiences to which Lawrence Hillyer was subjected: some light, I think, is thrown on the problem by the strange adventure of Mr. Smith of Wimbledon, as I have called him; the gentleman who, paying a chance visit to his favourite seaside town found to his horror and indignation the Green Round, the peaceful retreat on the sand-dunes, turned into a sort of 'Fun City', vile with the dissonant jargon of the jazz band struggling against the shriek and clangour of roundabouts, jigging with dancers of uncouth measures, a centre of vulgar and raucous merriment. The newspaper discussion which his letter set going went off very quickly into all sorts of foolishness and irrelevance; and nobody seemed to notice the very vital point, that the Town Clerk of the Welsh watering-place in question wrote a formal and full denial of Mr. Smith's story. The Town Clerk said that there was no jazz band on the dunes or anywhere near them. He denied the band, the roundabouts, the Palais de Danse, the hard tennis courts, and all the riot of sound and sight that Smith described. He admitted a fair held by ancient charter in a field on the other side of the town; and he rather hinted at some indiscretion on the part of Mr. Smith, which had led that gentleman to mistake his right hand for his left. But the storm centre of the discussion had by this time deserted the dunes of Porth and the Green Round, and was occupied safely with odd obscenities in brick-sculpture and the new theatre at Stratford-on-

Avon. Mr. Smith, it is true, was still interested in his own experience and went down to Wales in indignation only to return to Wimbledon in confusion. He had both seen and heard, and now all had vanished without a trace, as if it had been Aladdin's palace in the Eastern Tale. We do not know what he made of it; but it is probable that his state of mind was not very different from that of Dr. William Brown after the "sitting" with Rudi Schneider; though Mr. Smith would not be able to express himself with the clarity of the man of science.

But here, in the Green Round by the shore of Porth, was evidently the source of all the strange trouble that befell Hillyer. Again, we must take refuge in those *lacunæ,* and profess our entire ignorance both of the nature and of the laws of the power that for a time at least had its centre in this place. We cannot pretend to determine, for instance, why one man was subject to the influence, while another was immune. Smith, on the face of it, was not a likely man to be affected. But it is quite possible that he had recovered from a bad attack of influenza a week or two before his visit; and his state of health may have laid him open to the attack of another enemy. The case of Hillyer is easier. He had been on the verge of a nervous breakdown in London immediately before his stay at Porth. No doubt he was benefited, as he says, by the sea air, the change of scene and the very different habit of life that he adopted for a time. Still, he was convalescent, not absolutely well. The walls of the fortress had been repaired and strengthened; but there seems reason to suppose that they were in no state to stand a siege. And, in fact, the enemy poured through the breach in a somewhat terrible manner. And in one respect at all events, Hillyer's affair stands alone, at least, that is my impression. There are, no doubt, many cases of a particular locality harbouring forces unbenignant to man, and so constituting what is commonly called a "haunted" house or a "haunted" wood; but at the moment I cannot recall any instance of these obscure and nameless energies following a man home, as it were, and harassing him at a distance from the place of their awful habitation. There is, for example, the book called *An Adventure,* the extraordinary story of what happened to Miss Ann Moberly and Miss Eleanor F. Jourdain at Versailles. For them, the clock was put back; time was no more. They were no longer in the twentieth century. They were rapt back into the eighteenth. They became witnesses of events that happened at Versailles, so far as time is concerned, on a particular day in the course of the French Revolution; and the trees, the lawns, the bridges were as they were in the Versailles of 1789. And such is the clear veracity of the record of these ladies' experiences, that I have never known any person who has read it be anything but perfectly convinced that every word is true. But let this be noted: once the ladies were without the walls of Versailles, the powers that were within ceased to operate or to manifest. Those that had seen the evidence of their presence, saw it no more when once the gates were passed. And, so far as I am informed, the like rule obtained in the following experience, which appeared in *Light*—issue of May 23rd, 1931—which is quoted here, *in extenso,* by the kind permission of my friend, Mr. David Gow, Advisory Editor of *Light.* It is entitled "A Mountain Adventure". "J. C. P.", the author, is stated to be a woman in a responsible and dignified position. Her story, like the story of the ladies of Versailles, gives me the impression of absolute and scrupulous veracity.

"About the twentieth of July, 1929, while climbing the mountain, Nephin, in the west of Ireland above Lough Conn, we had the following curious experience.

"The six, who climbed the mountain on one of the clearest of July days, consisted of three women and three men; one of the party—a girl—had an injured knee, and so did not go further than the place at which we stopped for lunch.

"The ascent was started about eleven o'clock. After climbing for an hour, through very heavy heather, we stopped beside a burn for lunch. After lunch we continued up the mountain, the girl with the injured knee going back to the cottage at which we had left the car, to wait for our return. We reached the top of the mountain about a quarter to three, and sat for a while looking at the surrounding country.

"We started down at about three, or a little after, in groups and singly, my husband by himself, F. H., James and myself together, and the other man quite a bit ahead of us. Suddenly F. H. turned away, and vanished over the shoulder of the mountain. Little was said, for she often took her own way down the various mountains we climbed during the summer. James and I continued our way for a while, then turned to each other and said: 'Something has happened to F. H.!' We felt so sure of this that we called to the other two men, who returned.

We agreed that they should go back to the mountain to where she was last seen, and search for her, while I should continue down and meet them at the cottage.

"Now this I did not know till afterwards, but F. H. does not know, cannot possibly imagine, what happened to her. She can only say that it was as though she had lapsed into complete unconsciousness, and all the while thought she was walking beside us. She was in reality walking straight away from us. She does not know what it was that 'took' her suddenly; she said it was as though there were *no Time* for a moment, and some strange force were pulling her away. Then she realised that we were not there, and heard the crying of voices. She went in the direction of the sound, thinking she would find some one; on crossing a ravine the voices were still audible, and she heard some one blowing a horn, but no one was in sight. Then she thought she saw a small person beyond and below her, possibly a child; she went down towards it but on crossing another ravine, found no one, though the voices still continued. After this she realised she was lost, and headed for the white roadway below her, and walked about eight miles to a police-barracks, where we later found her.

"Now, when I left the men I went down the mountain. When I was half-way down I decided to look for F. H. on my lower level. I walked along, falling twice up to my waist into caves that were hidden beneath the heather. Presently I sat down and had no sooner done that than I heard crying behind me—a funny kind of crying, like a child that was lost—very distinctly. Looking around I saw, a long distance above me, some one I took to be James, waving. I waved back, got up, crossed a couple of hillocks, and looked for James again. No one was there. I sat down again, and was admiring the view when, directly behind me, some one laughed. Looking around I saw no one for a moment; then above me in almost the same place, I thought I saw James again.

"Getting up once more, I went straight up the mountain in his direction. In crossing a small burn I lost sight of him, and when I came out of the stream-bed I found no one. After this I went down the mountain to the cottage, expecting to find the girl with the injured knee there, but the cottage people told me she had not been there all the afternoon. Presently she came in, very angry, saying that early in the afternoon I had come down the mountain and waved to her, but had not waited for her to come up. (She had not gone up very far as she stumbled into a bog, and found the walking too hard.) Obviously I had not done any such thing.

"By 7.30 P.M. the men came back, exhausted, and without F. H. James had a curious story. Twice he had seen, out of the tail of his eye, a club coming down on him. So strong had been the impression that he had jumped considerable distances down the mountain on each occasion. We were very worried by this time about F. H.'s disappearance. I asked the man of the cottage what there was to fall into on the mountain.

"'Quarries?' I suggested.

"'Nothing,' he said.

"'Children on the mountain?' I asked.

"'No, they're in school,' he said.

"'What about the Little People?'

"He became very severe, and turned to go out, saying:

"'We do not talk about that.'

"We now took the car to search along the roads at the foot of the mountain, and so came upon F. H. at the police station."

Here again, the adventure ended at the foot of the mountain. The party were not pursued to their homes, as was Lawrence Hillyer. There are, indeed, likenesses between the two cases; notably, in the triviality of the annoyances inflicted. It is trivial and childish to make a woman lose her way on a mountain, to afflict a man with the sense that somebody is flinging clubs after him. It is trivial and childish to cause a man to be harried and seized by an angry and unreasoning officer and his stupid friends. It is even more trivial and childish to strew his track with broken chairs and shattered mirrors. But whatever this other side of things may be in itself, I have often noticed that its manifestations on this side are apt to be trifling and meaningless. The apparition recorded by the Psychical Research Society are mostly insignificant, without purpose: a miller sees the ghost of a farmer, a mere casual acquaintance; and nothing happens. One of the most remarkable instances of the predictive faculty, combined with "clear sight" is contained. in Mr. Theodore Besterman's book on Crystal gazing. A lady looking in the crystal at a house near Salisbury one morning saw Lady

Barnby (wife of "For all the Saints" Barnby) washing her hands in a bedroom with an open door, in a Folkestone Hotel, about three and a half hours afterwards. This was verified in an extraordinary manner afterwards by Sir Joseph Barnby, who was present at the crystal gazing. I have no doubt that the story is veridical; but the prophetic gift has been employed on more tremendous issues. But as to what is, or should be, the main question: what, who are the powers or forces that were manifested on Mount Nephin and in the Green Round? The Little People, the Fairies?

I believe there is no answer. We had better say, with the man of the cottage: "We do not talk about that."

The Compliments of the Season

You know," said Tyndall to his quiet friend Andrews, "that I have long felt that there is only one citadel to be captured. If we can take that, we've won, and rationalism will be the only possible attitude for sane men to adopt."

"That sounds excellent," said Andrews, "but I don't quite follow you. One citadel? Is there anything that depends on one citadel? You mean, I suppose, one particular centre of argument?"

"If you like to put it like that. But I'll shew you what I mean. You know the enemy have taken refuge in the arts, the aesthetic impulses, and their results. You can corner them, you can say, 'Here's this religion of yours, with its doctrines and its dogmas, its emotions and its prayers, its rites and its ceremonies and the rest of it. Very good; but can you give any rational account of it? Can you offer any intelligible reason for going to Mass or meeting or wherever you do go? As the Balliol don said to the undergraduate: can you *think* it?"

"I think that's very good, very strongly put indeed, as far as it goes," said Andrews thoughtfully. "After all, you know, 'the enemy', as you call them, are always insisting—to use a favourite phrase of theirs—that every good gift is from above. And, I take it, that they can't deny that the intellect is a good gift: no, they could scarcely do that. They couldn't have the face to say that the perfect man is a being who has completely sterilised and stifled all his intellectual faculties. So, if they have to confess that this religious business of theirs can't stand the examination of the intellect, and mustn't be asked to give a rational account of itself; well, really, I should have thought you had them already."

"We used to think so. But, then, they've lugged in the arts. They say frankly that they can't give a logical and rational intelligible account of their spiritual universe; and, by the way, it's rather convenient for us that they don't turn round and ask us to give a rational account of our physical universe. But they don't do that. They say: 'All right; if you like, we don't know why we go to Mass, and we can't put that revival feeling into a series of logical propositions. But can *you* explain why you go to concerts, and why you become hysterical, or almost hysterical, over this soprano and that violinist? You have written libraries of books and spent millions of money over what is nothing more nor less than a lot of noises. Men have passed their lives in daubing canvasses with coloured earths, and other men have spent their fortunes in buying these canvasses. How much money has been poured out in the last hundred years in buying Keats's poems? How many hours have been spent in reading them? Where's the intellectual justification for all this? And, anyhow, what does *faery lands forlorn* mean? Where are they? You see the argument: 'If you do things which you can't explain logically; why shouldn't we?' That is, they ask us to accept the existence of super-rational faculties and emotions peculiar to man. And that won't do."

Andrews looked thoughtful.

"I see your point; as you say, it won't do. We should have them praying all over the place, as the verger at the Abbey said. I see; that's what you meant by 'the citadel'. Well?"

"I've taken it," said Tyndall, and stuffed his pipe, and lit it, and blew a triumphant blast. "It's ours. They're done."

"You know," Andrews murmured in his quiet way, "in spite of what has been said in favour of vintage wines, and Brillat Savarin and Alpine climbing, and bridge and all sorts of things; there are very few pleasures to beat a clean demonstration. That Eureka feeling."

"I agree with you. Well, I found out the right line to take with these people in an odd sort of way. Some one sent me that Frenchman's book about birds; the second book he's written about birds. An English translation appeared in the autumn.

"It's not my subject; but I read it with a good deal of interest: plenty of keen observation; a bit flowery and fanciful for my taste, but still, an intelligent book. There was one thing that caught my attention particularly: the Frenchman described certain birds, two or three sorts, I believe, that have the curious habit of sticking bright flowers and feathers into their nests; nobody knows why. Queer, isn't it? As the author points out, the bird that sticks bright objects into its nest makes it conspicuous, and most birds do their best in the opposite direction.

He didn't attempt to explain the difficulty. It's a minor difficulty, no doubt, and after all we can't expect to understand everything."

Andrews looked up at this. His expression was somewhat whimsical.

Tyndall went on:

"I just thought of it as a queer exception to the rule, and let it drop. About a fortnight ago, I went down to stay with some friends in Pembrokeshire, the Voyles of Penyrhaul. They've got a beautiful place in a sheltered cove, facing due south: much better climate than the Riviera, if people would only believe it. They hadn't been touched by the frost there; there were roses and snapdragons and chrysanthemums and hollyhocks still lingering, and the spring flowers, violets and primroses and primulas, getting into blossom. In the greenhouse they had some splendid early lilies; really noble specimens. One day Mrs. Voyle was shaking her head over them. 'We usually keep the door locked,' she said, 'but Friday was so fine that we left it open in the middle of the day, and when I came to lock up, two of the finest lilies had gone—snapped off.' She shewed me the stems. 'Those little Morgans, I am afraid. Bad boys!'

"It really is a wonderful climate. What sort of weather did you have in town last Monday?"

"Old-fashioned fog; black frost."

"Do you know, at Penyrhaul the sun was absolutely hot in the morning: the sky deep blue. I thought I would stroll down to the beach and sit by the sea; the family had all gone out somewhere. As I was walking through the little brake at the bottom of the garden, I heard the most extraordinary twittering and whistling of birds; and I went very softly, thinking I should see a very odd sight. I have read about small birds mobbing an enemy, an owl or a weasel. I came to a turn of the path, and peeped round the corner. I could scarcely believe my eyes."

"What was happening?"

"There is a prehistoric stone, a menhir, beside the path. The flat limestone was nearly covered with green moss, and as I looked, about half a dozen small birds came flying with moss in their beaks, and filled up a bare patch. They had made—I saw it, mind you, and I saw sparrows putting the last touches to it—a perfect little figure, like a doll, lying in a cradle of moss; made out of twigs of evergreens, and bits of straw, and reeds, and flowers. And on each side of this doll, they had stuck those two lilies from Mrs. Voyle's greenhouse. They looked like candles. And hundreds of birds fluttering and flying in a circle above it, and singing on the boughs of the brake.

"There was my Eureka! There was the origin of the aesthetic faculty. Purely animal, purely material. The French naturalist had seen a mere hint; I had observed the whole process. No doubt a simple seasonal impulse, with definite biological ends."

"A seasonal impulse," said Andrews thoughtfully. "Yes. No doubt. Last Monday you said, didn't you?"

"Last Monday."

"That was Christmas Day."

N

I

They were talking about old days and old ways and all the changes that have come on London in the last weary years; a little party of three of them, gathered for a rare meeting in Perrott's rooms.

One man, the youngest of the three, a lad of fifty-five or so, had begun to say:

"I know every inch of that neighbourhood, and I tell you there's no such place."

His name was Harliss; and he was supposed to have something to do with chemicals and carboys and crystals.

They had been recalling many London vicissitudes, these three; and it must be noted that the boy of the party, Harliss, could remember very well the Strand as it used to be, before they spoilt it all. Indeed, if he could not have gone as far back as the years of those doings, it is doubtful whether Perrott would have let him into the meeting in Mitre Place, an alley which was an entrance of the inn by day, but was blind after nine o'clock at night, when the iron gates were shut, and the pavement grew silent. The rooms were on the second floor, and from the front windows could be seen the elms in the inn garden, where the rooks used to build before the war. Within, the large, low room was softly, deeply carpeted from wall to wall; the winter night, with a bitter dry wind rising, and moaning even in the heart of London, was shut out by thick crimson curtains, and the three men sat about a blazing fire in an old fireplace, a fireplace that stood high from the hearth, with hobs on each side of it, and a big kettle beginning to murmur on one of them. The armchairs on which the three sat were of the sort that Mr. Pickwick sits on for ever in his frontispiece.

The round table of dark mahogany stood on one leg, very deeply and profusely carved, and Perrott said it was a George IV table, though the third friend, Arnold, held that William IV, or even very early Victoria, would have been nearer the mark. On the dark red wall-paper there were eighteenth-century engravings of Durham Cathedral and Peterborough Cathedral, which shewed that, in spite of Horace Walpole and his friend Mr. Gray, the eighteenth century couldn't draw a Gothic building when its towers and traceries were before its eyes: "because they couldn't see it", Arnold had insisted, late one night, when the gliding signs were far on in their course, and the punch in the jar had begun to thicken a little on its spices. There were other engravings of a later date about the walls, things of the thirties and forties by forgotten artists, known well enough in their day; landscapes of the Valley of the Usk, and the Holy Mountain, and Llanthony: all with a certain enchantment and vision about them, as if their domed hills and solemn woods were more of grace than of nature. Over the hearth was *Bolton Abbey in the Olden Time.*

Perrott would apologise for it.

"I know," he would say. "I know all about it. It is a pig, and a goat, and a dog, and a damned nonsense—he was quoting a Welsh story— but it used to hang over the fire in the dining-room at home. And I often wish I had brought along *Te Deum Laudamus* as well."

"What's that?" Harliss asked.

"Ah, you're too young to have lived with it. It depicts three choirboys in surplices; one singing for his life, and the other two looking about them—just like choir-boys. And we were always told that the busy boy was hanged at last. The companion picture shewed three charity girls, also singing. This was called *Te Dominum Confitemur.* I never heard their story."

"I know." Harliss brightened. "I came upon them both in lodgings near the station at Brighton, in Mafeking year. And, a year or two later, I saw *Sherry, Sir* in an hotel at Tenby."

"The finest wax fruit I ever saw," Arnold joined in, "was in a window in the King's Cross Road."

So they would maunder along, about the old-fashioned rather than the old. And so on this winter night of the cold wind they lingered about the London streets of forty, forty-five, fifty-five years ago.

One of them dilated on Bloomsbury, in the days when the bars were up, and the Duke's porters had boxes beside the gates, and all was peace, not to say profound dulness, within those solemn boundaries. Here was the high vaulted church of a strange sect, where, they said, while the smoke of incense fumed about a solemn rite, a wailing voice would suddenly rise up with the sound of an incantation in magic. Here, another church, where Christina Rossetti bowed her head; all about, dim squares where no one walked, and the leaves of the trees were dark with smoke and soot.

"I remember one spring," said Arnold, "when they were the brightest green I ever saw. In Bloomsbury Square. Long ago."

"That wonderful little lion stood on the iron posts in the pavement in front of the British Museum," Perrott put in. "I believe they have kept a few and hidden them in museums. That's one of the reasons why the streets grow duller and duller. If there is anything curious, anything beautiful in a street, they take it away and stick it in a museum. I wonder what has become of that odd little figure, I think it was in a cocked hat, that stood by the bar-parlour door in the courtyard of the bell in Holborn."

They worked their way down by Fetter Lane, and lamented Dryden's house—"I think it was in '87 that they pulled it down"—and lingered on the site of Clifford's Inn—"you could walk into the seventeenth century"—and so at last into the Strand.

"Some one said it was the finest street in Europe."

"Yes, no doubt—in a sense. Not at all in the obvious sense; it wasn't *belle architecture de ville*. It was of all ages and all sizes and heights and styles: a unique enchantment of a street; an incantation, full of words that meant nothing to the uninitiated."

A sort of Litany followed.

"The Shop of the Pale Puddings, where little David Copperfield might have bought his dinner."

"That was close to Bookseller's Row—sixteenth-century houses."

"And 'Chocolate as in Spain'; opposite Charing Cross."

"The *Globe* office, where one sent one's early turnovers."

"The narrow alleys with steps going down to the river."

"The smell of making soap from the scent shop."

"Nutt's bookshop, near the Welsh mutton butcher's, where the street was narrow."

"The *Family Herald* office; with a picture in the window of an early type-setting machine, shewing the operator working a contraption with long arms, that hovered over the case."

"And Garden House in the middle of a lawn, in Clement's Inn."

"And the flicker of those old yellow gas-lamps, when the wind blew up the street, and the people were packing into that passage that led to the Lyceum pit."

One of them, his ear caught by a phrase that another had used, began to murmur verses from "Oh, plump head waiter at the Cock."

"What chops they were!" sighed Perrott. And he began to make the punch, grating first of all the lumps of sugar against the lemons; drawing forth thereby the delicate, aromatic oils from the rind of the Mediterranean fruit. Matters were brought forth from cupboards at the dark end of the room: rum from the Jamaica Coffee House in the City, spices in blue china boxes, one or two old bottles containing secret essences. The kettle boiled, the ingredients were dusted in and poured into the red-brown jar, which was then muffled and set to digest on the hearth, in the heat of the fire.

"Misce, fiat mistura," said Harliss.

"Very well," answered Arnold. "But remember that all the true matters of the work are invisible."

Nobody minded him or his alchemy; and after a due interval, the glasses were held over the fragrant steam of the jar, and then filled. The three sat round the fire, drinking and sipping with grateful hearts.

II

Let it be noted that the glasses in question held no great quantity of the hot liquor. Indeed, they were what used to be called rummers; round, and of a bloated aspect, but of comparatively small capacity. Therefore, nothing injurious to the clearness of those old heads is to be inferred, when it is said that between the third and fourth filling, the talk drew away from central London and the lost, beloved Strand and began to go farther afield, into stranger, less-known territories. Perrott began it, by tracing a curious passage he had once made northward, dodging by the Globe and the Olympic theatres into the dark labyrinth of Clare Market, under arches and by alleys, till he came into Great

Queen Street, near the Freemason's Tavern and Inigo Jones's red pilasters. Another took up the tale, and drifting into Holborn by Whet-
stone's Park, and going astray a little to visit Kingsgate Street—"just
like Phiz's plate: mean, low, deplorable; but I wish they hadn't pulled it
down"—finally reached Theobald's Road. There, they delayed a little,
to consider curiously decorated leaden water-cisterns that were once to
be seen in the areas of a few of the older houses, and also to speculate
on the legend that an ancient galleried inn, now used as a warehouse,
had survived till quite lately at the back of Tibbles Road—for so they
called it. And thence, northward and eastward, up the Gray's Inn
Road, crossing the King's Cross Road, and going up the hill.

"And here," said Arnold, "we begin to touch on the conjectured.
We have left the known world behind us."

Indeed, it was he who now had the party in charge.

"Do you know," said Perrott, "that sounds awful rot, but it's true;
at least so far as I am concerned. I don't think I ever went beyond
Holborn Town Hall, as it used to be—I mean walking. Of course, I've
driven in a hansom to King's Cross Railway Station, and I went once
or twice to the Military Tournament, when it was at the Agricultural
Hall, in Islington; but I don't remember how I got there."

Harliss said he had been brought up in North London, but much
farther north—Stoke Newington way.

"I once knew a man," said Perrott, "who knew all about Stoke
Newington; at least he ought to have known about it. He was a Poe
enthusiast, and he wanted to find out whether the school where Poe
boarded when he was a little boy was still standing. He went again and
again; and the odd thing is that, in spite of his interest in the matter, he
didn't seem to know whether the school was still there, or whether he
had seen it. He spoke of certain survivals of the Stoke Newington that
Poe indicates in a phrase or two in 'William Wilson': the dreamy village, the misty trees, the old rambling red-brick houses, standing in
their gardens, with high walls all about them. But though he declared
that he had gone so far as to interview the vicar, and could describe
the old church with the dormer windows, he could never make up his
mind whether he had seen Poe's school."

"I never heard of it when I lived there," said Harliss. "But I came
of business stock. We didn't gossip much about authors. I have a

vague sort of notion that I once heard somebody speak of Poe as a notorious drunkard—and that's about all I ever heard of him till a good deal later."

"It is queer, but it's true," Arnold broke in, "that there's a general tendency to seize on the accidental, and ignore the essential. You may be vague enough about the treble works, the vast designs of the laboured rampart lines; but at least you knew that the Duke of Wellington had a very big nose. I remember it on the tins of knife polish."

"But that fellow I was speaking of," said Perrott, going back to his topic, "I couldn't make him out. I put it to him, 'Surely you know one way or the other: this old school is still standing—or was still standing—or not: you either saw it or you didn't: there can't be any doubt about the matter.' But we couldn't get to negative or positive. He confessed that it was strange; 'But upon my word I don't know. I went once, I think, about '95, and then, again, in '99—that was the time I called on the vicar; and I have never been since.' He talked like a man who had gone into a mist, and could not speak with any certainty of the shapes he had seen in it.

"And that reminds me. Long after my talk with Hare—that was the man who was interested in Poe—a distant cousin of mine from the country came up to town to see about the affairs of an old aunt of his who had lived all her life somewhere Stoke Newington way, and had just died. He came in here one evening to look me up—we had not met for many years—and he was saying, truly enough, I am sure, how little the average Londoner knew of London, when you once took him off his beaten track. 'For example,' he said to me, 'have you ever been in Stoke Newington?' I confessed that I hadn't, that I had never had any reason to go there. 'Exactly; and I don't suppose you've ever even heard of Canon's Park?' I confessed ignorance again. He said it was an extraordinary thing that such a beautiful place as this, within four or five miles of the centre of London, seemed absolutely unknown and unheard of by nine Londoners out of ten."

"I know every inch of that neighbourhood," broke in Harliss.

"I was born there and lived there till I was sixteen. There's no such place anywhere near Stoke Newington."

"But, look here, Harliss," said Arnold. "I don't know that you're really an authority."

"Not an authority on a place I knew backwards for sixteen years? Besides, I represented Crosbies in that district later, soon after I went into business."

"Yes, of course. But—I suppose you know the Haymarket pretty well, don't you?"

"Of course I do; both for business and pleasure. Everybody knows the Haymarket."

"Very good. Then tell me the way to St. James's Market."

"There's no such market."

"We have him," said Arnold, with bland triumph. "Literally, he is correct: I believe it's all pulled down now. But it was standing during the war: a small open space with old, low buildings in it, a stone's throw from the back of the tube station. You turned to the right, as you walked down the Haymarket."

"Quite right," confirmed Perrott. "I went there, only once, on the business of an odd magazine that was published in one of those low buildings. But I was talking of Canon's Park, Stoke Newington—"

"I beg your pardon," said Harliss. "I remember now. There is a part in Stoke Newington or near it called Canon's Park. But it isn't a park at all; nothing like a park. That's only a builder's name. It's just a lot of streets. I think there's a Canon's Square, and a Park Crescent, and an Esplanade: there are some decent shops there. But it's all quite ordinary; there's nothing beautiful about it."

"But my cousin said it was an amazing place. Not a bit like the ordinary London parks or anything of the kind he'd seen abroad. You go in through a gateway, and he said it was like finding yourself in another country. Such trees, that must have been brought from the end of the world: there were none like them in England, though one or two reminded him of trees in Kew Gardens; deep hollows with streams running from the rocks; lawns all purple and gold with flowers, and golden lilies too, towering up into the trees, and mixing with the crimson of the flowers that hung from the boughs. And here and there, there were little summer-houses and temples, shining white in the sun, like a view in China, as he put it."

Harliss did not fail with his response, "I tell you there's no such place."

And he added:

"And, anyhow, it all sounds a bit too flowery. But perhaps your cousin was that sort of man: ready to be enthusiastic over a patch of dandelions in a back-garden. A friend of mine once sent me a wire to 'come at once: most important: meet me St. John's Wood Station'. Of course I went, thinking it must be really important; and what he wanted was to shew me the garden of a house to let in Grove End Road, which was a blaze of dandelions."

"And a very beautiful sight," said Arnold, with fervour.

"It was a fine sight; but hardly a thing to wire a man about. And I should think that's the secret of all this stuff your cousin told you, Perrott. There used to be one or two big well-kept gardens at Stoke Newington; and I suppose he strolled into one of them by mistake, and then got rather wildly enthusiastic about what he saw."

"It's possible, of course," said Perrott, "but in a general way he wasn't that sort of man. He had an experimental farm, not far from Wells, and bred new kinds of wheat, and improved grasses. I have heard him called stodgy, though I always found him pleasant enough when we met."

"Well, I tell you there's no such place in Stoke Newington or anywhere near it. I ought to know."

"How about St. James's Market?" asked Arnold.

Then, they "left it at that". Indeed, they had felt for some time that they had gone too far away from their known world, and from the friendly tavern fires of the Strand, into the wild no man's land of the north. To Harliss, of course, those regions had once been familiar, common, and uninteresting: he could not revisit them in talk with any glow of feeling. The other two held them unfriendly and remote; as if one were to discourse of Arctic explorations, and lands of everlasting darkness.

They all returned with relief to their familiar hunting-grounds, and saw the play in theatres that had been pulled down for thirty-five years or more, and had steaks and strong ale afterwards, in the box by the fire, by the fire that had been finally raked out soon after the new law courts were opened.

III

So, at least, it appeared at the time; but there was something in the tale of this suburban park that remained with Arnold and beset him, and sent him at last to the remote north of the story. For, as he was meditating on this vague attraction, he chanced to light on a shabby brown book on his untidy shelves; a book gathered from a stall in Farringdon Street, where the manuscript of Traherne's *Centuries of Meditations* had been found. So far, Arnold had scarcely glanced at it. It was called, *A London Walk: Meditations in the Streets of the Metropolis.* The author was the Reverend Thomas Hampole, and the book was dated 1853. It consisted for the most part of moral and obvious reflections, such as might be expected from a pious and amiable clergyman of the day. In the middle of the nineteenth century, the relish of moralising which flourished so in the age of Addison and Pope and Johnson, which made the *Rambler* a popular book, and gave fortunes to the publishers of sermons, had still a great deal of vigour. People liked to be warned of the consequences of their actions, to have lessons in punctuality, to learn about the importance of little things, to hear sermons from stones, and to be taught that there were gloomy reflections to be drawn from almost everything. So then, the Reverend Thomas Hampole stalked the London streets with a moral and monitory glance in his eye: saw Regent Street in its early splendour and thought of the ruins of mighty Rome, preached on the text of solitude in a multitude as he viewed what he called the teeming myriads, and allowed a desolate, half-ruinous house "in Chancery" to suggest thoughts of the happy Christmas parties that had once thoughtlessly revelled behind the crumbling walls and broken windows.

But here and there, Mr. Hampole became less obvious, and perhaps more really profitable. For example, there is a passage—it has already been quoted, I think, by some modern author—which seems curious enough.

> Has it ever been your fortune, courteous reader [Mr. Hampole enquired] to rise in the earliest dawning of a summer day, ere yet the radiant beams of the sun have done more than touch with light the domes and spires of the great city? . . . If this has been your lot, have you not observed that magic powers have apparently been at work? The accustomed scene has

lost its familiar appearance. The houses which you have passed daily, it may be for years, as you have issued forth on your business or on your pleasure, now seem as if you beheld them for the first time. They have suffered a mysterious change, into something rich and strange. Though they may have been designed with no extraordinary exertion of the art of architecture . . . yet you have been ready to admit that they now "stand in glory, shine like stars, apparelled in a light serene". They have become magical habitations, supernal dwellings, more desirable to the eye than the fabled pleasure dome of the Eastern potentate, or the bejewelled hall built by the Genie for Aladdin in the Arabian tale.

A good deal in this vein; and then, when one expected the obvious warning against putting trust in appearances, both transitory and delusory, there came a very odd passage:

Some have declared that it lies within our own choice to gaze continually upon a world of equal or even greater wonder and beauty. It is said by these that the experiments of the alchemists of the Dark Ages . . . are, in fact, related, not to the transmutation of metals, but to the transmutation of the entire Universe. . . . This method, or art, or science, or whatever we choose to call it (supposing it to exist, or to have ever existed), is simply concerned to restore the delights of the primal Paradise; to enable men, if they will, to inhabit a world of joy and splendour. It is perhaps possible that there is such an experiment, and that there are some who have made it.

The reader was referred to a note—one of several—at the end of the volume, and Arnold, already a good deal interested by this unexpected vein in the Reverend Thomas, looked it up. And thus it ran:

I am aware that these speculations may strike the reader as both singular and (I may, perhaps, add) chimerical; and, indeed, I may have been somewhat rash and ill-advised in committing them to the printed page. If I have done wrong, I hope for pardon; and, indeed, I am far from advising anyone who may read these lines to engage in the doubtful and difficult experiment which they adumbrate. Still; we are bidden to be seekers of the truth: *veritas contra mundum.*

I am strengthened in my belief that there is at least some foundation for the strange theories at which I have hinted, by an experience that befell me in the early days of my ministry. Soon after the termination of my first curacy, and after I had been admitted to Priest's Orders, I spent some months in London, living with relations in Kensington. A college friend of mine, whom I will call the Reverend Mr. S——, was, I was aware, a curate in a suburb of the north of London, S.N. I wrote to him, and afterwards called at his lodgings at his invitation. I found S—— in a state of some perturbation. He was threatened, it seemed, with an affection of the lungs, and his medical adviser was insistent that he should leave London for awhile, and spend the four months of the winter in the more genial climate of Devonshire. Unless this were done, the doctor declared, the consequences to my friend's health might be of a very serious kind. S—— was very willing to act on this advice, and indeed, anxious to do so; but, on the other hand, he did not wish to resign his curacy, in which, as he said, he was both happy and, he trusted, useful. On hearing this, I at once proffered my services, telling him that if his Vicar approved, I should be happy to do his duty till the end of the ensuing March; or even later, if the physicians considered a longer stay in the south would be advisable. S—— was overjoyed. He took me at once to see the Vicar; the fitting enquiries were made, and I entered on my temporary duties in the course of a fortnight.

It was during this brief ministry in the environs of London, that I became acquainted with a very singular person, whom I shall call Glanville. He was a regular attendant at our services, and, in the course of my duty, I called on him, and expressed my gratification at his evident attachment to the Liturgy of the Church of England. He replied with due politeness, asked me to sit down and partake with him of the soothing cup, and we soon found ourselves engaged in conversation. I discovered early in our association that he was conversant with the reveries of the German Theosophist, Behmen, and the later works of his English disciple, William Law; and it was clear to me that he looked on these labyrinths of mystical theology with a friendly eye. He was a middle-aged man, spare of habit, and of a dark complexion; and his face was illuminated in a very impressive manner, as he discussed the speculations which had evidently occupied his thoughts for many years. Based as these theories were on the doctrines (if we may call them by that name) of Law and Behmen, they struck me as of an extremely fantastic, I would even say fabulous, nature, but I confess that I listened with a considerable degree of interest, while making it evident that as a Minister of the Church of England I was far from giving my free assent to the propositions that were placed before me. They were not, it is true, manifestly and certainly opposed to orthodox belief, but they were assuredly strange, and as such to be received with salutary caution. As an example of the ideas which beset a mind which was ingenious, and I may say, devout, I may mention that Mr. Glanville often dwelt on a consequence, not generally acknowledged, of the Fall of Man. "When man yielded," he would say, "to the mysterious temptation intimated by the figurative language of Holy Writ, the universe, originally fluid and the servant of his spirit, became solid, and crashed down upon him overwhelming him beneath its weight and its dead mass." I requested him to furnish me with more light on this remarkable belief; and I found that in his opinion that which we now regard as stubborn matter was, primally, to use his singular phraseology, the Heavenly Chaos, a soft and ductile substance, which could be moulded by the imagination of uncorrupted man into whatever forms he chose it to assume. "Strange as it may seem," he added, "the wild inventions (as we consider them) of the Arabian Tales give us some notion of the powers of the *homo protoplastus*. The prosperous city becomes a lake, the carpet transports us in an instant of time, or rather without time, from one end of the earth to another, the palace rises at a word from nothingness. Magic, we call all this, while we deride the possibility of any such feats; but this magic of the East is but a confused and fragmentary recollection of operations which were of the first nature of man, and of the *fiat* which was then entrusted to him."

I listened to this and other similar expositions of Mr. Glanville's extraordinary beliefs with some interest, as I have remarked. I could not but feel that such opinions were in many respects more in accordance with the doctrine I had undertaken to expound than much of the teaching of the philosophers of the day, who seemed to exalt rationalism at the expense of Reason, as that divine faculty was exhibited by Coleridge. Still, when I assented, I made it clear to Glanville that my assent was qualified by my firm adherence to the principles which I had solemnly professed at my ordination.

The months went by in the peaceful performance of the pastoral duties of my office. Early in March, I received a letter from my friend Mr. S——, who informed me that he had greatly benefited by the air of Torquay, and that his medical adviser had assured him that he need no longer hesitate to resume his duties in London. Consequently, S—— proposed to return at once, and, after warmly expressed thanks for my extreme kindness, as he called it, he announced his wish to perform his part in the Church services on the following Sunday. Accordingly, I paid my final visits to those of the parishioners with whom I had more particularly associated, reserving my call on Mr. Glanville for the last day of my residence at S.N. He was sorry, I think, to hear of my impending departure, and told me that he would always recollect our conversational exchanges with much pleasure.

"I, too, am leaving S.N.," he added. "Early next week I sail for the East, where my stay may be prolonged for a considerable period."

After mutual expressions of polite regret, I rose from my chair, and was about to make my farewells, when I observed that Glanville was gazing at me with a fixed and singular regard.

"One moment," he said, beckoning me to the window, where he was standing. "I want to shew you the view. I don't think you have seen it."

The suggestion struck me as peculiar, to say the least of it. I was, of course, familiar with the street in which Glanville resided, as with most of the S.N. streets; and he on his side must have been well aware that no prospect that his window might command could shew me anything that I had not seen many times during my four months' stay in the parish. In addition to this, the streets of our London suburbs do not often offer a spectacle to engage the amateur of landscape and the picturesque. I was hesitating, hardly knowing whether to comply with Glanville's request, or to treat it as a piece of pleasantry, when it struck me that it was possible that his first-floor window might afford a distant view of St. Paul's Cathedral; I accordingly stepped to his side, and waited for him to indicate the scene which he, presumably, wished me to admire.

His features still wore the odd expression which I have already remarked.

"Now," said he, "look out and tell me what you see."

Still bewildered, I looked through the window, and saw exactly that which I had expected to see: a row or terrace of neatly designed residences, separated from the highway by a parterre or miniature park, adorned with trees and shrubs. A road, passing to the right of the terrace, gave a view of streets and crescents of more recent construction, and of some degree of elegance. Still, in the whole of the familiar spectacle I saw nothing to warrant any particular attention; and, in a more or less jocular manner, I said as much to Glanville.

By way of reply, he touched me lightly with his finger-tips on the shoulder, and said:

"Look again."

I did so. For a moment, my heart stood still, and I gasped for breath. Before me, in place of the familiar structures, there was disclosed a panorama of unearthly, of astounding beauty. In deep dells, bowered by overhanging trees, there bloomed flowers such as only dreams can shew; such deep purples that yet seemed to glow like precious stones with a hidden but ever-present radiance, roses whose hues outshone any that are to be seen in our gardens, tall lilies alive with light, and blossoms that were as beaten gold. I saw well-shaded walks that went down to green hollows bordered with thyme; and here and there the grassy eminence above, and the bubbling well below, were crowned with architecture of fantastic and unaccustomed beauty, which seemed to speak of fairyland itself. I might almost say that my soul was ravished by the spectacle displayed before me. I was possessed by a degree of rapture and delight such as I had never experienced. A sense of beatitude pervaded my whole being; my bliss was such as cannot be expressed by words. I uttered an inarticulate cry of joy and wonder. And then, under the influence of a swift revulsion of terror, which even now I cannot explain, I turned and rushed from the room and from the house, without one word of comment or farewell to the extraordinary man who had done—I knew not what.

In great perturbation and confusion of mind, I made my way into the street. Needless to say, no trace of the phantasmagoria that had been displayed before me remained. The familiar street had resumed its usual aspect, the terrace stood as I had always seen it, and the newer buildings beyond, where I had seen oh! what dells of delight, what blossoms of glory, stood as before in their neat, though unostentatious order. Where I had seen valleys embowered in green leafage, waving gently in the sunshine and the summer breeze, there were now boughs bare and black, scarce shewing so much as a single bud. As I have mentioned, the season was early in March, and a black frost which had set in ten days or a fortnight before still constrained the earth and its vegetation.

I walked hurriedly away to my lodgings, which were some distance from the abode of Glanville. I was sincerely glad to think that I was leaving the neighbourhood on the following day. I may say that up to the present moment I have never revisited S.N.

Some months later I encountered my friend Mr. S——, and under cover of asking about the affairs of the parish in which he still ministered, I enquired after Glanville, with whom (I said) I had made acquaintance. It seemed he had fulfilled his intention of leaving the neighbourhood within a few days of my own departure. He had not confided his destination or his plans for the future to anyone in the parish.

"My acquaintance with him," said S——, "was of the slightest, and I do not think that he made any friends in the locality, though he had resided in S.N. for more than five years."

It is now some fifteen years since this most strange experience befell me; and during that period I have heard nothing of Glanville. Whether he is still alive in the distant Orient, or whether he is dead, I am completely ignorant.

IV

Arnold was generally known as an idle man; and, as he said himself, he hardly knew what the inside of an office was like. But he was laborious in his idleness, and always ready to take any amount of pains, over anything in which he was interested. And he was very much interested in this Canon's Park business. He felt sure that there was a link between Mr. Hampole's odd story—"more than odd", he meditated—and the experience of Perrott's cousin, the wheat-breeder from the west country. He made his way to Stoke Newington, and strolled up and down it, looking about him with an inquisitive eye. He found Canon's Park, or what remained of it, without any trouble. It was pretty well as Harliss had described it: a neighbourhood laid out in the twenties or thirties of the last century for City men of comfortable down to tolerable incomes.

Some of these houses remained, and there was an attractive row of old-fashioned shops still surviving. Again, in one place there was the modest cot of late Georgian or early Victorian design, with its trellised porch of faded blue-green paint, its patterned iron balcony, not displeasing, its little garden in the front, and its walled garden at the back; a small coach-house, a small stable. In another, something more exuberant and on a much larger scale: ambitious pilasters and stucco, broad lawns and sweeping drives, towering shrubs, and glass in the back premises. But on all the territory modernism had delivered its assault. The big houses remaining had been made into maisonettes, the small ones were down-at-heel, no longer objects of love; and everywhere there were blocks of flats in wicked red brick, as if Mrs. Todgers had given Mr. Pecksniff her notion of an up-to-date gaol, and he had worked out her design. Opposite Canon's Park, and occupying the site on which Mr. Glanville's house must have stood, was a technical college; next to it a school of economics. Both buildings curdled the blood: in their purpose and in their architecture. They looked as if Mr. H. G. Wells's bad dreams had come true.

In none of this, whether moderately ancient or grossly modern, could Arnold see anything to his purpose. In the period of which Mr. Hampole wrote, Canon's Park may have been tolerably pleasant; it was now becoming intolerably unpleasant. But at its best, there could not have been anything in its aspect to suggest the wonderful vision which the clergyman thought he had seen from Glanville's window. And suburban gardens, however well kept, could not explain the farmer's rhapsodies. Arnold repeated the sacred words of the explanation formula: telepathy, hallucination, hypnotism; but felt very little easier. Hypnotism, for example: that was commonly used to explain the Indian rope trick. There was no such trick, and in any case, hypnotism could not explain that or any other marvel seen by a number of people at once, since hypnotism could only be applied to individuals, and with their full knowledge, consent, and conscious attention. Telepathy might have taken place between Glanville and Hampole; but whence did Perrott's cousin receive the impression that he not only saw a sort of Kubla Khan, or Old Man of the Mountain paradise, but actually walked abroad in it? The S.P.R. had, one might say, discovered telepathy, and had devoted no small part of their energies for the last forty-five years or more to a minute and thoroughgoing investigation of it; but, to the best of his belief, their recorded cases gave no instance of anything so elaborate as this business of Canon's Park. And again; so far as he could remember, the appearances ascribed to a telepathic agency were all personal; visions of people, not of places: there were no telepathic landscapes. And as for hallucination: that did not carry one far. That stated a fact, but offered no explanation of it. Arnold had suffered from liver trouble: he had come down to breakfast one morning and had been vexed to see the air all dancing with black specks. Though he did not smell the nauseous odour of a smoky chimney, he made no doubt at first that the chimney had been smoking, or that the black specks were floating soot. It was some time before he realised that, objectively, there were no black specks, that they were optical illusions, and that he had been hallucinated. And no doubt the parson and the farmer had been hallucinated: but the cause, the motive power, was to seek. Dickens told how, waking one morning, he saw his father sitting by his bedside, and wondered what he was doing there. He addressed the old man, and got no answer, put out his hand to touch him: and there was no such thing. Dickens was hallucinated; but since his father was perfectly well at the time, and in no sort of trouble, the mystery remained insoluble, unaccountable. You had to accept it; but there was no rationale of it. It was a problem that had to be given up.

But Arnold did not like giving problems up. He beat the coverts of Stoke Newington, and dived into pubs of promising aspect, hoping to meet talkative old men, who might remember their fathers' stories and repeat them. He found a few, for though London has always been a place of restless, migratory tribes, and shifting populations; and now more than ever before; yet there still remains in many places, and above all in the remoter northern suburbs, an old fixed element, which can go back in memory sometimes for a hundred, even a hundred and fifty years. So in a venerable tavern—it would have been injurious and misleading to call it a pub—on the borders of Canon's Park he found an ancient circle that gathered nightly for an hour or two in a snug, if dingy, parlour. They drank little and that slowly, and went early home. They were small tradesmen of the neighbourhood, and talked their business and the changes they had seen, the curse of multiple shops, the poor stuff sold in them, and the cutting of prices and profits. Arnold edged into the conversation by degrees, after one or two visits—"Well, sir, I am very much obliged to you, and I won't refuse"—and said that he thought of settling in the neighbourhood: it seemed quiet. "Best wishes, I'm sure. Quiet; well it was, once; but not much of that now in Stoke Newington. All pride and dress and bustle now; and the people that had the money and spent it, they're gone, long ago."

"There were well-to-do people here?" asked Arnold, treading cautiously, feeling his way, inch by inch.

"There were, I assure you. Sound men—warm men, my father used to call them. There was Mr. Tredegar, head of Tredegar's Bank. That was amalgamated with the City and National many years ago: nearer fifty than forty, I suppose. He was a fine gentleman, and grew beautiful pineapples. I remember his sending us one, when my wife was poorly all one summer. You can't buy pineapples like that now."

"You're right, Mr. Reynolds, perfectly right. I have to stock what they call pineapples, but I wouldn't touch them myself. No scent, no flavour. Tough and hard; you can't compare a crab-apple with a Cox's pippin."

There was a general assent to this proposition; and Arnold felt that it was slow work.

And even when he got to his point, there was not much gained. He said he had heard that Canon's Park was a quiet part; off the main track.

"Well, there's something in that," said the ancient who had accepted the half-pint. "You don't get very much traffic there, it's true: no trams or buses or motor coaches. But they're pulling it all to pieces; building new blocks of flats every few months. Of course, that might suit your views. Very popular these flats are, no doubt, with many people; most economical, they tell me. But I always liked a house of my own, myself."

"I'll tell you one way a flat is economical," the greengrocer said with a preparatory chuckle. "If you're fond of the wireless, you can save the price and the licence. You'll hear the wireless on the floor above, and the wireless on the floor below, and one or two more besides when they've got their windows open on summer evenings."

"Very true, Mr. Batts, very true. Still, I must say, I'm rather partial to the wireless myself. I like to listen to a cheerful tune, you know, at tea time."

"You don't tell me, Mr. Potter, that you like that horrible jazz, as they call it?"

"Well, Mr. Dickson, I must confess . . ." and so forth, and so forth. It became evident that there were modernists even here: Arnold thought that he heard the term "hot blues" distinctly uttered. He forced another half-pint—"very kind of you; mild this time, if you don't mind"—on his neighbour, who turned out to be Mr. Reynolds, the pharmaceutical chemist, and tried back.

"So you wouldn't recommend Canon's Park as a desirable residence."

"Well, no, sir; not to a gentleman who wants quiet, I should not. You can't have quiet when a place is being pulled down about your ears, as you may say. It certainly was quiet enough in former days. Wouldn't you say so, Mr. Batts?"—breaking in on the musical discussion—"Canon's Park was quiet enough in our young days, wasn't it? It would have suited this gentleman then, I'm sure."

"Perhaps so," said Mr. Batts. "Perhaps so, and perhaps not. There's quiet, and quiet."

And a certain stillness fell upon the little party of old men. They seemed to ruminate, to drink their beer in slower sips.

"There was always something about the place I didn't altogether like," said one of them at last. "But I'm sure I don't know why."

"Wasn't there some tale of a murder there, a long time ago? Or was it a man that killed himself, and was buried at the crossroads by the green, with a stake through his heart?"

"I never heard of that, but I've heard my father say that there was a lot of fever about there formerly."

"I think you're all wide of the mark, gentlemen, if you'll excuse my saying so"—this from an elderly man in a corner, who had said very little hitherto. "I wouldn't say Canon's Park had a bad name, far from it. But there certainly was something about it that many people didn't like; fought shy of, you may say. And it's my belief that it was all on account of the lunatic asylum that used to be there, awhile ago."

"A lunatic asylum was there?" Arnold's particular friend asked. "Well, I think I remember hearing something to that effect in my very young days, now you recall the circumstances. I know we boys used to be very shy of going through Canon's Park after dark. My father used to send me on errands that way now and again, and I always got another boy to come along with me if I could. But I don't remember that we were particularly afraid of the lunatics either. In fact, I hardly know what we were afraid of, now I come to think of it."

"Well, Mr. Reynolds, it's a long time ago; but I do think it was that madhouse put people off Canon's Park in the first place. You know where it was, don't you?"

"I can't say I do."

"Well, it was that big house right in the middle of the park, that had been empty years and years—forty years, I dare say, and going to ruin."

"You mean the place where Empress Mansions are now? Oh, yes, of course. Why they pulled it down more than twenty years ago, and then the land was lying idle all through the war and long after. A dismal-looking old place it was; I remember it well: the ivy growing over the chimney-pots, and the windows smashed, and the 'To Let' boards smothered in creepers. Was that house an asylum in its day?"

"That was the very house, sir. Himalaya House, it was called. In the first place it was built on to an old farmhouse by a rich gentleman from India, and when he died, having no children, his relations sold the property to a doctor. And he turned it into a madhouse. And as I was saying, I think people didn't much like the idea of it. You know, those places weren't so well looked after as they say they are now, and some very unpleasant stories got about; I'm not sure if the doctor didn't get mixed up in a lawsuit over a gentleman, of good family, I believe, who had been shut up in Himalaya House by his relations for years, and as sensible as you or me all the time. And then there was that young fellow that managed to escape: that was a queer business. Though there was no doubt that he was mad enough for anything."

"One of them got away, did he?" Arnold enquired, wishing to break the silence that again fell on the circle.

"That was so. I don't know how he managed it, as they were said to be very strictly kept, but he contrived to climb out or creep out somehow or other, one evening about tea time, and walked as quietly as you please up the road, and took lodgings close by here, in that row of old red-brick houses that stood where the technical college is now. I remember well hearing Mrs. Wilson that kept the lodgings—she lived to be a very old woman—telling my mother that she never saw a nicer-looking, better-spoken young man than this Mr. Vallance—I think he called himself: not his real name, of course. He told her a proper story enough about coming from Norwich, and having to be very quiet on account of his studies and all that. He had his carpet-bag in his hand, and said the heavy luggage was coming later, and paid a fortnight in advance, quite regular. Of course, the doctor's men were after him directly and making enquiries in all directions, but Mrs. Wilson never thought for a moment that this quiet young lodger of hers was the missing madman. Not for some time, that is."

Arnold took advantage of a rhetorical pause in the story. He leaned forward to the landlord, who was leaning over the bar, and listening like the rest. Presently orders round were solicited, and each of the circle voted for a small drop of gin, feeling "mild" or even "bitter" to be inadequate to the crisis of such a tale. And then, with courteous expressions, they drank the health of "our friend sitting by our friend Mr. Reynolds". And one of them said:

"So she found out, did she?"

"I believe," the narrator continued, "that it was a week or thereabouts before Mrs. Wilson saw there was something wrong. It was when she was clearing away his tea, he suddenly spoke up, and says:

"'What I like about these apartments of yours, Mrs. Wilson, is the amazing view you have from your windows.'

"Well, you know, that was enough to startle her. We all of us know what there was to see from the windows of Rodman's Row: Fothergill Terrace, and Chatham Street, and Canon's Park: very nice properties, no doubt, all of them, but nothing to write home about, as the young people say. So Mrs. Wilson didn't know how to take it quite, and thought it might be a joke. She put down the tea-tray, and looked the lodger straight in the face.

"'What is it, sir, you particularly admire, if I might ask?'

"'What do I admire?' said he. 'Everything.' And then, it seems, he began to talk the most outrageous nonsense about golden and silver and purple flowers, and the bubbling well, and the walk that went under the trees right into the wood, and the fairy house on the hill; and I don't know what. He wanted Mrs. Wilson. to come to the window and look at it all. She was frightened, and took up her tray, and got out of the room as quick as she could; and I don't wonder at it. And that night, when she was going up to bed, she passed her lodger's door, and heard him talking out loud, and she stopped to listen. Mind you, I don't think you can blame the woman for listening. I dare say she wanted to know who and what she had got in her house. At first she couldn't make out what he was saying. He was jabbering in what sounded like a foreign language; and then he cried out in plain English as if he were talking to a young lady, and making use of very affectionate expressions.

"That was too much for Mrs. Wilson, and she went off to bed with her heart in her boots, and hardly got to sleep all through the night. The next morning the gentleman seemed quiet enough, but Mrs. Wilson knew he wasn't to be trusted, and directly after breakfast she went round to the neighbours, and began to ask questions. Then, of course, it came out who her lodger must be, and she sent word round to Himalaya House. And the doctor's men took the young fellow back. And, bless my soul, gentlemen; it's close on ten o'clock."

The meeting broke up in a kind of cordial bustle. The old man who had told the story of the escaped lunatic had remarked, it appeared, the very close attention that Arnold had given to the tale. He was evidently gratified. He shook Arnold warmly by the hand, remarking: "So you see, sir, the grounds I have for my opinion that it was that madhouse that gave Canon's Park rather a bad name in our neighbourhood."

And Arnold, revolving many things, set out on the way back to London. Much seemed heavily obscure, but he wondered whether Mrs. Wilson's lodger was a madman at all; any madder than Mr. Hampole, or the farmer from Somerset or Charles Dickens, when he saw the appearance of his father by his bed.

V

Arnold told the story of his researches and perplexities at the next meeting of the three old friends in the quiet court leading into the inn. The scene had changed into a night in June, with the trees in the inn garden fluttering in a cool breeze, that wafted a vague odour of hayfields far away into the very heart of London. The liquor in the brown jar smelt of Gascon vineyards and herb-gardens, and ice had been laid about it, but not for too long a time.

Harliss's word all through Arnold's tale was:

"I know every inch of that neighbourhood, and I told you there was no such place."

Perrott was judicial. He allowed that the history was a remarkable one: "You have three witnesses," Arnold had pointed out.

"Yes," said Perrott, "but have you allowed for the marvellous operation of the law of coincidences? There's a case, trivial enough, perhaps you may think, that made a deep impression on me when I read it, a few years ago. Forty years before, a man had bought a watch in Singapore—or Hong Kong, perhaps. The watch went wrong, and he took it to a shop in Holborn to be seen to. The man who took it from him over the counter was the man who had sold him the watch in the East all those years before. You can never put coincidence out of court, and dismiss it as an impossible solution. Its possibilities are infinite."

Then Arnold told the last broken, imperfect chapter of the story.

"After that night at the King of Jamaica," he began, "I went home and thought it all over. There seemed no more to be done. Still, I felt as if I would like to have another look at this singular park, and I went up there one dark afternoon. And then and there I came upon the young man who had lost his way, and had lost—as he said—the one who lived in the white house on the hill. And I am not going to tell you about her, or her house, or her enchanted gardens. But I am sure that the young man was lost also—and for ever."

And after a pause, he added:

"I believe that there is a perichoresis, an interpenetration. It is possible, indeed, that we three are now sitting among desolate rocks, by bitter streams.

". . . And with what companions?"

The Exalted Omega

I

One darkening autumn evening, not long ago, a man stopped a moment in his quarter-deck walk up and down his sitting-room in Gray's Inn Square and gazed out of the window at the trees, tossing and restless before the west wind, with a look of vague perplexity, in which there was a hint of slight uneasiness. Not more than a hint; it was rather the air of a man who is confronted by a minor difficulty or obstacle in some little plans he is making, or in the train of thought he is following; and to be precise, with J. F. Mansel, the personage in question, it was hardly so large a matter as that. The fact was that Mansel had been a good deal struck by an odd book he had once read, the "Adventure" of two English ladies in the gardens of Versailles. Most people, I suppose, have read the book in question, and have puzzled their heads over it, and tried to find some plausible explanation of its story: a day in the French Revolution returning over the gulf of years; the image of the lady sketching in the garden, the lady who must have been Marie Antoinette, the hurrying messengers, perturbed footmen, stolid gardeners; all, as it appeared, going about their affairs, quiet or unquiet, as they had gone about them on that October day in 1789.

But Mansel was not thinking, as he stared out of the window, of the men and women whose apparitions, as it seemed, had been called up to puzzle the two scholastic Englishwomen and their readers. For the moment, it was not the ghostly people, but the ghostly landscape of the vision—or whatever it was—that slightly troubled him. He recollected that either Miss Moberly or Miss Jourdain—or was it both ladies?—had noted at the time of the strange experience, as they walked by woods and groves that are not marked in the modern maps of Versailles, since they have long ceased to exist, that the scene had something unusual in its aspect, that the trees were more like the pictured trees in a tapestry, objects on the flat, than the stout growth of the common wood. And, as it happened, Mansel looking out of his window on that familiar scene—the plane trees of the Inn Garden, and the turf beneath, and a glimpse here and there of Raymond Buildings on the other side of the lawn—was reminded of the Versailles manifestation. There was, he hesitated, something not altogether solid and satisfactory in the sight before him. It looked, he felt, as though leafage and tree trunks, green turf and grey bricks of Raymond Buildings wavered together, as he had seen vistas and towers wavering on the theatre backcloth, in the old days when things, perhaps, were generally more cheerful, and he had been used to go to the play. He glanced again, and doubtfully supposed it was all right, because it must be all right; and then turned from the window to the fireplace, and sat down in the ugly, comfortable arm-chair, which he had brought up from his old home in the west, quite a long time ago. There was a little round table beside the chair, one of those papier mâché pieces of the 'thirties and 'forties, that people are beginning to esteem curious. It had a painting of woods, and a lake, and distant mountains on it, with an inlay of mother-of-pearl and a cusped and gilded edge. It had been in his Aunt Eleanor's drawing-room at the Garth. Aunt Eleanor's work-box usually stood on it, and obstructed the view of the painted scene, somewhat to the distress of Johnny—as they called him then. He wanted to stand by the gleaming lake, where the sunset light shone on the water through a cleft in the trees. He desired also to track a path— he saw the entrance and the beginning of it—that wound through the dark, rich wood; there to gather unknown purple flowers that drooped in the shade, and at last, perhaps, to come out and ascend the shining mountain-tops: which he called The Land that is Very Far Off.

The work-box had vanished long ago; he thought that Cousin Emma had taken it away with her after the funeral; and when Emma died thirty—or forty?—years ago, there had been a sale and everything was scattered. He rather missed the work-box now, and wished he had secured it; but Durham was a long journey. There was a book on the table, the *Secret Counsels of a Certain Exile*. He laid a hand on it as if to take it up, but let it stay beside the lake, and sat back in his chair, and half-dozed and half-waked, and scarcely distinguished between a broken dream and a confused waking. Outside, the September evening darkened, and the leaves stilled as the west wind sank to peace. The jangle of the 'buses, the cry of the newsboys, the traffic of Theobald's Road, sounded very faintly; now and again there was a dull thud as the last clerks to go banged the outer doors of the lawyers' offices on the stairs. The place grew heavy with silence, and the lamps began to flicker in the square.

Mansel lay back in the soft comfort of his arm-chair. When he woke, or half-woke, he found his room dark about him, and didn't trouble to light the candles—he had never used gas or electricity in his rooms. He would soon get up and light the two candles on the mantelshelf; but, as he considered, there was nothing particular to do, and he might have supper instead of dinner; there was a 'bus that would take him from the corner of Theobald's Road down to Shaftesbury Avenue. He thought of the jolly hours when, perhaps, "things had been more cheerful", long ago, soon after he had come to live in the inn: great evenings at the Café de l'Europe in its golden days. Indeed; why shouldn't he go there to-night for his supper? It might be, likely enough, that he might meet Tom, or Dick, or Harry there; or, perhaps, all three of them; and the old quartet would be assembled again, and the old jokes and passwords recalled, and the band in its balcony would play the tunes from *The Belle of New York*. The recollection merged into a dream: there he was at the table in the corner, with his old friends about him, and nothing said about his long absence, and the band blared away as in the merry time. Then there was the question of a dream within the dream. For as he sat and talked and laughed with his friends, it suddenly struck him that, after all, it was not as it had been: there was a sad and heavy background, or a cloud that drifted across his happiness, that he had known nothing of long ago. Long ago: but, what if he had dreamed all those years of heaviness, as he slept in his chair in the inn? They had never been, perhaps; he had met Tom, and Dick, and Harry last night, and he would meet them to-morrow. He shook his head, as if to drive the shadow away, and rattled the lid of his *krug*, and left it open, to shew the waiter that he wanted more Munich beer. He had quite forgotten that Tom, and Dick, and Harry had been dead for years, that friendship had failed before life failed; and that the Café de l'Europe had closed its doors twenty years before.

The scene of the café had dissolved, and formless sleep had come heavily upon him, when he started up, roused by a woman's voice, raw and raucous. As he woke, he heard the words:

"Quiet? Mahvlessly quiet, I'm sure. In fact, I should call it bloody quiet." She shrieked like a macaw.

The voice burst through his head, like an express train whirling and thundering through a station. He staggered up out of his chair, and stared, distraught, about him. For a moment, swift and gone as a flash, though he had not lit those candles after all, the room seemed glaring bright, and all disturbed and quaking, till his chairs and tables and bookcases shivered and settled down into their accustomed places. They were his chairs and tables? The garden was in moonlight; and he crept cautiously about the room, and satisfied himself that each piece was in its accustomed place.

Mansel had long been aware that the sharp outlines of life and time and daily event were becoming blurred and indistinct for him. He was apt, he knew quite well, to confuse the years and those who passed through them. He would assign in thought this or that friend to a year long before the time when the two first met; he would think of men talking together who, in fact, had never encountered; a whole group of interests were antedated or post-dated. Edwardians wandered back into the Victorian years and sometimes a young countryman of his boyhood in the west would stray into the café and seem familiar with the place and with those other men whom he had never met, or even heard of. And, then, Mansel would question himself. "After all, wasn't there a night when Vaughan joined us and came up to my rooms afterwards? He did come up to town once, I'm sure. Or, did I dream it all?" He was never quite sure. He felt that his lonely habit and silent days were more and more closing in upon him like a cloud; but by the time that he had realised the danger—if it were a danger—his resolution and will to live clearly and in the light of the day had weakened and dissolved. Once or twice, old friends had looked him up and tried to rouse him and to renew laughter and life within him. But it would not do. Mansel remembered very well who they were, or rather, who they had been; for they had become strangers, or ghosts that spoke of ghostly meetings that had lost all savour. The talk would die down, the man would feel his cheerful intent sink away from him, and go as quickly as he could, and hardly summon a conventional smile as Mansel closed his outer door.

"Poor Mansel!" he might say afterwards. "I could do nothing with him. He's not interested in anything. I tried him with the sort of talk that used to set him on fire; but no good. He might as well be dead, it seems to me."

So, one by one, his friends dropped away and left him alone, wondering what had happened to dry up all the springs of joy. Indeed, the question was an obscure one. There had been no tragedy, no violent disappointment or loss, no specific malady of mind or body, to be ascertained, defined, and encountered with remedies. He had been conscious of a savour gradually departing from the whole body of life, so that a grave book or a gay gathering had become alike flat and meaningless. Walking up and down his rooms, laying down the law, arguing, growing heated about the essence of poetry or the demerits of Meredith: that had been fine, relishing sport once on a time: and now it was nothing. He would look at old note-books he had filled, and wonder what possessed him to write down all those futilities. And then; the last cheerful evening that he had attempted with his old friends, who drank a little and laughed a great deal; that held no cheerfulness for Mansel. He asked with Johnson: "Where's the merriment?" and stole away home very sadly, and sat alone in the dark room. And one of these old friends talking to another, said: "I don't know what's happened to Mansel. He may have sinned against the light or he may be suffering from some obscure form of liver. I feel sure he hasn't taken to drinking methylated."

Mansel was a good deal vexed with that sudden shriek of a woman's voice that had made him start up from his dreams and drowsy recollections. He could not make it out. There was nobody in any one of his three rooms; he was sure of that. He found his outer door shut fast. The only other person to have a key was his laundress, and she only came in the morning. Besides; she did not talk like that. Her voice was soft and heavy and suety; and she was particular as to what she said, in the presence of her clients, at all events. The voice could not have come across the landing; where the rooms were inhabited by another lonely bachelor. It might have been somebody wandering about the place, looking for rooms, and standing on the landing itself. There was certainly that small opening contrived in the wall, by the door, to enable the tenant, summoned by a knock, to stand in the darkness and inspect his caller, displayed in the light of the window or the lamp. The raucous cry that had roused him might, perhaps, have penetrated through the hole in the wall. He hoped that no such company might come about his stairs again.

But here he was disappointed. Again and again, and constantly, his journeys into the past, and dreams and meditations were broken by a hubbub of voices, shouts of laughter, always accompanied by that glare of light in the moment of awakening, the sense of disturbance and confusion in the objects about him. He was perplexed and frightened, and wondered whether he were going mad, for it was clear that there was no ordinary explanation of the strange trouble. He thought of consulting a doctor, but he knew he could never summon up the resolution for such an encounter. And so he grew into the sense of being hemmed about by these dismal visitants, creatures, he supposed, of his own morbid fancies or diseased body. They were not real; he was sure of that. In the darkness of the night, as he came up from the wood of the purple flowers, and stood in the sunlight on a shining, happy hill—perhaps the true Land that was Very Far Off—a shriek of laughter would shatter his dreams, and he would start up in terror, and his gloomy bedroom would be ablaze.

And, then, the trouble began to beset his day-dreams in another form, without the violence of the awaking. He heard the woman, her voice subdued, though it still grated on his ears, murmuring, murmuring, and a gruff man's tones, assenting or objecting or denying. It would seem that this muffled talk went on, day after day, night after night; and by degrees Mansel got the impression that he was listening to the plot of a deadly business. There were mysterious allusions to "a bottle party", which conveyed nothing to him; and someone called "Cousin Jerome" was to get a drink from the right bottle; and the man's voice, answering, it seemed, a question, said "eighty thousand at least, perhaps more". And, then, again the words came: "No danger, no danger. No weed killer for me, no fly-papers, or any damn childish tricks of that sort. You have only to hang the leg of mutton long enough; and the juice of it will have no taste or smell or colour. The place will be all shut while we are away in the country. If anything gets through closed doors and windows; I dare say rats die under the floor now and then."

And one . . . night or day, he could hardly tell which; as if the low voice were speaking in his very ear: "Old Mansel will never tell." And then they laughed, quite quietly for once: and those five words struck through his soul with unutterable horror.

He thought that one misty evening he must have left his rooms and wandered out of the inn to escape that instant horror that beset him. He could not tell the way he took, but he thought he remembered crossing a bridge, and straying on through unknown places, till he found himself in a maze of streets almost deserted; streets of little houses; dismal, monotonous, and yet pretentious. There was one house with a great green bush growing up from the area, and here he stopped, and somehow found himself within it. He was in a small room on the ground floor; a shabby and flashy room with flaring, foolish ornaments above the empty grate, and a gaudy linoleum on the floor. At the gimcrack table there sat a party of seven people; there were six men and women; three on each side; and at one end, a stout, dark, middle-aged woman, with black and greasy hair elaborately done in a sort of structure on top of her head. She wore a black and shiny and belaced dress, shabby and pretentious like all else in that place. The others bent their heads in an attitude of profound attention; the woman at the head of the table seemed to gaze before her, as if she saw nothing. She held up her hands in the Jewish attitude of prayer; and began to sway gently to and fro. The light was dim, for there was only one gas jet burning, and that was turned low, but Mansel noted big rings studded with apparent emeralds, rubies, and diamonds thick on her fingers. One of the men at the table got up and sat down again, and a gramophone began to discourse, "Abide With Me".

The dark woman spoke in a thick, unctuous voice:

"I get a message for Sam. Is there anyone here named Samuel?"

A man looked up eagerly, and stuttered, as he answered.

"I haven't been called Samuel since I was a nipper nine years old. My name is Albert Samuel Morton, right enough, but I always call myself Albert Morton. Who can it be?"

"I get a message for Sam. Ask him if he remembers Aunt Clara. Clara? Clara? I am not certain about this name."

"It's not Clara," said the man, excitedly. "I had an Aunt Sarah, all right."

"It comes through clearly now. Ask him if he remembers his Aunt Sarah, and her china dogs."

"So she had!" exclaimed the man. "On her mantelpiece in the parlour. I can remember them. It's wonderful."

"The message says: 'Look after the pence, and the pounds will look after themselves!'"

"That's Aunt Sarah, right enough!" The man bubbled with amazement and delight. "Why, that was a regular saying of hers. My dad always called her 'Saving Sarah'! Isn't it wonderful? Well, I'm glad to think she's not forgotten me."

There were more messages of much the same character. Most of them seemed to find an echo in the breasts of those present. There was one woman who could not remember any "Cousin Joshua", who seemed distressed about some matter which he said she would understand. The woman reflected, and said: No. No, she couldn't recollect any Cousin Joshua.

"Perhaps," said the lady at the head of the table, "he died when you were very young. There may have been something painful, which prevented his friends talking about him."

The woman's face was blank; then she started slightly, and kept silence; looking a little frightened.

There was a pause. The gramophone had run down. The dark woman had seemed to deliver her last message with a certain difficulty. Her voice faltered; she paled through her paint. There was silence in the dim room.

The woman shuddered as if an electric shock had passed through her. She shook from head to foot. Her face was twisted all awry. And then she suddenly bent forward, and began to scribble with a pencil on a piece of paper that lay on the table before her. Her crooked face was all ghastly and twitching, as she rather struck with the pencil than wrote; and in a few seconds, it seemed, there was a harsh noise in her throat, and she fell sideways from her chair to the floor, in some kind of fit or seizure, that was very dreadful to behold.

The clients started in alarm from their places. Someone turned up the gas, and the two women of the party approached the epileptic fearfully. A bell was rung, and a timid, shadowy little man came running upstairs and looked into the room, a sluttish servant following on his heels. Two or three of the party carried out the dark woman, still struggling and foaming. One of those who was left picked up the paper that had fallen to the floor. He scanned it curiously under the gas, now flaring.

"You can't get much out of that," he said, in a disappointed tone. "A lot of marks that don't look as if they meant anything, and something about 'grows my spirit', and more marks. The fit was on her, no doubt."

He laid down the paper on the table, and turned to go.

Mansel, vague as usual, supposed he must have found his way out with the rest of the party. No doubt, he mused and wondered over the strange ending of the evening as he made his way back to the inn, and took no note of the streets through which he passed; for his next impression was of the familiar room. It was silent at first; and then he caught once more the mutter of those evil voices.

II

There can be no doubt, I am afraid, that Mrs. Ladislaw sometimes cheated. Her mediumship had often been assailed, and not merely by the incredulous outsiders who take a pleasure in turning on their torches at inopportune moments, and in grasping at ectoplasm and giving it another name. Eminent Spiritualists had exposed her in their papers. It is true, that other eminent Spiritualists had at first taken her part, and had called for justice and for the spirit of English fair play. There had been the spirit paintings, for example, which were supposed to blaze out suddenly on a blank sheet of paper. It seemed all right at first. There was the paper lying white and virgin, on the table before Mrs. Ladislaw; and half a dozen coloured chalks beside it. She would lay a large, fat hand upon it and the chalks, and go into a mild trance: then, the hand was lifted, and a glowing work of art appeared on the page. But an elderly and honoured Spiritualist first of all recognised the picture submitted to him as an indifferent copy of a coloured plate that had appeared in a Christmas Number many years before. There was a controversy about this in the *Metapsychical Review* and in *Daybreak*. It was pointed out that the subject matter of the picture was beside the point: the question was, how it had appeared on a piece of blank paper in the course of a few seconds. How, if not through the agency of Red Bull, Mrs. Ladislaw's control? This question was answered before long in a sense which seemed to make the aid of Red Bull superfluous and unnecessary. Then, there were questions on slips of paper, which were placed in a casket, and duly sealed by one of the sitters, who had brought with him an old armorial signet ring, with an elaborate coat engraved on it. At the next séance, the casket was passed round, and it was clear that the seal had not been tampered with in any way. It was then solemnly broken by the owner of the jewel; and inside the box, there were the slips of paper with the questions, and answers, more or less coherent, written beneath in scrawling, untidy script. This interesting manifestation was repeated several times and made a considerable impression. It seemed quite clear that on each occasion the seal was absolutely undisturbed; and people of some intelligence were beginning to be interested, when one of these thought of turning the mysterious casket upside down, and discovered the secret in the construction of the bottom of the box. It slid open, in response to judicious pressure on one of the four knobs or feet on which it rested. So, on the whole, it was felt in the higher circles of Spiritualism that Mrs. Ladislaw must be dropped; that she must be seen no more at the College of Research, or at the Spiritualist Institute. So she carried on her business in some obscure street in south London, and, on the whole, satisfied her local clients very well. They were not critical; they had never heard of the *Metapsychical Review*, they accepted the messages they received, and when the lights were turned quite out, they enjoyed the marvellous things that happened. None of them carried an electric torch to the dark séance; none of them raised objections if the spirit of a Roman Cardinal uttered the blessed word "Benedictine". So Mrs. Ladislaw sank to the lower levels of necromantic culture, and was heard of no more amongst literate Spiritualists. And yet, a few who had seen her in her more prosperous days maintained that, in spite of all, there was something strange about the woman, something not altogether explicable. They confessed that she was, beyond doubt, an arrant cheat: "there can be no doubt that Eusapia Palladino cheated, and cheated almost openly at times", one of them reminded me, and he went on: "Mrs. Ladislaw's childish tricks didn't deceive me for a moment. They were old tricks that were going in the 'sixties, as you can see if you look up the newspaper files of the time. They were exposed then, and were forgotten, and this woman, whose mother may have been in the business for anything I know, brought them up again, and ran them till they were exposed a second time. But it wasn't all cheating; not quite all. I remember sitting with her at the Institute, seven or eight years ago. It was a summer afternoon, and the séance room was in full light. There were about a dozen people there. Mrs. Ladislaw was doing the Red Bull act. She had passed round the half-sheet of note-paper that was to shew the picture in a minute or two, so that everybody might see that it was absolutely blank and clean. It went round from hand to hand, and people looked at it hard, and held it up to the light, and felt the texture of the paper to be sure that it was one piece, not two. One man pulled out a magnifying-glass from his pocket, and went over the surface inch by inch. Two or three were trying what they could make of the coloured chalks, turning them over, and weighing them in their hands: I don't know what they thought that would do, I am sure. I wasn't bothering about the chalks or the paper myself, you see, because I know how it is done.

"Anyhow; pretty well everybody was busy investigating and testing and the rest of it, with their eyes fixed on the table, or the paper going its round, and two or three of them were arguing in low voices about the fluidity of matter.

"You don't know Séance Room 5 at the Institute? Well, the table runs down the room between the fire-place and the window. I was sitting half-way down with my back to the fire-place. I was looking at Mrs. Ladislaw, dark and greasy, who was sitting straight up with her fat hands flat on the table before her. She was doing the dignified and impassive very fairly well: presently, as I knew, when those keen fellows had finished investigating, she would begin her trick.

"Her face changed. She turned her head a little, and I saw her staring at the wall behind me. She went white. Her mouth dropped open. She was glaring with terror at something that was happening at the back of my head. Naturally, I looked round to see what had frightened the woman.

"In the middle of the mantelshelf behind me was one of those infernal Greek Temple clocks, in black and green marble, with rows of pillars and gilding where it had no business; an ugly, heavy thing. It was at this clock that Mrs. Ladislaw was staring: frozen with fright. And then I saw the clock rise high from the mantelpiece and sail gently down on to the floor. Mrs. Ladislaw fell forward with her face on the table, in a faint.

"The séance broke up in confusion. The women looked after Mrs. Ladislaw. In the process, the picture was to have appeared if things had gone better fluttered from somewhere on to the floor, and there was some argument as to what this proved. I got up, and looked at the clock, which was sitting on the carpet. I lifted it up—heavy goods— and put it back in its place. No; no wire, or thread, or anything of the sort, and if there had been, it wouldn't have accounted for anything. If that lumping thing had been twitched from the mantelpiece, it would have fallen with a crash. It *sailed* down, quite gently, like a feather. You can call it a Poltergeist case, if you think that makes it any clearer. I don't. I don't know in the least how it was done. But, as I was saying, I've always thought since then that there was something odd about the old swindler that she didn't understand herself I never saw anybody look so frightened as she did."

It is to be presumed that this tinge of interest in "the old swindler" led this cautious and sceptical investigator of obscure things to keep in some sort of touch with her down in the lower levels to which she had drifted. Anyhow, it was through this man, Welling, that I was made acquainted with a very queer business, in which Mrs. Ladislaw played a part—a principal part perhaps it might be called, but I don't know about that.

A month or so before, Welling had sent me a singular script, an example, as he said, of what is called "automatic writing". A lady living in a small town in Somerset had discovered that she possessed this gift. She had sat down at her desk with pencil and paper before her, intending to make a list of goods she required from the grocer. She took the pencil in her hand, and, as she declared, it "ran away with her", and proceeded to scrawl and scribble away at a great rate. The slip of paper was soon exhausted, Miss Tuke supplied another, and again the pencil raced away. It had covered six or seven sheets before the impulse or whatever it is ceased. And this had happened several times when Miss Tuke communicated with my acquaintance, Welling, and asked his opinion: should she persist, or resist the impulse when it next occurred?

"I told her," said Welling, "to go on if she liked; provided she regarded it as a parlour game, without any consequence, and quite devoid of any sort of authority. The scripts? Oh, the usual thing: pious exclamations—I understand Miss Tuke is a Wesleyan—and moral maxims, and all sorts of vagueness, and words running into each other, and some repeated three or four times. But this last thing she sent me is a bit of a curiosity; it seems to be Latin tied into knots. I haven't time to disentangle them. But the lady assures me that she doesn't understand it, as she knows no language but her own."

I took the slip home, and found it was much as Welling said: scraps of Latin that read as if they had been taken down from dictation by somebody ignorant of Latin. I corrected the text without much difficulty, and it gave up a number of admirable sentences that might have been extracted from the Fathers: "Jordan was driven back that Israel might enter the land of promise: in like manner it is necessary that the river of our sins be turned back if we would come into that holy land of our inheritance": and a good deal more in that vein. How Miss Tuke came by it all, we never knew. I gathered from Welling that there was no reason to doubt her word, that she knew no Latin. He was inclined to think that she had read it all without understanding it when she was a child, and that it had been preserved, imperfectly enough, in her subconscious memory: a guess, nothing more. And soon after, Welling told me that Miss Tuke had written to him to say that she had given up her "sittings" with pencil and paper, as she thought it was an unsuitable employment for a middle-aged woman.

And all this leads up to something much more significant; at least, so it strikes me. One day, not long ago, Welling called on me, and began at once on Miss Tuke's Latin script.

"You know how you made sense of that stuff. Well, look here. This is worse, and I wonder whether you will be able to make anything of it. Here you are; see what you can do." And he handed me a sheet of paper that gave the effect of a child's scribble.

"And what is one to make of that trident thing or whatever it is?"

He was evidently a good deal interested. And I was more than interested when I saw the device which he had called, "that trident thing".

It was the oddest looking document. At the head of the paper, the word "quotient" was repeated six times. Then came "poison" scrawled in large, loose letters. Then the word "ore" was written twice, followed by "or", and then "oar" was written three times. Then "quite" and finally, the words, "grows my spirit".

It was not difficult. It was, clearly, an attempt at a familiar phrase in *Hamlet*, "the potent poison quite o'ercrows my spirit"; written, apparently, by a person in delirium. "Quotient" for "potent" was odd; but there were similar mistakes in the more subdued scripts of Miss Tuke: the effect being, as I noted in some of her communications, that of a dictation taken down by somebody who failed to catch the exact sound of individual words, and had no notion of the meaning of the complete sentence.

But all this was a very minor matter. It was the symbol that I found exciting. It was dashed all over the paper, sometimes obscuring the writing. It was not exactly a trident. I should have described it as a small Greek omega, at the end of a stick. The two outer lines of the letter were curved inwardly; the middle line, which in a trident is equal in length to the others, was barely indicated. The "stick", as I have called it, was about an inch and a half long.

"Now," said I to Welling, "would you tell me all about it, and where it comes from?"

"Well, it's rather queer. You remember me talking to you about that medium, Mrs. Ladislaw, and the clock business? Well, for that reason I kept something of an eye on her doings. You know she's been down in the world some time now. She lives somewhere in Stockwell, and has séances there, and makes what she can; the old game, the old tricks. There was one of these séances a week ago; and people were getting messages from Aunt This and Uncle That, and they were satisfied, and everything was going all right, when quite suddenly, Mrs. Ladislaw began to twist her face about and scribble away on this bit of paper. And then she went into a fit, and a pretty bad one. A man I know was there, and brought this along, thinking it might interest me. What do you think of it?"

I told him that, apart from the *Hamlet* quotation, there were some interesting points that I should like to go into at leisure. I promised to let him know if there were anything of real consequence involved, and so sent him on his way.

It was the omega mark that concerned me. About twenty-five years ago, I was living in Verulam Buildings, Gray's Inn. In summer, it was often my habit to take a turn about the Square, on fine nights, after the gates were shut; and I soon became aware of a small nocturnal population, who were never seen about the inn in daytime. There were three or four—perhaps five or six—of them; and they prowled in a hapless, aimless, hesitating fashion; stopping now and then and looking vaguely about them, and then moving on, dragging one foot slowly after another. They never spoke to each other, or seemed aware of one another in any sort of way. It is a race that has long been familiar in the Inns of Court. Dickens, who knew all about them, thought that it was the gloom and isolation of the sets of the inns that had reduced them to their dismal apathy and misery. It may be so, or it is possible that the solemn air of antiquity and retirement in the heart of London appeals to men of retired and melancholy habit. I have been long absent from the courts and squares and buildings, and I do not know whether the silent men still resort in these places.

It was an accident that introduced me to one of them. One June night, about ten o'clock, when the sky was still luminous, I was strolling round the Square, and was just passing one of the brotherhood of the night, when he slipped on something on the pavement, and fell sideways, very awkwardly. I helped him up at once, and put him on his feet, and he gave a cry of pain as I did so. He had sprained or strained his ankle muscle, and was evidently in anguish when he tried to set the foot on the ground. I told him to lean on me, and I would see him home. He said his name was Mansel, and he gave me his number; one of the top sets on the west side of the Square. I got him up the stairs with a good deal of difficulty, took his key and supported him to his arm-chair by the fire-place. Then I suggested fetching the doctor from Warwick Place; but he wouldn't hear of that. "We will see how it feels after a good night's rest. I don't like sending for the doctor; you never know what they may say."

I expressed my doubts as to the effects of the night's rest, and proposed that I should leave him in his candle-lit room.

"I wish you would sit down and keep me company for an hour, if you can spare the time. Light your pipe—I've seen you smoking in the Square—and if you don't mind going to that cupboard, I think you'll find some whiskey there, and glasses, and a jug of water."

The whiskey bottle was unopened and dusty, and I searched at his direction in a drawer for the corkscrew. I set a glass beside him, and was about to pour, when he checked me with a gesture, and a "help yourself". And then, relenting, he said: "I think I will have a little to-night. I am still feeling rather shaky." But he stopped me when about a tablespoonful had gone into the glass, and added water largely, and so made himself a ghostly and ineffectual drink.

We began to talk. He told me he had been living in the inn for four or five years; he didn't seem certain as to the precise duration of his residence.

"One gets a little vague, don't you think, living in these old rooms, looking down on the trees," he apologised, "and, somehow, I have rather fallen out of the way of seeing people, and getting about, and so forth, and so forth. One drifts along from day to day, rather sluggishly and ineffectually, I'm afraid . . . and, the edges get dulled, I suppose."

He was a man in the early or middle thirties by his looks: a slight, dark man, with small features, and nothing very distinctive or distinguished about him.

He was difficult to talk to. He never read the papers, he told me. He spoke with a glint of fervour about his old home in the west, of waterbrooks in still hidden valleys, of the wild outlands where no one came, of the sun shining on the bracken on the mountain-side, of the grove of ash trees and their magic.

"Hic vox sine clamore sonat; hic saltat et cantat chorus nympharum eternus." He spoke as if he were quoting some familiar text.

He drifted on, in his own terms, rather sluggishly and ineffectually. I noted that book-cases, well filled, took up a great part of the wall space.

"You have at least good company there," I said, pointing to the shelves.

"Well, I have read a good deal in my time. Yes; I used to be a considerable reader—of a very unsystematic kind, I may say. I never read a book that I didn't want to read. Nobody shall shove books down my throat. . . . But I find myself losing the habit of reading; I can't get the relish that I used to find in it. What did I say just now? The edges are dulled. . . . When a man finds *Tristram Shandy* flat, you know? I remember when I first read it, and for long after that, it was pure sorcery to me; a spell, a spell."

He took up the book from the little table by his chair, and handed it to me as if in illustration of what he had just said. It was an early nineteenth century edition, rather shabbily printed.

I turned over the leaves of the great fantasy, and something on the fly-leaf caught my attention: an odd mark or symbol; the mark that I have described as an omega on a stick. We talked a little longer, and then I left him, with the hope that he might find the remedy of a night's rest efficient in the cure of the twisted ankle. He looked a disconsolate figure in his chair in the dim room, with the misty night in the plane trees of the inn garden as a background.

The next day my business took me up north, among the singing voices of Northumberland. I was away for nearly a week, and when I got back there were evening engagements and amusements to occupy me. It must have been ten days before leisure and a pale green sky led me to take my stroll about the Square. Three or four of the usual nocturnal company were dawdling and creeping round the pavement in the usual manner; but there was no sign of Mansel. I knew it would be of no use to ask about him from these men; it was not likely that any one of them would know his name. I went up his stair, and knocked at the black door. There was no reply, no sound. I waited and knocked again and louder: still, nothing. For a third time I beat my summons, and then there were slow footsteps sounding along the passage. The door was opened; and there stood Mansel, carrying a candle; and the light of it shewed a face of strong distaste for the caller; for any caller. But he relaxed a little when he saw me, and asked me to follow him. He was still limping from the injury of ten days before. No doubt, he had tried neither care nor cure.

"It hasn't troubled me much," he remarked when we sat down. "If I had wanted to get about it would have been tiresome, I dare say. But then, I never do want to get about. I hardly ever go beyond the inn gates. I have seen it all, I don't want to see it again."

He spoke a little of his reading, which had become, he repeated, distasteful to him.

"You get to the end of it all," he murmured. "Or, so I have found. Everywhere, you come to a blank wall. Every path and track you take ends with a blank wall. Not read everything? No indeed; I have neglected vast deserts of dulness. Would you advise me to try Mommsen, or Professor Freeman, or Darwin? Science deals with surfaces; what have I to do with surfaces?"

I was saying that Dickens knew about the solitaries of the Inns of Court. As Mansel was talking his weary nonsense, about coming to the end of everything, of being brought up by a blank wall whatever track he took, I was reminded very strongly of Mr. Parkle's friend in "Chambers".

"One dry hot autumn evening at twilight, this man, being then turned of fifty, looked in upon Parkle in his usual lounging way, with his cigar in his mouth as usual, and said: 'I am going out of town.' As he never went out of town Parkle said: 'Oh, indeed! At last?' 'Yes,' says he, 'at last. For what is a man to do? London is so small! If you go west, you come to Hounslow. If you go east, you come to Bow. If you go south, there's Brixton or Norwood. If you go north, you can't get rid of Barnet.'"

It struck me as odd that two such different people as the actual Mansel and the Dickens character should reach the same end by their varying ways. The blank wall loomed equally before them. I hoped that Mansel would not find at last the same end as Parkle's friend; the end of a suicide's rope.

I tried to stir the man a little out of his apathy. I misquoted a well-known passage of a well-known writer; and he flickered into a faint gleam of interest.

"Not quite that, is it? 'We are all as God made us, and many of us a great deal worse.' Surely, 'and *often* a great deal worse'? Would you mind verifying? There's the book, at the end of the second shelf."

I verified the *Don Quixote* quotation; and he nodded a very brief satisfaction at having the phrase correctly. I was putting the book back in its place, and it slipped from my hand to the floor. As I picked it up, I noticed again the mark of the omega; this time on the title-page.

"May I ask," I said, "if this odd omega in your books has any particular meaning?"

He smiled faintly. "That," he explained, "is a bit of schoolboy nonsense. I don't recollect whether it was because I was proud of having learnt the Greek alphabet; but I got into the way of putting that thing in my books instead of my name or initials, and I kept it up afterwards. You would find it in every book on the shelves, and sometimes I've used it to mark a passage, in the margin. Indeed, I used to sign my letters to old friends with the Omega Exalted, as I called it."

I stayed on at Gray's Inn for the next six or seven months, and I suppose I repeated my visit to Mansel three or four times. I could not say that I was welcome, but I was not exactly unwelcome. It was a pang for him to open his door, but he was not displeased to let me in. There was no change in him, no sign that he would revive, and live again like other men. Then I left London, and remained away for many years, and I cannot say that Mansel was much more than a dim image in my memory. On my return, finding myself one day in Holborn, it struck me that I might make some enquiries. They told me in the inn that Mr. Mansel was understood to be very infirm; that he had not been seen outside his chambers for years and years. I thought I had better not look him up; he would not remember me or desire to do so.

A year ago his laundress found him dead in his chair next to the fireplace. It appeared on examination that his heart had given out. He had left his money and his goods to a distant cousin in the west, who came up to town, did what was necessary, and went down again to some obscure retreat by the sunset. Mansel's books and furniture—there was nothing of value—were sold and dispersed.

The inn painted and papered the set of rooms on the top floor of the Square, and made them look as gay as they could look. But they did not let readily. There were plenty of applicants, but I gathered that people who came in a hurry to secure chambers giving on the Garden, drew back when they were taken into the set. Something seemed amiss; they could not say what. They didn't "fancy" the place. Everything in the way of decoration, it was allowed, was extremely bright and cheerful; but . . . there was something, and that something was far from cheerful. One prospective tenant, a lady, was seized with a fit of shivering and said she felt as if icy water were trickling down her spine. It must have been nine or ten months after Mansel's death that the set was taken by a young couple, who seemed to think themselves lucky, and made no complaint as to "something" or anything. The gentleman was connected with finance, and the lady was gaiety itself. She had a loud and cheerful voice, and a louder laugh, and expressed herself, so it was said, with considerable freedom. These people laid themselves out to brighten things. They gave frequent parties, a little on the loud side, it was thought, for the Inn, and the porters at the Holborn Gate were busy long after midnight.

And then, all this liveliness came to an end in a very tragic manner. In the middle of a "bottle party", when everything was at a high pitch, one of the guests, a Mr. Jerome Platt, understood to be a cousin of the host's, suddenly complained of agonising internal pains. He was taken to the hotel where he was staying, and doctors were summoned, and everything done that could be done. But Mr. Platt died the next day; of acute ptomaine poisoning as the evidence at the inquest demonstrated. He had dined at a fashionable West End restaurant before going on to the party at Gray's Inn. There were no complaints from any other of the diners.

By the end of the month, old Mansel's rooms were again vacant. The bright tenants, very naturally, as people said, felt they could not go on living in a place where such a terrible thing had happened. They were supposed to have gone abroad within three weeks of the disastrous "bottle party".

And as to that very different party given by Mrs. Ladislaw, and the end of it, and the scribble on the paper? So far as I can make out from what Welling has told me, the Ladislaw séance must have taken place a day, or perhaps two days, before that grim gathering in Gray's Inn. Mansel had been dead for many months: what are we to infer? Had he anything to do with the seizure of the medium, and with what was written by her?

There is one point that should not be forgotten. I noted that, in Welling's opinion, the corrupt Latin "messages" written by Miss Tuke might very well be subconscious memories, imperfectly preserved, of something which she had read without understanding years before, and which had entirely disappeared from her conscious mind. So, perhaps, with the "exalted omega". Mansel's books had been dispersed.

None of them was of any interest to the big second-hand booksellers, to the dealers in rarities; the volumes would therefore tend to find their way to the small shops and the poorer neighbourhoods. Mrs. Ladislaw might very well have passed such shops on her marketing rounds; she might have turned over the books in the threepenny and sixpenny boxes—and she might easily have seen old Mansel's omega mark; very likely without consciously noting it.

It is distinctly possible that this is the solution of the problem; though here also there are lurking difficulties and obscurities.

The Children of the Pool

A couple of summers ago I was staying with old friends in my native county, on the Welsh border. It was in the heat and drought of a hot and dry year, and I came into those green, well-watered valleys with a sense of a great refreshment. Here was relief from the burning of London streets, from the close and airless nights, when all the myriad walls of brick and stone and concrete and the pavements that are endless give out into the heavy darkness the fires that all day long have been drawn from the sun. And from those roadways that have become like railways, with their changing lamps, and their yellow globes, and their bars and studs of steel; from the menace of instant death if your feet stray from the track: from all this what a rest to walk under the green leaf in quiet, and hear the stream trickling from the heart of the hill.

My friends were old friends, and they were urgent that I should go my own way. There was breakfast at nine, but it was equally serviceable and excellent at ten; and I could be in for something cold for lunch, if I liked; and if I didn't like I could stay away till dinner at half past seven; and then there was all the evening for talks about old times and about the changes, with comfortable drinks, and bed soothed by memories and tobacco, and by the brook that twisted under dark alders through the meadow below. And not a red bungalow to be seen for many a mile around! Sometimes, when the heat even in that green land was more than burning, and the wind from the mountains in the west ceased, I would stay all day under shade on the lawn, but more often I went afield and trod remembered ways, and tried to find new ones, in that happy and bewildered country. There, paths go wandering into undiscovered valleys, there from deep and narrow lanes with over-shadowing hedges, still smaller tracks that I suppose are old bridle-paths, creep obscurely, obviously leading nowhere in particular.

It was on a day of cooler air that I went adventuring abroad on such an expedition. It was a "day of the veil". There were no clouds in the sky, but a high mist, grey and luminous, had been drawn all over it. At one moment, it would seem that the sun must shine through, and the blue appear; and then the trees in the wood would seem to blossom, and the meadows lightened; and then again the veil would be drawn. I struck off by the stony lane that led from the back of the house up over the hill; I had last gone that way a-many years ago, of a winter afternoon, when the ruts were frozen into hard ridges, and dark pines on high places rose above snow, and the sun was red and still above the mountain. I remembered that the way had given good sport, with twists to right and left, and unexpected descents, and then risings to places of thorn and bracken, till it darkened to the hushed stillness of a winter's night, and I turned homeward reluctant. Now I took another chance with all the summer day before me, and resolved to come to some end and conclusion of the matter.

I think I had gone beyond the point at which I had stopped and turned back as the frozen darkness and the bright stars came on me. I remembered the dip in the hedge, from which I saw the round tumulus on high at the end of the mountain wall; and there was the white farm on the hillside, and the farmer was still calling to his dog, as he— or his father—had called before, his voice high and thin in the distance. After this point, I seemed to be in undiscovered country; the ash trees grew densely on either side of the way and met above it: I went on and on into the unknown in the manner of the only good guidebooks, which are the tales of old knights.

The road went down, and climbed, and again descended, all through the deep of the wood. Then, on both sides, the trees ceased, though the hedges were so high that I could see nothing of the way of the land about me. And just at the wood's ending, there was one of those tracks or little paths of which I have spoken, going off from my lane on the right, and winding out of sight quickly under all its leafage of hazel and wild rose, maple and hornbeam, with a holly here and there, and honeysuckle golden, and dark briony shining and twining everywhere. I could not resist the invitation of a path so obscure and uncertain, and set out on its track of green and profuse grass, with the ground beneath still soft to the feet, even in the drought of that fiery summer. The way wound, as far as I could make out, on the slope of a hill, neither ascending nor descending, and after a mile or more of this rich walking, it suddenly ceased, and I found myself on a bare hillside, on a rough track that went down to a grey house. It was now a farm by its looks and surroundings, but there were signs of old state about it: good sixteenth-century mullioned windows and a Jacobean porch projecting from the centre, with dim armorial bearings mouldering above the door.

It struck me that bread and cheese and cider would be grateful, and I beat upon the door with my stick, and brought a pleasant woman to open it.

"Do you think," I began, "you could be so good as . . ."

And then came a shout from somewhere at the end of the stone passage, and a great voice called:

"Come in, then, come in, you old scoundrel, if your name is Meyrick, as I'm sure it is."

I was amazed. The pleasant woman grinned and said:

"It seems you are well known here, sir, already. But perhaps you had heard that Mr. Roberts was staying here."

My old acquaintance, James Roberts, came tumbling out from his den at the back. He was a man whom I had known a long time, but not very well. Our affairs in London moved on different lines, and so we did not often meet. But I was glad to see him in that unexpected place: he was a round man, always florid and growing redder in the face with his years. He was a countryman of mine, but I had hardly known him before we both went to town, since his home had been at the northern end of the county.

He shook me cordially by the hand, and looked as if he would like to smack me on the back—he was, a little, that kind of man—and repeated his "Come in, come in!" adding to the pleasant woman: "And bring you another plate, Mrs. Morgan, and all the rest of it. I hope you've not forgotten how to eat Caerphilly cheese, Meyrick. I can tell you, there is none better than Mrs. Morgan's making. And, Mrs. Morgan, another jug of cider, and *seidr dda*, mind you."

I never knew whether he had been brought up as a boy to speak Welsh. In London he had lost all but the faintest trace of accent, but down here in Gwent the tones of the country had quickly returned to him; and he smacked as strongly of the land in his speech as the cheerful farmer's wife herself. I judged his accent was a part of his holiday.

He drew me into the little parlour with its old furniture and its pleasant old-fashioned ornaments and faintly flowering wallpaper, and set me in an elbow-chair at the round table, and gave me, as I told him, exactly what I had meant to ask for: bread and cheese and cider. All very good; Mrs. Morgan, it was clear, had the art of making a Caerphilly cheese that was succulent—a sort of white *bel paese*—far different from those dry and stony cheeses that often bring dishonour on the Caerphilly name. And afterwards there was gooseberry jam and cream. And the tobacco that the country uses: Shag-on-the-Back, from the Welsh Back, Bristol. And then there was gin.

This last we partook of out of doors, in an old stone summer-house, in the garden at the side. A white rose had grown all over the summer-house, and shaded and glorified it. The water in the big jug had just been drawn from the well in the limestone rock—and I told Roberts gratefully that I felt a great deal better than when I had knocked at the farmhouse door. I told him where I was staying—he knew my host by name—and he, in turn, informed me that it was his first visit to Lanypwll, as the farm was called. A neighbour of his at Lee had recommended Mrs. Morgan's cooking very highly: and, as he said, you couldn't speak too well of her in that way or any other.

We sipped and smoked through the afternoon in that pleasant retreat under the white roses. I meditated gratefully on the fact that I should not dare to enjoy Shag-on-the-Back so freely in London: a potent tobacco, of full and ripe savour, but not for the hard streets.

"You say the farm is called Lanypwll," I interjected, "that means 'by the pool,' doesn't it? Where is the pool? I don't see it."

"Come you," said Roberts, "and I will shew you."

He took me by a little gate through the garden hedge of laurels, thick and high, and round to the left of the house, the opposite side to that by which I had made my approach. And there we climbed a green rounded bastion of the old ages, and he pointed down to a narrow valley, shut in by steep wooded hills. There at the bottom was a level, half marshland and half black water lying in still pools, with green islands of iris and of all manner of rank and strange growths that love to have their roots in slime.

"There is your pool for you," said Roberts.

It was the most strange place, I thought, hidden away under the hills as if it were a secret. The steeps that went down to it were a tangle of undergrowth, of all manner of boughs mingled with taller trees rising above the mass, and down at the edge of the marsh some of these had perished in the swampy water, and stood white and bare and ghastly, with leprous limbs.

"An ugly looking place," I said to Roberts.

"I quite agree with you. It is an ugly place enough. They tell me at the farm it's not safe to go near it, or you may get fever and I don't know what else. And, indeed, if you didn't go down carefully and watch your steps, you might easily find yourself up to the neck in that black muck there."

We turned back into the garden and to our summer-house, and soon after, it was time for me to make my way home.

"How long are you staying with Nichol?" Roberts asked me as we parted. I told him, and he insisted on my dining with him at the end of the week.

"I will 'send' you," he said. "I will take you by a short cut across the fields and see that you don't lose your way. Roast duck and green peas," he added alluringly, "and something good for the digestion afterwards."

It was a fine evening when I next journeyed to the farm, but indeed we got tired of saying "fine weather" throughout that wonderful summer. I found Roberts cheery and welcoming, but, I thought, hardly in such rosy spirits as on my former visit. We were having a cocktail of his composition in the summer-house, as the famous duck gained the last glow of brown perfection; and I noticed that his speech was not bubbling so freely from him as before. He fell silent once or twice and looked thoughtful. He told me he'd ventured down to the pool, the swampy place at the bottom. "And it looks no better when you see it close at hand. Black, oily stuff that isn't like water, with a scum upon it, and weeds like a lot of monsters. I never saw such queer, ugly plants. There's one rank-looking thing down there covered with dull crimson blossoms, all bloated out and speckled like a toad."

"You're no botanist," I remarked.

"No, not I. I know buttercups and daisies and not much more. Mrs. Morgan here was quite frightened when I told her where I'd been. She said she hoped I mightn't be sorry for it. But I feel as well as ever. I don't think there are many places left in the country now where you can get malaria."

We proceeded to the duck and the green peas and rejoiced in their perfection. There was some very old ale that Mr. Morgan had bought when an ancient tavern in the neighbourhood had been pulled down; its age and original excellence had combined to make a drink like a rare wine. The "something good for the digestion" turned out to be a mellow brandy that Roberts had brought with him from town. I told him that I had never known a better hour. He warmed up with the good meat and drink and was cheery enough; and yet I thought there was a reserve, something obscure at the back of his mind that was by no means cheerful.

We had a second glass of the mellow brandy, and Roberts, after a moment's indecision, spoke out. He dropped his holiday game of Welsh countryman completely.

"You wouldn't think, would you," he began, "that a man would come down to a place like this to be blackmailed at the end of the journey?"

"Good Lord!" I gasped in amazement, "I should think not indeed. What's happened?"

He looked very grave. I thought even that he looked frightened.

"Well, I'll tell you. A couple of nights ago, I went for a stroll after my dinner; a beautiful night, with the moon shining, and a nice, clean breeze. So I walked up over the hill, and then took the path that leads down through the wood to the brook. I'd got into the wood, fifty yards or so, when I heard my name called out: 'Roberts! James Roberts!' in a shrill, piercing voice, a young girl's voice, and I jumped pretty well out of my skin, I can tell you. I stopped dead and stared all about me. Of course I could see nothing at all—bright moonlight and black shadow and all those trees—anybody could hide. Then it came to me that it was some girl of the place having a game with her sweetheart: James Roberts is a common enough name, especially in this part of the country. So I was just going on, not bothering my head about the local love-affairs, when that scream came right in my ear: 'Roberts! Roberts!

James Roberts!'—and then half a dozen words that I won't trouble you with; not yet, at any rate."

I have said that Roberts was by no means an intimate friend of mine. But I had always known him as a genial, cordial fellow, a thoroughly good-natured man; and I was sorry and shocked, too, to see him sitting there wretched and dismayed. He looked as if he had seen a ghost; he looked much worse than that. He looked as if he had seen terror.

But it was too early to press him closely. I said:

"What did you do then?"

"I turned about, and ran back through the wood, and tumbled over the stile. I got home here as quick as ever I could, and shut myself up in this room, dripping with fright and gasping for breath. I was almost crazy, I believe. I walked up and down. I sat down in the chair and got up again. I wondered whether I should wake up in my bed and find I'd been having a nightmare. I cried at last. I'll tell you the truth: I put my head in my hands, and the tears ran down my cheeks. I was quite broken."

"But, look here," I said, "isn't this making a great to-do about very little? I can quite see it must have been a nasty shock. But, how long did you say you had been staying here; ten days, was it?"

"A fortnight, to-morrow."

"Well; you know country ways as well as I do. You may be sure that everybody within three or four miles of Lanypwll knows about a gentleman from London, a Mr. James Roberts, staying at the farm. And there are always unpleasant young people to be found, wherever you go. I gather that this girl used very abusive language when she hailed you. She probably thought it was a good joke. You had taken that walk through the wood in the evening a couple of times before? No doubt, you had been noticed going that way, and the girl and her friend or friends planned to give you a shock. I wouldn't think any more of it, if I were you."

He almost cried out.

"Think any more of it! What will the world think of it?" There was an anguish of terror in his voice. I thought it was time to come to cues. I spoke up pretty briskly:

"Now, look here, Roberts, it's no good beating about the bush.

Before we can do anything, we've got to have the whole tale, fair and square. What I've gathered is this: you go for a walk in a wood near here one evening, and a girl—you say it was a girl's voice—hails you by your name, and then screams out a lot of filthy language. Is there anything more in it than that?"

"There's a lot more than that. I was going to ask you not to let it go any further; but as far as I can see, there won't be any secret in it much longer. There's another end to the story, and it goes back a good many years—to the time when I first came to London as a young man. That's twenty-five years ago."

He stopped speaking. When he began again, I could feel that he spoke with unutterable repugnance. Every word was a horror to him.

"You know as well as I do that there are all sorts of turnings in London that a young fellow can take; good, bad, and indifferent. There was a good deal of bad luck about it. I do believe, and I was too young to know or care much where I was going; but I got into a turning with the black pit at the end of it."

He beckoned me to lean forward across the table, and whispered for a minute or two in my ear. In my turn, I heard not without horror. I said nothing.

"*That* was what I heard shrieked out in the wood. What do you say?"

"You've done with all that long ago?"

"It was done with very soon after it was begun. It was no more than a bad dream. And then it all flashed back on me like deadly lightning. What do you say? What can I do?"

I told him that I had to admit that it was no good to try to put the business in the wood down to accident, the casual filthy language of a depraved village girl. As I said, it couldn't be a case of a bow drawn at a venture.

"There must be somebody behind it. Can you think of anybody?"

"There may be one or two left. I can't say. I haven't heard of any of them for years. I thought they had all gone; dead, or at the other side of the world."

"Yes; but people can get back from the other side of the world pretty quickly in these days. Yokohama is not much farther off than Yarmouth. But you haven't heard of any of these people lately?"

"As I said, not for years. But the secret's out."

"But, let's consider. Who is this girl? Where does she live? We must get at her, and try if we can't frighten the life out of her. And, in the first place, we'll find out the source of her information. Then we shall know where we are. I suppose you have discovered who she is?"

"I've not a notion of who she is or where she lives."

"I dare say you wouldn't care to ask the Morgans any questions. But to go back to the beginning: you spoke of blackmail. Did this damned girl ask you for money to shut her mouth?"

"No; I shouldn't have called it blackmail. She didn't say anything about money."

"Well; that sounds more helpful. Let's see; to-night is Saturday. You took this unfortunate walk of yours a couple of nights ago; on Thursday night. And you haven't heard anything more since. I should keep away from that wood, and try to find out who the young lady is. That's the first thing to be done, clearly."

I was trying to cheer him up a little; but he only stared at me with his horror-stricken eyes.

"It didn't finish with the wood," he groaned. "My bedroom is next door to this room where we are. When I had pulled myself together a bit that night, I had a stiff glass, about double my allowance, and went off to bed and to sleep. I woke up with a noise of tapping at the window, just by the head of the bed. Tap, tap, tap, it went. I thought it might be a bough beating on the glass. And then I heard that voice calling me: 'James Roberts: open, open!'

"I tell you, my flesh crawled on my bones. I would have cried out, but I couldn't make a sound. The moon had gone down, and there's a great old pear tree close to the window, and it was quite dark. I sat up in my bed, shaking for fear. It was dead still, and I began to think that the fright I had got in the wood had given me nightmare. Then the voice called again, and louder:

"'James Roberts! Open. Quick.'

"And I had to open. I leaned half out of bed, and got at the latch, and opened the window a little. I didn't dare to look out. But it was too dark to see anything in the shadow of the tree. And then she began to talk to me. She told me all about it from the beginning. She knew all the names. She knew where my business was in London, and where I lived, and who my friends were. She said that they should all know.

And she said: 'And you yourself shall tell them, and you shall not be able to keep back a single word!'"

The wretched man fell back in his chair, shuddering and gasping for breath. He beat his hands up and down, with a gesture of hopeless fear and misery; and his lips grinned with dread.

I won't say that I began to see light. But I saw a hint of certain possibilities of light or—let us say—of a lessening of the darkness. I said a soothing word or two, and let him get a little more quiet. The telling of this extraordinary and very dreadful experience had set his nerves all dancing; and yet, having made a clean breast of it all, I could see that he felt some relief. His hands lay quiet on the table, and his lips ceased their horrible grimacing. He looked at me with a faint expectancy, I thought; as if he had begun to cherish a dim hope that I might have some sort of help for him. He could not see himself the possibility of rescue; still, one never knew what resources and freedoms the other man might bring.

That, at least, was what his poor, miserable face seemed to me to express; and I hoped I was right, and let him simmer a little, and gather to himself such twigs and straws of hope as he could. Then, I began again:

"This was on the Thursday night. And last night? Another visit?"

"The same as before. Almost word for word."

"And it was all true, what she said? The girl was not lying?"

"Every word of it was true. There were some things that I had forgotten myself; but when she spoke of them, I remembered at once. There was the number of a house in a certain street, for example. If you had asked me for that number a week ago I should have told you, quite honestly, that I knew nothing about it. But when I heard it, I knew it in the instant: I could see that number in the light of a street lamp. The sky was dark and cloudy, and a bitter wind was blowing, and driving the leaves on the pavement—that November night."

"When the fire was lit?"

"That night. When they appeared."

"And you haven't seen this girl? You couldn't describe her?'"

"I was afraid to look; I told you. I waited when she stopped speaking. I sat there for half an hour or an hour. Then I lit my candle and shut the window-latch. It was three o'clock and growing light."

I was thinking it over. I noted that Roberts confessed that every word spoken by his visitant was true. She had sprung no surprises on him; there had been no suggestion of fresh details, names, or circumstances. That struck me as having a certain—possible—significance; and the knowledge of Roberts's present circumstances, his City address, and his home address, and the names of his friends: that was interesting, too.

There was a glimpse of a possible hypothesis. I could not be sure; but I told Roberts that I thought something might be done. To begin with, I said, I was going to keep him company for the night. Nichol would guess that I had shirked the walk home after nightfall; that would be quite all right. And in the morning he was to pay Mrs. Morgan for the two extra weeks he had arranged to stay, with something by way of compensation. "And it should be something handsome," I added with emotion, thinking of the duck and the old ale. "And then," I finished, "I shall pack you off to the other side of the island."

Of that old ale I made him drink a liberal dose by way of sleeping-draught. He hardly needed a hypnotic; the terror that he had endured and the stress of telling it had worn him out. I saw him fall into bed and fall asleep in a moment, and I curled up, comfortably enough, in a roomy arm-chair. There was no trouble in the night, and when I writhed myself awake, I saw Roberts sleeping peacefully. I let him alone, and wandered about the house and the shining morning garden, till I came upon Mrs. Morgan, busy in the kitchen.

I broke the trouble to her. I told her that I was afraid that the place was not agreeing at all with Mr. Roberts. "Indeed," I said, "he was taken so ill last night that I was afraid to leave him. His nerves seem to be in a very bad way."

"Indeed, then, I don't wonder at all," replied Mrs. Morgan, with a very grave face. But I wondered a good deal at this remark of hers, not having a notion as to what she meant.

I went on to explain what I had arranged for our patient, as I called him: east-coast breezes, and crowds of people, the noisier the better, and, indeed, that was the cure that I had in mind. I said that I was sure Mr. Roberts would do the proper thing.

"That will be all right, sir, I am sure: don't you trouble yourself about that. But the sooner you get him away after I have given you both your breakfasts, the better I shall be pleased. I am frightened to death for him, I can tell you."

And she went off to her work, murmuring something that sounded like *"Plant y pwll, plant y pwll."*

I gave Roberts no time for reflection. I woke him up, bustled him out of bed, hurried him through his breakfast, saw him pack his suitcase, make his farewells to the Morgans, and had him sitting in the shade on Nichol's lawn well before the family were back from church. I gave Nichol a vague outline of the circumstances—nervous breakdown and so forth—introduced them to one another, and left them talking about the Black Mountains, Roberts's land of origin. The next day I saw him off at the station, on his way to Great Yarmouth, via London. I told him with an air of authority that he would have no more trouble, "from any quarter," I emphasised. And he was to write to me at my town address in a week's time.

"And, by the way," I said, just before the train slid along the platform, "here's a bit of Welsh for you. What does *'plant y pwll'* mean? Something of the pool?"

"Plant y pwll," he explained, "means 'children of the pool.'"

When my holiday was ended, and I had got back to town, I began my investigations into the case of James Roberts and his nocturnal visitant. When he began his story I was extremely distressed—I made no doubt as to the bare truth of it, and was shocked to think of a very kindly man threatened with overwhelming disgrace and disaster. There seemed nothing impossible in the tale stated at large, and in the first outline. It is not altogether unheard of for very decent men to have had a black patch in their lives, which they have done their best to live down and atone for and forget. Often enough, the explanation of such misadventure is not hard to seek. You have a young fellow, very decently but very simply brought up among simple country people, suddenly pitched into the labyrinth of London, into a maze in which there are many turnings, as the unfortunate Roberts put it, which lead to disaster, or to something blacker than disaster. The more experienced man, the man of keen instincts and perceptions, knows the aspect of these tempting passages and avoids them; some have the wit to turn back in time; a few are caught in the trap at the end. And in some cases, though there may be apparent escape, and peace and security for many years, the teeth of the snare are about the man's leg all the while, and close at last on highly reputable chairmen and churchwardens and pillars of all sorts of seemly institutions. And then gaol, or at best, hissing and extinction.

So, on the first face of it, I was by no means prepared to pooh-pooh Roberts's tale. But when he came to detail, and I had time to think it over, that entirely illogical faculty, which sometimes takes charge of our thoughts and judgments, told me that there was some huge flaw in all this, that somehow or other, things had not happened so. This mental process, I may say, is strictly indefinable and unjustifiable by any laws of thought that I have ever heard of. It won't do to take our stand with Bishop Butler, and declare with him that probability is the guide of life; deducing from this premise the conclusion that the improbable doesn't happen. Any man who cares to glance over his experience of the world and of things in general is aware that the most wildly improbable events are constantly happening. For example, I take up to-day's paper, sure that I shall find something to my purpose, and in a minute I come across the headline: "Damaging a Model Elephant." A father, evidently a man of substance, accuses his son of this strange offence. Last summer, the father told the court, his son constructed in their front garden a large model of an elephant, the material being bought by witness. The skeleton of the elephant was made of tubing, and it was covered with soil and fibre, and held together with wire netting. Flowers were planted on it, and it cost £3 5s.

A photograph of the elephant was produced in court, and the clerk remarked: "It is a fearsome-looking thing."

And then the catastrophe. The son got to know a married woman much older than himself, and his parents frowned, and there were quarrels. And so, one night, the young man came to his father's house, jumped over the garden wall and tried to push the elephant over. Failing, he proceeded to disembowel the elephant with a pair of wire clippers.

There! Nothing can be much more improbable than that tale, but it all happened so, as the *Daily Telegraph* assures me, and I believe every word of it. And I have no doubt that if I care to look I shall find something as improbable, or even more improbable, in the newspaper columns three or perhaps four times a week. What about the old man, unknown, unidentified, found in the Thames: in one pocket, a stone Buddha; in the other, a leather wallet, with the inscription: "The hen that sits on the china egg is best off."

The improbable happens and is constantly happening; but, using that faculty which I am unable to define, I rejected Roberts's girl of the wood and the window. I did not suspect him for a moment of leg-pulling of an offensive and vicious kind. His misery and terror were too clearly manifest for that, and I was certain that he was suffering from a very serious and dreadful shock—and yet I didn't believe in the truth of the story he had told me. I felt convinced that there was no girl in the case; either in the wood or at the window. And when Roberts told me, with increased horror, that every word she spoke was true, that she had even reminded him of matters that he had himself forgotten, I was greatly encouraged in my growing surmise. For, it seemed to me at least probable that if the case had been such as he supposed it, there would have been new and damning circumstances in the story, utterly unknown to him and unsuspected by him. But, as it was, everything that he was told he accepted; as a man in a dream accepts without hesitation the wildest fantasies as matters and incidents of his daily experience. Decidedly, there was no girl there.

On the Sunday that he spent with me at the Wern, Nichol's place, I took advantage of his calmer condition—the night's rest had done him good—to get some facts and dates out of him, and when I returned to town, I put these to the test. It was not altogether an easy investigation since, on the surface, at least, the matters to be investigated were eminently trivial; the early days of a young man from the country up in London in a business house; and twenty-five years ago. Even really exciting murder trials and changes of ministries become blurred and uncertain in outline, if not forgotten, in twenty-five years, or in twelve years for that matter: and compared with such events, the affair of James Roberts seemed perilously like nothing at all.

However, I had made the best use I could of the information that Roberts had given me; and I was fortified for the task by a letter I received from him. He told me that there had been no recurrence of the trouble (as he expressed it), that he felt quite well, and was enjoying himself immensely at Yarmouth. He said that the shows and entertainments on the sands were doing him "no end of good. There's a retired executioner who does his old business in a tent, with the drop and everything. And there's a bloke who calls himself Archbishop of London, who fasts in a glass case, with his mitre and all his togs on." Certainly, my patient was either recovered, or in a very fair way to recovery: I could set about my researches in a calm spirit of scientific curiosity, without the nervous tension of the surgeon called upon at short notice to perform a life-or-death operation.

As a matter of fact it was all more simple than I thought it would be. True, the results were nothing, or almost nothing, but that was exactly what I had expected and hoped. With the slight sketch of his early career in London, furnished me by Roberts, the horrors omitted by my request; with a name or two and a date or two, I got along very well. And what did it come to? Simply this: here was a lad—he was just seventeen—who had been brought up amongst lonely hills and educated at a small grammar school, furnished through a London uncle with a very small stool in a City office. By arrangement, settled after a long and elaborate correspondence, he was to board with some distant cousins, who lived in the Cricklewood–Kilburn–Brondesbury region, and with them he settled down, comfortably enough, as it seemed, though Cousin Ellen objected to his learning to smoke in his bedroom, and begged him to desist. The household consisted of Cousin Ellen, her husband, Henry Watts, and the two daughters, Helen and Justine. Justine was about Roberts's own age; Helen three or four years older. Mr. Watts had married rather late in life, and had retired from his office a year or so before. He interested himself chiefly in tuberous-rooted begonias, and in the season went out a few miles to his cricket club and watched the game on Saturday afternoons. Every morning there was breakfast at eight, every evening there was high tea at seven, and in the meantime young Roberts did his best in the City, and liked his job well enough. He was shy with the two girls at first, but Justine was lively, and couldn't help having a voice like a peacock, and Helen was adorable. And so things went on very pleasantly for a year or perhaps eighteen months; on this basis, that Justine was a great joke, and that Helen was adorable. The trouble was that Justine didn't think she was a great joke.

For, it must be said that Roberts's stay with his cousins ended in disaster. I rather gather that the young man and the quiet Helen were guilty of—shall, we say—amiable indiscretions, though without serious consequences. But it appeared that Cousin Justine, a girl with black eyes and black hair, made discoveries which she resented savagely, denouncing the offenders at the top of that piercing voice of hers, in the waste hours of the Brondesbury night, to the immense rage, horror, and consternation of the whole house. In fact, there was the devil to pay, and Mr. Watts then and there turned young Roberts out of the house. And there is no doubt that he should have been thoroughly ashamed of himself. But young men . . .

Nothing very much happened. Old Watts had cried in his rage that he would let Roberts's chief in the City hear the whole story; but, on reflection, he held his tongue. Roberts roamed about London for the rest of the night, refreshing himself occasionally at coffee-stalls. When the shops opened, he had a wash and brush-up, and was prompt and bright at his office. At midday, in the underground smoking-room of the tea-shop, he conferred with a fellow clerk over their dominoes, and arranged to share rooms with him out Norwood way. From that point onwards, the career of James Roberts had been eminently quiet, uneventful, successful.

Now, everybody, I suppose, is aware that in recent years the silly business of divination by dreams has ceased to be a joke and has become a very serious science. It is called "Psycho-analysis"; and is compounded, I would say, by mingling one grain of sense with a hundred of pure nonsense. From the simplest and most obvious dreams, the psycho-analyst deduces the most incongruous and extravagant results. A black savage tells him that he has dreamed of being chased by lions, or, maybe, by crocodiles: and the psycho man knows at once that the black is suffering from the Œdipus complex. That is, he is madly in love with his own mother, and is, therefore, afraid of the vengeance of his father. Everybody knows, of course, that "lion" and "crocodile" are symbols of "father". And I understand that there are educated people who believe this stuff.

It is all nonsense, to be sure; and so much the greater nonsense inasmuch as the true interpretation of many dreams—not by any means of all dreams—moves, it may be said, in the opposite direction to the method of psycho-analysis. The psycho-analyst infers the monstrous and abnormal from a trifle; it is often safe to reverse the process. If a man dreams that he has committed a sin before which the sun hid his face, it is often safe to conjecture that, in sheer forgetfulness, he wore a red tie, or brown boots with evening dress. A slight dispute with the vicar may deliver him in sleep into the clutches of the Spanish Inquisition, and the torment of a fiery death. Failure to catch the post with a rather important letter will sometimes bring a great realm to ruin in the world of dreams. And here, I have no doubt, we have the explanation of part of the explanation of the Roberts affair. Without question, he had been a bad boy; there was something more than a trifle at the heart of his trouble. But his original offence, grave as we may think it, had, in his hidden consciousness, swollen and exaggerated itself into a monstrous mythology of evil. Some time ago, a learned and curious investigator demonstrated how Coleridge had taken a bald sentence from an old chronicler, and had made it the nucleus of *The Ancient Mariner.* With a vast gesture of the spirit, he had unconsciously gathered from all the four seas of his vast reading all manner of creatures into his net: till the bare hint of the old book glowed into one of the great masterpieces of the world's poetry. Roberts had nothing in him of the poetic faculty, nothing of the shaping power of the imagination, no trace of the gift of expression, by which the artist delivers his soul of its burden. In him, as in many men, there was a great gulf fixed between the hidden and the open consciousness; so that which could not come out into the light grew and swelled secretly, hugely, horribly in the darkness. If Roberts had been a poet or a painter or a musician; we might have had a masterpiece. As he was neither: we had a monster. And I do not at all believe that his years had consciously been vexed by a deep sense of guilt. I gathered in the course of my researches that not long after the flight from Brondesbury, Roberts was made aware of unfortunate incidents in the Watts saga—if we may use this honoured term—which convinced him that there were extenuating circumstances in his offence, and excuses for his wrongdoing. The actual fact had, no doubt, been forgotten or remembered very slightly, rarely, casually, without any sense of grave moment or culpability attached to it; while, all the while, a pageantry of horror was being secretly formed in the hidden places of the man's soul. And at last, after the years of growth and swelling in the darkness; the monster leapt into the light, and with such violence that to the victim it seemed an actual and objective entity.

And, in a sense, it had risen from the black waters of the pool. I was reading a few days ago, in a review of a grave book on psychology, the following very striking sentences:

> The things which we distinguish as qualities or values are inherent in the real environment to make the configuration that they do make with our sensory response to them. There is such a thing as a "sad" landscape, even when we who look at it are feeling jovial; and if we think it is "sad" only because we attribute to it something derived from our own past associations with sadness, Professor Koffka gives us good reason to regard the view as superficial. That is not imputing human attributes to what are described as "demand characters" in the environment, but giving proper recognition to the other end of a nexus, of which only one end is organised in our own mind.

Psychology is, I am sure, a difficult and subtle science, which, perhaps naturally, must be expressed in subtle and difficult language. But so far as I can gather the sense of the passage which I have quoted, it comes to this: that a landscape, a certain configuration of wood, water, height and depth, light and dark, flower and rock, is, in fact, an objective reality, a thing; just as opium and wine are things, not clotted fancies, mere creatures of our make-believe, to which we give a kind of spurious reality and efficacy. The dreams of De Quincey were a synthesis of De Quincey, *plus* opium; the riotous gaiety of Charles Surface and his friends was the product and result of the wine they had drunk, *plus* their personalities. So, the profound Professor Koffka—his book is called *Principles of Gestalt Psychology*—insists that the "sadness" which we attribute to a particular landscape is really and efficiently in the landscape and not merely in ourselves; and consequently that the landscape can affect us and produce results in us, in precisely the same manner as drugs and meat and drink affect us in their several ways. Poe, who knew many secrets, knew this, and taught that landscape gardening was as truly a fine art as poetry or painting; since it availed to communicate the mysteries to the human spirit.

And perhaps Mrs. Morgan of Lanypwll Farm put all this much better in the speech of symbolism, when she murmured about the children of the pool. For if there is a landscape of sadness, there is certainly also a landscape of a horror of darkness and evil; and that black and oily depth, overshadowed with twisted woods, with its growth of foul weeds and its dead trees and leprous boughs, was assuredly potent in terror. To Roberts it was a strong drug, a drug of evocation; the black deep without calling to the black deep within, and summoning the inhabitant thereof to come forth. I made no attempt to extract the legend of that dark place from Mrs. Morgan; and I do not suppose that she would have been communicative if I had questioned her. But it has struck me as possible and even probable that Roberts was by no means the first to experience the power of the pool.

Old stories often turn out to be true.

The Bright Boy

I

Young Joseph Last, having finally gone down from Oxford, wondered a good deal what he was to do next and for the years following next. He was an orphan from early boyhood, both his parents having died of typhoid within a few days of each other when Joseph was ten years old, and he remembered very little of Dunham, where his father ended a long line of solicitors, practising in the place since 1707. The Lasts had once been very comfortably off. They had intermarried now and again with the gentry of the neighbourhood and did a good deal of the county business, managing estates, collecting rents, officiating as stewards for several manors, living generally in a world of quiet but snug prosperity, rising to their greatest height, perhaps, during the Napoleonic Wars and afterwards. And then they began to decline, not violently at all, but very gently, so that it was many years before they were aware of the process that was going on, slowly, surely. Economists, no doubt, understand very well how the country and the country town gradually became less important soon after the Battle of Waterloo; and the causes of the decay and change which vexed Cobbett so sadly, as he saw, or thought he saw, the life and strength of the land being sucked up to nourish the monstrous excrescence of London. Anyhow, even before the railways came, the assembly rooms of the country towns grew dusty and desolate, the county families ceased to come to their "town houses" for the winter season, and the little theatres, where Mrs. Siddons and Grimaldi had appeared in their divers arts, rarely opened their doors, and the skilled craftsmen, the clock-makers and the furniture makers and the like began to drift away to the big towns and to the capital city. So it was with Dunham. Naturally the fortunes of the Lasts sank with the fortunes of the town;

and there had been speculations which had not turned out well, and people spoke of a heavy loss in foreign bonds. When Joseph's father died, it was found that there was enough to educate the boy and keep him in strictly modest comfort and not much more.

He had his home with an uncle who lived at Blackheath, and after a few years at Mr. Jones's well-known preparatory school, he went to Merchant Taylors and thence to Oxford. He took a decent degree (2nd in Greats) and then began that wondering process as to what he was to do with himself. His income would keep him in chops and steaks, with an occasional roast fowl, and three or four weeks on the Continent once a year. If he liked, he could do nothing, but the prospect seemed tame and boring. He was a very decent Classical scholar, with something more than the average schoolmaster's purely technical knowledge of Latin and Greek and professional interest in them: still, schoolmastering seemed his only clear and obvious way of employing himself. But it did not seem likely that he would get a post at any of the big public schools. In the first place, he had rather neglected his opportunities at Oxford. He had gone to one of the obscurer colleges, one of those colleges which you may read about in memoirs dealing with the first years of the nineteenth century as centres and fountains of intellectual life; which for some reason or no reason have fallen into the shadow. There is nothing against them in any way; but nobody speaks of them any more. In one of these places Joseph Last made friends with good fellows, quiet and cheerful men like himself; but they were not, in the technical sense of the term, the "good friends" which a prudent young man makes at the University. One or two had the Bar in mind, and two or three the Civil Service; but most of them were bound for country curacies and country offices. Generally, and for practical purposes, they were "out of it": they were not the men whose whispers could lead to anything profitable in high quarters. And then, again, even in those days, games were getting important in the creditable schools; and there, young Last was very decidedly out of it. He wore spectacles with lenses divided in some queer manner: his athletic disability was final and complete.

He pondered, and thought at first of setting up a small preparatory school in one of the well-to-do London suburbs; a day-school where parents might have their boys well-grounded from the very beginning, for comparatively modest fees, and yet have their upbringing in their own hands. It had often struck Last that it was a barbarous business to send a little chap of seven or eight away from the comfortable and affectionate habit of his home to a strange place among cold strangers; to bare boards, an inky smell, and grammar on an empty stomach in the morning. But consulting with Jim Newman of his old college, he was warned by that sage to drop his scheme and leave it on the ground. Newman pointed out in the first place that there was no money in teaching unless it was combined with hotel-keeping. That, he said, was all right, and more than all right; and he surmised that many people who kept hotels in the ordinary way would give a good deal to practise their art and mystery under Housemaster's Rules. "You needn't pay so very much for your furniture, you know. You don't want to make the boys into young sybarites. Besides, there's nothing a healthy-minded boy hates more than stuffiness: what he likes is clean fresh air and plenty of it. And, you know, old chap, fresh air is cheap enough. And then with the food, there's apt to be trouble in the ordinary hotel if it's uneatable; but in the sort of hotel we're talking of, a little accident with the beef or mutton affords a very valuable opportunity for the exercise of the virtue of self-denial."

Last listened to all this with a mournful grin.

"You seem to know all about it," he said. "Why don't you go in for it yourself?"

"I couldn't keep my tongue in my cheek. Besides, I don't think it's fair sport. I'm going out to India in the autumn. What about pig-sticking?"

"And there's another thing," he went on after a meditative pause. "That notion of yours about a day prep. school is rotten. The parents wouldn't say thank you for letting them keep their kids at home when they're all small and young. Some people go so far as to say that the chief purpose of schools is to allow parents a good excuse for getting rid of their children. That's nonsense. Most fathers and mothers are very fond of their children and like to have them about the house; when they're young, at all events. But somehow or other, they've got it into their heads that strange schoolmasters know more about bringing up a small boy than his own people; and there it is. So, on all counts, drop that scheme of yours."

Last thought it over, and looked about him in the scholastic world, and came to the conclusion that Newman was right. For two or three years he took charge of reading parties in the long vacation. In the winter he found occupation in the coaching of backward boys, in preparing boys not so backward for scholarship examinations; and his little text-book, *Beginning Greek,* was found quite useful in Lower School. He did pretty well on the whole, though the work began to bore him sadly, and such money as he earned, added to his income, enabled him to live in the way he liked, comfortably enough. He had a couple of rooms in one of the streets going down from the Strand to the river, for which he paid a pound a week, had bread and cheese and odds and ends for lunch, with beer from his own barrel in the cellar, and dined simply but sufficiently now in one, now in another of the snug taverns which then abounded in the quarter. And, now and again, once a month or so, perhaps, instead of the tavern dinners, there was the play at the Vaudeville or the Olympic, the Globe or the Strand, with supper and something hot to follow. The evening might turn into a little party: old Oxford friends would look him up in his rooms between six and seven; Zouch would gather from the Temple and Medwin from Buckingham Street, and possibly Garraway, taking the Yellow Albion 'bus, would descend from his remote steep in the northern parts of London, would knock at 14, Mowbray Street, and demand pipes, porter, and the pit at a good play. And, on rare occasions, another member of the little society, Noel, would turn up. Noel lived at Turnham Green in a red brick house which was then thought merely old-fashioned, which would now—but it was pulled down long ago—be distinguished as choice Queen Anne or Early Georgian. He lived there with his father, a retired official of the British Museum, and through a man whom he had known at Oxford, he had made some way in literary journalism, contributing regularly to an important weekly paper. Hence the consequence of his occasional descents on Buckingham Street, Mowbray Street, and the Temple. Noel, as in some sort a man of letters, or, at least, a professional journalist, was a member of Blacks' Club, which in those days had exiguous premises in Maiden Lane. Noel would go round the haunts of his friends, and gather them to stout and oysters, and guide them into some neighbouring theatre pit, whence they viewed excellent acting and a cheerful, nonsensical play, enjoyed both, and were ready for supper at the Tavistock. This done, Noel would lead the party to Blacks', where they, very likely, saw some of the actors who had entertained them earlier in the evening, and Noel's friends, the journalists and men of letters, with a painter and a black-and-white man here and there. Here, Last enjoyed himself very much, more especially among the actors, who seemed to him more genial than the literary men. He became especially friendly with one of the players, old Meredith Mandeville, who had talked with the elder Kean, was reliable in the smaller Shakespearean parts, and had engaging tales to tell of early days in county circuits. "You had nine shillings a week to begin with. When you got to fifteen shillings you gave your landlady eight or nine shillings, and had the rest to play with. You felt a prince. And the county families often used to come and see us in the Green Room: most agreeable."

With this friendly old gentleman, whose placid and genial serenity was not marred at all by incalculable quantities of gin, Last loved to converse, getting glimpses of a life strangely remote from his own: vagabondage, insecurity, hard times, and jollity; and against it all as a background, the lighted murmur of the stage, voices uttering tremendous things, and the sense of moving in two worlds. The old man, by his own account, had not been eminently prosperous or successful, and yet he had relished his life, and drew humours from its disadvantages, and made hard times seem an adventure. Last used to express his envy of the player's career, dwelling on the dull insignificance of his own labours, which, he said, were a matter of tinkering small boys' brains, teaching older boys the tricks of the examiners, and generally doing things that didn't matter.

"It's no more education than bricklaying is architecture," he said one night. "And there's no fun in it."

Old Mandeville, on his side, listened with interest to these revelations of a world as strange and unknown to him as the life of the floats was to the tutor. Broadly speaking, he knew nothing of any books but play books. He had heard, no doubt, of things called examinations, as most people have heard of Red Indian initiations; but to him one was as remote as the other. It was interesting and strange to him to be sitting at Blacks' and actually talking to a decent young fellow who was seriously engaged in this queer business. And there were—Last noted with amazement—points at which their two circles touched, or so it seemed. The tutor, wishing to be agreeable, began one night to talk about the origins of *King Lear*. The actor found himself listening to Celtic legends which to him sounded incomprehensible nonsense. And when it came to the Knight who fought the King of Fairyland for the hand of Cordelia till Doomsday, he broke in: "*Lear* is a pill; there's no doubt of that. You're too young to have seen Barry O'Brien's *Lear*: magnificent. The part has been attempted since his day. But it has never been played. I have depicted the Fool myself, and, I must say, not without some meed of applause. I remember once at Stafford . . ." and Last was content to let him tell his tale, which ended, oddly enough, with a bullock's heart for supper.

But one night when Last was grumbling, as he often did, about the fragmentary, desultory, and altogether unsatisfactory nature of his occupation, the old man interrupted him in a wholly unexpected vein.

"It is possible," he began, "mark you, I say possible, that I may be the means of alleviating the tedium of your lot. I was calling some days ago on a cousin of mine, a Miss Lucy Pilliner, a very agreeable woman. She has a considerable knowledge of the world, and, I hope you will forgive the liberty, but I mentioned in the course of our conversation that I had lately become acquainted with a young gentleman of considerable scholastic distinction, who was somewhat dissatisfied with the too abrupt and frequent entrances and exits of his present tutorial employment. It struck me that my cousin received these remarks with a certain reflective interest, but I was not prepared to receive this letter."

Mandeville handed Last the letter. It began: "My dear Ezekiel," and Last noted out of the corner of his eye a glance from the actor which pleaded for silence and secrecy on this point. The letter went on to say in a manner almost as dignified as Mandeville's, that the writer had been thinking over the circumstances of the young tutor, as related by her cousin in the course of their most agreeable conversation of Friday last, and she was inclined to think that she knew of an educational position shortly available in a private family, which would be of a more permanent and satisfactory nature. "Should your friend feel interested," Miss Pilliner ended, "I should be glad if he would communicate with me, with a view to a meeting being arranged, at which the matter could be discussed with more exact particulars."

"And what do you think of it?" said Mandeville, as Last returned Miss Pilliner's letter.

For a moment Last hesitated. There is an attraction and also a repulsion in the odd and the improbable, and Last doubted whether educational work obtained through an actor at Blacks' and a lady at Islington—he had seen the name at the top of the letter—could be altogether solid or desirable. But brighter thoughts prevailed, and he assured Mandeville that he would be only too glad to go thoroughly into the matter, thanking him very warmly for his interest. The old man nodded benignly, gave him the letter again that he might take down Miss Pilliner's address, and suggested an immediate note asking for an appointment.

"And now," he said, "despite the carping objections of the Moody Prince, I propose to drink your jocund health to-night."

And he wished Last all the good luck in the world with hearty kindliness.

In a couple of days Miss Pilliner presented her compliments to Mr. Joseph Last and begged him to do her the favour of calling on her on a date three days ahead, at noon, "if neither day nor hour were in any way incompatible with his convenience". They might then, she proceeded, take advantage of the occasion to discuss a certain proposal, the nature of which, she believed, had been indicated to Mr. Last by her good cousin, Mr. Meredith Mandeville.

Corunna Square, where Miss Pilliner lived, was a small, almost a tiny, square in the remoter parts of Islington. Its two-storied houses of dim, yellowish brick were fairly covered with vines and clematis and all manner of creepers. In front of the houses were small paled gardens, gaily flowering, and the square enclosure held little else besides a venerable, wide-spreading mulberry, far older than the buildings about it. Miss Pilliner lived in the quietest corner of the square. She welcomed Last with some sort of compromise between a bow and a curtsey, and begged him to be seated in an upright arm-chair, upholstered in horsehair. Miss Pilliner, he noted, looked about sixty, and was, perhaps, a little older. She was spare, upright, and composed; and yet one might have suspected a lurking whimsicality. Then, while the weather was discussed, Miss Pilliner offered a choice of port or sherry, sweet biscuits or plum cake. And so to the business of the day.

"My cousin, Mr. Mandeville, informed me," she began, "of a young friend of great scholastic ability, who was, nevertheless, dissatisfied with the somewhat casual and occasional nature of his employment. By a singular coincidence, I had received a letter a day or two before from a friend of mine, a Mrs. Marsh. She is, in fact, a distant connection, some sort of cousin, I suppose, but not being a Highlander or a Welshwoman, I really cannot say how many times removed. She was a lovely creature; she is still a handsome woman. Her name was Manning, Arabella Manning, and what possessed her to marry Mr. Marsh I really cannot say. I only saw the man once, and I thought him her inferior in every respect, and considerably older. However, she declares that he is a devoted husband and an excellent person in every respect. They first met, odd as it must seem, in Pekin, where Arabella was governess in one of the Legation families. Mr. Marsh, I was given to understand, represented highly important commercial interests at the capital of the Flowery Land, and being introduced to my connection, a mutual attraction seems to have followed. Arabella Manning resigned her position in the attaché's family, and the marriage was solemnised in due course. I received this intelligence nine years ago in a letter from Arabella, dated at Pekin, and my relative ended by saying that she feared it would be impossible to furnish an address for an immediate reply, as Mr. Marsh was about to set out on a mission of an extremely urgent nature on behalf of his firm, involving a great deal of travelling and frequent changes of address. I suffered a good deal of uneasiness on Arabella's account, it seemed such an unsettled way of life, and so unhomelike. However, a friend of mine who is in the City assured me that there was nothing unusual in the circumstances, and that there was no cause for alarm. Still, as the years went on, and I received no further communication from my cousin, I made up my mind that she had probably contracted some tropical disease which had carried her off, and that Mr. Marsh had heartlessly neglected to communicate to me the intelligence of the sad event. But a month ago, almost to the day"—Miss Pilliner referred to an almanac on the table beside her—"I was astonished and delighted to receive a letter from Arabella. She wrote from one of the most luxurious and exclusive hotels in the West End of London, announcing the return of her husband and herself to their native land after many years of wandering.

Mr. Marsh's active concern in business had, it appeared, at length terminated in a highly prosperous and successful manner, and he was now in negotiation for the purchase of a small estate in the country, where he hoped to spend the remainder of his days in peaceful retirement."

Miss Pilliner paused and replenished Last's glass.

"I am so sorry," she continued, "to trouble you with this long narrative, which, I am sure, must be a sad trial of your patience. But, as you will see presently, the circumstances are a little out of the common, and as you are, I trust, to have a particular interest in them, I think it is only right that you should be fully informed—fair and square, and all above board, as my poor father used to say in his bluff manner.

"Well, Mr. Last, I received, as I have said, this letter from Arabella with its extremely gratifying intelligence. As you may guess, I was very much relieved to hear that all had turned out so felicitously. At the end of her letter, Arabella begged me to come and see them at Billing's Hotel, saying that her husband was most anxious to have the pleasure of meeting me."

Miss Pilliner went to a drawer in a writing-table by the window and took out a letter.

"Arabella was always considerate. She says: 'I know that you have always lived very quietly, and are not accustomed to the turmoil of fashionable London. But you need not be alarmed. Billing's Hotel is no bustling modern caravanserai. Everything is very quiet, and, besides, we have our own small suite of apartments. Herbert—her husband, Mr. Last—positively insists on your paying us a visit, and you must not disappoint us. If next Thursday, the 22nd, suits you, a carriage shall be sent at four o'clock to bring you to the hotel, and will take you back to Corunna Square, after you have joined us in a little dinner.'

"Very kind, most considerate; don't you agree with me, Mr. Last? But look at the postscript."

Last took the letter, and read in a tight, neat script: "PS. We have a wonderful piece of news for you. It is too good to write, so I shall keep it for our meeting."

Last handed back Mrs. Marsh's letter. Miss Pilliner's long and ceremonious approach was lulling him into a mild stupor; he wondered faintly when she would come to the point, and what the point would be like when she came to it, and, chiefly, what on earth this rather dull family history could have to do with him.

Miss Pilliner proceeded.

"Naturally, I accepted so kindly and urgent an invitation. I was anxious to see Arabella once more after her long absence, and I was glad to have the opportunity of forming my own judgment as to her husband, of whom I knew absolutely nothing. And then, Mr. Last, I must confess that I am not deficient in that spirit of curiosity, which gentlemen have scarcely numbered with female virtues. I longed to be made partaker in the wonderful news which Arabella had promised to impart on our meeting, and I wasted many hours in speculating as to its nature.

"The day came. A neat brougham with its attendant footman arrived at the appointed hour, and I was driven in smooth luxury to Billing's Hotel in Manners Street, Mayfair. There a major-domo led the way to the suite of apartments on the first floor occupied by Mr. and Mrs. Marsh. I will not waste your valuable time, Mr. Last, by expatiating on the rich but quiet luxury of their apartments; I will merely mention that my relative assured me that the Sèvres ornaments in their drawing-room had been valued at nine hundred guineas. I found Arabella still a beautiful woman, but I could not help seeing that the tropical countries in which she had lived for so many years had taken their toll of her once resplendent beauty; there was a weariness, a lassitude in her appearance and demeanour which I was distressed to observe. As to her husband, Mr. Marsh, I am aware that to form an unfavourable judgment after an acquaintance which has only lasted a few hours is both uncharitable and unwise; and I shall not soon forget the discourse which dear Mr. Venn delivered at Emmanuel Church on the very Sunday after my visit to my relative: it really seemed, and I confess it with shame, that Mr. Venn had my own case in mind, and felt it his bounden duty to warn me while it was yet time. Still, I must say that I did not take at all to Mr. Marsh. I really can't say why. To me he was most polite; he could not have been more so. He remarked more than once on the extreme pleasure it gave him to meet at last one of whom he had heard so much from his dear Bella; he trusted that now his wandering days were over, the pleasure might be frequently repeated; he omitted nothing that the most genial courtesy might suggest. And yet, I cannot say that the impression I received was a favourable one. However; I dare say that I was mistaken."

There was a pause. Last was resigned. The point of the long story seemed to recede into some far distance, into vanishing prospective.

"There was nothing definite?" he suggested.

"No; nothing definite. I may have thought that I detected a lack of candour, a hidden reserve behind all the generosity of Mr. Marsh's expressions. Still; I hope I was mistaken.

"But I am forgetting in these trivial and I trust erroneous observations, the sole matter that is of consequence; to you, at least, Mr. Last. Soon after my arrival, before Mr. Marsh had appeared, Arabella confided to me her great piece of intelligence. Her marriage had been blessed by offspring. Two years after her union with Mr. Marsh, a child had been born, a boy. The birth took place at a town in South America, Santiago de Chile—I have verified the place in my atlas—where Mr. Marsh's visit had been more protracted than usual. Fortunately, an English doctor was available, and the little fellow throve from the first, and as Arabella, his proud mother, boasted, was now a beautiful little boy, both handsome and intelligent to a remarkable degree. Naturally, I asked to see the child, but Arabella said that he was not in the hotel with them. After a few days it was thought that the dense and humid air of London was not suiting little Henry very well; and he had been sent with a nurse to a resort in the Isle of Thanet, where he was reported to be in the best of health and spirits.

"And now, Mr. Last, after this tedious but necessary preamble, we arrive at that point where you, I trust, may be interested. In any case, as you may suppose, the life which the exigencies of business compelled the Marshes to lead, involving as it did almost continual travel, would have been little favourable to a course of systematic education for the child. But this obstacle apart, I gathered that Mr. Marsh holds very strong views as to the folly of premature instruction. He declared to me his conviction that many fine minds had been grievously injured by being forced to undergo the process of early stimulation; and he pointed out that, by the nature of the case, those placed in charge of very young children were not persons of the highest acquirements and the keenest intelligence. 'As you will readily agree, Miss Pilliner,' he remarked to me, 'great scholars are not employed to teach infants their alphabet, and it is not likely that the mysteries of the multiplication table will be imparted by a master of mathematics.' In consequence, he urged, the young and budding intelligence is brought into contact with dull and inferior minds, and the damage may well be irreparable."

There was much more, but gradually light began to dawn on the dazed man. Mr. Marsh had kept the virgin intelligence of his son Henry undisturbed and uncorrupted by inferior and incompetent culture. The boy, it was judged, was now ripe for true education, and Mr. and Mrs. Marsh had begged Miss Pilliner to make enquiries, and to find, if she could, a scholar who would undertake the whole charge of little Henry's mental upbringing. If both parties were satisfied, the engagement would be for seven years at least, and the appointments, as Miss Pilliner called the salary, would begin with five hundred pounds a year, rising by an annual increment of fifty pounds. References, particulars of University distinctions would be required: Mr. Marsh, long absent from England, was ready to proffer the names of his bankers. Miss Pilliner was quite sure, however, that Mr. Last might consider himself engaged, if the position appealed to him.

Last thanked Miss Pilliner profoundly. He told her that he would like a couple of days in which to think the matter over. He would then write to her, and she would put him into communication with Mr. Marsh. And so he went away from Corunna Square in a mood of great bewilderment and doubt. Unquestionably, the position had many advantages. The pay was very good. And he would be well lodged and well fed. The people were wealthy, and Miss Pilliner had assured him: "You will have no cause to complain of your entertainment." And from the educational point of view, it would certainly be an improvement on the work he had been doing since he left the University. He had been an odd-job man, a tinker, a patcher, a cobbler of other people's work; here was a chance to shew that he was a master craftsman. Very few people, if any, in the teaching profession had ever enjoyed such an opportunity as this. Even the sixth-form masters in the big public schools must sometimes groan at having to underpin and relay the bad foundations of the fifth and fourth. He was to begin at the beginning, with no false work to hamper him: "from A B C to Plato,

Æschylus, and Aristotle," he murmured to himself. Undoubtedly it was a big chance.

And on the other side? Well, he would have to give up London, and he had grown fond of the homely, cheerful London that he knew; his comfortable rooms in Mowbray Street, quiet enough down by the unfrequented Embankment, and yet but a minute or two from the ringing Strand. Then there were the meetings with the old Oxford friends, the nights at the theatre, the snug taverns with their curtained boxes, and their good chops and steaks and stout, and chimes of midnight and after, heard in cordial company at Blacks': all these would have to go. Miss Pilliner had spoken of Mr. Marsh as looking for some place a considerable distance from town, "in the real country". He had his eye, she said, on a house on the Welsh border, which he thought of taking furnished, with the option of buying, if he eventually found it suited him. You couldn't look up old friends in London and get back the same night, if you lived somewhere on the Welsh border. Still, there would be the holidays, and a great deal might be done in the holidays.

And yet; there was still debate and doubt within his mind, as he sat eating his bread and cheese and potted meat, and drinking his beer in his sitting-room in peaceful Mowbray Street. He was influenced, he thought, by Miss Pilliner's evident dislike of Mr. Marsh, and though Miss Pilliner talked in the manner of Dr. Johnson, he had a feeling that, like a lady of the Doctor's own day, she had a bottom of good sense. Evidently she did not trust Mr. Marsh overmuch. Yet, what can the most cunning swindler do to his resident tutor? Give him cold mutton for dinner or forget to pay his salary? In either case, the remedy was simple: the resident tutor would swiftly cease to reside, and go back to London, and not be much the worse. After all, Last reflected, a man can't compel his son's tutor to invest in Uruguayan Silver or Java Spices or any other fallacious commercial undertaking, so what mattered the supposed trickiness of Marsh to him?

But again, when all had been summed up and considered, for and against; there was a vague objection remaining. To oppose this, Last could bring no argument, since it was without form of words, shapeless, and mutable as a cloud.

However, when the next morning came, there came with it a couple of letters inviting him to cram two young dunderheads with facts

and figures and verbs in *mi*. The prospect was so terribly distasteful
that he wrote to Miss Pilliner directly after breakfast, enclosing his College Testimonials and certain other commendatory letters he had in his
desk. In due course, he had an interview with Mr. Marsh at Billing's
Hotel. On the whole, each was well-enough pleased with the other.
Last found Marsh a lean, keen, dark man in later middle age; there was
a grizzle in his black hair above the ears, and wrinkles seamed his face
about the eyes. His eyebrows were heavy, and there was a hint of a
threat in his jaw, but the smile with which he welcomed Last lit up his
grimmish features into a genial warmth. There was an oddity about his
accent and his tone in speaking; something foreign, perhaps? Last remembered that he had journeyed about the world for many years, and
supposed that the echoes of many languages sounded in his speech.
His manner and address were certainly suave, but Last had no prejudice against suavity, rather, he cherished a liking for the decencies of
common intercourse. Still, no doubt, Marsh was not the kind of man
Miss Pilliner was accustomed to meet in Corunna Square society or
among Mr. Venn's congregation. She probably suspected him of having been a pirate.

And Mr. Marsh on his side was delighted with Last. As appeared
from a letter addressed by him to Miss Pilliner—"or, may I venture to
say, Cousin Lucy?"—Mr. Last was exactly the type of man he and Arabella had hoped to secure through Miss Pilliner's recommendation.
They did not want to give their boy into the charge of a flashy man of
the world with a substratum of learning. Mr. Last was, it was evident, a
quiet and unworldly scholar, more at home among books than among
men; the very tutor Arabella and himself had desired for their little
son. Mr. Marsh was profoundly grateful to Miss Pilliner for the great
service she had rendered to Arabella, to himself, and to Henry.

And, indeed, as Mr. Meredith Mandeville would have said, Last
looked the part. No doubt, the spectacles helped to create the remote,
retired, Dominie Sampson impression.

In a week's time it was settled, he was to begin his duties. Mr.
Marsh wrote a handsome cheque, "to defray any little matters of outfit,
travelling expenses, and so forth; nothing to do with your salary". He
was to take train to a certain large town in the west, and there he
would be met and driven to the house, where Mrs. Marsh and his pupil

were already established—"beautiful country, Mr. Last; I am sure you will appreciate it".

There was a famous farewell gathering of the old friends. Zouch and Medwin, Garraway and Noel came from near and far. There was grilled sole before the mighty steak, and a roast fowl after it. They had decided that as it was the last time, perhaps, they would not go to the play, but sit and talk about the mahogany. Zouch, who was understood to be the ruler of the feast, had conferred with the head waiter, and when the cloth was removed, a rare and curious port was solemnly set before them. They talked of the old days when they were up at Wells together, pretended—though they knew better—that the undergraduate who had cut his own father in Piccadilly was a friend of theirs, re-told jokes that must have been older than the wine, related tales of Moll and Meg, and the famous history of Melcombe, who screwed up the dean in his own rooms. And then there was the affair of the Poses Plastiques. Certain lewd fellows, as one of the Dons of Wells College expressed it, had procured scandalous figures from the wax-work booth at the fair, and had disposed them by night about the fountain in the college garden in such a manner that their scandal was shamefully increased. The perpetrators of this infamy had never been discovered: the five friends looked knowingly at each other, pursed their lips, and passed the port.

The old wine and the old stories blended into a mood of gentle meditation; and then, at the right moment, Noel carried them off to Blacks' and new company. Last sought out old Mandeville and related, with warm gratitude, the happy issue of his intervention.

The chimes sounded, and they all went their several ways.

II

Though Joseph Last was by no means a miracle of observation and deduction, he was not altogether the simpleton among his books that Mr. Marsh had judged him. It was not so very long before a certain uneasiness beset him in his new employment.

At first everything had seemed very well. Mr. Marsh had been right in thinking that he would be charmed by the scene in which the White

House was set. It stood, terraced on a hillside, high above a grey and silver river winding in esses through a lonely, lovely valley. Above it, to the east, was a vast and shadowy and ancient wood, climbing to the high ridge of the hill, and descending by height and by depth of green to the level meadows and to the sea. And, standing on the highest point of the wood above the White House, Last looked westward between the boughs and saw the lands across the river, and saw the country rise and fall in billow upon billow to the huge dim wall of the mountain, blue in the distance, and white farms shining in the sun on its vast side. Here was a man in a new world. There had been no such country as this about Dunham in the Midlands, or in the surroundings of Blackheath or Oxford; and he had visited nothing like it on his reading parties. He stood amazed, enchanted under the green shade, beholding a great wonder. Close beside him the well bubbled from the grey rocks, rising out of the heart of the hill.

And in the White House, the conditions of life were altogether pleasant. He had been struck by the dark beauty of Mrs. Marsh, who was clearly, as Miss Pilliner had told him, a great many years younger than her husband. And he noted also that effect which her cousin had ascribed to years of living in the tropics, though he would hardly have called it weariness or lassitude. It was something stranger than that; there was the mark of flame upon her, but Last did not know whether it were the flame of the sun, or the stranger fires of places that she had entered, perhaps long ago.

But the pupil, little Henry, was altogether a surprise and a delight. He looked rather older than seven, but Last judged that this impression was not so much due to his height or physical make as to the bright alertness and intelligence of his glance. The tutor had dealt with many little boys, though with none so young as Henry; and he had found them as a whole a stodgy and podgy race, with faces that recorded a fixed abhorrence of learning and a resolution to learn as little as possible. Last was never surprised at this customary expression. It struck him as eminently natural. He knew that all elements are damnably dull and difficult. He wondered why it was inexorably appointed that the unfortunate human creature should pass a great portion of its life from the very beginning in doing things that it detested; but so it was, and now for the syntax of the optative.

But there were no such obstinate entrenchments in the face or the manner of Henry Marsh. He was a handsome boy, who looked brightly and spoke brightly, and evidently did not regard his tutor as a hostile force that had been brought against him. He was what some people would have called, oddly enough, old-fashioned; child-like, but not at all childish, with now and then a whimsical turn of phrase more suggestive of a humorous man than a little boy. This older habit was no doubt to be put down partly to the education of travel, the spectacle of the changing scene and the changing looks of men and things, but very largely to the fact that he had always been with his father and mother, and knew nothing of the company of children of his own age.

"Henry has had no playmates," his father explained. "He's had to be content with his mother and myself. It couldn't be helped. We've been on the move all the time; on shipboard or staying at cosmopolitan hotels for a few weeks, and then on the road again. The little chap had no chance of making any small friends."

And the consequence was, no doubt, that lack of childishness that Last had noted. It was, probably, a pity that it was so. Childishness, after all, was a wonder world, and Henry seemed to know nothing of it: he had lost what might be, perhaps, as valuable as any other part of human experience, and he might find the lack of it as he grew older. Still, there it was; and Last ceased to think of these possibly fanciful deprivations, when he began to teach the boy, as he had promised himself, from the very beginning. Not quite from the beginning; the small boy confessed with a disarming grin that he had taught himself to read a little: "But please, sir, don't tell my father, as I know he wouldn't like it. You see, my father and mother had to leave me alone sometimes, and it was so dull, and I thought it would be such fun if I learnt to read books all by myself."

Here, thought Last, is a lesson for schoolmasters. Can learning be made a desirable secret, an excellent sport, instead of a horrible penance? He made a mental note, and set about the work before him. He found an extraordinary aptitude, a quickness in grasping his indications and explanations such as he had never known before—"not in boys twice his age, or three times his age, for the matter of that", as he reflected. This child, hardly removed from strict infancy, had something almost akin to genius—so the happy tutor was inclined to believe.

Now and again, with his, "Yes, sir, I see. And then, of course . . ." he would veritably take the coming words out of Last's mouth, and anticipate what was, no doubt, logically the next step in the demonstration. But Last had not been accustomed to pupils who anticipated anything—save the hour for putting the books back on the shelf. And above all, the instructor was captured by the eager and intense curiosity of the instructed. He was like a man reading *The Moonstone*, or some such sensational novel, and unable to put the book down till he had read to the very last page and found out the secret. This small boy brought just this spirit of insatiable curiosity to every subject put before him. "I wish I had taught him to read," thought Last to himself. "I have no doubt he would have regarded the alphabet as we regard those entrancing and mysterious cyphers in Edgar Allan Poe's stories. And, after all, isn't that the right and rational way of looking at the alphabet?"

And then he went on to wonder whether curiosity, often regarded as a failing, almost a vice, is not, in fact, one of the greatest virtues of the spirit of man, the key to all knowledge and all the mysteries, the very sense of the secret that must be discovered.

With one thing and another: with this treasure of a pupil, with this enchantment of the strange and beautiful country about him, and with the extreme kindness and consideration shewn him by Mr. and Mrs. Marsh, Last was in rich clover. He wrote to his friends in town, telling them of his happy experiences, and Zouch and Noel, meeting by chance at the Sun, the Dog, or the Triple Tun, discussed their friend's felicity.

"Proud of the pup," said Zouch.

"And pleased with the prospect," responded Noel, thinking of Last's lyrics about the woods and the waters, and the scene of the White House. "Still, *timeo Hesperides et dona ferentes*. I mistrust the west. As one of its own people said, it is a land of enchantment and illusion. You never know what may happen next. It is a fortunate thing that Shakespeare was born within the safety line. If Stratford had been twenty or thirty miles farther west . . . I don't like to think of it. I am quite sure that only fairy gold is dug from Welsh gold-mines. And you know what happens to that."

Meanwhile, far from the lamps and rumours of the Strand, Last continued happy in his outland territory, under the great wood. But before long he received a shock. He was strolling in the terraced garden one afternoon between tea and dinner, his work done for the day; and feeling inclined for tobacco with repose, drifted towards the stone summer-house—or, perhaps, gazebo—that stood on the verge of the lawn in a coolness of dark ilex-trees. Here one could sit and look down on the silver winding of the river, crossed by a grey bridge of ancient stone. Last was about to settle down when he noticed a book on the table before him. He took it up, and glanced into it, and drew in his breath, and turning over a few more pages, sank aghast upon the bench. Mr. Marsh had always deplored his ignorance of books. "I knew how to read and write and not much more," he would say, "when I was thrown into business—at the bottom of the stairs. And I've been so busy ever since that I'm afraid it's too late now to make up for lost time." Indeed, Last had noted that though Marsh usually spoke carefully enough, perhaps too carefully, he was apt to lapse in the warmth of conversation: he would talk of "fax", meaning "facts". And yet, it seemed, he had not only found time for reading, but had acquired sufficient scholarship to make out the Latin of a terrible Renaissance treatise, not generally known even to collectors of such things. Last had heard of the book; and the few pages he had glanced at shewed him that it thoroughly deserved its very bad character.

It was a disagreeable surprise. He admitted freely to himself that his employer's morals were no business of his. But why should the man trouble to tell lies? Last remembered queer old Miss Pilliner's account of her impressions of him; she had detected "a lack of candour", something reserved behind a polite front of cordiality. Miss Pilliner was, certainly, an acute woman: there was an undoubted lack of candour about Marsh.

Last left the wretched volume on the summer-house table, and walked up and down the garden, feeling a good deal perturbed. He knew he was awkward at dinner, and said he felt a bit seedy, inclined to a headache. Marsh was bland and pleasant as usual, and Mrs. Marsh sympathised with Last. She had hardly slept at all last night, she complained, and felt heavy and tired. She thought there was thunder in the air. Last, admiring her beauty, confessed again that Miss Pilliner had been right. Apart from her fatigue of the moment, there was a certain tropical languor about her, something of still, burning nights and the odour of strange flowers.

Marsh brought out a very special brandy which he administered with the black coffee; he said it would do both the invalids good, and that he would keep them company. Indeed, Last confessed to himself that he felt considerably more at ease after the good dinner, the good wine, and the rare brandy. It was humiliating, perhaps, but it was impossible to deny the power of the stomach. He went to his room early and tried to convince himself that the duplicity of Marsh was no affair of his. He found an innocent, or almost innocent explanation of it before he had finished his last pipe, sitting at the open window, hearing faintly the wash of the river and gazing towards the dim lands beyond it.

"Here," he meditated, "we have a modified form of Bounderby's Disease. Bounderby said that he began life as a wretched, starved, neglected little outcast. Marsh says that he was made into an office boy or something of the sort before he had time to learn anything. Bounderby lied, and no doubt Marsh lies. It is the trick of wealthy men; to magnify their late achievements by magnifying their early disadvantages."

By the time he went to sleep he had almost decided that the young Marsh had been to a good grammar school, and had done well.

The next morning, Last awoke almost at ease again. It was no doubt a pity that Marsh indulged in a subtle and disingenuous form of boasting, and his taste in books was certainly deplorable: but he must look after that himself. And the boy made amends for all. He shewed so clean a grasp of the English sentence, that Last thought he might well begin Latin before very long. He mentioned this one night at dinner, looking at Marsh with a certain humorous intention. But Marsh gave no sign that the dart had pricked him.

"That shews I was right," he remarked. "I've always said there's no greater mistake than forcing learning on children before they're fit to take it in. People will do it, and in nine cases out of ten the children's heads are muddled for the rest of their lives. You see how it is with Henry; I've kept him away from books up to now, and you see for yourself that I've lost him no time. He's ripe for learning, and I shouldn't wonder if he got ahead better in six months than the ordinary, early-crammed child would in six years."

It might be so, Last thought, but on the whole he was inclined to put down the boy's swift progress rather to his own exceptional intelligence than to his father's system, or no system. And in any case, it was a great pleasure to teach such a boy. And his application to his books had certainly no injurious effect on his spirits. There was not much society within easy reach of the White House, and, besides, people did not know whether the Marshes were to settle down or whether they were transient visitors: they were chary of paying their calls while there was this uncertainty. However, the rector had called; first of all the rector and his wife, she cheery, good-humoured and chatty; he somewhat dim and vague. It was understood that the rector, a high wrangler in his day, divided his time between his garden and the invention of a flying machine. He had the character of being slightly eccentric. He came not again, but Mrs. Winslow would drive over by the forest road in the governess car with her two children; Nancy, a pretty fair girl of seventeen, and Ted, a boy of eleven or twelve, of that type which Last catalogued as "stodgy and podgy", broad and thick set, with bulgy cheeks and eyes, and something of the determined expression of a young bulldog. After tea Nancy would organise games for the two boys in the garden and join in them herself with apparent relish. Henry, who had known few companions besides his parents, and had probably never played a game of any kind, squealed with delight, ran here and there and everywhere, hid behind the summer-house and popped out from the screen of the French beans with the greatest gusto, and Ted Winslow joined in with an air of protest. He was on his holidays, and his expression signified that all that sort of thing was only fit for girls and kids. Last was delighted to see Henry so ready and eager to be amused; after all, he had something of the child in him. He seemed a little uncomfortable when Nancy Winslow took him on her knee after the sports were over; he was evidently fearful of Ted Winslow's scornful eye. Indeed, the young bulldog looked as if he feared that his character would be compromised by associating with so manifest and confessed a kid. The next time Mrs. Winslow took tea at the White House, Ted had a diplomatic headache and stayed at home. But Nancy found games that two could play, and she and Henry were heard screaming with joy all over the gardens. Henry wanted to shew Nancy a wonderful well that he had discovered in the forest; it came, he said, from under the roots of a great yew tree. But Mrs. Marsh seemed to think that they might get lost.

Last had got over the uncomfortable incident of that villainous book in the summer-house. Writing to Noel, he had remarked that he feared his employer was a bit of an old rascal in some respects, but all right so far as he was concerned; and there it was. He got on with his job and minded his own business. Yet, now and again, his doubtful uneasiness about the man was renewed. There was a bad business at a hamlet a couple of miles away, where a girl of twelve or thirteen, coming home after dusk from a visit to a neighbour, had been set on in the wood and very vilely misused. The unfortunate child, it would appear, had been left by the scoundrel in the black dark of the forest, at some distance from the path she must have taken on her way home. A man who had been drinking late at the Fox and Hounds heard crying and screaming, "like someone in a fit", as he expressed it, and found the girl in a terrible state, and in a terrible state she had remained ever since. She was quite unable to describe the person who had so shamefully maltreated her; the shock had left her beside herself; she cried out once that something had come behind her in the dark, but she could say no more, and it was hopeless to try to get her to describe a person that, most likely, she had not even seen. Naturally, this very horrible story made something of a feature in the local paper, and one night, as Last and Marsh were sitting smoking after dinner, the tutor spoke of the affair; said something about the contrast between the peace and beauty and quiet of the scene and the villainous crime that had been done hard by. He was surprised to find that Marsh grew at once ill at ease. He rose from his chair and walked up and down the room muttering "horrible business, shameful business"; and when he sat down again, with the light full on him, Last saw the face of a frightened man. The hand that Marsh laid on the table was twitching uneasily; he beat with his foot on the floor as he tried to bring his lips to order, and there was a dreadful fear in his eyes.

Last was shocked and astonished at the effect he had produced with a few conventional phrases. Nervously, willing to tide over a painful situation, he began to utter something even more conventional to the effect that the loveliness of external nature had never conferred immunity from crime, or some stuff to the same inane purpose. But

Marsh, it was clear, was not to be soothed by anything of the kind. He started again from his chair and struck his hand upon the table, with a fierce gesture of denial and refusal.

"Please, Mr. Last, let it be. Say no more about it. It has upset Mrs. Marsh and myself very much indeed. It horrifies us to think that we have brought our boy here, to this peaceful place as we thought, only to expose him to the contagion of this dreadful affair. Of course we have given the servants strict orders not to say a word about it in Henry's presence; but you know what servants are, and what very sharp ears children have. A chance word or two may take root in a child's mind and contaminate his whole nature. It is, really, a very terrible thought. You must have noticed how distressed Mrs. Marsh has been for the last few days. The only thing we can do is to try and forget it all, and hope no harm has been done."

Last murmured a word or two of apology and agreement, and the talk moved off into safer country. But when the tutor was alone, he considered what he had seen and heard very curiously. He thought that Marsh's looks did not match his words. He spoke as the devoted father, afraid that his little boy should overhear nauseous and offensive gossip and conjecture about a horrible and obscene crime. But he looked like a man who had caught sight of a gallows, and that, Last felt, was altogether a very different kind of fear. And, then, there was his reference to his wife. Last had noticed that since the crime in the forest there had been something amiss with her; but, again, he mistrusted Marsh's comment. Here was a woman whose usual habit was a rather lazy good humour; but of late there had been a look and an air of suppressed fury, the burning glance of a jealous woman, the rage of despised beauty. She spoke little, and then as briefly as possible; but one might suspect flames and fires within. Last had seen this and wondered, but not very much, being resolved to mind his own business. He had supposed there had been some difference of opinion between her and her husband; very likely about the rearrangement of the drawing-room furniture and hiring a grand piano. He certainly had not thought of tracing Mrs. Marsh's altered air to the villainous crime that had been committed. And now Marsh was telling him that these glances of concealed rage were the outward signs of tender maternal anxiety; and not one word of all that did he believe. He put Marsh's half-hidden terror beside his wife's half-hidden fury; he thought of the book in the summer-house and things that were being whispered about the horror in the wood: and loathing and dread possessed him. He had no proof, it was true; merely conjecture, but he felt no doubt. There could be no other explanation. And what could he do but leave this terrible place?

Last could get no sleep. He undressed and went to bed, and tossed about in the half-dark of the summer night. Then he lit his lamp and dressed again, and wondered whether he had better not steal away without a word, and walk the eight miles to the station, and escape by the first train that went to London. It was not merely loathing for the man and his works; it was deadly fear, also, that urged him to fly from the White House. He felt sure that if Marsh guessed at his suspicions of the truth, his life might well be in danger. There was no mercy or scruple in that evil man. He might even now be at his door, listening, waiting. There was cold terror in his heart, and cold sweat pouring at the thought. He paced softly up and down his room in his bare feet, pausing now and again to listen for that other soft step outside. He locked the door as silently as he could, and felt safer. He would wait till the day came and people were stirring about the house, and then he might venture to come out and make his escape.

And yet when he heard the servants moving over their work, he hesitated. The light of the sun was shining in the valley, and the white mist over the silver river floated upward and vanished; the sweet breath of the wood entered the window of his room. The black horror and fear were raised from his spirit. He began to hesitate, to suspect his judgment, to enquire whether he had not rushed to his black con-clusions in a panic of the night. His logical deductions at midnight seemed to smell of nightmare in the brightness of that valley; the song of the aspiring lark confuted him. He remembered Garraway's great argument after a famous supper at the Turk's Head: that it was always unsafe to make improbability the guide of life. He would delay a little, and keep a sharp look-out, and be sure before taking sudden and vio-lent action. And perhaps the truth was that Last was influenced very strongly by his aversion from leaving young Henry, whose extraordi-nary brilliance and intelligence amazed and delighted him more and more.

It was still early when at last he left his room, and went out into the fine morning air. It was an hour or more before breakfast-time, and he set out on the path that led past the wall of the kitchen garden up the hill and into the heart of the wood. He paused a moment at the upper corner, and turned round to look across the river at the happy country shewing its morning magic and delight. As he dawdled and gazed, he heard soft steps approaching on the other side of the wall, and low voices murmuring. Then, as the steps drew near, one of the voices was raised a little, and Last heard Mrs. Marsh speaking:

"Too old, am I? And thirteen is too young. Is it to be seventeen next when you can get her into the wood? And after all I have done for you, and after what you have done to me."

Mrs. Marsh enumerated all these things without remission, and without any quiver of shame in her voice. She paused for a moment. Perhaps her rage was choking her; and there was a shrill piping cackle of derision, as if Marsh's voice had cracked in its contempt.

Very softly, but very swiftly, Last, the man with the grey face and the staring eyes, bolted for his life, down and away from the White House. Once in the road, free from the fields and brakes, he changed his run into a walk, and he never paused or stopped, till he came with a gulp of relief into the ugly streets of the big industrial town. He made his way to the station at once, and found that he was an hour too soon for the London Express. So there was plenty of time for breakfast; which consisted of brandy.

III

The tutor went back to his old life and his old ways, and did his best to forget the strange and horrible interlude of the White House. He gathered his podgy pups once more about him; crammed and coached, read with undergraduates during the long vacation, and was moderately satisfied with the course of things in general. Now and then, when he was endeavouring to persuade the podges against their deliberate judgment that Latin and Greek were languages once spoken by human beings, not senseless enigmas invented by demons, he would think with a sigh of regret of the boy who understood and longed to understand. And he wondered whether he had not been a coward to leave that enchanting child to the evil mercies of his hideous parents. But what could he have done? But it was dreadful to think of Henry, slowly or swiftly corrupted by his detestable father and mother, growing up with the fat slime of their abominations upon him.

He went into no detail with his old friends. He hinted that there had been grave unpleasantness, which made it impossible for him to remain in the west. They nodded, and perceiving that the subject was a sore one, asked no questions, and talked of old books and the new steak instead. They all agreed, in fact, that the steak was far too new, and William was summoned to explain this horror. Didn't he know that beefsteak, beefsteak meant for the consumption of Christian men, as distinguished from Hottentots, required hanging just as much as game? William the ponderous and benignant, tasted and tested, and agreed; with sorrowful regret. He apologised, and went on to say that as the gentlemen would not care to wait for a fowl, he would suggest a very special, tender, and juicy fillet of roast veal, then in cut. The suggestion was accepted, and found excellent. The conversation turned to Choric Metres and Florence St. John at the Strand. There was port later.

It was many years afterwards, when this old life, after crumbling for a long while, had come down with a final crash, that Last heard the real story of his tutorial engagement at the White House. Three dreadful people were put in the dock at the Old Bailey. There was an old man, with the look of a deadly snake; a fat, sloppy, deplorable woman with pendulous cheeks and a faint hint of perished beauty in her eyes; and to the utter blank amazement of those who did not know the story, a wonderful little boy. The people who saw him in court said he might have been taken for a child of nine or ten; no more. But the evidence that was given shewed that he must be between fifty and sixty at the least; perhaps more than that.

The indictment charged these three people with an unspeakable and hideous crime. They were charged under the name of Mailey, the name which they had borne at the time of their arrest; but it turned out at the end of the trial that they had been known by many names in the course of their career: Mailey, Despasse, Lartigan, Delarue, Falcon, Lecossic, Hammond, Marsh, Haringworth. It was established that the apparent boy, whom Last had known as Henry Marsh, was no relation of any kind to the elder prisoners. "Henry's" origins were deeply obscure. It was conjectured that he was the illegitimate son of a very high Englishman, a diplomatist, whose influence had counted for a great deal in the Far East. Nobody knew anything about the mother. The boy shewed brilliant promise from very early years, and the father, a bachelor, and disliking what little he knew of his relations, left his very large fortune to his son. The diplomatist died when the boy was twelve years old; and he had been aged, and more than aged when the child was born. People remarked that Arthur Wesley, as he was then called, was very short for his years, and he remained short, and his face remained that of a boy of seven or eight. He could not be sent to a school, so he was privately educated. When he was of age, the trustees had the extraordinary experience of placing a very considerable property in the hands of a young man who looked like a little boy. Very soon afterwards, Arthur Wesley disappeared. Dubious rumours spoke of reappearances, now here, now there, in all quarters of the world. There were tales that he had "gone fantee" in what was then unknown Africa, when the Mountains of the Moon still lingered on the older maps. It was reported, again, that he had gone exploring in the higher waters of the Amazon, and had never come back; but a few years later a personage that must have been Arthur Wesley was displaying unpleasant activities in Macao. It was soon after this period, according to the prosecution, that—in the words of counsel—he realised the necessity of "taking cover". His extraordinary personality, naturally enough, drew attention to him and his doings, and these doings being generally or always of an infamous kind, such attention was both inconvenient and dangerous. Somewhere in the East, and in very bad company, he came upon the two people who were charged with him. Arabella Manning, who was said to have respectable connections in Wiltshire, had gone out to the East as a governess, but had soon found other occupations. Meers had been a clerk in a house of business at Shanghai. His very ingenious system of fraud obtained his discharge, but, for some reason or other, the firm refused to prosecute, and Meers went— where Arthur Wesley found him. Wesley thought of his great plan. Manning and Meers were to pretend to be Mr. and Mrs. Marsh—that seemed to have been their original style—and he was to be their little boy. He paid them well for their various services: Arabella was his mistress-in-chief, the companion of his milder moments, for some years. Occasionally, a tutor was engaged to make the situation more plausible. In this state, the horrible trio peregrinated over the earth.

The court heard all this, and much more, after the jury had found the three prisoners guilty of the particular offence with which they were charged. This last crime—which the press had to enfold in paraphrase and periphrase—had been discovered, strange as it seemed, largely as a result of the woman's jealousy. Wesley's . . . affections, let us call them, were still apt to wander, and Arabella's jealous rage drove her beyond all caution and all control. She was the weak joint in Wesley's armour, the rent in his cover. People in court looked at the two; the debauched, deplorable woman with her flagging, sagging cheeks, and the dim fire still burning in her weary old eyes, and at Wesley, still, to all appearance, a bright and handsome little boy; they gasped with amazement at the grotesque, impossible horror of the scene. The judge raised his head from his notes, and gazed steadily at the convicted persons for some moments; his lips were tightly compressed.

The detective drew to the end of his portentous history. The track of these people, he said, had been marked by many terrible scandals, but till quite lately there had been no suspicion of their guilt. Two of these cases involved the capital charge: but formal evidence was lacking.

He drew to his close.

"In spite of his diminutive stature and juvenile appearance, the prisoner, Charles Mailey, *alias* Arthur Wesley, made a desperate resistance to his arrest. He is possessed of immense strength for his size, and almost choked one of the officers who arrested him."

The formulas of the court were uttered. The judge, without a word of comment, sentenced Mailey, or Wesley, to imprisonment for life, John Meers to fifteen years' imprisonment, Arabella Manning to ten years' imprisonment.

The old world, it has been noted, had crashed down. Many, many years had passed since Last had been hunted out of Mowbray Street, that went down dingily, peacefully from the Strand. Mowbray Street was now all blazing office buildings. Later, he had been driven from one nook and corner and snug retreat after another as new London rose in majesty and splendour. But for a year or more he had lain hidden in a by-street that had the advantage of leading into a disused graveyard near the Gray's Inn Road. Medwin and Garraway were dead; but Last summoned Zouch and Noel to his abode one night; and then and there made punch, and good punch for them.

"It's so jolly it must be sinful," he said, as he pared his lemons, "but up to the present I believe it is not illegal. And I still have a few bottles of that port I bought in 'ninety-two."

And then he told them for the first time all the whole story of his engagement at the White House.

The Tree of Life

I

The Morgans of Llantrisant were regarded for many centuries as among the most considerable of the landed gentry of South Wales. They had been called Reformation *parvenus,* but this was a piece of unhistorical and unjust abuse. They could trace their descent back, without doubt, certainly as far as Morgan ab Ifor, who fought and, no doubt, flourished in his way c. 980. He, in his turn, was always regarded as of the tribe of St. Teilo; and the family kept, as a most precious relic, a portable altar which was supposed to have belonged to the saint. And for many hundred years, the eldest son had borne the name of Teilo. They had intermarried, now and again, with the Normans, and lived in a thirteenth-century castle, with certain additions for comfort and amenity made in the reign of Henry VII, whose cause they had supported with considerable energy. From Henry, they had received grants of forfeited estates, both in Monmouthshire and Glamorganshire. At the dissolution of the religious houses, the Sir Teilo of the day was given Llantrisant Abbey with all its possessions. The monastic church was stripped of its lead roof, and soon fell into ruin, and became a quarry for the neighbourhood. The abbot's lodging and other of the monastic buildings were kept in repair, and being situated in a sheltered valley, were used by the family as a winter residence in preference to the castle, which was on a bare hill, high above the abbey. In the seventeenth century, Sir Henry Morgan—his elder brother had died young—was a Parliament man. He changed his opinions, and rose for the King in 1648; and, in consequence, had the mortification of seeing the outer wall of the castle on the hill, not razed to the ground, but carefully reduced to a height of four or five feet by the Cromwellian major-general commanding in the west. Later in the century, the Morgans became Whigs, and later still were able to support Mr. Gladstone, up to the Home Rule Bill of 1886. They still held most of the lands which they had gathered together gradually for eight or nine hundred years. Many of these lands had been wild, remote, and mountainous, of little use or profit save for the sport of hunting the hare; but early in the nineteenth century mining experts from the north, Fothergills and Renshaws, had found coal, and pits were sunk in the wild places, and the Morgans became wealthy in the modern way. By consequence, the bad seasons of the late 'seventies and the agricultural depression of the early 'eighties hardly touched them. They reduced rents and remitted arrears and throve on their mining royalties: they were still great people of the county. It was a very great pity that Teilo Morgan of Llantrisant was an invalid and an enforced recluse; especially as he was devoted to the memories of his house, and to the estate, and to the interests of the people on it.

The Llantrisant Abbey of his day had been so altered from age to age that the last abbot would certainly have seen little that was familiar to his eyes. It was set in rich and pleasant meadow-land, with woods of oak and beech and ash and elm all about it. Through the park ran the swift, clear river, Avon Torfaen, the stone or boulder-crusher, so named from its furious courses in the mountains where it rose. And the hills stood round the Abbey on every side. Here and there in the southern-facing front of the house, there could be seen traces of fifteenth-century building; but on this had been imposed the Elizabethan gables of the first lay resident, and Inigo Jones was said to have added the brick wing with the Corinthian pilasters, and there was a stuccoed projection in the sham Gothic of the time of George II. It was architecturally ridiculous, but it was supposed to be the warmest part of the house, and Teilo Morgan occupied a set of five or six rooms on the first floor, and often looked out on the park, and opened the windows to hear the sound of the pouring Avon, and the murmur of the wood-pigeons in the trees, and the noise of the west wind from the mountain. He longed to be out among it all, running as he saw boys running on the hillside through a gap in the wood; but he knew that there was a gulf fixed between him and that paradise. There was, it seemed, no specific disease but a profound weakness, a *marasmus* that had stopped short of its term, but kept the patient chronically incapable of any physical exertion, even the slightest. They had once tried taking him out on a very fine day in the park, in a wheeled chair; but even that easy motion was too much for him. After ten minutes, he had fainted, and lay for two or three days on his back, alive, but little more than alive. Most of his time was spent on a couch. He would sit up for his meals and to interview the estate agent; but it was effort to do so much as this. He used to read in county histories and in old family records of the doings of his ancestors; and wonder what they would have said to such a successor. The storming of castles at dead darkness of night, the firing of them so that the mountains far away shone, the arrows of the Gwent bowmen darkening the air at Crécy, the battle of the dawn by the river, when it was seen scarlet by the first light in the east, the drinking of Gaston wine in hall from moonrise to sunrise; he was no figure for the old days and works of the Morgans.

It was probable that his feeble life was chiefly sustained by his intense interest in the doings of the estate. The agent, Captain Vaughan, a keen, middle-aged man, had often told him that a monthly interview would be sufficient and more than sufficient. "I'm afraid you find all this detail terribly tiring," he would say. "And you know it's not really necessary. I've one or two good men under me, and between us we manage to keep things in very decent order. I do assure you, you needn't bother. As a matter of fact; if I brought you a statement once a quarter, it would be quite enough."

But Teilo Morgan would not entertain any such laxity.

"It doesn't tire me in the least," he always replied to the agent's remonstrances. "It does me good. You know a man must have exercise in some form or another. I get mine on your legs. I'm still enjoying that tramp of yours up to Castell-y-Bwch three years ago. You remember?"

Captain Vaughan seemed at a loss for a moment.

"Let me see," he said. "Three years ago? Castell-y-Bwch? Now, what was I doing up there?"

"You can't have forgotten. Don't you recollect? It was just after the great snowstorm. You went up to see that the roof was all right, and fell into a fifteen-foot drift on the way."

"I remember now," said Vaughan. "I should think I do remember. I don't think I've been so cold and so wet before or since—worse than the Balkans. I wasn't prepared for it. And when I got through the snow, there was an infernal mountain stream still going strong beneath it all."

"But there was a good fire at the pub when you got there?"

"Half-way up the chimney; coal and wood mixed; roaring, I've never seen such a blaze: six foot by three, I should think. And I told them to mix it strong."

"I wish I'd been there," said the squire. "Let me see; you recommended that some work should be done on the place, didn't you? Re-roofing, wasn't it?"

"Yes, the slates were in a bad way, and in the following March we replaced them by stone tiles, extra heavy. Slates are not good enough, half-way up the mountain. To the west, of course, the place is more or less protected by the wood, but the south-east pine end is badly exposed and was letting the wet through, so I ran up an oak frame, nine inches from the wall, and fixed tiles on that. You remember passing the estimate?"

"Of course, of course. And it's done all right? No trouble since?"

"No trouble with wind or weather. When I was there last, the fat daughter was talking about going to service in Cardiff. I don't think Mrs. Samuel fancied it much. And young William wants to go down the pit when he leaves school."

"Thomas is staying to help his father with the farm, I hope? And how is the farm doing now?"

"Fairly well. They pay their rent regularly, as you know. In spite of what I tell them, they will try to grow wheat. It's much too high up."

"How do the people on the mountain like the new parson?"

"They get on with him all right. He tries to persuade them to come to Mass, as he calls it, and they stay away and go to meeting. But quite on friendly terms—out of business hours."

"I see. I should think he would be more at home in one of the Cardiff parishes. We must see if it can't be worked somehow. And how about those new pigsties at Ty, Captain? Have you got the estimate with you? Read it out, will you? My eyes are tired this morning. You went to Davies for the estimate? That's right: the policy of the estate is, always encourage the small man. Have you looked into that business of the marsh?"

"The marsh? Oh, you mean at Kemeys? Yes, I've gone into it. But I don't think it would pay for draining. You'd never see your money back."

"You think not? That's a pity."

Teilo Morgan seemed depressed by the agent's judgment on the Kemeys marshland. He weighed the matter.

"Well; I suppose you are right. We mustn't go in for fancy farming. But look here! It's just struck me. Why not utilise the marsh for growing willows? We could run a sluice from the brook right across it. It might be possible to start basket-making—in a small way, of course, at first. What do you think?"

"That wants looking into," said Captain Vaughan. "I know a place in Somerset where they are doing something of the kind. I'll go over on Wednesday and see if I can get some useful information. I hardly think the margin of profit would be a big one. But you would be satisfied with two per cent?"

"Certainly. And here's a thing I've been wanting to talk to you about for a long time—for the last three or four Mondays—and I've always forgotten. You know the Graeg on the home farm? A beautiful southern exposure, and practically wasted. I feel sure that egg-plants would do splendidly there. Could you manage to get out some figures for next Monday? There's no reason why the egg-plant shouldn't become as popular as the tomato and the banana; if a cheap supply were forthcoming. You will see to that, won't you? If you're busy, you might put off going to Somerset till next week: no hurry about the marsh."

"Very good. The Graeg: egg-plants." The agent made an entry in his note-book, and took his leave soon afterwards. He paced a long corridor till he came to the gallery, from which the main staircase of the Abbey went down to the entrance hall. There he encountered an important-looking personage, square-chinned, black-coated, slightly grizzled.

"As usual, I suppose?" the personage enquired.

"As usual."

"What was it this time?"

"Egg-plants."

The important one nodded, and Captain Vaughan went on his way.

II

As soon as the agent had gone, Teilo Morgan rang a bell. His man came, and lifted him skilfully out of the big chair, and laid him on the day-bed by the window, propping him with cushions behind his back.

"Two cushions will be enough," said the squire. "I'm rather tired this morning."

The man put the bell within easy reach, and went out softly. Teilo Morgan lay back quite still; thinking of old days, and of happy years, and of the bad season that followed them. His first recollections were of a little cottage, snow-white, high upon the mountain, a little higher than the hamlet of Castell-y-Bwch, of which he had been talking to the agent. The shining walls of the cottage, freshly whitened every Easter, were very thick, and sloped outward to the ground: the windows were deep-set in the wall. By the porch which sheltered the front door from the great winds of the mountain, were two shrubs, one on each side, that were covered in their season with orange-coloured flowers, as round as oranges, and these golden flowers were, in his memory, tossed and shaken to and fro, in the breeze that always blew in that high land, when every leaf and blossom of the lower slopes was still. About the house was the garden, and a rough field, and a small cherry orchard, in a sheltered dip of land, and a well dripping from the grey rock with water very clear and cold. Above the cottage and its small demesne came a high bank, with a hedge of straggling, wind-beaten trees and bramble thickets on top of it, and beyond, the steep and wild ascent of the mountain, where the dark green whin bushes bore purple berries, where white cotton grew on the grass, and the bracken shimmered in the sun, and the imperial heather glowed on golden autumn days. Teilo remembered well how, a long age ago, he would stand in summer weather by the white porch, and look down on the great territory, as if on the whole world, far below: wave following wave of hill and valley, of dark wood and green pastures and cornfields, pale green or golden, the white farms shining, the mist of blue smoke above the Roman city, and to the right, the far waters of the yellow sea. And then there were the winter nights: all the air black as pitch, and a noise of tumult and battle, when the great winds and driving rain beat upon wall and window; and it was praise and thanksgiving to lie safe and snug in a cot by the settle near the light and the warmth of the fire, while without the heavens and the hills were confounded together in the roaring darkness.

In the white cottage on the high land, Teilo had lived with his mother and grandmother, very old, bent and wrinkled; with a sallow face, and hair still black in spite of long years. But he was a very small boy, when a gentleman who had often been there before, came and took his mother and himself away, down into the valley; and his next memories were of the splendours of Llantrisant Abbey, where the three of them lived together, and were waited on by many servants, and he found that the gentleman was his father: a cheerful man, always laughing, with bright blue eyes and a thick, tawny moustache, that drooped over his chin. Here Teilo ran about the park, and raced sticks in the racing Avon, and climbed up the steep hill they called the Graeg, and liked to be there because with the shimmering, sweet-scented bracken it was like the mountain-side. His walks and runs and climbs did not last long. The strange illness that nobody seemed to understand struck him down, and when after many weeks of bitter pains and angry, fiery dreams, the anguish of day and night left him; he was weak and helpless, and lay still, waiting to get well, and never got well again. Month after month he lay there in his bed, able to move his hands faintly, and no more. At the end of a year he felt a little stronger and tried to walk, and just managed to get across the room, helping himself from chair to chair. There was one thing that was for the better: he had been a silent child, happy to sit all by himself hour after hour on the mountain and then on the steep slope of the Graeg, without uttering a word or wanting anyone to come and talk to him. Now, in his weakness, he chattered eagerly, and thought of admirable things. He would tell his father and mother all the schemes and plans he was making; and he wondered why they looked so sadly at him.

And then, disaster. His father died, and his mother and he had to leave Llantrisant Abbey; they never told him why. They went to live in a grey, dreary street somewhere in the north of London. It was a place full of ugly sights and sounds, with a stench of burning bones always in the heavy air, and an unseemly litter of egg-shells and torn paper and cabbage-stalks about the gutters, and screams and harsh cries fouling the ears at midnight. And in winter, the yellow sulphur mist shut out the sky and burned sourly in the nostrils. A dreadful place, and the exile was long there. His mother went out on most days soon after breakfast, and often did not come back till ten, eleven, twelve at night, tired to death, as she said, and her dark beauty all marred and broken. Two or three times, in the course of the day, a neighbour from the floor below would come in and see if he wanted anything; but, except for these visits, he lay alone all the hours, and read in the few old books that they had in the room. It was a life of bewildered misery. There was not much to eat, and what there was seemed not to have the right taste or smell; and he could not understand why they should have to live in the horrible street, since his mother had told him that now his father was dead, he was the rightful master of Llantrisant Abbey and should be a very rich man. "Then why are we in this dreadful place?" he asked her; and she only cried.

And then his mother died. And a few days after the funeral, people came and took him away; and he found himself once more at Llantrisant, master of it all, as his mother had told him he should be. He made up his mind to learn all about the lands and farms that he owned, and got them to bring him the books of the estate, and then Captain Vaughan began to come and see him, and tell him how things were going on, and how this farmer was the best tenant in the county, and how that man had nothing but bad luck, and John Williams would put gin in his cider, and drive breakneck down steep, stony lanes on market nights, standing up in the cart like a Roman charioteer. He learnt about all these works and ways, and how the land was farmed, and what was done and what was needed to be done in the farmhouses and farm-buildings, and asked the agent about all his visits of inspection and enquiry, till be felt that he knew every field and footpath on the Llantrisant estate, and could find his way to every farm-house and cottage chimney corner from the mountain to the sea. It was the absorbing interest and the great happiness of his life; and he was proud to think of all he had done for the land and for the people on it. They were excellent people, farmers, but apt to be too conservative, too much given to stick in the old ruts that their fathers and grandfathers had made, obstinately loyal to old methods in a new world. For example, there was Williams, Penyrhaul, who almost refused to grow roots, and Evan Thomas, Glascoed, who didn't believe in drainpipes, and tried to convince Vaughan that bush drainage was better for the land, and half a dozen, at least, who were sure that all artificials exhausted the soil, and the silly fellow who had brought his black Castle Martins with him from Pembrokeshire, and turned up his nose at Shorthorns and Herefords. Still, Vaughan had as way with him, and made most of them see reason sooner or later; and they all knew that there was not another estate in England or Wales that was so ready to meet its tenants halfway, and do repairs and build new barns and cowsheds very often before they were asked. Teilo Morgan gave his agent all the credit he deserved, but at the same time he could not help feeling that in spite of his disabilities, of the weakness that kept him a prisoner to these four or five rooms, so that he had not once gone over the rest of the Abbey since his return to it; in spite of his invalid and stricken days, a great deal was owing to himself and to the fresh ideas that he had brought to the management of the estate. He took in the farming journals, and was thoroughly well read in the latest literature that dealt with the various branches of agriculture, and he knew in consequence that he was well in advance of his time, in advance even of the most forward agriculturalists of the day.

There were methods and schemes and ideas in full course of practical and successful working on the Llantrisant property that were absolutely unheard of on any other estate in the country. He had wanted to discuss some of these ideas in the Press; but Vaughan had dissuaded him; he said that for the present the force of prejudice was too strong. Vaughan was possibly right; all the same Teilo Morgan knew that he was making agricultural history. In the meantime, he was jotting down careful and elaborate notes on the experiments that were being tried, and in a year or two he intended to put a book on the stocks: *The Llantrisant Estates: a New Era in Farming.*

He was pondering happily in this strain, when, in a flash, a brilliant, a dazzling notion came to him. He drew a long breath of delighted wonder; then rang his hand-bell, and told the man that he might now put in the third cushion—"and give me my writing things". A handy contraption, with paper, ink and the rest was adjusted before him, and as soon as the servant was gone, Teilo began a letter, his eyes bright with excitement.

"DEAR VAUGHAN,

"I know you think I'm inclined to be rather too experimental in my farming; I believe that this time you will agree that I have hit on a great idea. Don't say a word to anybody about it. I am astonished that it hasn't been thought of long ago, and my only fear is that we may be forestalled. I suppose the fact is that it has been staring us all in the face so long that we haven't noticed it!

"My idea is simply this; a plantation, or orchard, if you like, of the Arbor Vitæ; and I know the exact place for it. You have often told me how Jenkins of the Garth insists on having those fields of his by the Soar down in potatoes, a most unsuitable place for such a crop. I want you to go and see him as soon as you have time, and tell him we want the use of the fields—about five acres, if I remember. Of course, he must be compensated, and, within reason, you can be as liberal as you like. I have understood from you that the soil is a deep, rich loam, in very good heart; it should be an ideal position for the culture I intend. I believe that the Arbor Vitæ will flourish anywhere, and is practically indifferent to climatic conditions: 'makes its own climate', as one writer rather poetically expresses it. Still, its culture in this county is an experiment; and I am sure Mharadwys—I think that's the old name of those fields by the Soar—is the very spot.

"The land must be thoroughly trenched. Get this put in hand as soon as you can possibly manage it. Let them leave it in ridges, so that the winter frosts can break it up. Then, if we give it a good dressing of superphosphate of time and bone meal in the spring, and plough in September, everything will be ready for the autumn planting. You know I always insist on shallow planting; don't bury the roots in a hole; spread them out evenly within five or six inches of the surface; let them feel the sun. And when it comes to staking; mind that each tree has two stakes, crossed at the top, with the points driven into the ground at a good distance from the roots. I am sure that the single stake, close to the tree stem, with its point driven through the roots is very bad practice.

"Of course, you will appreciate the importance of this new culture. The twelve distinct kinds of fruit produced by this extraordinary tree, all of them of delicious flavour, render it absolutely unique. Whatever the cost of the experiment may be, I am sure it will be made good in a very short time. And it must be remembered that while the name, *Tous les mois,* given to a kind of strawberry cultivated on the continent, really only implies that the plants fruit all through the summer and early autumn, in the case of the Arbor Vitæ, the claim may be made with literal truth. As the old writers say: 'The Arbor yielded her fruit every month.' No other cropper, however heavy, can be compared with it. And in addition to all this, the leaves are said to possess the most valuable therapeutic qualities.

"Don't you agree with me that this will prove by far the most important and far-reaching of all our experiments?

"I remain,

"Yours sincerely,

"TEILO MORGAN.

"P.S. On consideration; I think it might be better to keep the dressing of super and bone meal till the autumn, just before ploughing.

"And you might as well begin to look up the Nurserymens' Catalogues. As we shall be giving a large order, you may have to place it with two or three firms. I think you will find the Arbor Vitæ listed with the Coniferæ."

III

Long years after all this, two elderly men were talking together in a club smoking-room. They had the place almost to themselves; most of the members, having lunched and taken their coffee and cigarettes, had strolled away. There was a small knot of men with their heads close together over the table, chuckling and relating and hearing juicy gossip. Two or three others were dotted about the solemn, funebrous room, each apart with his paper, deep in his arm-chair. Our two were in a retired corner, which might have been called snug in any other place. They were old friends, it appeared, and one, the less elderly, had returned not long before from some far place, after an absence of many years.

"I haven't seen anything of Harry Morgan since I've been home," he remarked. "I suppose he's still in town."

"Still in Beresford Street. But he doesn't get out so much now.

He's getting a bit stiff in the joints. A good ten years older than I am."

"I should like to see him again. I always thought him a very good fellow."

"A first-rate fellow. You know that story about Bartle Frere? Man was sent to meet him at the station, and asked how he should know him. They told him to look out for an old gentleman with grey whiskers helping somebody—and he found Frere helping an old woman with a big basket out of a third-class carriage. Harry Morgan was like that—except for the whiskers."

There was a pause; and then the man who had retold the old Sir Bartle Frere story began again.

"I don't suppose you ever heard the kindest thing Morgan ever did—one of the kindest things I've ever heard of. You know I come from his part of the country: my people used to have Plas Henoc, only a few miles from Llantrisant Abbey, the Morgans' place. My father told me all about it; Harry kept the thing very dark. Upon my word! what is it about a man not letting his left hand know what his right hand is about? Morgan has lived up to that if any man ever did. Well, it was like this:

"Have you ever heard of old Teilo Morgan? He was a bit before our day. Not an old man, by the way; I don't suppose he was much over forty when he died. Well, he went the pace in the old style. He was very well known in town, not in society, or rather in damned bad society, and not far from here either. They had a picture of him in some low print of the time, with those long whiskers that used to be worn then. They didn't give his name; just called it, 'The Hero of the Haymarket'. You wouldn't believe it, would you, but in those days the Haymarket was the great place for night-houses—Kate Hamilton and all that lot. Morgan was in the thick of it all; but that picture annoyed him; he had those whiskers of his cut off at Truefitt's the very next day. He was the sort of man they got the silver dinner service out for, when he entertained his friends at Cremorne. And 'Judge and Jury', and the *poses plastiques,* and that place in Windmill Street where they fought without the gloves—and all the rest of it.

"And it was just as bad down in the country. He used to take his London friends, male and female, down there, and lead the sort of life he lived in town, as near as he could make it. They used to tell a story, true very likely, of how he and half a dozen rapscallions like himself were putting away the port after dinner, and making a devil of a noise, all talking and shouting and cursing at the top of their voices, when Teilo seemed to pull himself together and get very grave all in a minute. 'Silence! gentlemen!' he called out. The rest of them took no notice; one of them started a blackguard song, and the others got ready to join in the chorus. 'Hold your damned tongues, damn you!' Morgan bawled at them, and smashed a, big decanter on the table. 'D'you think,' he said, 'that that's the sort of thing for youngsters to listen to? Have you no sense of decency? Didn't I tell you that the children were coming down to dessert?' With that, he rang a bell that was by him on the table and—so the story goes—six young fellows and six girls came trooping down the big staircase: without a single stitch on them, calling out in squeaky voices: 'Oh, dear Papa, what have you done to dear Mamma?' And the rest of it."

The phrase was evidently an inclusive, vague, but altogether damnatory clause with this teller of old tales.

"Well," he continued, "you can imagine what the county thought of all that sort of thing. Teilo Morgan made Llantrisant Abbey stink in their nostrils. Naturally, none of them would go near the place. The women, who were, perhaps, rather more particular about such matters than they are now, simply wouldn't have Morgan's name mentioned in their presence. The Duke cut him dead in the street. His subscription to the Hunt was returned. I don't think he cared. You know Garden Parties were beginning to get fashionable then, and they say Morgan sent out engraved invitation cards, with a picture of a Nymph and a Satyr on them that some artist fellow had done for him—not a nice picture at all according to county standards. And what d'ye think he had at the bottom of the card instead of R.S.V.P.?—'No clothes by request.' He was a damned impudent fellow, if you like. I believe the party came off all right, with more friends from town, and most unusual games and sports on the lawn and in the shrubberies. It was said that Treowen, the Duke's son, was there; but he always swore through thick and thin that it was a lie. But it was brought up against him afterwards when he stood with Herbert for the county.

"And what d'ye think happened next? A most extraordinary thing. Nobody was prepared for it. Everyone said he would just drink and devil and wench himself to death, and a damned good riddance. Well, I'll tell you. There was one thing, you know, that everybody had to confess: in his very worst days Teilo Morgan always left the country girls alone. Never interfered with the farmers' daughters or cottage girls or anything in that way. And then, one fine day when he was up with a keeper looking after a few head of grouse he had on the mountain, what should he do but fall in love with a girl of fifteen, who lived with her mother or grandmother, I don't know which, in a cottage right up there. Mary Trevor, I believe her name was. My father had seen her once or twice afterwards driving with Morgan in his tandem: he said she was a most beautiful creature, a perfectly lovely woman. She was a type that you see sometimes in Wales: very dark, black eyes, black hair, oval face, skin a pale olive—not at all unlike those girls that used to prance up and down Arles in Southern France, with their hair done up in velvet ribbons; I don't know whether you've ever been there? There's something Oriental about that style of beauty; it doesn't last long.

"Anyhow, Teilo Morgan fell flat on the spot. He went straight down to the Abbey and packed the whole company back to town— told them they could go to hell, or bloody Jerusalem, or the Haymarket, for all he cared. As soon as they'd all gone, he was off to the mountain again. He wasn't seen at the Abbey for weeks. I am sure I don't know why he didn't marry the girl straight away; nobody knew. She said that he did marry her; but we shall come to that presently. In due course, the baby came along, and Morgan wanted to pension off the old lady and take the mother and child down to Llantrisant. But the doctors advised against it. I believe Morgan got some very good men down, and they were all inclined to shake their heads over the child. I don't think they committed themselves or named any distinct disease or anything of that kind; but they were all agreed that there was a certain delicacy of constitution, and that the boy would have a much better chance if they kept him up in the mountain air for the first few years of his life. Llantrisant Abbey, I should tell you, is right down in the valley by the river, with woods and hills all round it; fine place, but rather damp and relaxing, I dare say. So, the long and short of it was that young Teilo stayed up with his mother and the old woman, and old Teilo used to come and see them for week-ends, as they say now, till the boy was four or five years old; and then the old lady was looked after somewhere or other, and the mother and son went to live at the Abbey.

"Everything went on all right—except that the county people kept away—for three or four years. The child seemed well and strong, and the tutor they got in for him said he was a tremendous fellow with his books, well in advance of his age, unusually interested in his work and all that. Then he got ill, very ill indeed. I don't know what it was; some brain trouble, I should think, meningitis or something of that sort. It was touch and go for weeks, and it left the unfortunate little chap an absolute wreck at the end of it. For a long time they thought he was paralysed; all the strength had gone out of his limbs. And the worst of it was, the mind was affected. He seemed bright enough, mind you; nothing dull or heavy about him; and I'm told you might listen to him chattering away for half an hour on end, and go away thinking he was a perfect phenomenon of a child for intelligence. But if you listened long enough, you'd hear something that would pull you up with a jerk. Crazy?—yes, and worse than crazy—mixed up in a way with a kind of sense, so that you might begin to wonder which was queer, yourself or the boy. It was a dreadful grief to the parents, especially to his father. He used to talk about his sins finding him out. I don't know, there may have been something in that. 'Whips to scourge us'—perhaps so.

"They got the tutor back after some time; the child begged so hard for him that they were afraid he'd worry himself into another brain fever if they didn't give way. So he came along with instructions to make the lessons as much a farce as he liked, and the more the better; not on any account to press the boy over his work. And from what my father told me, young Teilo nearly drove the poor man off his head. He was far sharper in a way than he'd ever been before, with a memory like Macaulay's—once read, never forgotten—and an amazing appetite for learning. But then the twist in the brain would come out. Mathematics brilliant; and at the end of the lesson he'd frighten that tutor of his with a new theory of figures, some notion of the figures that we don't know of, the numbers that are between the others, something rather more than one and less than two, and so forth. It was the same with everything: there was the Secret Conquest of England a hundred years ago, that nobody was allowed to mention, and the squares that were always changing their shape in geometry, and the great continent that was hidden because Africa was on top of it, so that you couldn't see it. Then, when it came to the classics, there were fresh cases for the nouns and new moods for the verbs: and all the rest of it. Most extraordinary, and very sad for his father and mother. The poor little fellow took a tremendous interest in the family history and in the property; but I believe he hashed all that up in some infernal way. Well; it seemed there was nothing to be done.

"Then his father died. Of course, the question of the succession came up at once. Poor Mrs. Morgan, as she called herself to the last, swore she was married to Teilo, but she couldn't produce any papers—any papers that were evidence of a legal marriage anyhow. I fancy the truth was that they were married in some forgotten little chapel up in the mountains by a hedge preacher or somebody of that kind, who didn't know enough to get in the registrar. Of course, Teilo ought to have known better, but probably he didn't bother at the time so long as he satisfied the girl. He may have meant to make it all right eventually, and left it too late: I don't know. Anyhow, Payne Llewellyn, the family solicitor, gave the poor woman to understand that she and the boy would have to leave Llantrisant Abbey, and off they went. They had one room in a miserable back street in Islington or Barnsbury or some such God-forsaken place and she earned a bare living in a sweater's workshop.

"Meanwhile, the property had passed to a cousin; Harry Morgan. And he hadn't been heard of, or barely heard of, for some years. He had gone off exploring Central Asia or the sources of the Amazon when Teilo Morgan was in his glory—if you can put it that way. He hadn't heard a word of Teilo's reformation or of Mary Trevor and her boy; and when old Llewellyn was able to get at him after considerable difficulty and delay, he never mentioned the woman or her son. When Morgan did come home at last, he found he didn't fancy the old family place; called it a dismal hole, I believe. Anyhow, he let it on a longish lease to a mental specialist—mad doctors, they called them then—and he turned the Abbey into a lunatic asylum.

"Then somebody told Harry about Mary Trevor, and the poor child, and the marriage or no-marriage. He was furious with Llewellyn. He had a search made, and when he found them, it was just too late so

far as Mary Trevor was concerned. She had died, of grief and hard
work and semi-starvation, no doubt. But Harry took the boy away, and
finding how he was longing to go back to the Abbey—he was quite
convinced, you see, that he was the owner of it and of all the Morgan
estates—Harry got the doctor who was running the place to take Teilo
as a patient. He was given a set of rooms to himself in a wing, right
away from the other patients. Everything was done to encourage him
in his notion that he was Teilo Morgan of Llantrisant Abbey. Going
back to the old place had stirred up all his enthusiasm for the family,
and the property, and the management of the estates, and it became
the great interest of his life. He quite thought he was making it the
best-managed estate in the county: inaugurating a new era in English
farming, and all the rest of it. Harry Morgan instructed Captain
Vaughan, the Estate Agent, to see Teilo once a week, and enter into all
his schemes and pretend to carry them out, and I believe Vaughan
played up extremely well, though he sometimes found it difficult to
keep a straight face. You see, that twist in the brain wasn't getting any
better, and when it went to work on practical farming it produced
some amazing results. Vaughan would be told to get this bit of land
ready for pineapples, and somewhere else they were to grow olives;
and what about zebras for haulage? But it kept him happy to the last.
D'you know, the very day he died, he wrote a long letter of instructions to Vaughan. What d'you think it was about? You won't guess. He
told Vaughan to plant the Tree of Life in a potato patch by the Soar,
and gave full cultural directions."

"God bless me! You don't say so?"

The Major, who had listened to the long story, ruminated awhile.
He had been brought up in an old-fashioned Evangelical household,
and had always loved "Revelation". The text burned and glowed into
his memory, and he said in a strong voice:

"'In the midst of the street of it, and on either side of the river,
was there the tree of life, which bare twelve manner of fruits, and
yielded her fruit every month: and the leaves of the tree were for the
healing of the nations.'"

There was only one man beside our two friends left in the darkening
room; and he had fallen fast asleep in his arm-chair, with his paper on

the ground before him. The Major's clear intonation woke him with a crash, and when he heard the words that were being uttered, he was seized with unspeakable and panic terror, and ran out of the room, howling (more or less) for the Committee.

But the Major having ended his text, said:

"I always thought Harry Morgan was a good fellow. But I didn't know he was such a thundering good fellow as that."

And that was his Amen.

Out of the Picture

I

In the old days—which means anything from ten to thirty years ago—there was a question which used to be asked now and then at studio parties and Chelsea pubs. The question was:

"But who was the twisted man?"

And it was often followed by another:

"But where did M'Calmont take himself off to?"

Neither interrogation ever got an answer; save that to the second query, a young man in very full dark green corduroy trousers is reported to have said once upon a time:

"Somebody told me he had been seen in Quito."

But to this neither credit or attention was given. And it is probable from what follows that the double enigma is to be reckoned with that question as to what song the Sirens sang; if, indeed, it is not past all solution.

Going back, then, to those old days aforesaid, and rather to the earlier portion of them, when, as a journalist, I saw many strange things and people; I was once sent to view an exhibition of pictures at the Molyneux Galleries in Danby Place. Perhaps the event may be sufficiently dated by saying that the Exhibition was opened somewhere between the Battle of Sidney Street and the Coronation of King George V; and I have a feeling that it was a misty May morning when I went to see it. It was not a large exhibition: all the pictures were contained in two sizeable rooms, and as soon as I got into them I saw at once that I could make nothing of it—that is, from any serious standpoint. I cared nothing; my point of view in that instance, as in all others like it, was that if the paper chose to send an outsider and an ignoramus to criticise works of art—especially the works of a new and tentative and experimental school—then, on the head of the paper let the just doom fall. And the school represented on this particular occasion at the Molyneux Galleries evidently represented a fierce revolt against the traditions and conventions of the elders. To begin with, my eye was caught by "The Old Harbour". There were buildings in vertical perspective, their walls appearing to incline together and to aspire to meet in the upper part of the canvas, and with a sense about them as if the whole mass were unstable, impermanent, void of true solidity and settlement on the earth. A mystic once told me that after he had finished his meditation and gone out into the street, he had seen the grey bulk of the houses opposite suddenly melt, evaporate, go up like smoke, leaving void nothingness in their place. And so the painter with his art had made these warehouses and Customs buildings, or whatever they were, in such a fashion that they seemed as if they also were on the very point to turn to mist, to float into the air, and to disappear. And then, for the rest, there was grey water, and segments, and portions, and particles of keels, sails, masts, ropes, decks, and deck furniture, not cohering, or fitting together, but dispersed and apart. Here, I could see, was choice matter on which the expert and art critic could exercise their knowledge and judgement. As I had neither, I made an experiment or two, and was able to inform the readers of the paper that if you walked briskly past the picture, winking both eyes as fast as possible, you really got a sort of impression of movement and activity, of ships and boats coming into harbour and sailing out of it, of sails lowered and hoisted, of an uncertain background, now obscured, now left visible as a ship in full sail passed before it. It struck me that, in my hands, art criticism was in a fair way to become a popular sport.

And then there was another picture that both attracted and distracted me. It was a big canvas, and the subject was a number of geometrical figures of all kinds, most ingeniously fitted into one another, and rainbow painted, no doubt on some occult principle of contrast and complement and correspondence. It was called "King Solomon's Cargoes". I murmured: "Gold and silver and ivory and apes and peacocks," and looked for them. I could not see any of them, and I thought I would go back to Fleet Street, relying on my impressions of "The Old Harbour", which would just fill the "two sticks" that had been allotted to the story. It was, decidedly, a case of least said, soonest mended. In spite of the defence which, as I have mentioned, I had ready; I felt I was on unsafe and treacherous ground. Who was I to sit in judgment on the work of painters? No doubt, I might say that I had looked for apes and peacocks in that picture and had found none; and, likely enough, that remark might merely serve to display my utter ignorance of the subject I was pretending to treat. But it was not written that I should escape "King Solomon's Cargoes" so easily.

It was some years after the exhibition at the Molyneux Galleries that I found myself in a various company one evening. I saw a few people that I knew, and was talking to one of them, when the friend who had brought me along came and said:

"Do you mind if I introduce you to a man? It's M'Calmont, the painter, who says he's been wanting to meet you for years. Some criticism of yours that he read seems to have made a great impression on him."

He took me up to a dark, slight man with a black moustache, and left me. M'Calmont made room on the settee, and began at once:

"I've been wanting to thank you for a long time for that notice you wrote in your paper about the Exhibition in the Molyneux Galleries. You'll remember? It was in Coronation year."

I told him I thought I did remember something about it. But I wondered, internally, what sort of thanks I was going to get from a painter for my vain ribaldry. He went on:

"I said to myself at the time: 'This A.M., whoever he may be, has got an eye to detect the falsities and fallacies, and I'd like to have a talk with him.' Then somebody told me your name, but I left town soon after, and this is the first chance I've had."

And, finally, it came to this: that the falsities and fallacies were the picture of "The Old Harbour", by Frank Guildford, and M'Calmont had enjoyed the way I had stuck my knife into the fellow.

I explained. I said I knew nothing about painting, and had been afraid that I had been guilty of ill-placed and unmannerly humour. He wouldn't hear of this.

"It was just instinct, pure instinct. You may not have the technical knowledge, but you know a silly man when you see him."

I asked what had become of this unhappy man.

"He's what they call a fashionable painter, and makes his eight thousand a year by painting grocers and their wives—damn him!"

And he went on:

"I don't know whether you happened to see a thing I had in that Exhibition? I called it 'King Solomon's Cargoes'. "

I lied. I dwelt again and more forcibly on the utter unscrupulousness of my character when simulating an art critic. I said I had not seen his canvas. I had just dashed into the galleries, invented my silly game with the ships in the harbour, and run out again as soon as I had got material for my two or three paragraphs. But, in fact, I remembered those purple squares, scarlet triangles, sky-blue circles very well.

M'Calmont nodded his head gloomily.

"I'm glad it didn't catch your eye. You might have had something to say to me too. You'd have been right, and you'd have been wrong. I was never a faker like Guildford. I never pretended that if you painted a bit of mast here and a scrap of a sail there and a deck in another part of the canvas you could call it painting a ship. But I did believe in abstract painting—and I do still in a way."

I asked him to tell me all about it.

"I'd like to explain what I was after in those days. You say you know nothing about the technical side of painting. You won't want to know anything about it: it's not a technical question. It's behind all that and beyond it. But you can't talk sense in the middle of all these havers. Come away."

I followed him out, and by devious and obscure ways he led me to an obscure tavern, where we sat down together in a quiet corner of a bulging and old-fashioned bar. They spoke his language there, since his order for "two wee halfyins" was fulfilled without comment. But I looked at the stuff in my glass, and remembered how the poet had said that the half is greater than the whole—"greater," I corrected mentally, "than the double." I added water.

"Don't kill good drink," M'Calmont said reproachfully. "*Scelus est jugulare Falernum,* and this is better. It's the genuine Lagavulin, not the trash they sell in London for whiskey. But you were asking about abstract painting. It will be necessary to go back and away a little if we're to see what we're after. They say distance lends enchantment to the view; I'd put it myself, 'lends vision', *theoria.* It may turn out, of course, that when you do see, you see enchantment, but that is just secondary;

a kind of by-product, you might say, of the proposition. I'll ask you, then, if you know anything about the Kabbala of the Hebrews?"

Whatever I knew of that matter, I dissembled. I am a lover of the rich improbabilities, and I would not check this rare manifestation of them.

"Well, I don't want you to feel like a cow in a fremd loaming; so we won't go too deeply into those dark mysteries. But the Kabbalists tell us that at the Fall of Man, the Serpent did not ascend to Kether in the Tree of Life. It stopped at Daath. And that's their way of saying that the nature of man was not entirely corrupted. The Serpent poisoned and infected the logical understanding, but there was a pure, spiritual region above that which remained untouched.

"Very good. You see that? And there you have the reason why a man that's sunk deep in the blackest mud of materialism may very possibly be overcome with delight at the Fugues of Bach. You see how that may be? That's absolute music. It has nothing to do with Daath, the logical understanding. I'm speaking, you understand, of the pattern of sounds that reaches the ears of the hearer; just the ordered noise that he hears, if you like to put it that way. In the making of the music, no doubt, in the technical part of the creation, the understanding had its share, as the slave of the spirit. If you want to build Jerusalem with its Temple you must have your hewers of wood and stone and drawers of water. You're a writer yourself, and you know you can't do much in that way without calling in the aid of the pen-makers and the ink manufacturers and paper merchants; but you don't allow them to teach you how to turn the phrase.

"But the way the thing is fashioned is nothing to do with us. What we're concerned with is the thing we hear; and with that thing the logical understanding has just no concern at all. You'll note there's no tongue or language in which we can speak of it. There's no answer to the question: 'But what does it mean?' when that question is asked of pure music. Bach, you may say, had the gift of tongues; but in his case there's no legitimate gift of the interpretation of tongues. It's impossible to translate the language of Kether into the speech of Daath. I remember well going to hear *Lohengrin,* and there was a manner of commentary attached to the bill of the opera. I just glanced at it and saw that when the overture began I was to picture to myself a blue sky, and then to watch the wee white clouds forming on it. There you have your music critic calling in nature, and I saw in the paper, there was another of them puzzling his head over Berlioz, and decided that he was a 'pictural', not a 'linear' composer—calling in the terms of another art. And you'll hear often enough of the 'magnificent colour' of this or that passage of music. And I don't say they can do better. But it proves what I am telling you: that the understanding has nothing to do with absolute music, and nothing to say to it.

"Aye, and what about painting? That's the question I asked myself years ago. You know Aristotle says that all art is imitation. It's a very questionable pronouncement. If I'm not mistaken he had the drama chiefly in his mind when he made it. But the drama is just an impure or mixed development of the dance. In its primitive, original form, the dance was not an imitation of anything. It was, like music, an expression of something; but that's different. You may say that the drama of the Greeks was the dance set to words. And then, there's architecture. You can't say that the Parthenon is an imitation of anything, or that Rheims Cathedral is an imitation of anything. And literature. I shan't need to tell you that all the things we value most in the finest literature are just the things that soar above the sense—that is the logical understanding of it. If you turn to the Book and read Second Samuel, one, seventeen, you'll find a statement to the effect that David lamented the decease of Saul and Jonathan; but you'll not tell me that the vital interest and value of that proposition is to be discovered in the logical sense of it. And if you read Coleridge's *Kubla Khan,* I think you'll be puzzled to find out the logical sense in it and to tell me what it is. But there you have literature almost becoming music.

"And now you see what I've been getting at all the while."

I did not; but I forbore to say so.

"It was just this: that I asked myself why should there not be abstract or absolute painting, as well as absolute music and architecture? In the past, painting has been almost entirely Aristotelian, imitative. Why should it continue wholly on those lines? And you'll have gathered that I don't consider you solve the problem by cracking an object up into bits and scraps and pieces, and then painting the bits as they lie abroad. And if you paint a man's hands three times their natural size and draw a jackass with five legs, I'm not thinking you're any nearer to a solution. And that's how I came to paint the picture that I sent into those Galleries, that I'm glad now you didn't see. I was on the wrong track."

He lapsed at last into silence. I broke it by making a proposition remote from pure aesthetics. He declined to accede to it.

"No, no," said M'Calmont, "I'll not hear of it. In the 'Crown and Thistle', I'm in Scotland, and you're my guest. Where's the Macfarlane creature?"

When we parted soon after, he wrote his address on a scrap of paper torn from his note-book, and begged me to come and see him one evening.

"I'd like to shew you the new track I've found," he said, and vanished into the night, as we came out together.

II

It may be as well to make it clear at once that I am not the man to be daunted by the unusual. I have seen too much of it for that. I know that there are quarters, and very influential quarters, in which it is considered improper to mention such things. Every age has its conventions of propriety and impropriety: every age and every race. The missionary's wife in Africa shocked her two black servants horribly and unspeakably when she said that she was afraid the fruit was too green for a tart. Her husband's name was Green, and every (black) body knows that for a wife to utter her husband's name is both impious and obscene in the highest degree. We talk quite freely in the drawing-room in a style that would have made Dickens run out of the smoking-room, and when we write books we set down boldly words that were only forced out of the policeman of yesterday by the strict order of the Bench. It is all a matter of convention and taboo, and perhaps it is idle to ask for reasons. Mrs. Green, I dare say, couldn't understand why on earth she shouldn't utter the word "green"; and I suppose I am in much the same case when I say that I have no notion why I shouldn't mention the unusual, the odd, the extraordinary when I come across it. At any rate, I propose to defy this particular convention, here and elsewhere and always. As I was saying, I have seen too much of it to affect disbelief in its existence. I heard from the brassfounders of Clerkenwell about a former member of their craft who had confuted Darwin by the Hebrew alphabet and by the stars, and had buried the pot of gold in a field, where it was found by the navvies who were making the cutting for the Midland Railway. I have discussed with a solicitor, in his London office, the affairs of the J.H.V.S. Syndicate, who were seeking for the Ark of the Covenant from the directions of a cypher contained in that chapter of the Prophet Ezekiel which is called Mercabah. I know all about Campo Tosto, of Burnt Green, near Reigate, who defended his treasures with the bow and arrow. Why, then, should I hush up M'Calmont the painter, who drew his artistic principles from the Hebrew Kabbala?

As a matter of fact, I thought him an interesting man, and determined that I would see more of him. And so, one windy night in October, a few weeks after our meeting, I set out from somewhere in the west and made up the Gray's Inn Road. I am not certain by which street I turned from it. I think, but I am not sure, that it was by Acton Street. I know that I had gone too far north, and that when I came to the bottom of the street, and traversed the King's Cross Road, I found out my mistake, and had to incline somewhat to the right in climbing the hill. It is a district both devious and obscure, and I suppose that its twisting streets and unexpected squares of dusty trees will all come to ruin before they are intelligently explored. I had trod these mazes before, and thought I knew them tolerably well, but it was some years since I had been in that region, and I found myself perplexed and at fault, while the great wind blew the leaves of shadowy trees about my head and at my feet. At last I entered a black passage at a venture, and came down a short flight of steps into an irregular open space, on which there abutted a chapel of the Countess of Huntingdon's Connexion. I went round and about this square or triangle or trapezium, which was sparsely lit, till I found the green door in a wall to which I was directed, and rang the bell under the name M'Calmont. It was M'Calmont who opened the door and, taking hold of my arm, led me down a passage, past a house all lit up, where they were singing, and so to his studio, with trees all about it, bending and tossing and straining in the wind. Inside, there was a hanging lamp, and though it was not cold, the blaze of the fire was cheerful; and lamplight and firelight glittered on the carved and gilded frames of the pictures that hung on the walls. We sat down on a big settee at a comfortable distance from the fire; and he pressed on my attention what he called "Eela"—which is spelt, I found, "Islay".

And then there was more of it. Not of the spirit of the western isle, but of art, as he expounded it. It seemed that he had been forced to modify, one might say, to abandon his earlier views.

"I found out, and I was not so long about it, that you can't have absolute painting any more than you can have absolute literature. There are people, as you know, who are trying their hands at that—by writing gibberish without grammar. And *that* won't do. And I discovered that my endeavours in the direction of pure painting wouldn't do either. The principle of it is all right; but it's not for pigments. If you would carry it out, you must turn Eastern carpet-maker. And I'll maintain that there are Persian carpets as fine as any symphony of Beethoven's. They are the very analogy in colour and form of pure music.

"As it seemed that I couldn't go forward, I went back. And there, as you'll no doubt be well aware, I was in the height of the fashion. The sculptors and painters too have been trying back for the last quarter of a century. There are men who do their best to forget all the bare elements of their art, their drawing and their perspective and all the rest of it, that they may paint as if they were five years old. Another lot are off to Borrioboolah Gha, to learn the principles of sculpture from black savages. And I've no doubt there's a weary band trying to tramp back all the way to the Stone Age to see what they can find there. It's all very interesting. I'd like it fine—if they'd not call their imitations of barbarism Modern Art. And now I shall shew you where I've gone back myself, so as to be in the movement."

He barked derisively, and turning up the lamp a little, proceeded to guide me round the studio. And I felt as helpless and as futile as I had been in the old days, when I was an art critic *pour rire*.

For I was not at all sure where he had gone back, to use his own phrase. The pictures were all landscapes, painted, I conjecture, in the manner of the eighteenth century. There seemed to me, the uninstructed, as it were a dark shadow that hung over them all. Now and again there were patches of an intense and glowing blue in M'Calmont's skies; but these were contrasted with purple cloud masses rimmed with fire, with huge white clouds blown up into the sky by gathering thunder, with cloudy walls of black streaked with coppery flame. The green of the trees and of the grass was dark and livid, and the water of the pools and streams reflected something of the threat of the skies. M'Calmont had depicted open spaces in the midst of mysterious woods, narrow valleys edged with grim rocks, paths that wound in and out by lonely lands to shattered walls on a far height, trees of strange growth hanging over a well, glades glooming with twilight and the coming storm. There was an enchantment; but the incantation was of oppression and terror. There were three things that I noticed as curious: the first was that in every picture M'Calmont had introduced fire: logs burning under a broken wall, flames breaking out of yellowish smoke in the forest clearing, a fire by the well, a fire on the far hillside. Water, also, was represented in each canvas; well, or brook, or pool in the woods; and in every one of them there was the figure of a man, the same man, so far as I could judge. The figure was roughly dressed in the costume of an eighteenth-century countryman, in ragged clothes, with a scarlet cap on his head. He was depicted as tending the invariable fire, perhaps, or leaning on his staff, or half-hidden behind the trunk of a tree, or crouching among thorns on the border of a broken road. As I passed slowly from picture to picture, I noticed that the figure became more prominent. At first, it was barely seen in the background. Then it came forward into the middle distance, and at the end of the tour, the recently painted pictures, as M'Calmont told me, it was prominent in the foreground. In one picture he led a procession of torch-bearers into a wood as the night came on; but mostly he was alone in these desolate places that M'Calmont had made. And there was about this figure an impression of distortion. There was no specific deformity, as of hunched back or misshapen limbs, but yet a distinct sense of a form twisted and awry. And the face, where it could be clearly seen, was at once piteous and malignant, as of a stricken snake, wounded and dying.

Whatever my feelings about this odd gallery of paintings may have been, I kept it to myself. I reminded M'Calmont that I was an outsider and (perhaps exaggerating a little) that I could never be an admirer of the famous slaughterhouse, since it told no story.

"You're an awful liar," he said with engaging directness as we sat down again, "but let that flea stick to the wa'. I told you I was going back, like the rest, but not to the ignorance of childhood or savagery. I'm returning to a great art, and exploring its possibilities. You know that the Gothic architecture was the result of the builders, first of the Dark Ages and then of the Middle Ages, exploring the possibilities of the architecture of the Romans?"

"I have heard that theory advanced," I said, "but I don't know that it holds the field so decisively as you seem to think. I believe that some authorities would tell you that the gothicosity of the Gothic derives, to a great extent at least, from the East."

"I wouldn't believe a word of that tale—not that it signifies one way or the other in the argument. But I've seen churches down on the Rhone where the Gothic seems growing out of the Classic before your very eyes. There's one such at Valence: a regular Classic pediment, and all the detail of it one would call Norman, if one saw it in England. And anyone who will cast an eye over a First Pointed capital will see in a moment that it's a Corinthian capital in disguise; especially if it's got the square abacus."

"Very good, then," I assented, "let us grant your doctrine of Gothic. You're applying it to painting?"

"That is so. As I said; I'm exploring the possibilities of an old school of landscape. I don't know whether it's ever struck you; but there's no doubt that some of the painters of that age anticipated the world that came to Coleridge and Wordsworth. The eighteenth-century literature was Pope. It belonged to Daath, the region of the logical understanding. To the men of that age, the poetry of the six-teenth century and the first half of the seventeenth century was just Egyptian hieroglyphics. They could not interpret a single word of it; they'd forgotten what it meant. And, naturally, they could not dream of what was to come after them. But if you look at some of their painting, you'll see the landscapes of *Kubla Khan*—the awe, and the terror, and the hidden mysteries of earth and air, water and fire. And I just meant to find out what's beyond the turn of those paths they made."

He paused for a moment. "But that's not painter's talk," he went on. "I mean, of course, that I've taken a certain school of landscape painting as my starting-point; and I will see if I can't develop it on its own lines. I hope to draw something new out of the old."

"You have a figure, I notice, in all your pictures."

"You must have the human figure. Without that all your scenery would dissolve and melt away. It would be just nothing at all."

I did not ask if it was necessary that this human figure should be abhorrent of aspect. For that, I was certain, would not be painter's talk. And soon after, I went out into the labyrinth on the hillside. It was late, and the night had grown misty, and the sound of the streets below came faintly, with strange voices.

III

I remember being told a good many years ago in the course of a cheerful evening that the one thing fatal to an actor was intelligence.

"Or if you like it better," said the speaker, "I will say intellect. Or, better still, that something or other in a man that can pick a character to pieces, and analyse it, and find out why it does this, that, or the other, and relate it to the plot and the other parts in the cast; and then, continuing the process, build up by careful reasoning, the impersonation out of tones of the voice, facial expression, gesture, habit of body, and so forth."

"But," said a gentleman in the company, "isn't that the way to act? I thought that was how it was done."

"That's how I do it," replied the lecturer. "But I haven't any illusions. The man who depicts by that method will never be a 'feerst actor', as the German producer called it when I was in *Old Heidelberg* with Alexander. You know the story of Irving and poor Bill Terriss. Bill was ponging away for all he was worth as Henry VIII. Irving stopped him.

"'Very good, Terriss; very good indeed. I suppose you don't understand the meaning of one single word that you have uttered?'

"'No, guv'nor,' said Terriss, not in the least put out. 'But it'll go all right on the night.'

"That's the way to act."

"But, excuse me," said the man who wanted to know, "I'm afraid I don't quite grasp your meaning. *What* is the way to act?"

"You begin by not being able to give a single reason for anything you do or for your particular style of doing it. The rest comes along by itself. And I think I will help myself to another drink ere I go to that bourne . . . I don't want to miss the twelve-forty."

It was probable, I considered, that the old actor—a dignified Priest in *Hamlet*—was right in the main. Creative work, even such secondary creative work as the actor's, is not achieved by theories or by taking thought. A man must know the grammar of his business, whatever it is; the rest, if it is to be of the first order, must be the work of the hidden flame within. And, therefore, I had grave doubts of the validity of M'Calmont's art, when I thought of the elaboration of his theories. I remembered Claude Lantier in *L'Œuvre*. He made up his mind to be a stark realist, to paint bunches of carrots with sincerity. But he listened to theories, and ended by hanging himself before his symbolical picture of Paris as a nude woman, whose flesh glowed with jewels, like a Byzantine icon. It was some time before I went to see him again in that retired and secret studio. I met him in Holborn a few weeks after my visit, and he asked me in a very cheerful manner whether I was recovering from his pictures by degrees—giving his short bark of laughter. I told him that I had been allowed out for the last week.

"But," said I, willing to continue the vein of mild facetiousness, "you know art without a story is no good to me. Do tell me the story of that figure in all your paintings—the figure of the twisted man."

He stared at me blankly as if he hadn't a notion what I was talking about. Then he caught sight of an east-bound 'bus in a slowly moving press of traffic, ran for it, and shook a jocular fist at me from the top of the stair. And that was the last I saw of M'Calmont for a considerable time.

I was occupied as a matter of fact all through that winter with affairs and interests of my own. What is generally and conveniently known as psychical research has always had a strong attraction for me, in spite, or perhaps because, of the obscurities, difficulties and drawbacks of the pursuit. I must say, that the usual demand of the men of physical science does not strike me as in the least rational. This demand is, I believe, that psychical phenomena should be made to conform to the laws of the laboratory experiment. The man of science says: "I can make hydrogen by a simple process of mixing acid and water and zinc. If you don't believe me, come along now to my laboratory, and I will make hydrogen in three or four minutes, and shew you how it is done, so that you can make it yourself—and blow yourself up, too, if you don't follow the directions. Or, if you like, I will make hydrogen to-morrow morning at eleven, or to-morrow night at twelve, or on Saturday by written appointment." You confess your belief in the validity and efficacy of the hydrogen process; and your scientific friend goes on: "Very good; but you were telling me of a woman who looked in a crystal one morning, and saw and foretold correctly certain things that happened fifty miles away four hours later. Then, find that woman and bring her along to the laboratory, and let me see and hear her doing it again, and let her explain to me how she does it." And here, I say, physical science strikes me as profoundly irrational. A great poet cannot guarantee a masterpiece to be written on demand, under the eye of an observer, by 6.50 p.m. Shillaker, the famous bat, would never undertake to reproduce his 250 not out and no chances given, against the Patagonians. He knows that when he next meets that famous eleven, he may be out for a duck in the first over. And what painter can explain how he does it? Can Dick, Tom, and Harry go to the Master, listen to a demonstration, and come away, fully prepared to equal his immortal works? Clearly, men are capable of all sorts of performances of body and spirit which are not in the least amenable to the law of the laboratory. Let us remember the historic case of one of whom it is recorded: "at tip-cheese, or odd and even, his hand is out". If Master Tommy Bardell had been required to demonstrate his skill at tip-cheese then and there in Court, under the immediate eye of Mr. Justice Stareleigh, he would, very likely, have made a miserable fiasco.

So I have always ruled out the scientific demand and its implied conclusion as void and vain and foolish. The real difficulties in these enquiries are to be found, partly in the exquisite skill to which the art of the conjurer is sometimes brought, partly to the rarity of the faculty of keen and clear observation, partly to inaccurate and unreliable memory, a little to the commonness of lying: but most of all to the vast and bottomless credulity of the race of men. It is not a case of a plausible tale deceiving a simpleton; it is a case of homely strangers going to a hotel in a busy seaside town, telling the managing director of the concern that they are leaving him a couple of million in their wills, and living at the hotel free of payment for eight or nine months. What is to be expected when the managing director—the type is common—devotes his talents to psychical research?

Still, with all this in my mind, I persevered; perhaps not altogether

displeased at the thought that, so far as clear and final and general conclusions were concerned, the quest was a hopeless one. After all, there
is something eminently human in the desire of impossible things. To
seek for possibilities is rather the business of the lower animals than of
man. To be more specific: it had often struck me that from the singular
phenomena grouped together under the heading of *poltergeist* there
might, possibly or even probably, emerge a good deal of light on the doings and showings of modern spiritualism. In both cases, naturally, a
huge discount has to be made. No doubt, the *poltergeist* was often a bad
child, delighting in annoying, alarming, and humbugging its elders, delighting also in playing the leading part in the comedy. Sometimes, hysteria was to be expected; and hysteria is capable of anything. But it seems
to me that there was a very considerable remnant of *poltergeist* cases in
which mischief and trickery and ordinary hysteria were necessarily excluded from consideration. As to the other end of the enquiry, spiritualism; its history might, in a sense, be called a sad one. The last time I
looked into the leading spiritualist journal I saw on one page a description of the unpleasing methods by which the medium had hidden the
flowers that were to drop later from the spirit world on to the séance
table; on another page was a brief announcement that an eminent spiritualist had declared the equally eminent Mr. X, the spirit photographer,
to be a highly fraudulent person. For the time, at all events, I decided
on occupying myself with the manifestations of the simple *poltergeist*.

And, as it happened, a favourable opportunity came in my way.
Soon after my encounter with M'Calmont in Holborn, I ran across an
old acquaintance of mine, Manning, who was something in the British
Museum. A few years before, when he had been a lodger in a Bloomsbury street, I had been accustomed to see a good deal of him; but he
had married and gone to live with his wife on some remote heights up
at Hornsey, and we had not encountered one another for some time.
We found a nook in which we could exchange such news as we had,
and I heard a good deal about the fine old garden, "above the London
smoke," and of great success with roses. Then came something interesting.

"Six months ago," Manning began, "we took a boarder. He's a boy
of fifteen, and his father, Richards, an old friend of mine, has got a job
in the East, which will keep him there for some years. He asked me if

my wife and I would take charge of the lad for the next year or two, anyhow. The mother is dead, and, as Richards put it, he didn't want to leave his son with strangers. The young fellow is a day boy at Westminster, so we don't see too much of him, in term-time at all events.

"Well, he came along and seemed a decent young chap enough, and didn't give any trouble—till the last week or so. And now we don't know what to do about him."

"What's wrong?" I asked. "Stays out late at night and comes home drunk? That sort of thing?"

"Not a bit of it. He sticks to his work all of the evening and goes to bed soon after ten. But, wherever he is, things go smash. It began with a stone coming through the dining-room window. I thought, naturally, some hooligan had thrown it from the street, and rushed out. The only people near enough to have done it were a couple of quiet old ladies walking along and chatting to each other about the vicar. Another night the clock jumped from the shelf onto the table. Then he went into the kitchen to get me a box of matches, and the plates on the dresser began falling about. It worries my wife—and it bothers me too. Young Richards says he doesn't do it. No doubt he does, all the same, but I haven't succeeded in catching him at it, so far. I suppose I shall have to write to his father, and that won't be pleasant."

I saw my chance. I told Manning that young Richards must be regarded, not as an infernal nuisance, but as an interesting case. On my earnest petition, Mrs. Manning being, I believe, rather glad to have another man on the premises, I became the second paying guest at the Hornsey house, promising myself important and first-hand evidence. And I had better say at once that I was disappointed. As young Richards pored over his home-work at a side table, I saw a small piece of Samian ware rise up from the table at the other end of the room, hover, or seem to hover, for an instant, and then fall to the floor, breaking into fragments. I could not see how Richards could possibly be the conscious agent in this event. There was, certainly, no apparatus of threads or wires concerned in the destruction of the Samian bowl. The boy looked frightened and furious; and I found out that he had been thrashed at his preparatory school for "wilful destruction". But, from the enquirer's point of view, "what next?" It seemed that one was reduced to posit an unknown force, devoid of conscious or intelligent direction, and wholly outside and beyond the sphere of physical science. And yet, this was something.

Richards in himself was an entirely ordinary and normal boy, a very decent fellow, I should say, neither too stupid nor too intelligent. It was only in his appearance that there was something not quite ordinary. I do not know that he was short for his age, but his breadth of chest made him appear short, and gave a certain vague impression of deformity, and also of considerable strength.

I had been staying with the Mannings for six or seven weeks, and it was drawing towards the darkest and shortest days in the year. There was a succession of heavy fogs, and it was after one of these that the "Horrible Dwarf" scare began its course in the papers. A small child, living with its parents in a back street of Westminster, had been sent on some errand to a shop round the corner. The fog was thick down there by the river, but the distance was short, the little girl went to the shop for her mother every other day, and there were no roads to be crossed. She came back crying, and evidently badly frightened, having dropped the sixpenn'orth of tea, or whatever it was. When she had been soothed into coherence, she told a tale of a "dreadful little man", who came out of a passage, and bent down with all his teeth shewing, and put out his hands as if he would take her by the throat and kill her—and then disappeared into the fog, without saying a word. Of course the neighbours came swarming to hear all about it, and deafened each other with conjectures of an impossible kind, and proposed moves and measures which led nowhere. On the whole, it was to be gathered that the horrible little man must be a stranger, since no dwarfs were known to inhabit the neighbourhood. The police were called in, and made very little of the business, ranking the offender with those tiresome but not dangerous semi-lunatics who cut off girls' hair on the 'bus, or slash their clothes in the street. The paragraphs in the press were brief, and some people were inclined to think that the small messenger had let the tea or sugar spill into the gutter and had invented the dwarf in order to escape punishment. But, then, in a couple of days, there was something more serious. Late on a dismal afternoon, a man who was taking a short cut through an unfrequented by-street off the Tottenham Court Road, felt, as he said, a violent punch in the back, and found himself at the bottom of a flight of area stairs.

He was bruised and shaken, but conscious, and as he looked up, he saw an ugly little man grinning at him through the railings. He struggled to his feet, and ran up the steps, shouting: "Stop, thief!" There were two or three people about, who came running; but they had seen nothing. Then, on another evening, five or six days later, a girl looking into a shop window in Camden Town became aware that there was a short man, "with a nasty look on his face", standing beside her, and the next moment she felt a piercing pain in her arm, screamed out in agony and fear, and fainted. There was hurry and bustle, shouting and confusion, running here and there from all quarters, but by the time the girl had come to herself and was able to say what had happened to her, the assailant had disappeared. A doctor came up and found a long needle almost buried in her arm. The newspaper paragraphs had become half-columns, and people began to be afraid. And the next outrage of the "Horrible Dwarf" was again at Westminster, and close to the place where the small messenger had been frightened. Again there was a dense fog; rather a thick white mist, deadening to sound, so that in those narrow streets where there is little wheeled traffic on the brightest days, such noises as these could hardly be heard, and seemed dull and muffled as if they came from a place far off. But through this thick, stilled silence there broke a lamentable complaint. A man, making his way homeward, cautiously, warily, and slowly, passed through one of these by-streets where, for some years, there had been a patch of wretched and wasted land. Four or five cottages had been pulled down, and for some reason or another the plans for re-building had fallen through, and the plot where the houses stood lay as the house-breakers had left it. There were cavernous remains of underground rooms or cellars, brickbat mountains, plaster valleys, all scattered over with fragments of mouldering beams and jagged with slates; a very dismal and ruined place, separated from the pavement by a line of broken-down palings. As the homeward-bound man felt his way along the street, he thought he heard a noise of crying, a very faint, sad sound. He stopped and listened by a window, where the light from within was barely apparent through the thick, white folds of mist, and wondered whether the sound came from a child, shut up alone and frightened. He could not satisfy himself that this was so, and walked on a few paces, still listening, and thinking that he was drawing nearer to the noise of crying. He was now by the palings that hedged off the waste land, and he became sure that here was the scene of the trouble. He broke through the rotten fence, and went prowling and stumbling about, well aware, as he had often passed that way, that he might very well come to grief himself in the broken-down ruin and confusion of the place. But, with good fortune, he came without disaster to a wretched child lying on his back amidst the rubbish, sobbing and wailing most piteously. The man gave him a cheerful "What's the matter, Tommy? Come along, and we'll make it all right," and tried to lift the child to his feet. But the poor misery cried out in sharper anguish, and the man raised him as gently as he could and bore him away, dreadfully afraid all the while that he might stumble and fall and, as he said afterwards, do the poor little beggar in.

However, he brought his burden safely out of the horrible pits, and rang the bell at the first house he came to. The rescuer and the people of the house saw a terrible sight. It was a poor place, with a bed in the sitting-room, and on this they laid the wreckage. It was a boy of nine or ten. One leg seemed bent under him, and when they tried to straighten it the child screamed with pain. But it was the boy's face that frightened them. It was all swollen and bloody, and black with bruises, and the blood was still gushing from the nostrils, which were as if they had been stamped on by the hoof of a horse. One went out and shouted through the fog for the police; and in time the poor boy was taken in an ambulance to the hospital. In a day or two, a little mended and recovered, he told his tale of a twisted man that came out of the mist, and took him up as if he would have broken him, and carried him over the fence and threw him down, and then stamped with his feet on his face.

The newspapers altered their headline to "Devilish Dwarf", and cursed the police—and so forth.

And it was after this most detestable outrage that Manning horrified me one night, as we sat by the fire with the rest of the house abed. He told me that he was seriously afraid that young Richards was guilty of these abominations. He urged that they had all taken place at a time when the boy was on his way from Westminster to Hornsey, that he had certainly been late home on the occasions of the first and last of the outrages. He dwelt on his dwarfish appearance, on his great strength, but above all on those abnormal activities which had interested me in the first place.

"You know yourself there's something queer about the fellow. Upon my word, I'm afraid he's the man. And if we don't do something, it will come to murder."

I was, indeed, horrified for a moment when he began, but at the end I laughed, I am glad to remember. I told him that the fog would amply account for Richards's late return on the two occasions he had mentioned; that to the best of my recollection he had been back in good time on the other two evenings of outrage; and finally, and most conclusively, that he was talking nonsense. "Excepting only that singular faculty or fatality of his, he's a very ordinary boy, and a good sort."

In short, I laughed him out of it. Happily, there were no more horrors of the "Devilish Dwarf" order for the rest of the winter. They stopped as suddenly as they had begun; and in the succeeding calm somebody found sense enough to write an article pointing out the helplessness of the police when confronted with the motiveless outrages of a maniac. The new generation heard all about the doings of Jack the Ripper, and the analogy seemed fair enough. And at the same time—it was, of course, pure coincidence—the *poltergeist* activity, or possession, or whatever it was, of young Richards dwindled and ceased. The house on the Hornsey heights was in all respects at peace with itself when I left it for the valley of London in the early spring.

IV

Extract from a letter received about eighteen months after "the early spring" mentioned above.

... Now, as to this M'Calmont business. In your place, I should certainly go no farther—or "further"—I never know which is right and which is wrong. There's no question of bringing the story to its logical conclusion, because there isn't one. Your theories and conjectures and the rest of it may be all right—and they may be all wrong. And just remember that for all we know M'Calmont may turn up any day, and that might be a nasty business for you. I remember Sandy M'Calmont very well, and he always struck me as a man who would be extremely (shall we say) tenacious, if he got in a temper.

I note what you say about your visit to his studio in the spring of last year. In the first place; as to the man himself. You say he struck you as very much changed: "silent, morose, and apparently not in the least glad to see me". And I gather that the Lagavulin touch was conspicuous by its absence. I don't think there's much significance in that. There are genial Scotchmen and frozen Scotchmen, and sometimes and naturally enough you have samples of both temperaments in one man. And, as I've just said, he always struck me as having a reserve of grimness. One of his race gave me a most cordial invitation to dine with him at his club, and when the evening came, I was going to say, he didn't speak half a dozen words. That's a figure of speech; but, to be strictly accurate, if he had been "measured up", I don't think his remarks all through the evening would have exceeded a hundred words. He was all right the next time we met. Some of them are like that.

You say that all the pictures you had seen when you went to the studio the autumn before had been cleared away, and that there was a new lot on the walls. The change you noticed is certainly interesting: the seduction of the elaborate landscapes into mere backgrounds, the trees barely indicated, the detail shadowy, and so forth: the Twisted Man promoted from a sort of super to be the real subject of the picture—"a devilish figure", as you say, with, I gather, minor demons grouped about him, being instructed in strange traps and chases, in obscure employments, in pastimes that did not strike you as too agreeable. I was rather reminded of an old lacquer bureau I grew up with. I remember one of the drawers was decorated with a design of a golden garden of unearthly trees, in which Chinamen in golden robes tormented a porcupine with long wands of gold. All this was certainly very odd. You didn't like M'Calmont's manner when he said: "You asked me for the story of the Twisted Man and here it is"? I don't see much in that. But that particular gesture in one of the pictures: the man pointing to an indistinct figure on the ground, and lifting up his foot above it: well . . . Still, as you can see for yourself, there's nothing you can fasten on in that. You can't charge a painter with the crimes he chooses to paint. And that's the fatal flaw in the whole of your case; if you think you have a case.

Of course I remember that awful business of the poor girl in the July following. It was one of the most hideous and revolting things that have happened in my time; and I think that we should both agree that Fleet Street, with all its faults, rendered a public service by its suppression of most of the facts. I knew Selwyn of the *Gazette*, who was put on the country end of the story. He managed to see a sort of diary the girl had kept—about her visits to London and all that. I don't care to recall what he told me. But there again, when you try to put two and two together, you'll find it can't be done. There was nothing in those papers that Selwyn looked at to connect the unfortunate wretch with the studio. As you say, that square in Bloomsbury where the body was found is not a great distance off, but that's nothing to go on.

And, after all, it seems to me that either way, you would be well advised to let it alone. The man has gone away, and it seems likely that he will stay away, so there's no fear of any recurrence of these abominations. But, on the other hand, he *may* come back, and if he did, you might find yourself in the dock on a charge of criminal libel. And I don't think that such evidence as you have is anything like strong enough for you to put up a good defence. I say again: drop it.

I took this advice, so far as making any representations to the police authorities was concerned. After some years—nine, getting on for ten—nothing has been heard of M'Calmont. A cousin of his eventually received authority to deal with the pictures in the studio. Some of the earlier canvases appeared in due course in the dealers' shops round St. James's and Bond Street, and others went to the auction rooms and realised very fair prices. There is a movement, I have gathered, in certain circles of art criticism, to appreciate M'Calmont's work very highly. One critic wrote lately: "It is all old school, if you like, but there is something there that the old school never had; and I don't think that any of us quite know what it is. And I am convinced that collectors, public and private, will do well to keep a very keen eye on M'Calmont. At the present prices they are undoubted bargains."

And the studios are still asking where M'Calmont got his model for the wonderful Twisted Man.

There was one circumstance which I failed to mention, when I consulted the friend who wrote me the letter of advice. I am not sure why I left it out of my story; possibly from a whimsical dislike of making the case too complete, possibly from a feeling, equally whimsical, that it was as well to keep one card at least safe and secret in my own hand.

But, two nights after the discovery of the package in Irving Square, when horror was still black and raging, I felt that I must visit that secret studio on the hillside. It was a clear night with a red moon, just past the full, rising out of a low band of clouds, and this time I found my way without any difficulty. And just as I came down the flight of steps that led into the open square, I saw the green door of M'Calmont's studio open, very cautiously at first, inch by inch, and then wider, and a figure, vague against the darkness behind it, seemed to peer about for a moment. Then, the door was opened wide, and as quickly shut, and I saw a man, all twisted and bent so as to be dwarf-like, go capering with fantastic and extravagant gestures across the scene of light, and vanish into a narrow passage which led down the hill between garden walls and the shadowy boughs of trees. I stood still, beaten back into the shelter of my steps, drawing a long breath. I had recognised very well that dancing and terrible figure, and I was quite overcome by the utter impossibility of that which I had certainly seen. I had been living for some time with gathering suspicions of some dreadful and mysterious connection between the work of the studio and the horror of the waste place in Westminster; but they had been vague surmises and unshapen fears. But this was delirium; nightmare walking visibly abroad. I shook myself out of my terror and went briskly up to the studio door and rang the bell.

The door was opened by M'Calmont's handy man whom I had seen pottering about on my last visit. I asked him if Mr. M'Calmont were at home.

"Not at the moment, sir," he replied. "But please to step in. Mr. M'Calmont told me he'd be back in a minute; he's only gone to post a letter—and I'm sure he'd be very sorry to miss you."

I followed the man to the studio, which was all lit up. I stood there in a great bewilderment.

"But, William," I said, "I saw somebody come out by that door just as I was coming down the steps. But it was a twisted sort of man, like that man in all Mr. M'Calmont's pictures. I thought it must be the model." The notion had flashed into my mind that moment, as with a deep sigh of relief.

William looked puzzled.

"It must have been Mr. M'Calmont, sir. There's nobody else been here to-night. He went out a couple of minutes ago."

"But the man I saw was twisted, crooked. And he was dancing about like a lunatic."

'Then, sir, I think that was Mr. M'Calmont all right. I expect he was doing what he calls his Physical Jerks, thinking there would be nobody about to see him. He says it's strongly recommended by the doctors. But do be seated, sir, if you please."

I was staring at a great sheet of paper on an easel. It was covered with black charcoal outlines, to me significant and most awful. I had heard something of the contents of the package that had been found under the bushes of Irving Square.

I told the man I really could not wait. I hurried out of the place, and struck away up to the north, and made as quickly as I could for the broad and jangling streets, and so got home at last, avoiding dark narrows and short cuts all the way.

I do not know how long William waited for his master to return. But he waited vainly.

Change

H ere," said old Mr. Vincent Rimmer, fumbling in the pigeon-holes of his great ancient bureau, "is an oddity which may interest you."

He drew a sheet of paper out of the dark place where it had been hidden, and handed it to Reynolds, his curious guest. The oddity was an ordinary sheet of notepaper, of a sort which has long been popular; a bluish grey with slight flecks and streaks of a darker blue embedded in its substance. It had yellowed a little with age at the edges. The outer page was blank; Reynolds laid it open and spread it out on the table beside his chair. He read something like this:

> a aa e ee i e ee
> aa i i o e ee o
> ee ee i aa o oo o
> a o a a e i ee
> e o i ee a e i

Reynolds scanned it with stupefied perplexity.

"What on earth is it?" he said. "Does it mean anything? Is it a cypher, or a silly game, or what?"

Mr. Rimmer chuckled. "I thought it might puzzle you," he remarked. "Do you happen to notice anything about the writing; anything out of the way at all?"

Reynolds scanned the document more closely.

"Well, I don't know that there is anything out of the way in the script itself. The letters are rather big, perhaps, and they are rather clumsily formed. But it's difficult to judge handwriting by a few letters, repeated again and again. But, apart from the writing, what is it?"

"That's a question that must wait a bit. There are many strange things related to that bit of paper. But one of the strangest things about it is this; that it is intimately connected with the Darren Mystery."

"What Mystery did you say? The Darren Mystery? I don't think I ever heard of it."

"Well, it was a little before your time. And, in any case, I don't see how you could have heard of it. There were, certainly, some very curious and unusual circumstances in the case, but I don't think that they were generally known, and if they were known, they were not understood. You won't wonder at that, perhaps, when you considered that the bit of paper before you was one of those circumstances."

"But what exactly happened?"

"That is largely a matter of conjecture. But, anyhow, here's the outside of the case, for a beginning. Now, to start with, I don't suppose you've ever been to Meirion? Well, you should go. It's a beautiful county, in West Wales, with a fine sea-coast, and some very pleasant places to stay at, and none of them too large or too popular. One of the smallest of these places, Trenant, is just a village. There is a wooded height above it called the Allt; and down below, the church, with a Celtic cross in the churchyard, a dozen or so of cottages, a row of lodging-houses on the slope round the corner, a few more cottages dotted along the road to Meiros, and that's all. Below the village are marshy meadows where the brook that comes from the hills spreads abroad, and then the dunes, and the sea, stretching away to the Dragon's Head in the far east and enclosed to the west by the beginnings of the limestone cliffs. There are fine, broad sands all the way between Trenant and Porth, the market-town, about a mile and a half away, and it's just the place for children.

Well, just forty-five years ago, Trenant was having a very successful season. In August there must have been eighteen or nineteen visitors in the village. I was staying in Porth at the time, and, when I walked over, it struck me that the Trenant beach was quite crowded—eight or nine children castle-building and learning to swim, and looking for shells, and all the usual diversions. The grown-up people sat in groups on the edge of the dunes and read and gossiped, or took a turn towards Porth, or perhaps tried to catch prawns in the rock-pools at the other end of the sands. Altogether a very pleasant, happy scene in its simple way, and, as it was a beautiful summer, I have no doubt they all enjoyed themselves very much. I walked to Trenant and back three or four times, and I noticed that most of the children were more or less in charge of a very pretty dark girl, quite young, who seemed to advise in laying out the ground-plan of the castle, and to take off her stockings and tuck up her skirts—we thought a lot of Legs in those days—when the bathers required supervision. She also indicated the kinds of shells which deserved the attention of collectors: an extremely serviceable girl.

It seemed that this girl, Alice Hayes, was really in charge of the children—or of the greater part of them. She was a sort of nursery-governess or lady of all work to Mrs. Brown, who had come down from London in the early part of July with Miss Hayes and little Michael, a child of eight, who refused to recover nicely from his attack of measles. Mr. Brown had joined them at the end of the month with the two elder children, Jack and Rosamund. Then, there were the Smiths, with their little family, and the Robinsons with their three; and the fathers and mothers, sitting on the beach every morning, got to know each other very easily. Mrs. Smith and Mrs. Robinson soon appreciated Miss Hayes's merits as a child-herd; they noticed that Mrs. Brown sat placid and went on knitting in the sun, quite safe and unperturbed, while they suffered from recurrent alarms. Jack Smith, though barely fourteen, would be seen dashing through the waves to swim to the Dragon's Head, about twenty miles away, or Jane Robinson, in bright pink, would reappear suddenly right way among the rocks of the points, ready to vanish into the perilous unknown round the corner. Hence, alarums and excursions, tiresome expeditions of rescue and remonstrance, through soft sand or over slippery rocks under a hot sun. And then these ladies would discover that certain of their offspring had entirely disappeared or were altogether missing from the landscape; and dreadful and true tales of children who had driven tunnels into the sand and had been overwhelmed therein rushed to the mind. And all the while Mrs. Brown sat serene, confident in the overseership of her Miss Hayes. So, as was to be gathered, the other two took counsel together. Mrs. Brown was approached, and something called an arrangement was made, by which Miss Hayes undertook the joint mastership of all three packs, greatly to the ease of Mrs. Smith and Mrs. Robinson.

It was about this time, I suppose, that I got to know this group of holiday-makers. I had met Smith, whom I knew slightly in town, in the streets of Porth, just as I was setting out for one of my morning walks. We strolled together to Trenant on the firm sand down by the water's edge, and introductions went round, and so I joined the party, and sat with them, watching the various diversions of the children and the capable superintendence of Miss Hayes.

"Now there's a queer thing about his little place," said Brown, a genial man, connected, I believe, with Lloyd's. "Wouldn't you say this was as healthy a spot as any you could find? Well sheltered from the north, southern aspect, never too cold in winter, fresh sea-breeze in summer: what could you have more?"

"Well," I replied, "it always agrees with me very well: a little relaxing, perhaps, but I like being relaxed. Isn't it a healthy place, then? What makes you think so?"

"I'll tell you. We have rooms on Govan Terrace, up there on the hillside. The other night I woke up with a coughing fit. I got out of bed to get a drink of water, and then had a look out of the window to see what sort of night it was. I didn't like the look of those clouds in the south-west after sunset the night before. As you can see, the upper windows of Govan Terrace command a good many of the village houses. And, do you know, there was a light in almost every house? At two o'clock in the morning. Apparently the village is full of sick people. But who would have thought it?"

We were sitting a little apart from the rest. Smith had brought a London paper from Porth and he and Robinson had their heads together over the City article. The three women were knitting and talking hard, and down by the blue, creaming water Miss Hayes and her crew were playing happily in the sunshine.

"Do you mind," I said to Brown, "if I swear you to secrecy? A limited secrecy: I don't want you to speak of this to any of the village people. They wouldn't like it. And have you told your wife or any of the party about what you saw?"

"As a matter of fact, I haven't said a word to anybody. Illness isn't a very cheerful topic for a holiday, is it? But what's up? You don't mean to say there's some sort of epidemic in the place that they're keeping dark? I say! That would be awful. We should have to leave at once. Think of the children."

"Nothing of the kind. I don't think that there's a single case of illness in the place unless you count old Thomas Evans, who has been in what he calls a decline for thirty years. You won't say anything? Then I'm going to give you a shock. The people have a light burning in their houses all night to keep out the fairies."

I must say it was a success. Brown looked frightened. Not of the fairies; most certainly not; rather at the reversion of his established order of things. He occupied his business in the City; he lived in an extremely comfortable house at Addiscombe; he was a keen though sane adherent of the Liberal Party; and in the world between these points there was no room at all either for fairies or for people who believed in fairies. The latter were almost as fabulous to him as the former, and still more objectionable.

"Look here!" he said at last. "You're pulling my leg. Nobody believes in fairies. They haven't for hundreds of years. Shakespeare didn't believe in fairies. He says so."

I let him run on. He implored me to tell him whether it was typhoid, or only measles, or even chicken-pox. I said at last:

"You seem very positive on the subject of fairies. Are you sure there are no such things?"

"Of course I am," said Brown, very crossly.

"How do you know?"

It is a shocking thing to be asked a question like that, to which, be it observed, there is no answer. I left him seething dangerously.

"Remember," I said, "not a word of lit windows to anybody; but if you are uneasy as to epidemics, ask the doctor about it."

He nodded his head glumly. I knew he was drawing all sorts of false conclusions; and for the rest of our stay I would say that he did not seek me out—until the last day of his visit. I had no doubt that he put me down as a believer in fairies and a maniac; but it is, I consider, good for men who live between the City and Liberal Politics and Addiscombe to be made to realise that there is a world elsewhere. And, as it happens, it was quite true that most of the Trenant people believed in the fairies and were horribly afraid of them.

But this was only an interlude. I often strolled over and joined the party. And I took up my freedom with the young members by contributing posts and a tennis net to the beach sports. They had brought down rackets and balls, in the vague idea that they might be able to get a game somehow and somewhere, and my contribution was warmly welcomed. I helped Miss Hayes to fix the net, and she marked out the court, with the help of many suggestions from the elder children, to which she did not pay the slightest attention. I think the constant disputes as to whether the ball was "in" or "out" brightened the game, though Wimbledon would not have approved. And sometimes the elder children accompanied their parents to Porth in the evening and watched the famous Japanese Jugglers or Pepper's Ghost at the Assembly Rooms, or listened to the Mysterious Musicians at the De Barry Gardens—and altogether everybody had, you would say, a very jolly time.

It all came to a dreadful end. One morning when I had come out on my usual morning stroll from Porth, and had got to the camping ground of the party at the end of the dunes, I found somewhat to my surprise that there was nobody there. I was afraid that Brown had been in part justified in his dread of concealed epidemics, and that some of the children had "caught something" in the village. So I walked up in the direction of Govan Terrace, and found Brown standing at the bottom of his flight of steps, and looking very much upset.

I hailed him.

"I say," I began, "I hope you weren't right, after all. None of the children down with measles, or anything of that sort?"

"It's something worse than measles. We none of us know what has happened. The doctor can make nothing of it. Come in, and we can talk it over."

Just then a procession came down the steps leading from a house a few doors further on. First of all there was the porter from the station, with a pile of luggage on his truck. Then there came the two elder Smith children, Jack and Millicent, and finally, Mr. and Mrs. Smith. Mr. Smith was carrying something wrapped in a bundle in his arms.

"Where's Bob?" He was the youngest; a brave, rosy little man of five or six.

"Smith's carrying him," murmured Brown.

"What's happened? Has he hurt himself on the rocks? I hope it's nothing serious."

I was going forward to make my enquiries, but Brown put a hand on my arm and checked me. Then I looked at the Smith party more closely, and I saw at once that there was something very much amiss.

The two elder children had been crying, though the boy was doing his best to put up a brave face against disaster—whatever it was. Mrs. Smith had drawn her veil over her face, and stumbled as she walked, and on Smith's face there was a horror as of ill dreams.

"Look," said Brown in his low voice.

Smith had half-turned, as he set out with his burden to walk down the hill to the station. I don't think he knew we were there; I don't think any of the party had noticed us as we stood on the bottom step, half-hidden by a blossoming shrub. But as he turned uncertainly, like a man in the dark, the wrappings fell away a little from what he carried, and I saw a little wizened, yellow face peering out; malignant, deplorable.

I turned helplessly to Brown, as that most wretched procession went on its way and vanished out of sight.

"What on earth has happened? That's not Bobby. Who is it?"

"Come into the house," said Brown, and he went before me up the long flight of steps that led to the terrace.

There was a shriek and a noise of thin, shrill, high-pitched laughter as we came into the lodging-house.

"That's Miss Hayes in blaspheming hysterics," said Brown grimly. "My wife's looking after her. The children are in the room at the back. I daren't let them go out by themselves in this awful place." He beat with his foot on the floor and glared at me, awestruck, a solid man shaken.

"Well," he said at last, "I'll tell you what we know; and as far as I can make out, that's very little. However ... You know Miss Hayes, who helps Mrs. Brown with the children, had more or less taken over the charge of the lot; the young Robinsons and the Smiths, too. You've seen how well she looks after them all on the sands in the morning. In the afternoon she's been taking them inland for a change. You know there's beautiful country if you go a little way inland; rather wild and woody; but still very nice; pleasant and shady. Miss Hayes thought that the all-day glare of the sun on the sands might not be very good for the small ones, and my wife agreed with her. So they took their teas with them and picnicked in the woods and enjoyed themselves very much, I believe. They didn't go more than a couple of miles or three at the outside; and the little ones used to take turns in a go-cart. They never seemed too tired.

"Yesterday at lunch they were talking about some caves at a place called the Darren, about two miles away. My children seemed very anxious to see them, and Mrs. Probert, our landlady, said they were quite safe, so the Smiths and Robinsons were called in, and they were enthusiastic, too; and the whole party set off with their tea-baskets, and candles and matches, in Miss Hayes's charge. Somehow they made a later start than usual, and from what I could make out they enjoyed themselves so much in the cool dark cave, first of all exploring, and then looking for treasure, and winding up with tea by candlelight, that they didn't notice how the time was going—nobody had a watch—and by the time they'd packed up their traps and come out from under-ground, it was quite dark. They had a little trouble making out the way at first, but not very much, and came along in high spirits, tumbling over molehills and each other, and finding it all quite an adventure.

"They had got down in the road there, and were sorting them-selves out into the three parties, when somebody called out: 'Where's Bobby Smith?' Well, he wasn't there. The usual story; everybody thought he was with somebody else. They were all mixed up in the dark, talking and laughing and shrieking at the top of their voices, and taking everything for granted—I suppose it was like that. But poor lit-tle Bob was missing. You can guess what a scene there was. Everybody was much too frightened to scold Miss Hayes, who had no doubt been extremely careless, to say the least of it—not like her. Robinson pulled us together. He told Mrs. Smith that the little chap would be perfectly all right: there were no precipices to fall over and no water to fall into, the way they'd been, that it was a warm night, and the child had had a good stuffing tea, and he would be as right as rain when they found him. So we got a man from the farm, with a lantern, and Miss Hayes to shew us exactly where they'd been, and Smith and Robinson and I went off to find poor Bobby, feeling a good deal better than at first. I noticed that the farm man seemed a good deal put out when we told him what had happened and where we were going. 'Got lost in the Darren,' he said, 'indeed that is a pity.' That set Smith off at once; and he asked Williams what he meant; what was the matter with the place? Williams said there was nothing the matter with it at all whatever but it was 'a tiresome place to be in after dark'. That reminded me of what you were saying a couple of weeks ago about the people here. 'Some damned superstitious nonsense,' I said to myself, and thanked God it was nothing worse. I thought the fellow might be going to tell us of a masked bog or something like that. I gave Smith a hint in a whisper as to where the land lay; and we went on, hoping to come on little Bob any minute. Nearly all the way we were going through open fields without any cover or bracken or anything of that sort, and Williams kept twirling his lantern, and Miss Hayes and the rest of us called out the child's name; there didn't seem much chance of missing him.

"However, we saw nothing of him—till we got to the Darren. It's an odd sort of place, I should think. You're in an ordinary field, with a gentle upward slope, and you come to a gate, and down you go into a deep, narrow valley; a regular nest of valleys as far as I could make out in the dark, one leading into another, and the sides covered with trees. The famous caves were on one of these steep slopes, and, of course, we all went in. They didn't stretch far; nobody could have got lost in them, even if the candles gave out. We searched the place thoroughly, and saw where the children had had their tea; no signs of Bobby. So we went on down the valley between the woods, till we came to where it opens out into a wide space, with one tree growing all alone in the middle. And then we heard a miserable whining noise, like some little creature that's got hurt. And there under the tree was—what you saw poor Smith carrying in his arms this morning.

"It fought like a wild cat when Smith tried to pick it up, and jabbered some unearthly sort of gibberish. Then Miss Hayes came along and seemed to soothe it; and it's been quiet ever since. The man with the lantern was shaking with terror; the sweat was pouring down his face."

I stared hard at Brown. "And," I thought to myself, "you are very much in the same condition as Williams." Brown was obviously overcome with dread.

We sat there in silence.

"Why do you say 'it'?" I asked. "Why don't you say 'him'?"

"You saw."

"Do you mean to tell me seriously that you don't believe that child you helped to bring home was Bobby? What does Mrs. Smith say?"

"She says the clothes are the same. I suppose it must be Bobby. The doctor from Porth says the child must have had a severe shock. I don't think he knows anything about it."

He stuttered over his words, and said at last:

"I was thinking of what you said about the lighted windows. I hoped you might be able to help. Can you do anything? We are leaving this afternoon; all of us. Is there nothing to be done?"

"I'm afraid not."

I had nothing else to say. We shook hands and parted without more words.

The next day I walked over to the Darren. There was something fearful about the place, even in the haze of a golden afternoon. As Brown had said, the entrance and the disclosure of it were sudden and abrupt. The fields of the approach held no hint of what was to come. Then, past the gate, the ground fell violently away on every side, grey rocks of an ill shape pierced through it, and the ash trees on the steep slopes overshadowed all. The descent was into silence, without the singing of a bird, into a wizard shade. At the farther end, where the wooded heights retreated somewhat, there was the open space, or circus, of turf; and in the middle of it a very ancient, twisted thorn tree, beneath which the party in the dark had found the little creature that whined and cried out in unknown speech. I turned about, and on my way back I entered the caves, and lit the carriage candle I had brought with me. There was nothing much to see—I never think there is much to see in caves. There was the place where the children and others before them had taken their tea, with a ring of blackened stones within which many fires of twigs had been kindled. In caves or out of caves, townsfolk in the country are always alike in leaving untidy and unseemly litter behind; and here with the usual scraps of greasy paper, daubed with smears of jam and butter, the half-eaten sandwich, and the gnawed crust. Amidst all this nastiness I saw a piece of folded notepaper, and in sheer idleness picked it up and opened it. You have just seen it. When I asked you if you saw anything peculiar about the writing, you said that the letters were rather big and clumsy. The reason of that is that they were written by a child. I don't think you examined the back of the second leaf. Look: 'Rosamund'—Rosamund Brown, that is. And beneath; there, in the corner."

Reynolds looked, and read, and gaped aghast.

"That was—her other name; her name in the dark."

"Name in the dark?"

"In the dark night of the Sabbath. That pretty girl had caught them all. They were in her hands, those wretched children, like the clay images she made. I found one of those things, hidden in a cleft of the rocks, near the place where they had made their fire. I ground it into dust beneath my feet."

"And I wonder what her name was?"

"They called her, I think, the Bridegroom and the Bride."

"Did you ever find out who she was, or where she came from?"

"Very little. Only that she had been a mistress at the Home for Christian Orphans in North Tottenham, where there was a hideous scandal some years before."

"Then she must have been older than she looked, according to your description."

"Possibly."

They sat in silence for a few minutes. Then Reynolds said:

"But I haven't asked you about this formula, or whatever you may call it—all these vowels, here. Is it a cypher?"

"No. But it is really a great curiosity, and it raises some extraordinary questions, which are outside this particular case. To begin with—and I am sure I could go much farther back than my beginning, if I had the necessary scholarship—I once read an English rendering of a Greek manuscript of the second or third century—I won't be certain which. It's a long time since I've seen the thing. The translator and editor of it was of the opinion that it was a Mithraic Ritual; but I have gathered that weightier authorities are strongly inclined to discredit this view. At any rate, it was no doubt an initiation rite into some mystery; possibly it had Gnostic connections; I don't know. But our interest lies in this, that one of the stages or portals, or whatever you call them, consisted, almost exactly, of that formula you have in your hand. I don't say that the vowels and double vowels are in the same order; I don't think the Greek manuscript has any *aes* or *aas*. But it is perfectly clear that the two documents are of the same kind and have the same purpose. And, advancing a little in time from the Greek manuscript, I don't think it is very surprising that the final operation of an incantation in mediaeval and later magic consisted of this wailing on vowels arranged in a certain order.

"But here is something that is surprising. A good many years ago I strolled one Sunday morning into a church in Bloomsbury, the head-quarters of a highly respectable sect. And in the middle of a very digni-fied ritual, there rose quite suddenly, without preface or warning, this very sound, a wild wail on vowels. The effect was astounding, anyhow; whether it was terrifying or merely funny, is a matter of taste. You'll have guessed what I heard: they call it 'speaking with tongues', and they believe it to be a heavenly language. And I need scarcely say that they mean very well. But the problem is: how did a congregation of solid Scotch Presbyterians hit upon that queer, ancient and not over-sanctified method of expressing spiritual emotion? It is a singular puzzle.

"And that woman? That is not by any means so difficult. The good Scotchmen—I can't think how they did it—got hold of something that didn't belong to them: she was in her own tradition. And, as they say down there: *asakai dasa:* the darkness is undying."

The Dover Road

The disappearance of Sir Halliday Stuart, the well-known antiquary, was really a very puzzling affair. And even the solution of it is in itself something of a puzzle.

Some of the circumstances that surrounded and involved this singular business were recalled by the painstaking though futile attempt undertaken by the B.B.C. to pin down a ghost that was supposed to haunt an old manor house in an out-of-the-way part of Kent. The B.B.C. people, it will be remembered, put themselves in the hands of a recognised expert. This gentleman took the precautions which considerable experience of sprites, some of them exceedingly tricky, suggested as necessary. He sealed the doors with a special seal, he established microphones at critical points. In that quarter which was supposed to be afflicted now and again by icy draughts of air he set up an automatic temperature registering instrument. A watch went on guard outside the house, and patrolled the ground from eight o'clock to a quarter to twelve. Then the expert and four or five others sat down to watch and listen.

Everything, in short, that could be done was done. And nothing, or next to nothing, happened. The instrument that registered the temperature shewed some odd alternations, moving up and down within four or five degrees Fahrenheit, but there was no indication of the blasts of ice-cold air of which the legends spoke. Beyond this, there was nothing, and the expert and his assessors broke off the enquiry, observing very sensibly that the local ghost in particular and ghosts in general had neither been proved nor disproved by the proceedings of the night.

Very much the same kind of thing happened at an earlier investigation of a supposed case of haunting, which was conducted without the aid or countenance of Broadcasting House. In this case, the building supposed to be haunted was an old manor house called Morton Grange, situated in Essex, fourteen or fifteen miles from London, to the north-east. In those days, it might fairly be said to be in the country, but now it stands, if it does stand at all, in the very middle of the Morton Grange Estate, a sad grey rock in a red suburban sea. At the time of the experiment in ghost-detection, the Grange was not only in the country, but lonely—for a house within reasonable distance from Liverpool Street. Following the main road, dotted here and there with pleasant old cottages, and not unpleasant oldish villas—the sort of villa that has a trellised porch, a verandah, and a curving penthouse over a window here and there—one came to the hamlet of Morton; a whole row of cottages, a Queen Anne house for a doctor, a public-house with dim green seats and tables before it, the rectory, with a drive, behind shrubs and elms, and a small, unrestored church. At the end of all this, a yellow-washed farmhouse, with famous barns, red brick, half-timber, and dipping roof-trees, and a bare quarter of a mile farther, on the other side of the road, and some way from it, where the land rose up in a slope, Morton Grange, a confused appearance of buildings, part stucco and part stone, and altogether of a neglected aspect.

It was approached, in spite of what must have been its former dignity, by a lane that could hardly have been a formal drive in its best days, since it had rough high banks with old timber growing on them. Then, a stone wall with good iron-work gates, beginning to rust away, and a grove of dark ilexes. Before the front of the house, a lawn sloped down to a sunken fence or ha-ha: there were remnants of flower beds, their edges vague and overgrown with grass and weeds, remnants of a rosary, in which the suckers of the wild stock had overpowered the cultivated flowers, and grown into matted and thorny thickets. A leaden statue, with one arm missing, stood in the midst of a stagnant pool; some grey stone urns on pillars shewed vague and mouldering indications of stone garlands.

Where the stucco had begun to peel away on the right, as you faced the house, the architecture looked early Georgian; the left, the grey stone portion, was a good deal older, though the mullions had been knocked out of most of the windows. At the back: kitchens, pantries, butteries, brew-house, and the rest smacked of the sixteenth century; low, solid, cavernous places. The living-rooms were dank and damp; the gorgeous Chinese paper of the drawing-room was smeared with grey shapes of rising wet, the heavy crimson flock paper of the dining-room was beginning to peel and rip from the sweating wall. In three or four of the rooms there was a skeleton furnishing: cheap modern stuff, shabby after forty, fifty years of little use and long neglect. And the usual story was told about the house. It was empty because no one could live in it. It was haunted.

Of course, there was a legend; and here again it was the usual legend; more or less. I believe there was a Monk who was looking for treasure, and might have had some difficulty in explaining his *locus standi,* if he could have been brought to book, since the Grange had never been a religious house. There was a Priest, who had been stifled in his hiding-hole, contrived in the hall chimney. And there was a Cavalier, who perished in some very unhappy manner. These three stock phantoms hovered about the legend of the Grange; now one troubled the peace of its inhabitants, now another. There was every reason to suppose that all three of them were invented some time in the 'thirties or 'forties of the last century, together with the Mysterious Terror of Glamis Castle, and the *chère reine* of Charing.

Yet, though the Monk and the Priest and the Cavalier were, doubtless, idle and late inventions; there was a certain remnant of strangeness about Morton Grange, which, it seemed, could not be explained as the result of natural and normal causes. Andrew Lang, if I remember, was taken into counsel over the place, and on hearing of some of the alleged abnormal phenomena, was inclined to suggest rats and defective waterpipes. There was also a singular moaning sound, distinct and different from the whine of the wind in the chimneys; and Lang advised a close structural examination of the other parts of the house; it was possible, he thought, that there might be a tunnel or vent in the thickness of the walls, which might catch the wind blowing from a particular quarter.

This surmise, I believe, was justified on examination, such a tunnel was found in the old brew-house at the back of the Grange. But, beyond the moans and whines and sighs, there were other manifestations of a more difficult order. There was a cellar door which persisted in staying open, whatever you did with it. A new lock was affixed, the bolt turned, and the other two keys taken away in the occupant's pocket; but when he came back from London in the evening, the door was wide open. The man, not to be beaten, had another and a very special mechanism, with an alphabetical combination, affixed, but again the door was opened—somehow. Lang confessed that he could not account for this circumstance; and there the matter rested until Professor Warburton took the Grange in hand ten or a dozen years ago.

Warburton was a distinguished man of science, and a strong exponent of the purely materialistic theory of the universe; he was even reckoned by some of his own school as a little old-fashioned in this respect. I am not sure that the particular instance applied in his case; but he was certainly with the older men who held that the stigmata—for example—were lies and impostures and didn't happen, rather than on the side of the younger scientists, who would discuss cases of the stigmata that they had observed in the hospital wards, and shew that they had no more spiritual significance than carbuncles.

Somehow, this very valiant and determined man heard of the Morton Grange puzzle, and felt certain that either trickery or a purely mechanical cause was the only agent. He made up his mind to investigate, not without hesitation, since he held that the man of science should hardly partake so far of the evil thing—which he sometimes called Mysticism and sometimes Spiritualism—as to admit that it required investigation. However, in this case, the end seemed to justify the means; and the professor began to make his arrangements. The then occupant of the Grange, who seldom occupied it, made no difficulties; and Professor Warburton chose as assistants three or four friends and acquaintances: Rodney, the biologist, W. K. Forster, a Chancery barrister, Sir Charles Lemon, the throat specialist, and Ian Tallent, who was supposed to have inherited a good share of the Andrew Lang mantle, and had a very ingenious hypothesis as to the fire-walking problem.

The night of the inquest was fixed, the caretaker and his wife were warned to get in sufficient fuel and have a fire burning all day in the room nearest to the cellar stairs, and to await the party at eight o'clock, thereafter to betake themselves to the village inn, where a room had been ordered for them. On the morning of the appointed day, Professor Warburton was sitting in his study at his house in Philpot Crescent, Kensington, contemplating the campaign of Morton Grange, when his servant announced a caller. The Professor knew the name, Sir Halliday

Stuart, the famous antiquary, very well, though he had never met the man. Sir Halliday was asked to come up, and the two eminent personages met with grave courtesy. After a phrase of apology, the caller came directly to his point.

"I understand," he said, "that you are going down this evening to investigate certain phenomena which are alleged to take place at Morton Grange, in Essex. Well, if I may venture, I would put it that you would do me a very great favour, if you would allow me to be of your party. Do you think you could stretch a point?"

Warburton was agreeably impressed by the antiquary. He was of a dark, agreeable presence, and his face lit up with a very engaging smile, as he made his apology and petition.

"We shall all be most pleased, I am sure," he said, "and honoured too by your company. But I didn't know that Spiritualism was much in your line."

"It's not, not a bit of it," said Sir Halliday. "And if you'll forgive me, I've always understood that it was still less in yours."

The Professor explained.

"You're perfectly right. Thirty years ago I shouldn't have dreamed of having anything to do with such unmitigated nonsense. There were exceptions, of course—there was Crookes—but men of science wouldn't hear of such stuff or of any approach to it. They didn't refute it. They didn't know it was there. And any scientist who was suspected of having any kind of interest in all this mystical humbug would have forfeited the respect of his colleagues.

"But the War had changed everything. It was, no doubt, a very severe national shock. It has had all sorts of bad effects and repercussions; and one of the worst, in my opinion, is this hysterical credulity that one sees everywhere. There's no tale too monstrous to be believed. We're threatened with the return of the most childish superstitions of the Middle Ages. Here's an instance: this tale of a door that can't be kept shut whatever locks you put on it. And there are people of supposed intelligence who are ready to discuss this nonsense seriously! I feel it's my duty to expose the trick, whatever it is. It will be 'doing my bit', as the men used to say in the War."

"I quite understand," said Sir Halliday, "and I may as well explain my interest in the matter. I made a study of Morton Grange some years ago and included it in my *Essex Manor Houses and Halls*. There are some extremely interesting features in the building. The vaulting in the cellar is, in my opinion, unquestionably Roman, though Markham won't admit it. I think there is a very strong evidence that the Grange cellar was, originally, a Mithrian temple. I should like to have the opportunity of making a re-examination. And it also occurred to me that my knowledge of the structure of the place might possibly be of some service to you in your investigation."

Sir Halliday Stuart was cordially included in the party of ghost-hunters. He refused with thanks the offer of a seat in Warburton's car: he was going down earlier, he explained, as he wished to have another look at the very singular squint in the Grange brew-house: an undoubted thirteenth-century building, he explained, the original lancets having been replaced by square headed windows of 1530–40.

"And for this I shall want daylight. So you will find me at the Grange when you arrive. It is extremely kind of you to let me join your party."

Warburton was pleased with this addition to his committee of investigation. There was a genial gravity about the antiquary that won favour; and he was evidently a man of an accurate habit of mind, accustomed to careful observation, a minute weighing of evidence, the very man for the occasion. The Professor told the others about the inclusion of Stuart, when they all met at his house in the late afternoon, and they agreed he would be valuable. They all knew him by reputation, and Tallent had read his revised edition of *Isca Silurum* with very great interest. When the cars drew up before the door of Morton Grange that evening, Stuart was waiting on the steps. He was mildly excited.

"I've examined that squint very minutely," he said to Warburton. "I have Markham at my mercy."

The introductions were made, and the party entered the house. Warburton had brought down flasks of strong coffee, and the caretaker, having set cups and saucers on the table, departed with his wife. Warburton locked the front door, the back door, and the door communicating with the brew-house, and put the keys in his pocket. A systematic tour and search of the mouldering and desolate house was made. The cellar came last in the inspection, and Professor Warburton pointed out the bolts he had added to the alphabet lock.

"One top, one bottom," he said. "The best steel, fitted under my supervision."

The door stood open; a powerful lamp was fixed above it, and another on the other side, within the cellar. Sir Halliday Stuart went in eagerly, and peered about him.

"Look at the entablatures," he said. "There's no room for doubt."

Warburton called him out, adjusted the lock, and shot the bolts. The party went up the steps of the winding stair, and sat down to their hot coffee, while Warburton explained his plan.

"One of us," he said, "is to be on guard at the bottom of the cellar stair, by the door, the whole evening from eight to twelve-fifteen. The watch will be for an hour; I will take the first watch, and Rodney will relieve me at nine. The door at the top of the stairs will be open, and the door of this room will be open. The instruction to the man on guard is: to call out at the top of his voice if he sees or hears anything in the least out of the way. That is understood? Very good. It is now half-past seven; perhaps Sir Halliday will tell us something about the history of Morton Grange while we are drinking our coffee?"

Sir Halliday cordially assented, and proceeded to deliver a bristling lecture. He merely touched on the evidences for stone and bronze age occupation, was diffused and elaborate on the Roman period; thinning again with the Saxon invasion; but becoming merciless from Doomsday Book to the end of the seventeenth century. Strange terms and allusions were heard; *inquisitis post mortem,* Fine and Recovery, *diem clausit extremum, mortuus sine prole,* Pipe Rolls, vert, a chevron or. Some of these terms awoke memories in Forster, the barrister; to the rest they were as the hooting of owls. The Monk, the Priest, and the Cavalier were mentioned only to be puffed away like thistledown.

"So you see," said the antiquary, "the place has a very ordinary history; the typical history, in fact, of the East Anglian manor house. So far as I know, apart from certain remarkable features in construction, which I have explained to you as well as I can, the only point of interest I can recall in the history of the Grange is the discovery, a few years ago, of a hiding-place in the chimney of the great hall, used from 1690 onwards as a brew-house. A workman employed in putting right some loose bricks, found a small oak chest in a place contrived in the thickness of the chimney. The contents were legal documents, of the late sixteenth and early seventeenth centuries, relating to the passing of the manor and estate from the Mullins Moleyno family to the Roches."

At eight o'clock, punctually, the watch was set, Warburton went down, impressing on the others that they were to join him at top speed if he called out. The two doors: the sitting-room door, and the door at the top of the stairs, were left open as arranged. The party in the room broached another flask of coffee, smoked a little, and talked a little in low tones. Some of them thought they were making fools of themselves, and were sorry they had come.

The hours went by without event. The antiquary, having delivered his lecture, seemed to sink into a gentle abstraction, from which he roused himself now and again to make remarks which seemed to be dictated by a sense of conversational duty, rather than by interest in the (possible) ghost. He pulled out his watch, looked at it and observed with bland satisfaction, "We are keeping good time, I think." Warburton, who had just come up from his turn at the door, assured him that the timetable was being strictly adhered to. Sir Halliday nodded, and again became quiescent.

Nothing happened. Rodney had crept like a snail down the stairs on hearing Warburton's summons. The barrister, Forster, succeeded the biologist. Sir Halliday, brightening once more, said it was a calm night, at all events, "and that's in our favour". People were puzzled for a moment, and then concluded that he meant that their observations were not to be confused by the noises of high wind and restless trees. Sir Charles Lemon took up his position at the bottom of the stairs at eleven. The low-voiced conversation flagged. Most of the men looked tired and bored to the extreme. Sir Halliday's head shook and nodded, not with sleep, but rather as if he were following a train of reasoning, an argument with an imaginary opponent, dissenting and agreeing by turns. Finally, as Lemon's watch drew on and midnight was at hand, the antiquary, feeling, perhaps, that he had cultivated silence at the expense of courtesy, remarked in a very amiable manner:

"Well, I suppose Dover *is* rather a hole. But I must say I've always liked it; Strond Street and the old harbour; all that part, you know."

The company in general, who were longing to make an end of a tiresome and futile sitting, as they considered it, looked up crossly, and wondered what on earth Stuart thought he was talking about. Tallent chuckled quietly; the key word of Sir Halliday's sentence, and its lack of precise relevance to the business in hand, had reminded him of a certain immortal axiom relating to milestones on the Dover Road, but he speculated also as to whether Sir Halliday's intellect was quite the keen instrument of their belief.

It was on the first stroke of twelve that at last something happened. Lemon, who had by this time quite made up his mind that he had wasted the evening, was just calling on Ian Tallent to take his place, when the summons changed to a dismal sound, something inarticulate, between a croak and a cry. The whole company in the sitting-room jumped up and pelted out of the door, and jammed in the narrow stair. Sir Charles, gasping, with a grey-white face, was hauled up, on the verge of a fainting fit, to the higher region. Brandy was administered, and he was soon able to say, rather tartly, that beyond damned foul air, he had nothing to report. They were all yawning and looking at their watches and agreeing that there was nothing to be done but to go home, when Warburton, glancing from one to another, said with a jerk:

"Where's Stuart?"

And, in a second or two, it was evident that he had asked a question that nobody could answer. Sir Halliday Stuart was not there, nowhere in the room at all. They bustled into the passage, went again, not quite so madly, down the stair to the cellar; presently explored every room in the house with the aid of electric torches, returned, looking helpless, to the room where they had held their session. They had not found a trace of the antiquary. And Warburton, who had the keys of every exit in his pocket, knew perfectly well that he must be in the house—somewhere. Then a notion struck him.

"Will you all stay in this room?" he said. "I should think it would be as well if you sat down. It has just struck me as possible that Sir Halliday is in the cellar, examining those accursed entablatures of his. I can't think how he can have got there, if he is there, without knowing the lock combination—but perhaps there is some trickery about that door which circumstances have prevented us from detecting so far. At any rate, I am going to make sure that Sir Halliday has not been caught in some sort of trap. May I ask you again to keep your positions exactly as you are at present?"

Warburton was absent for seven or eight minutes. His face was blank when he returned.

"I've been over every inch of the cellar," he said. "There's no one there. I've put out the lights and refastened the door. We mustn't leave a bolt-hole. Not that I would suggest for a moment that Stuart could or would desire to bolt; of course that's absurd. Still . . . what on earth can have become of the man? I was standing just behind him when the doctor gave the alarm, and we all ran down. Did anybody else notice him, then or afterwards?"

Nobody had. They were all staring at Sir Charles Lemon. They saw nothing else during the critical moments.

"There is nothing to be done," concluded Professor Warburton after some minutes of perplexed meditation, "but to make a thorough and systematic search of the whole house. Perhaps we were a little haphazard before. I will take Forster with me, and we will go over every room in the house."

The two went off with their torches. They were away for half an hour. They had failed to discover Sir Halliday, or any trace or hint of his presence. It was evident that there was nothing more to be done. Tallent put the position of affairs to himself that Sir Halliday was both in the Grange and not in the Grange at the same time; he remembered having seen something of the kind in Eastern philosophy. But he kept the contradiction to himself, not thinking it suitable for the company. He substituted the sagacious and commonsensical remark:

"A difficult thing to be sure you've gone into every nook and cupboard of an old place like this. A little chap of Stuart's build could pack himself away in a very small space."

"Little chap?" said Forster. "I should have said that Sir Halliday was above the average height."

Finally, they all returned to town in a condition of stupefied bewilderment.

The first thing, the next morning, Professor Warburton found out Sir Halliday Stuart's address. He had a place in Oxfordshire, it appeared, but when in town he occupied a suite of rooms in service chambers near St. James's. Warburton went there at once and saw the management. Sir Halliday had been in residence for five or six weeks, the manager told him.

"Yesterday morning, soon after twelve, he came round to the offices and handed in his key. He said he might be away for some little time. I was not at all surprised; there was nothing unusual in the proceeding. Sir Halliday often went away without giving us notice in advance. He would be out of town for a week, a month, even three months. Sometimes he would send a postcard announcing his return; but as a rule he merely walked in and asked for his key."

"And there is no address to which I could write?"

"You might try Sir Halliday Stuart's Oxfordshire address. I can give you that: 'Campden House, High Street—the name of the village, I understand—Oxfordshire.' It is possible that Sir Halliday is there."

The professor went home and wrote two letters. One to Sir Halliday, politely begging to be reassured as to his safety, asking no questions, going into no detail. This letter he put into a small envelope, which was enclosed in a large envelope, addressed "Occupant", with a letter begging for Sir Halliday's present address. The large envelope, marked "Urgent Immediate", was despatched by registered post. There was an answer by return. M. Timpson begged to say that Sir Halliday Stuart was at present residing in his London chambers, the address of which was enclosed.

Meanwhile, Professor Warburton had taken counsel with the friends who had been with him in the strange adventure of Morton Grange. They had all agreed together that it would be well to keep the whole affair in strict secrecy. It was clear, they decided, that in some way or another, Sir Halliday Stuart had contrived to get out of the house in the midst of the confusion over Lemon's collapse. Nobody could suggest how he made his exit or why he made it; but it was evident that he *had* made it. One of them, given on the quiet to the reading of very old-fashioned fiction, babbled of sliding panels and secret passages. But Warburton, who had reluctantly thought of this, had paid another visit to the Grange, going there in broad daylight, and taking with him an expert with a foot-rule, who tapped and measured and surveyed within and without, and gave it as his technical and considered opinion that in this case, at all events, the notion of sliding panels, hidden doors, and secret passages was bunkum. There was nothing to be said; they all felt that they had come to a blank and intolerable wall. And if, by some unconjectured way and dark passage,

Sir Halliday had got out of Morton Grange, where was he?

No doubt they all tried their best to keep the secret, but Sir Halliday, it seemed, had an aunt, very old and energetic, and this lady, hearing that her nephew was not to be found, went to the police, and the constables of Essex called in Scotland Yard, which was interested by the peculiar circumstances of the disappearance.

Now, there is nothing illegal about disappearing. Hundreds, or dozens at any rate, of people disappear every year, and nobody bothers about them. Night by night, "Time, Weather, and News", on the wireless is prefaced by one, two or three S O S's: "S O S Lawkins. Will Thomas Lawkins, last heard of about five years ago in Dulverton, go to Hampstead Heath Hospital, Hampstead, London, where his father Albert Lawkins, is dangerously ill." Clearly, Thomas Lawkins disappeared five years ago or more, and did so in perfect peace. A few years since, a man was found murdered in a car on the highway; and even the violent notoriety of his death did not suffice to identify him, he also must have disappeared, leaving neither trace nor enquiry behind him. But, presumably, Lawkins and the murdered man and men like them have been undistinguished and obscure people, who for one reason or another have shed relations and connections, and have left no great curiosity as to their whereabouts behind them. But Sir Halliday Stuart was none such: he was highly distinguished, a figure in his own world, a man of many friends and colleagues. Moreover, there were the peculiar circumstances, and other people, also well-known, were, one must not say involved, but at any rate present on the occasion when Sir Halliday, as it appeared, was last seen by his fellow-men. Ten days after this event, Professor Warburton received a call from a high official of Scotland Yard, purely in search of exact information. The Professor gave it, told the whole story, gave the name of the men who were associated with him in the affair, and at the end said very frankly:

"And I should be very much obliged to you, sir, if you would tell me what has happened to Sir Halliday Stuart."

The Scotland Yard man said that that was a question which could not be answered off-hand. Enquiries of the most searching nature would be made: there must be a flaw somewhere, a weak spot, in the statement he had just heard, and, no doubt, a trained man would be able to put his finger on it—in time. They would send their own experts to make a special examination of Morton Grange; they might find something.

"Here's a possibility, now, that has just occurred to me. It's not uncommon to come across old, disused wells in such houses as Morton Grange. They are sometimes in the most unexpected places; at the end of dark passages, in a corner at the bottom of a staircase: you never know where to look for them. And the covering, the trap at the top, has sometimes gone rotten. The solution may lie in that direction; though I sincerely hope it doesn't. And in the meantime, would you give me the addresses of your friends who were engaged with you in this business? They may give us some help; you never know. And would you let me have the best description you can manage of Sir Halliday Stuart's personal appearance? Height, fair or dark, colour of hair and eyes, fat or thin, any peculiarities, facial or otherwise; scars; you know the sort of thing?"

The four men were run down at once; they were all Londoners. Each had been asked to give the best description he could of the missing man, together with his account of what had happened, as each had observed the events of that singular night. By the evening, the shorthand notes had been transcribed, and were laid before the personage at the Yard.

"Now, look here," he said to his lieutenant. "This is going to be a very complicated business. For the moment we won't bother about the accounts of the proceedings at this dam' silly business of theirs. I've run through them and compared them with what I got from Professor Warburton this morning, and as far as I can make out they all agree as to the main facts. There are no important discrepancies, anyhow. It's these descriptions of Sir Halliday's personal appearance that are bothering me. Here, you see, is the stuff we got from two of his most intimate friends: Dr. Manning, of Brasenose, and Lord John Ashley of Queen's Row. You see they agree practically in every particular: height, about 5 ft. 7 ins; hair, dark brown, thinning; eyes, grey;—Lord John Ashley says blue—nose aquiline; short upper lip—Manning doesn't mention that—thin; white scar on forefinger of right hand; chestnut eyebrows; and so forth and so forth. As I say, the two descriptions agree."

"By the way," said the lieutenant, "no photographs?"

"He hasn't been photographed for twenty years. There's a sketch in black and white, but I don't think it's going to be of much use. But here's the important point. Look at these descriptions of Sir Halliday by Professor Warburton and his four friends: you see, they don't agree. One man says short, another tall; the professor says hair black; Forster, light brown. They're all at odds. Yet by their own account they were sitting with Sir Halliday and talking to him for four hours on end. What do you make of it?"

The other man studied the documents carefully.

"It's a pity," he said, "that detective fiction is so seldom of much use to detectives. You remember, 'The Murders in the Rue Morgue', the witnesses differing about the language which they had heard the unseen murderer speaking? The Frenchman thought it was English—he didn't know any English. The overwrought Dutchman held it to be Russian; the Englishman, who was ignorant of French, was sure it was French. The deduction to be drawn was that the murderer wasn't speaking any language at all; that he was an ape, and merely gibbering. But I don't see how we can apply Poe's invention to our difficulty."

"No, I don't think we can," said the chief with some dryness and a touch of impatience.

"Unless," said the lieutenant, "we argue that there was nobody there—no Sir Charles Halliday, I mean. That seems the legitimate conclusion; and, obviously, it won't do."

Then the chief said that it was a serious business and they must go about it seriously. He had put a man who knew his job into the Grange, and had told him to go over every inch of it. And if he wanted to do any digging outside, he was to telephone for help.

"You don't think so?"

"No, I don't; but it may perhaps be as well to make sure."

The problem remained the secret of Scotland Yard, and of a circle that was moderately small, considering all things. It was kept out of the Press; and the enquiries went on without result for a month, less three or four days, when a solution was given in a very singular manner. The scene returns to Professor Warburton's study. The Professor is discovered at his bureau, trying hard to occupy himself with his proper business, but wondering at intervals when he would be arrested for the murder of Sir Halliday Stuart. That was what he told his friends later, as a matter of fact he was not beset at all by any such nonsensical fears;

but he was still intensely puzzled by the antiquary's disappearance, and intensely curious to know what had really happened. And while he was in this state of mind, his man brought in a card. Warburton took it impatiently; he didn't want to be bothered by anybody. He read: *Sir Halliday Stuart.*

He stared at the servant with an expression that the man found dreadful in its sheer amazement. He gave the necessary order with difficulty, and got up from his chair and stood waiting, in such surprise and confusion of mind as made him realise for the first time that he had never thought to see Sir Halliday again amongst living men.

The door opened, and the servant announced the visitor. A middle-aged, baldish man with a beaky nose entered the room, and, smiling, confronted the bewildered Professor.

"I gather that you wish to see me, Professor Warburton," he began. "When I got back to High Street yesterday, my housekeeper handed me this envelope, with the enclosure addressed to me. You ask"—he took out his glasses—"to be reassured as to my safety. I hope you will excuse me: but I assure you that I haven't the remotest notion of what you mean."

Warburton feebly motioned the visitor to a chair, and sat down himself, so far incapable of coherent speech.

"You see," Sir Halliday went on, "I don't think I've had the pleasure of meeting you till the present moment, and I, naturally, feel a little puzzled. Is it possible that there has been some mistake, some confusion possibly on the part of your secretary? Were you by any chance mixing me up with Mackinlay Stuart, the Science Don? You know him, no doubt?"

Warburton felt that he was sinking into yet deeper and dimmer depths of confusion. "Not had the pleasure of meeting you till the present moment," he quoted helplessly to himself, and though not deeply versed in Holy Writ, he thought of somebody who could have roared for the very disquietness of his heart. He gaped at the man sitting before him, amazed at his barefaced denial of their former encounter, and of the hours they had spent together at the Grange. "Is it possible," he asked himself, "that he doesn't recognise me as I recognise him?"

He scrutinised Sir Halliday's features more intently, and then realised, astonished, that the Sir Halliday of a month ago compared with the Sir Halliday now in presence, was rather like an old, yellowed, and blurred photograph in an ancient album, put beside a clean, recent likeness; or, one might say, a first sketch contrasted with the finished drawing. One saw the resemblance, of course, but the Sir Halliday of the Grange had been, as it were, faint.

But how did that help? Not in the least. It rather added confusion to a business that was already utterly confounded. But after a long silence, Warburton struggled from his morass of dazed perplexity and climbed his way into speech. On the whole, he did not do badly; he told Sir Halliday the story of his morning call and evening's occupation, finishing with his mysterious disappearance from Morton Grange.

"And at the present moment," he ended, "Scotland Yard are looking for you. Unless, of course, they have heard of your return."

And it was hard to say which of the two were the more astounded. Warburton, by telling it, had revived all his first amazement when Sir Halliday could not be found. Sir Halliday could not control himself as he heard an account of his movements on a particular day in October which he knew to be at total variance with the facts. He looked hard at Warburton. There is always a certain way of escape open, when a man is confronted with an incredible and intolerable statement. That is, to hold the person who makes the statement to be a liar. And, undoubtedly, this is often the right solution of such problems. But the antiquary, scanning the visage of the man of exact science, measuring the manner of his utterance, felt that, in this case, mere lying was not the required answer to the riddle. And, besides . . .

"There were four men with you, you said. Who were they?"

Professor Warburton gave the names.

"They're responsible men," he said. "All of them of a certain distinction."

"And they all share your impressions of what happened that night?"

"Absolutely. We are all agreed; I think I may say in every detail."

He suppressed the fact that there had been some discussion and divergence in the party as to Sir Halliday's build and appearance; firstly, because it seemed personal, and then, because he thought very few men were capable of exact observation and subsequent description, and lastly, because he was still puzzled by the difference he had just observed between the look and show of Sir Halliday on his former and his latter visits, and didn't know what to say or think about it.

Sir Halliday pondered. He knew the names of the people who had been associated with Warburton, and, as the professor had observed, they were responsible men. None of them was at all likely to conspire in the concoction of an aimless and preposterous fiction. To believe that would be simply to substitute one incredible story for another. He would take it, then, that the whole five of them supposed that they were telling the truth. He broke his silence.

"I really don't know what to say. The absolute antinomy between your statement and what I know to be the facts as to my doings on the day in question is quite overwhelming. But I'll tell you what really happened, so far as I am concerned, and I hope you'll forgive the small quantity of shop I may have to introduce.

"Well, then. You may be aware that a few years ago there was a good deal of discussion in the press as to certain discoveries in Central France of objects in baked clay which were said to belong to a very remote period. There were considerable names in favour of their antiquity. However, in the long run, evidence of a destructive character was produced, and in spite of a very spirited defence, the verdict was that the supposed prehistoric pottery was nothing more or less than a modern forgery. Naturally, therefore, we were inclined to treat reports of similar finds with a good deal of distrust, and it was some time before I paid any attention to accounts of discoveries of very early pottery at a place near Loches, in the department of Indre-et-Loire. However, on the morning of October 13th last—your date, I think, Professor—there was an article in *The Times*, which seemed to leave no room for suspicion. I felt I must see for myself: the occurrence of the maze of labyrinth pattern on Neolithic objects struck me as of very great significance and importance.

"I left my chambers late in the morning, took a long walk out into the country, dined in some strange place in Soho, and left London by the night service. I got to Paris the next morning, caught the *Rapide* to Tours, and stayed the night at Loches. Next day, I walked through the forest to the village of Genille, and through the courtesy of M. Pic-Paris, the distinguished French antiquary, whom I had met before, I was able to make a thorough examination of the objects discovered in the rock caves, a short distance from the village. In this case, I may say, I am convinced of the entire genuineness of the find—but that doesn't concern our present purpose. After a week of very close study and of conferences with M. Pic-Paris and other French colleagues, I went on to Tours; a most agreeable city. I left Tours for England a couple of days ago. I should be glad to shew you my hotel bills."

There was a pause. Very evidently and certainly Professor Warburton considered within himself, the man was telling the truth. Then Sir Halliday began talking again, with a sudden plunge.

"But here's a very odd thing, which has just struck me. It is the case that some years ago Morton Grange engaged a good deal of my attention. I made a special study of it for a book of mine, called *Essex Manor Houses and Halls.*"

Warburton interrupted, "You told me that before—the last time you were here."

Sir Halliday choked down an inarticulate noise in his throat.

"And you were a good deal interested in something you called a squint in the brew-house at the Grange. Also in the vaulting of the cellar. You said, I think, that you were convinced that the cellar had been originally a temple of Mithras."

The effect of this utterance on the two men was tremendous. It was the great name of Mithras that produced this effect. Sir Halliday had been shaken by Warburton's, "You told me that before." He took his host for a truthful man; his familiarity with *Essex Manor Houses* title was, therefore, not a feigned one. And it might be taken as certain that this physiologist, or physicist, or whatever he was, had never so much as seen the publication in question—a subscription book issued to the members of a learned society—and yet he talked of the cellar vaulting and the brew-house squint. But the matter of Mithras! That was a secret, held in reserve, not breathed to his nearest associates. The evidence for the Mithraic origin and use of that Morton Grange cellar, drawn from many sources and accumulating for years, was almost ready to be welded into a demonstration. Other affairs had pressed on Stuart, and he had not been able to bring this matter to an absolute conclusion; he had been waiting for time and opportunity to make one more visit to the Grange, to satisfy himself by a final and meticulous

examination of certain details that his theory was well-founded and assured. And here was this man speaking as easily of the great secret of
Mithras as of cucumbers in June. He was astounded and confounded:
and he looked it.

And Warburton on his side marked the effect he had produced.
He did not altogether understand the full force of his own words, but
he noted the shock, and interpreted it in his own manner. He thought
that the antiquary must be one of those unfortunate people who suffer
from lapses of memory; that he had honestly forgotten his call of a
month ago, and his subsequent visit to the Grange; and that the mention of his researches and theories had suddenly recalled the lost
memories. The next thing would be that he would explain how he got
away, unobserved, from the Grange; very likely it would turn out to be
quite simple. Very possibly, he had really been to France on the business he had specified; he had merely antedated his journey by a day.
Warburton was going to hint, very gently, something of all this to Sir
Halliday, but his guest forestalled him.

"You will excuse me, I am sure," he said, "but I think I had better
leave you. I do not think that we can do any good by discussing this
subject further. I do not know how you feel, but to me it is intolerable.
Something very awful must have happened. I do not dare to think
what it can have been. I am afraid—I am afraid that I must be on the
other side of death."

He stumbled out of the room. Warburton, going to the window,
saw the unfortunate man swaying and staggering like a drunkard, as he
picked his blind way along the pavement.

The Professor went down thoughtfully to his lunch. He felt sure
that he had been right in his theory. Loss of memory; or perhaps it
might be a case of double personality. He had heard, somewhat doubtfully, of such cases. It had struck him as rather fanciful, but men of
good scientific repute were said to have been convinced, and to have
undoubted evidence in favour of the doctrine. Well, one or the other,
at all events he was afraid that Sir Halliday had been very much upset.

Warburton, on the other hand, was immensely relieved by the solution he had propounded to himself. He was an extremely worthy man,
but a materialist and a rationalist to the core; the determined and unre-
lenting foe of all mysteries. If you had told him that a man of sense

passes his whole life in wondering awe and amazement before the mysteries which perpetually confront him, he would have thought you either a madman, or else an intolerable and pretentious humbug. He dismissed the whole affair from his mind, and lived in extreme comfort for the remainder of his days.

It was Ian Tallent who provided an hypothesis, extravagant and improbable in the highest degree, no doubt, and yet the only tolerable solution of a most difficult problem. He conferred with Professor Warburton, and had the story of his conferences with Sir Halliday out of him, noting his point of view, the loss of memory or if you like— double personality—theory, and leaving him to enjoy it. He had more trouble with Sir Halliday Stuart, who had gone down to his retreat in Oxfordshire in sorry condition, and was making a slow recovery there, restoring himself to a normal state by degrees as he found that the common processes of life still continued in their usual order. At first, Sir Halliday refused Tallent's petitions for an audience with the driest negative; he said that he wished to dismiss "the wretched business" entirely from his thoughts. But Tallent persisted. He had got from Warburton an account of the shattered condition in which Sir Halliday had left him; but, naturally, Warburton had given his own reasons, as he had conceived them, for the shock which the antiquary had very evidently received.

"You see," Warburton had explained, "my reference to the conversation we had had together on his former visit brought the whole thing back to him. It made him aware that for a whole month there had been a lapse in his personality; the transactions of a day and a night had been blotted out as if they had never existed. He was prepared to deny, as he did deny, that he had ever seen me before, that he had visited Morton Grange in our company, and had somehow or other succeeded in avoiding our observation and getting away from the place. And it was then, in my opinion, that the break in consciousness occurred. He got home to his chambers, I don't pretend to say how, in a dazed, confused state, went to bed, and woke up next morning— with the whole of the previous day missing from his memory. And it was no doubt a very startling and a very painful shock when he realised from my remarks the true state of the case."

Tallent heard all this and seemed to accept Warburton's theory.

Indeed, it might be true; but he did not think so. He had a dim glimmering in his mind of possibilities far stranger than this; but he felt that he must talk to the antiquary, with whom the secret must rest. He saw that Warburton, pleased with his solution of the problem, was willing to treat the manner in which Sir Halliday had withdrawn himself inexplicably from their midst as an affair of secondary importance. But to Tallent, this appeared of vital moment: he could not let it go by as a trifle. And if it had happened as he began to dream it might have happened: then, by all means he must see Sir Halliday. But he let him rest a little, and gather his broken forces together, and refit. Then, in a couple of weeks, he wrote again, urging a meeting which might do a great deal, he said, to clear up a very obscure business.

After a few days, he got a letter of reluctant consent, and Tallent went down to High Street, and found Sir Halliday obviously in much better condition than that described by Warburton. And Warburton, it should be said, had not mentioned the odd impression he had received on the antiquary's last visit; the feeling that his visitor's aspect was more fully defined, more sharply "bitten in" than before. This circumstance had become negligible; indeed it was dismissed as a passing fancy—since it did not minister to the master theory of the loss of memory and the consequent annihilation of a day. But Tallent in his turn was impressed in much the same fashion. Sir Halliday looked worn and anxious; but he was distinct and present, as he had not been at the Grange. As Tallent put it to himself: a faint mist seemed to have cleared away from before him.

There was something of a nervous air in Sir Halliday's welcome; a suggestion of disquiet and almost of fear, as if he dreaded a renewal of the very painful and terrifying sensations that had sent him trembling from Warburton's presence a few weeks before. Tallent moved tactfully; he had come prepared to avoid any rough-and-ready handling of this very delicate and difficult case. He made no secret of his interest in the affair, he admitted that there were extraordinary complications and obstacles in the way of a clear issue.

"But before we go down into the deep waters," he added, "there are one or two trifling matters that I believe you would be able to clear up without any trouble. I don't know that they're of much consequence; still, it's as well to start fair. Now, Warburton tells me that on the night of October 13th you went to Paris?"

"I most certainly did," said Sir Halliday, with the strongest emphasis.

"By what route? Dover–Calais?"

"By Dover–Calais. I'm an extremely bad sailor, and I always shorten my discomfort as much as possible. Luckily, it was a calm night. I remember remarking on that fact with considerable satisfaction to a fellow-traveller."

Tallent all but smacked his lips. He remembered the sentence: "It's a calm night, at all events; and that's in our favour."

"Well," he said, "you're meeting me half-way. All these little impressions and recollections of the journey down to Dover: that's exactly what I want you to tell me, if you will. They're trifles, no doubt, but we may possibly find a use for them. Go ahead, sir."

"Really, there's very little to tell: London–Dover isn't generally very eventful. There were two other people in the carriage with me; a middle-aged man and a youngish man. For a good part of the way, I was reading some papers that I had brought with me. And that does remind me of something: I found myself distracted to a certain extent in my reading—somewhat technical matter, I may say—by what struck me as a hum of low-voiced conversation. An odd effect; as if one were listening at one end of a large room to three or four men talking quietly together at the other end. I could just distinguish, as I thought, one man speaking and then another; but I couldn't make out a word they were saying. It quite worried me at last. So far as I've observed, I don't think one hears one's neighbours in the next compartment talking; but I supposed that that was where the sound came from. So, at last I got up from my place and strolled up and down the corridor for a few minutes; and the queer thing was that one of the compartments next to us was empty, and in the other there were two men fast asleep. So I went back to my place and shut the door after me. I took up my papers again, but the hum of talk went on, and it bothered me so much that I gave up the attempt, and began to talk myself to the young man opposite me—the youngish fellow."

Tallent heard Sir Halliday intently.

"And where were these people talking, do you think?" he asked.

"I haven't a notion. I know nothing whatever about acoustics, and I may be talking great nonsense; but I wondered whether by any possibility the sound may have been somehow transmitted from a remote carriage to my own. Sound does play very odd tricks sometimes."

"Whispering galleries? Echoes? That kind of thing, you mean? Well, I don't know. But . . . did you distinguish one voice from another? Do you think you could recognise them if you heard them again?"

"I don't know about that," said Sir Halliday, doubtfully. "But, as you ask me, I must say that your own voice reminds me a good deal of one of these unseen conversationalists. One of them spoke on a slightly higher pitch than the others; and really, the tone was very like yours."

"That's odd, indeed. So you gave up trying to read, and began talking to one of the men in the carriage. Just about the weather and the news, I suppose; things in general?"

"That sort of thing. Then, if I remember, he propounded his solution for the unemployment problem; he would provide work for the workless by pulling down all the old buildings in the country and running up new ones, constructed on purely functional lines, and adapted to the needs of the age. As you may imagine, I don't often hear that sort of talk at the Antiquaries, and I was a good deal amused. I tried to argue with him. I asked him if he didn't take a certain pleasure in looking at an old church or an old house.

"'No more pleasure than you would take,' he replied, 'if you were speeding and saw a heap of old stones and rubbish in the middle of the road, right in front of your car. Old churches, old houses, old castles; they're obstructive rubbish, nothing more or less.'

"Well, he went on at a great rate in this style, and I put in an objection now and again, without any effect, I must confess. We were getting near Dover by this time, and the young iconoclast began to abuse that harmless old place; he said it was a hole. I stuck up for it, and told him that I liked Dover, especially Strond Street and the old harbour."

Tallent remembered this utterance very well.

"And that's all, I suppose. You got out of the train and got on board the boat—and I hope you had a good crossing?"

"Perfectly calm, I am glad to say. But, since you mention it, getting on board was not quite so quiet a business as usual. There seemed a good deal of pushing and excitement; I am sure I don't know what about.

There was plenty of time, of course; but people positively plunged down the gangway; it was almost an ugly rush. But I am afraid I have bored you terribly with all these trivial details. Still, I warned you that you can hardly expect very exciting adventures on the Dover boat-train."

Then the wild hypothesis stood fully confirmed; so Tallent murmured in his mind. "And now," he said to himself, "for the deep waters." He had not only obtained matter of extraordinary value and significance from Sir Halliday's recital of his traveller's trivialities—as he thought them—but the simple story of the Dover boat-train had been soothing to the teller of it. Tallent put his question:

"Professor Warburton," he began, "gave me to understand that you seemed a good deal put out when you left him, after your talk together a few weeks ago. Now, we want to clear things up; and I feel quite sure that it would help very much if you would tell me the exact reason of the distress which I am afraid you experienced."

Sir Halliday Stuart rose from his chair and began to pace slowly up and down the room, evidently in deep and perplexed consideration. At the end of a few minutes, he stopped and faced Tallent.

"I think you are right. Apart from any question of clearing or elucidating a most perplexing business, which I am sure is most desirable, I feel that I shall be the better for plain talk. At the moment, I certainly received a hideous shock."

Tallent perceived that the hour of the forceps had come.

"Tell me exactly what it was."

"It was this. I knew and I know exactly how I had spent that particular day. I knew and I know how every hour of it had been occupied. I knew and I know that I had never set eyes on Professor Warburton before the visit I paid him a few weeks ago. But . . . from certain things that he said, I also knew and know that I had seen him before and told him my most reserved secrets."

He sat down, and covered his face with his hands, bowing his head.

Then Tallent said:

"Do you know that your casual remark about your liking for Dover was heard that night in a room in Morton Grange, where Warburton and the rest of us were sitting? And do you know that you, to all appearance, were sitting also in that room, and that we saw you as you spoke? So it was."

He was met by a blank stare; uncomprehending, utterly incredulous.

"That is quite impossible," said Sir Halliday, quietly and finally.

"There are very few things that are impossible," Tallent replied. "In pure mathematics, perhaps, there may be; though I believe that of late even these eternal canons—as we used to think them—have begun to admit of doubts and uncertainties. Still, I hope we shall not be required to admit the possibility of three-sided squares and two-sided triangles. But, once outside these regions, can we dare to talk of impossibility at all? We can use the word, of course, and I have no doubt that we shall continue to use it; but I think we shall all have to recognise the fact that when we say any event is impossible, we merely mean that we've never heard of such a thing before, and that we don't begin to understand how it can happen so. That is very well, and very applicable to your own case, for I don't think I have ever heard of anything quite on all fours with the extraordinary manifestation in which you were concerned. And I certainly don't begin to understand how it could happen so.

"But, look here; I've just remembered something. I mentioned mathematics just now: I take it you believe there are such things as lines, don't you? Well, have you ever seen one? If so, I should be interested to hear how *that* happened; how length without breadth became visible to the human eye. If you think it over, I believe you will recognise that there are more evident impossibilities lurking in this elementary axiom of geometry than in your own—adventure, shall we call it?"

Sir Halliday was dazed and amazed, and yet attentive. Tallent thought he could hold him, and went on:

"As I said, I think that there are circumstances in your case that are unique; but in the main outlines it falls under a well-ascertained category. There have been many instances of what used to be called Doubles, but are now generally known as Apparitions of Phantasms of the Living. In its early years, the Society for Psychical Research published a thick volume of such cases, all carefully examined and well attested. If I remember, a number of these appearances were of people at the point of death, and the large majority of them were, so far as can be seen, purposeless.

"I remember one case, which might be called typical. A Berkshire farmer, coming down to breakfast one morning, sees on the stairs a Buckinghamshire miller, a market acquaintance, no more, coming up to meet him. The farmer is astonished to see him; and as he stares, the miller is not there. The miller, it was found, was dying at the time, but nobody could guess why he had projected this image of himself into the consciousness of a man with whom he had been barely on nodding terms."

"But, you see," broke in Sir Halliday, "I wasn't dying, or anything like it. I was perfectly well at the time, and that must be seven weeks ago."

"Quite so, but these appearances are by no means invariably the images of the moribund. Indeed, I think that the most remarkable case I know of is a man who was perfectly well and at ease when he became apparent—can we say?—where he was not. This is not one of the Psychical Researchers' cases, it is recorded by Charles Dickens. I have it in my notebook, and here it is—

"'I once saw the apparition of my father at this hour (the early morning). He was alive and well, and nothing ever came of it, but I saw him in the daylight, sitting with his back towards me, on a seat that stood beside my bed. His head was resting on his hand, and whether he was slumbering or grieving, I could not discern. Amazed to see him there, I sat up, moved my position, leaned out of bed, and watched him. As he did not move, I spoke to him more than once. As he did not move then, I became alarmed and laid my hand upon his shoulder—as I thought—and there was no such thing.'

"You see? There you have the apparently purposeless projection of the image of a man in good health. And I think I may say that in the Psychical Research records, there is hardly a single case—if there is such a case—where the apparition was anything but purposeless. To quote a passage from one of the publications of the S.P.R.: 'One has to admit a total absence of any apparent aim or of any intelligent action on the part of phantoms.' We may venture, then, to say that this is the rule: that the apparition or projection of the image is not (in our modern jargon) a 'wish-fulfilment' on the part of the projector. The miller did not want to see the farmer; old Mr. Dickens did not want to see his son.

"Here is where your case parts company from all the others on record. We know that you had made a special study of Morton Grange, and I gathered from Warburton that for some time you had wished to revisit the place, to make a further examination of certain details of importance. That is so, isn't it?"

"Yes, that is quite true. There were points on which I wished to satisfy myself by a second inspection, before finishing some work I had in hand."

"Exactly; and there, I believe, we have the distinction between your particular case and all the others that we have been considering. You say you had a fixed purpose to revisit Morton Grange, in order that you might satisfy yourself finally on certain matters which to you were of the first importance? Good. Then, I think, having established that distinction—the purpose behind the projection—we come, not unnaturally, to the other distinction or difference—the superior intensity of the image projected. The normal phantasy of the living manifests and vanishes. It does not speak, it does not abide our question, its visibility is its only energy, and that is rapidly exhausted and dispersed. In your case, on the other hand, the phantasm was in all respects like an ordinary human being; it was both persistent and energetic; to all apparent intents and purposes it was yourself as you sit there before me.

"Beyond the extraordinary character of the whole manifestation, there are one or two very curious points. For instance. While the phantasm was with us, we saw nothing, as I have just intimated, at all peculiar or out of the way about it. But when it had disappeared, and we were wondering what on earth had happened, it came out accidentally that the figure—I was going to say, 'you'—had not impressed us all in the same way. One man thought Sir Halliday was short and small, another described him as above the average height. And another thing: when I came into this room about an hour ago, I noticed at once the difference between Sir Halliday of Campden House and the Sir Halliday of Morton Grange: the former figure was by far more definite and vivid than the latter. You know in the old Christmas Ghost stories, the apparition is often described as 'a shadowy figure'. A traditional phrase, no doubt, and an instance, as I think, of the fact that tradition often tells the truth under the form of a picturesque symbolism. We couldn't see the furniture through the phantasm of Sir Halliday; but, in a sense, the image was certainly shadowy, indeterminate.

"And again: here is a puzzle. As you sat in the train on the way to Dover, you heard the murmur of the conversation in the room at Morton Grange. You recognised my voice just now. And, on the other hand, we heard some—not all—of your remarks to your fellow-travellers in the carriage. Of course we thought you were speaking to us. These are difficulties which I do not attempt to explain. But I hope that on the whole you are relieved."

Sir Halliday Stuart had listened in a deep, meditative silence; assenting, now and again, with a nod of the head, when Tallent appealed to him.

"'Journeying very far, I found what I had not sought,'" he murmured to himself, sighing, in great wonder.

"Well, yes," he said aloud. "In a way, I suppose you have relieved me—of the sense of an intolerable contradiction."

"Well, I am glad," said Tallent, rising. "Though I believe it may be held at last that true wisdom consists in accepting contradictions and rejoicing in them greatly."

Ritual

Once upon a time, as we say in English, or *olim*, as the Latins said in their more austere and briefer way, I was sent forth on a May Monday to watch London being happy on their Whitsun holiday. This is the sort of appointment that used to be known in newspaper offices as an annual; and the difficulty for the men engaged in this business is to avoid seeing the same sights as those witnessed a year before and saying much the same things about them as were said on Whit-Monday twelvemonth. Queuing up for Madame Tussaud's waxworks, giving buns to diverse creatures in the Zoo, gazing at those Easter Island gods in the portico of the British Museum, waiting for all sorts of early doors to open; all these are spectacles of the day. And the patient man who boards the buses from suburbs may chance to hear a lady from Hornsey expounding to her neighbour on the seat, an inhabitant of Enfield Wash, the terrible gaieties that Piccadilly Circus witnesses when the electric signs are fairly lit.

On the Whit-Monday in question I saw and recorded some of these matters; and then strolled westward along Piccadilly, by the palings of the Green Park. The conventional business of the day had been more or less attended to: now for the unsystematic prowl: one never knows where one may find one's goods. And then and there, I came across some boys, half-a-dozen or so of them, playing what struck me as a very queer game on the fresh turf of the Park, under the tender and piercing green of the young leaves. I have forgotten the preliminary elaborations of the sport; but there seemed to be some sort of dramatic action, perhaps with dialogue, but this I could not hear. Then one boy stood alone, with the five or six others about him. They pretended to hit the solitary boy, and he fell to the ground and lay motionless, as if dead. Then the others covered him up with their coats, and ran away. And then, if I remember, the boy who had been ritually smitten, slaughtered, and buried, rose to his feet, and the very odd game began all over again.

Here, I thought, was something a little out of the way of the accustomed doings and pleasures of the holiday crowds, and I returned to my office and embodied an account of this Green Park sport in my tale of Whit-Monday in London; with some allusion to the curious analogy between the boys' game and certain matters of a more serious nature. But it would not do. A spectacled Reader came down out of his glass cage, and held up a strip of proof.

"Hiram Abiff?" he queried in a low voice, as he placed the galley-slip on my desk, and pointed to the words with his pen. "It's not usual to mention these things in print."

I assured the Reader that I was not one of the Widow's offspring, but he still shook his head gravely, and I let him have his way, willing to avoid all *admiratio*. It was, I thought, a curious little incident, and to this day I have never heard an explanation of the coincidence—mere chance, very likely—between the pastime in the Park and those matters which it is not usual to mention in print.

But a good many years later, this business of the Green Park was recalled to me by a stranger experience in a very different part of London. A friend of mine, an American, who had travelled in many outland territories of the earth, asked me to shew him some of the less known quarters of London.

"Do not misunderstand me, sir," he said, in his measured, almost Johnsonian manner, "I do not wish to see your great city in its alleged sensational aspects. I am not yearning to probe the London underworld, nor do I wish to view any opium joints or blind-pigs for cocaine addicts. In such matters, I have already accumulated more than sufficient experience in other quarters of the world. But if you would just shew me those aspects which are so ordinary that nobody ever sees them, I shall be greatly indebted to you."

I remember how I had once awed two fellow-citizens of his by taking them to a street not very far from King's Cross Station, and shewing them how each house was guarded by twin plaster sphinxes of a deadly chocolate-red, which crouched on either side of the flights of steps leading to the doorways. I remembered how the late Arnold Bennett had come exploring in this region, and seen the sphinxes and had noted them in his diary with a kind of dumb surmise, venturing no comment. So I said that I thought I understood. We set out, and soon we were deep in that unknown London which is at our very doors.

"Dickens had been here," I said in my part as Guide and Interpreter. "You know *Little Dorrit?* Then this might be Mr. Casby's very street, which set out meaning to run down into the valley and up again to the top of the hill, but got out of breath and stopped still after twenty yards."

The American gentleman relished the reference and his surroundings. He pointed out to me curious work in some of the iron balconies before the first floor windows in the grey houses, making a rough sketch of the design of one of them in his note-book. We wandered here and there, and up and down at haphazard, by strange wastes and devious ways, till I, in spite of my fancied knowledge, found myself in a part that I did not remember to have seen before. There were timber yards with high walls about them. There were cottages that seemed to have strayed from the outskirts of some quiet provincial town, off the main road. One of these lay deep in the shadow of an old mulberry, and ripening grapes hung from a vine on a neighbouring wall. The hollyhocks in the neat little front gardens were almost over; there were still brave displays of snapdragons and marigolds. But round the corner, barrows piled with pale bananas and flaming oranges filled the roadway, and the street market resounded with raucous voices, praise of fruit and fish, and loud bargainings, and gossip at its highest pitch. We pushed our way through the crowd, and left the street of the market, and presently came into the ghostly quiet of a square: high, severe houses, built of whitish bricks, complete in 1840 Gothic, all neat and well-kept, and for all sign of life or movement, uninhabited.

And then, when we had barely rested our ears from the market jangle, there came what I suppose was an overflow from that region. A gang of small boys surged into the square and broke its peace. There were about a dozen of them, more or less, and I took it that they were playing soldiers. They marched, two and two, in their dirty and shabby order, apparently under the command of a young ruffian somewhat bigger and taller than the rest. Two of them banged incessantly with bits of broken wood on an old meat tin and a battered iron tea tray, and all of them howled as barbarously as any crooner, but much louder. They went about and about, and then diverged into an empty road that looked as if it led nowhere in particular, and there drew up, and formed themselves into a sort of hollow square, their captain in the middle. The tin pan music went on steadily, but less noisily; it had become a succession of slow beats, and the howls had turned into a sort of whining chant.

But it remained a very horrible row, and I was moving on to get away from the noise, when my American interposed.

"If you wouldn't mind our tarrying here for a few moments," he said apologetically. "This pastime of your London boys interests me very much. You may think it strange, but I find it more essentially exciting than the Eton and Harrow Cricket Match of which I witnessed some part a few weeks ago."

So we looked on from an unobtrusive corner. The boys, evidently, agreed with my friend, and found their game absorbing. I don't think that they had noticed us or knew that we were there.

They went through their queer performance. The bangs or beats on the tin and the tray grew softer and slower, and the yells had died into a monotonous drone. The leader went inside the square, from boy to boy, and seemed to whisper into the ear of each one. Then he passed round a second time, standing before each, and making a sort of summoning or beckoning gesture with his hand. Nothing happened. I did not find the sport essentially exciting; but looking at the American, I observed that he was watching it with an expression of the most acute interest and amazement. Again the big boy went around the square. He stopped dead before a little fellow in a torn jacket. He threw out his arms wide, with a gesture of embrace, and then drew them in. He did this three times, and at the third repetition of the ceremony, the little chap in the torn jacket cried out with a piercing scream and fell forward as if dead.

The banging of the tins and the howl of the voices went up to heaven with a hideous dissonance.

My American friend was gasping with astonishment as we passed on our way.

"This is an amazing city," he said. "Do you know, sir, that those boys were acting all as if they'd been Asiki doing their Njoru ritual. I've seen it in East Africa. But there the black man that falls down stays down. He's dead."

A week or two later, I was telling the tale to some friends. One of them pulled an evening paper out of his pocket.

"Look at that," said he, pointing with his finger. I read the head-lines:

MYSTERY DEATH IN NORTH LONDON SQUARE

HOME OFFICE DOCTOR PUZZLED

HEART VESSELS RUPTURED

"PLAYING SOLDIERS"

BOY FALLS DEAD

CORONER DIRECTS OPEN VERDICT

Appendix

Introduction to *The Angels of Mons*

I have been asked to write an introduction to the story of "The Bowmen", on its publication in book form together with three other tales of similar fashion. And I hesitate. This affair of "The Bowmen" has been such an odd one from first to last, so many queer complications have entered into it, there have been so many and so divers currents and cross-currents of rumour and speculation concerning it, that I honestly do not know where to begin. I propose, then, to solve the difficulty by apologising for beginning at all.

For, usually and fitly, the presence of an introduction is held to imply that there is something of consequence and importance to be introduced. If, for example, a man has made an anthology of great poetry, he may well write an introduction justifying his principle of selection, pointing out here and there, as the spirit moves him, high beauties and supreme excellencies, discoursing of the magnates and lords and princes of literature, whom he is merely serving as groom of the chamber. Introductions, that is, belong to the masterpieces and classics of the world, to the great and ancient and accepted things; and I am here introducing a short, small story of my own which appeared in *The Evening News* about ten months ago.

I appreciate the absurdity, nay, the enormity of the position in all its grossness. And my excuse for these pages must be this: that though the story itself is nothing, it has yet had such odd and unforeseen consequences and adventures that the tale of them may possess some interest. And then, again, there are certain psychological morals to be drawn from the whole matter of the tale and its sequel of rumours and discussions that are not, I think, devoid of consequence; and so to begin at the beginning.

* * *

This was in last August; to be more precise, on the last Sunday of last August. There were terrible things to be read on that hot Sunday morning between meat and mass. It was in *The Weekly Dispatch* that I saw the awful account of the retreat from Mons. I no longer recollect the details; but I have not forgotten the impression that was then made on my mind. I seemed to see a furnace of torment and death and agony and terror seven times heated, and in the midst of the burning was the British Army. In the midst of the flame, consumed by it and yet aureoled in it, scattered like ashes and yet triumphant, martyred and for ever glorious. So I saw our men with a shining about them, so I took these thoughts with me to church, and, I am sorry to say, was making up a story in my head while the deacon was singing the Gospel.

This was not the tale of "The Bowmen". It was the first sketch, as it were, of "The Soldiers' Rest", which is reprinted in this volume. I only wish I had been able to write it as I conceived it. The tale as it stands is, I think, a far better piece of craft than "The Bowmen", but the tale that came to me as the blue incense floated above the Gospel Book on the desk between the tapers: that indeed was a noble story— like all the stories that never get written. I conceived the dead men coming up through the flames and in the flames, and being welcomed in the Eternal Tavern with songs and flowing cups and everlasting mirth. But every man is the child of his age, however much he may hate it; and our popular religion has long determined that jollity is wicked. As far as I can make out modern Protestantism believes that Heaven is something like Evensong in an English cathedral, the service by Stainer and the Dean preaching. For those opposed to dogma of any kind—even the mildest—I suppose it is held that a Course of Ethical Lectures will be arranged.

Well, I have long maintained that on the whole the average church, considered as a house of preaching, is a much more poisonous place than the average tavern; still, as I say, one's age masters one, and clouds and bewilders the intelligence, and the real story of "The Soldiers' Rest", with its "sonus epulantium in æterno convivio", was ruined at the moment of its birth, and it was some time later that the actual story, as here printed, got written. And in the meantime the plot of "The Bowmen" occurred to me. Now it has been murmured and hinted and suggested and whispered in all sorts of quarters that before I wrote the tale I had heard something. The most decorative of these legends is also the most precise: "I know for a fact that the whole thing was given him in typescript by a lady-in-waiting." This was not the case; and all vaguer reports to the effect that I had heard some rumours or hints of rumours are equally void of any trace of truth.

Again I apologise for entering so pompously into the minutiæ of my bit of a story, as if it were the lost poems of Sappho; but it appears that the subject interests the public, and I comply with my instructions. I take it, then, that the origins of "The Bowmen" were composite. First of all, all ages and nations have cherished the thought that spiritual hosts may come to the help of earthly arms, that gods and heroes and saints have descended from their high immortal places to fight for their worshippers and clients. Then Kipling's story of the ghostly Indian regiment got in my head and got mixed with the mediævalism that is always there; and so "The Bowmen" was written. I was heartily disappointed with it, I remember, and thought it—as I still think it—an indifferent piece of work. However, I have tried to write for these thirty-five long years, and if I have not become practised in letters, I am at least a past master in the Lodge of Disappointment. Such as it was, "The Bowmen" appeared in *The Evening News* of September 29th, 1914.

Now the journalist does not, as a rule, dwell much on the prospect of fame; and if he be an evening journalist, his anticipations of immortality are bounded by twelve o'clock at night at the latest; and it may well be that those insects which begin to live in the morning and are dead by sunset deem themselves immortal. Having written my story, having groaned and growled over it and printed it, I certainly never thought to hear another word of it. My colleague "The Londoner" praised it warmly to my face, as his kindly fashion is; entering, very properly, a technical caveat as to the language of the battle-cries of the bowmen. "Why should English archers use French terms?" he said. I replied that the only reason was this—that a "Monseigneur" here and there struck me as picturesque; and I reminded him that, as a matter of cold historical fact, most of the archers of Agincourt were mercenaries from Gwent, my native country, who would appeal to Mihangel and to saints not known to the Saxons—Teilo, Iltyd, Dewi, Cadwaladyr Vendigeid. And I thought that that was the first and last discussion of "The Bowmen". But in a few days from its publication the editor of

The Occult Review wrote to me. He wanted to know whether the story had any foundation in fact. I told him that it had no foundation in fact of any kind or sort; I forget whether I added that it had no foundation in rumour, but I should think not, since to the best of my belief there were no rumours of heavenly interposition in existence at that time. Certainly I had heard of none. Soon afterwards the editor of *Light* wrote asking a like question, and I made him a like reply. It seemed to me that I had stifled any "Bowmen" mythos in the hour of its birth.

A month or two later, I received several requests from editors of parish magazines to reprint the story. I—or, rather, my editor—readily gave permission; and then, after another month or two, the conductor of one of these magazines wrote to me, saying that the February issue containing the story had been sold out, while there was still a great demand for it. Would I allow them to reprint "The Bowmen" as a pamphlet, and would I write a short preface giving the exact authorities for the story? I replied that they might reprint in pamphlet form with all my heart, but that I could not give my authorities, since I had none, the tale being pure invention. The priest wrote again, suggesting—to my amazement—that I must be mistaken, that the main "facts" of "The Bowmen" must be true, that my share in the matter must surely have been confined to the elaboration and decoration of a veridical history. It seemed that my light fiction had been accepted by the congregation of this particular church as the solidest of facts; and it was then that it began to dawn on me that if I had failed in the art of letters, I had succeeded, unwittingly, in the art of deceit. This happened, I should think, some time in April, and the snowball of rumour that was then set rolling has been rolling ever since, growing bigger and bigger, till it is now swollen to a monstrous size.

It was at about this period that variants of my tale began to be told as authentic histories. At first, these tales betrayed their relation to their original. In several of them the vegetarian restaurant appeared, and St. George was the chief character. In one case an officer—name and address missing—said that there was a portrait of St. George in a certain London restaurant, and that a figure, just like the portrait, appeared to him on the battlefield, and was invoked by him, with the happiest results. Another variant—this, I think, never got into print—told how dead Prussians had been found on the battlefield with arrow wounds in their bodies. This notion amused me, as I had imagined a scene, when I was thinking out the story, in which a German general was to appear before the Kaiser to explain his failure to annihilate the English.

"All-Highest," the general was to say, "it is true, it is impossible to deny it. The men were killed by arrows; the shafts were found in their bodies by the burying parties."

I rejected the idea as over-precipitous even for a mere fantasy. I was therefore entertained when I found that what I had refused as too fantastical for fantasy was accepted in certain occult circles as hard fact.

Other versions of the story appeared in which a cloud interposed between the attacking Germans and the defending British. In some examples the cloud served to conceal our men from the advancing enemy; in others, it disclosed shining shapes which frightened the horses of the pursuing German cavalry. St. George, it will be noted, has disappeared—he persisted some time longer in certain Roman Catholic variants—and there are no more bowmen, no more arrows. But so far angels are not mentioned; yet they are ready to appear, and I think that I have detected the machine which brought them into the story.

In "The Bowmen" my imagined soldier saw "a long line of shapes, with a shining about them". And Mr. A. P. Sinnett, writing in the May issue of *The Occult Review,* reporting what he had heard, states that "those who could see said they saw 'a row of shining beings' between the two armies". Now I conjecture that the word "shining" is the link between my tale and the derivative from it. In the popular view shining and benevolent supernatural beings are angels and nothing else, and must be angels, and so, I believe, the Bowmen of my story have become "the Angels of Mons". In this shape they have been received with respect and credence everywhere, or almost everywhere.

And here, I conjecture, we have the key to the large popularity of the delusion—as I think it. We have long ceased in England to take much interest in saints, and in the recent revival of the cultus of St. George, the saint is little more than a patriotic figurehead. And the appeal to the saints to succour us is certainly not a common English practice; it is held Popish by most of our countrymen. But angels, with certain reservations, have retained their popularity, and so, when it was settled that the English army in its dire peril was delivered by angelic aid, the way was clear for general belief, and for the enthusiasms of the religion of the man in the street. And so soon as the legend got the title "The Angels of Mons" it became impossible to avoid it. It permeated the Press: it would not be neglected; it appeared in the most unlikely quarters—in *Truth* and *Town Topics, The New Church Weekly* (Swedenborgian) and *John Bull.* The editor of *The Church Times* has exercised a wise reserve: he awaits that evidence which so far is lacking; but in one issue of the paper I noted that the story furnished a text for a sermon, the subject of a letter, and the matter for an article. People send me cuttings from provincial papers containing hot controversy as to the exact nature of the appearances; the "Office Window" of *The Daily Chronicle* suggests scientific explanations of the hallucination; the *Pall Mall* in a note about St. James says he is of the brotherhood of the Bowmen of Mons—this reversion to the bowmen from the angels being possibly due to the strong statements that I have made on the matter. The pulpits both of the Church and of Nonconformity have been busy: Bishop Welldon, Dean Hensley Henson (a disbeliever), Bishop Taylor Smith (the Chaplain-General), and many other clergy have occupied themselves with the matter. Dr. Horton preached about the "angels" at Manchester; Sir Joseph Compton Rickett (President of the National Federation of Free Church Councils) stated that the soldiers at the front had seen visions and dreamed dreams, and had given testimony of powers and principalities fighting for them or against them. Letters come from all the ends of the earth to the Editor of *The Evening News* with theories, beliefs, explanations, suggestions. It is all somewhat wonderful; one can say that the whole affair is a psychological phenomenon of considerable interest, fairly comparable with the great Russian delusion of last August and September.

*   *   *

Now it is possible that some persons, judging by the tone of these remarks of mine, may gather the impression that I am a profound disbeliever in the possibility of any intervention of the superphysical order in the affairs of the physical order. They will be mistaken if they make this inference; they will be mistaken if they suppose that I think miracles in Judæa credible but miracles in France or Flanders incredible. I hold no such absurdities. But I confess, very frankly, that I credit none of the "Angels of Mons" legends, partly because I see, or think I see, their derivation from my own idle fiction, but chiefly because I have, so far, not received one jot or tittle of evidence that should dispose me to belief. It is idle, indeed, and foolish enough for a man to say: "I am sure that story is a lie, because the supernatural element enters into it"; here, indeed, we have the maggot writhing in the midst of corrupted offal denying the existence of the sun. But if this fellow be a fool—as he is—equally foolish is he who says, "If the tale has anything of the supernatural it is true, and the less evidence the better"; and I am afraid this tends to be the attitude of many who call themselves occultists. I hope that I shall never get to that frame of mind. So I say, not that super-normal interventions are impossible, not that they have not happened during this war—I know nothing as to that point, one way or the other—but that there is not one atom of evidence (so far) to support the current stories of the angels of Mons. For, be it remarked, these stories are specific stories. They rest on the second, third, fourth, fifth hand stories told by "a soldier", by "an officer", by "a Catholic correspondent", by "a nurse", by any number of anonymous people. Indeed, names have been mentioned. A lady's name has been drawn, most unwarrantably as it appears to me, into the discussion, and I have no doubt that this lady has been subject to a good deal of pestering and annoyance. She has written to the Editor of *The Evening News* denying all knowledge of the supposed miracle. The Psychical Research Society's expert confesses that no real evidence has been proffered to her Society on the matter. And then, to my amazement, she accepts as fact the proposition that some men on the battlefield have been "hallucinated", and proceeds to give the theory of sensory hallucination. She forgets that, by her own showing, there is no reason to suppose that anybody has been hallucinated at all. Someone (unknown) has met a nurse (unnamed) who has talked to a soldier (anonymous) who has seen angels. But that is not evidence; and not even Sam Weller at his gayest would have dared to offer it as such in the Court of Common Pleas. So far, then, nothing remotely approaching proof has been offered as to any supernatural intervention during the Retreat from Mons. Proof may come; if so, it will be interesting and more than interesting.

*   *   *

But, taking the affair as it stands at present, how is it that a nation plunged in materialism of the grossest kind has accepted idle rumours and gossip of the supernatural as certain truth? The answer is contained in the question: it is precisely because our whole atmosphere is materialist that we are ready to credit anything—save the truth. Separate a man from good drink, he will swallow methylated spirit with joy. Man is created to be inebriated; to be "nobly wild, not mad". Suffer the Cocoa Prophets and their company to seduce him in body and spirit, and he will get himself stuff that will make him ignobly wild and mad indeed. It took hard, practical men of affairs, business men, advanced thinkers, Freethinkers, to believe in Madame Blavatsky and Mahatmas and the famous message from the Golden Shore: "Judge's plan is right; follow him and *stick*."

And the main responsibility for this dismal state of affairs undoubtedly lies on the shoulders of the majority of the clergy of the Church of England. Christianity, as Mr. W. L. Courtney has so admirably pointed out, is a great Mystery Religion; it is *the* Mystery Religion. Its priests are called to an awful and tremendous hierurgy; its pontiffs are to be the pathfinders, the bridge-makers between the world of sense and the world of spirit. And, in fact, they pass their time in preaching, not the eternal mysteries, but a twopenny morality, in changing the Wine of Angels and the Bread of Heaven into gingerbeer and mixed biscuits: a sorry transubstantiation, a sad alchemy, as it seems to me.

The Coming of the Terror

After two years we are turning once more to the morning's news with a sense of appetite and glad expectation. There were thrills at the beginning of the war, the thrill of horror and of a doom that seemed at once incredible and certain. This was when Namur fell, and the German host swelled like a flood over the French fields, and drew very near to the walls of Paris. Then we felt the thrill of exultation when the good news came that the awful tide had been turned back, that Paris and the world were safe, for a while, at all events.

Then for days we hoped for more news as good as this or better. Has Kluck been surrounded? Not to-day, but perhaps he will be surrounded to-morrow. But the days became weeks, the weeks drew out to months; the battle in the West seemed frozen. People speculated as to the reason of this inaction: the hopeful said that Joffre had a plan, that he was "nibbling"; others declared that we were short of munitions, others again that the new levies were not yet ripe for battle. So the months went by, and almost two years of war had been completed before the motionless English line began to stir and quiver as if it awoke from a long sleep, and began to roll onward, overwhelming the enemy.

The secret of the long inaction of the British armies has been well kept. On the one hand it was rigorously protected by the censorship, which, severe, and sometimes severe to the point of absurdity, became in this particular matter ferocious. As soon as the real significance of that which was happening was perceived by the authorities, an under-lined circular was issued to the newspaper proprietors of Great Britain and Ireland. It warned each proprietor that he might impart the contents of this circular to one other person only, such person being the responsible editor of his paper, who was to keep the communication secret under the severest penalties. The circular forbade any mention of certain events that had taken place, that might take place; it forbade any kind of reference to these events or any hint of their existence. The subject was not to be referred to in conversation, it was not to be hinted at, however obscurely, in letters; the very existence of the circular, its subject apart, was to be a dead secret.

Now, a censorship that is sufficiently minute and utterly remorseless can do amazing things in the way of hiding what it wants to hide. Once one would have thought otherwise; one would have said that, censor or no censor, the fact of the murder at X—— would certainly become known, if not through the press, at all events through rumor and the passage of the news from mouth to mouth. And this would be true of England three hundred years ago. But we have grown of late to such a reverence for the printed word and such a reliance on it that the old faculty of disseminating news by word of mouth has become atrophied. Forbid the press to mention the fact that Jones has been murdered, and it is marvelous how few people will hear of it, and of those who hear how few will credit the story that they have heard.

And, then, again, the very fact of these vain rumors and fantastic tales having been so widely believed for a time was fatal to the credit of any stray mutterings that may have got abroad.

Before the secret circular had been issued my curiosity had somehow been aroused by certain paragraphs concerning a "Fatal Accident to Well-known Airman." The propeller of the airplane had been shattered, apparently by a collision with a flight of pigeons; the blades had been broken, and the machine had fallen like lead to the earth. And soon after I had seen this account, I heard of some very odd circumstances relating to an explosion in a great munition factory in the Midlands. I thought I saw the possibility of a connection between two very different events.

It has been pointed out to me by friends who have been good enough to read this record that certain phrases I have used may give the impression that I ascribe all the delays of the war on the Western front to the extraordinary circumstances which occasioned the issue of the secret circular. Of course this is not the case; there were many reasons for the immobility of our lines from October, 1914, to July, 1916. We could undertake to supply the defects of our army both in men and munitions *if* the new and incredible danger could be overcome. It has been overcome,—rather, perhaps, it has ceased to exist,—and the secret may now be told.

I have said my attention was attracted by an account of the death of a well-known airman. I have not the habit of preserving cuttings, I am sorry to say, so that I cannot be precise as to the date of this event. To the best of my belief it was either toward the end of May or the beginning of June, 1915. The manner in which Western-Reynolds met his death struck me as extraordinary. He was brought down by a flight of pigeons, as appeared by what was found on the blood-stained and shattered blades of the propeller. An eyewitness of the accident, a fellow-officer, described how Western-Reynolds set out from the aërodrome on a fine afternoon, there being hardly any wind. He was going to France.

"'Wester' rose to a great height at once, and we could scarcely see the machine. I was turning to go when one of the fellows called out: 'I say! What's this?' He pointed up, and we saw what looked like a black cloud coming from the south at a tremendous rate. I saw at once it wasn't a cloud; it came with a swirl and a rush quite different from any cloud I've ever seen. It turned into a great crescent, and wheeled and veered about as if it was looking for something. The man who had called out had got his glasses, and was staring for all he was worth. Then he shouted that it was a tremendous flight of birds, 'thousands of them.' They went on wheeling and beating about high up in the air, and we were watching them, thinking it was interesting, but not supposing that they would make any difference to 'Wester,' who was just about out of sight. Then the two arms of the crescent drew in as quick as lightning, and these thousands of birds shot in a solid mass right up there across the sky, and flew away. Then Henley, the man with the glasses, called out, 'He's down!' and started running, and I went after him. We got a car, and as we were going along Henley told me that he'd seen the machine drop dead, as if it came out of that cloud of birds. We found the propeller-blades all broken and covered with blood and pigeon-feathers, and carcasses of the birds had got wedged in between the blades and were sticking to them."

It was, I think, about a week or ten days after the airman's death that my business called me to a Northern town, the name of which, perhaps, had better remain unknown. My mission was to inquire into certain charges of extravagance which had been laid against the munition-workers of this special town. I found, as usual, that there was a mixture of truth and exaggeration in the stories that I had heard.

"And how can you be surprised if people will have a bit of a fling?" a worker said to me. "We're seeing money for the first time in our lives, and it's bright. And we work hard for it, and we risk our lives to get it. You've heard of explosion yonder?"

He mentioned certain works on the outskirts of the town. Of course neither the name of the works nor that of the town had been printed; there had been a brief notice of "Explosion at Munition Works in the Northern District: Many Fatalities." The working-man told me about it, and added some dreadful details.

"They wouldn't let their folks see bodies; screwed them up in coffins as they found them in shop. The gas had done it."

"Turned their faces black, you mean?"

"Nay. They were all as if they had been bitten to pieces."

This was a strange gas.

I asked the man in the Northern town all sorts of questions about the extraordinary explosion of which he had spoken to me, but he had very little more to say. As I have noted already, secrets that may not be printed are often deeply kept; last summer there were very few people outside high official circles who knew anything about the "tanks," of which we have all been talking lately, though these strange instruments of war were being exercised and tested in a park not far from London.

I gave him up, and took a tram to the district of the disaster, a sort of industrial suburb, five miles from the center of the town. When I asked for the factory, I was told that it was no good my going to it, as there was nobody there. But I found it, a raw and hideous shed, with a walled yard about it, and a shut gate. I looked for signs of destruction, but there was nothing. The roof was quite undamaged; and again it struck me that this had been a strange accident. There had been an explosion of sufficient violence to kill people in the building, but the building itself showed no wounds or scars.

A man came out of the gate and locked it behind him. I began to ask him some sort of question, or, rather, I began to "open" for a question with "A terrible business here, they tell me," or some such phrase of convention. I got no further. The man asked me if I saw a policeman walking down the street. I said I did, and I was given the choice of getting about my business forthwith or of being instantly given in charge as a spy. "Th' 'ast better be gone, and quick about it," was, I think, his final advice, and I took it.

It was a day or two later that the accident to the airman Western-Reynolds came into my mind. For one of those instants which are far shorter than any measure of time there flashed out the possibility of a link between the two disasters. But here was a wild impossibility, and I drove it away. And yet I think that the thought, mad as it seemed, never left me; it was the secret light that at last guided me through a somber grove of enigmas.

It was about this time, so far as the date can be fixed, that a whole district, one might say a whole county, was visited by a series of extraordinary and terrible calamities, which were the more terrible inasmuch as they continued for some time to be inscrutable mysteries. It is indeed doubtful whether these awful events do not still remain mysteries to many of those concerned; for before the inhabitants of this part of the country had time to join one link of evidence to another the circular was issued, and thenceforth no one knew how to distinguish undoubted fact from wild and extravagant surmise.

The district in question is in the far west of Wales; I shall call it, for convenience, Meirion. Here, then, one sees a wild and divided and scattered region, a land of outland hills and secret and hidden valleys.

Such, then, in the main is Meirion, and on this land in the early summer of last year terror descended—a terror without shape, such as no man there had ever known.

It began with the tale of a little child who wandered out into the lanes to pick flowers one sunny afternoon, and never came back to the cottage on the hill. It was supposed that she must have crossed the road and gone to the cliff's edge, possibly in order to pick the sea-pinks that were then in full blossom. She must have slipped, they said, and fallen into the sea, two hundred feet below. It may be said at once that there was no doubt some truth in this conjecture, though it stopped far short of the whole truth. The child's body must have been carried out by the tide, for it was never found.

The conjecture of a false step or of a fatal slide on the slippery turf that slopes down to the rocks was accepted as being the only explanation possible. People thought the accident a strange one, because, as a rule, country children living by the cliffs and the sea become wary at an early age, and the little girl was almost ten years old. Still, as the neighbors said, "That's how it must have happened; and it's a great pity, to be sure." But this would not do when in a week's time a strong young laborer failed to come to his cottage after the day's work. His body was found on the rocks six or seven miles from the cliffs where the child was supposed to have fallen; he was going home by a path that he had used every night of his life for eight or nine years, that he used on dark nights in perfect security, knowing every inch of it. The police asked if he drank, but he was a teetotaler; if he was subject to fits, but he wasn't. And he was not murdered for his wealth, since agricultural laborers are not wealthy. It was only possible again to talk of slippery turf and a false step; but people began to be frightened. Then a woman was found with her neck broken at the bottom of a disused quarry near Llanfihangel, in the middle of the county. The false-step theory was eliminated here, for the quarry was guarded by a natural hedge of gorse. One would have to struggle and fight through sharp thorns to destruction in such a place as this; and indeed the gorse was broken, as if some one had rushed furiously through it, just above the place where the woman's body was found. And this also was strange: there was a dead sheep lying beside her in the pit, as if the woman and the sheep together had been chased over the brim of the quarry. But chased by whom or by what? And then there was a new form of terror.

This was in the region of the marshes under the mountain. A man and his son, a lad of fourteen or fifteen, set out early one morning to work, and never reached the farm whence they were bound. Their way skirted the marsh, but it was broad, firm, and well metalled, and it had been raised about two feet above the bog. But when search was made in the evening of the same day, Phillips and his son were found dead in the marsh, covered with black slime and pond-weed. And they lay some ten yards from the path, which, it would seem, they must have left deliberately. It was useless, of course, to look for tracks in the black ooze, for if one threw a big stone into it, a few seconds removed all marks of the disturbance. The men who found the two bodies beat about the verges and purlieus of the marsh in hope of finding some trace of the murderers; they went to and fro over the rising ground where the black cattle were grazing, they searched the alder-thickets by the brook: but they discovered nothing.

Most horrible of all these horrors, perhaps, was the affair of the Highway, a lonely and unfrequented by-road that winds for many miles on high and lonely land. Here, a mile from any other dwelling, stands a cottage on the edge of a dark wood. It was inhabited by a laborer named Williams, his wife, and their three children. One hot summer's evening a man who had been doing a day's gardening at a rectory three or four miles away passed the cottage, and stopped for a few minutes to chat with Williams, who was pottering about his garden, while the children were playing on the path by the door. The two talked of their neighbors and of the potatoes till Mrs. Williams appeared at the door-way and said supper was ready, and Williams turned to go into the house. This was about eight o'clock, and in the ordinary course the family would have had their supper and be in bed by nine, or by half-past nine at the latest. At ten o'clock that night the local doctor was driving home along the Highway. His horse shied violently and then stopped dead just opposite the gate to the cottage. The doctor got down, and there on the roadway lay Williams, his wife, and the three children, stone-dead. Their skulls were battered in as if by some heavy iron instrument; their faces were beaten into a pulp.

It is not easy to make any picture of the horror that lay dark on the hearts of the people of Meirion. It was no longer possible to believe or to pretend to believe that these men and women and children had met their deaths through strange accidents. For a time people said that there must be a madman at large, a sort of country variant of Jack the Ripper, some horrible pervert who was possessed by the passion of death, who prowled darkling about that lonely land, hiding in woods and in wild places, always watching and seeking for the victims of his desire.

Indeed, Dr. Lewis, who found poor Williams, his wife, and children, was convinced at first that the presence of a concealed madman in the country-side offered the only possible solution to the difficulty.

"I felt sure," he said to me afterward, "that the Williamses had been killed by a homicidal maniac. It was the nature of the poor creatures' injuries that convinced me that this was the case. Those poor people had their heads smashed to pieces by what must have been a storm of blows. Any one of them would have been fatal, but the murderer must have gone on raining blows with his iron hammer on people who were already stone-dead. And *that* sort of thing is the work of a madman, and nothing but a madman. That's how I argued the matter out to myself just after the event. I was utterly wrong, monstrously wrong; hut who could have suspected the truth?"

I quote Dr. Lewis, or the substance of him, as representative of most of the educated opinion of the district at the beginnings of the terror. People seized on this theory largely because it offered at least the comfort of an explanation, and any explanation, even the poorest, is better than an intolerable and terrible mystery. Resides, Dr. Lewis's theory was plausible; it explained the lack of purpose that seemed to characterize the murders.

And yet there were difficulties even from the first. It was hardly possible that a strange madman would be able to keep hidden in a countryside where any stranger is instantly noted and noticed; sooner or later he would be seen as he prowled along the lanes or across the wild places.

Then another theory, or, rather, a variant of Dr. Lewis's theory, was started. This was to the effect that the person responsible for the outrages was indeed a madman, but a madman only at intervals. It was one of the members of the Porth Club, a certain Mr. Remnant, who was supposed to have originated this more subtle explanation. Mr. Remnant was a middle-aged man who, having nothing particular to do, read a great many books by way of conquering the hours. He talked to the club—doctors, retired colonels, parsons, lawyers—about "personality," quoted various psychological text-books in support of his contention that personality was sometimes fluid and unstable, went back to "Dr. Jekyll and Mr. Hyde" as good evidence of this proposition, and laid stress on *Dr. Jekyll's* speculation that the human soul, so far from being one and indivisible, might possibly turn out to be a mere polity, a state in which dwelt many strange and incongruous citizens, whose characters were not merely unknown, but altogether unsurmised by that form of consciousness which rashly assumed that it was not only the president of the republic, but also its sole citizen.

However, Mr. Remnant's somewhat crazy theory became untenable when two more victims of an awful and mysterious death were offered up in sacrifice, for a man was found dead in the Llanfihangel quarry where the woman had been discovered, and on the same day a girl of fifteen was found broken on the jagged rocks under the cliffs near Porth. Now, it appeared that these two deaths must have occurred at about the same time, within an hour of one another, certainly, and the distance between the quarry and the cliffs by Black Rock is certainly twenty miles.

And now a fresh circumstance or set of circumstances became manifest to confound judgment and to awaken new and wild surmises; for at about this time people realized that none of the dreadful events that were happening all about them was so much as mentioned in the press. Horror followed on horror, but no word was printed in any of the local journals. The curious went to the newspaper offices,—there were two left in the county,—but found nothing save a firm refusal to discuss the matter. Then the Cardiff papers were drawn and found blank, and the London press was apparently ignorant of the fact that crimes that had no parallel were terrorizing a whole country-side. Everybody wondered what could have happened, what was happening; and then it was whispered that the coroner would allow no inquiry to be made as to these deaths of darkness.

Clearly, people reasoned, these government restrictions and prohibitions could only refer to the war, to some great danger in connection with the war. And that being so, it followed that the outrages which must be kept so secret were the work of the enemy; that is, of concealed German agents.

It is time, I think, for me to make one point clear. I began this history with certain references to an extraordinary accident to an airman whose machine fell to the ground after collision with a huge flock of pigeons, and then to an explosion in a Northern munition factory of a very singular kind. Then I deserted the neighborhood of London and the Northern district, and dwelt on a mysterious and terrible series of events which occurred in the summer of 1915 in a Welsh county, which I have named for convenience Meirion.

Well, let it be understood at once that all this detail that I have given about the occurrences in Meirion does not imply that the county in Wales was alone or specially afflicted by the terror that was over the land. They tell me that in the villages about Dartmoor the stout Devonshire hearts sank as men's hearts used to sink in the time of plague and pestilence. There was horror, too, about the Norfolk Broads, and far up by Perth no one would venture on the path that leads by Scone to the wooded heights above the Tay. And in the industrial districts. I met a man by chance one day in an odd London corner who spoke with horror of what a friend had told him.

"'Ask no questions, Ned,' he says to me, 'but I tell yow a was in Bairnigan t' other day, and a met a pal who'd seen three hundred coffins going out of a works not far from there.'"

Then there was the vessel that hovered outside the mouth of the Thames with all sails set, and beat to and fro in the wind, and never answered any signals and showed no light. The forts shot at her, and brought down one of the masts; but she went suddenly about, stood down channel, and drove ashore at last on the sand-banks and pine-woods of Arcachon, and not a man alive on her, but only rattling heaps of bones! That last voyage of the *Semiramis* would be something horribly worth telling; but I heard it only at a distance as a yarn, and believed it only because it squared with other things that I knew for certain.

This, then, is my point: I have written of the terror as it fell on Meirion simply because I have had opportunities of getting close there to what really happened.

Well, I have said that the people of that far Western county realized not only that death was abroad in their quiet lanes and on their peaceful hills, but that for some reason it was to be kept secret. And so they concluded that this veil of secrecy must somehow be connected with the war; and from this position it was not a long way to a further inference that the murderers of innocent men and women and children were either Germans or agents of Germany. It would be just like the Huns, everybody agreed, to think out such a devilish scheme as this; and they always thought out their schemes beforehand.

It all seemed plausible enough; Germany had by this time perpetrated so many horrors and had so excelled in devilish ingenuities that no abomination seemed too abominable to be probable or too ingeniously wicked to be beyond her tortuous malice. But then came the questions as to who the agents of this terrible design were, as to where they lived, as to how they contrived to move unseen from field to field, from lane to lane. All sorts of fantastic attempts were made to answer these questions, but it was felt that they remained unanswered. Some suggested that the murderers landed from submarines, or flew from hiding-places on the west coast of Ireland, coming and going by night; but there were seen to be flagrant impossibilities in both these suggestions. Everybody agreed that the evil work was no doubt the work of Germany; but nobody could begin to guess how it was done.

It was, I suppose, at about this time when the people were puzzling their heads as to the secret methods used by the Germans or their agents to accomplish their crimes that a very singular circumstance became known to a few of the Porth people. It related to the murder of the Williams family on the Highway in front of their cottage door. I do not know that I have made it plain that the old Roman road called the Highway follows the course of a long, steep hill that goes steadily westward till it slants down toward the sea. On each side of the road the ground falls away, here into deep shadowy woods, here into high pastures, but for the most part into the wild and broken land that is characteristic of Arfon.

Now, on the lower slopes of it, beneath the Williams cottage, some three or four fields down the hill, there is a military camp. The place has been used as a camp for many years, and lately the site has been extended and huts have been erected; but a considerable number of the men were under canvas here in the summer of 1915.

On the night of the Highway murder this camp, as it appeared afterward, was the scene of the extraordinary panic of horses.

A good many men in the camp were asleep in their tents soon after 9:30. They woke up in panic. There was a thundering sound on the steep hillside above them, and down upon the tents came half a dozen horses, mad with fright, trampling the canvas, trampling the men, bruising dozens of them, and killing two.

Everything was in wild confusion, men groaning and screaming in the darkness, struggling with the canvas and the twisted ropes, and some of them, raw lads enough, shouting out that the Germans had at last landed.

Some of the men had seen the horses galloping down the hill as if terror itself was driving them. They scattered off into the darkness, and somehow or other found their way. back in the night to their pasture above the camp. They were grazing there peacefully in the morning, and the only sign of the panic of the night before was the mud they had scattered all over themselves as they pelted through a patch of wet ground. The farmer said they were as quiet a lot as any in Meirion; he could make nothing of it.

Then two or three other incidents, quite as odd and incomprehensible, came to be known, borne on chance trickles of gossip that came into the towns from outland farms. And in such ways it came out that up at Plas Newydd there had been a terrible business over swarming the bees; they had turned as wild as wasps and much more savage. They had come about the people who were taking the swarms like a cloud. They settled on one man's face so that you could not see the flesh for the bees crawling over it, and they had stung him so badly that the doctor did not know whether he would get well; they had chased a girl who had come out to see the swarming, and settled on her and stung her to death. Then they had gone off to a brake below the farm and got into a hollow tree, and it was not safe to go near it, for they would come out at you by day or by night.

And much the same thing had happened, it seemed, at three or four farms and cottages where bees were kept. And there were stories, hardly so clear or so credible, of sheep-dogs, mild and trusted beasts, turning as savage as wolves and injuring the farm boys in a horrible manner, in one case, it was said, with fatal results. It was certainly true that old Mrs. Owens's favorite Dorking cock had gone mad. She came into Porth one Saturday morning with her face and her neck all bound up and plastered. She had gone out to her bit of field to feed the poultry the night before, and the bird had flown at her and attacked her most savagely, inflicting some very nasty wounds before she could beat it off.

"There was a stake handy, lucky for me," she said, "and I did beat him and beat him till the life was out of him. But what is come to the world, whatever?"

Now Remnant, the man of theories, was also a man of extreme leisure. He was no more brutal than the general public, which revels in the details of mysterious crime; but it must be said that the terror, black though it was, was a boon to him. He peered and investigated and poked about with the relish of a man to whose life a new zest has been added. He listened attentively to the strange tales of bees and dogs and poultry that came into Porth with the country baskets of butter, rabbits, and green peas, and he evolved at last a most extraordinary theory. He went one night to see Dr. Lewis.

"I want to talk to you," he said to the doctor, "about what I have called provisionally the Z-ray."

Dr. Lewis, smiling indulgently, and quite prepared for some monstrous piece of theorizing, led Remnant into the room that overlooked the terraced garden and the sea.

"I suppose, Lewis, you've heard these extraordinary stories of bees and dogs and things that have been going about lately?"

"Certainly I have heard them. I was called in at Plas Newydd. and treated Thomas Trevor, who's only just out of danger, by the way. I certified for the poor child, Mary Trevor. She was dying when I got to the place."

"Well, then there are the stories of good-tempered old sheep-dogs turning wicked and 'savaging' children."

"Quite so. I haven't seen any of these cases professionally; but I believe the stories are accurate enough."

"And the old woman assaulted by her own poultry?"

"That's perfectly true."

"Very good," said Mr. Remnant. He spoke now with an italic impressiveness, *"Don't you see the link between all this and the horrible things that have been happening about here for the last month?"*

Lewis stared at Remnant in amazement. He lifted his red eyebrows and lowered them in a kind of scowl. His speech showed traces of his native accent.

"Great burning!" he exclaimed, "what on earth are you getting at now? It is madness. Do you mean to tell me that you think there is some connection between a swarm or two of bees that have turned nasty, a cross dog, and a wicked old barn-door cock, and these poor people that have been pitched over the cliffs and hammered to death on the road? There's no sense in it, you know."

"I am strongly inclined to believe that there is a great deal of sense in it," replied Remnant, with extreme calmness. "Look here, Lewis, I saw you grinning the other day at the club when I was telling the fellows that in my opinion all these outrages had been committed, certainly by the Germans, but by some method of which we have no conception. Do you see my point?"

"Well, in a sort of way. You mean there's an absolute originality in the method? I suppose that is so. But what next?"

Remnant seemed to hesitate, partly from a sense of the portentous nature of what he was about to say, partly from a sort of half-unwillingness to part with so profound a secret.

"Well," he said, "you will allow that we have two sets of phenomena of a very extraordinary kind occurring at the same time. Don't you think that it's only reasonable to connect the two sets with one another?"

"So the philosopher of Tenterden steeple and the Goodwin Sands thought, certainly," said Lewis. "But what is the connection? Those poor folks on the Highway weren't stung by bees or worried by a dog. And horses don't throw people over cliffs or stifle them in marshes."

"No; I never meant to suggest anything so absurd. It is evident to me that in all these cases of animals turning suddenly savage the cause has been terror, panic, fear. The horses that went charging into the camp were mad with fright, we know. And I say that in the other instances we have been discussing the cause was the same. The creatures were exposed to an infection of fear, and a frightened beast or bird or insect uses its weapons, whatever they may be. If, for example, there had been anybody with those horses when they took their panic, they would have lashed out at him with their heels."

"Yes, I dare say that that is so. Well?" demanded the doctor.

"Well, my belief is that the Germans have made an extraordinary discovery. I have called it the Z-ray. You know that the ether is merely an hypothesis; we have to suppose that it's there to account for the passage of the Marconi current from one place to another. Now, suppose that there is a psychic ether as well as a material ether, suppose that it is possible to direct irresistible impulses across this medium, suppose that these impulses are toward murder or suicide; then I think that you have an explanation of the terrible series of events that have been happening in Meirion for the last few weeks. And it is quite clear to my mind that the horses and the other creatures have been exposed to this Z-ray, and that it has produced on them the effect of terror, with ferocity as the result of terror. Now, what do you say to that? Telepathy, you know, is well established; so is hypnotic suggestion.

Now don't you feel that putting telepathy and suggestion together, as it were, you have more than the elements of what I call the Z-ray? I feel that I have more to go on in making my hypothesis than the inventor of the steam-engine had in making his hypothesis when he saw the lid of the kettle bobbing up and down. What do you say?"

Dr. Lewis made no answer. He was watching the growth of a new, unknown tree in his garden.

It was a dark summer night. The moon was old and faint above the Dragon's Head, on the opposite side of the bay, and the air was very still. It was so still that Lewis had noted that not a leaf stirred on the very tip of a high tree that stood out against the sky; and yet he knew that he was listening to some sound that he could not determine or define. It was not the wind in the leaves, it was not the gentle wash of the water of the sea against the rocks; that latter sound he could distinguish easily. But there was something else. It was scarcely a sound; it was as if the air itself trembled and fluttered, as the air trembles in a church when they open the great pedal pipes of the organ.

The doctor listened intently. It was not an illusion, the sound was not in his own head, as he had suspected for a moment; but for the life of him he could not make out whence it came or what it was. He gazed down into the night, over the terraces of his garden, now sweet with the scent of the flowers of the night; tried to peer over the tree-tops across the sea toward the Dragon's Head. It struck him suddenly that this strange, fluttering vibration of the air might be the noise of a distant aëroplane or airship; there was not the usual droning hum, but this sound might be caused by a new type of engine. A new type of engine? Possibly it was an enemy airship; their range, it had been said, was getting longer, and Lewis was just going to call Remnant's attention to the sound, to its possible cause, and to the possible danger that might be hovering over them, when he saw something that caught his breath and his heart with wild amazement and a touch of terror.

He had been staring upward into the sky, and, about to speak to Remnant, he had let his eyes drop for an instant. He looked down toward the trees in the garden, and saw with utter astonishment that one had changed its shape in the few hours that had passed since the setting of the sun. There was a thick grove of ilexes bordering the lowest terrace, and above them rose one tall pine, spreading its head of sparse branches dark against the sky.

As Lewis glanced down over the terraces he saw that the tall pine-tree was no longer there. In its place there rose above the ilexes what might have been a greater ilex; there was the blackness of a dense growth of foliage rising like a broad, far-spreading, and rounded cloud over the lesser trees.

Dr. Lewis glared into the dimness of the night, at the great, spreading tree that he knew could not be there. And as he gazed he saw that what at first appeared the dense blackness of foliage was fretted and starred with wonderful appearances of lights and colors.

The night had gloomed over; clouds obscured the faint moon and the misty stars. Lewis rose, with some kind of warning and inhibiting gesture to Remnant, who, he was aware, was gaping at him in astonishment. He walked to the open French window, took a pace forward on the path outside, and looked very intently at the dark shape of the tree. He shaded the light of the lamp behind him by holding his hands on each side of his eyes.

The mass of the tree—the tree that couldn't be there—stood out against the sky, but not so clearly now that the clouds had rolled up. Its edges, the limits of its leafage, were not so distinct. Lewis thought that he could detect some sort of quivering movement in it, though the air was at a dead calm. It was a night on which one might hold up a lighted match and watch it burn without any wavering or inclination of the flame.

"You know," said Lewis, "how a bit of burned paper will sometimes hang over the coals before it goes up the chimney, and little worms of fire will shoot through it. It was like that, if you should be standing some distance away. Just threads and hairs of yellow light I saw, and specks and sparks of fire, and then a twinkling of a ruby no bigger than a pin-point, and a green wandering in the black, as if an emerald were crawling, and then little veins of deep blue. 'Woe is me!' I said to myself in Welsh. 'What is all this color and burning?'

"At that very moment there came a thundering rap at the door of the room inside, and there was my man telling me that I was wanted directly up at the Garth, as old Mr. Trevor Williams had been taken very bad. I knew his heart was not worth much, so I had to go off directly, and leave Remnant alone to make what he could of it all."

Dr. Lewis was kept some time at the Garth. It was past twelve when he got back to his house. He went quickly to the room that overlooked the garden and the sea, threw open the French window, and peered into the darkness. There, dim indeed against the dim sky, but unmistakable, was the tall pine, with its sparse branches, high above the dense growth of the ilex-trees. The strange boughs which had amazed him had vanished; there was no appearance of colors or of fires.

The doctor did not say anything about the strange tree to Remnant. When they next met, he said that he had thought there was a man hiding among the bushes. This was in explanation of that warning gesture he had used, and of his going out into the garden and staring into the night. He concealed the truth because he dreaded the Remnant doctrine that would undoubtedly be produced; indeed, he hoped that he had heard the last of the theory of the Z-ray. But Remnant firmly reopened this subject.

"We were interrupted just as I was putting my case to you," he said. "And to sum it all up, it amounts to this: the Huns have made one of the great leaps of science. They are sending 'suggestions' (which amount to irresistible commands) over here, and the persons affected are seized with suicidal or homicidal mania. In my opinion Evans was the murderer of the Williams family. You know he said he stopped to talk to Williams. It seems to me simple. And as for the animals,—the horses, dogs, and so forth,—they, as I say, were no doubt panic-stricken by the ray, and hence driven to frenzy."

"Why should Evans have murdered Williams instead of Williams murdering Evans? Why should the impact of the ray affect one and not the other?"

"Why does one man react violently to a certain drug, while it makes no impression on another man? Why is A able to drink a bottle of whisky and remain sober, while B is turned into something very like a lunatic after he has drunk three glasses?"

"It is a question of idiosyncrasy," said the doctor.

Lewis escaped from the club and from Remnant. He did not want to hear any more about that dreadful ray, because he felt sure that the ray was all nonsense. But asking himself why he felt this certitude in the matter, he had to confess that he didn't know. An aëroplane, he reflected, was all nonsense before it was made.

But he thought with fervor of the extraordinary thing he had seen in his own garden with his own eyes. How could one fail to be afraid with great amazement at the thought of such a mystery?

Dr. Lewis's thoughts were distracted from the incredible adventure of the tree by the visit of his sister and her husband. Mr. and Mrs. Merritt lived in a well-known manufacturing town of the Midlands, which was now, of course, a center of munition work. On the day of their arrival at Porth, Mrs. Merritt, who was tired after the long, hot journey, went to bed early, and Merritt and Lewis went into the room by the garden for their talk and tobacco. They spoke of the year that had passed since their last meeting, of the weary dragging of the war, of friends that had perished in it, of the hopelessness of an early ending of all this misery. Lewis said nothing of the terror that was on the land. One does not greet with a tale of horror a tired man who is come to a quiet, sunny place for relief from black smoke and work and worry. Indeed, the doctor saw that his brother-in-law looked far from well. He seemed "jumpy"; there was an occasional twitch of his mouth that Lewis did not like at all.

"Well," said the doctor, after an interval of silence and port wine, "I am glad to see you here again. Porth always suits you. I don't think you're looking quite up to your usual form; but three weeks of Meirion air will do wonders."

"Well, I hope it will," said the other. "I am not up to the mark. Things are not going well at Midlingham."

"Business is all right, isn't it?"

"Yes; but there are other things that are all wrong. We are living under a reign of terror. It comes to that."

"What on earth do you mean?"

"It's not much. I didn't dare write it. But do you know that at every one of the munition-works in Midlingham and all about it there's a guard of soldiers with drawn bayonets and loaded rifles day and night? Men with bombs, too. And machine-guns at the big factories."

"German spies?"

"You don't want machine-guns and bombs to fight spies with."

"But what against?"

"Nobody knows. Nobody knows what is happening," Merritt repeated, and he went on to describe the bewilderment and terror that hung like a cloud over the great industrial city in the Midlands; how the feeling of concealment, or some intolerable secret danger that must not be named, was worst of all.

Merritt made a sort of picture of the great town cowering in its fear of an unknown danger.

"There's a queer story going about," he said, "as to a place right out in the country, over the other side of Midlingham. They've built one of the new factories out there, a great red brick town of sheds. About two hundred yards from this place there's an old footpath through a pretty large wood, most of it thick undergrowth. It's a black place of nights.

"A man had to go this way one night. He got along all right till he came to the wood, and then he said his heart dropped out of his body. It was awful to hear the noises in that wood. Thousands of men were in it, he swears. It was full of rustling, and pattering of feet trying to go dainty, and the crack of dead boughs lying on the ground as some one trod on them, and swishing of the grass, and some sort of chattering speech going on that sounded, so he said, as if the dead sat in their bones and talked! He ran for his life, anyhow, across fields, over hedges, through brooks. He must have run, by his tale, ten miles out of his way before he got home to his wife, beat at the door, broke in, and bolted it behind him."

"There is something rather alarming about any wood at night," said Dr. Lewis.

Merritt shrugged his shoulders.

"People say that the Germans have landed, and that they are hiding in underground places all over the country."

Lewis gasped for a moment, silent in contemplation of the magnificence of rumor. The Germans already landed, hiding underground, striking by night, secretly, terribly, at the power of England! It was monstrous, and yet—

"People say they've got a new kind of poison-gas," continued Merritt. "Some think that they dig underground places and make the gas there, and lead it by secret pipes into the shops; others say that they throw gas bombs into the factories. It must be worse than anything they've used in France, from what the authorities say."

"The authorities? Do *they* admit that there are Germans in hiding about Midlingham?"

"No. They call it 'explosions.' But *we* know it isn't explosions. We know in the Midlands what an explosion sounds like and looks like. And we know that the people killed in these 'explosions' are put into their coffins in the works. Their own relations are not allowed to see them."

"And do you believe in the German theory?"

"If I do, it's because one must believe in something. Some say they've seen the gas. I heard that a man living in Dunwich saw it one night like a black cloud, with sparks of fire in it, floating over the tops of the trees by Dunwich Common."

The light of an ineffable amazement came into Lewis's eyes. The night of Remnant's visit, the trembling vibration of the air, the dark tree that had grown in his garden since the setting of the sun, the strange leafage that was starred with burning, and all vanished away when he returned from his visit to the Garth; and such a leafage had appeared as a burning cloud far in the heart of England. What intolerable mystery, what tremendous doom was signified in this? But one thing was clear and certain: the terror of Meirion was also the terror of the Midlands.

Merritt told the story of how a Swedish professor, Huvelius, had sold to the Germans a plan for filling England with German soldiers. Land was to be bought in certain suitable and well-considered places, Englishmen were to be bought as the apparent owners of such land, and secret excavations were to be made, till the country was literally undermined. A subterranean Germany, in fact, was to be dug under selected districts of England; there were to be great caverns, underground cities, well drained, well ventilated, supplied with water, and in these places vast stores both of food and of munitions were to be accumulated year after year till "the Day" dawned. And then, warned in time, the secret garrison would leave shops, hotels, offices, villas, and vanish underground, ready to begin their work of bleeding England at the heart.

"Well," said Lewis, "of course, it may be so. If it is so, it is terrible beyond words."

Indeed, he found something horribly plausible in the story. It was an extraordinary plan, of course, an unheard-of scheme; but it did not seem impossible. It was the Trojan Horse on a gigantic scale. And this theory certainly squared with what one had heard of German preparations in Belgium and in France.

And it seemed from that wonder of the burning tree that the enemy mysteriously and terribly present at Midlingham was present also in Meirion. Yet, he thought again, there was but little harm to be done in Meirion to the armies of England or to their munitionment. They were working for panic terror. Possibly that might be so; but the camp under the Highway? That should be their first object, and no harm had been done there.

Lewis did not know that since the panic of the horses men had died terribly in that camp; that it was now a fortified place, with a deep, broad trench, a thick tangle of savage barbed wire about it, and a machine-gun planted at each corner.

One evening the doctor was summoned to a little hamlet on the outskirts of Porth. In one of the cottages the doctor found a father and mother weeping and crying out to "Doctor Bach, Doctor Bach," two frightened children, and one little body, still and dead.

The doctor found that the child had been asphyxiated. His clothes were dry; it was not a case of drowning. There was no mark of strangling. He asked the father how it had happened, and father and mother, weeping most lamentably, declared they had no knowledge of how their child had been killed, "unless it was the People that had done it." The Celtic fairies are still malignant. Lewis asked what had happened that evening; where had the child been?

"Was he with his brother and sister?" asked the doctor. "Don't they know anything about it?"

The children had been playing in the road at dusk, and just as their mother called them in one child had heard Johnnie cry out:

"Oh, what is that beautiful, shiny thing over the stile?"

They found the little body, under the ash-grove in the middle of the field. He was quite still and dead, so still that a great moth had settled on his forehead, fluttering away when they lifted him up.

Dr. Lewis heard this story. There was nothing to be done, little to be said to these most unhappy people.

"Take care of the two that you have left to you," said the doctor as he went away. "Don't let them out of your sight if you can help it. It is dreadful times that we are living in."

About ten days later a young farmer had been found by his wife lying in the grass close to the castle, with no scar on him or any mark of violence, but stone-dead.

Lewis was sent for, and knew at once, when he saw the dead man, that he had perished in the way that the little boy had perished, whatever that awful way might be.

It seemed that he had gone out at about half -past nine to look after some beasts. He told his wife he would be back in a quarter of an hour or twenty minutes. He did not return, and when he had been gone for three quarters of an hour Mrs. Cradock went out to look for him. She went into the field where the beasts were, and everything seemed all right; but there was no trace of Cradock. She called out; there was no answer.

She told the doctor:

"There was something that I could not make out at all. It seemed to me that the hedge did look different from usual. To be sure, things do look different at night, and there was a bit of sea mist about; but somehow it did look odd to me, and I said to myself, 'Have I lost my way, then?'"

She declared that the shape of the trees in the hedge appeared to have changed, and besides, it had a look "as if it was lighted up, somehow," and so she went on toward the stile to see what all this could be; and when she came near, everything was as usual. She looked over the stile and called, hoping to see her husband coming toward her or to hear his voice; but there was no answer, and glancing down the path, she saw, or thought she saw, some sort of brightness on the ground, "a dim sort of light, like a bunch of glow-worms in a hedge-bank.

"And so I climbed over the stile and went down the path, and the light seemed to melt away; and there was my poor husband lying on his back, saying not a word to me when I spoke to him and touched him."

So for Lewis the terror blackened and became altogether intolerable, and others, he perceived, felt as he did. He did not know, he never asked, whether the men at the club had heard of these deaths of the child and the young farmer; but no one spoke of them. Indeed, the change was evident; at the beginning of the terror men spoke of nothing else; now it had become all too awful for ingenious chatter or labored and grotesque theories. And Lewis had received a letter from his brother-in-law, who had gone back to Midlingham: it contained the sentence, "I am afraid Fanny's health has not greatly benefited by her visit to Porth; there are still several symptoms I don't at all like." This told him, in a phraseology that the doctor and Merritt had agreed upon, that the terror remained heavy in the Midland town.

It was soon after the death of Cradock that people began to tell strange tales of a sound that was to be heard of nights about the hills and valleys to the northward of Porth. A man who had missed the last train from Meiros and had been forced to tramp the ten miles between Meiros and Porth seems to have been the first to hear it. He said he had got to the top of the hill by Tredonoc, somewhere between half-past ten and eleven, when he first noticed an odd noise that he could not make out at all; it was like a shout, a long drawn-out, dismal wail coming from a great way off. He stopped to listen, thinking at first that it might be owls hooting in the woods; but it was different, he said, from that. He could make nothing of it, and feeling frightened, he did not quite know of what, he walked on briskly, and was glad to see the lights of Porth station. Then others heard it.

Let it be remembered again and again that all the while that the terror lasted there was no common stock of information as to the dreadful things that were being done. The press had not said one word upon it, there was no criterion by which the mass of the people could separate fact from mere vague rumor, no test by which ordinary misadventure or disaster could be distinguished from the achievements of the secret and awful force that was at work. And since the real nature of all this mystery of death was unknown, it followed easily that the signs and warnings and omens of it were all the more unknown. Here was horror, there was horror; but there were no links to join one horror with another, no common basis of knowledge from which the connection between this horror and that horror might be inferred.

The sound had been heard for three or perhaps four nights, when the people coming out of Tredonoc church after morning service on Sunday noticed that there was a big yellow sheep-dog in the church-yard. The dog, it appeared, had been waiting for the congregation; for it at once attached itself to them, at first to the whole body, and then to a group of half a dozen who took the turning to the right till they came to a gate in the hedge, whence a roughly made farm-road went through the fields, and dipped down into the woods and to Treff Loyne farm.

Then the dog became like a possessed creature. He barked furiously. He ran up to one of the men and looked up at him, "as if he were begging for his life," as the man said, and then rushed to the gate and stood by it, wagging his tail and barking at intervals. The men stared.

"Whose dog will that be?" said one of them.

"It will be Thomas Griffith's, Treff Loyne," said another.

"Well, then, why doesn't he go home? Go home, then!" He went through the gesture of picking up a stone from the road and throwing it at the dog. "Go home, then! Over the gate with you!"

But the dog never stirred. He barked and whined and ran up to the men and then back to the gate. The farmer shook the dog off, and the four went on their way, and the dog stood in the road and watched them, and then put up its head and uttered a long and dismal howl that was despair.

Then it occurred to somebody. so far as I can make out with no particular reference to the odd conduct of the Treff Loyne sheep-dog, that Thomas Griffith had not been seen for some time past.

One September afternoon, therefore, a party went up to discover what had happened to Griffith and his family. There were half a dozen farmers, a couple of policemen, and four soldiers, carrying their arms; those last had been lent by the officer commanding at the camp. Lewis, too, was of the party; he had heard by chance that no one knew what had become. of Griffith and his family, and he was anxious about a young fellow, a painter, of his acquaintance who had been lodging at Treff Loyne all the summer.

They came to the gate in the hedge where the farm-road led down to Treff Loyne. Here was the farm inclosure, the outlying walls of the yard and the barns and sheds and outhouses. One of the farmers threw open the gate and walked into the yard, and forthwith began bellowing at the top of his voice:

"Thomas Griffith! Thomas Griffith! Where are you, Thomas Griffith?"

The rest followed him. The corporal snapped out an order over his shoulder, and there was a rattling metallic noise as the men fixed their bayonets.

There was no answer to this summons; but they found poor Griffith lying on his face at the edge of the pond in the middle of the yard. There was a ghastly wound in his side, as if a sharp stake had been driven into his body.

It was a still September afternoon. No wind stirred in the hanging woods that were dark all about the ancient house of Treff Loyne; the only sound in the dim air was the lowing of the cattle. They had wandered, it seemed, from the fields and had come in by the gate of the farmyard and stood there melancholy, as if they mourned for their dead master. And the horses, four great, heavy, patient-looking beasts, were there, too, and in the lower field the sheep were standing, as if they waited to be fed.

Lewis knelt down by the dead man and looked closely at the gaping wound in his side.

"He's been dead a long time," he said. "How about the family? How many are there of them? I never attended them."

"There was Griffith, and his wife, his son Thomas, and Mary Griffith, his daughter. And I do think there was a gentleman lodging with them this summer."

That was from one of the farmers. They all looked at one another, this party of rescue, who knew nothing of the danger that had smitten this house of quiet people, nothing of the peril which had brought them to this pass of a farm-yard, with a dead man in it, and his beasts standing patiently about him as if they waited for the farmer to rise up and give them their food. Then the party turned to the house. The windows were shut tight. There was no sign of any life or movement about the place. The party of men looked at one another.

They did not know what the danger was or where it might strike them or whether it was from without or from within. They stared at the murdered man, and gazed dismally at one another.

"Come," said Lewis, "we must do something. We must get into the house and see what is wrong."

"Yes, but suppose they are at us while we are getting in?" said the sergeant. "Where shall we be then, Doctor Lewis?"

The corporal put one of his men by the gate at the top of the farm-yard, another at the gate by the bottom, and told them to challenge and shoot. The doctor and the rest opened the little gate of the front garden and went up to the porch and stood listening by the door. It was all dead silence. Lewis took an ash stick from one of the farmers and beat heavily three times on the old, black, oaken door studded with antique nails.

There was no answer from within. He beat again, and still silence.

He shouted to the people within, but there was no answer. They all turned and looked at one another. There was an iron ring on the door. Lewis turned it, but the door stood fast; it was evidently barred and bolted. The sergeant of police called out to open, but again there was no answer.

They consulted together. There was nothing for it but to blow the door open, and some one of them called in a loud voice to those that might be within to stand away from the door or they would be killed. And at this very moment the yellow sheep-dog came bounding up the yard from the woods and licked their hands and fawned on them and bared joyfully.

"Indeed, now," said one of the farmers, "he did know that there was something amiss. A pity it was, Thomas Williams, that we did not follow him when he implored us last Sunday."

The corporal disengaged his bayonet and shot into the keyhole, calling out once more before he fired. He shot and shot again, so heavy and firm was the ancient door, so stout its bolts and fastenings. At last he had to fire at the massive hinges, and then they all pushed together, and at that the door lurched open suddenly and fell forward.

Young Griffith was lying dead before the hearth. They went on toward the parlor, and in the doorway of the room was the body of the artist Secretan, as if he had fallen in trying to get to the kitchen. Upstairs the two women, Mrs. Griffith and her daughter, a girl of eighteen, were lying together on the bed in the big bedroom, clasped in each other's arms.

They went about the house, searched the pantries, the back kitchen, and the cellars; there was no life in it. There was no bread in the place, no milk. No water.

The group of men stood in the big kitchen and stared at one another, a dreadful perplexity in their eyes. The old man had been killed with the piercing thrust of some sharp weapon; the rest had perished, it seemed probable, of thirst; but what possible enemy was this that besieged the farm and shut in its inhabitants? There was no answer.

The sergeant of police spoke of getting a cart and taking the bodies into Porth, and Dr. Lewis went into the parlor that Secretan had used as a sitting-room, intending to gather any possessions or effects of the dead artist that he might possibly find there. Half a dozen portfolios were piled up in one corner, there were some books on a side-table, a fishing-rod and basket behind the door; that seemed all. Lewis was about to rejoin the rest of the party in the kitchen, when he looked down at some scattered papers lying with the books on the side-table. On one of the sheets he read, to his astonishment, the words, "Dr. James Lewis, Porth." This was written in a staggering, trembling scrawl.

The table stood in a dark corner of the room, and Lewis gathered up the sheets of paper and took them to the window and began to read this:

> I do not think that I can last much longer. We shared out the last drops of water a long time ago. I do not know how many days ago. We fall asleep and dream and walk about the house in our dreams, and I am often not sure whether I am awake or still dreaming, and so the days and nights are confused in my mind. I awoke not long ago, at least I suppose I awoke, and found I was lying in the passage.
>
> There seems no hope for any of us. We are in the dream of death.

Here the manuscript became unintelligible for half a dozen lines. There was a fresh start, as it were, and the writer began again, in ordinary letter-form:

DEAR LEWIS:

> I hope you will excuse all this confusion and wandering. I intended to begin a proper letter to you, and now I find all that stuff that you have been reading, if this ever gets into your hands. I have not the energy even to tear it up. If you read it you will know to what a sad pass I had come when it was written.
>
> I have said of what I am writing, "if this ever gets into your hands," and I am not at all sure that it ever will. If what is happening here is happening everywhere else, then, I suppose, the world is coming to an end. I cannot understand it; even now I can hardly believe it.
>
> And then there's another thing that bothers me. Now and then I wonder whether we are not all mad together in this house. Despite what I see and know, or, perhaps, I should say, because what I see and know is so impossible, I wonder whether we are not all suffering from a delusion. Perhaps we are our own jailers, and we are really free to go out and live. Perhaps what we think we see is not there at all. I wonder now and then whether we are all like this in Treff Loyne; yet in my heart I feel sure that it is not so.
>
> Still, I do not want to leave a madman's letter behind me, and so I will not tell you the full story of what I have seen or believe I have seen. If I

am a sane man, you will be able to fill in the blanks for yourself from your own knowledge. If I am mad, burn the letter and say nothing about it.

I think that it was on a Tuesday that we first noticed that there was something queer about. I came home about five or six o'clock and found the family at Treff Loyne laughing at old Tiger, the sheep-dog. He was making short runs from the farm-yard to the door of the house, barking, with quick, short yelps. Mrs. Griffith and Miss Griffith were standing by the porch, and the dog would go to them, look into their faces, and then run up the farm-yard to the gate, and then look back with that eager, yelping bark, as if he were waiting for the women to follow him. Then, again and again he ran up to them and tugged at their skirts, as if he would pull them by main force away from the house.

The dog barked and yelped and whined and scratched at the door all through the evening. They let him in once, but he seemed to have become quite frantic. He ran up to one member of the family after another; his eyes were bloodshot, and his mouth was foaming, and he tore at their clothes till they drove him out again into the darkness. Then he broke into a long, lamentable howl of anguish, and we heard no more of him.

It was soon after dawn when I finally roused myself. The people in the house were talking to each other in high voices, arguing about something that I did not understand.

"It is those damned Gipsies. I tell you," said old Griffith.

"What would they do a thing like that for?" asked Mrs. Griffith. "If it was stealing, now—"

They seemed puzzled and angry, so far as I could make out, but not at all frightened. I got up and began to dress. I don't think I looked out of the window. The glass on my dressing-table is high and broad, and the window is small; one would have to poke one's head round the glass to see anything.

The voices were still arguing down-stairs. I heard the old man say, "Well, here's for a beginning, anyhow," and then the door slammed.

A minute later the old man shouted, I think, to his son. Then there was a great noise which I will not describe more particularly, and a dreadful screaming and crying inside the house and a sound of rushing feet. They all cried out at once to each other. I heard the daughter crying: "It is no good, Mother; he is dead. Indeed they have killed him," and Mrs. Griffith screaming to the girl to let her go. And then one of them rushed out of the kitchen and shot the great bolts of oak across the door just as something beat against it with a thundering crash.

I ran down-stairs. I found them all in wild confusion, in an agony of grief and horror and amazement. They were like people who had seen something so awful that they had gone mad.

I went to the window looking out on the farm-yard. I won't tell you all that I saw, but I saw poor old Griffith lying by the pond, with the blood pouring out of his side.

I wanted to go out to him and bring him in. But they told me that he must be stone-dead, and such things also that it was quite plain that any one who went out of the house would not live more than a moment. We could not believe it even as we gazed at the body of the dead man; but it was there. I used to wonder sometimes what one would feel like if one saw an apple drop from the tree and shoot up into the air and disappear. I think I know now how one would feel.

Even then we couldn't believe that it would last. We were not seriously afraid for ourselves. We spoke of getting out in an hour or two, before dinner, anyhow. It couldn't last, because it was impossible. Indeed, at twelve o'clock young Griffith said he would go down to the well by the back way and draw another pail of water. I went to the door and stood by it. He had not gone a dozen yards before they were on him. He ran for his life, and we had all we could do to bar the door in time. And then I began to get frightened.

But day followed day, and it was still there. I went to Treff Loyne because it was buried in the narrow valley under the ash-trees, far away from any track. There was not so much as a footpath that was near it; no one ever came that way.

And now this thought came back without delight, with terror. Griffith thought that a shout might be heard on a still night up away on the Allt, "if a man was listening for it," he added doubtfully. My voice was clearer and stronger than his, and on the second night I said I would go up to my bedroom and call for help through the open window. I waited till it was all dark and still, and looked out through the window before opening it. And then I saw over the ridge of the long barn across the yard what looked like a tree, though I knew there was no tree there. It was a dark mass against the sky, with wide-spread boughs, a tree of thick, dense growth. I wondered what this could be, and I threw open the window not only because I was going to call for help, but because I wanted to see more clearly what the dark growth over the barn really was.

I saw in the depth of it points of fire, and colors in light, all glowing and moving, and the air trembled. I stared out into the night, and the dark tree lifted over the roof of the barn, rose up in the air, and floated toward me. I did not move till it was close to the house; and then I saw what it was, and banged the window down only just in time. I had to fight, and I saw the tree that was like a burning cloud rise up in the night and settle over the barn.

Another day went by, and at dusk I looked out, but the eyes of fire were watching me. I dared not open the window. And then I thought of another plan. There was the great old fireplace, with the round Flemish chimney going high above the house. If I stood beneath it and shouted, I thought perhaps the sound might be carried better than if I called out of the window; for all I knew the round chimney might act as a sort of megaphone. Night after night, then, I stood on the hearth and called for help from nine o'clock to eleven.

But we had drunk up the beer, and we would let ourselves have water only by little drops, and on the fourth night my throat was dry, and I began to feel strange and weak; I knew that all the voice I had in my lungs would hardly reach the length of the field by the farm.

It was then we began to dream of wells and fountains, and water coming very cold, in little drops, out of rocky places in the middle of a cool wood. We had given up all meals; now and then one would cut a lump from the sides of bacon on the kitchen wall and chew a bit of it, but the saltness was like fire.

And then we began to dream, as I say. And one day I dreamed that there was a bubbling well of cold, clear water in the cellar, and I had just hollowed my hand to drink it when I woke. I went into the kitchen and told young Griffith. I said I was sure there was water there. He shook his head, but he took up the great kitchen poker and we went down to the old cellar. I showed him the stone by the pillar, and he raised it up. But there was no well. Later I came upon young Griffith one evening evidently trying to make a subterranean passage under one of the walls of the house. I knew he was mad, as he knew I was mad when he saw me digging for a well in the cellar; but neither said anything to the other.

Now we are past all this. We are too weak. We dream when we are awake and when we dream we think we wake. Night and day come and go, and we mistake one for another.

Only a little while ago I heard a voice which sounded as if it were at my very ears, but rang and echoed and resounded as if it were rolling and reverberated from the vault of some cathedral, chanting in terrible modulations. I heard the words quite clearly, "Incipit liber iræ Domini Dei nostri" ("Here beginneth The Book of the Wrath of the Lord our God").

And then the voice sang the word *Aleph*, prolonging it, it seemed through ages, and a light was extinguished as it began the chapter:

"In that day, saith the Lord, there shall be a cloud over the land, and in the cloud a burning and a shape of fire, and out of the cloud shall issue forth my messengers; they shall run all together, they shall not turn aside; this shall be a day of exceeding bitter-

ness, without salvation. And on every high hill, saith the Lord of Hosts, I will set my sentinels, and my armies shall encamp in the place of every valley: in the house that is amongst rushes I will execute judgment, and in vain shall they fly for refuge to the munitions of the rocks. In the groves of the woods, in the places where the leaves are as a tent above them, they shall find the sword of the slayer: and they that put their trust in walled cities shall be confounded. Woe unto the armed man, woe unto him that taketh pleasure in the strength of his artillery, for a little thing shall smite him, and by one that hath no might shall he be brought down into the dust. That which is low shall be set on high; I will make the lamb and the young sheep to be as the lion from the swellings of Jordan; they shall not spare, saith the Lord, and the doves shall be as eagles on the hill Engedi: none shall be found that may abide the onset of their battle."

Here the manuscript lapsed again and finally into utter, lamentable confusion of thought.

Dr. Lewis maintained that we should never begin to understand the real significance of life until we began to study just those aspects of it which we now dismiss and overlook as utterly inexplicable and therefore unimportant.

We were discussing a few months ago the awful shadow of the terror which at length had passed away from the land. I had formed my opinion, partly from observation, partly from certain facts which had been communicated to me, and the passwords having been exchanged, I found that Lewis had come by very different ways to the same end.

"And yet," he said, "it is not a true end, or, rather, it is like all the ends of human inquiry—it leads one to a great mystery. We must confess that what has happened might have happened at any time in the history of the world. It did not happen till a year ago, as a matter of fact and therefore we made up our minds that it never could happen; or, one would better say, it was outside the range even of imagination. But this is our way. Most people are quite sure that the Black Death— otherwise the Plague—will never invade Europe again. They have made up their complacent minds that it was due to dirt and bad drainage. As a matter of fact the Plague had nothing to do with dirt or with drains, and there is nothing to prevent its ravaging England tomorrow. But if you tell people so, they won't believe you."

I agreed with all this. I added that sometimes the world was incapable of seeing, much less believing, that which was before its own eyes.

"Look," I said, "at any eighteenth-century print of a Gothic cathedral. You will find that the trained artistic eye even could not behold in any true sense the building that was before it. I have seen an old print of Peterborough Cathedral that looks as if the artist had drawn it from a clumsy model, constructed of bent wire and children's bricks."

"Exactly; because Gothic was outside the esthetic theory, and therefore vision, of the time. You can't believe what you don't see; rather, you can't see what you don't believe.

"You must not suppose that my experiences of that afternoon at Treff Loyne had afforded me the slightest illumination. Indeed, if it had not been that I had seen poor old Griffith's body lying pierced in his own farm-yard, I think I should have been inclined to accept one of Secretan's hints, and to believe that the whole family had fallen a victim to a collective delusion or hallucination, and had shut themselves up and died of thirst through sheer madness. I think there have been such cases. But I had seen the body of the murdered man and the wound that had killed him.

"Did the manuscript left by Secretan give me no hint? Well, it seemed to me to make confusion worse confounded. You see, Secretan, in writing that extraordinary document, almost insisted on the fact that he was not in his proper senses; that for days he had been part asleep, part awake, part delirious. How was one to judge his statement, to separate delirium from fact? In one thing he stood confirmed; you remember he speaks of calling for help up the old chimney of Treff Loyne; that did seem to fit in with the tales of a hollow, moaning cry that had been heard upon the Allt. So far one could take him as a recorder of actual experiences. And I looked in the old cellars of the farm and found a frantic sort of rabbit-hole dug by one of the pillars; again he was confirmed. But what was one to make of that story of the chanting voice and the letters of the Hebrew alphabet and the chapter out of some unknown minor prophet? When one has the key it is easy enough to sort out the facts or the hints of facts from the delusions; but I hadn't the key on that September evening. I was forgetting the 'tree' with lights and fires in it; that, I think, impressed me more than anything with the feeling that Secretan's story was in the main a true story. I had seen a like appearance down there in my own garden; but what was it?

"Now, I was saying that, paradoxically, it is only by the inexplicable things that life can be explained. We are apt to say, you know, 'a very odd coincidence,' and pass the matter by, as if there were no more to be said or as if that were the end of it. Well, I believe that the only real path lies through the blind alleys."

"How do you mean?"

"Well, this is an instance of what I mean. I was talking with Merritt, my brother-in-law, about the strange things he had seen in a way that I thought all nonsense, and I was wondering how I was going to shut him up when a big moth flew into the room through that window, fluttered about, and succeeded in burning itself alive in the lamp. That gave me my cue. I asked Merritt if he knew why moths made for lamps or something of the kind; I thought it would be a hint to him that I was sick of his half-baked theories. So it was; he looked sulky and held his tongue.

"But a few minutes later I was called out by a man who had found his little boy dead in a field near his cottage about an hour before. The child was so still, they said, that a great moth had settled on his forehead and fluttered away only when they lifted up the body. It was absolutely illogical; but it was this odd 'coincidence' of the moth in my lamp and the moth on the dead boy's forehead that first set me on the track. I can't say that it guided me in any real sense; it was more like a great flare of red paint on a wall.

"But, as you will remember, from having read my notes on the matter, I was called in about ten days later to see a man named Cradock who had been found in a field near his farm quite dead. This also was at night. His wife found him, and there were some very queer things in her story. She said that the hedge of the field looked as if it were changed; she began to be afraid that she had lost her way and got into the wrong field.

"Then came that extraordinary business of Treff Loyne. I took it all home, and sat down for the evening before it. It appalled me not only by its horror, but here again by the discrepancy between its terms.

"It was, I believe, a sudden leap of the mind that liberated me from the tangle. It was quite beyond logic. I went back to that evening when Merritt was boring me, to the moth in the candle, and to the moth on the forehead of poor Johnnie Roberts. There was no sense in it; but I suddenly determined that the child and Joseph Cradock the farmer, and that unnamed Stratfordshire man, all found at night, all asphyxiated, had been choked by vast swarms of moths. I don't pretend even now that this is demonstrated, but I'm sure it's true.

"Now suppose you encounter a swarm of these creatures in the dark. Suppose the smaller ones fly up your nostrils. You will gasp for breath and open your mouth. Then, suppose some hundreds of them fly into your mouth, into your gullet, into your windpipe, what will happen to you? You will be dead in a very short time, choked, asphyxiated."

"But the moths would be dead, too. They would be found in the bodies."

"The moths? Do you know that it is extremely difficult to kill a moth with cyanide of potassium? Take a frog, kill it, open its stomach. There you will find its dinner of moths and small beetles, and the 'dinner' will shake itself and walk off cheerily, to resume an entirely active existence. No; that is no difficulty.

"Well, now I came to this. I was shutting out all the other cases. I was confining myself to those that came under the one formula.

"Then the next step. Of course we know nothing really about moths; rather, we know nothing of moth reality. For all I know there may be hundreds of books which treat of moths and nothing but moths. But these are scientific books, and science deals only with surfaces. It has nothing to do with realities. To take a very minor matter: we don't even know why the moth desires the flame. But we do know what the moth does not do; it does not gather itself into swarms with the object of destroying human life. But here, by the hypothesis, were cases in which the moth had done this very thing; the moth race had entered, it seemed, into a malignant conspiracy against the human race. It was quite impossible, no doubt,—that is to say, it had never happened before,—but I could see no escape from this conclusion.

"These insects, then, were definitely hostile to man; and then I stopped, for I could not see the next step, obvious though it seems to me now. If the moths were infected with hatred of men, and possessed the design and the power of combining against him, why not suppose this hatred, this design, this power shared by other non-human creatures?

"The secret of the Terror might be condensed into a sentence: the animals had revolted against men.

"Now, the puzzle became easy enough; one had only to classify. Take the cases of the people who met their deaths by falling over cliffs or over the edge of quarries. We think of sheep as timid creatures, who always run away. But suppose sheep that don't run away; and, after all. in reason why should they run away? Quarry or no quarry, cliff or no cliff, what would happen to you if a hundred sheep ran after you instead of running from you? There would be no help for it; they would have you down and beat you to death or stifle you. Then suppose man, woman, or child near a cliff's edge or a quarry-side, and a sudden rush of sheep. Clearly there is no help; there is nothing for it but to go over. There can be no doubt that that is what happened in all these cases.

"And again. You know the country and you know how a herd of cattle will sometimes pursue people through the fields in a solemn, stolid sort of way. They behave as if they wanted to close in on you. Townspeople sometimes get frightened and scream and run; you or I would take no notice, or, at the utmost, would wave our sticks at the herd, which would stop dead or lumber off. But suppose they don't lumber off? It was a quicker death for poor Griffith of Treff Loyne: one of his own beasts gored him to death with one sharp thrust of its horn into his heart. And from that morning those within the house were closely besieged by their own cattle and horses and sheep, and when those unhappy people within opened a window to call for help or to catch a few drops of rain-water to relieve their burning thirst, the cloud waited for them with its myriad eyes of fire. Can you wonder that Secretan's statement reads in places like mania? You perceive the horrible position of those people in Treff Loyne; not only did they see death advancing on them, but advancing with incredible steps, as if one were to die not only in nightmare, but by nightmare. But no one in his wildest, most fiery dreams had ever imagined such a fate. I am not astonished that Secretan at one moment suspected the evidence of his own senses, at another surmised that the world's end had come."

"And how about the Williamses who were murdered on the Highway near here?"

"The horses were the murderers, the horses that afterward stampeded the camp below. By some means which is still obscure to me they lured that family into the road and beat their brains out; their shod hoofs were the instruments of execution. The munition-works? Their enemy was rats. I believe that it has been calculated that in 'greater London' the number of rats is about equal to the number of human beings; that is, there are about seven millions of them. The proportion would be about the same in all the great centers of population; and the rat, moreover, is on occasion migratory in its habits. You can understand now that story of the *Semiramis* beating about the mouth of the Thames, and at last cast away by Arcachon, her only crew dry heaps of bones. The rat is an expert boarder of ships. And so one can understand the tale told by the frightened man who took the path by the wood that led up from the new munition-works. He thought he heard a thousand men treading softly through the wood and chattering to one another in some horrible tongue; what he did hear was the marshaling of an army of rats, their array before the battle.

"And conceive the terror of such an attack. Even one rat in a fury is said to be an ugly customer to meet; conceive, then, the irruption of these terrible, swarming myriads, rushing upon the helpless, unprepared, astonished workers in the munition-shops."

There can be no doubt, I think, that Dr. Lewis was entirely justified in these extraordinary conclusions. As I say, I had arrived at pretty much the same end, by different ways; but this rather as to the general situation, while Lewis had made his own particular study of those circumstances of the Terror that were within his immediate purview, as a physician in large practice in the southern part of Meirion. Of some of the cases which he reviewed he had, no doubt, no immediate or firsthand knowledge; but he judged these instances by their similarity to the facts which had come under his personal notice. He spoke of the affairs of the quarry at Llanfihangel on the analogy of the people who were found dead at the bottom of the cliffs near Porth, and he was no doubt justified in doing so. He told me that, thinking the whole matter over, he was hardly more astonished by the Terror in itself than by the strange way in which he had arrived at his conclusions.

"You know," he said, "those certain evidences of animal malevolence which we knew of, the bees that stung the child to death, the trusted sheep-dog's turning savage, and so forth. Well, I got no light whatever from all this; it suggested nothing to me. You do not believe; therefore you cannot see.

"And then, when the truth at last appeared, it was through the whimsical 'coincidence,' as we call such signs, of the moth in my lamp and the moth on the dead child's forehead. This, I think, is very extraordinary."

"And there seems to have been one beast that remained faithful—the dog at Treff Loyne. That is strange."

"That remains a mystery."

It would not be wise, even now, to describe too closely the terrible scenes that were to be seen in the munition areas of the North and the Midlands during the black months of the Terror. Out of the factories issued at black midnight the shrouded dead in their coffins, and their very kinsfolk did not know how they had come by their deaths. All the towns were full of houses of mourning, were full of dark and terrible rumors as incredible as the incredible reality. There were things done and suffered that perhaps never will be brought to light, memories and secret traditions of these things will be whispered in families, delivered from father to son, growing wilder with the passage of the years, but never growing wilder than the truth.

It is enough to say that the cause of the Allies was for a while in deadly peril. The men at the front called in their extremity for guns and shells. No one told them what was happening in the places where these munitions were made.

But, after the first panic, measures were taken. The workers were armed with special weapons, guards were mounted, machine-guns were placed in position, bombs and liquid flame were ready against the obscene hordes of the enemy, and the "'burning clouds" found a fire fiercer than their own. Many deaths occurred among the airmen; but they, too, were given special guns, arms that scattered shot broadcast, and so drove away the dark flight that threatened the airplanes.

And then, in the winter of 1915–16, the Terror ended suddenly as it had begun. Once more a sheep was a frightened beast that ran instinctively from a little child; the cattle were again solemn, stupid creatures, void of harm; the spirit and the convention of malignant design passed out of the hearts of all the animals. The chains that they had cast off for a while were thrown again about them.

And finally there comes the inevitable "Why?" Why did the beasts who had been humbly and patiently subject to man, or affrighted by his presence, suddenly know their strength and learn how to league together and declare bitter war against their ancient master?

It is a most difficult and obscure question. I give what explanation I have to give with very great diffidence, and an eminent disposition to be corrected if a clearer light can be found.

Some friends of mine, for whose judgment I have very great respect, are inclined to think that there was a certain contagion of hate. They hold that the fury of the whole world at war, the great passion of death that seems driving all humanity to destruction, infected at last these lower creatures, and in place of their native instinct of submission gave them rage and wrath and ravening.

This may be the explanation. I cannot say that it is not so, because I do not profess to understand the working of the universe. But I confess that the theory strikes me as fanciful. There may be a contagion of hate as there is a contagion of smallpox; I do not know, but I hardly believe it.

In my opinion, and it is only an opinion, the source of the great revolt of the beasts is to be sought in a much subtler region of inquiry. I believe that the subjects revolted because the king abdicated. Man has dominated the beasts throughout the ages, the spiritual has reigned over the rational through the peculiar quality and grace of spirituality that men possess, that makes a man to be that which he is. And when he maintained this power and grace, I think it is pretty clear that between him and the animals there was a certain treaty and alliance. There was supremacy on the one hand and submission on the other; but at the same time there was between the two that cordiality which exists between lords and subjects in a well-organized state. I know a socialist who maintains that Chaucer's "Canterbury Tales" give a picture of true democracy. I do not know about that, but I see that knight and miller were able to get on quite pleasantly together, just because the knight knew that he was a knight and the miller knew that he was a miller. If the knight had had conscientious objections to his knightly grade, while the miller saw no reason why he should not be a knight, I am sure that their intercourse would have been difficult, unpleasant, and perhaps murderous.

So with man. I believe in the strength and truth of tradition. A learned man said to me a few weeks ago: "When I have to choose between the evidence of tradition and the evidence of a document, I always believe the evidence of tradition. Documents may be falsified and often are falsified; tradition is never falsified." This is true; and therefore, I think, one may put trust in the vast body of folklore which asserts that there was once a worthy and friendly alliance between man and the beasts. Our popular tale of Dick Whittington and his cat no doubt represents the adaptation of a very ancient legend to a comparatively modern personage, but we may go back into the ages and find the popular tradition asserting that not only are the animals the subjects, but also the friends of man.

All that was in virtue of that singular spiritual element in man which the rational animals do not possess. Spiritual does not mean respectable, it does not even mean moral, it does not mean "good" in the ordinary acceptation of the word. It signifies the royal prerogative of man, differentiating him from the beasts.

For long ages he has been putting off this royal robe, he has been wiping the balm of consecration from his own breast. He has declared again and again that he is not spiritual, but rational; that is, the equal of the beasts over whom he was once sovereign. He has vowed that he is not Orpheus, but Caliban.

But the beasts also have within them something which corresponds to the spiritual quality in men; we are content to call it instinct. They perceived that the throne was vacant; not even friendship was possible between them and the self-deposed monarch. If he was not king, he was a sham, an impostor, a thing to be destroyed.

Hence, I think, the Terror. They have risen once; they may rise again.

Introduction to *The Shining Pyramid* (1925)

*T**he Shining Pyramid* is the result of a collaboration. Two years ago an American man-of-letters, full of industry, rummaged in old papers, magazines and manuscripts owing their origin to me, and produced as a result of his labours a volume published at Chicago, called *The Shining Pyramid.* The American gentleman, I may say, did not disturb my peace by consulting me as to the content of the book in question. Then, in 1924, pleased, I suppose, with the result of his toils, he rummaged a little more, and, using the same methods, produced a second volume of scraps and odds and ends from my workshop. This book he entitled *The Glorious Mystery.*

At length I thought I ought to take a hand in the business. It seemed to me that I was leaving too much to the American collector of fragments. I went through the two volumes, and, rejecting a good deal, have made them into one.

The contents of *The Shining Pyramid* are various enough. They are of many periods and of many manners. There are wonder-stories, bits of the breakages of unhappy failures of books, a literary-historical essay of some length, and two articles from the old *Academy,* one whimsical, the other venomous.

"The Shining Pyramid" which gives the book its title, was written, if I remember, in 1895. At that time my old friend, A. E. Waite, was editing a monthly magazine called *The Unknown World,* about which I must tell an entertaining story. The firm which published *The Unknown World,* amongst other things, was very largely supported financially by an English nobleman of ancient family, devoted to the occult arts. For one reason or another this support was at length withdrawn, and the publishing house found it necessary to suspend their business. There was, I believe, some difficulty in paying the rent due for the premises which they occupied. It was necessary to ask for a trifle of indulgence in this matter, and the firm wrote to this effect to their landlords, who occupied the lower part of the building.

Now at this point two odd circumstances met together. The landlords were, in fact, an Evangelical society of the strictest Protestant principles. That was one circumstance. The other was this: the firm wrote their letter begging for a slight delay on *Unknown World* letter paper, which displayed the magazine cover in miniature: a Pentacle of light, a strong Spirit proceeding from it, and, for all I remember, other apparatus of magic. And happy magic, indeed, resulted from this letter. The Evangelical society wrote in horror: they had never imagined that anything so dreadful was being done on their premises; they begged the publishers of *The Unknown World* not to speak of a trifle of rent owing, but to go forthwith in God's name. And the publishers went with happy hearts.

To *The Unknown World*, then, "The Shining Pyramid" was contributed. Reading it over, for the first time for nearly thirty years, I exclaimed to the Critic on the Hearth: "This is highly ingenious rubbish." The Critic, very properly, admitted the ingenuity, but denied the rubbish. But I adhere to my criticism. And I am reminded of the logical rule that A cannot be converted *simpliciter*. I have always maintained, and I maintain still, that all the good books have been written for fun, because the author wanted to write them. Now I wrote "The Shining Pyramid" purely for fun, to amuse myself. But one cannot change "All good books are written for fun" into "All books written for fun are good."

"Out of the Earth" and "The Happy Children" belong to a far later period, to the sad days of the war. The former centres round a wonderful headland in Pembrokeshire, called Old Castle Head, a prehistoric fort overlooking the sea. The latter derives from a night and morning spent at Whitby. I am glad to say that the scrap of an imaginary Ritual contained in "The Happy Children" deceived a liturgiologist of some experience.

I have already written, in the body of the book, an essay by way of preface to "The Secret of the Sangraal." This has always been a question of the keenest interest to me since my friend, A. E. Waite, whom I have already mentioned, directed my closer attention to it many years ago. It has the fascination of an insoluble problem; and I am happy to believe that it will always remain insoluble. I need scarcely say that I am under no delusions as to my own share in the Quest. I hope that I have thrown some light on one side of that great Figure "which no man can comprehend," which appears under five several manners. It is something to have done so much. I am sorry for one thing. In these later days this most deeply interesting subject seems in some danger of falling under the purview of the occult quack. There is no sadder fate. I can bear much more easily the attitude of the sham man of science, who knows that the Sangraal was merely an Irish feeding vessel: he does no harm, no harm, that is, to anybody who matters.

"The Mystic Speech" was, originally, a lecture delivered before the Quest Society, and so some traces of the lecture manner may still be found in it. One curious circumstance, I remember. In the course of the lecture I quoted (p. 143) a passage from a book of mine now known (or unknown!) as *Far Off Things*. When I had done, Mr. Mead, the founder, I believe, of the Quest Society, remarked that a passage very similar in feeling and even in expression to my quotation might be found in the prose works of seventeenth century Traherne. Now I have never read Traherne, but the other day I came upon the sentences of which Mr. Mead must have been thinking. The resemblance is amazing; so strong, indeed, that I am almost convinced that when I say that I have never read Traherne, I lie.

"In Convertendo" is a bit of wreckage from the latter part of *The Secret Glory*. All I can say of it is that it praises my country, Gwent, and that he who does this, does well in intent, if not in performance.

I think a very great deal is to be urged in favour of the thesis of "The Martyr." An eminent physician once said to me that the last superstition to perish would be the belief that medicine can make any man better. But when this foolery is ended, there will still be people found ready to declare that beef and beer do them good. The last article in the book speaks lightly of the Great Public Schools, and must be all wrong.

Bibliography

I. *Book Publications of Machen's Fiction*

The Chronicle of Clemendy. London: Privately Printed for the Society of Pantegruelists, [March 1888]. New York: Privately Printed for the Society of Pantegruelists [Boni & Liveright], 1923. London: Martin Secker, 1925. New York: Alfred A. Knopf, 1926. London: Martin Secker/Adelphi Library, 1927. London: Martin Secker/Adelphi Library, [1927].

The Great God Pan and The Inmost Light. London: John Lane; Boston: Roberts Brothers, 1894. Boston: Roberts Brothers, 1894. London: John Lane, 1895. London: Grant Richards, [1913]. London: Martin Secker/New Adelphi Library, 1926. [*Contents:* "The Great God Pan"; "The Inmost Light." The Secker edition adds "The Red Hand."]

The Three Impostors. London: John Lane; Boston: Roberts Brothers, 1895. New York: Alfred A. Knopf, 1923. London: Martin Secker/New Adelphi Library, 1926.

The House of Souls. London: E. Grant Richards, 1906. Boston: Dana Estes & Co., 1906. New York: Albert & Charles Boni, 1915. New York: Frank Shay, 1917. [*Contents:* "A Fragment of Life"; "The White People"; "The Great God Pan"; "The Inmost Light"; *The Three Impostors;* "The Red Hand."]

The Hill of Dreams. London: E. Grant Richards, 1907. Boston: Dana Estes, 1907. New York: Albert & Charles Boni, 1915. New York: Frank Shay, 1917. London: Martin Secker, 1922. New York: Alfred A. Knopf, 1923. London: Martin Secker, 1924. London: Secker & Warburg, 1927. [Serialised in *Horlick's Magazine* 2 (July 1904): 1–12; (August 1904): 129–39; (September 1904): 225–33; (October 1904): 353–62;

(November 1904): 417–27; (December 1904): 545–56 (as "The Garden of Avallaunius").]

The Angels of Mons: The Bowmen and Other Legends of the War. London: Simpkin, Marshall, Hamilton, Kent & Co., 1915 (2nd ed. 1915). New York: G. P. Putnam's Sons, 1915. [*Contents:* "The Bowmen"; "The Soldiers' Rest"; "The Monstrance"; "The Dazzling Light"; "The Bowmen and Other Noble Ghosts," by "The Londoner" (pseudonym of Oswald Barron, F. S. A.). Second edition adds the stories "The Little Nations" and "The Men from Troy."]

The Great Return. London: Faith Press, 1915.

The Great God Pan. London: Simpkin, Marshall, Hamilton, Kent & Co., 1916.

The Terror: A Fantasy. London: Duckworth, 1917. New York: Robert M. McBride & Co., 1917 (as *The Terror: A Mystery*). London: Duckworth, 1927.

The House of Souls. New York: Alfred A. Knopf, 1922. London: Grant Richards, 1923. [*Contents:* "A Fragment of Life"; "The White People"; "The Great God Pan"; "The Inmost Light."]

The Secret Glory. London: Martin Secker, 1922. New York: Alfred A. Knopf, 1922. London: Martin Secker, 1928. [Incorporates "The Marriage of Panurge," *Academy* 72 (22 June 1907): 607–9; *Wave* 1, no. 1 (January 1922): 2–7; in *Holy Terrors* (1946). "The Martyr," *Academy* 73 (20 July 1907): 702–4; in *The Shining Pyramid* (1923); in *The Shining Pyramid* (1925). "Levavi Oculos," *Academy* 73 (21 September 1907): 923–25. "The Parting," *Academy* 73 (23 November 1907): 166–69. "The Schoolmaster's Dream," *Academy* 74 (25 January 1908): 387–90. "Symbols," *Academy* 74 (23 May 1908): 808–10. "The Hidden Mystery," *Academy* 74 (6 June 1908): 856–58; in *The Shining Pyramid* (1923); In *Out of the Earth and Other Sketches* (1925?); in *The Cosy Room and Other Stories* (1936). "Enchanted Café," *Academy* 75 (27 June 1908): 927–28 (as part of the column "From a Notebook"). "In Convertendo," *Academy* 75 (15 August 1908): 157–58; in *The Shining Pyramid* (1923); in *The Shining*

Pyramid (1925). "The Secret Glory," *Gypsy* 1 (May 1915): 79–89; (May 1916): 139–45.]

Works (Caerleon Edition). London: Martin Secker; Edinburgh: Dunedin Press, 1923. 9 vols. [*Contents:* Vol. 1: "The Great God Pan," "The Inmost Light," "The Red Hand"; Vol. 2: *The Three Impostors;* Vol. 6: "A Fragment of Life," "The White People"; Vol. 7: *The Terror; The Bowmen and Other Legends of the War;* "The Great Return." Vols. 3–5, 8, and 9 contain no fiction.]

The Shining Pyramid. Edited by Vincent Starrett. Chicago: Covici-McGee, 1923. [*Contents* (fiction only): "The Shining Pyramid"; "Out of the Earth"; "The Lost Club"; "A Wonderful Woman."]

The Glorious Mystery. Edited by Vincent Starrett. Chicago: Covici-McGee, 1924. [*Contents* (fiction only): "The Rose Garden"; "Fragments of Paper" (i.e., "Psychology"); "The Holy Things"; "Scrooge: 1920."]

Ornaments in Jade. New York: Alfred A. Knopf, 1924. [*Contents:* "The Rose Garden"; "The Turanians"; "The Idealist"; "Witchcraft"; "The Ceremony"; "Psychology"; "Torture"; "Midsummer"; "Nature"; "The Holy Things."]

Tales of the Strange and the Supernatural. Girard, KS: Haldeman-Julius, [1925?]. [*Contents:* "The Priest and the Barber"; "The Lost Club"; "A Wonderful Woman"; "The Shining Pyramid."]

Out of the Earth and Other Sketches. Girard, KS: Haldeman-Julius, [1925?]. [*Contents* (fiction only): "Out of the Earth."]

The Shining Pyramid. London: Martin Secker, 1925. New York: Alfred A. Knopf, 1925. [*Contents* (fiction only): "The Shining Pyramid"; "Out of the Earth"; "The Happy Children."]

A Fragment of Life. London: Martin Secker, 1928. [*Contents:* "A Fragment of Life"; "The White People."]

The Green Round. London: Ernest Benn, 1933. Sauk City, WI: Arkham House, 1968.

The Children of the Pool and Other Stories. London: Hutchinson, 1936. [*Contents:* "The Exalted Omega"; "The Children of the Pool"; "The Bright Boy"; "The Tree of Life"; "Out of the Picture"; "Change."]

The Cosy Room and Other Stories. London: Rich & Cowan, 1936. [*Contents:* "A Double Return"; "A Wonderful Woman"; "The Lost Club"; "The Holy Things"; "Psychology"; "Torture"; "Witchcraft"; "The Turanians"; "The Rose Garden"; "The Ceremony"; "Midsummer"; "Nature"; "The Hidden Mystery"; "Munitions of War"; "Drake's Drum"; "A New Christmas Carol"; "The Islington Mystery"; "The Gift of Tongues"; "The Cosy Room"; "Awaking"; "Opening the Door"; "The Compliments of the Season"; "N."]

The Great God Pan and Other Weird Tales. New York: Editions for the Armed Services, [1943]. [*Contents:* "The Great God Pan"; "The White People"; "The Inmost Light"; "The Recluse of Bayswater" (segment of *The Three Impostors*).]

Holy Terrors. Harmondsworth: Penguin, 1946. [*Contents:* "The Bright Boy"; "The Tree of Life"; "Opening the Door"; "The Marriage of Panurge" (segment of *The Secret Glory*); "The Holy Things"; "Psychology"; "The Turanians"; "The Rose Garden"; "The Ceremony"; "The Soldiers' Rest"; "The Happy Children"; "The Cosy Room"; "Munitions of War"; "The Great Return."]

Tales of Horror and the Supernatural. New York: Alfred A. Knopf, 1948. London: Richards Press, 1949. [*Contents:* "Novel of the Black Seal"; "Novel of the White Powder"; "The Great God Pan"; "The White People"; "The Inmost Light"; "The Shining Pyramid"; "The Bowmen"; "The Great Return"; "The Happy Children"; "The Bright Boy"; "Out of the Earth"; "N"; "The Children of the Pool"; *The Terror.*]

II. Individual Publications of Short Stories

"Awaking: A Children's Story." In Lady Cynthia Asquith, ed. *The Children's Cargo.* London: Eyre & Spottiswoode, 1930. 29–36. In *The Cosy Room and Other Stories* (1936).

"The Bowmen." *Evening News* (London) (29 September 1914): 3. *Evening News* (London) (20 July 1915): 6. In *The Angels of Mons* (1915). In *Works,* Vol. 7 (1923). In *Tales of Horror and the Supernatural* (1948).

"The Bright Boy." In *The Children of the Pool and Other Stories* (1936). In *Holy Terrors* (1946). In *Tales of Horror and the Supernatural* (1948).

"Change." In *The Children of the Pool and Other Stories* (1936).

"The Children of the Pool." In *The Children of the Pool and Other Stories* (1936). In *Tales of Horror and the Supernatural* (1948).

"The Compliments of the Season." *Independent* 2 (13 January 1934): 24. In *The Cosy Room and Other Stories* (1936).

"The Cosy Room." In Cynthia Asquith, ed. *Shudders.* London: Hutchinson, 1928; New York: Scribner, 1929. 99–106. *John O'London's Weekly* 22 (14 December 1929): 433–34. In *The Cosy Room and Other Stories* (1936). In *Holy Terrors* (1946).

"The Dazzling Light." In *The Angels of Mons* (1915). In *Works,* Vol. 7 (1923).

"The Dover Road." In [Unsigned, ed.] *Missing from Their Homes.* London: Hutchinson, 1936. 235–72.

"The Exalted Omega." In *The Children of the Pool and Other Stories* (1936).

"The Ghost of Whit-Monday: After Charles Dickens." *Evening News* (London) (12 June 1916): 2.

"The Gift of Tongues." *T. P.'s and Cassell's Weekly* 9 (3 December 1927): 179–80. In *The Cosy Room and Other Stories* (1936).

"The Great Return." *Evening News* (London) (21 October 1915): 8; (25 October 1915): 2; (28 October 1915): 7; (3 November 1915): 3; (5 November 1915): 8; (10 November 1915): 8; (16 November 1915): 8. In *The Great Return* (1915). In *Works,* Vol. 7 (1923). In *Holy Terrors* (1946). In *Tales of Horror and the Supernatural* (1948).

"The Happy Children." In Sir J. A. Hammerton, ed. *The Masterpiece Library of Short Stories.* Volume 20. London: Educational Book Co., 1920. 148–52. In *The Shining Pyramid* (1925). In *Holy Terrors* (1946). In *Tales of Horror and the Supernatural* (1948).

"The Islington Mystery." In Lady Cynthia Asquith, ed. *The Black Cap: New Stories of Murder and Mystery.* London: Hutchinson, 1927. 134–48. New York: Scribner, 1928. In *The Cosy Room and Other Stories* (1936).

"Johnny Double." In Lady Cynthia Asquith, ed. *The Treasure Cave.* London: Jarrolds, 1928; New York: Scribner, 1928. 44–52.

"The Light That Can Never Be Put Out." *Evening News* (London) (14 February 1916): 2.

"The Little Nations." *Evening News* (London) (5 September 1915): 2 (as "What the Prebendary Saw"). In *The Angels of Mons,* 2nd ed. (1915).

"The Men from Troy." *Evening News* (London) (10 September 1915): 2. In *The Angels of Mons,* 2nd ed. (1915).

"The Monstrance." In *The Angels of Mons* (1915). In *Works,* Vol. 7 (1923).

"Munitions of War." In Lady Cynthia Asquith, ed. *The Ghost Book.* London: Hutchinson, 1926. 163–66. New York: Scribner, 1927. In *The Cosy Room and Other Stories* (1936). In *Holy Terrors* (1946).

"N." In *The Cosy Room and Other Stories* (1936). In *Tales of Horror and the Supernatural* (1948).

"A New Christmas Carol." *Evening News* (London) (28 December 1920): 2 (as "Scrooge: 1920"). In *The Cosy Room and Other Stories* (1936).

"Opening the Door." In Lady Cynthia Asquith, ed. *When Graveyards Yawn.* London: Hutchinson, 1931. 110–26. In *The Cosy Room and Other Stories* (1936). In *Holy Terrors* (1946).

"Out of the Earth." *T. P.'s Weekly* 26 (27 November 1915): 517–19. In *The Shining Pyramid* (1923). In *Out of the Earth and Other Sketches* (1925?). In *The Shining Pyramid* (1925). In *Tales of Horror and the Supernatural* (1946).

"Out of the Picture." In *The Children of the Pool and Other Stories* (1936).

"Ritual." In John Rowland, ed. *Path and Pavement: Twenty New Tales of Britain.* London: Eric Grant, 1937. 143–51.

"Scrooge and the Spirit of—Psycho-analysis." *T. P.'s and Cassell's Weekly* 1 (8 December 1923): 228.

"The Soldiers' Rest." *Evening News* (London) (20 October 1914): 4. In *The Angels of Mons* (1915). In *Works,* Vol. 7 (1923). In *Holy Terrors* (1946).

"Ten Thousand and One Nights." *Evening News* (London) (1 November 1911). *Reviewer* 4, No. 4 (July 1924): 263–65.

The Terror. Evening News (16 October 1916): 2; (17 October 1916): 2; (18 October 1916): 2; (19 October 1916): 5; (20 October 1916): 6; (21 October 1916): 2; (23 October 1916): 6; (24 October 1916): 5; (25 October 1916): 6; (26 October 1916): 6; (27 October 1916): 6; (28 October 1916): 2; (30 October 1916): 6; (31 October 1916): 6 (as "The Great Terror"). In *The Terror* (1917). In *Works,* Vol. 7 (1923). In *Tales of Horror and the Supernatural* (1948).

"The Tree of Life." In *The Children of the Pool and Other Stories* (1936). In *Holy Terrors* (1946).

"The Young Man in the Blue Serge Suit." *Evening News* (London) (29 December 1913): 6.

Appendix:

Introduction to *The Angels of Mons. The Angels of Mons: The Bowmen and Other Legends of the War.* London: Simpkin, Marshall, Hamilton, Kent & Co., 1915. 5–27.

"The Coming of the Terror." *Century Magazine* 94 (October 1917): 801–25. [Abridged edition of *The Terror.*]

Introduction to *The Shining Pyramid.* London: Martin Secker, 1925. 7–10.

www.ingramcontent.com/pod-product-compliance
Lightning Source LLC
Chambersburg PA
CBHW052346020726
47503CB00001B/123